A GAME OF THRONES

THE GRAPHIC NOVEL

VOLUME 1

GEORGE R. R. MARTIN

A GAME OF THRONES

THE GRAPHIC NOVEL

VOLUME 1

ADAPTED BY DANIEL ABRAHAM

ART BY TOMMY PATTERSON

COLORS BY IVAN NUNES

LETTERING BY MARSHALL DILLON

ORIGINAL SERIES COVER ART BY ALEX ROSS AND MIKE S. MILLER

BANTAM BOOKS • NEW YORK

Paintings on pages vi and xii by Alex Ross.
Paintings on pages 2, 32, 62, 92, 122, and 152 by Mike S. Miller.
Painting on page 182 by Michael Komark.

Published in the United States by Bantam Books, an imprint of the Random House Publishing Group, a division of Random House, Inc. New York.

Bantam Books is a registered trademark and the Bantam colophon is a trademark of Random House, Inc.

All characters featured in this book, and the distinctive names and likenesses thereof, and all related indicia are trademarks of George R.R. Martin.

ISBN 978-0-440-42321-8
eBook ISBN 978-0-345-53557-3

Printed in the United States of America on acid-free paper.

www.bantamdell.com

9 8 7

Graphic novel interior design by Foltz Design.

Visit us online at www.DYNAMITE.com
Follow us on Twitter @dynamitecomics
Like us on Facebook /Dynamitecomics
Watch us on YouTube /Dynamitecomics

Nick Barrucci, CEO / Publisher
Juan Collado, President / COO
Joe Rybandt, Senior Editor
Josh Johnson, Art Director
Rich Young, Director Business Development
Jason Ullmeyer, Senior Graphic Designer
Keith Davidsen, Marketing Manager
Josh Green, Traffic Coordinator
Chris Caniano, Production Assistant

CONTENTS

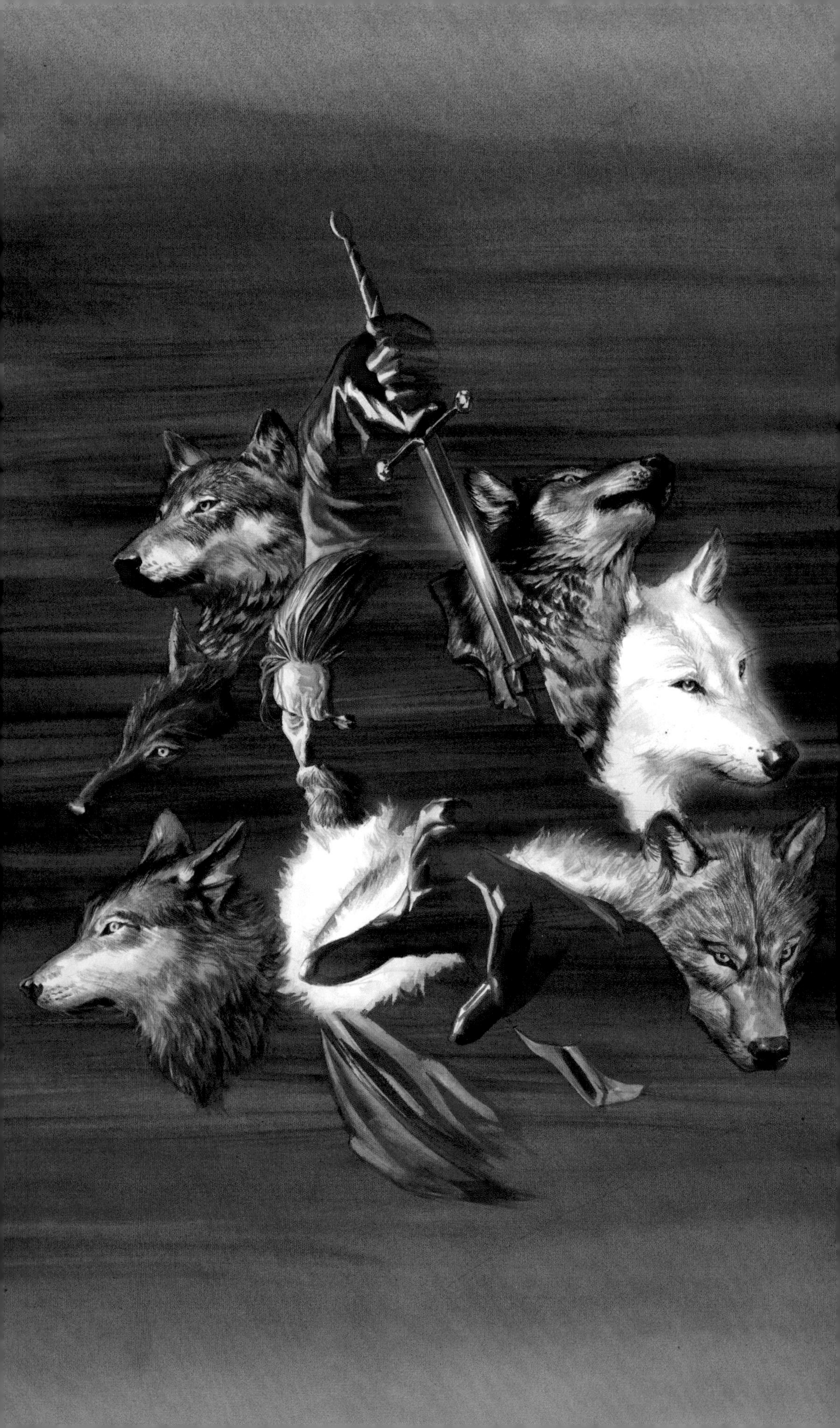

PREFACE

BY GEORGE R. R. MARTIN

Welcome to the first volume of the collected *A Game of Thrones,* a graphic novel based on my epic fantasy novel of the same name.

"Graphic novel" is what they call these things now. What they actually are, of course, are big fancy comic books published on glossy paper in hardcover or trade paperback format, and sold through bookshops rather than comic shops, news-stands, and candy-store spinner racks. Has a nice ring to it, "graphic novel." A nice, dignified, respectable name for an artistic medium that has traditionally gotten less respect than Rodney Dangerfield.

Which is all fine and good, I suppose…but my roots are in comics fandom, so they will always be comic books to me. They were never especially comedic (not intentionally, anyway), to be sure. That usage came over from newspaper comic *strips,* which had preceded comic books by decades. It makes more sense in that context; the majority of the newspaper strips were meant to be humorous, although even in the papers, there were plenty of exceptions, ranging from *Prince Valiant* to *Flash Gordon* to *Terry and the Pirates.* But "comic strips" was the term, and when the first publishers started collecting strips into flimsy little books printed on cheap paper and selling them for a dime, those became comic books.

When I was growing up in New Jersey in the 1950s, we called them all "funny books."

Some comics were actually intended to be funny, of course. Archie and his gang. Mickey and Donald and (best of the bunch) Uncle Scrooge. Casper the Friendly Ghost, Baby Huey, Little Lulu, Sugar and Spike, Beetle Bailey, Cosmo the Merry Martian, all those funny animals. Most of those were comics for little kids, though, way too young and silly for a serious comic-book fan like me. By the time I hit my serious comic-book-collecting phase, I was all of ten and eleven and then twelve, and spending my dimes on serious adult fare, like Batman and Superman and the Challengers of the Unknown, on war comics and Western comics and *Hot Rods and Racing Cars* (my family did not even own a car, but I liked to read about them), the horror and mystery and science-fiction titles from AMG and Charlton and the Company-Soon-to-Be-Marvel. A couple years later, I bought all the nascent Marvel superheroes too, Spider-Man and the Fantastic Four, the X-Men and Avengers, Thor and Iron Man and Ant-Man, and loved them so much I started writing to their letter columns. Some of my letters were published, which led to other comics fans contacting me and sending me their fanzines, which led to me writing stories for their fanzines, which led to…well, where I am today. But that's a story I've told before.

And then there were *Classics Illustrated.* Maybe those were the first graphic novels: seminal novels of Western literature (mixed in with some that were, ah, less seminal), adapted into comics. I did not collect *Classics Illustrated* comics as assiduously as I collected the Marvel and DC titles, but over the years I did buy quite a few of them. Later, in high school and college, I would read many of the original works on which the comics were based, but those experiences were years in my future. The funny books came first. *A Tale of Two Cities, The Time Machine, War of the Worlds, Great Expectations, Moby-Dick, Ivanhoe, The Iliad, The Last of the Mohicans, The House of the Seven Gables, The Three Musketeers, Arabian Nights,* even *Macbeth*…I read them first as funny books. Long years before I ever read a word of Dickens, Wells, Melville, Dumas, or Shakespeare, I encountered Sydney Carton, the Time Traveller, Captain Ahab, D'Artagnan, and Lady Macbeth slumming on pages made of newsprint and printed in four colors. And though I had not (yet) read the books, I devoured the stories.

Funny books were controversial in the 1950s. They were widely read, especially by kids (today's comic audience is much older, and much, much smaller). But they were not *approved of.* There was a psychiatrist named Fredric Wertham who claimed that comics caused juvenile delinquency, and hundreds of thousands of seemingly intelligent adults believed him. Teachers would confiscate your comics in school, and warn you that reading such stuff would "rot your mind." Mothers would throw away your collection the moment your back was turned (not MY mother, though, I'm pleased to say). Crime comics, horror comics, and even superhero comics were particularly reviled, almost certain to turn any healthy child into a violent criminal. Funny animal comics usually got a pass as harmless fun.

But the critics and the censors split on books like *Classics Illustrated.* Some allowed that they might be a good thing, seeing as how they helped to introduce kids to "real literature." Others insisted that a comic was a comic was a comic, that these adaptations did violence to the great books they were based on, cheapened them, robbed the reader of the delights of the original. The comic book of *Moby-Dick* was not Melville, they insisted.

They were right, of course. But they were wrong as well. No, the comic book of *Moby-Dick* was not Melville, could never be Melville...but the story was still there, and those of us who read that funny book were still richer for having sailed upon the *Pequod* and made the acquaintance of Ishmael, Queequeg, and Captain Ahab. For many, *Classics Illustrated* comics were the gateway drug, and led us on to the hard stuff—the original novels.

The comic book is not the book; the graphic novel is not the novel. The same, of course, is true of films and television. When we move a story from one medium to another, no matter how faithful we attempt to be, some changes are inevitable. Each medium has its own demands, its own restrictions, its own way of telling a story.

There are aspects of my epic fantasy series, A Song of Ice and Fire, that make it an especially difficult work to translate to any visual medium. The sheer scale of it. All those scenes. All those settings. A cast of thousands. The complexity of my plots and subplots. The structure: tight third-person narratives, interwoven from the viewpoint of many different characters. In the novels, I make free use of some techniques that work well in prose, and less well, or not at all, for a visual medium: internal monologues, flashbacks, unreliable narrators. I strive to put you inside the heads of my characters, make you privy to their thoughts, let you see the world through their eyes. Screenwriters and comic-book scriptors cannot do any of that, not without resorting to clumsy devices like voice-overs and thought balloons. For all these reasons, I went for years thinking that *A Game of Thrones* and its sequels would never be adapted. Not for film, not television, and certainly not for funny books. Just. Could. Not. Be. Done.

Shows you what I know.

As I write, the HBO television series *Game of Thrones* has just wrapped its second season, after a very successful premiere season that saw the show nominated for the Emmy, the Golden Globe, and a dozen other major awards. Reviews have been great, and so have the ratings.

And you hold the graphic novel in your hands.

Let me make one thing clear: This is not a tie-in to the television series. What you're about to read is an original adaptation of my novels. The creative teams responsible for these alternate versions of my tale—Daniel Abraham and Tommy Patterson for the comics, David Benioff and D. B. Weiss (aided and abetted by Bryan Cogman, Jane Espenson, and yours truly) for the TV show—worked from the same source material and faced some of the same challenges, but each had to deal with problems unique to their media as well. In some cases they may have hit on similar solutions; in others, they took very different approaches. But if you're a fan of the TV series, and you're wondering why the story lines are a little different, and the characters do not look like the actors you've seen on your flat screen…well, now you know.

For my part, I love the television series, and I love the comics…er, graphic novel…too. This is my world, these are my people, and this is still my story, now being told in a different way in a different medium, where a whole new audience can enjoy it.

Graphic stories are a collaborative medium, in much the same way as film and television; it takes a team to make a funny book worth reading. I have a lot of people to thank for the book you hold in your hands, starting with my publishers and editors, Anne Groell at Random House and Nick Barucci at Dynamite, who have shepherded this project through from start to finish. Thanks as well to our sensational cover artists, Alex Ross and Mike S. Miller and Michael Komarck, who have graced the monthly issues with some truly gorgeous artwork.

The interior art is from the gifted pencil of Tommy Patterson. We looked at dozens of different pencilers for this gig, talented artists from all over the world who sent in sample pages for our consideration. It was not at all an easy decision, but Tommy's samples stood out right from the first. He seemed to have a real feel for the world of Westeros and its denizens, and his passion for the project was second to none. And let's not forget the amazing work of Ivan Nunes on colors, and Marshall Dillon on letters.

Last, but most definitely not least, is Daniel Abraham, who did all the hard work of breaking down the novel into pages and panels, deciding what to cut and what to keep, doing all the scripting, the dialogue, the imagery. A former student and a close friend, Daniel is a triple-threat in his own right, writing epic fantasy under his real name, urban fantasy as M. L. N. Hanover, and science fiction (in collaboration with Ty Franck) as James S. A. Corey. He does all three superlatively. This comic...er, graphic novel...is as much his work as mine, and would not exist without him.

A series of novels. A television show. A comic book. Three different media, each with its own strengths and weaknesses, its own pleasure and frustrations...but all ultimately telling the same story. If you've enjoyed the books or the TV show, we hope you will like this version as well. And if you're new to A Song of Ice and Fire, I hope you'll enjoy visiting Westeros and Winterfell, and meeting Tyrion and Jon Snow and Arya and Ned and Cersei and Sansa and Bran and the rest of my cast of thousands. (But don't get too attached).

Maybe you will even want to read the original novels when you've finished the comic. That would be cool. Like those old *Classics Illustrated* com...er, graphic novels...this may be a gateway drug. Besides, comic books will rot your mind.

GEORGE R. R. MARTIN

Santa Fe
January 25, 2012

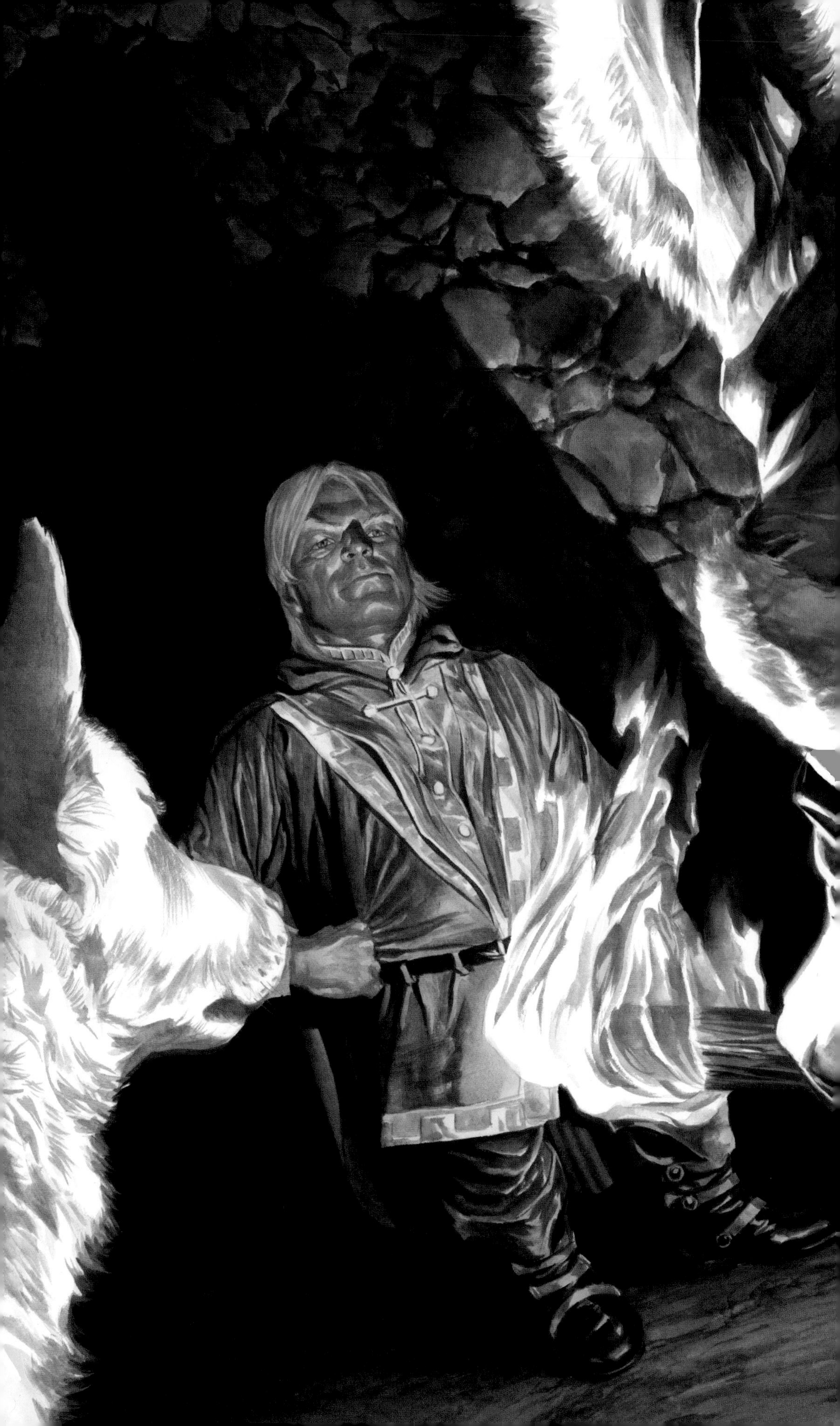

A GAME OF THRONES

THRONES

THE GRAPHIC NOVEL

VOLUME 1

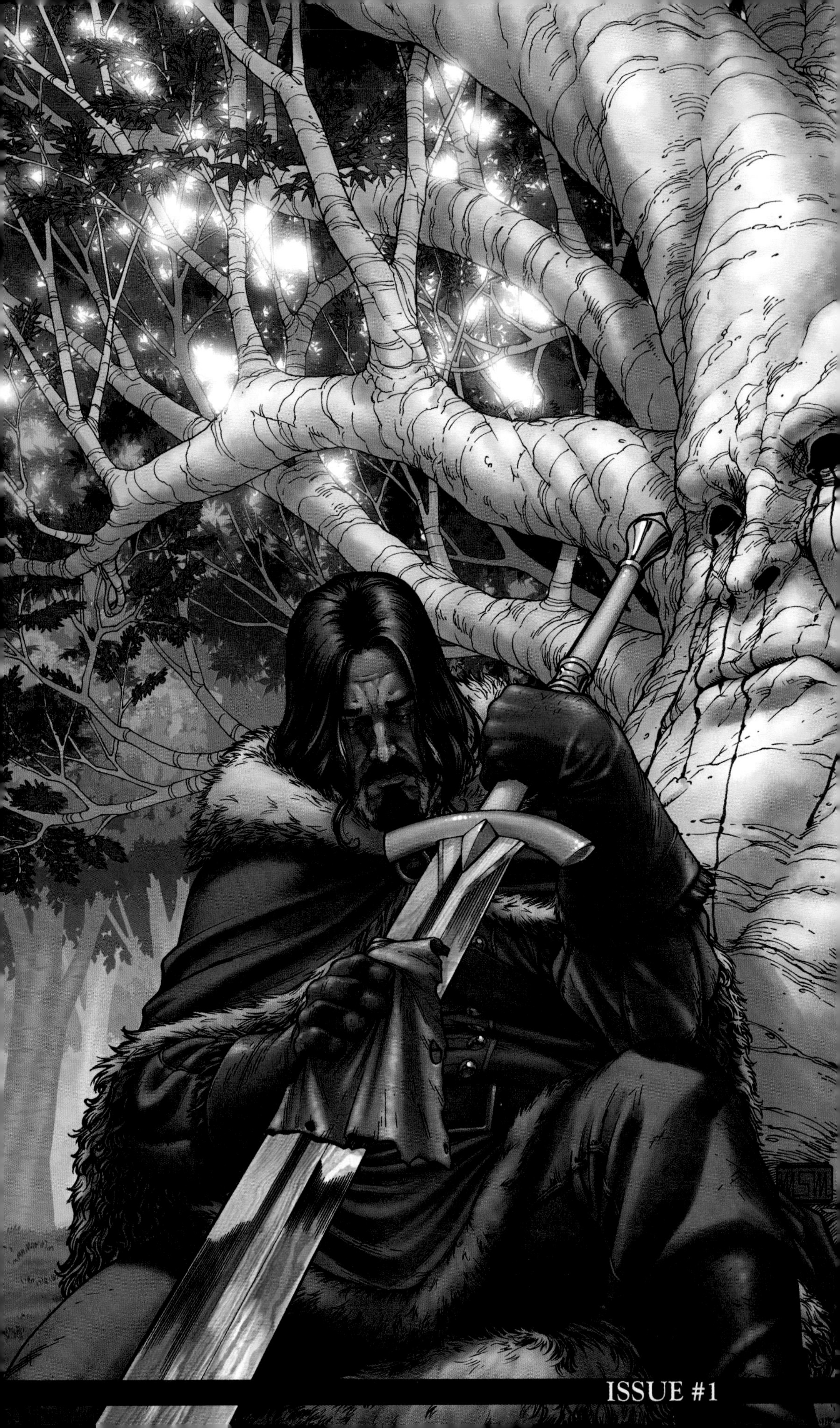
ISSUE #1

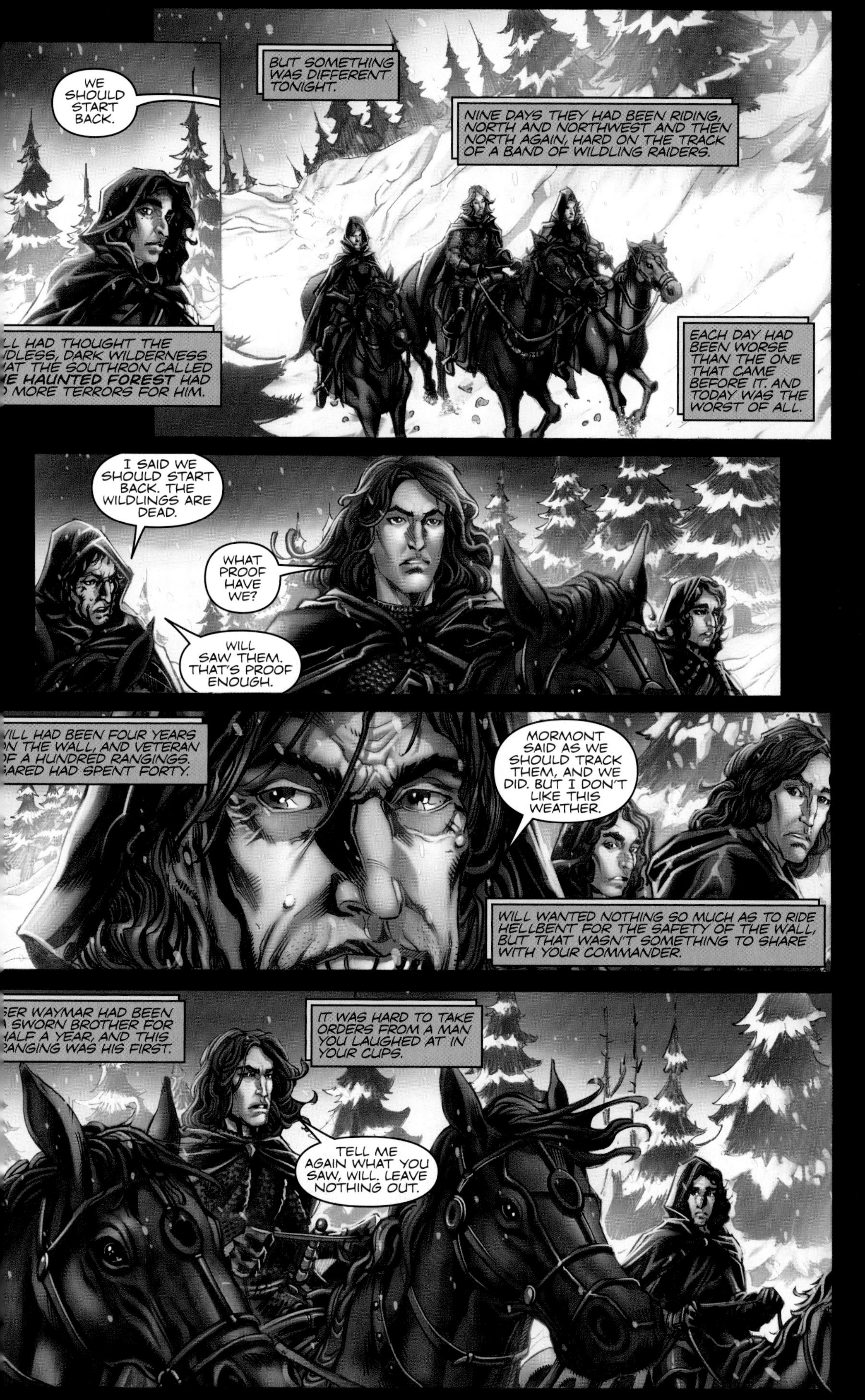
WE SHOULD START BACK.
BUT SOMETHING WAS DIFFERENT TONIGHT.
NINE DAYS THEY HAD BEEN RIDING, NORTH AND NORTHWEST AND THEN NORTH AGAIN, HARD ON THE TRACK OF A BAND OF WILDLING RAIDERS.
LL HAD THOUGHT THE NDLESS, DARK WILDERNESS AT THE SOUTHRON CALLED E HAUNTED FOREST HAD O MORE TERRORS FOR HIM.
EACH DAY HAD BEEN WORSE THAN THE ONE THAT CAME BEFORE IT. AND TODAY WAS THE WORST OF ALL.
I SAID WE SHOULD START BACK. THE WILDLINGS ARE DEAD.
WHAT PROOF HAVE WE?
WILL SAW THEM. THAT'S PROOF ENOUGH.
VILL HAD BEEN FOUR YEARS N THE WALL, AND VETERAN F A HUNDRED RANGINGS. GARED HAD SPENT FORTY.
MORMONT SAID AS WE SHOULD TRACK THEM, AND WE DID. BUT I DON'T LIKE THIS WEATHER.
WILL WANTED NOTHING SO MUCH AS TO RIDE HELLBENT FOR THE SAFETY OF THE WALL, BUT THAT WASN'T SOMETHING TO SHARE WITH YOUR COMMANDER.
SER WAYMAR HAD BEEN A SWORN BROTHER FOR HALF A YEAR, AND THIS RANGING WAS HIS FIRST.
IT WAS HARD TO TAKE ORDERS FROM A MAN YOU LAUGHED AT IN YOUR CUPS.
TELL ME AGAIN WHAT YOU SAW, WILL. LEAVE NOTHING OUT.

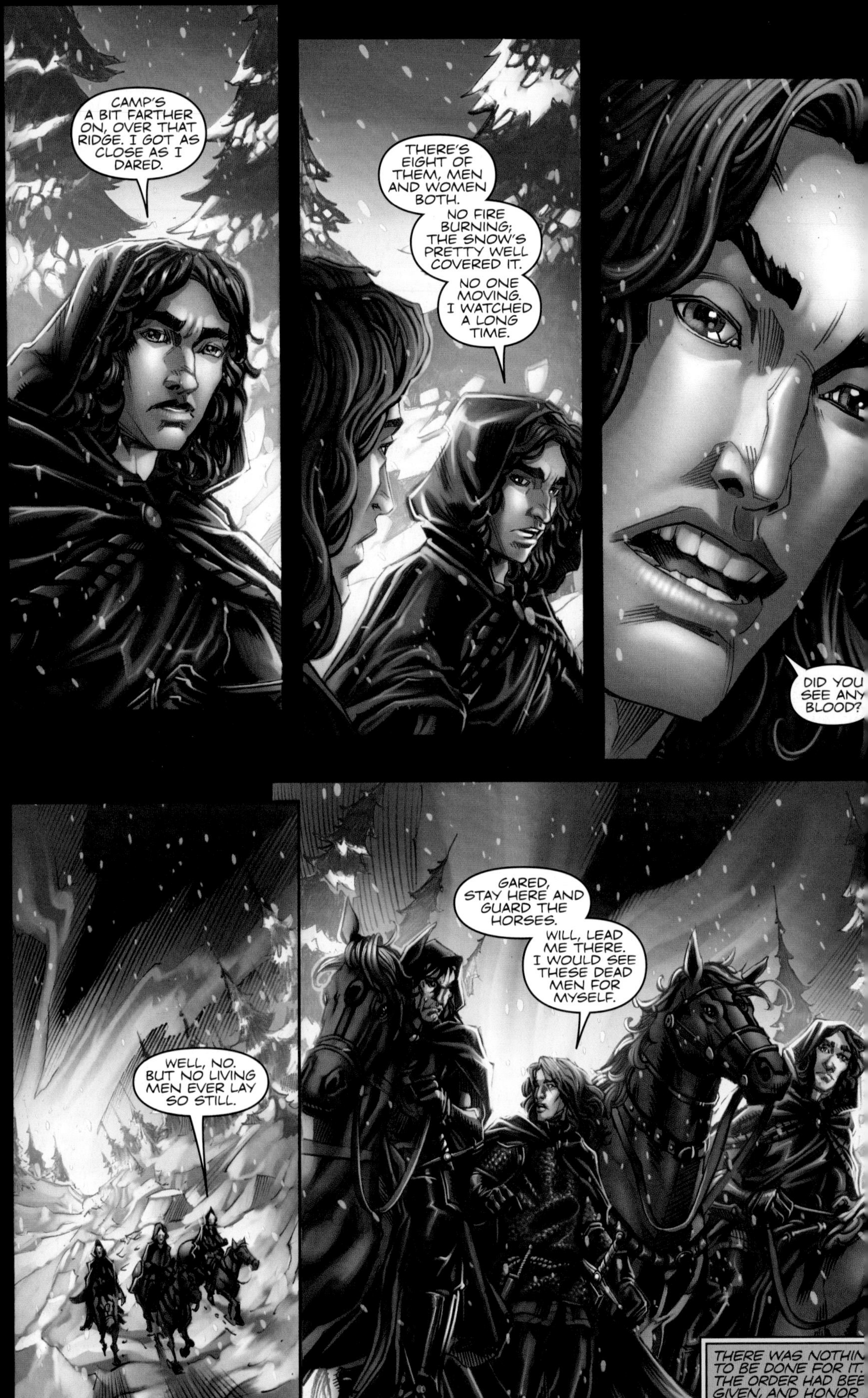
CAMP'S A BIT FARTHER ON, OVER THAT RIDGE. I GOT AS CLOSE AS I DARED.
THERE'S EIGHT OF THEM, MEN AND WOMEN BOTH.
NO FIRE BURNING; THE SNOW'S PRETTY WELL COVERED IT.
NO ONE MOVING. I WATCHED A LONG TIME.
DID YOU SEE ANY BLOOD?
WELL, NO. BUT NO LIVING MEN EVER LAY SO STILL.
GARED, STAY HERE AND GUARD THE HORSES.
WILL, LEAD ME THERE. I WOULD SEE THESE DEAD MEN FOR MYSELF.
THERE WAS NOTHIN TO BE DONE FOR IT. THE ORDER HAD BEE GIVEN, AND HONOR BOUND HIM TO OBE

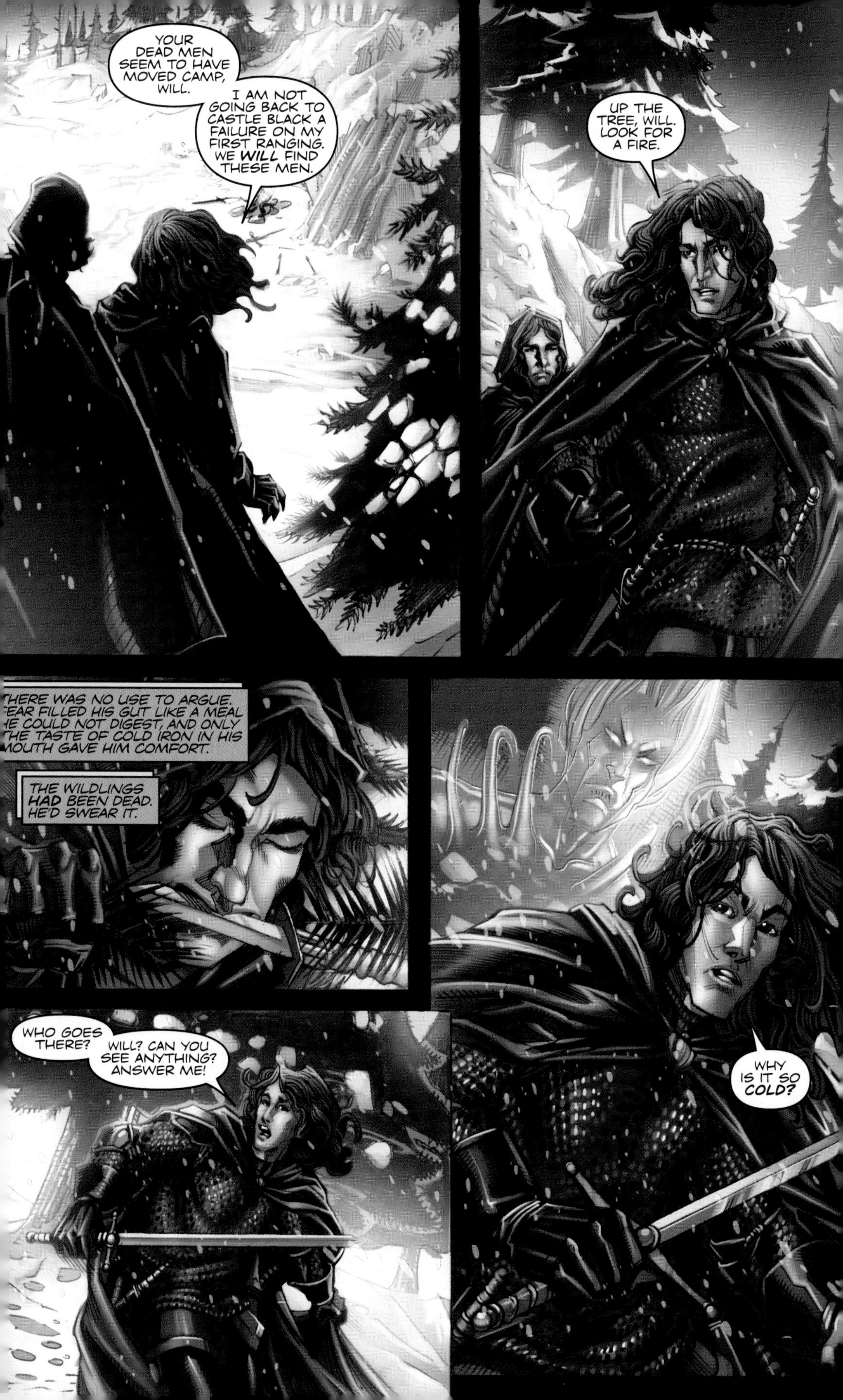
YOUR DEAD MEN SEEM TO HAVE MOVED CAMP, WILL.
I AM NOT GOING BACK TO CASTLE BLACK A FAILURE ON MY FIRST RANGING. WE **WILL** FIND THESE MEN.
UP THE TREE, WILL. LOOK FOR A FIRE.
THERE WAS NO USE TO ARGUE. FEAR FILLED HIS GUT LIKE A MEAL HE COULD NOT DIGEST, AND ONLY THE TASTE OF COLD IRON IN HIS MOUTH GAVE HIM COMFORT.
THE WILDLINGS **HAD** BEEN DEAD. HE'D SWEAR IT.
WHY IS IT SO **COLD?**
WHO GOES THERE?
WILL? CAN YOU SEE ANYTHING? ANSWER ME!

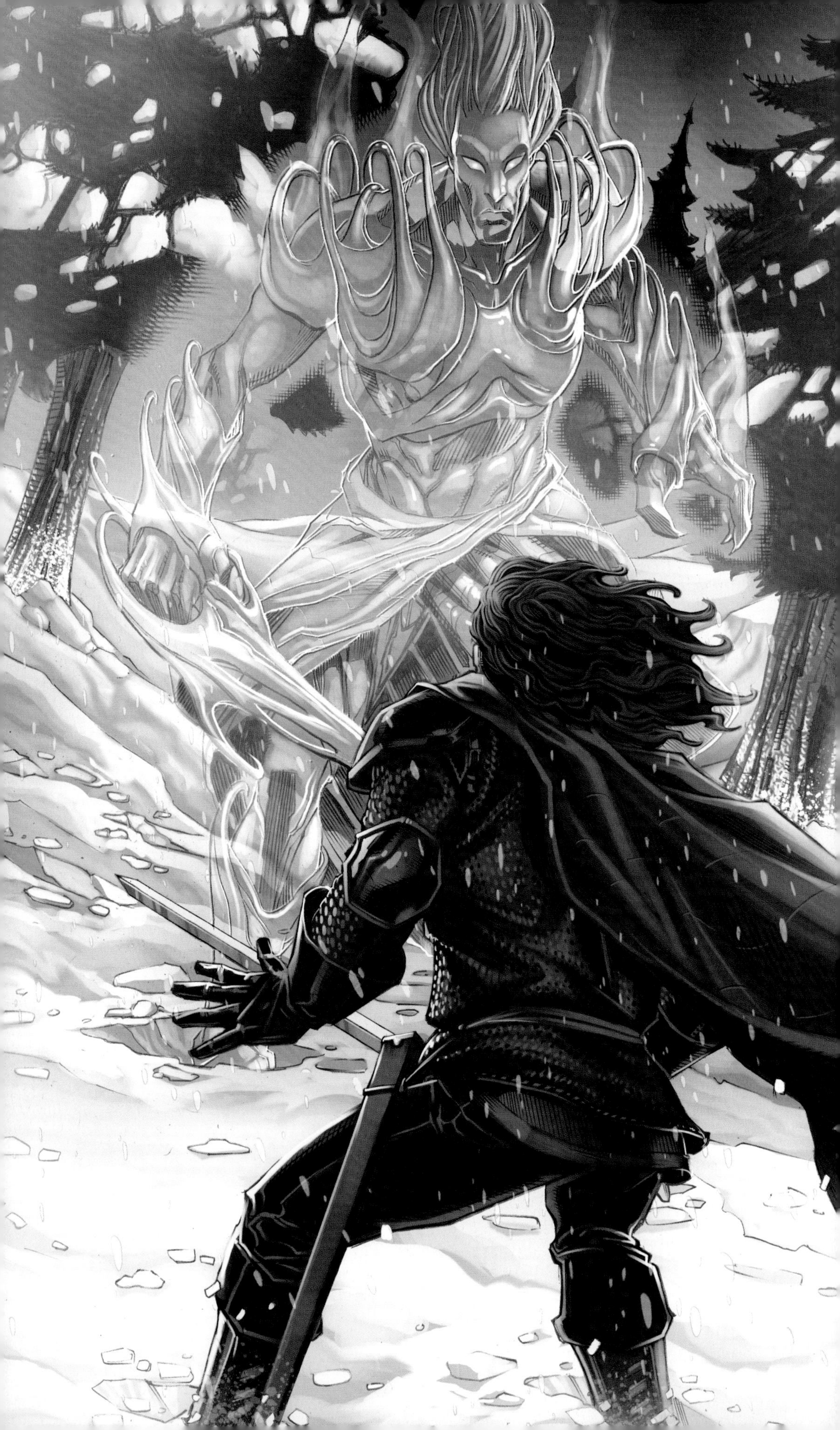

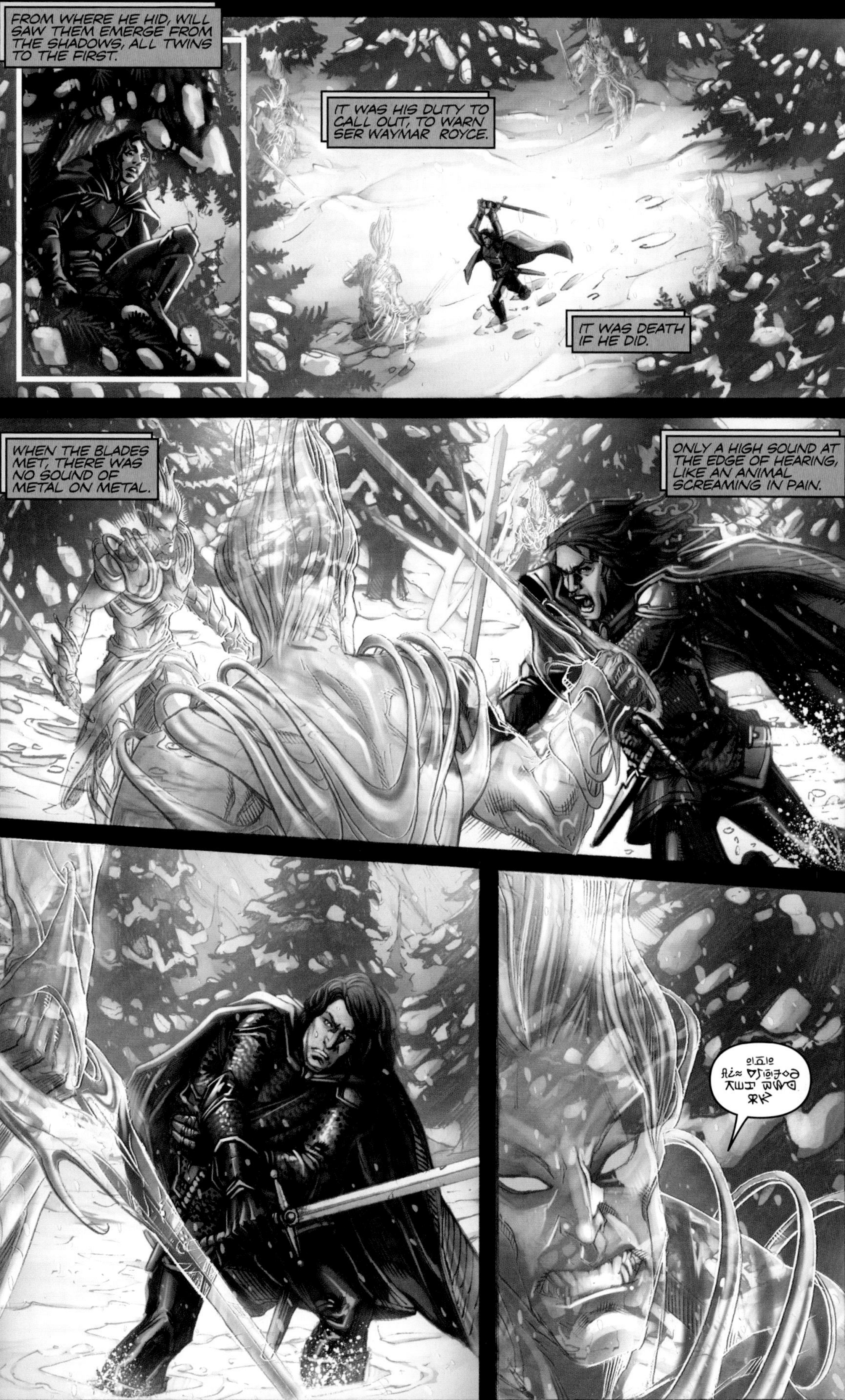
FROM WHERE HE HID, WILL SAW THEM EMERGE FROM THE SHADOWS, ALL TWINS TO THE FIRST.
IT WAS HIS DUTY TO CALL OUT, TO WARN SER WAYMAR ROYCE.
IT WAS DEATH IF HE DID.
WHEN THE BLADES MET, THERE WAS NO SOUND OF METAL ON METAL.
ONLY A HIGH SOUND AT THE EDGE OF HEARING, LIKE AN ANIMAL SCREAMING IN PAIN.

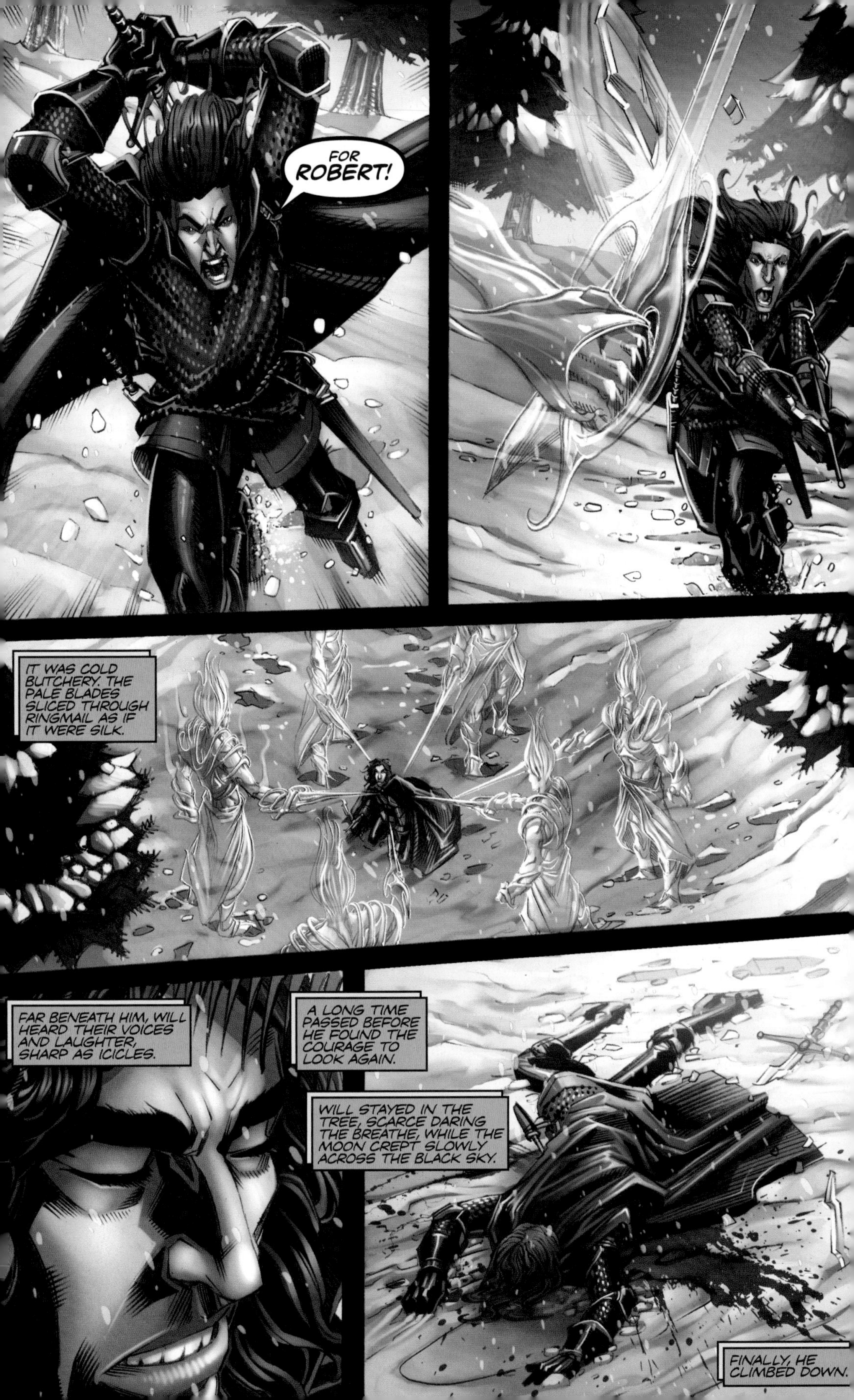
FOR ROBERT!
IT WAS COLD BUTCHERY. THE PALE BLADES SLICED THROUGH RINGMAIL AS IF IT WERE SILK.
FAR BENEATH HIM, WILL HEARD THEIR VOICES AND LAUGHTER, SHARP AS ICICLES.
A LONG TIME PASSED BEFORE HE FOUND THE COURAGE TO LOOK AGAIN.
WILL STAYED IN THE TREE, SCARCE DARING THE BREATHE, WHILE THE MOON CREPT SLOWLY ACROSS THE BLACK SKY.
FINALLY, HE CLIMBED DOWN.

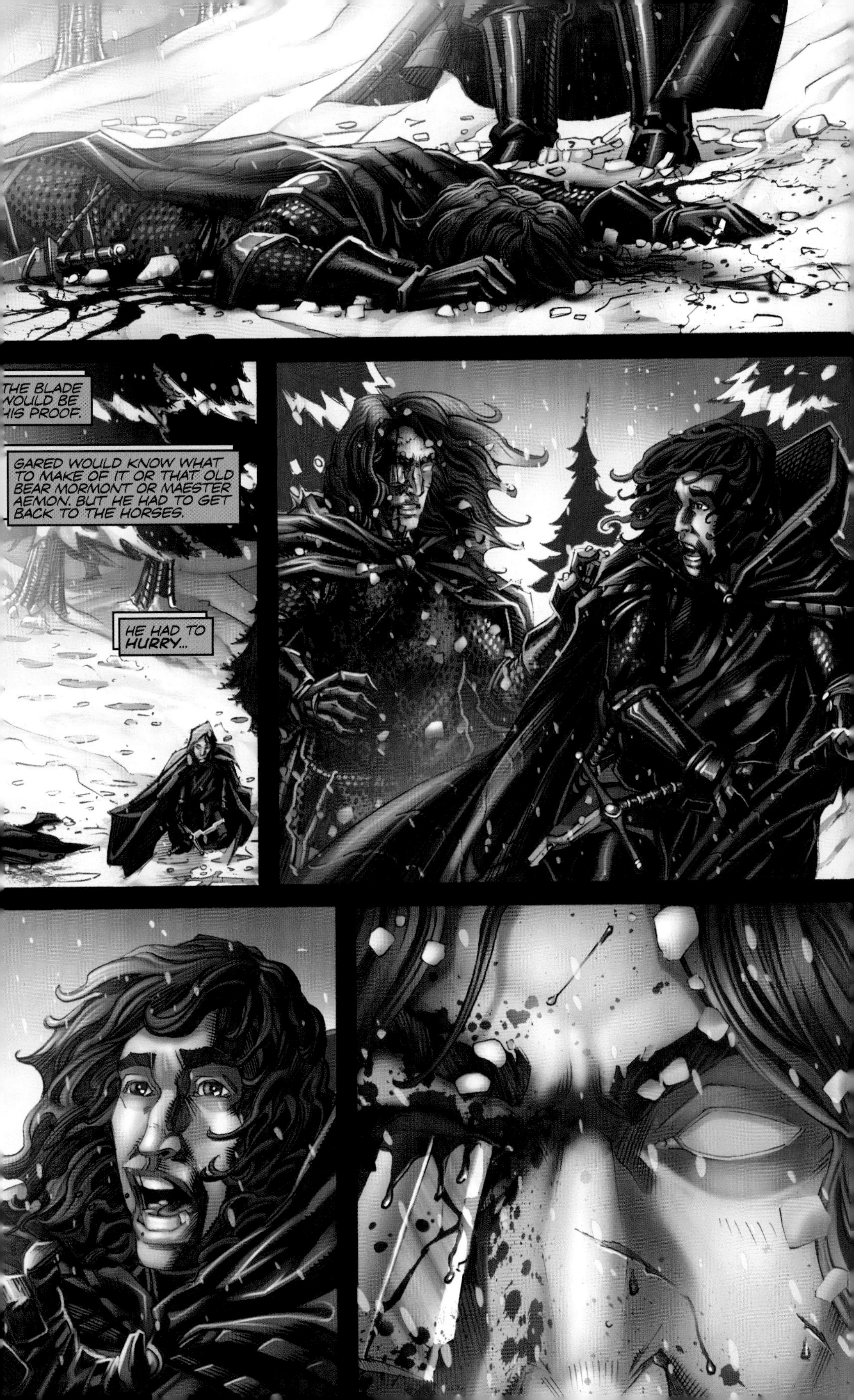

THE BLADE WOULD BE HIS PROOF.
GARED WOULD KNOW WHAT TO MAKE OF IT OR THAT OLD BEAR MORMONT OR MAESTER AEMON. BUT HE HAD TO GET BACK TO THE HORSES.
HE HAD TO HURRY...

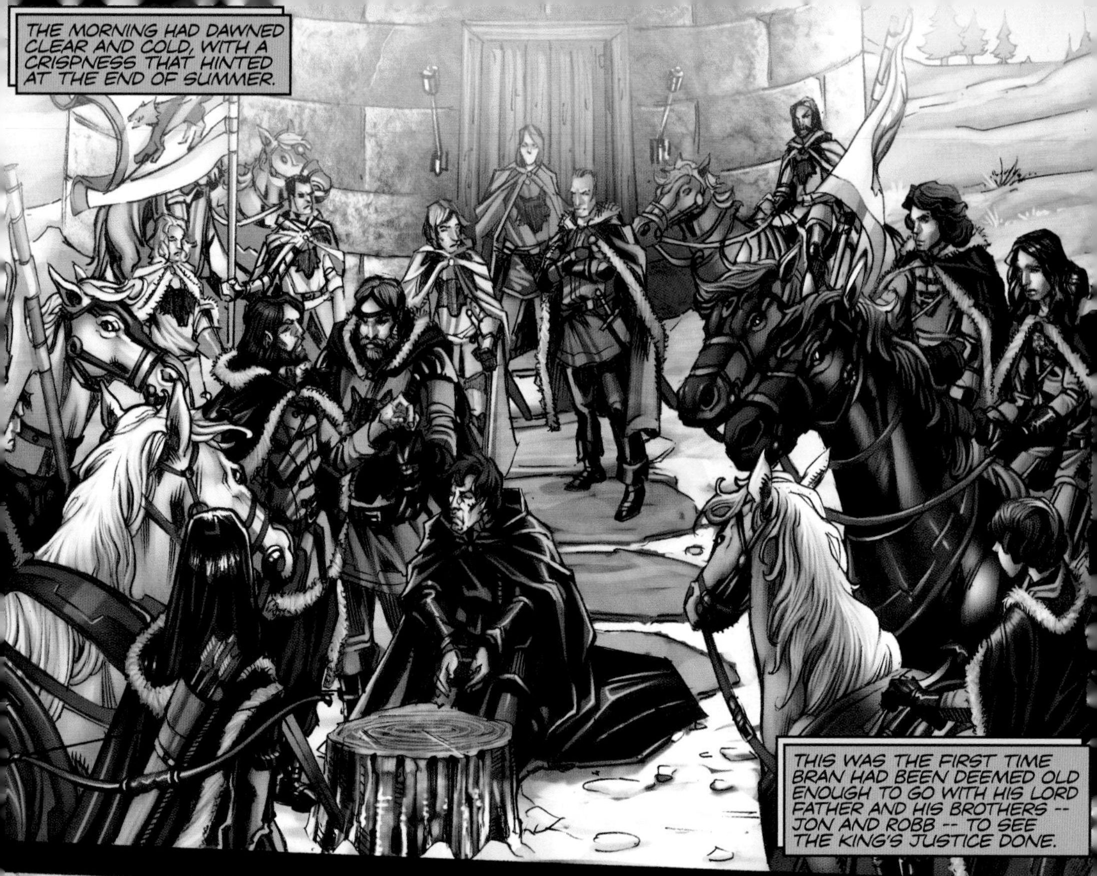
THE MORNING HAD DAWNED CLEAR AND COLD, WITH A CRISPNESS THAT HINTED AT THE END OF SUMMER.
THIS WAS THE FIRST TIME BRAN HAD BEEN DEEMED OLD ENOUGH TO GO WITH HIS LORD FATHER AND HIS BROTHERS -- JON AND ROBB -- TO SEE THE KING'S JUSTICE DONE.

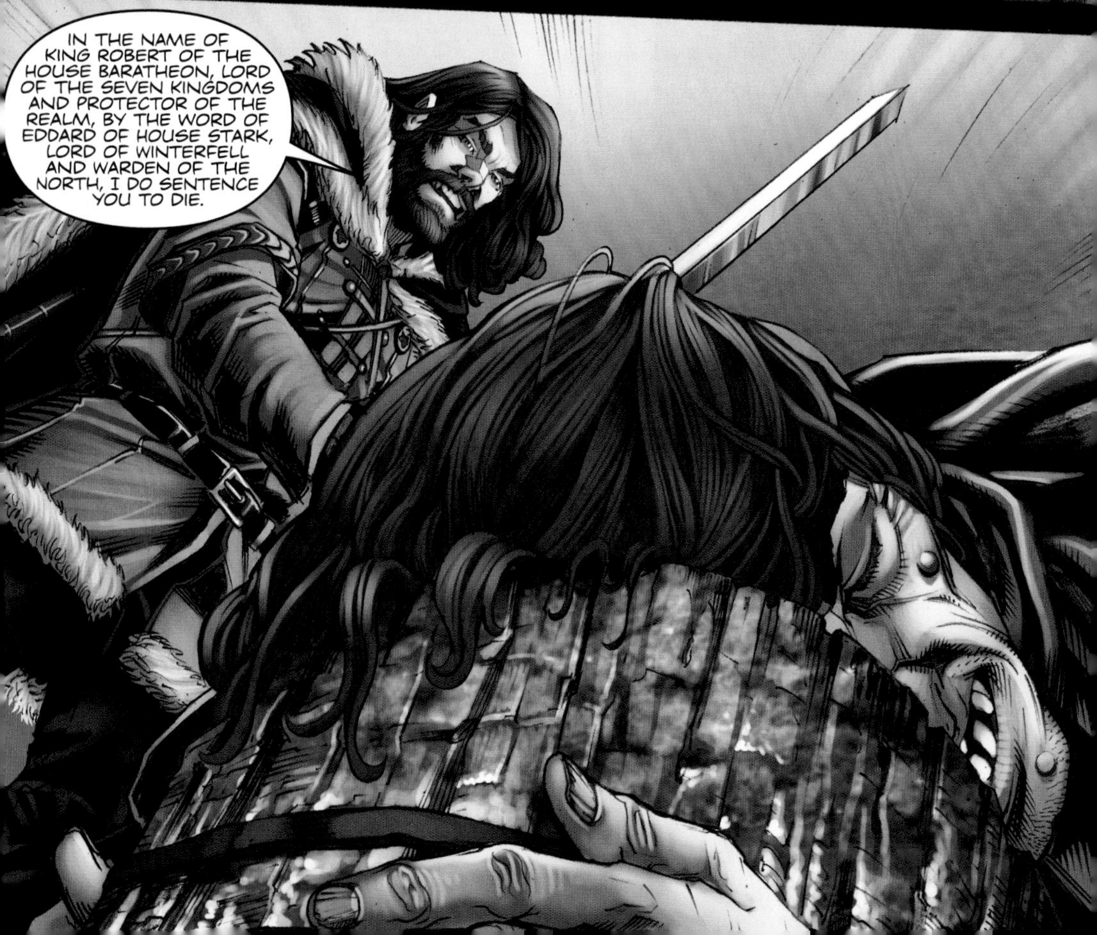
IN THE NAME OF KING ROBERT OF THE HOUSE BARATHEON, LORD OF THE SEVEN KINGDOMS AND PROTECTOR OF THE REALM, BY THE WORD OF EDDARD OF HOUSE STARK, LORD OF WINTERFELL AND WARDEN OF THE NORTH, I DO SENTENCE YOU TO DIE.

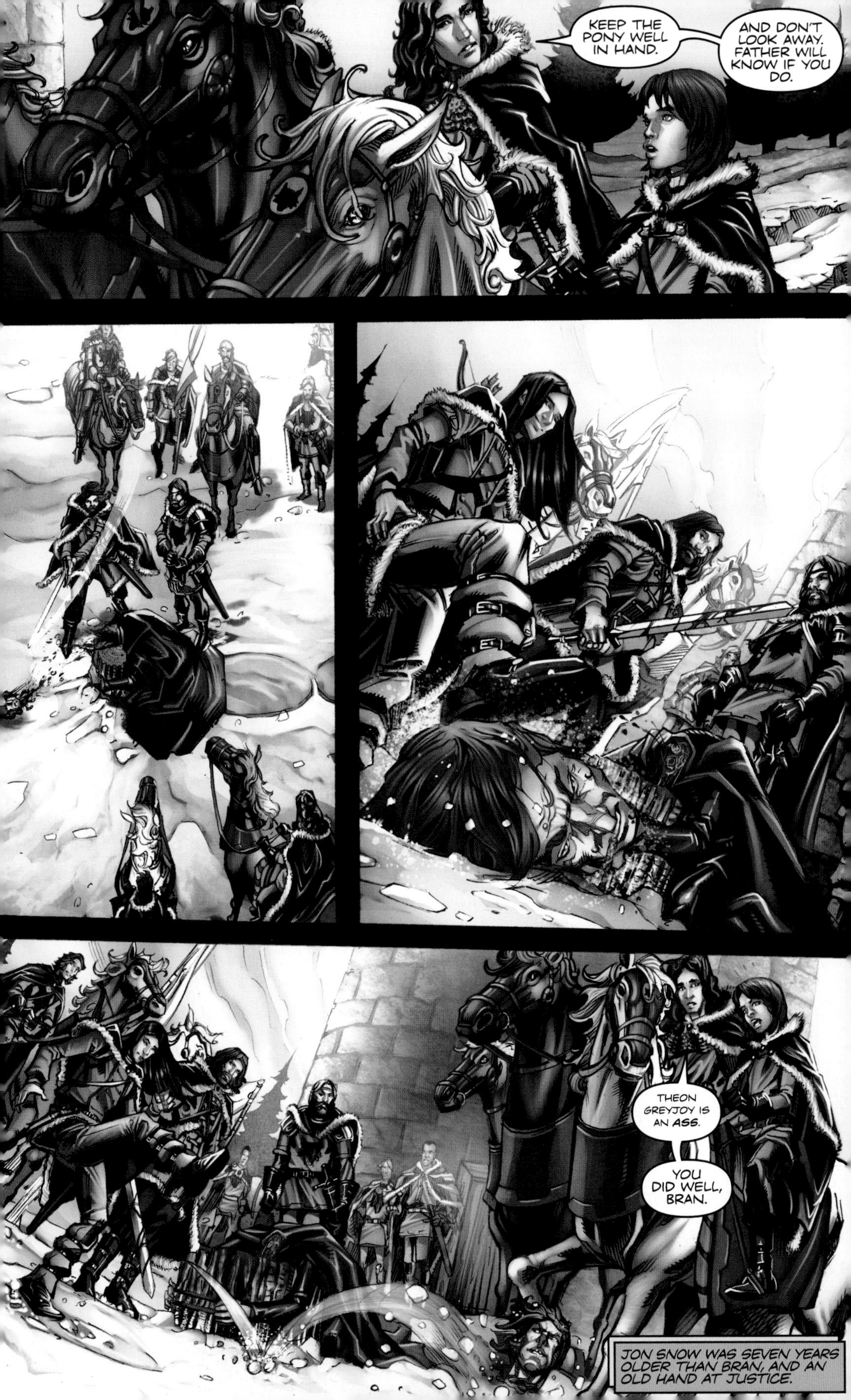
KEEP THE PONY WELL IN HAND.
AND DON'T LOOK AWAY. FATHER WILL KNOW IF YOU DO.
THEON GREYJOY IS AN ASS.
YOU DID WELL, BRAN.
JON SNOW WAS SEVEN YEARS OLDER THAN BRAN, AND AN OLD HAND AT JUSTICE.

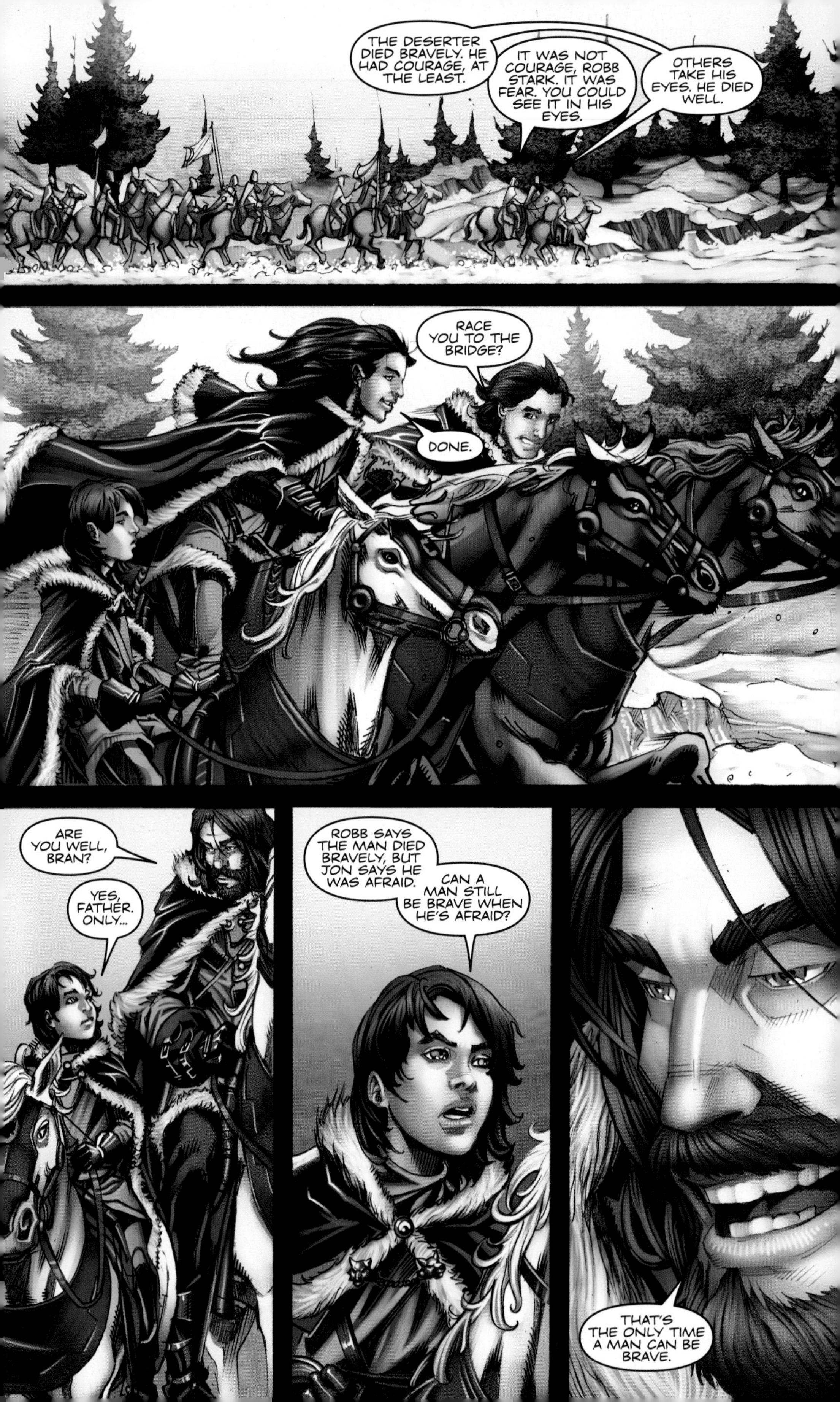
THE DESERTER DIED BRAVELY. HE HAD COURAGE, AT THE LEAST.
IT WAS NOT COURAGE, ROBB STARK. IT WAS FEAR. YOU COULD SEE IT IN HIS EYES.
OTHERS TAKE HIS EYES. HE DIED WELL.
RACE YOU TO THE BRIDGE?
DONE.
ARE YOU WELL, BRAN?
YES, FATHER. ONLY...
ROBB SAYS THE MAN DIED BRAVELY, BUT JON SAYS HE WAS AFRAID.
CAN A MAN STILL BE BRAVE WHEN HE'S AFRAID?
THAT'S THE ONLY TIME A MAN CAN BE BRAVE.

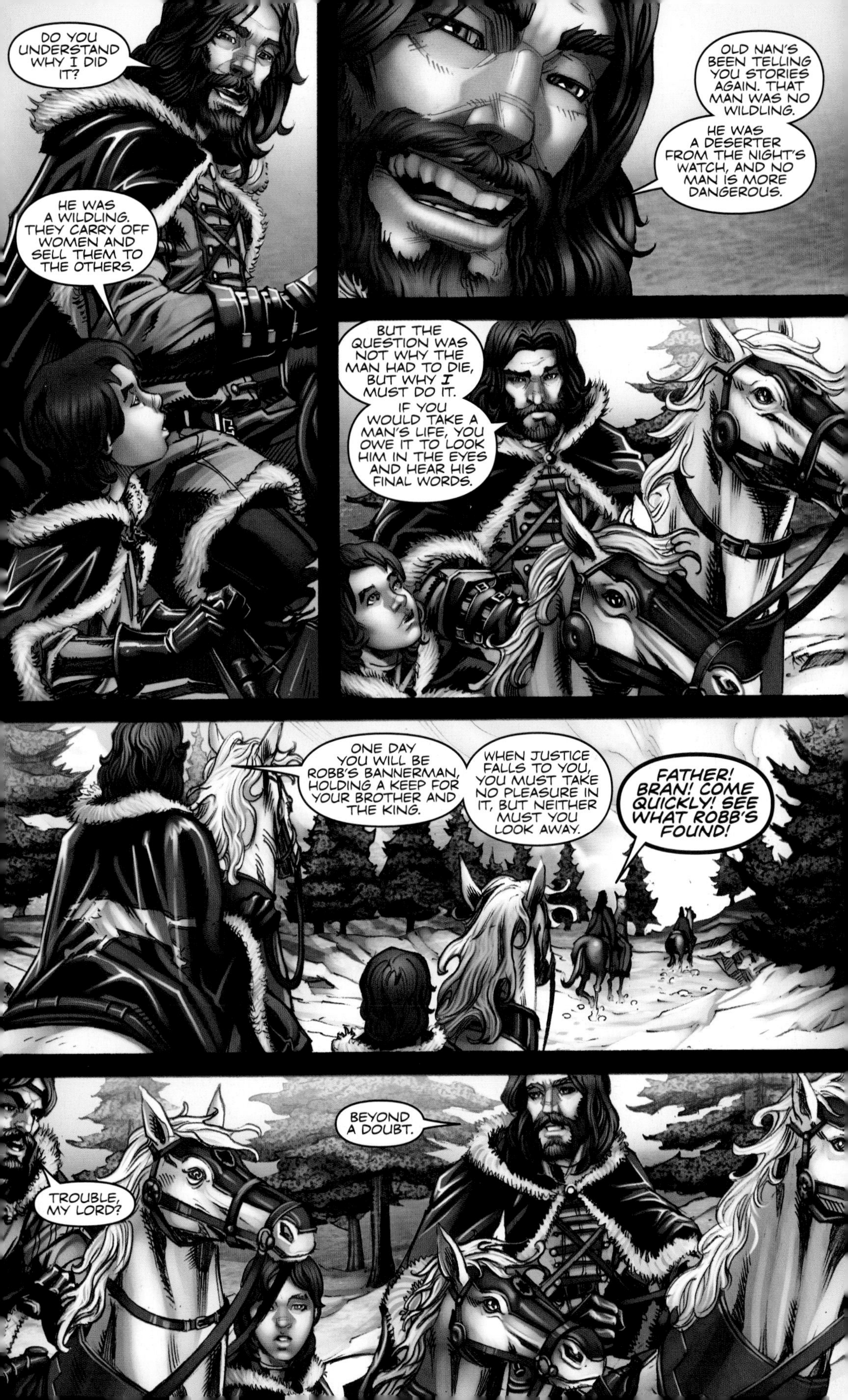

DO YOU UNDERSTAND WHY I DID IT?
HE WAS A WILDLING. THEY CARRY OFF WOMEN AND SELL THEM TO THE OTHERS.
OLD NAN'S BEEN TELLING YOU STORIES AGAIN. THAT MAN WAS NO WILDLING.
HE WAS A DESERTER FROM THE NIGHT'S WATCH, AND NO MAN IS MORE DANGEROUS.
BUT THE QUESTION WAS NOT WHY THE MAN HAD TO DIE, BUT WHY *I* MUST DO IT.
IF YOU WOULD TAKE A MAN'S LIFE, YOU OWE IT TO LOOK HIM IN THE EYES AND HEAR HIS FINAL WORDS.
ONE DAY YOU WILL BE ROBB'S BANNERMAN, HOLDING A KEEP FOR YOUR BROTHER AND THE KING.
WHEN JUSTICE FALLS TO YOU, YOU MUST TAKE NO PLEASURE IN IT, BUT NEITHER MUST YOU LOOK AWAY.
FATHER! BRAN! COME QUICKLY! SEE WHAT ROBB'S FOUND!
TROUBLE, MY LORD?
BEYOND A DOUBT.

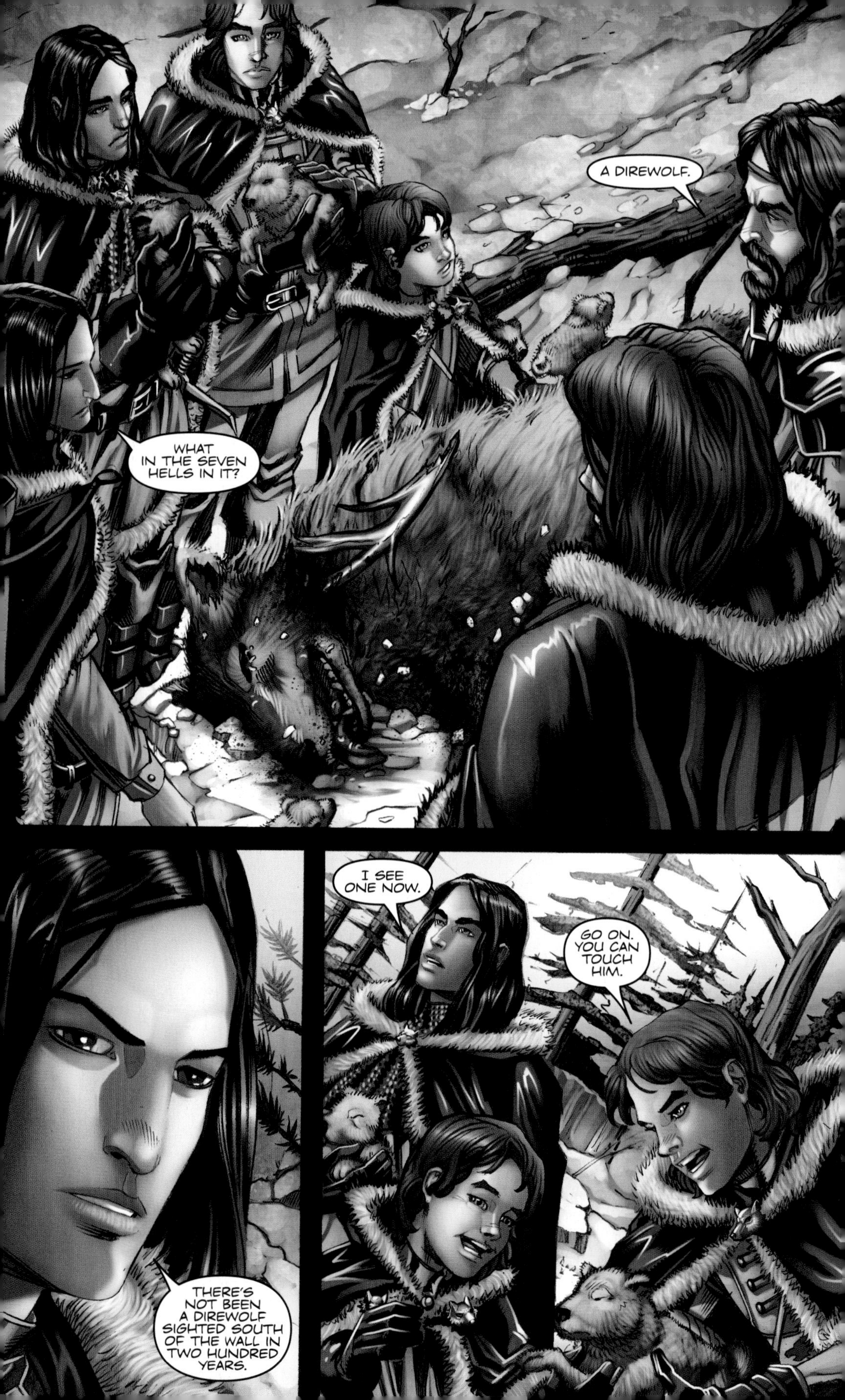
WHAT IN THE SEVEN HELLS IN IT?
A DIREWOLF.
THERE'S NOT BEEN A DIREWOLF SIGHTED SOUTH OF THE WALL IN TWO HUNDRED YEARS.
I SEE ONE NOW.
GO ON. YOU CAN TOUCH HIM.

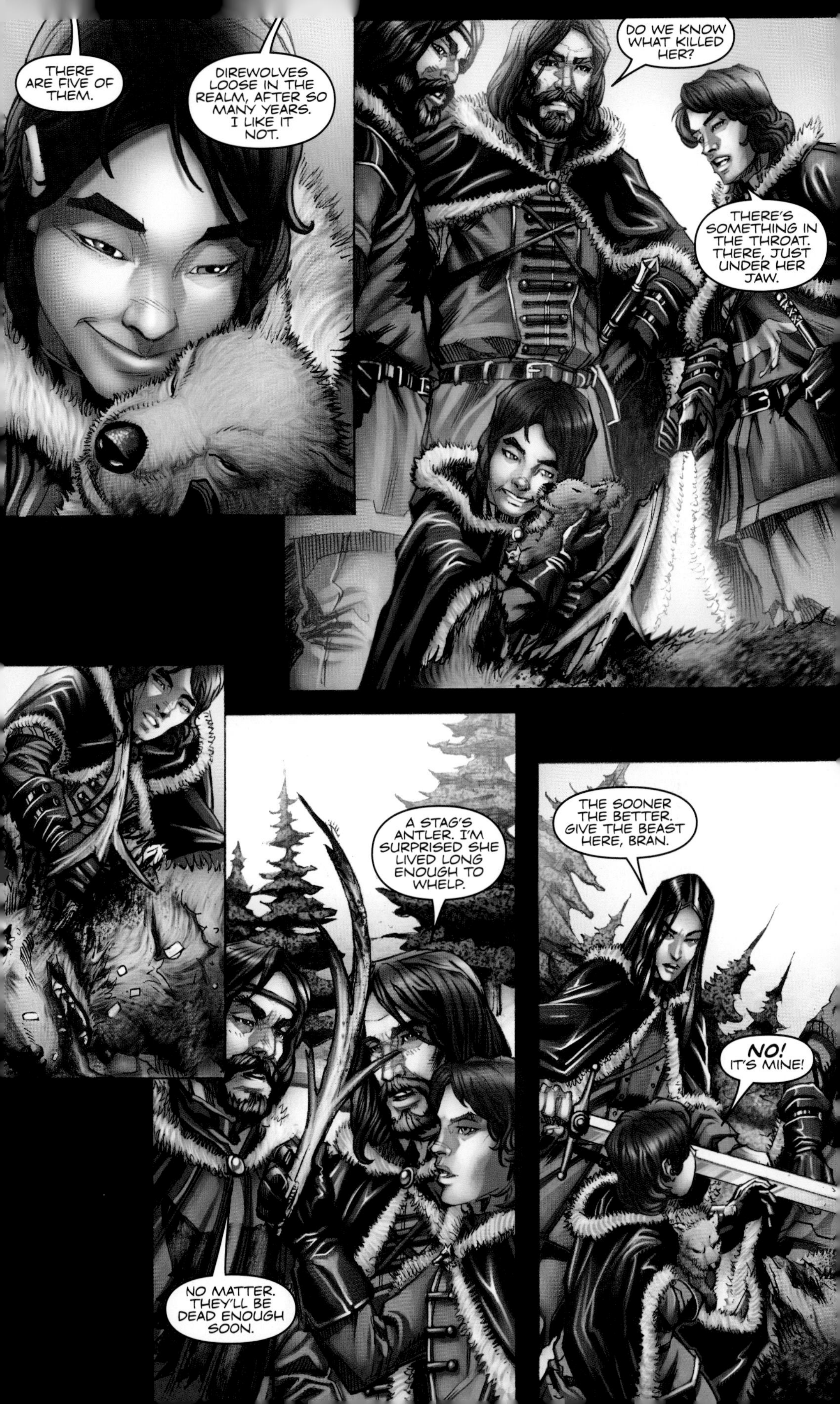
THERE ARE FIVE OF THEM.
DIREWOLVES LOOSE IN THE REALM, AFTER SO MANY YEARS. I LIKE IT NOT.
DO WE KNOW WHAT KILLED HER?
THERE'S SOMETHING IN THE THROAT. THERE, JUST UNDER HER JAW.
A STAG'S ANTLER. I'M SURPRISED SHE LIVED LONG ENOUGH TO WHELP.
NO MATTER. THEY'LL BE DEAD ENOUGH SOON.
THE SOONER THE BETTER. GIVE THE BEAST HERE, BRAN.
NO! IT'S MINE!

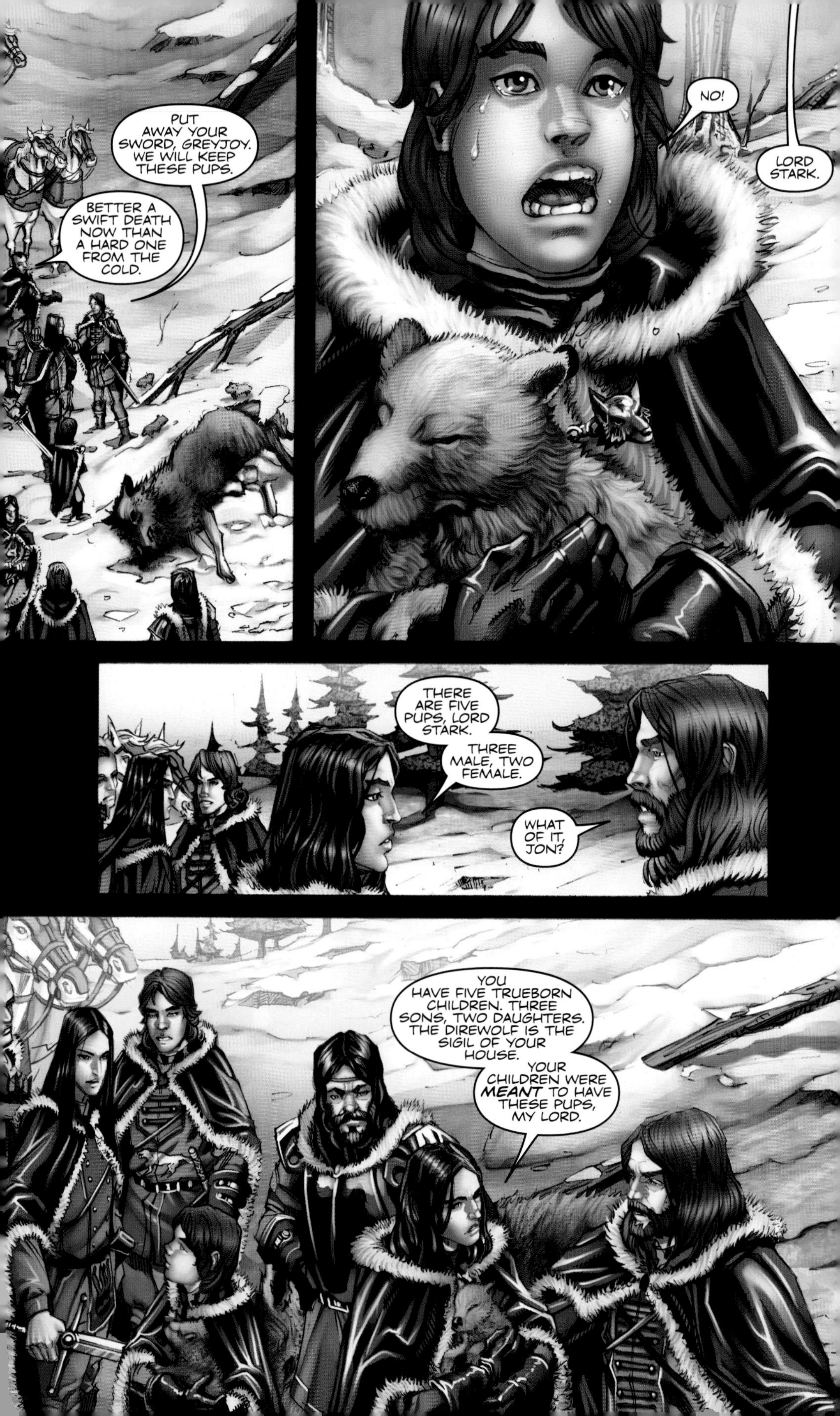
PUT AWAY YOUR SWORD, GREYJOY. WE WILL KEEP THESE PUPS.
BETTER A SWIFT DEATH NOW THAN A HARD ONE FROM THE COLD.
NO!
LORD STARK.
THERE ARE FIVE PUPS, LORD STARK.
THREE MALE, TWO FEMALE.
WHAT OF IT, JON?
YOU HAVE FIVE TRUEBORN CHILDREN. THREE SONS, TWO DAUGHTERS. THE DIREWOLF IS THE SIGIL OF YOUR HOUSE.
YOUR CHILDREN WERE *MEANT* TO HAVE THESE PUPS, MY LORD.

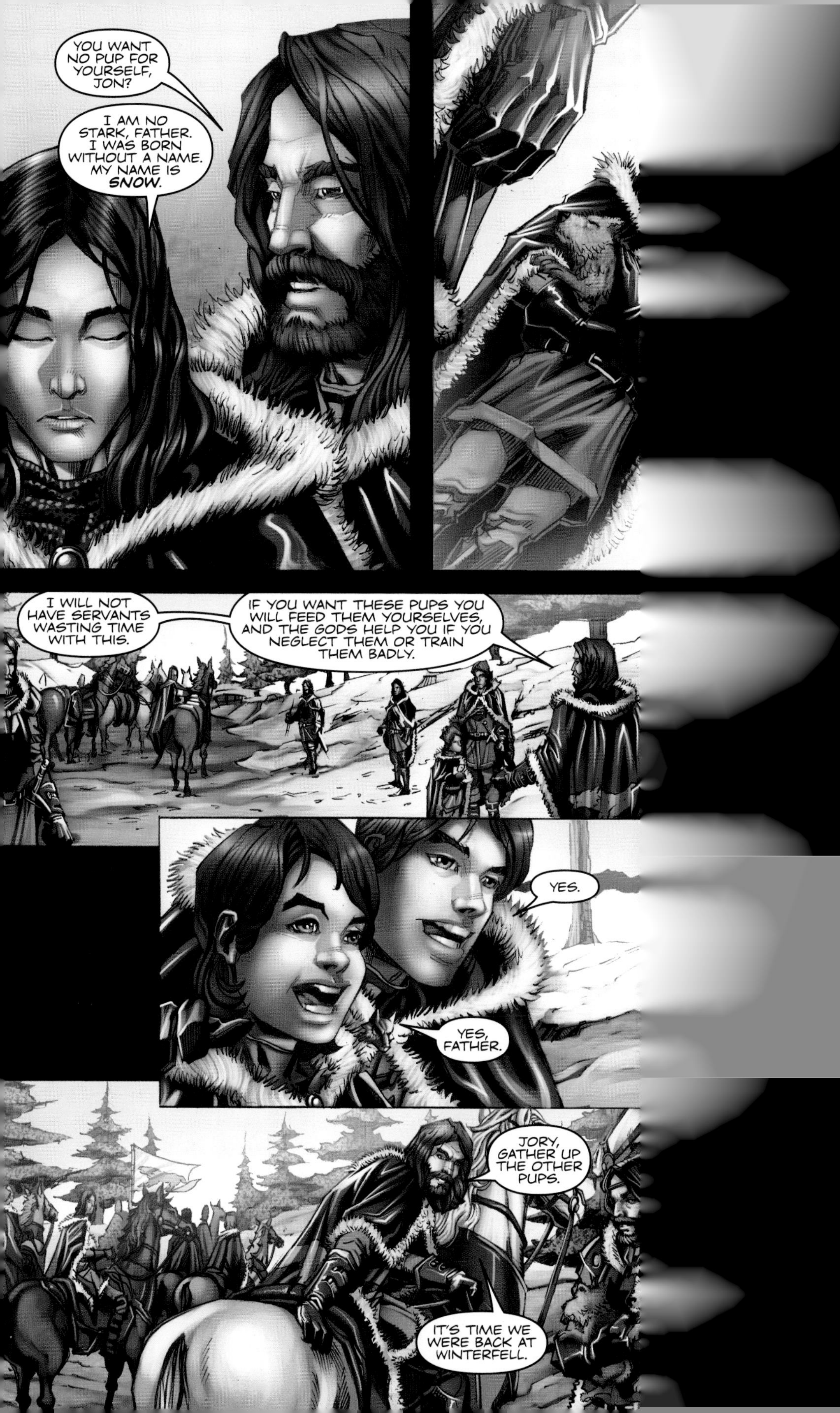
YOU WANT NO PUP FOR YOURSELF, JON?
I AM NO STARK, FATHER. I WAS BORN WITHOUT A NAME. MY NAME IS SNOW.
I WILL NOT HAVE SERVANTS WASTING TIME WITH THIS.
IF YOU WANT THESE PUPS YOU WILL FEED THEM YOURSELVES, AND THE GODS HELP YOU IF YOU NEGLECT THEM OR TRAIN THEM BADLY.
YES.
YES, FATHER.
JORY, GATHER UP THE OTHER PUPS.
IT'S TIME WE WERE BACK AT WINTERFELL.

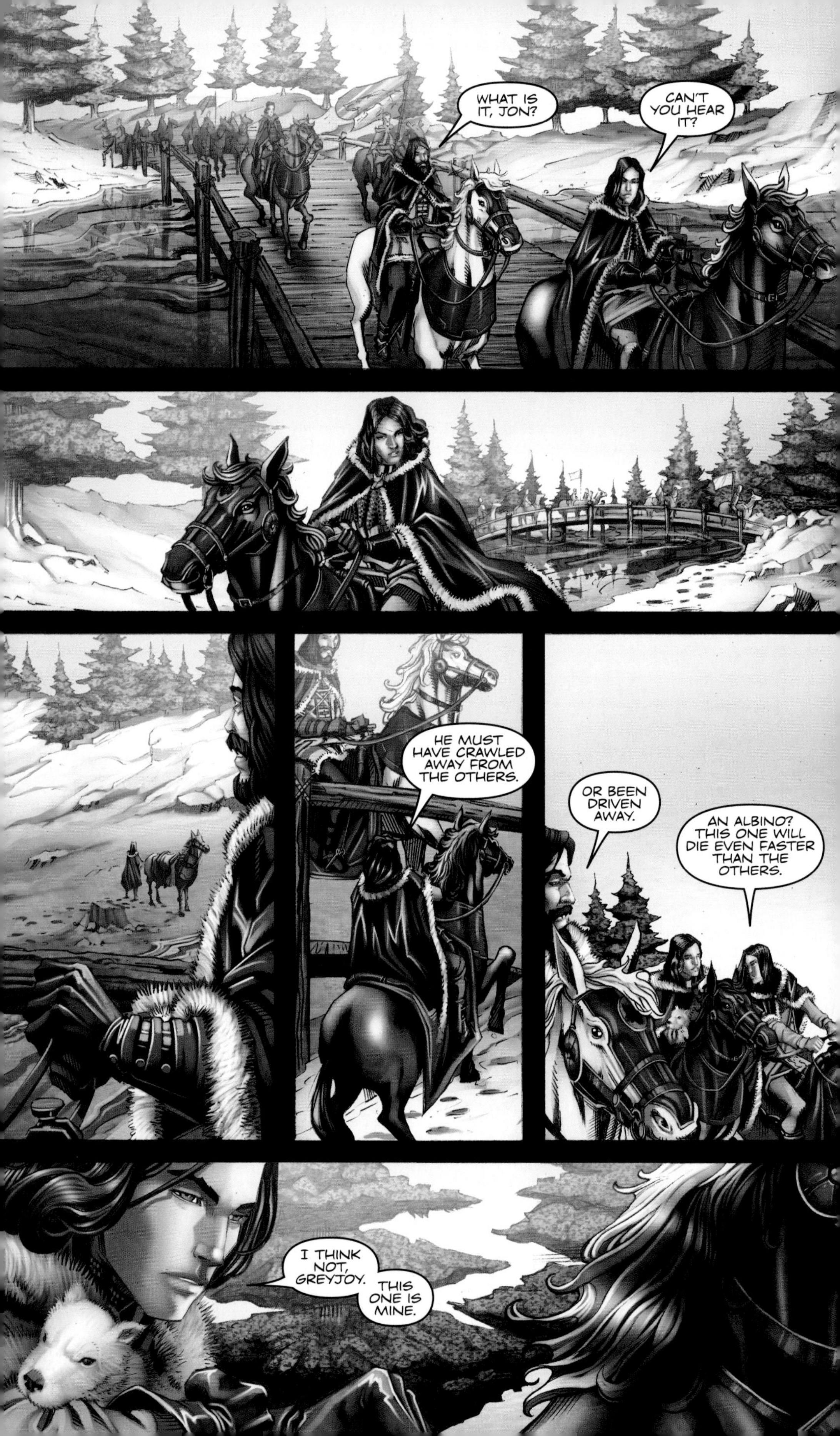
WHAT IS IT, JON?
CAN'T YOU HEAR IT?
HE MUST HAVE CRAWLED AWAY FROM THE OTHERS.
OR BEEN DRIVEN AWAY.
AN ALBINO? THIS ONE WILL DIE EVEN FASTER THAN THE OTHERS.
I THINK NOT, GREYJOY.
THIS ONE IS MINE.

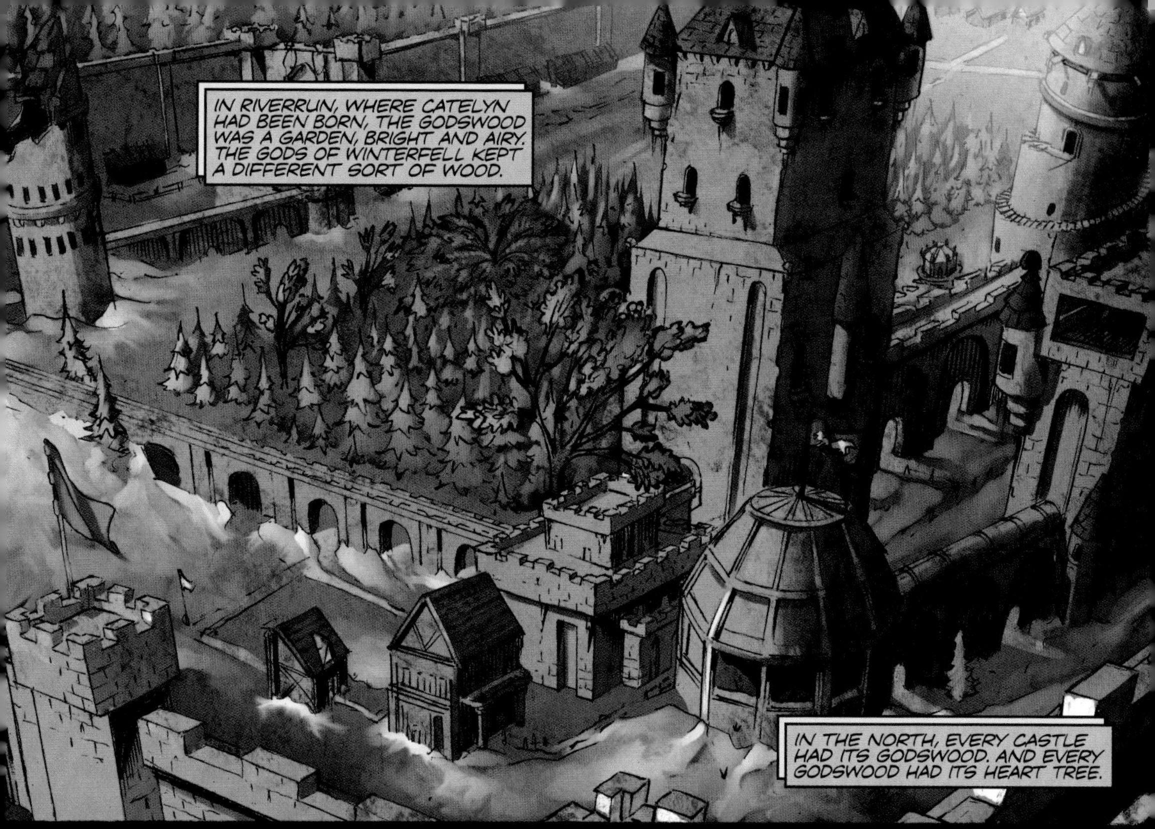
IN RIVERRUN, WHERE CATELYN HAD BEEN BORN, THE GODSWOOD WAS A GARDEN, BRIGHT AND AIRY. THE GODS OF WINTERFELL KEPT A DIFFERENT SORT OF WOOD.
IN THE NORTH, EVERY CASTLE HAD ITS GODSWOOD. AND EVERY GODSWOOD HAD ITS HEART TREE.

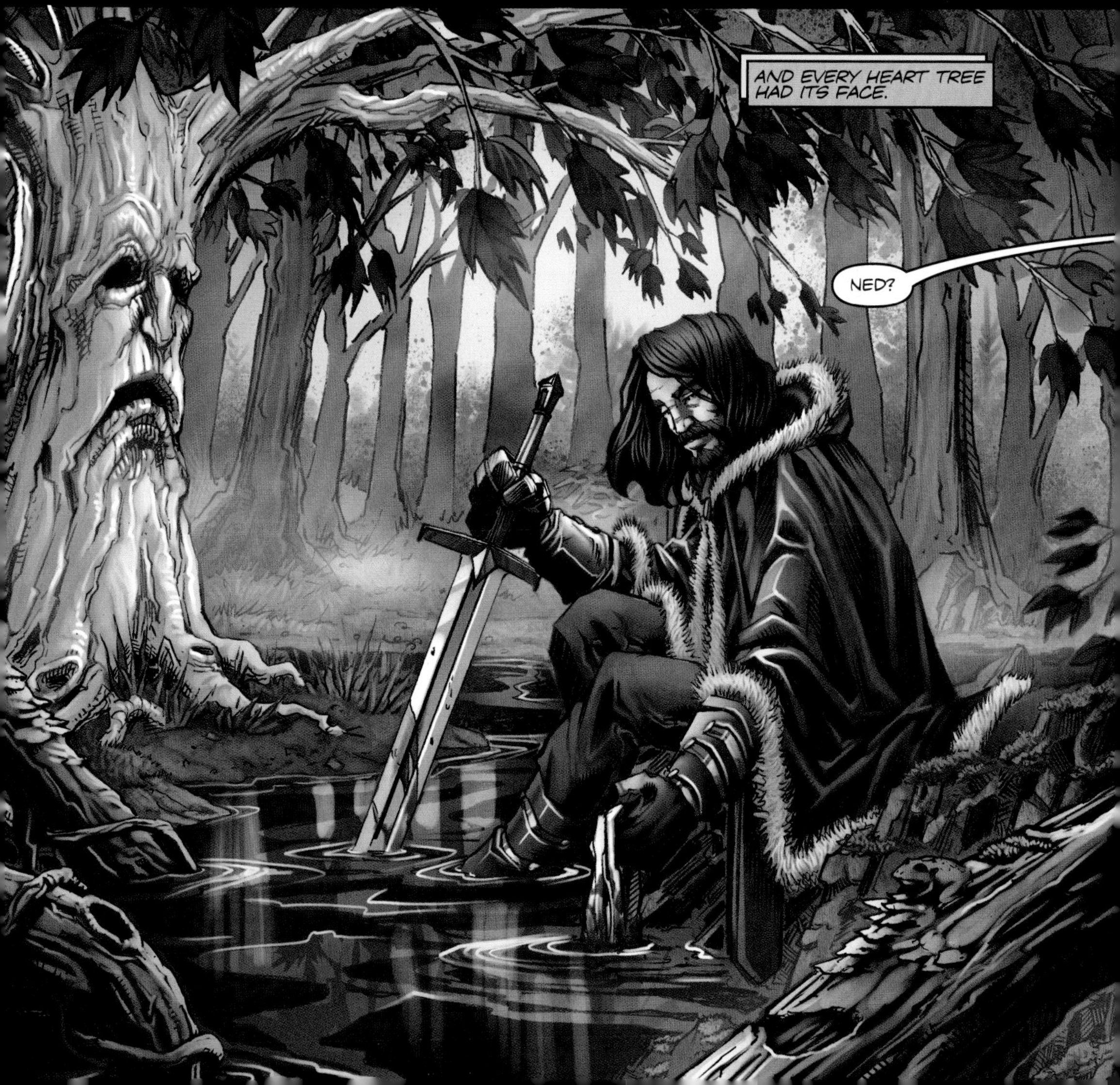
AND EVERY HEART TREE HAD ITS FACE.
NED?

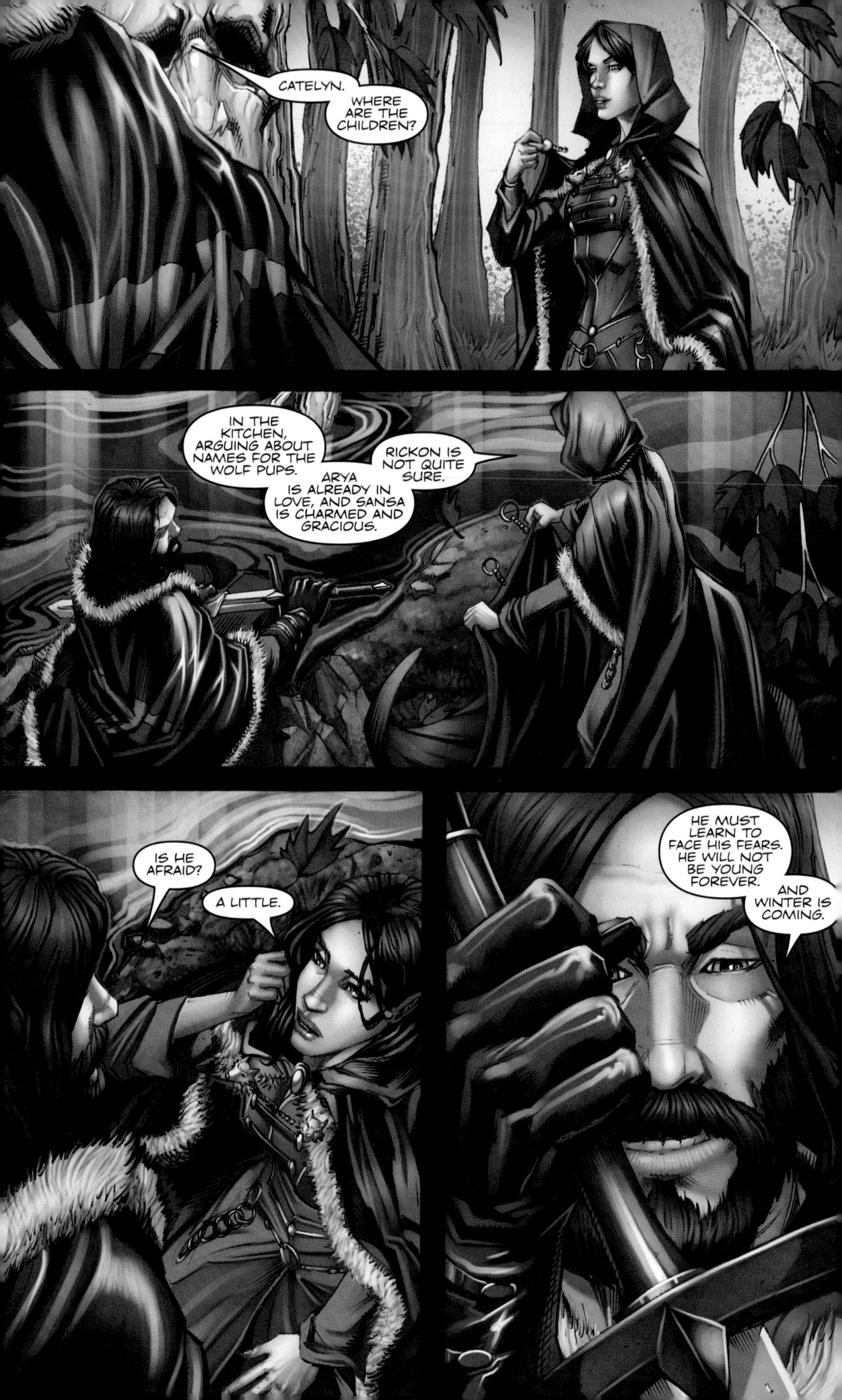
CATELYN.
WHERE ARE THE CHILDREN?
IN THE KITCHEN, ARGUING ABOUT NAMES FOR THE WOLF PUPS.
RICKON IS NOT QUITE SURE.
ARYA IS ALREADY IN LOVE, AND SANSA IS CHARMED AND GRACIOUS.
IS HE AFRAID?
A LITTLE.
HE MUST LEARN TO FACE HIS FEARS. HE WILL NOT BE YOUNG FOREVER.
AND WINTER IS COMING.

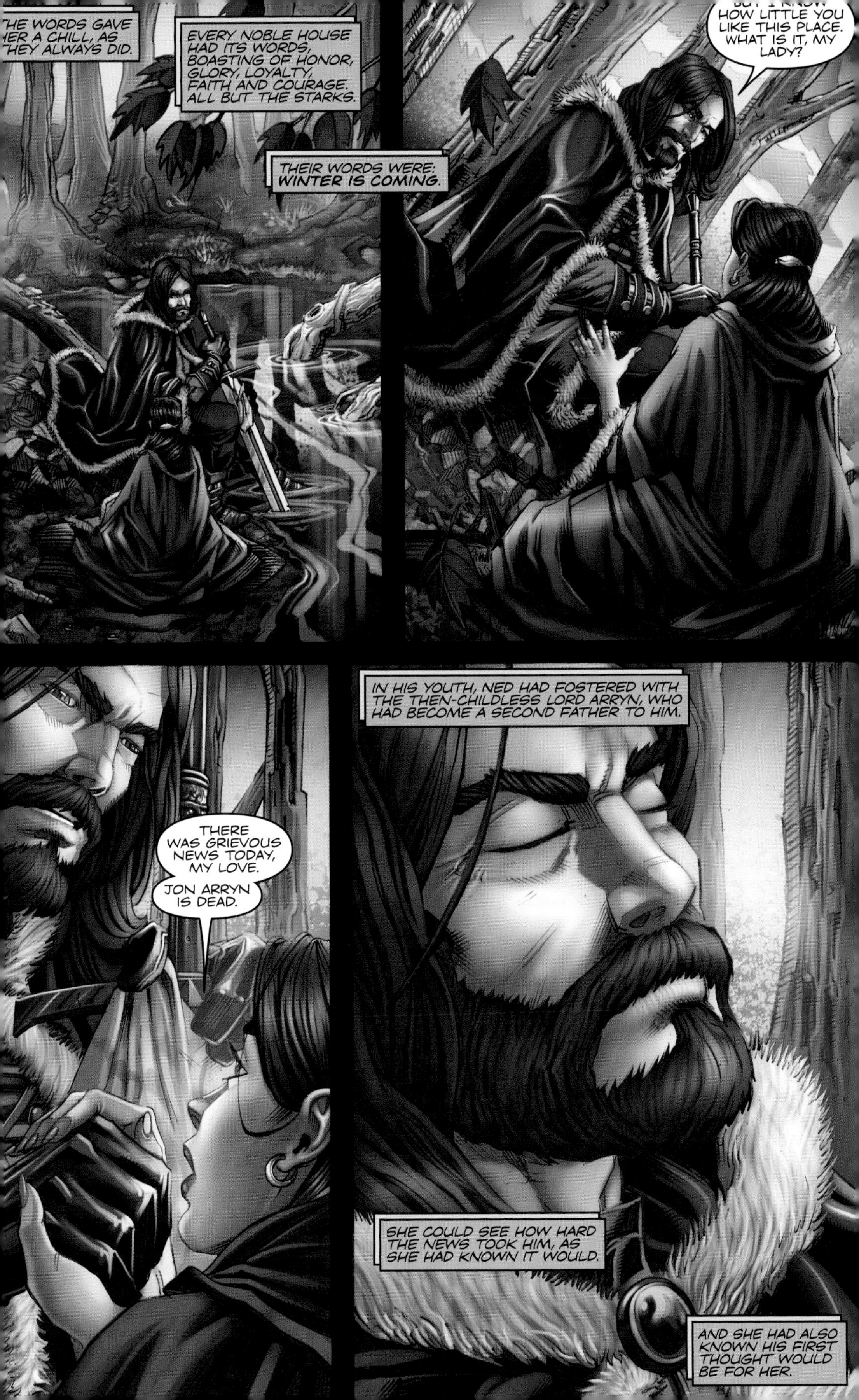
THE WORDS GAVE HER A CHILL, AS THEY ALWAYS DID.
EVERY NOBLE HOUSE HAD ITS WORDS, BOASTING OF HONOR, GLORY, LOYALTY, FAITH AND COURAGE. ALL BUT THE STARKS.
THEIR WORDS WERE: **WINTER IS COMING.**
HOW LITTLE YOU LIKE THIS PLACE. WHAT IS IT, MY LADY?
THERE WAS GRIEVOUS NEWS TODAY, MY LOVE.
JON ARRYN IS DEAD.
IN HIS YOUTH, NED HAD FOSTERED WITH THE THEN-CHILDLESS LORD ARRYN, WHO HAD BECOME A SECOND FATHER TO HIM.
SHE COULD SEE HOW HARD THE NEWS TOOK HIM, AS SHE HAD KNOWN IT WOULD.
AND SHE HAD ALSO KNOWN HIS FIRST THOUGHT WOULD BE FOR HER.

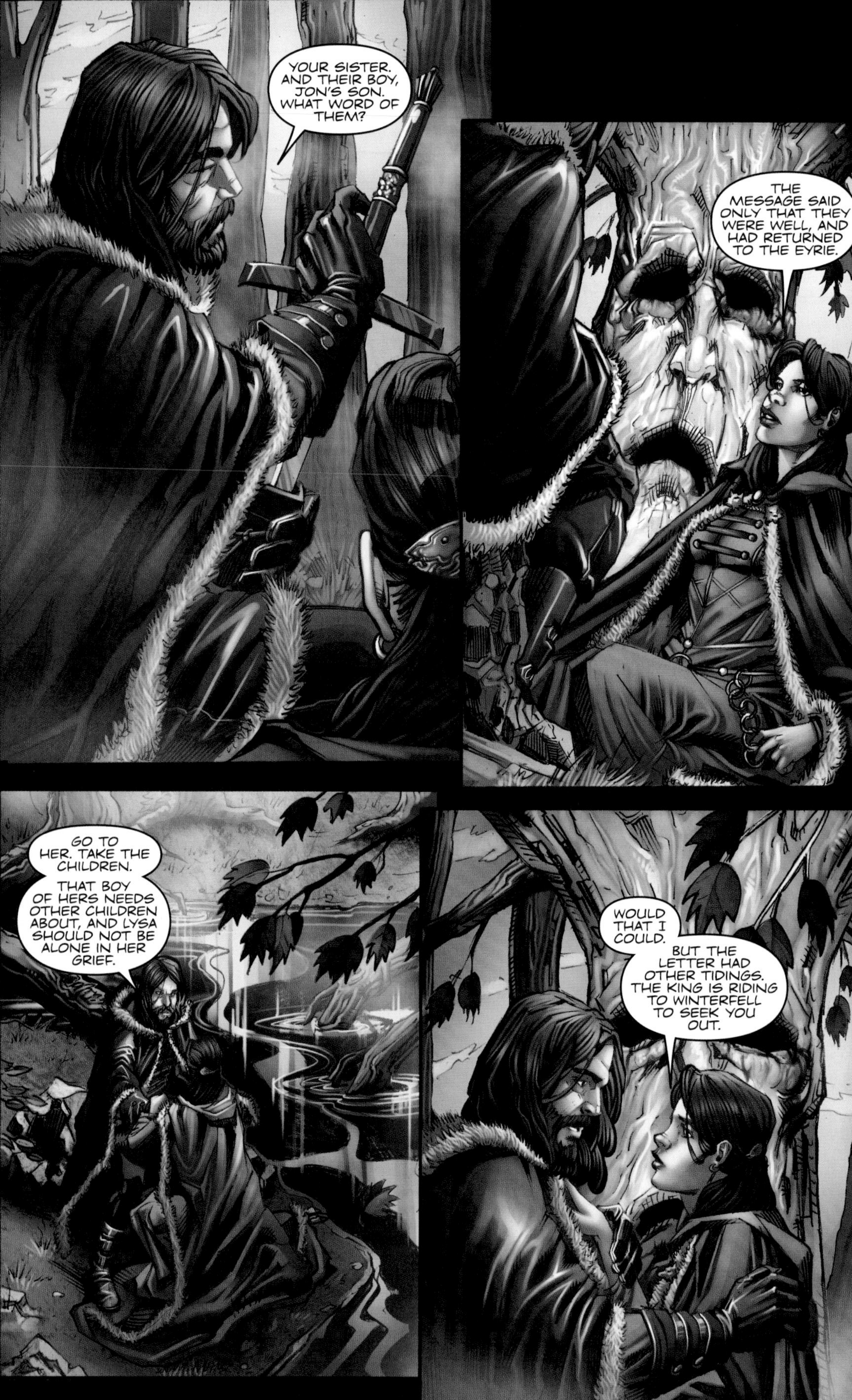
YOUR SISTER. AND THEIR BOY, JON'S SON. WHAT WORD OF THEM?
THE MESSAGE SAID ONLY THAT THEY WERE WELL, AND HAD RETURNED TO THE EYRIE.
GO TO HER. TAKE THE CHILDREN.
THAT BOY OF HERS NEEDS OTHER CHILDREN ABOUT, AND LYSA SHOULD NOT BE ALONE IN HER GRIEF.
WOULD THAT I COULD.
BUT THE LETTER HAD OTHER TIDINGS. THE KING IS RIDING TO WINTERFELL TO SEEK YOU OUT.

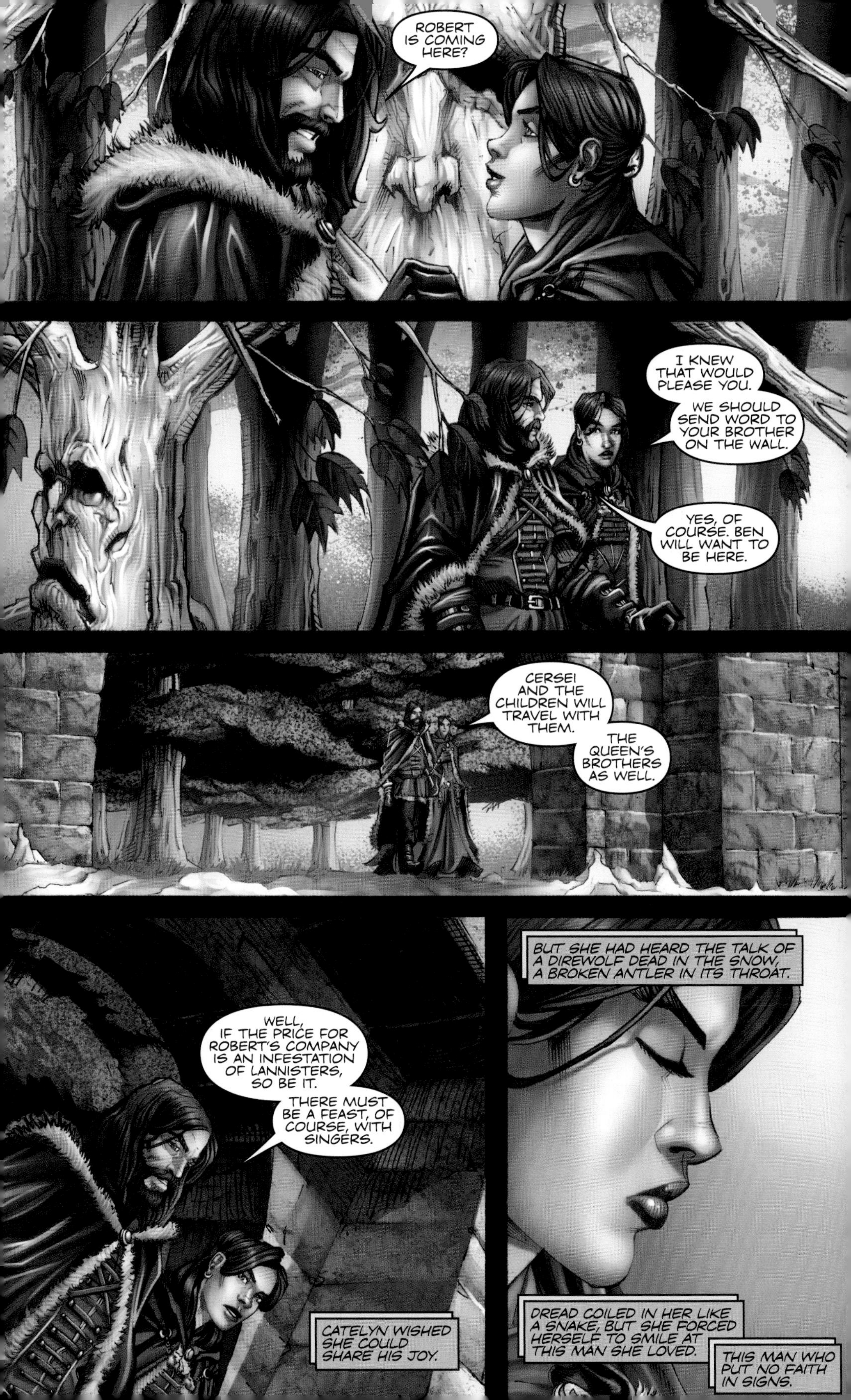
ROBERT IS COMING HERE?
I KNEW THAT WOULD PLEASE YOU.
WE SHOULD SEND WORD TO YOUR BROTHER ON THE WALL.
YES, OF COURSE. BEN WILL WANT TO BE HERE.
CERSEI AND THE CHILDREN WILL TRAVEL WITH THEM.
THE QUEEN'S BROTHERS AS WELL.
WELL, IF THE PRICE FOR ROBERT'S COMPANY IS AN INFESTATION OF LANNISTERS, SO BE IT.
THERE MUST BE A FEAST, OF COURSE, WITH SINGERS.
CATELYN WISHED SHE COULD SHARE HIS JOY.
BUT SHE HAD HEARD THE TALK OF A DIREWOLF DEAD IN THE SNOW, A BROKEN ANTLER IN ITS THROAT.
DREAD COILED IN HER LIKE A SNAKE, BUT SHE FORCED HERSELF TO SMILE AT THIS MAN SHE LOVED.
THIS MAN WHO PUT NO FAITH IN SIGNS.

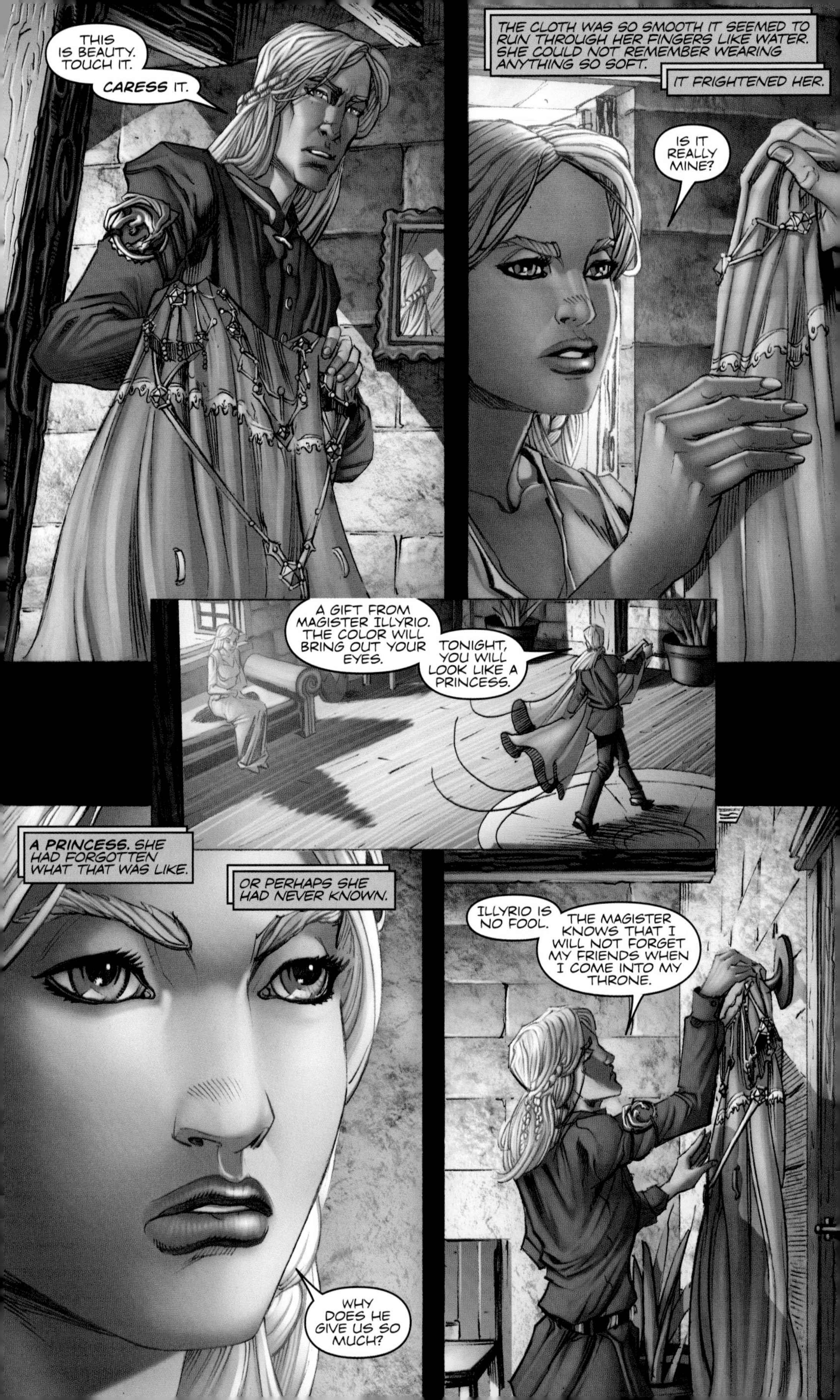
THIS IS BEAUTY. TOUCH IT.
CARESS IT.
THE CLOTH WAS SO SMOOTH IT SEEMED TO RUN THROUGH HER FINGERS LIKE WATER. SHE COULD NOT REMEMBER WEARING ANYTHING SO SOFT.
IT FRIGHTENED HER.
IS IT REALLY MINE?
A GIFT FROM MAGISTER ILLYRIO. THE COLOR WILL BRING OUT YOUR EYES.
TONIGHT, YOU WILL LOOK LIKE A PRINCESS.
A PRINCESS. SHE HAD FORGOTTEN WHAT THAT WAS LIKE.
OR PERHAPS SHE HAD NEVER KNOWN.
WHY DOES HE GIVE US SO MUCH?
ILLYRIO IS NO FOOL.
THE MAGISTER KNOWS THAT I WILL NOT FORGET MY FRIENDS WHEN I COME INTO MY THRONE.

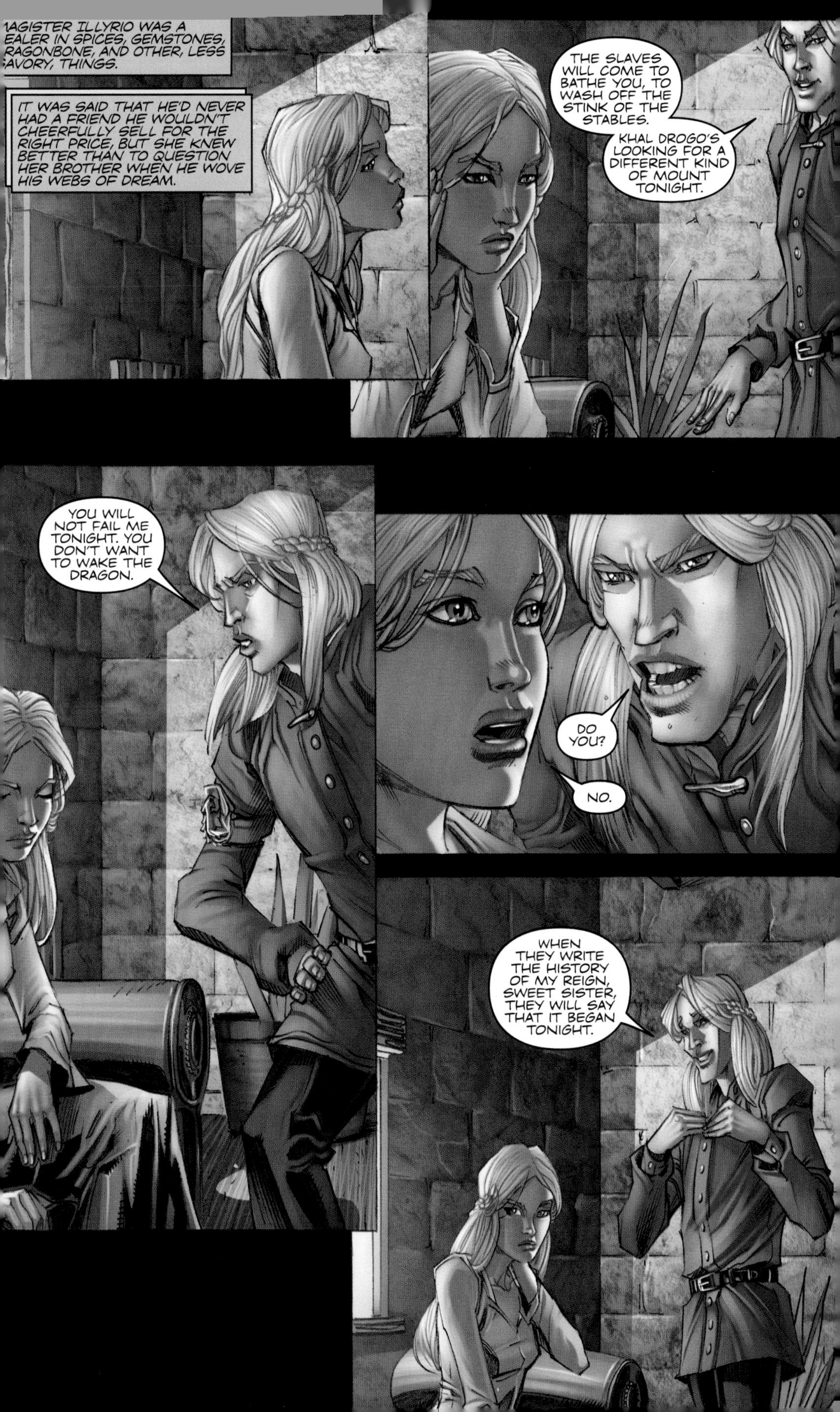

MAGISTER ILLYRIO WAS A DEALER IN SPICES, GEMSTONES, DRAGONBONE, AND OTHER, LESS SAVORY, THINGS.
IT WAS SAID THAT HE'D NEVER HAD A FRIEND HE WOULDN'T CHEERFULLY SELL FOR THE RIGHT PRICE, BUT SHE KNEW BETTER THAN TO QUESTION HER BROTHER WHEN HE WOVE HIS WEBS OF DREAM.
THE SLAVES WILL COME TO BATHE YOU, TO WASH OFF THE STINK OF THE STABLES.
KHAL DROGO'S LOOKING FOR A DIFFERENT KIND OF MOUNT TONIGHT.
YOU WILL NOT FAIL ME TONIGHT. YOU DON'T WANT TO WAKE THE DRAGON.
DO YOU?
NO.
WHEN THEY WRITE THE HISTORY OF MY REIGN, SWEET SISTER, THEY WILL SAY THAT IT BEGAN TONIGHT.

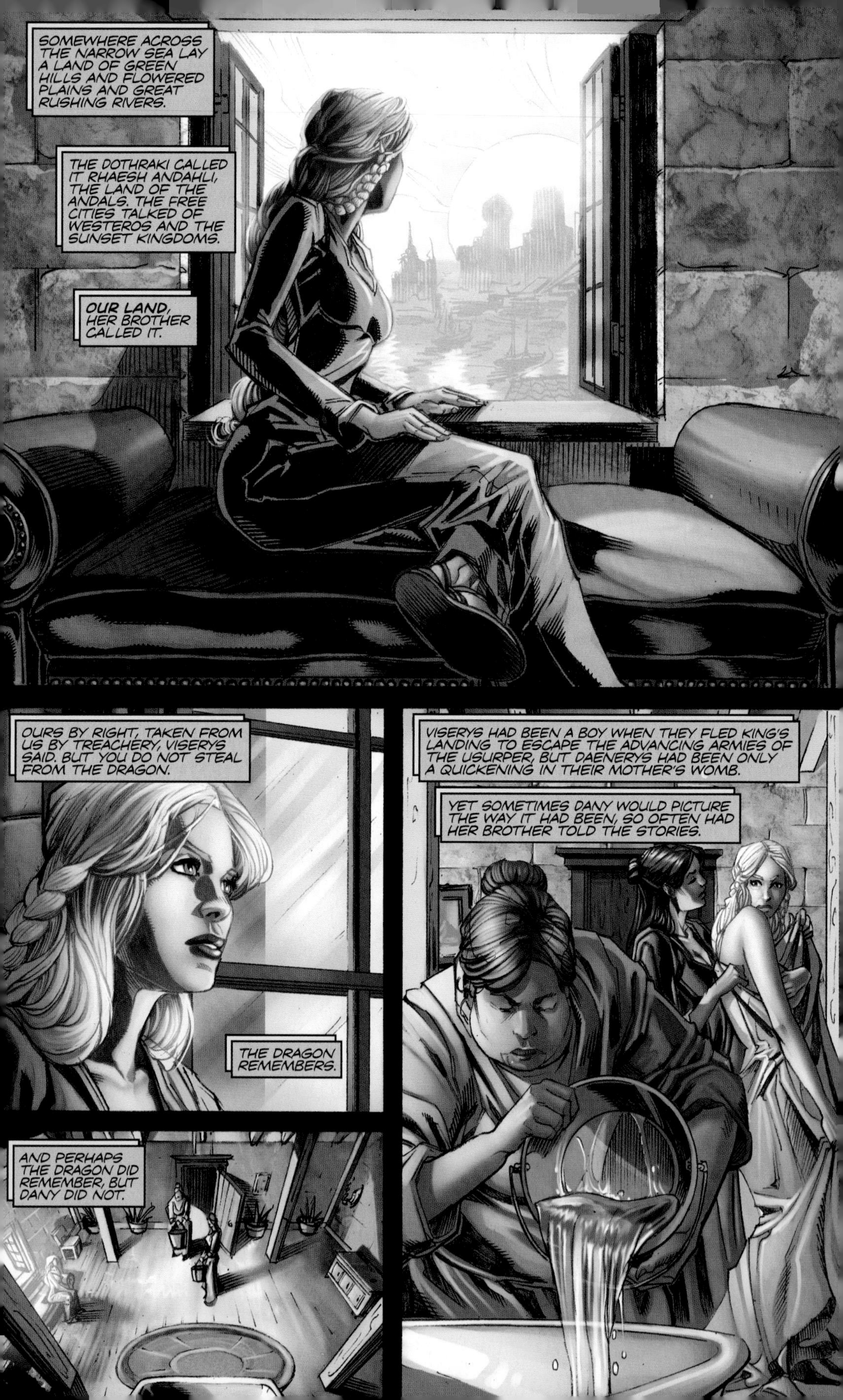
SOMEWHERE ACROSS THE NARROW SEA LAY A LAND OF GREEN HILLS AND FLOWERED PLAINS AND GREAT RUSHING RIVERS.
THE DOTHRAKI CALLED IT RHAESH ANDAHLI, THE LAND OF THE ANDALS. THE FREE CITIES TALKED OF WESTEROS AND THE SUNSET KINGDOMS.
OUR LAND, HER BROTHER CALLED IT.
OURS BY RIGHT, TAKEN FROM US BY TREACHERY, VISERYS SAID. BUT YOU DO NOT STEAL FROM THE DRAGON.
THE DRAGON REMEMBERS.
AND PERHAPS THE DRAGON DID REMEMBER, BUT DANY DID NOT.
VISERYS HAD BEEN A BOY WHEN THEY FLED KING'S LANDING TO ESCAPE THE ADVANCING ARMIES OF THE USURPER, BUT DAENERYS HAD BEEN ONLY A QUICKENING IN THEIR MOTHER'S WOMB.
YET SOMETIMES DANY WOULD PICTURE THE WAY IT HAD BEEN, SO OFTEN HAD HER BROTHER TOLD THE STORIES.

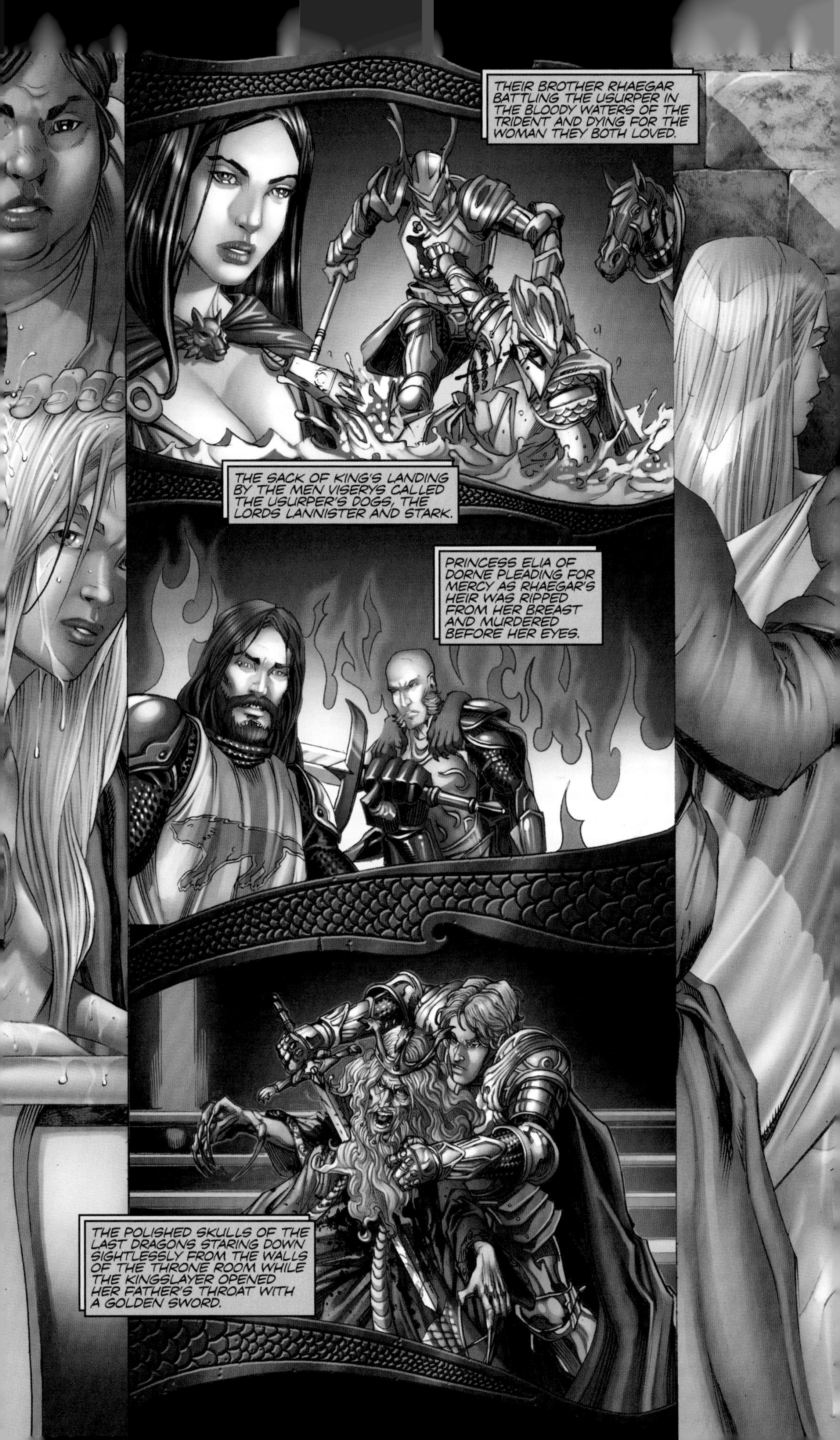
THEIR BROTHER RHAEGAR BATTLING THE USURPER IN THE BLOODY WATERS OF THE TRIDENT AND DYING FOR THE WOMAN THEY BOTH LOVED.
THE SACK OF KING'S LANDING BY THE MEN VISERYS CALLED THE USURPER'S DOGS, THE LORDS LANNISTER AND STARK.
PRINCESS ELIA OF DORNE PLEADING FOR MERCY AS RHAEGAR'S HEIR WAS RIPPED FROM HER BREAST AND MURDERED BEFORE HER EYES.
THE POLISHED SKULLS OF THE LAST DRAGONS STARING DOWN SIGHTLESSLY FROM THE WALLS OF THE THRONE ROOM WHILE THE KINGSLAYER OPENED HER FATHER'S THROAT WITH A GOLDEN SWORD.

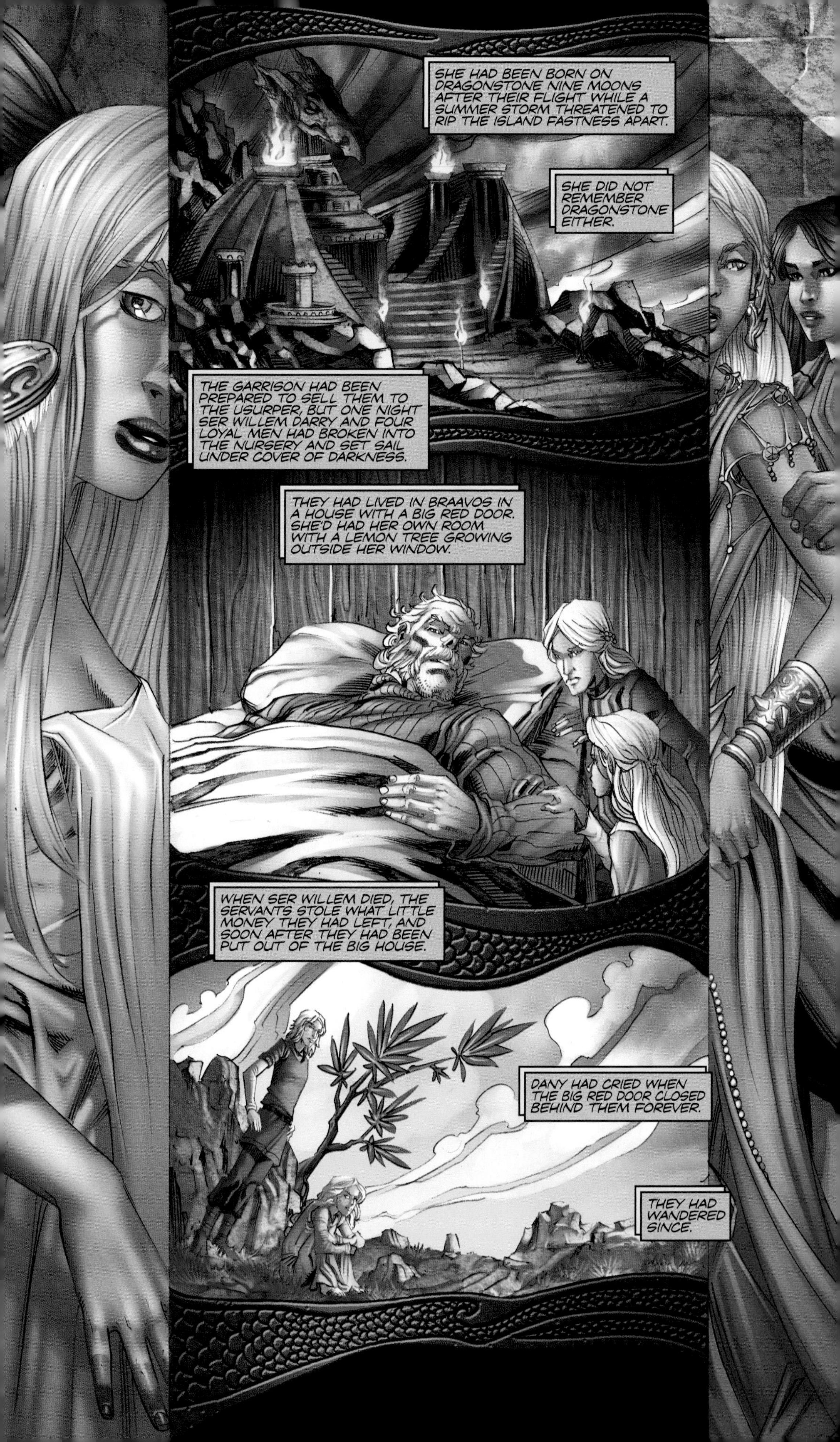
SHE HAD BEEN BORN ON DRAGONSTONE NINE MOONS AFTER THEIR FLIGHT WHILE A SUMMER STORM THREATENED TO RIP THE ISLAND FASTNESS APART.
SHE DID NOT REMEMBER DRAGONSTONE EITHER.
THE GARRISON HAD BEEN PREPARED TO SELL THEM TO THE USURPER, BUT ONE NIGHT SER WILLEM DARRY AND FOUR LOYAL MEN HAD BROKEN INTO THE NURSERY AND SET SAIL UNDER COVER OF DARKNESS.
THEY HAD LIVED IN BRAAVOS IN A HOUSE WITH A BIG RED DOOR. SHE'D HAD HER OWN ROOM WITH A LEMON TREE GROWING OUTSIDE HER WINDOW.
WHEN SER WILLEM DIED, THE SERVANTS STOLE WHAT LITTLE MONEY THEY HAD LEFT, AND SOON AFTER THEY HAD BEEN PUT OUT OF THE BIG HOUSE.
DANY HAD CRIED WHEN THE BIG RED DOOR CLOSED BEHIND THEM FOREVER.
THEY HAD WANDERED SINCE.

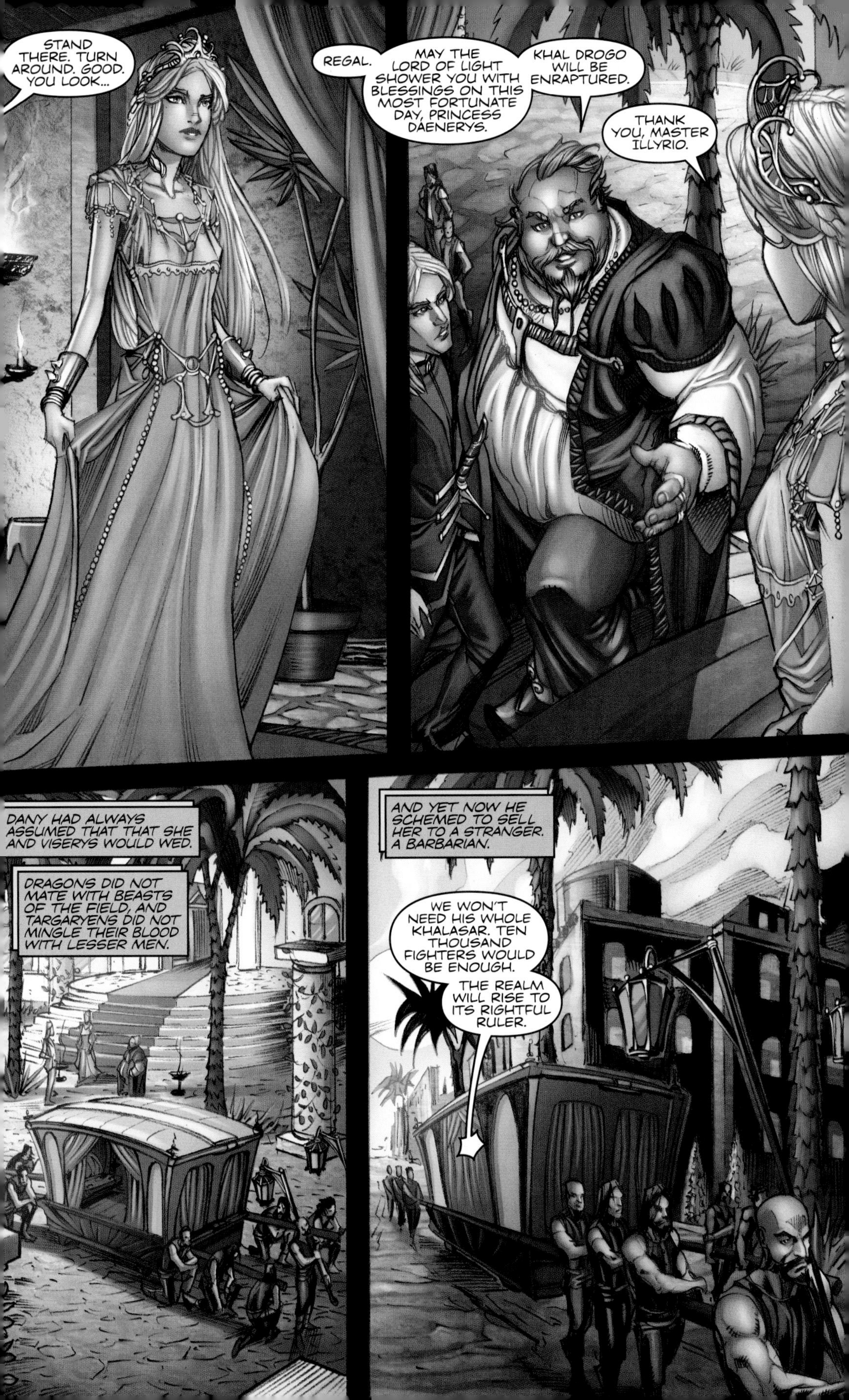
STAND THERE. TURN AROUND. GOOD. YOU LOOK...
REGAL.
MAY THE LORD OF LIGHT SHOWER YOU WITH BLESSINGS ON THIS MOST FORTUNATE DAY, PRINCESS DAENERYS.
KHAL DROGO WILL BE ENRAPTURED.
THANK YOU, MASTER ILLYRIO.
DANY HAD ALWAYS ASSUMED THAT THAT SHE AND VISERYS WOULD WED.
DRAGONS DID NOT MATE WITH BEASTS OF THE FIELD, AND TARGARYENS DID NOT MINGLE THEIR BLOOD WITH LESSER MEN.
AND YET NOW HE SCHEMED TO SELL HER TO A STRANGER. A BARBARIAN.
WE WON'T NEED HIS WHOLE KHALASAR. TEN THOUSAND FIGHTERS WOULD BE ENOUGH.
THE REALM WILL RISE TO ITS RIGHTFUL RULER.

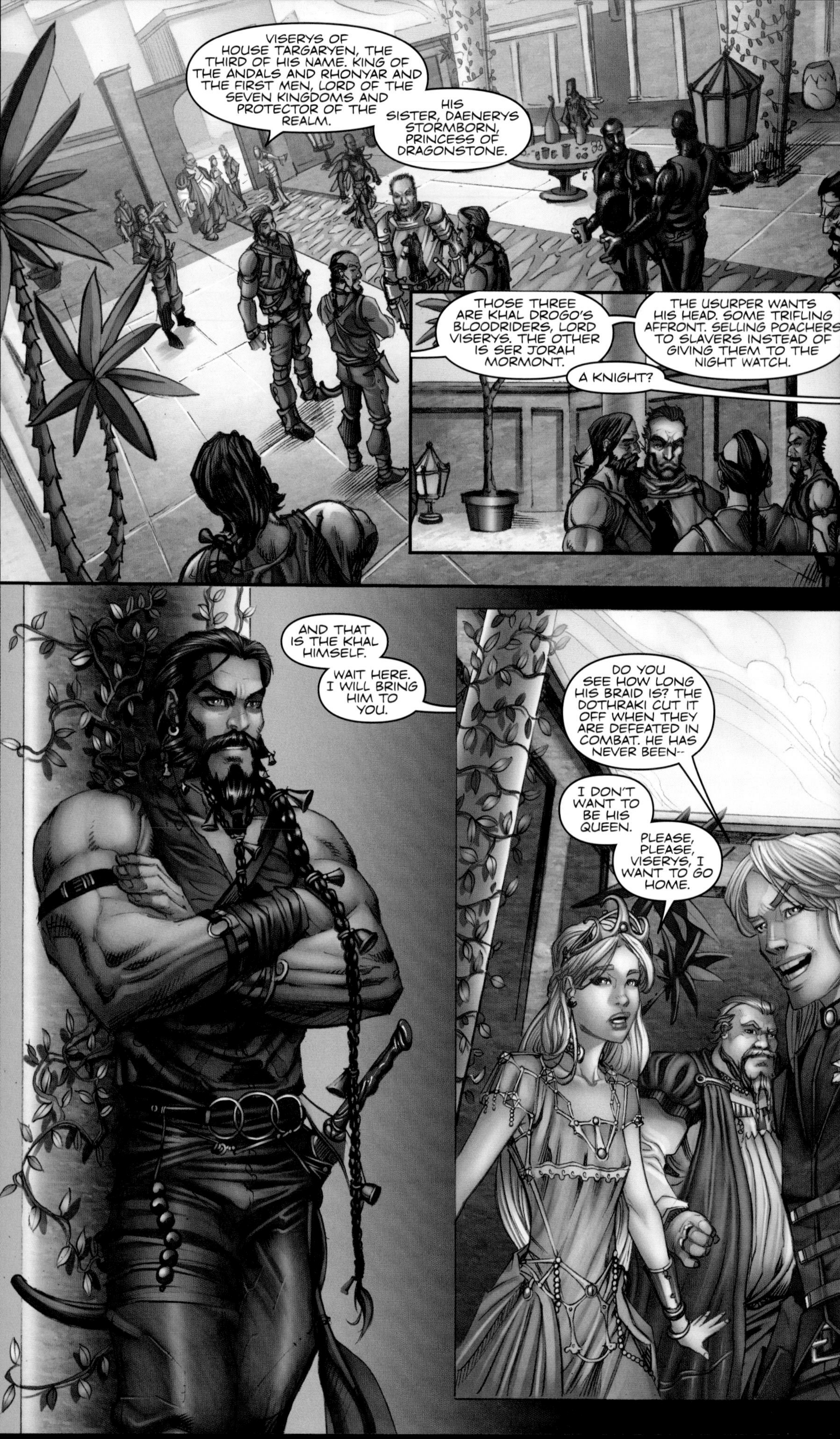
VISERYS OF HOUSE TARGARYEN, THE THIRD OF HIS NAME. KING OF THE ANDALS AND RHONYAR AND THE FIRST MEN, LORD OF THE SEVEN KINGDOMS AND PROTECTOR OF THE REALM.
HIS SISTER, DAENERYS STORMBORN, PRINCESS OF DRAGONSTONE.
THOSE THREE ARE KHAL DROGO'S BLOODRIDERS, LORD VISERYS. THE OTHER IS SER JORAH MORMONT.
THE USURPER WANTS HIS HEAD. SOME TRIFLING AFFRONT. SELLING POACHERS TO SLAVERS INSTEAD OF GIVING THEM TO THE NIGHT WATCH.
A KNIGHT?
AND THAT IS THE KHAL HIMSELF.
WAIT HERE. I WILL BRING HIM TO YOU.
DO YOU SEE HOW LONG HIS BRAID IS? THE DOTHRAKI CUT IT OFF WHEN THEY ARE DEFEATED IN COMBAT. HE HAS NEVER BEEN--
I DON'T WANT TO BE HIS QUEEN.
PLEASE, PLEASE, VISERYS, I WANT TO GO HOME.

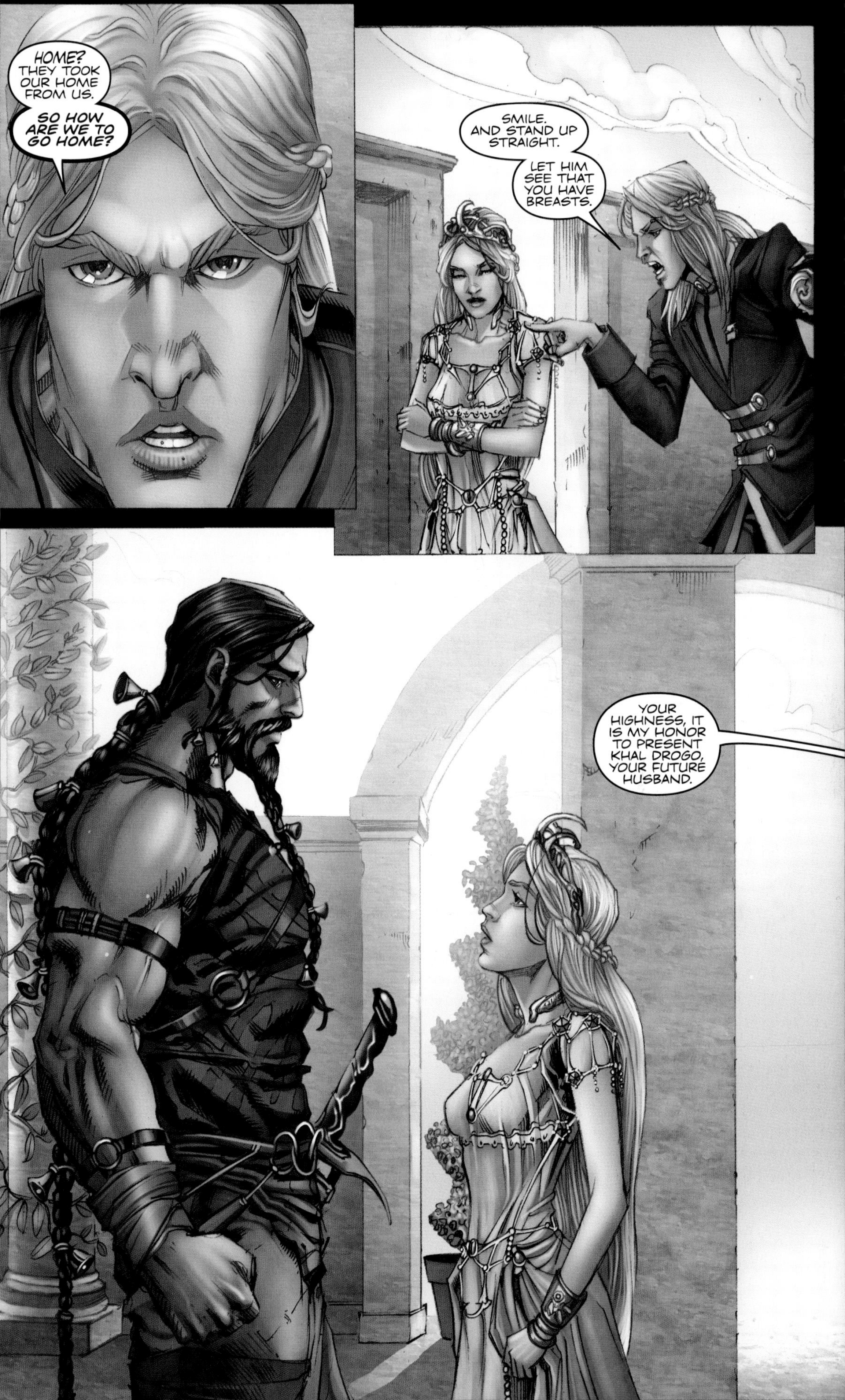
HOME? THEY TOOK OUR HOME FROM US.
SO HOW ARE WE TO GO HOME?
SMILE. AND STAND UP STRAIGHT.
LET HIM SEE THAT YOU HAVE BREASTS.
YOUR HIGHNESS, IT IS MY HONOR TO PRESENT KHAL DROGO, YOUR FUTURE HUSBAND.

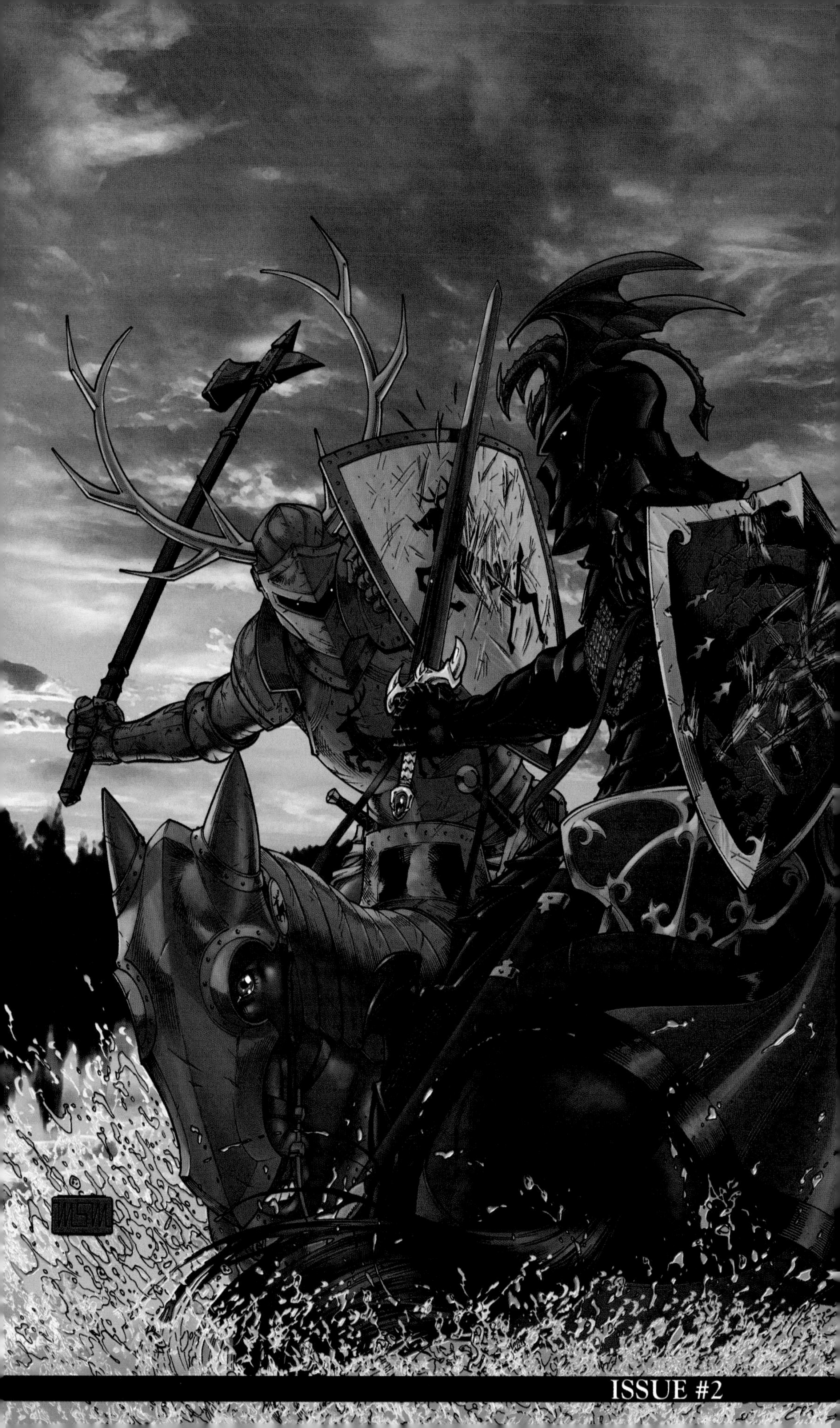

ISSUE #2

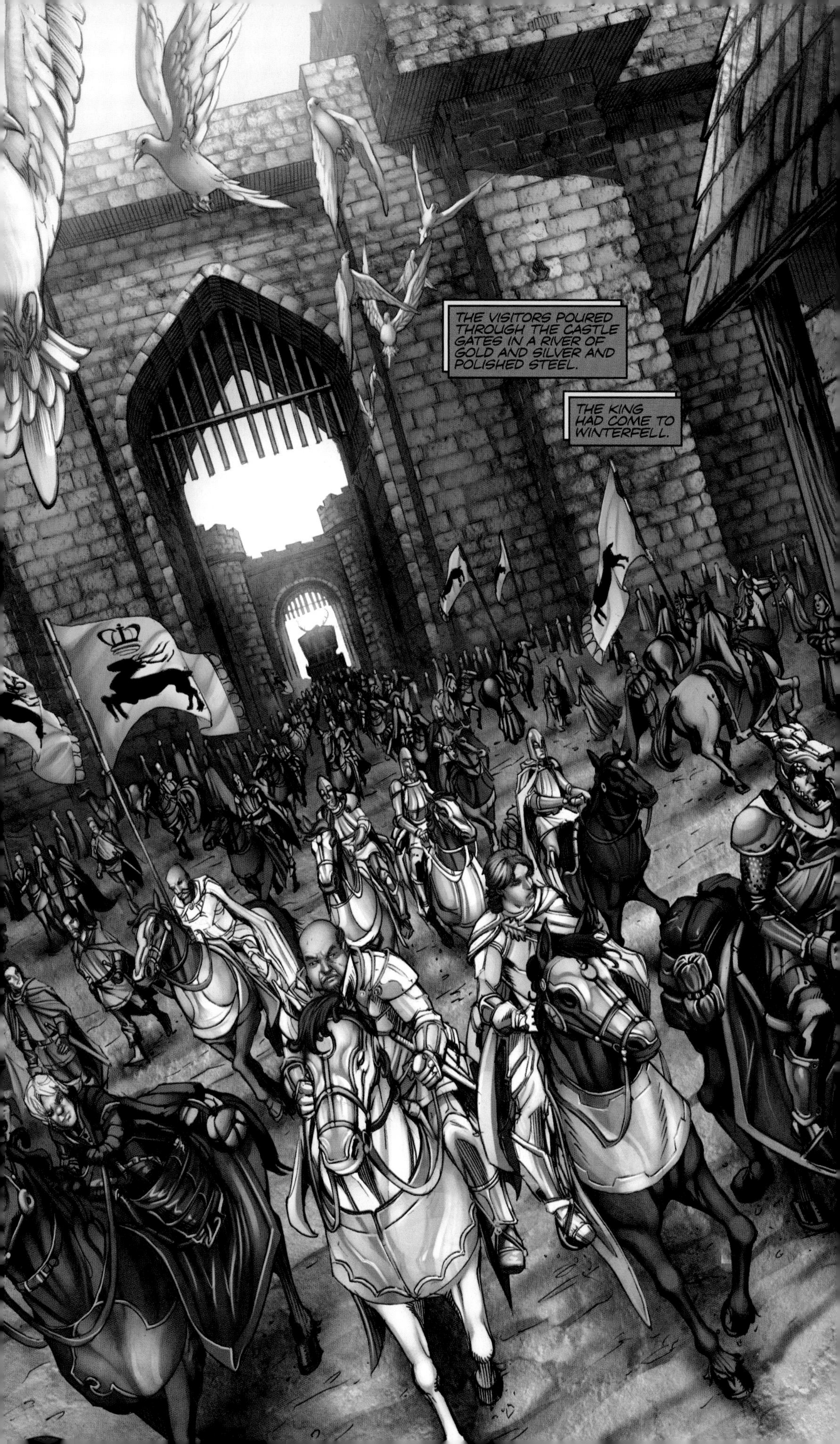
THE VISITORS POURED THROUGH THE CASTLE GATES IN A RIVER OF GOLD AND SILVER AND POLISHED STEEL.
THE KING HAD COME TO WINTERFELL.

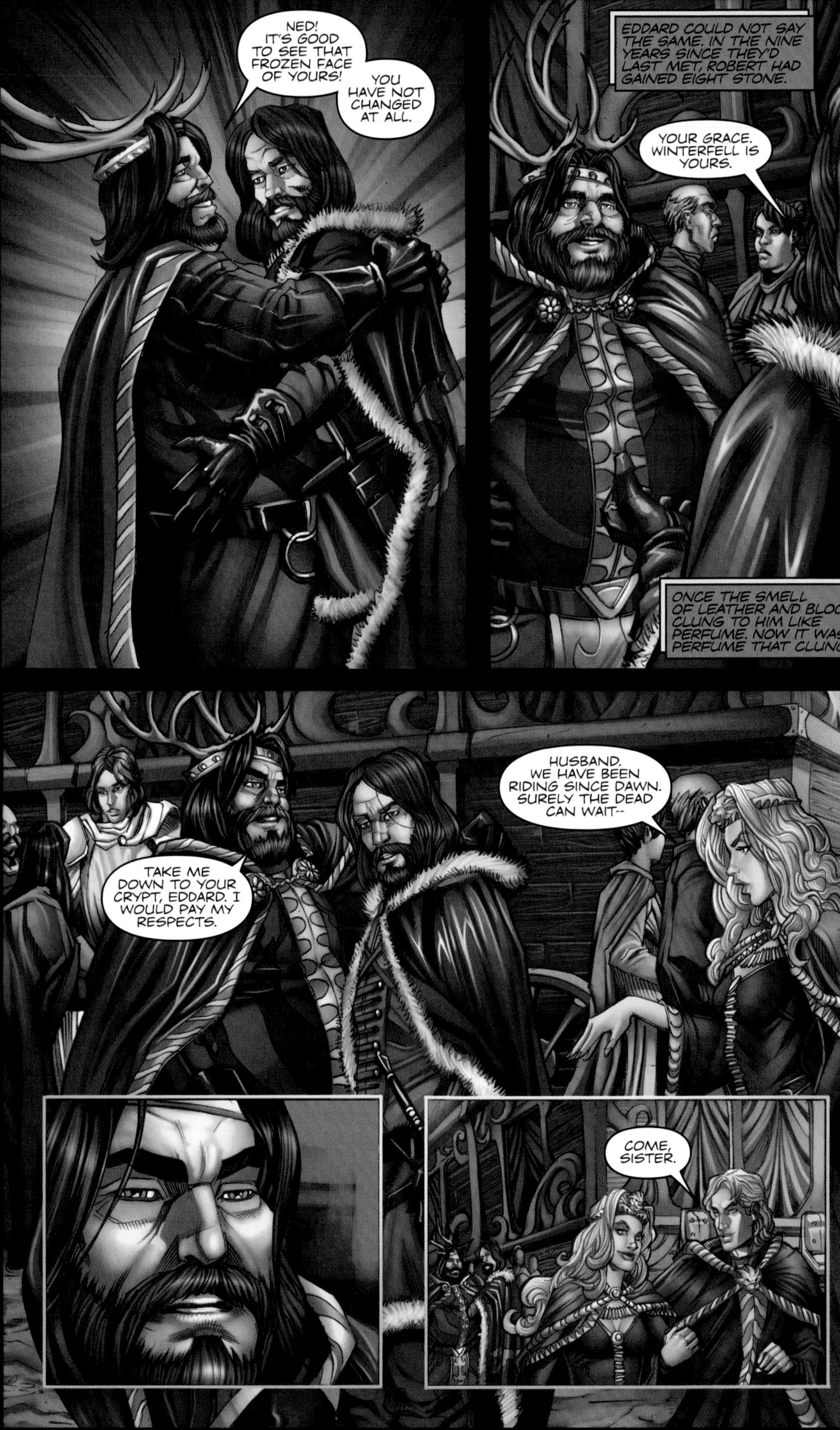
NED! IT'S GOOD TO SEE THAT FROZEN FACE OF YOURS!
YOU HAVE NOT CHANGED AT ALL.
EDDARD COULD NOT SAY THE SAME. IN THE NINE YEARS SINCE THEY'D LAST MET, ROBERT HAD GAINED EIGHT STONE.
YOUR GRACE. WINTERFELL IS YOURS.
ONCE THE SMELL OF LEATHER AND BLOO
CLUNG TO HIM LIKE PERFUME. NOW IT WAS PERFUME THAT CLUNG
TAKE ME DOWN TO YOUR CRYPT, EDDARD. I WOULD PAY MY RESPECTS.
HUSBAND. WE HAVE BEEN RIDING SINCE DAWN. SURELY THE DEAD CAN WAIT--
COME, SISTER.

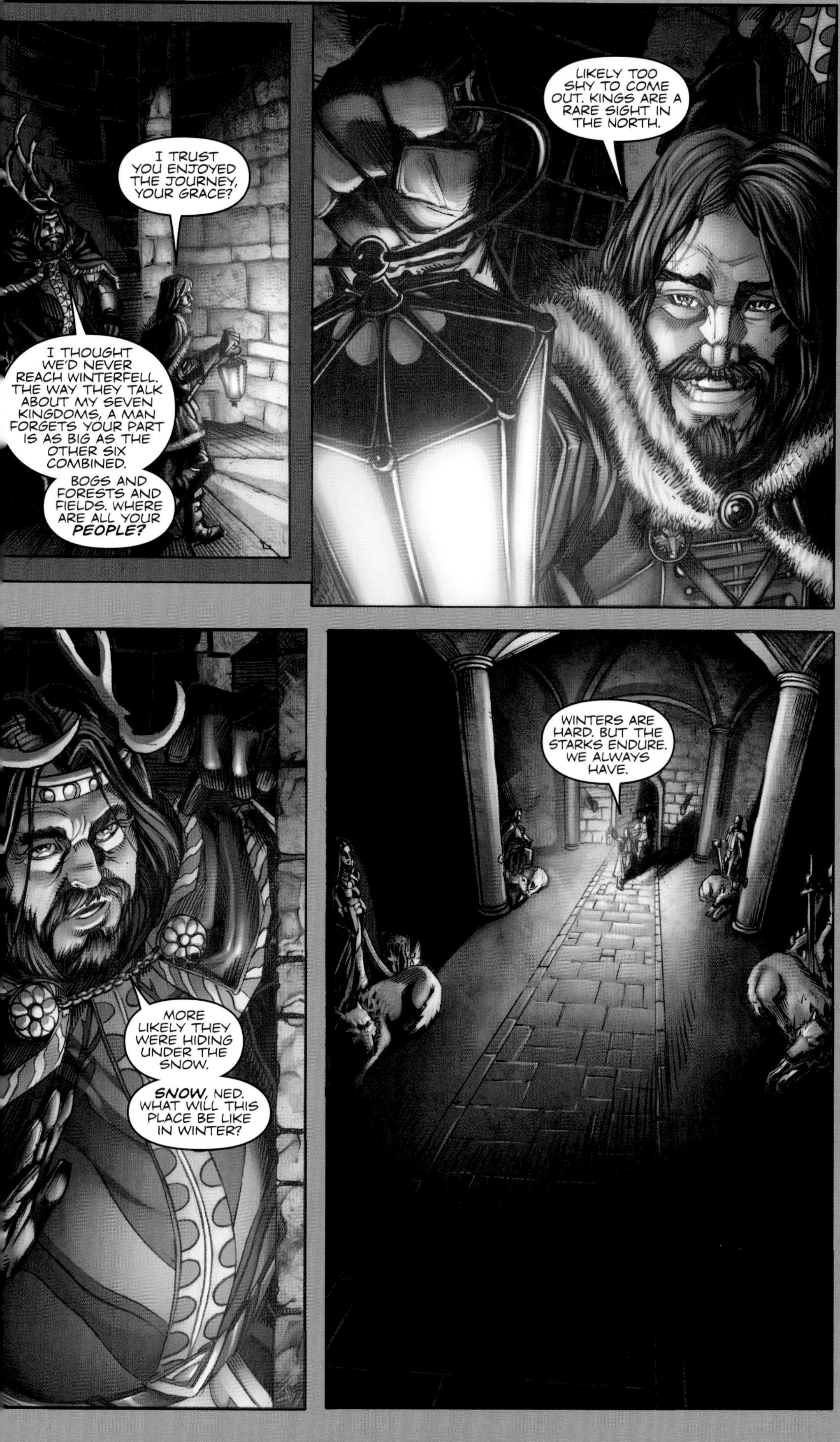
I TRUST YOU ENJOYED THE JOURNEY, YOUR GRACE?
I THOUGHT WE'D NEVER REACH WINTERFELL. THE WAY THEY TALK ABOUT MY SEVEN KINGDOMS, A MAN FORGETS YOUR PART IS AS BIG AS THE OTHER SIX COMBINED.
BOGS AND FORESTS AND FIELDS. WHERE ARE ALL YOUR **PEOPLE?**
LIKELY TOO SHY TO COME OUT. KINGS ARE A RARE SIGHT IN THE NORTH.
MORE LIKELY THEY WERE HIDING UNDER THE SNOW.
SNOW, NED. WHAT WILL THIS PLACE BE LIKE IN WINTER?
WINTERS ARE HARD. BUT THE STARKS ENDURE. WE ALWAYS HAVE.

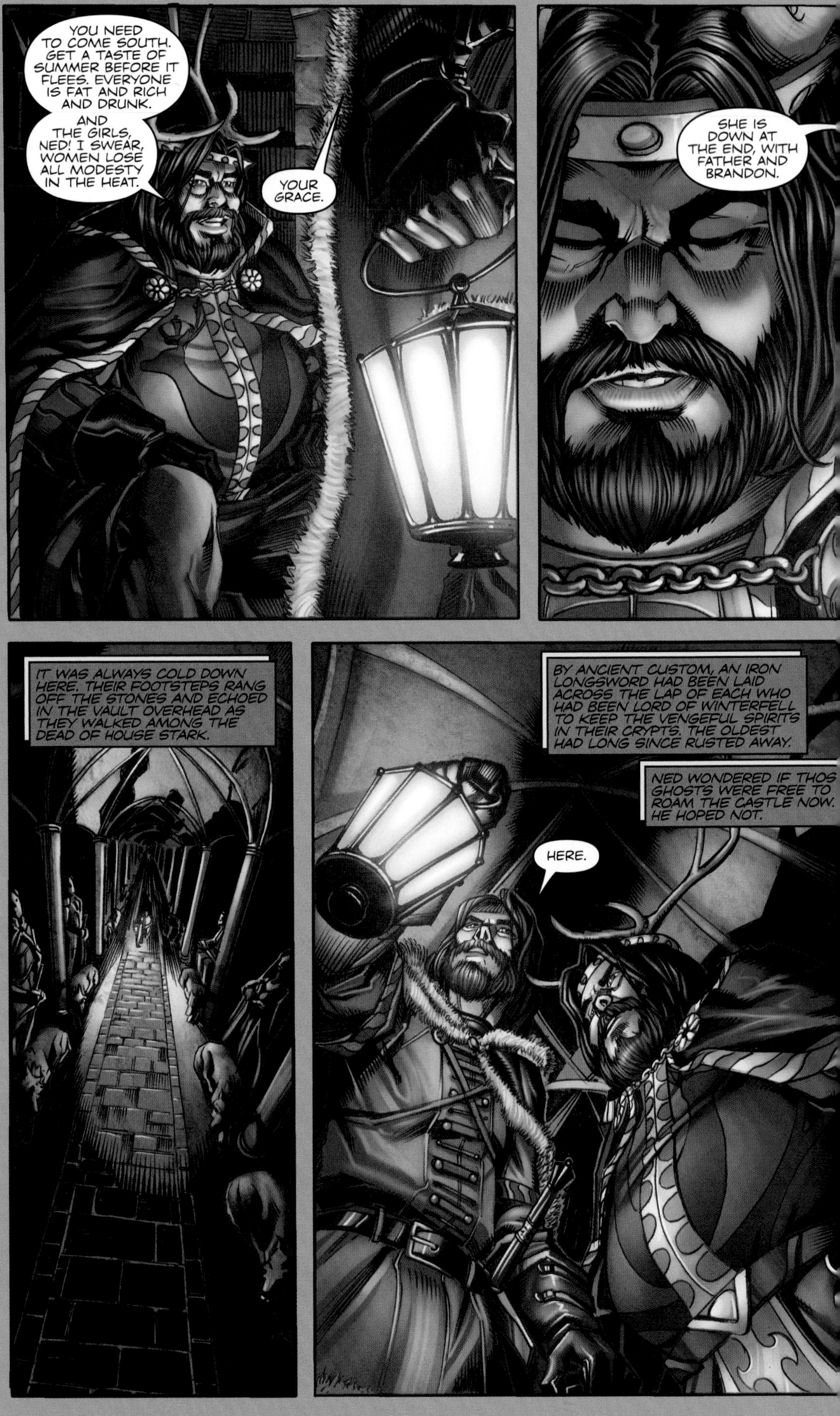
YOU NEED TO COME SOUTH. GET A TASTE OF SUMMER BEFORE IT FLEES. EVERYONE IS FAT AND RICH AND DRUNK.
AND THE GIRLS, NED! I SWEAR, WOMEN LOSE ALL MODESTY IN THE HEAT.
YOUR GRACE.
SHE IS DOWN AT THE END, WITH FATHER AND BRANDON.
IT WAS ALWAYS COLD DOWN HERE. THEIR FOOTSTEPS RANG OFF THE STONES AND ECHOED IN THE VAULT OVERHEAD AS THEY WALKED AMONG THE DEAD OF HOUSE STARK.
BY ANCIENT CUSTOM, AN IRON LONGSWORD HAD BEEN LAID ACROSS THE LAP OF EACH WHO HAD BEEN LORD OF WINTERFELL TO KEEP THE VENGEFUL SPIRITS IN THEIR CRYPTS. THE OLDEST HAD LONG SINCE RUSTED AWAY.
NED WONDERED IF THOS GHOSTS WERE FREE TO ROAM THE CASTLE NOW. HE HOPED NOT.
HERE.

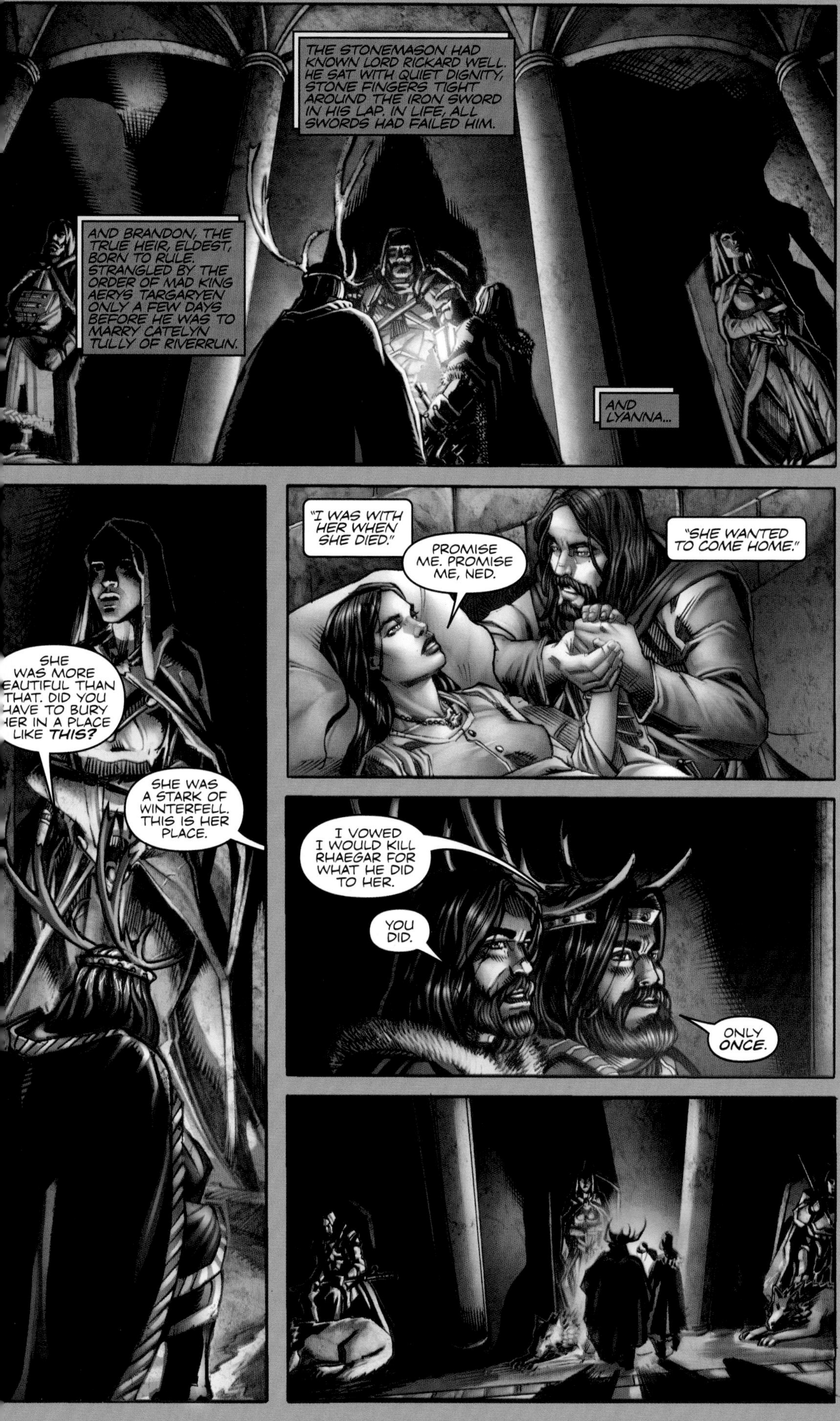
THE STONEMASON HAD KNOWN LORD RICKARD WELL. HE SAT WITH QUIET DIGNITY, STONE FINGERS TIGHT AROUND THE IRON SWORD IN HIS LAP. IN LIFE, ALL SWORDS HAD FAILED HIM.
AND BRANDON, THE TRUE HEIR, ELDEST, BORN TO RULE. STRANGLED BY THE ORDER OF MAD KING AERYS TARGARYEN ONLY A FEW DAYS BEFORE HE WAS TO MARRY CATELYN TULLY OF RIVERRUN.
AND LYANNA...
"I WAS WITH HER WHEN SHE DIED."
PROMISE ME. PROMISE ME, NED.
"SHE WANTED TO COME HOME."
SHE WAS MORE BEAUTIFUL THAN THAT. DID YOU HAVE TO BURY HER IN A PLACE LIKE **THIS?**
SHE WAS A STARK OF WINTERFELL. THIS IS HER PLACE.
I VOWED I WOULD KILL RHAEGAR FOR WHAT HE DID TO HER.
YOU DID.
ONLY **ONCE.**

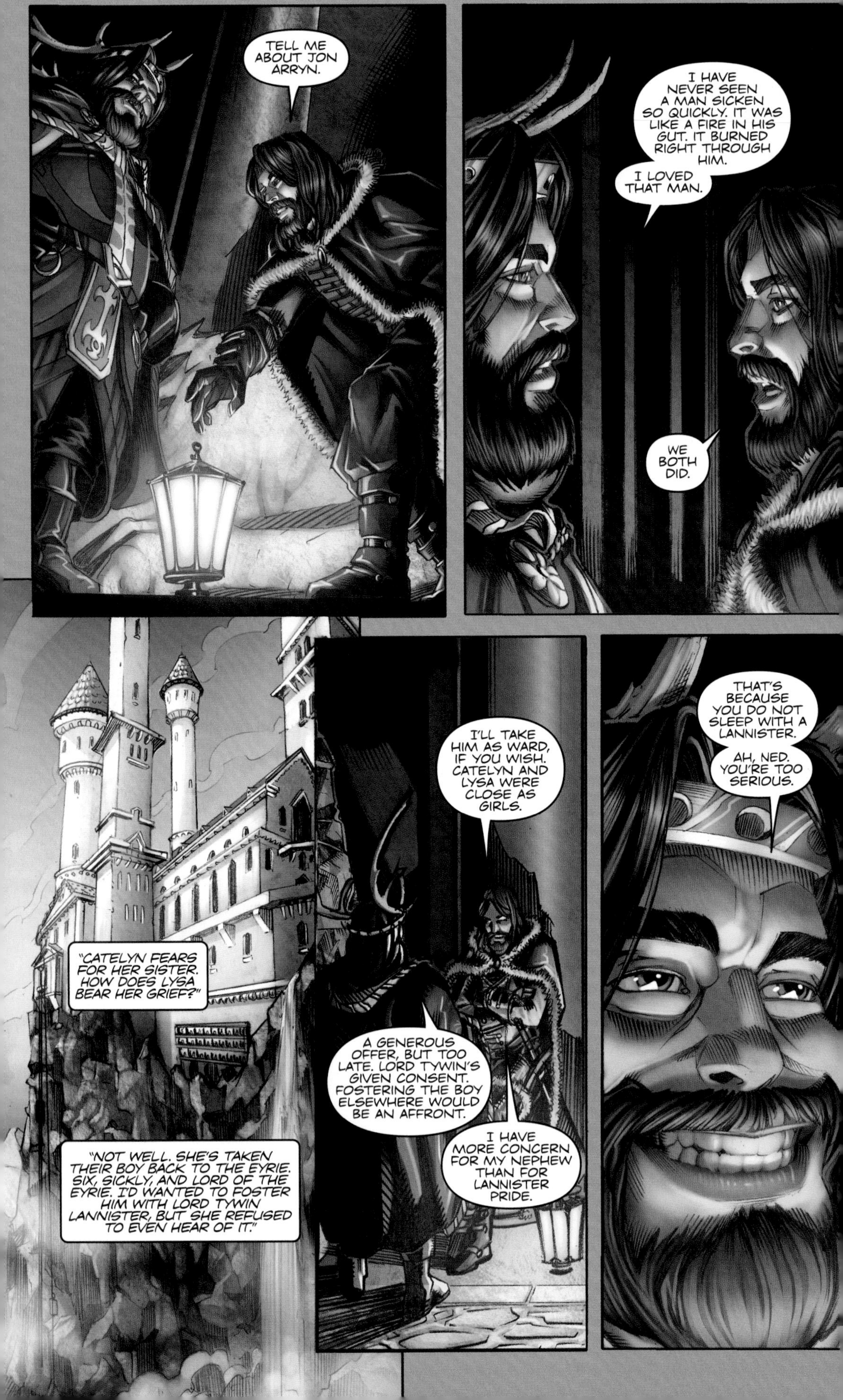
TELL ME ABOUT JON ARRYN.
I HAVE NEVER SEEN A MAN SICKEN SO QUICKLY. IT WAS LIKE A FIRE IN HIS GUT. IT BURNED RIGHT THROUGH HIM.
I LOVED THAT MAN.
WE BOTH DID.
"CATELYN FEARS FOR HER SISTER. HOW DOES LYSA BEAR HER GRIEF?"
"NOT WELL. SHE'S TAKEN THEIR BOY BACK TO THE EYRIE. SIX, SICKLY, AND LORD OF THE EYRIE. I'D WANTED TO FOSTER HIM WITH LORD TYWIN LANNISTER, BUT SHE REFUSED TO EVEN HEAR OF IT."
I'LL TAKE HIM AS WARD, IF YOU WISH. CATELYN AND LYSA WERE CLOSE AS GIRLS.
A GENEROUS OFFER, BUT TOO LATE. LORD TYWIN'S GIVEN CONSENT. FOSTERING THE BOY ELSEWHERE WOULD BE AN AFFRONT.
I HAVE MORE CONCERN FOR MY NEPHEW THAN FOR LANNISTER PRIDE.
THAT'S BECAUSE YOU DO NOT SLEEP WITH A LANNISTER.
AH, NED. YOU'RE TOO SERIOUS.

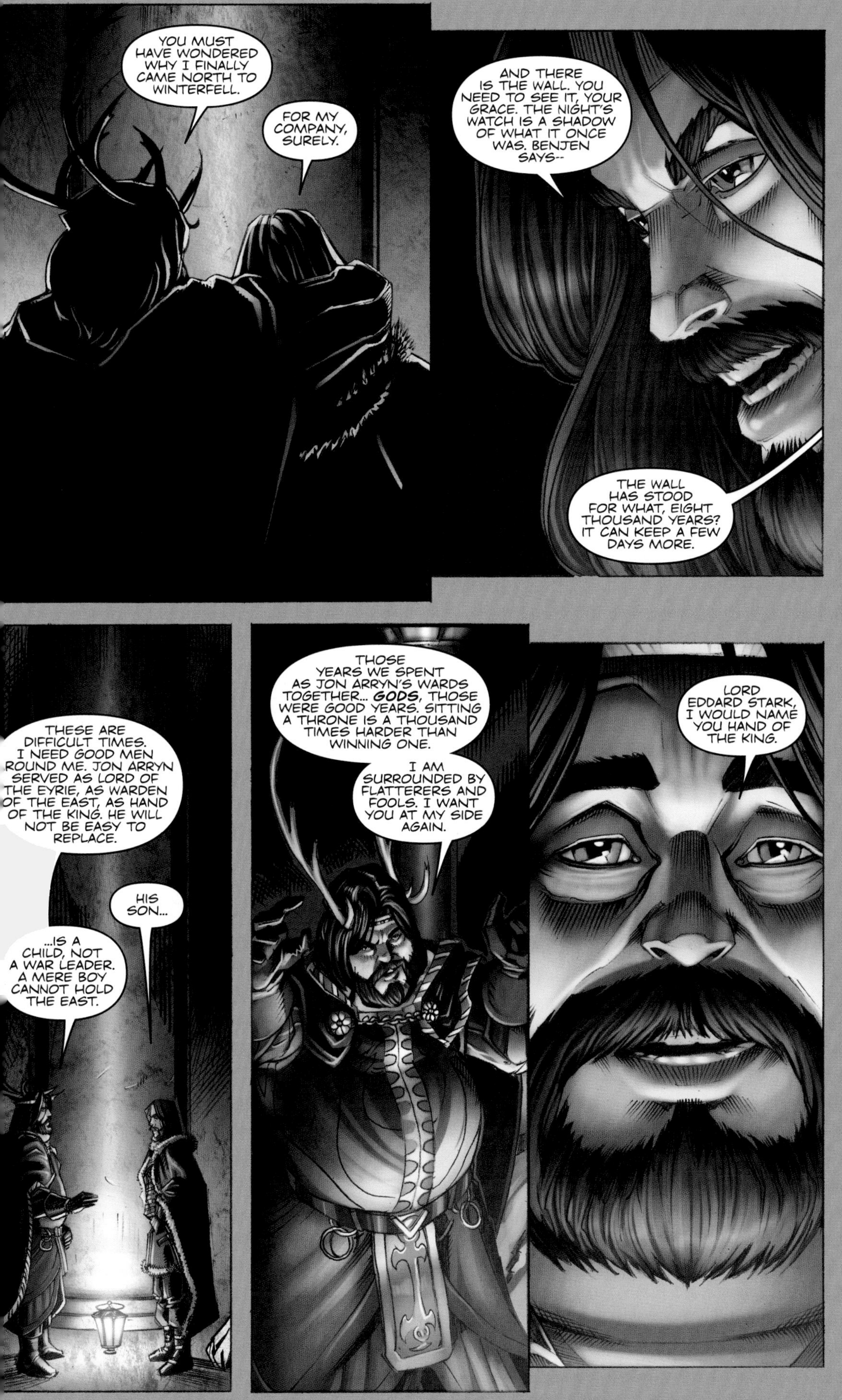
YOU MUST HAVE WONDERED WHY I FINALLY CAME NORTH TO WINTERFELL.
FOR MY COMPANY, SURELY.
AND THERE IS THE WALL. YOU NEED TO SEE IT, YOUR GRACE. THE NIGHT'S WATCH IS A SHADOW OF WHAT IT ONCE WAS. BENJEN SAYS--
THE WALL HAS STOOD FOR WHAT, EIGHT THOUSAND YEARS? IT CAN KEEP A FEW DAYS MORE.
THESE ARE DIFFICULT TIMES. I NEED GOOD MEN ROUND ME. JON ARRYN SERVED AS LORD OF THE EYRIE, AS WARDEN OF THE EAST, AS HAND OF THE KING. HE WILL NOT BE EASY TO REPLACE.
HIS SON...
...IS A CHILD, NOT A WAR LEADER. A MERE BOY CANNOT HOLD THE EAST.
THOSE YEARS WE SPENT AS JON ARRYN'S WARDS TOGETHER... **GODS**, THOSE WERE GOOD YEARS. SITTING A THRONE IS A THOUSAND TIMES HARDER THAN WINNING ONE.
I AM SURROUNDED BY FLATTERERS AND FOOLS. I WANT YOU AT MY SIDE AGAIN.
LORD EDDARD STARK, I WOULD NAME YOU HAND OF THE KING.

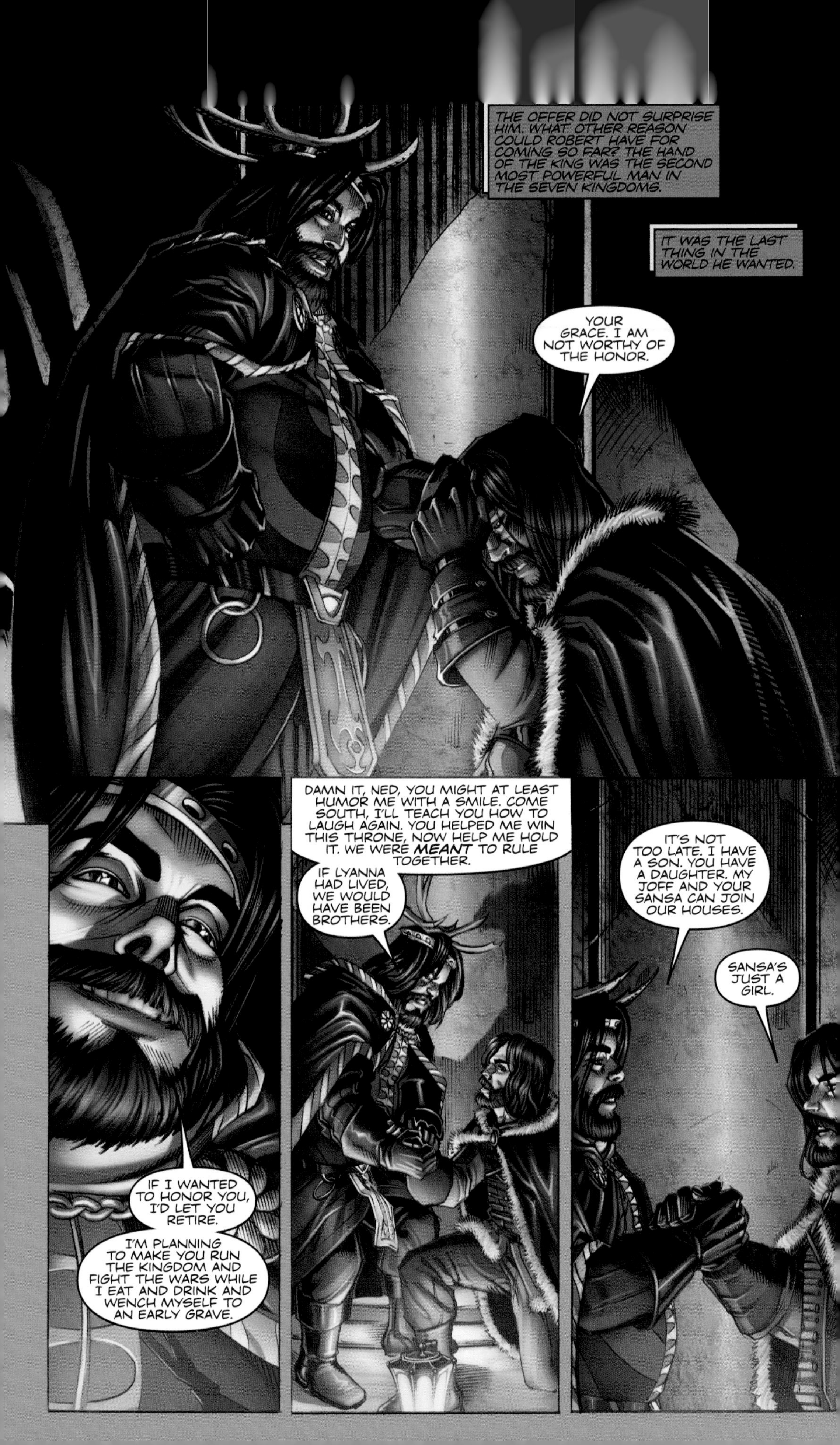
THE OFFER DID NOT SURPRISE HIM. WHAT OTHER REASON COULD ROBERT HAVE FOR COMING SO FAR? THE HAND OF THE KING WAS THE SECOND MOST POWERFUL MAN IN THE SEVEN KINGDOMS.
IT WAS THE LAST THING IN THE WORLD HE WANTED.
YOUR GRACE. I AM NOT WORTHY OF THE HONOR.
IF I WANTED TO HONOR YOU, I'D LET YOU RETIRE.
I'M PLANNING TO MAKE YOU RUN THE KINGDOM AND FIGHT THE WARS WHILE I EAT AND DRINK AND WENCH MYSELF TO AN EARLY GRAVE.
DAMN IT, NED, YOU MIGHT AT LEAST HUMOR ME WITH A SMILE. COME SOUTH, I'LL TEACH YOU HOW TO LAUGH AGAIN. YOU HELPED ME WIN THIS THRONE, NOW HELP ME HOLD IT. WE WERE MEANT TO RULE TOGETHER.
IF LYANNA HAD LIVED, WE WOULD HAVE BEEN BROTHERS.
IT'S NOT TOO LATE. I HAVE A SON. YOU HAVE A DAUGHTER. MY JOFF AND YOUR SANSA CAN JOIN OUR HOUSES.
SANSA'S JUST A GIRL.

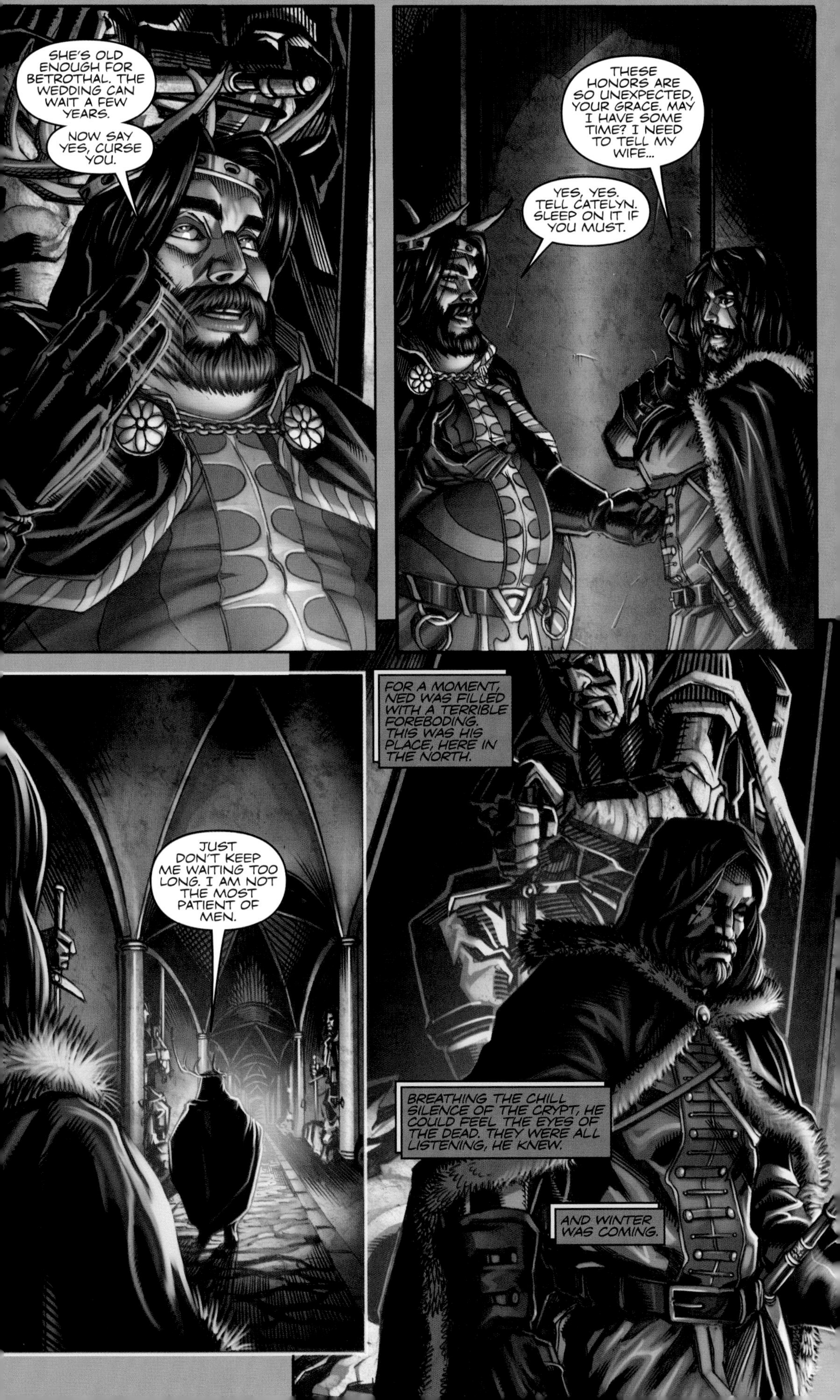
SHE'S OLD ENOUGH FOR BETROTHAL. THE WEDDING CAN WAIT A FEW YEARS.
NOW SAY YES, CURSE YOU.
THESE HONORS ARE SO UNEXPECTED, YOUR GRACE. MAY I HAVE SOME TIME? I NEED TO TELL MY WIFE...
YES, YES. TELL CATELYN. SLEEP ON IT IF YOU MUST.
JUST DON'T KEEP ME WAITING TOO LONG. I AM NOT THE MOST PATIENT OF MEN.
FOR A MOMENT, NED WAS FILLED WITH A TERRIBLE FOREBODING. THIS WAS HIS PLACE, HERE IN THE NORTH.
BREATHING THE CHILL SILENCE OF THE CRYPT, HE COULD FEEL THE EYES OF THE DEAD. THEY WERE ALL LISTENING, HE KNEW.
AND WINTER WAS COMING.

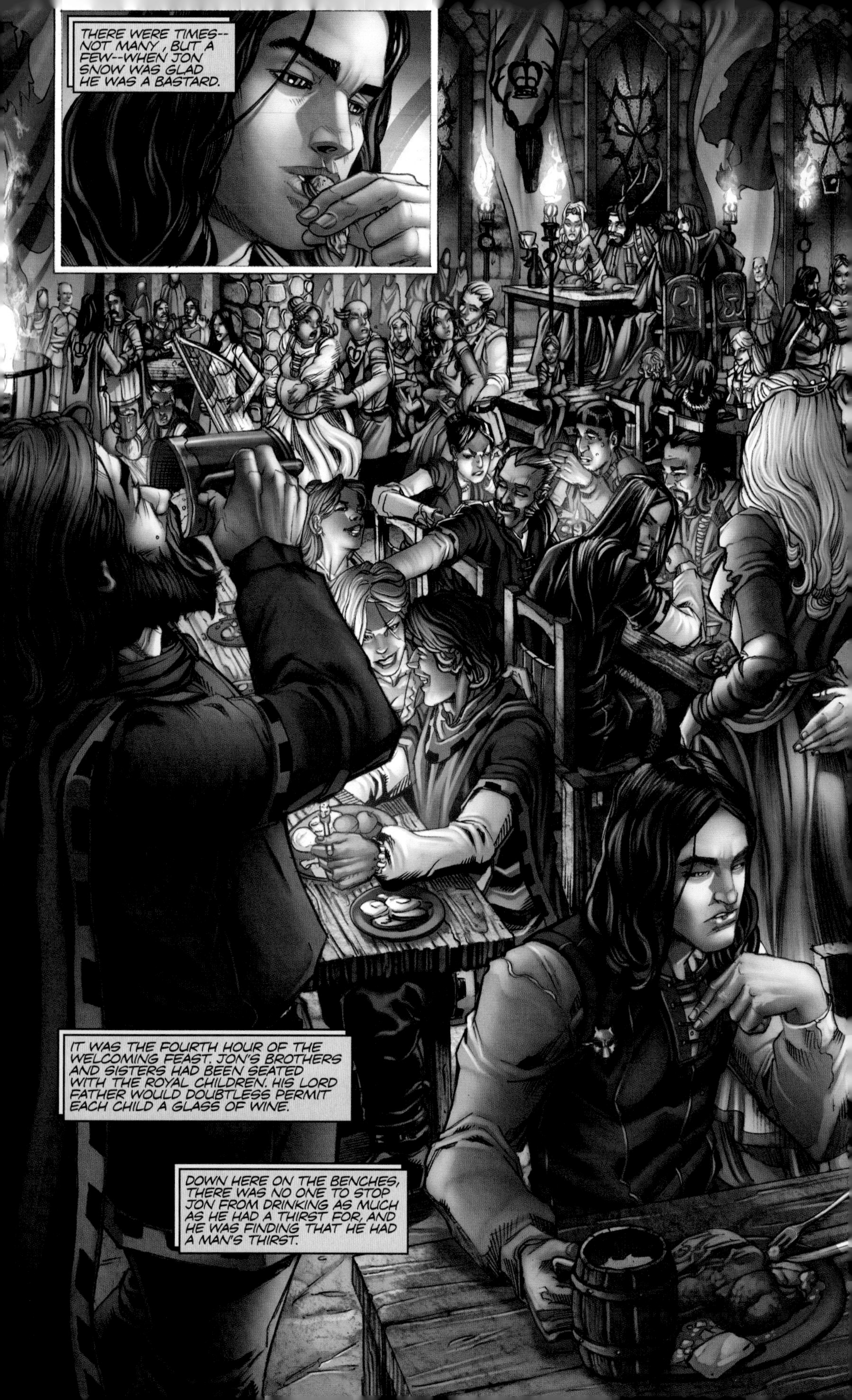
THERE WERE TIMES--NOT MANY, BUT A FEW--WHEN JON SNOW WAS GLAD HE WAS A BASTARD.
IT WAS THE FOURTH HOUR OF THE WELCOMING FEAST. JON'S BROTHERS AND SISTERS HAD BEEN SEATED WITH THE ROYAL CHILDREN. HIS LORD FATHER WOULD DOUBTLESS PERMIT EACH CHILD A GLASS OF WINE.
DOWN HERE ON THE BENCHES, THERE WAS NO ONE TO STOP JON FROM DRINKING AS MUCH AS HE HAD A THIRST FOR, AND HE WAS FINDING THAT HE HAD A MAN'S THIRST.

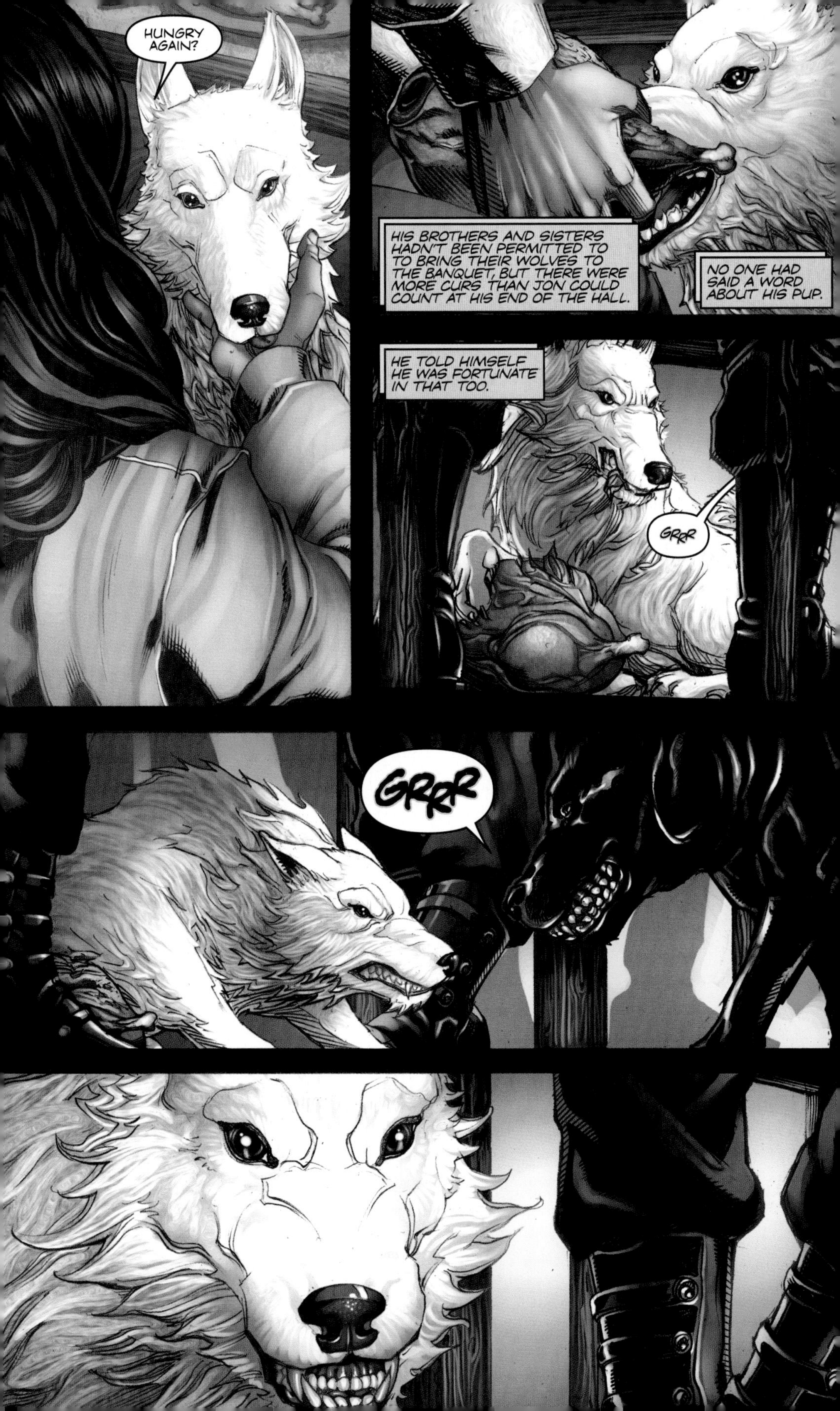
HUNGRY AGAIN?
HIS BROTHERS AND SISTERS HADN'T BEEN PERMITTED TO TO BRING THEIR WOLVES TO THE BANQUET, BUT THERE WERE MORE CURS THAN JON COULD COUNT AT HIS END OF THE HALL.
NO ONE HAD SAID A WORD ABOUT HIS PUP.
HE TOLD HIMSELF HE WAS FORTUNATE IN THAT TOO.
GRRR
GRRR

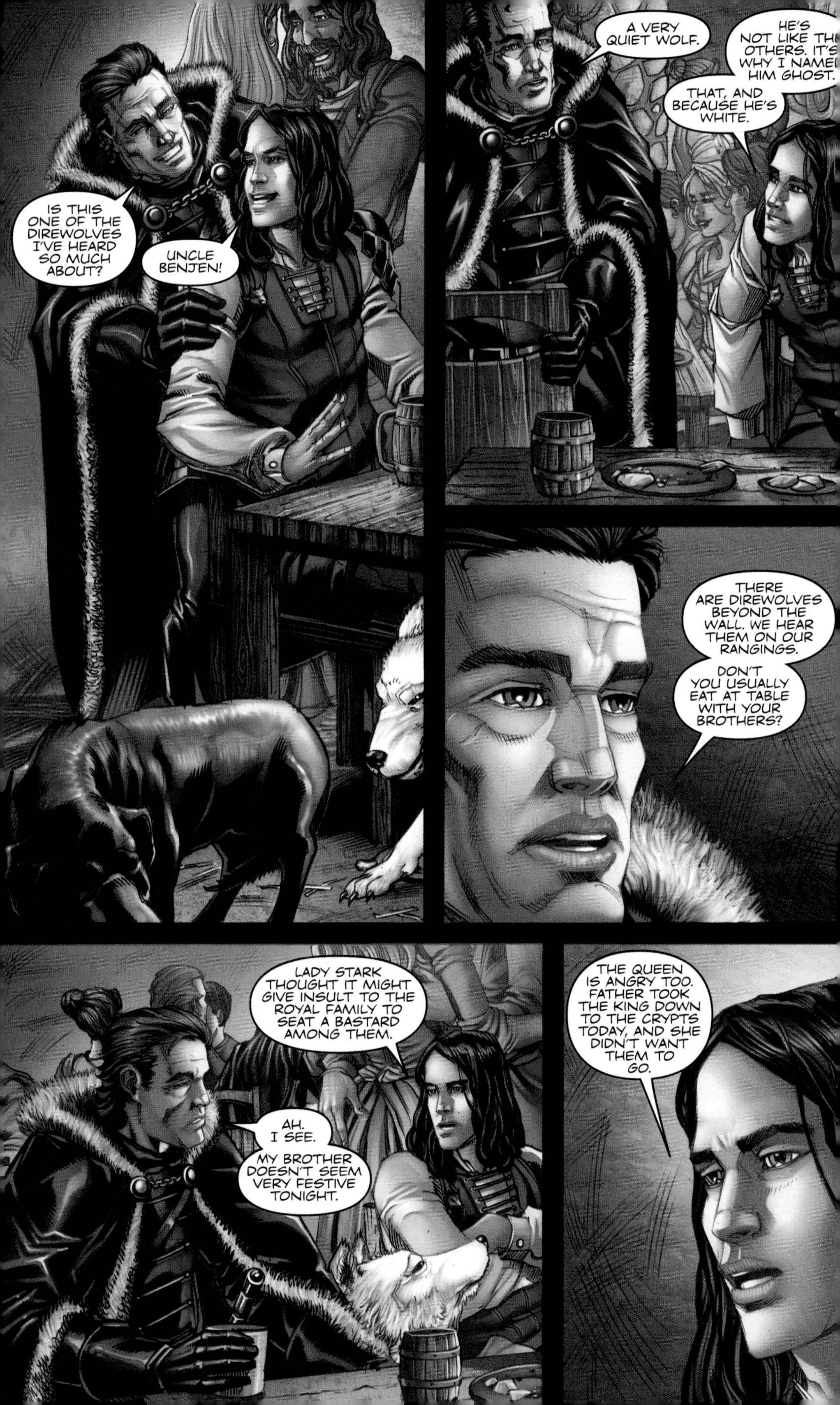
UNCLE BENJEN!
IS THIS ONE OF THE DIREWOLVES I'VE HEARD SO MUCH ABOUT?
A VERY QUIET WOLF.
HE'S NOT LIKE TH OTHERS. IT'S WHY I NAME HIM GHOST.
THAT, AND BECAUSE HE'S WHITE.
THERE ARE DIREWOLVES BEYOND THE WALL. WE HEAR THEM ON OUR RANGINGS.
DON'T YOU USUALLY EAT AT TABLE WITH YOUR BROTHERS?
LADY STARK THOUGHT IT MIGHT GIVE INSULT TO THE ROYAL FAMILY TO SEAT A BASTARD AMONG THEM.
AH. I SEE.
MY BROTHER DOESN'T SEEM VERY FESTIVE TONIGHT.
THE QUEEN IS ANGRY TOO. FATHER TOOK THE KING DOWN TO THE CRYPTS TODAY, AND SHE DIDN'T WANT THEM TO GO.

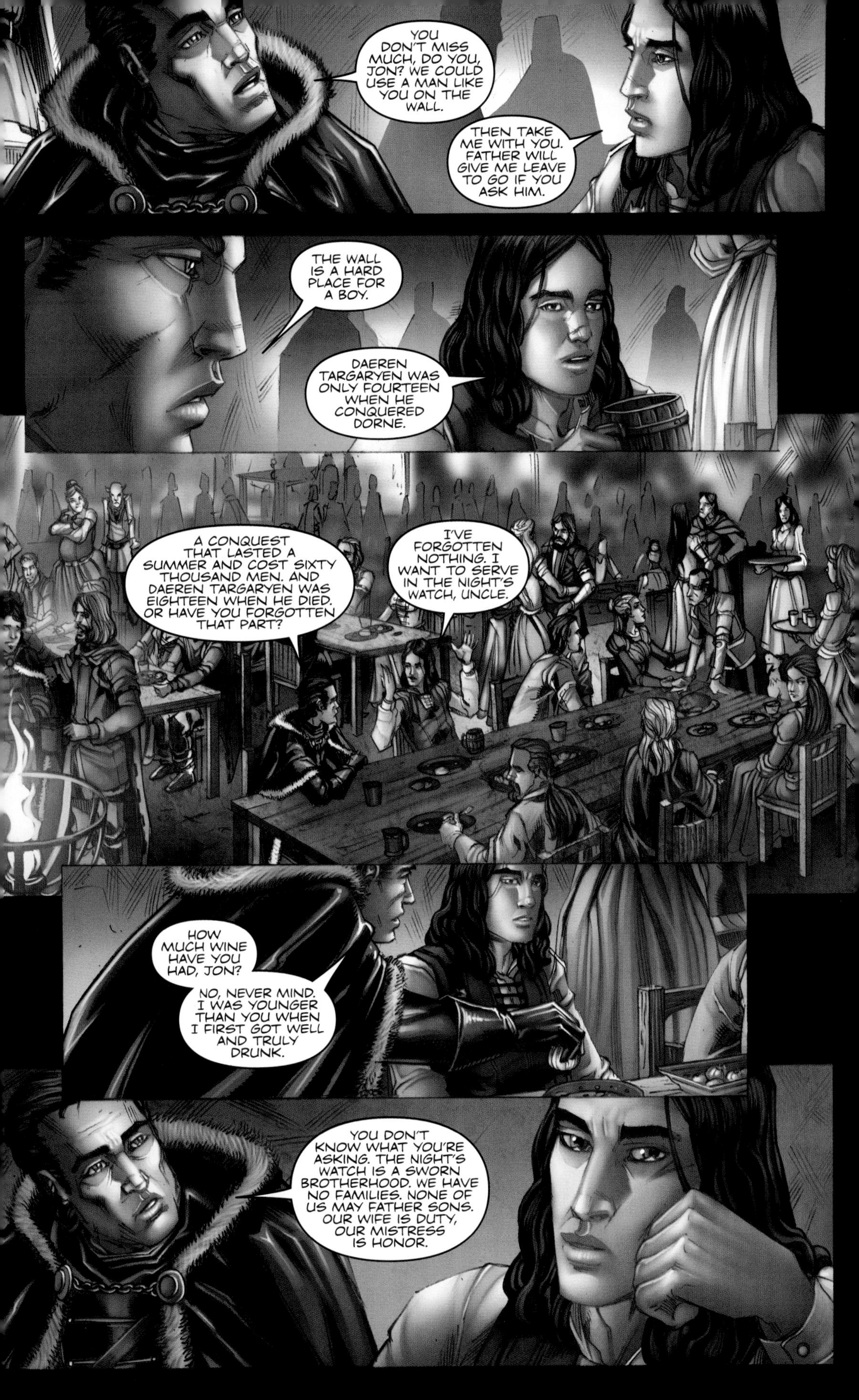
YOU DON'T MISS MUCH, DO YOU, JON? WE COULD USE A MAN LIKE YOU ON THE WALL.
THEN TAKE ME WITH YOU. FATHER WILL GIVE ME LEAVE TO GO IF YOU ASK HIM.
THE WALL IS A HARD PLACE FOR A BOY.
DAEREN TARGARYEN WAS ONLY FOURTEEN WHEN HE CONQUERED DORNE.
A CONQUEST THAT LASTED A SUMMER AND COST SIXTY THOUSAND MEN. AND DAEREN TARGARYEN WAS EIGHTEEN WHEN HE DIED. OR HAVE YOU FORGOTTEN THAT PART?
I'VE FORGOTTEN NOTHING. I WANT TO SERVE IN THE NIGHT'S WATCH, UNCLE.
HOW MUCH WINE HAVE YOU HAD, JON?
NO, NEVER MIND. I WAS YOUNGER THAN YOU WHEN I FIRST GOT WELL AND TRULY DRUNK.
YOU DON'T KNOW WHAT YOU'RE ASKING. THE NIGHT'S WATCH IS A SWORN BROTHERHOOD. WE HAVE NO FAMILIES. NONE OF US MAY FATHER SONS. OUR WIFE IS DUTY, OUR MISTRESS IS HONOR.

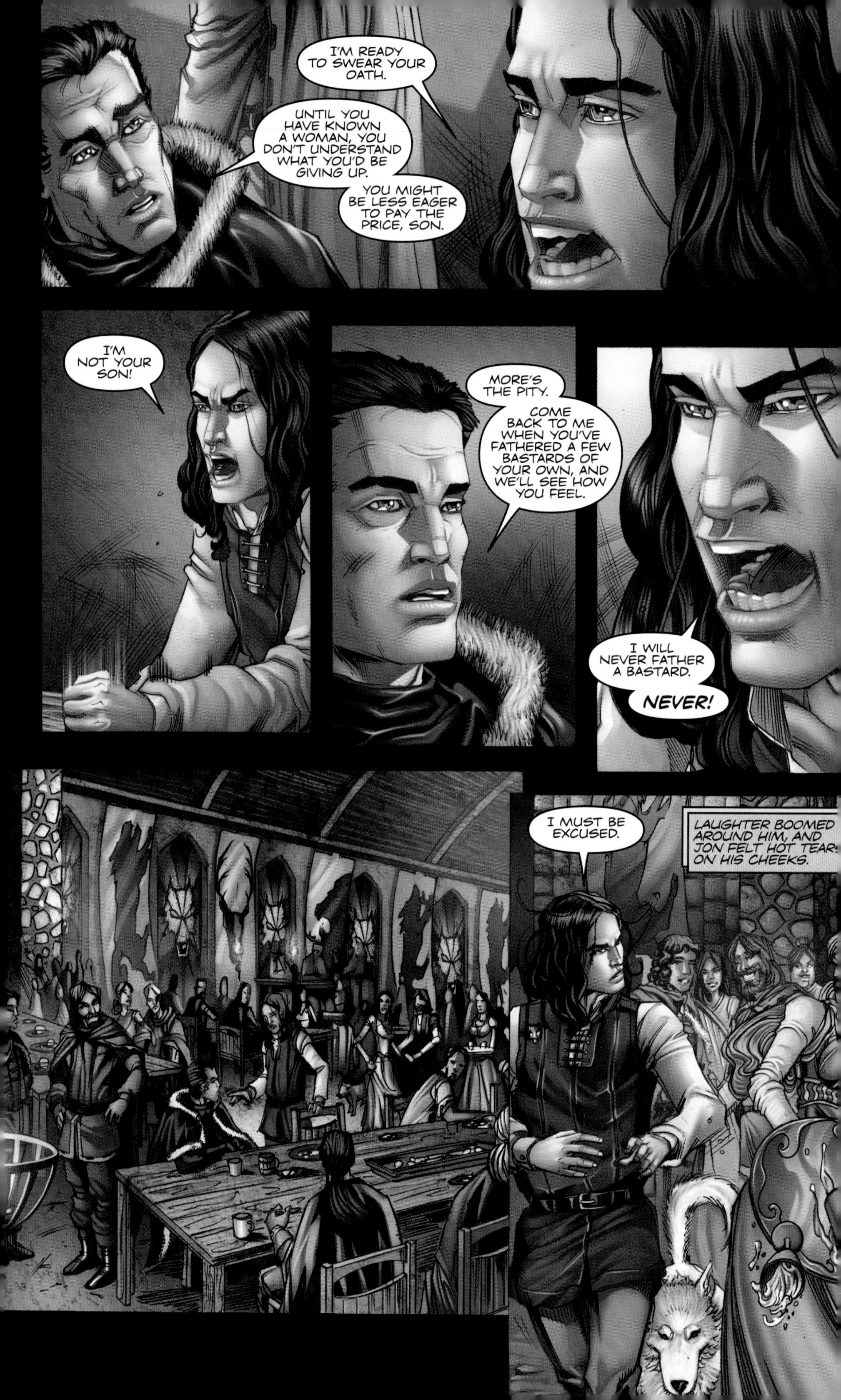
I'M READY TO SWEAR YOUR OATH.
UNTIL YOU HAVE KNOWN A WOMAN, YOU DON'T UNDERSTAND WHAT YOU'D BE GIVING UP.
YOU MIGHT BE LESS EAGER TO PAY THE PRICE, SON.
I'M NOT YOUR SON!
MORE'S THE PITY.
COME BACK TO ME WHEN YOU'VE FATHERED A FEW BASTARDS OF YOUR OWN, AND WE'LL SEE HOW YOU FEEL.
I WILL NEVER FATHER A BASTARD.
NEVER!
I MUST BE EXCUSED.
LAUGHTER BOOMED AROUND HIM, AND JON FELT HOT TEARS ON HIS CHEEKS.

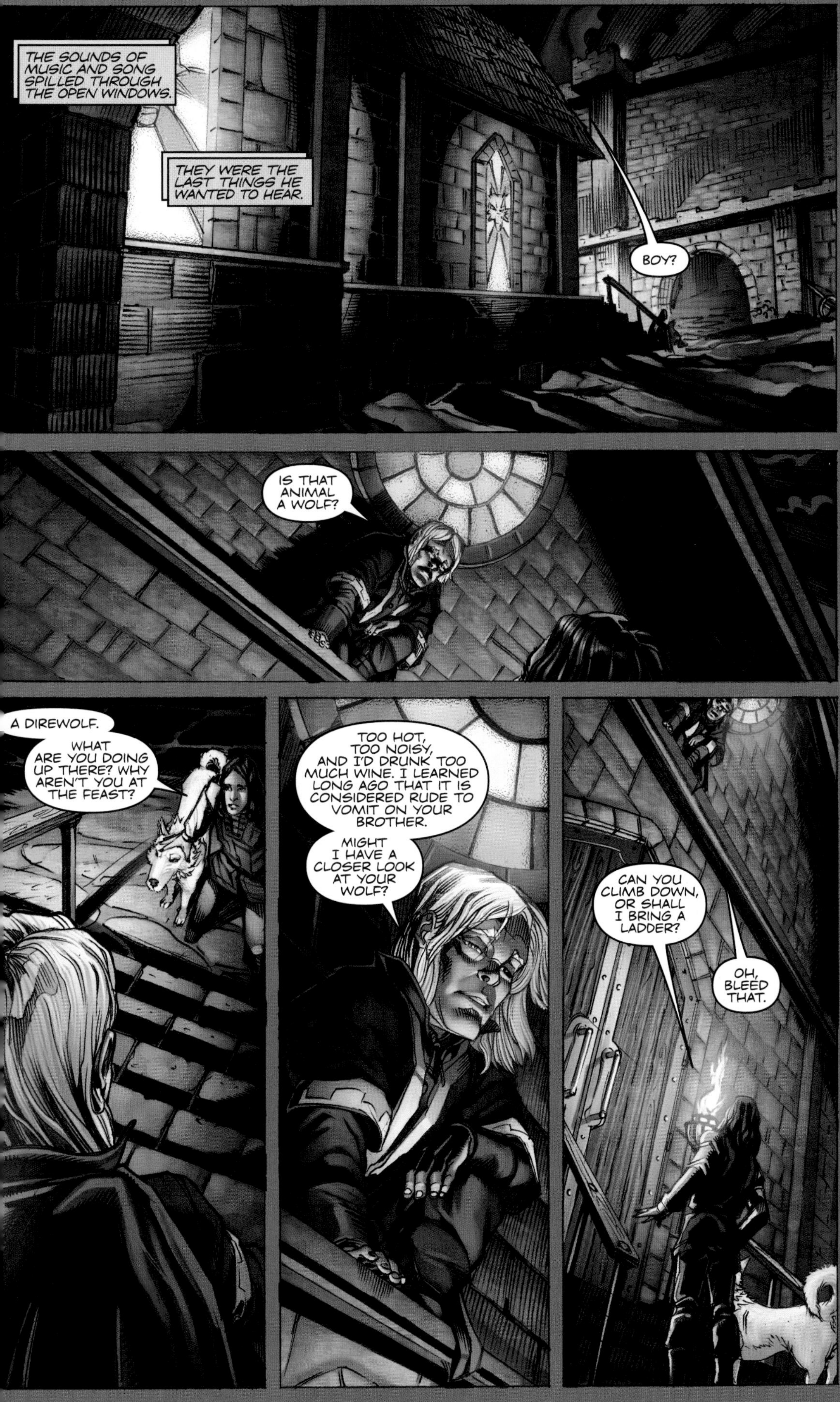
THE SOUNDS OF MUSIC AND SONG SPILLED THROUGH THE OPEN WINDOWS.
THEY WERE THE LAST THINGS HE WANTED TO HEAR.
BOY?
IS THAT ANIMAL A WOLF?
A DIREWOLF.
WHAT ARE YOU DOING UP THERE? WHY AREN'T YOU AT THE FEAST?
TOO HOT, TOO NOISY, AND I'D DRUNK TOO MUCH WINE. I LEARNED LONG AGO THAT IT IS CONSIDERED RUDE TO VOMIT ON YOUR BROTHER.
MIGHT I HAVE A CLOSER LOOK AT YOUR WOLF?
CAN YOU CLIMB DOWN, OR SHALL I BRING A LADDER?
OH, BLEED THAT.

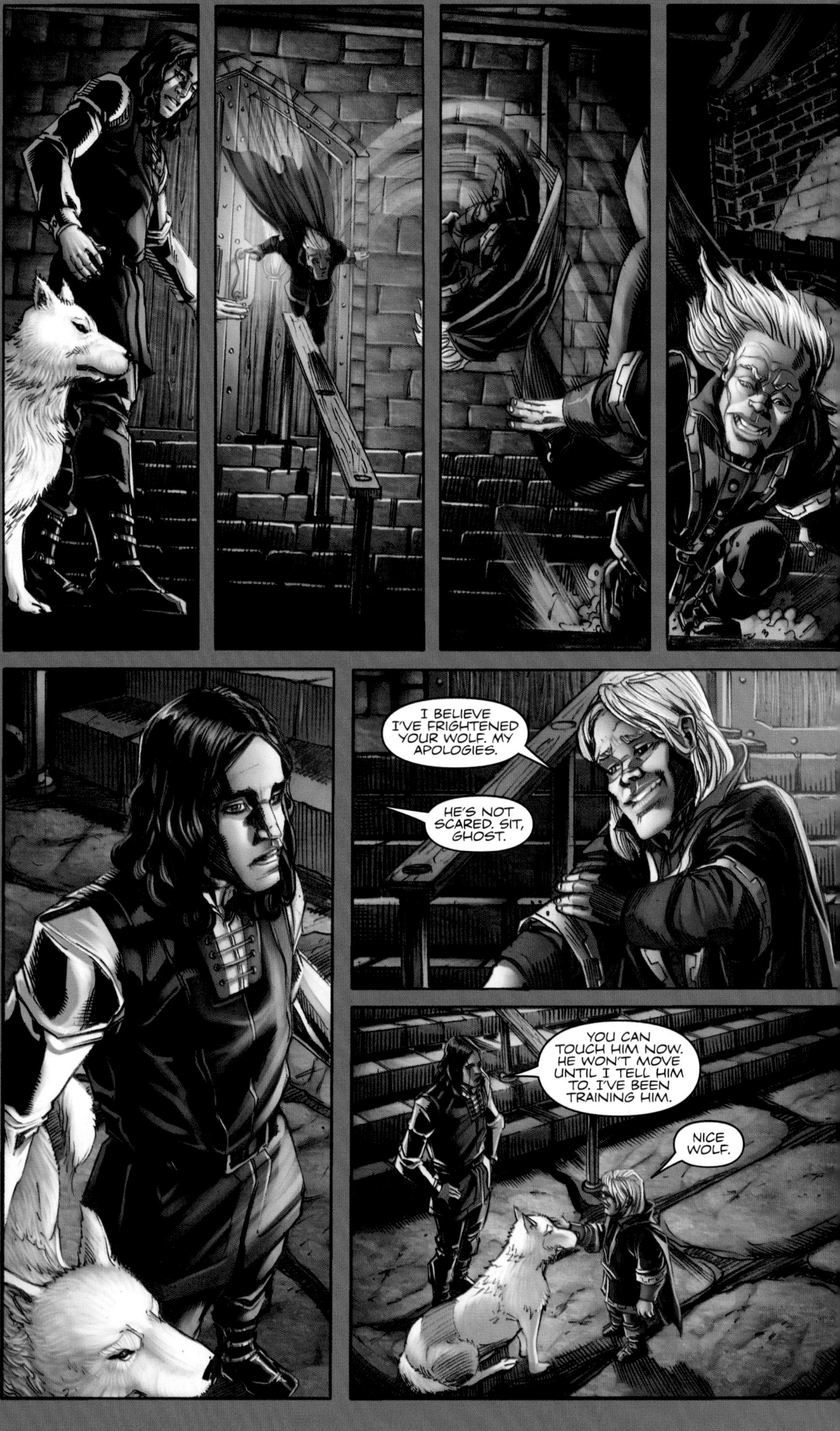
I BELIEVE I'VE FRIGHTENED YOUR WOLF. MY APOLOGIES.
HE'S NOT SCARED. SIT, GHOST.
YOU CAN TOUCH HIM NOW. HE WON'T MOVE UNTIL I TELL HIM TO. I'VE BEEN TRAINING HIM.
NICE WOLF.

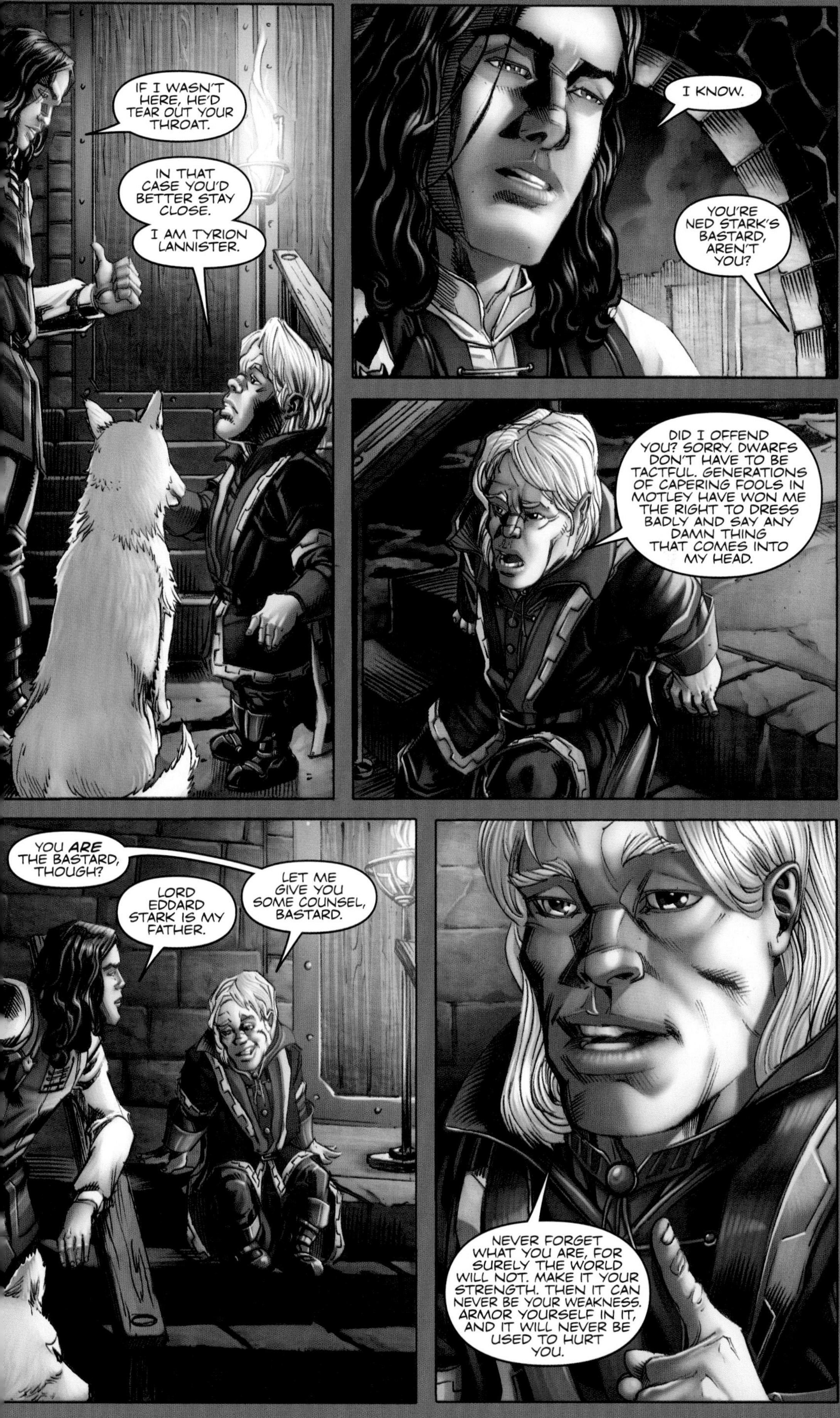
IF I WASN'T HERE, HE'D TEAR OUT YOUR THROAT.
IN THAT CASE YOU'D BETTER STAY CLOSE.
I AM TYRION LANNISTER.
I KNOW.
YOU'RE NED STARK'S BASTARD, AREN'T YOU?
DID I OFFEND YOU? SORRY. DWARFS DON'T HAVE TO BE TACTFUL. GENERATIONS OF CAPERING FOOLS IN MOTLEY HAVE WON ME THE RIGHT TO DRESS BADLY AND SAY ANY DAMN THING THAT COMES INTO MY HEAD.
YOU **ARE** THE BASTARD, THOUGH?
LORD EDDARD STARK IS MY FATHER.
LET ME GIVE YOU SOME COUNSEL, BASTARD.
NEVER FORGET WHAT YOU ARE, FOR SURELY THE WORLD WILL NOT. MAKE IT YOUR STRENGTH. THEN IT CAN NEVER BE YOUR WEAKNESS. ARMOR YOURSELF IN IT, AND IT WILL NEVER BE USED TO HURT YOU.

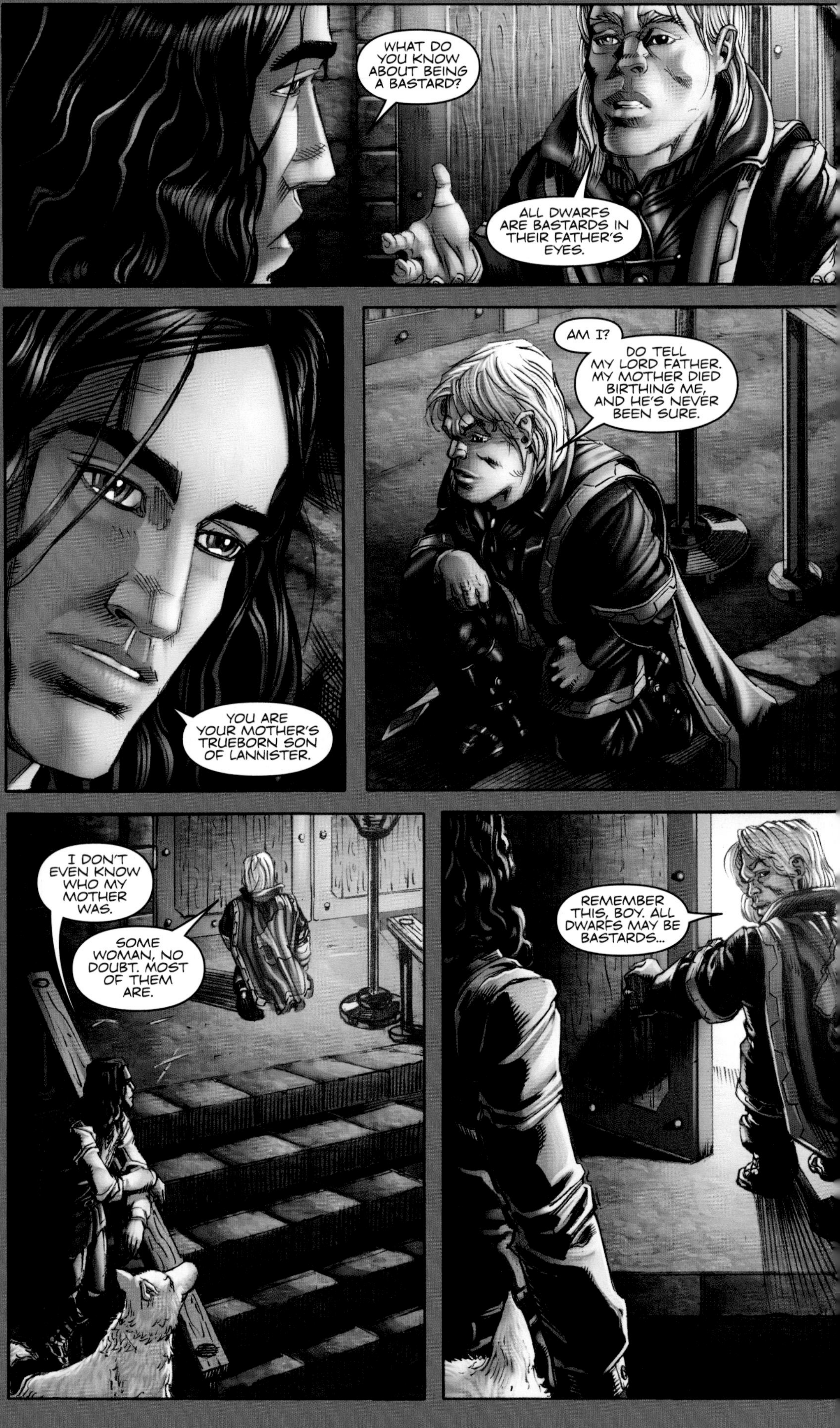
WHAT DO YOU KNOW ABOUT BEING A BASTARD?
ALL DWARFS ARE BASTARDS IN THEIR FATHER'S EYES.
YOU ARE YOUR MOTHER'S TRUEBORN SON OF LANNISTER.
AM I?
DO TELL MY LORD FATHER. MY MOTHER DIED BIRTHING ME, AND HE'S NEVER BEEN SURE.
I DON'T EVEN KNOW WHO MY MOTHER WAS.
SOME WOMAN, NO DOUBT. MOST OF THEM ARE.
REMEMBER THIS, BOY. ALL DWARFS MAY BE BASTARDS...

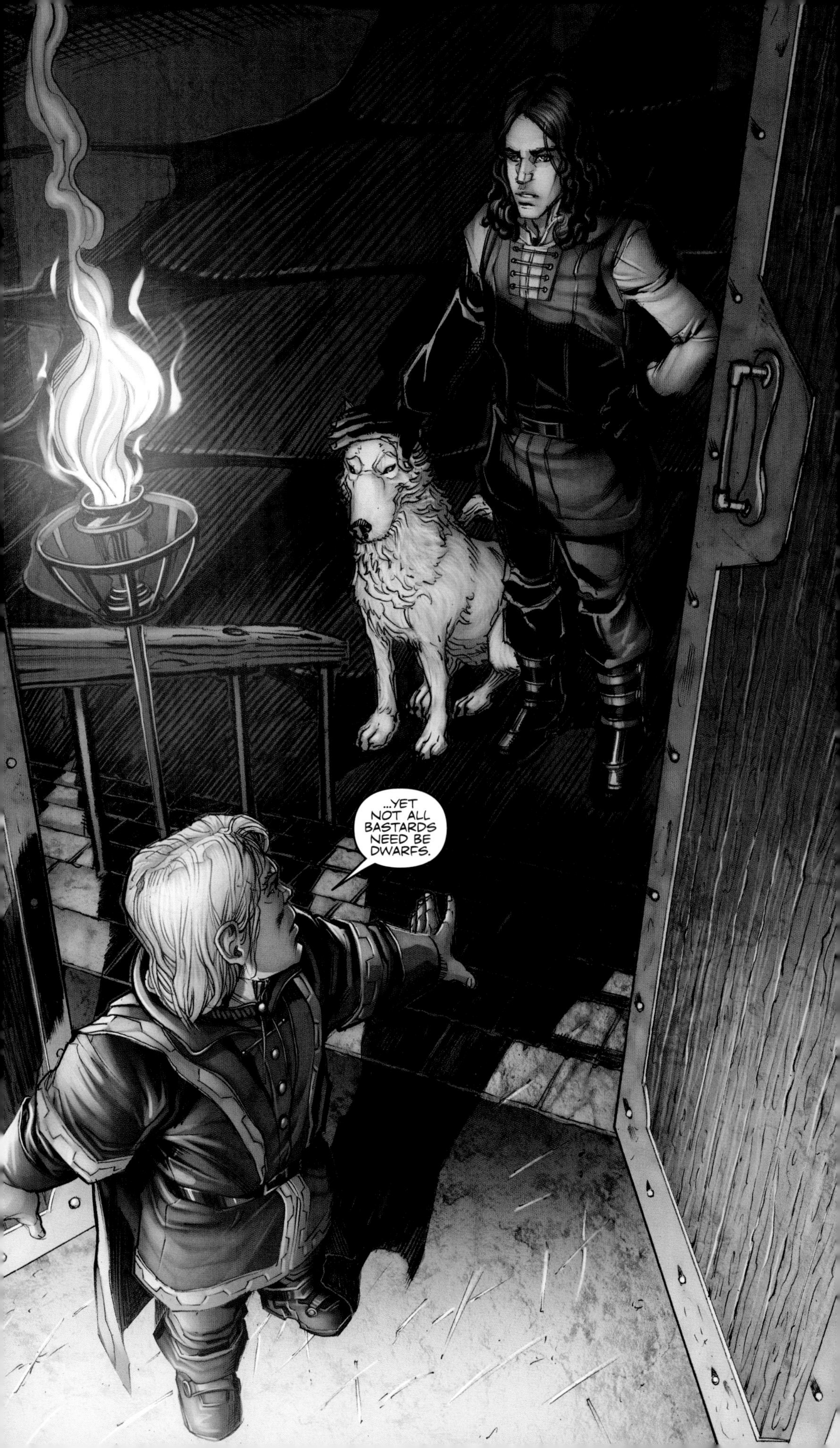
...YET NOT ALL BASTARDS NEED BE DWARFS.

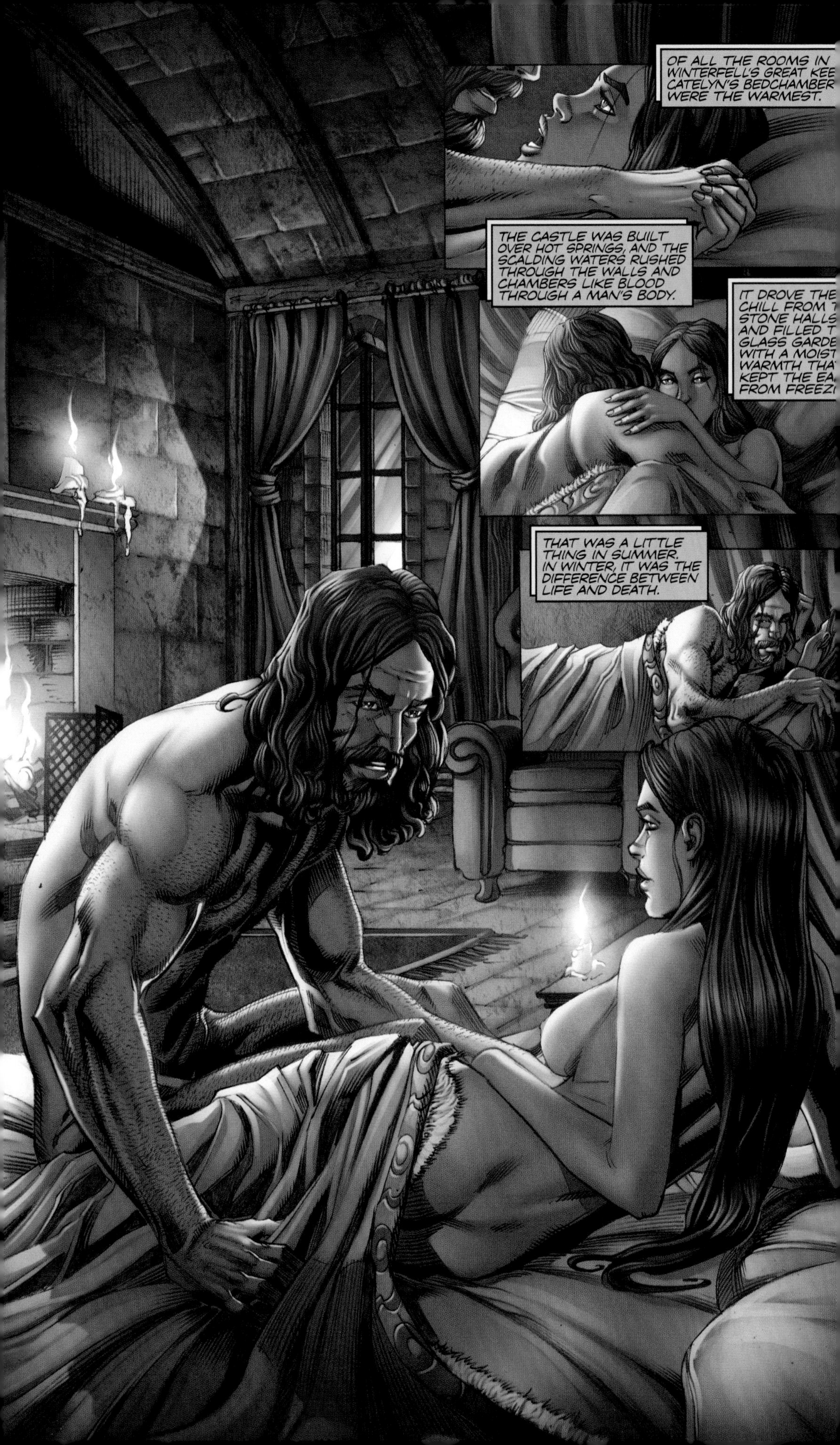
OF ALL THE ROOMS IN WINTERFELL'S GREAT KEE CATELYN'S BEDCHAMBER WERE THE WARMEST.
THE CASTLE WAS BUILT OVER HOT SPRINGS, AND THE SCALDING WATERS RUSHED THROUGH THE WALLS AND CHAMBERS LIKE BLOOD THROUGH A MAN'S BODY.
IT DROVE THE CHILL FROM T STONE HALLS AND FILLED T GLASS GARDE WITH A MOIST WARMTH THA KEPT THE EA FROM FREEZ
THAT WAS A LITTLE THING IN SUMMER. IN WINTER, IT WAS THE DIFFERENCE BETWEEN LIFE AND DEATH.

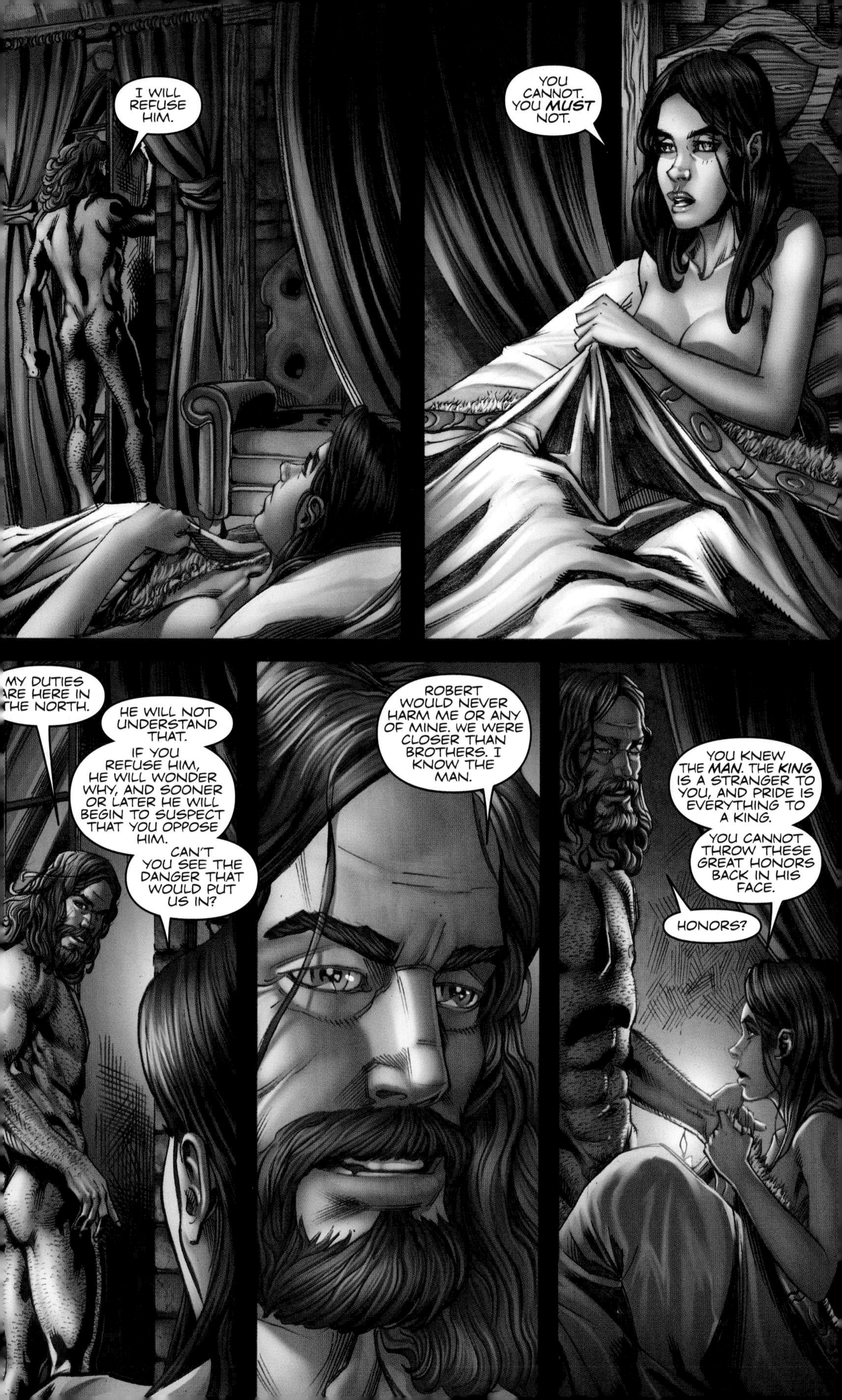

I WILL REFUSE HIM.
YOU CANNOT. YOU MUST NOT.
MY DUTIES ARE HERE IN THE NORTH.
HE WILL NOT UNDERSTAND THAT.
IF YOU REFUSE HIM, HE WILL WONDER WHY, AND SOONER OR LATER HE WILL BEGIN TO SUSPECT THAT YOU OPPOSE HIM.
CAN'T YOU SEE THE DANGER THAT WOULD PUT US IN?
ROBERT WOULD NEVER HARM ME OR ANY OF MINE. WE WERE CLOSER THAN BROTHERS. I KNOW THE MAN.
YOU KNEW THE MAN. THE KING IS A STRANGER TO YOU, AND PRIDE IS EVERYTHING TO A KING.
YOU CANNOT THROW THESE GREAT HONORS BACK IN HIS FACE.
HONORS?

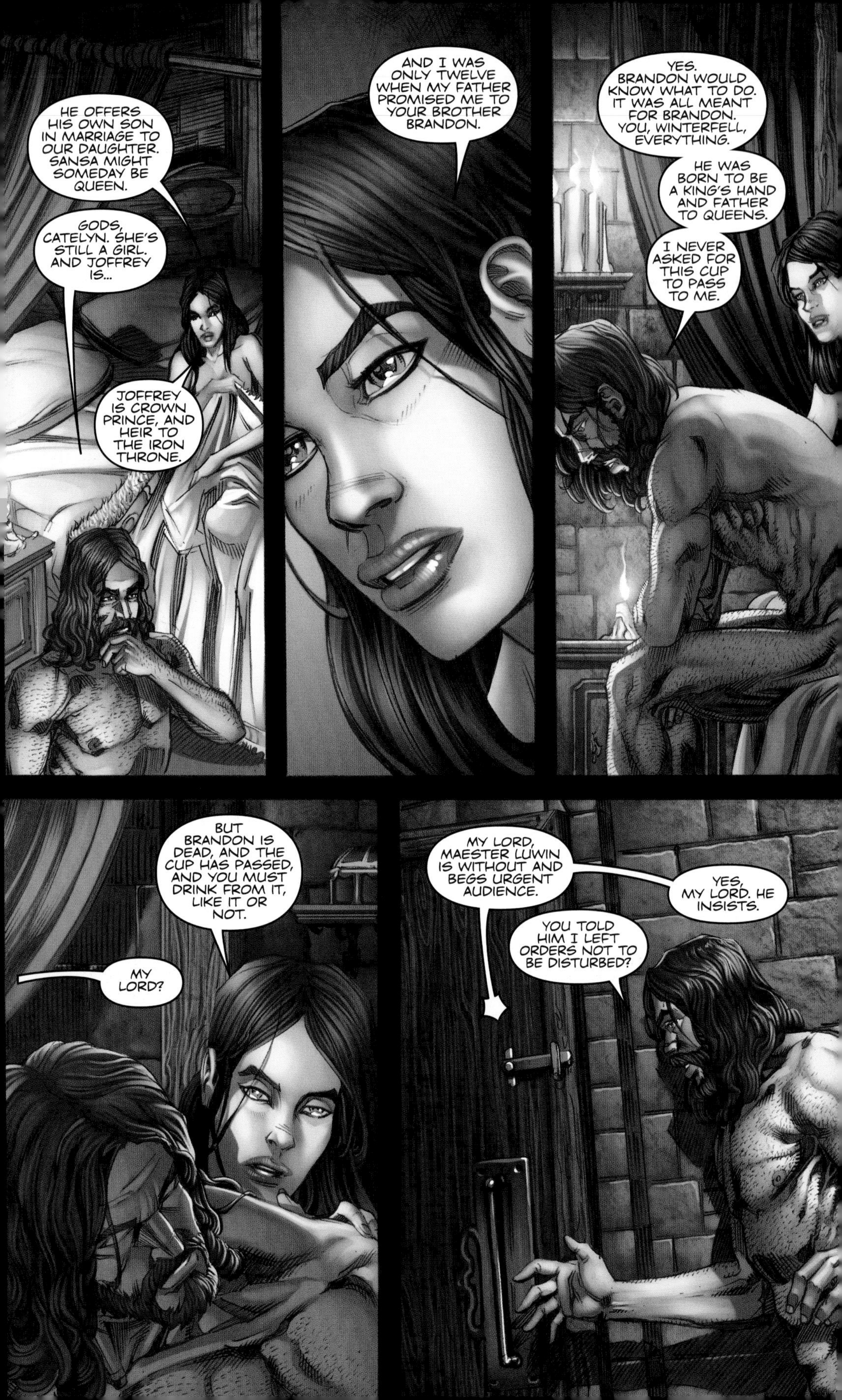
HE OFFERS HIS OWN SON IN MARRIAGE TO OUR DAUGHTER. SANSA MIGHT SOMEDAY BE QUEEN.
GODS, CATELYN. SHE'S STILL A GIRL. AND JOFFREY IS...
JOFFREY IS CROWN PRINCE, AND HEIR TO THE IRON THRONE.
AND I WAS ONLY TWELVE WHEN MY FATHER PROMISED ME TO YOUR BROTHER BRANDON.
YES. BRANDON WOULD KNOW WHAT TO DO. IT WAS ALL MEANT FOR BRANDON. YOU, WINTERFELL, EVERYTHING.
HE WAS BORN TO BE A KING'S HAND AND FATHER TO QUEENS.
I NEVER ASKED FOR THIS CUP TO PASS TO ME.
BUT BRANDON IS DEAD, AND THE CUP HAS PASSED, AND YOU MUST DRINK FROM IT, LIKE IT OR NOT.
MY LORD?
MY LORD, MAESTER LUWIN IS WITHOUT AND BEGS URGENT AUDIENCE.
YOU TOLD HIM I LEFT ORDERS NOT TO BE DISTURBED?
YES, MY LORD. HE INSISTS.

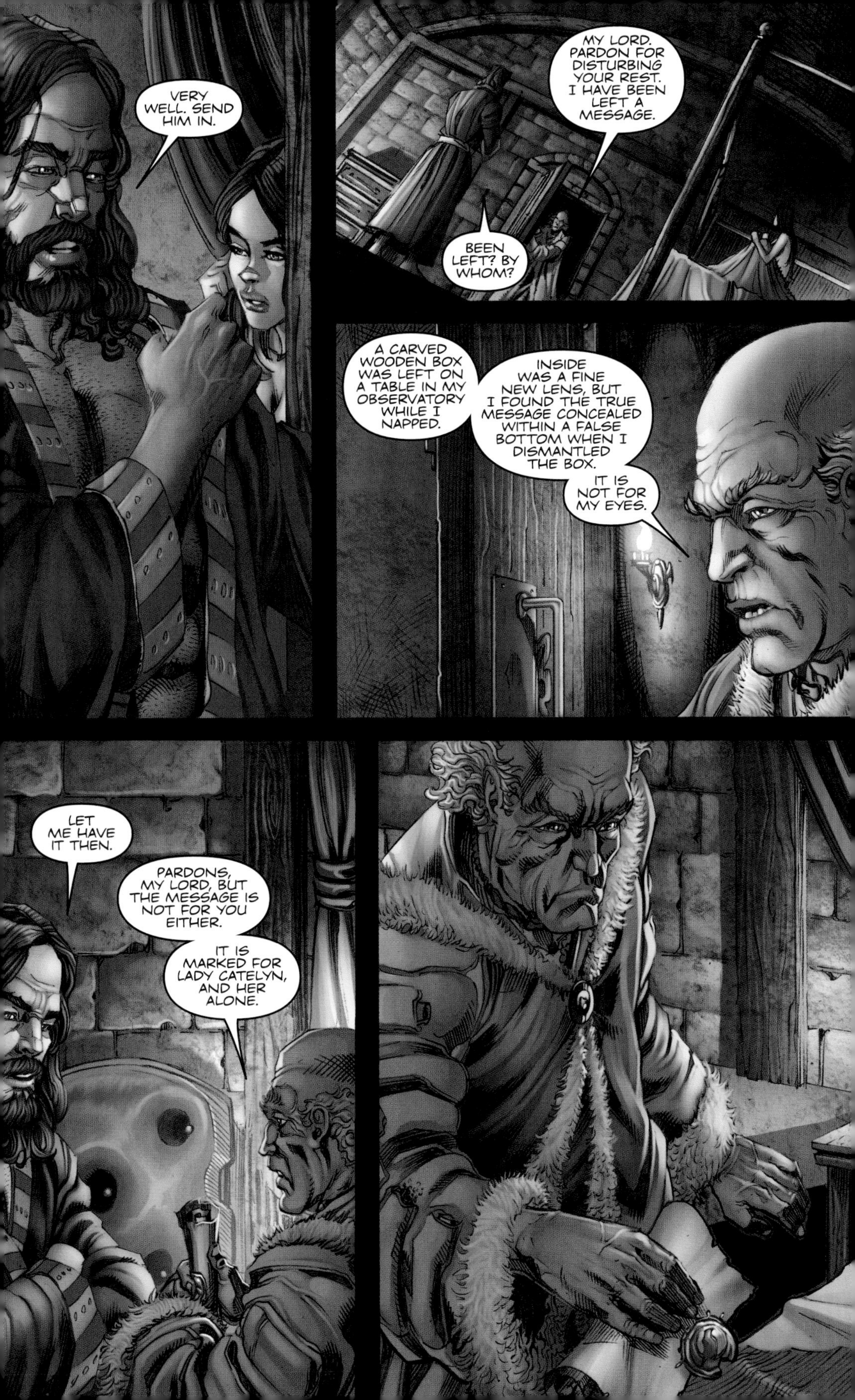
VERY WELL. SEND HIM IN.
MY LORD. PARDON FOR DISTURBING YOUR REST. I HAVE BEEN LEFT A MESSAGE.
BEEN LEFT? BY WHOM?
A CARVED WOODEN BOX WAS LEFT ON A TABLE IN MY OBSERVATORY WHILE I NAPPED.
INSIDE WAS A FINE NEW LENS, BUT I FOUND THE TRUE MESSAGE CONCEALED WITHIN A FALSE BOTTOM WHEN I DISMANTLED THE BOX.
IT IS NOT FOR MY EYES.
LET ME HAVE IT THEN.
PARDONS, MY LORD, BUT THE MESSAGE IS NOT FOR YOU EITHER.
IT IS MARKED FOR LADY CATELYN, AND HER ALONE.

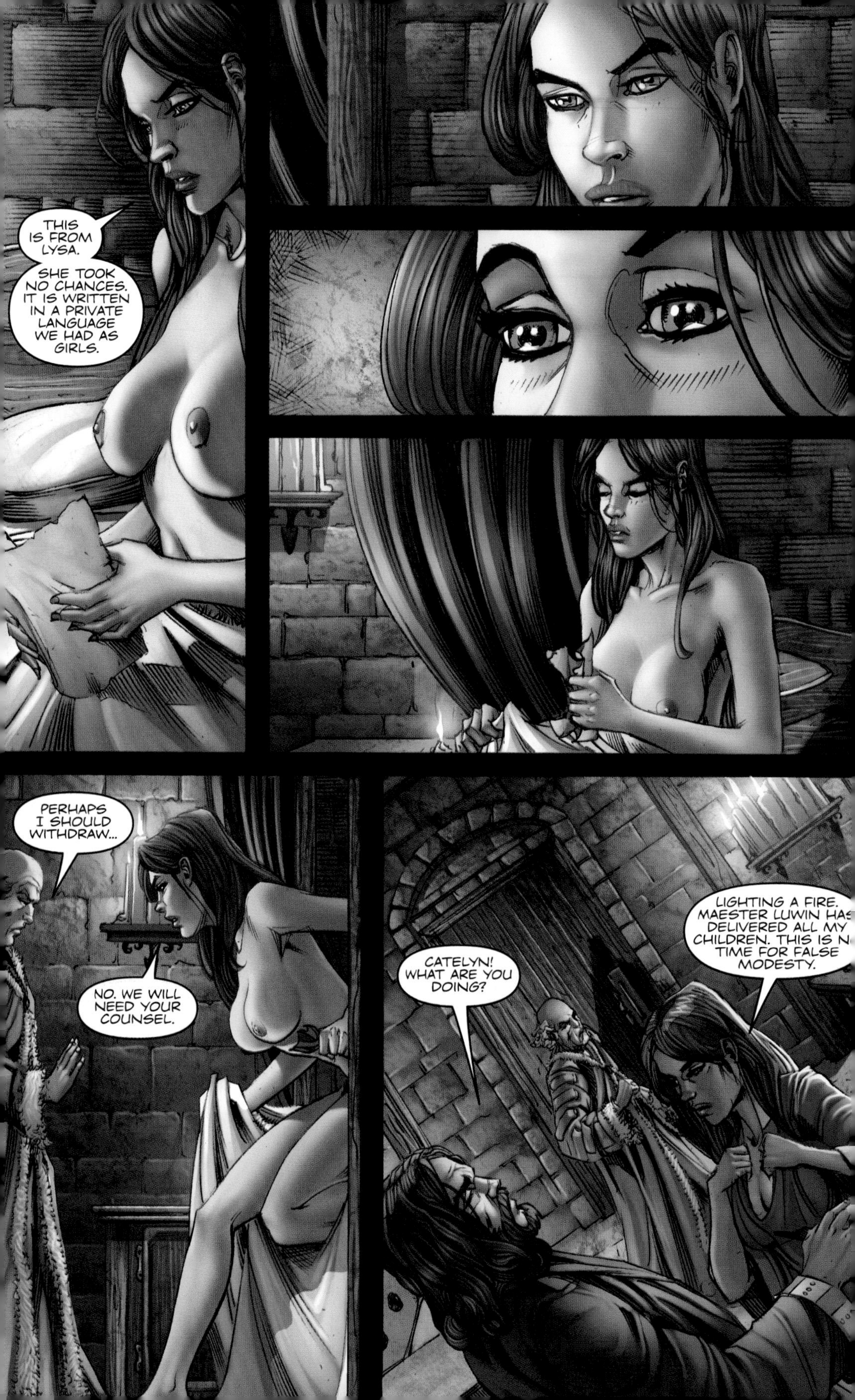
THIS IS FROM LYSA.
SHE TOOK NO CHANCES. IT IS WRITTEN IN A PRIVATE LANGUAGE WE HAD AS GIRLS.
PERHAPS I SHOULD WITHDRAW...
NO. WE WILL NEED YOUR COUNSEL.
CATELYN! WHAT ARE YOU DOING?
LIGHTING A FIRE. MAESTER LUWIN HAS DELIVERED ALL MY CHILDREN. THIS IS N TIME FOR FALSE MODESTY.

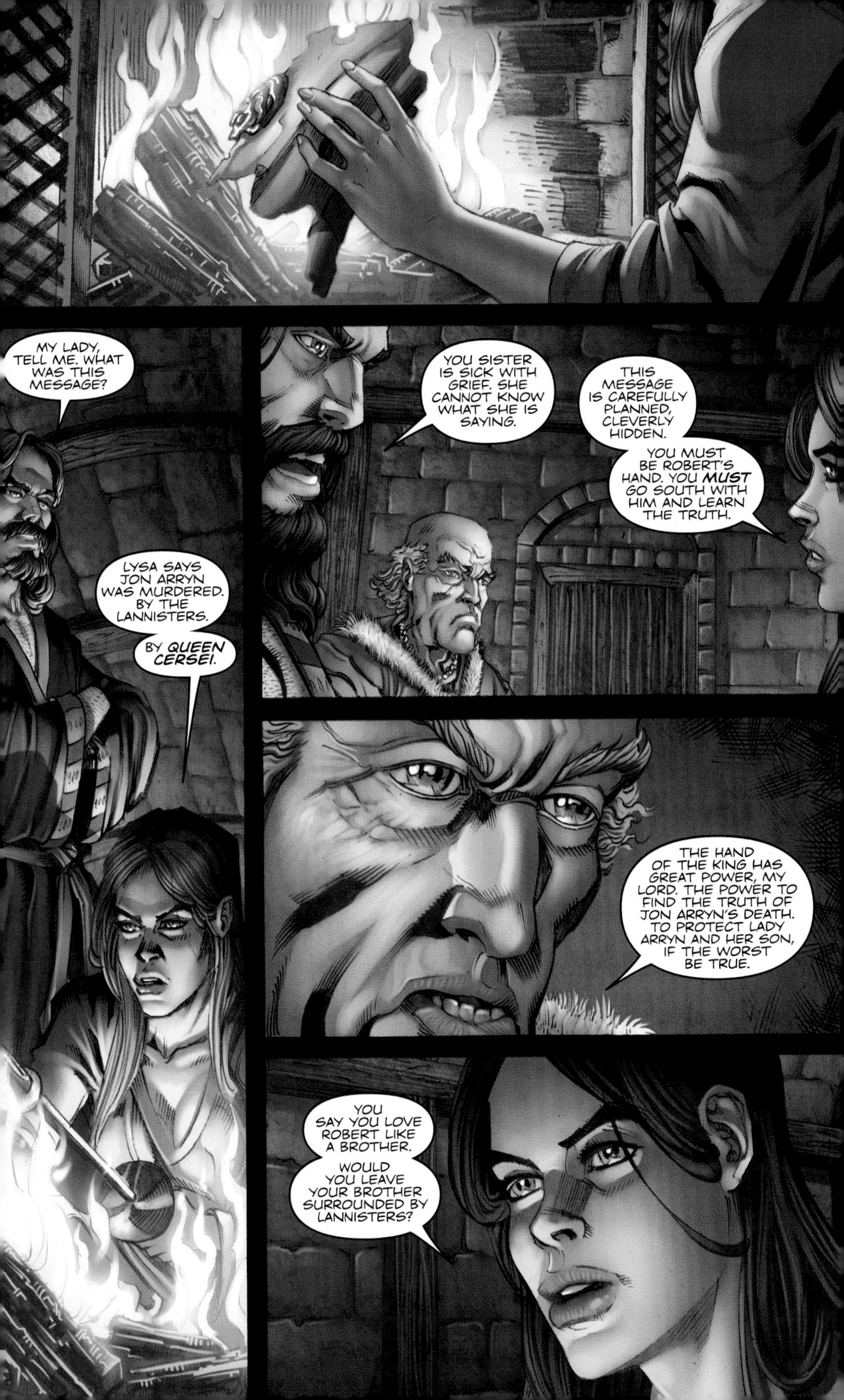
MY LADY, TELL ME. WHAT WAS THIS MESSAGE?
LYSA SAYS JON ARRYN WAS MURDERED. BY THE LANNISTERS.
BY QUEEN CERSEI.
YOU SISTER IS SICK WITH GRIEF. SHE CANNOT KNOW WHAT SHE IS SAYING.
THIS MESSAGE IS CAREFULLY PLANNED, CLEVERLY HIDDEN.
YOU MUST BE ROBERT'S HAND. YOU MUST GO SOUTH WITH HIM AND LEARN THE TRUTH.
THE HAND OF THE KING HAS GREAT POWER, MY LORD. THE POWER TO FIND THE TRUTH OF JON ARRYN'S DEATH. TO PROTECT LADY ARRYN AND HER SON, IF THE WORST BE TRUE.
YOU SAY YOU LOVE ROBERT LIKE A BROTHER.
WOULD YOU LEAVE YOUR BROTHER SURROUNDED BY LANNISTERS?

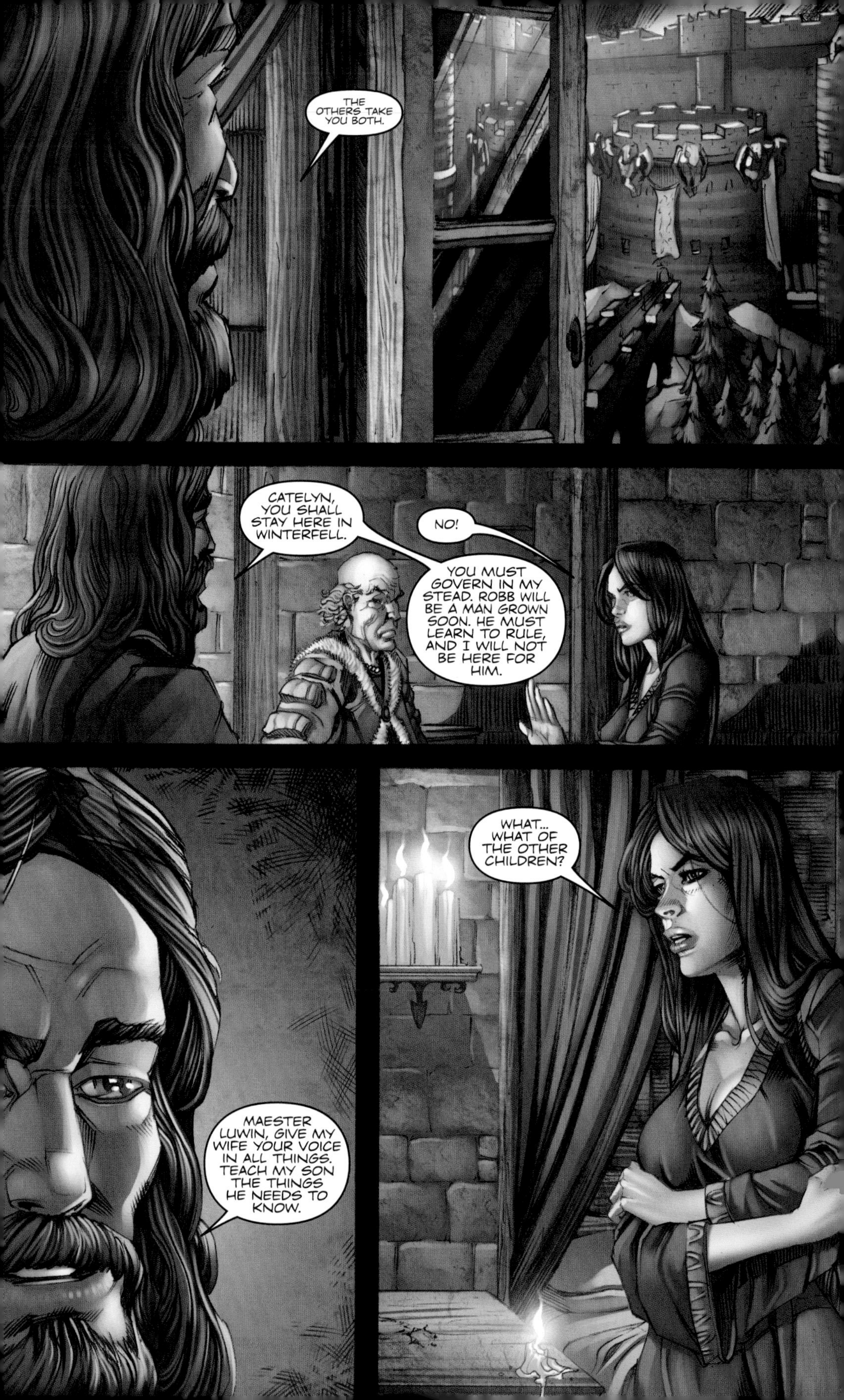
THE OTHERS TAKE YOU BOTH.
CATELYN, YOU SHALL STAY HERE IN WINTERFELL.
NO!
YOU MUST GOVERN IN MY STEAD. ROBB WILL BE A MAN GROWN SOON. HE MUST LEARN TO RULE, AND I WILL NOT BE HERE FOR HIM.
WHAT... WHAT OF THE OTHER CHILDREN?
MAESTER LUWIN, GIVE MY WIFE YOUR VOICE IN ALL THINGS. TEACH MY SON THE THINGS HE NEEDS TO KNOW.

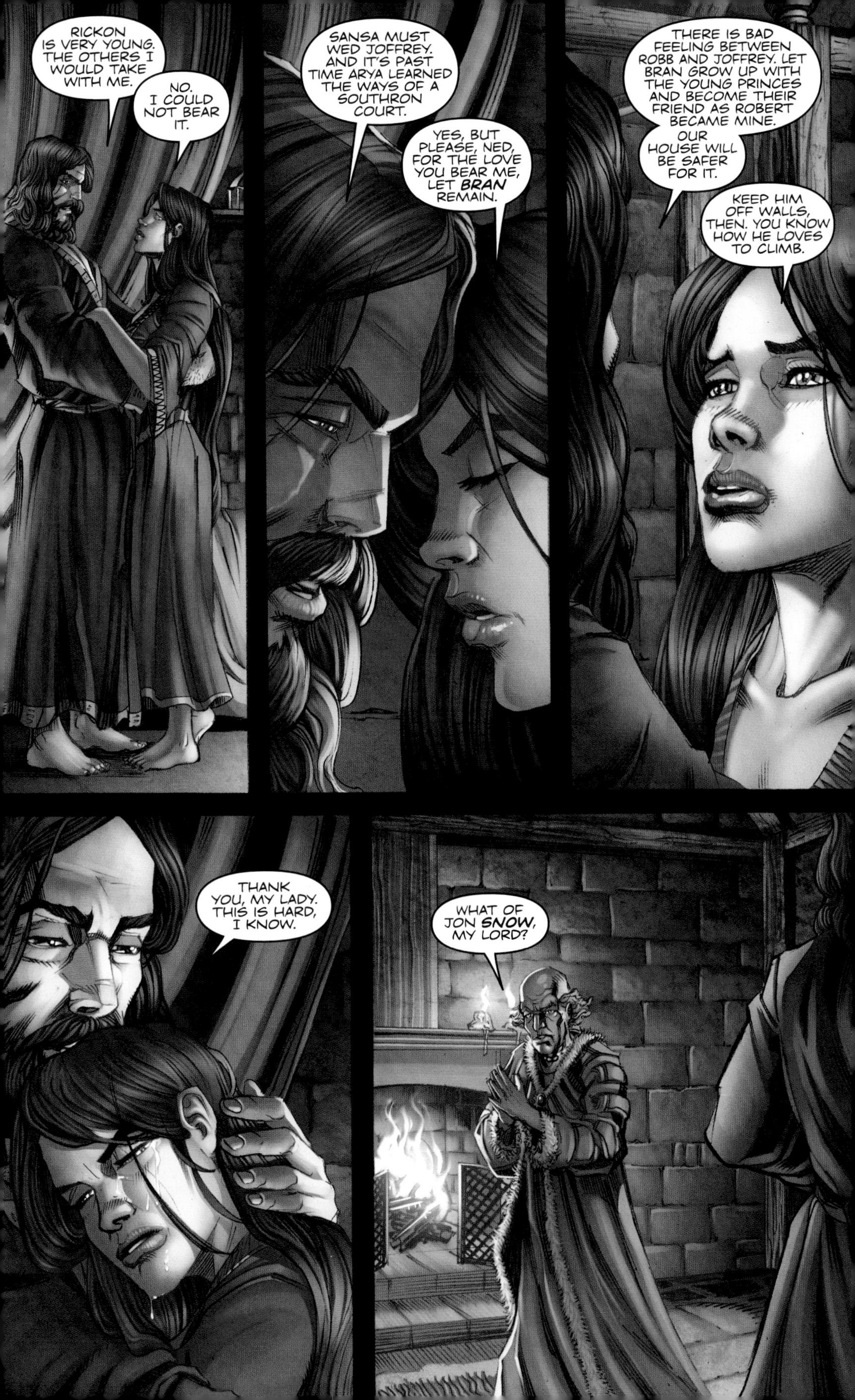
RICKON IS VERY YOUNG. THE OTHERS I WOULD TAKE WITH ME.
NO. I COULD NOT BEAR IT.
SANSA MUST WED JOFFREY. AND IT'S PAST TIME ARYA LEARNED THE WAYS OF A SOUTHRON COURT.
YES, BUT PLEASE, NED, FOR THE LOVE YOU BEAR ME, LET BRAN REMAIN.
THERE IS BAD FEELING BETWEEN ROBB AND JOFFREY. LET BRAN GROW UP WITH THE YOUNG PRINCES AND BECOME THEIR FRIEND AS ROBERT BECAME MINE.
OUR HOUSE WILL BE SAFER FOR IT.
KEEP HIM OFF WALLS, THEN. YOU KNOW HOW HE LOVES TO CLIMB.
THANK YOU, MY LADY. THIS IS HARD, I KNOW.
WHAT OF JON SNOW, MY LORD?

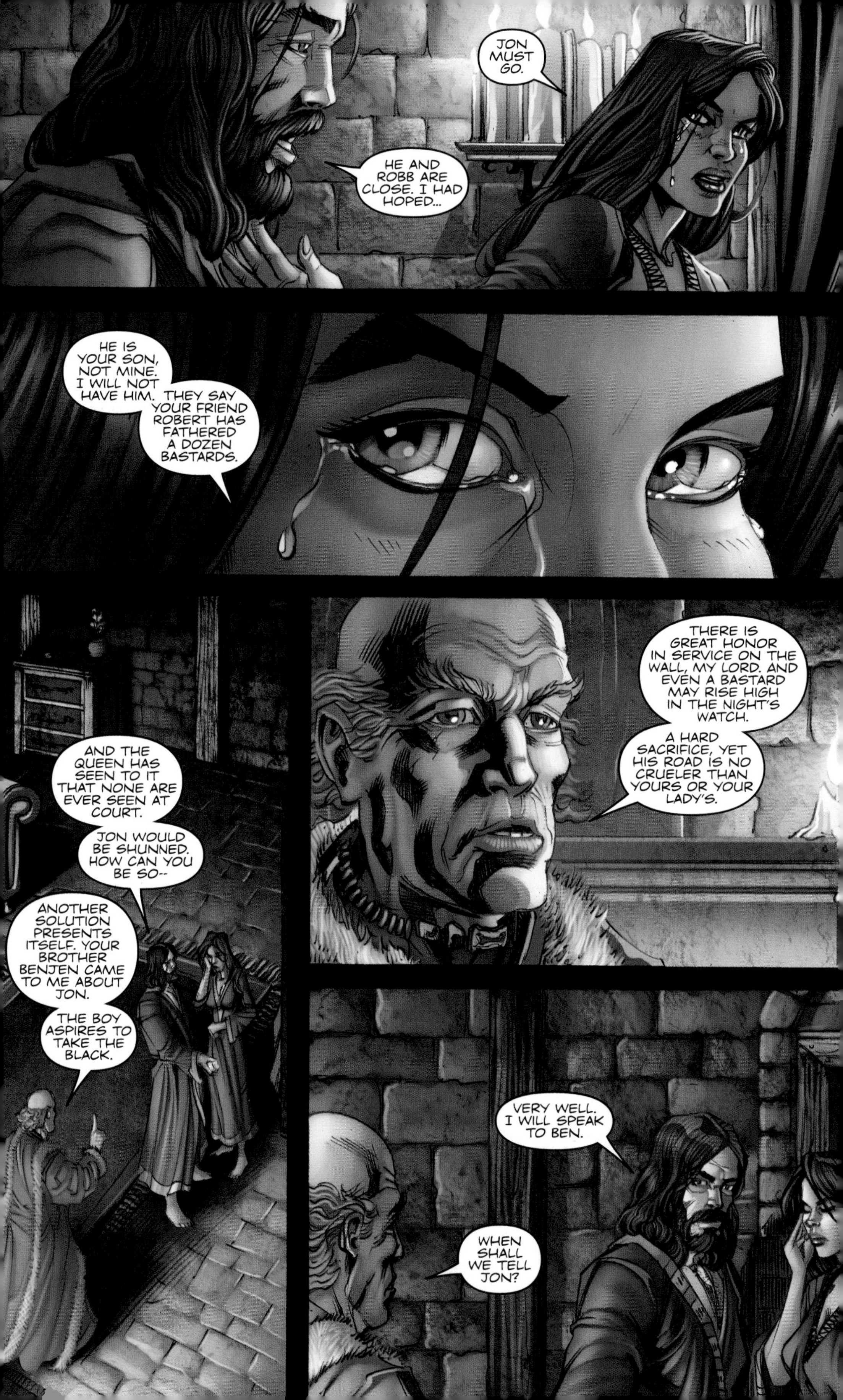

JON MUST GO.
HE AND ROBB ARE CLOSE. I HAD HOPED...
HE IS YOUR SON, NOT MINE. I WILL NOT HAVE HIM.
THEY SAY YOUR FRIEND ROBERT HAS FATHERED A DOZEN BASTARDS.
AND THE QUEEN HAS SEEN TO IT THAT NONE ARE EVER SEEN AT COURT.
JON WOULD BE SHUNNED. HOW CAN YOU BE SO--
ANOTHER SOLUTION PRESENTS ITSELF. YOUR BROTHER BENJEN CAME TO ME ABOUT JON.
THE BOY ASPIRES TO TAKE THE BLACK.
THERE IS GREAT HONOR IN SERVICE ON THE WALL, MY LORD. AND EVEN A BASTARD MAY RISE HIGH IN THE NIGHT'S WATCH.
A HARD SACRIFICE, YET HIS ROAD IS NO CRUELER THAN YOURS OR YOUR LADY'S.
VERY WELL. I WILL SPEAK TO BEN.
WHEN SHALL WE TELL JON?

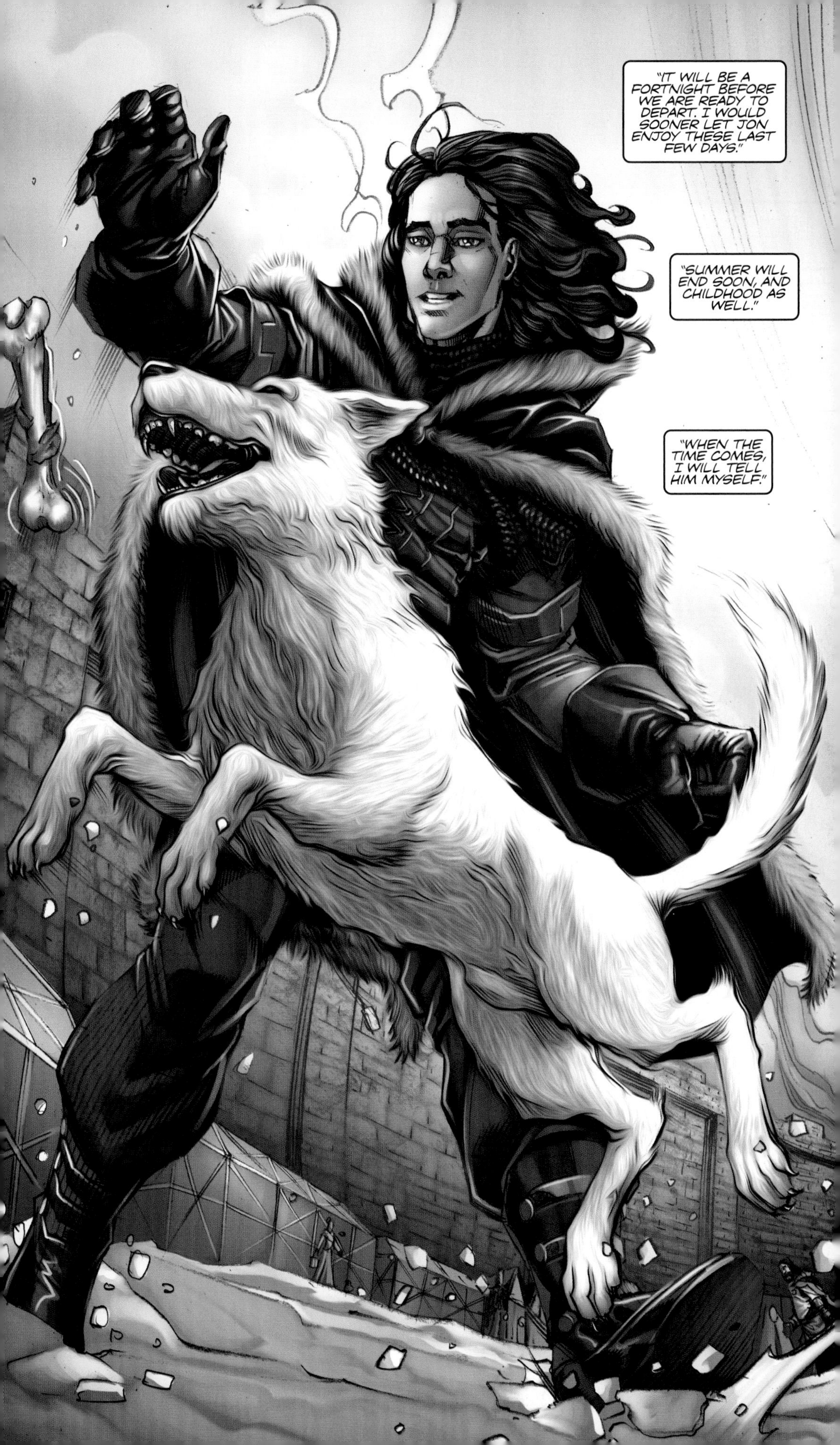
"IT WILL BE A FORTNIGHT BEFORE WE ARE READY TO DEPART. I WOULD SOONER LET JON ENJOY THESE LAST FEW DAYS."
"SUMMER WILL END SOON, AND CHILDHOOD AS WELL."
"WHEN THE TIME COMES, I WILL TELL HIM MYSELF."

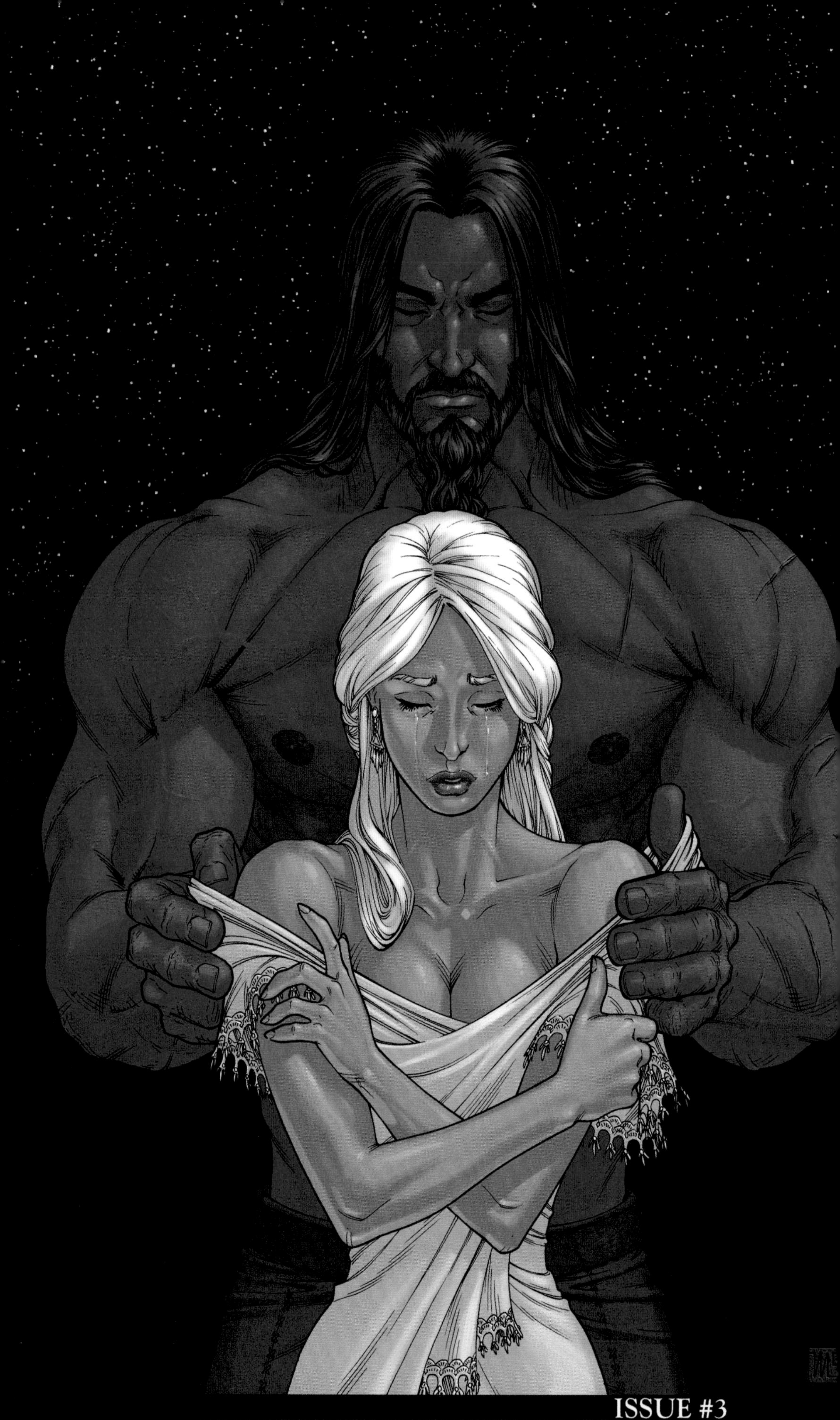

ISSUE #3

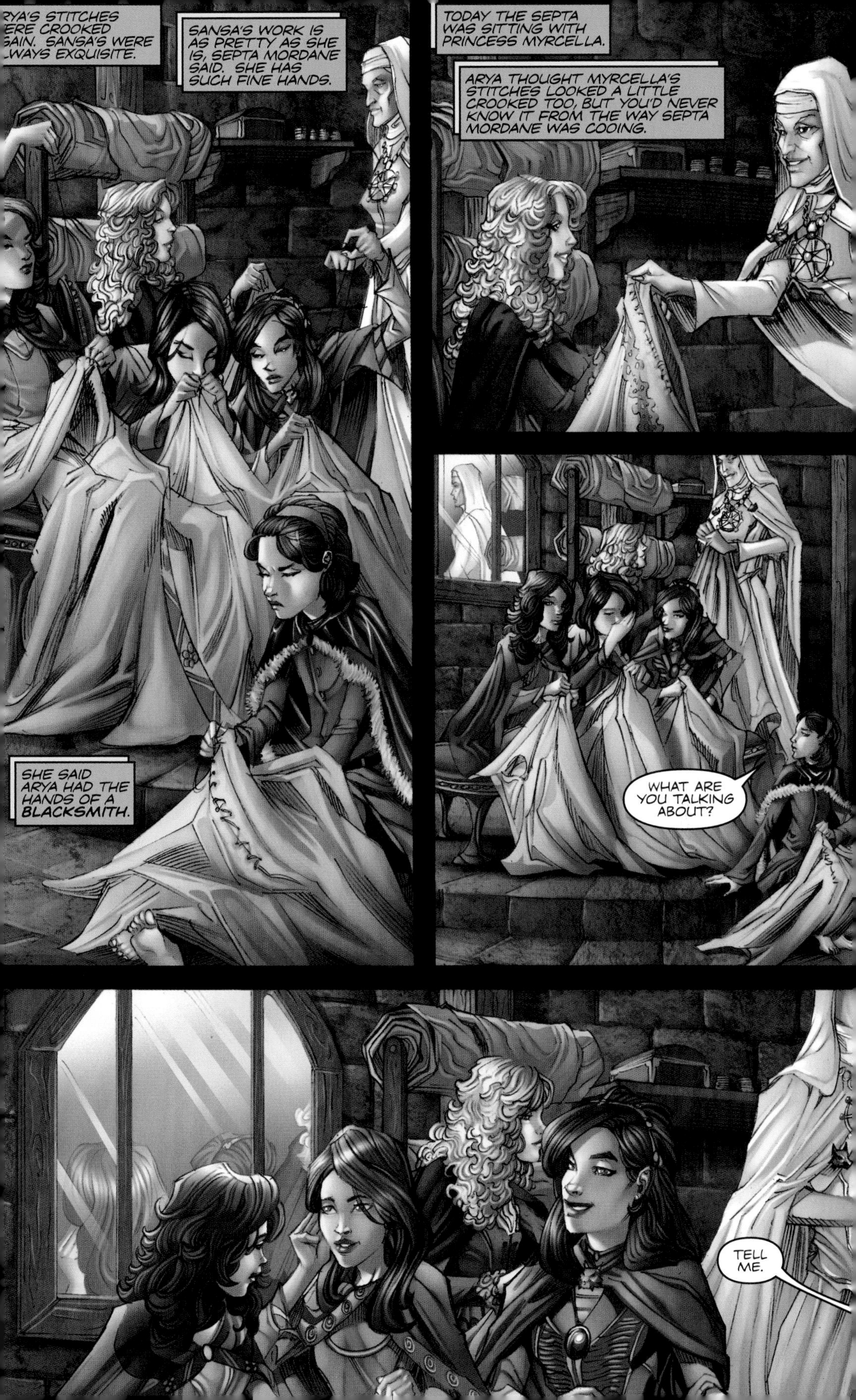
RYA'S STITCHES ERE CROOKED GAIN. SANSA'S WERE LWAYS EXQUISITE.
SANSA'S WORK IS AS PRETTY AS SHE IS, SEPTA MORDANE SAID. SHE HAS SUCH FINE HANDS.
SHE SAID ARYA HAD THE HANDS OF A BLACKSMITH.
TODAY THE SEPTA WAS SITTING WITH PRINCESS MYRCELLA.
ARYA THOUGHT MYRCELLA'S STITCHES LOOKED A LITTLE CROOKED TOO, BUT YOU'D NEVER KNOW IT FROM THE WAY SEPTA MORDANE WAS COOING.
WHAT ARE YOU TALKING ABOUT?
TELL ME.

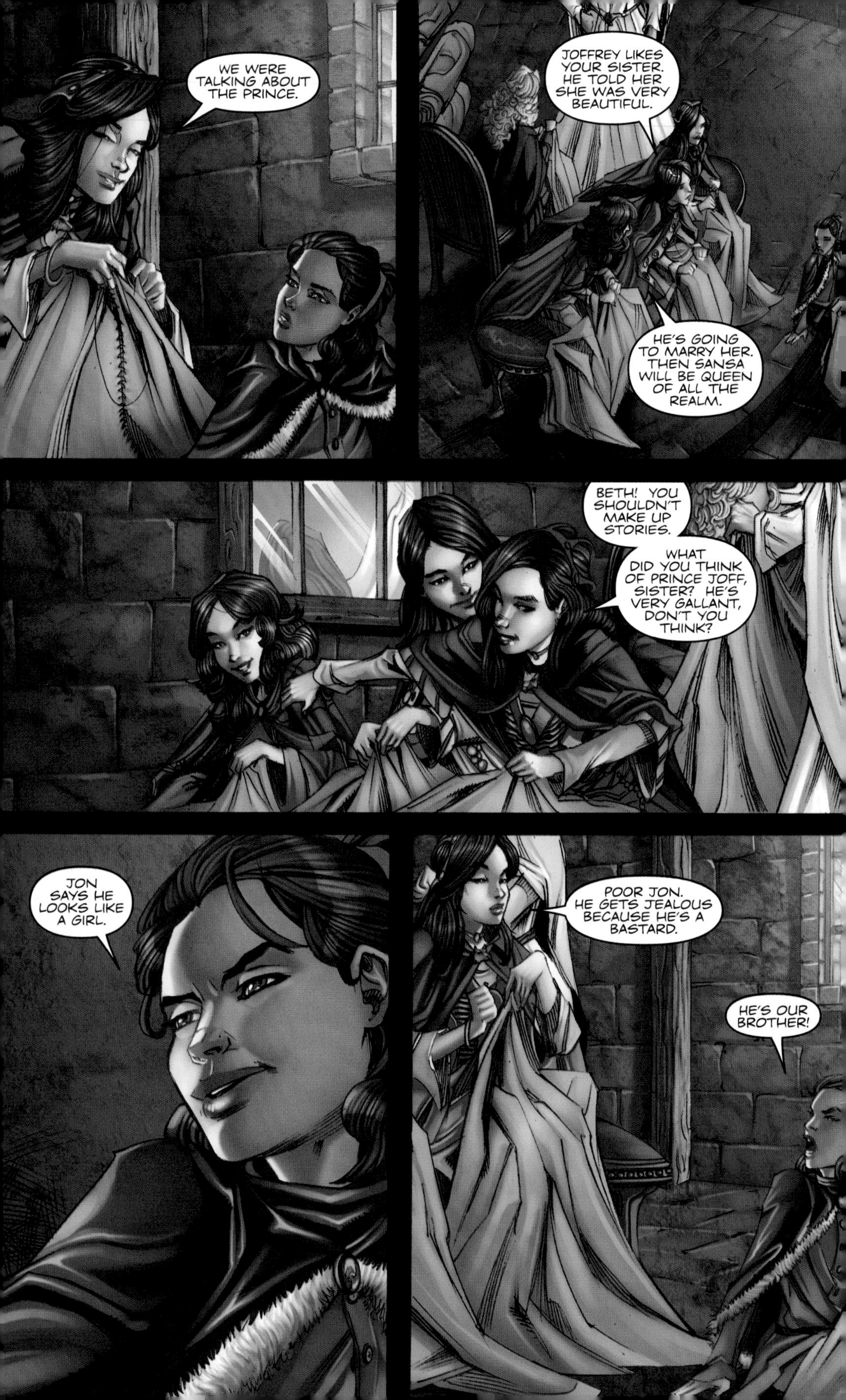
WE WERE TALKING ABOUT THE PRINCE.
JOFFREY LIKES YOUR SISTER. HE TOLD HER SHE WAS VERY BEAUTIFUL.
HE'S GOING TO MARRY HER. THEN SANSA WILL BE QUEEN OF ALL THE REALM.
BETH! YOU SHOULDN'T MAKE UP STORIES.
WHAT DID YOU THINK OF PRINCE JOFF, SISTER? HE'S VERY GALLANT, DON'T YOU THINK?
JON SAYS HE LOOKS LIKE A GIRL.
POOR JON. HE GETS JEALOUS BECAUSE HE'S A BASTARD.
HE'S OUR BROTHER!

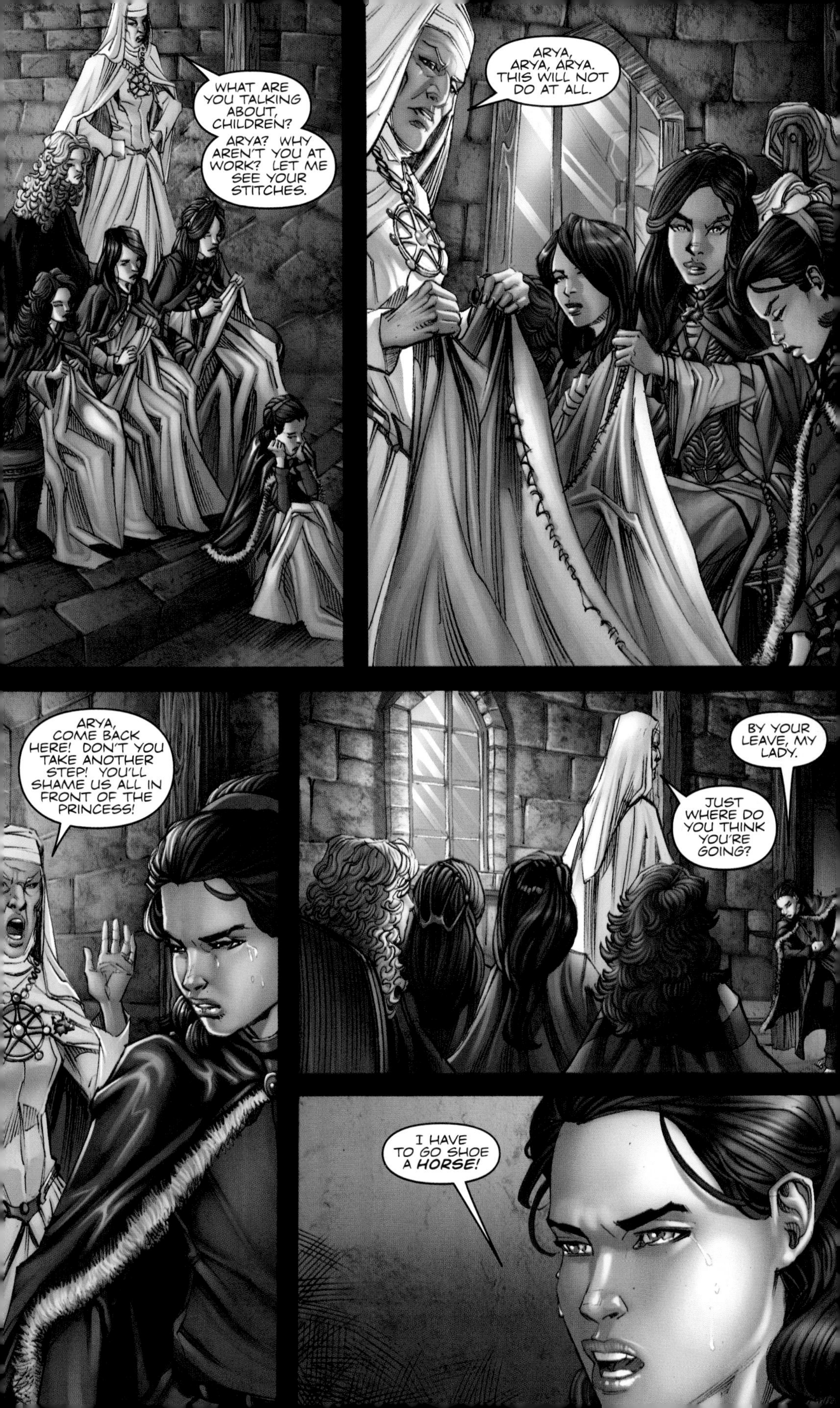
WHAT ARE YOU TALKING ABOUT, CHILDREN?
ARYA? WHY AREN'T YOU AT WORK? LET ME SEE YOUR STITCHES.
ARYA, ARYA, ARYA. THIS WILL NOT DO AT ALL.
ARYA, COME BACK HERE! DON'T YOU TAKE ANOTHER STEP! YOU'LL SHAME US ALL IN FRONT OF THE PRINCESS!
BY YOUR LEAVE, MY LADY.
JUST WHERE DO YOU THINK YOU'RE GOING?
I HAVE TO GO SHOE A HORSE!

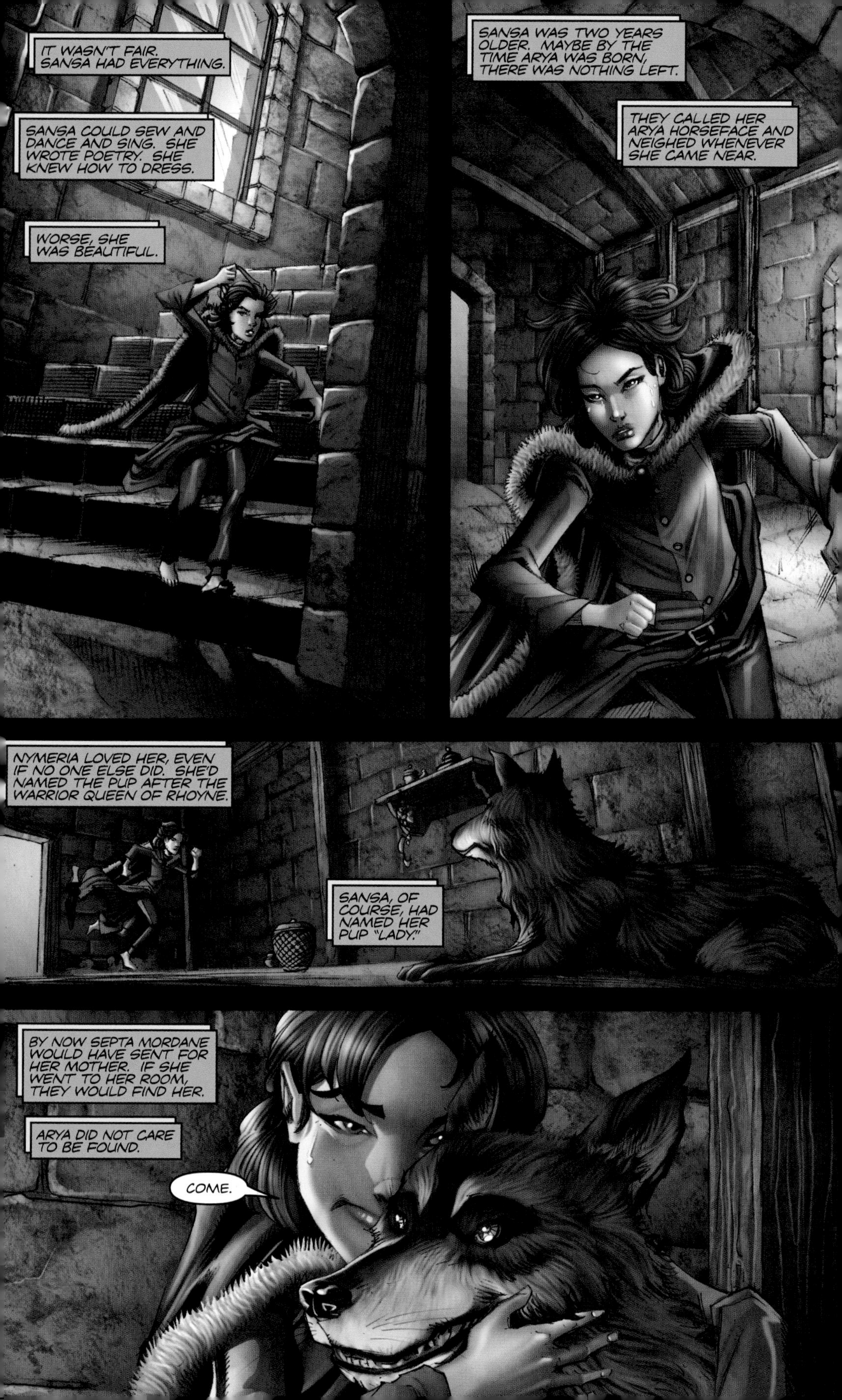

IT WASN'T FAIR. SANSA HAD EVERYTHING.
SANSA COULD SEW AND DANCE AND SING. SHE WROTE POETRY. SHE KNEW HOW TO DRESS.
WORSE, SHE WAS BEAUTIFUL.
SANSA WAS TWO YEARS OLDER. MAYBE BY THE TIME ARYA WAS BORN, THERE WAS NOTHING LEFT.
THEY CALLED HER ARYA HORSEFACE AND NEIGHED WHENEVER SHE CAME NEAR.
NYMERIA LOVED HER, EVEN IF NO ONE ELSE DID. SHE'D NAMED THE PUP AFTER THE WARRIOR QUEEN OF RHOYNE.
SANSA, OF COURSE, HAD NAMED HER PUP "LADY."
BY NOW SEPTA MORDANE WOULD HAVE SENT FOR HER MOTHER. IF SHE WENT TO HER ROOM, THEY WOULD FIND HER.
ARYA DID NOT CARE TO BE FOUND.
COME.

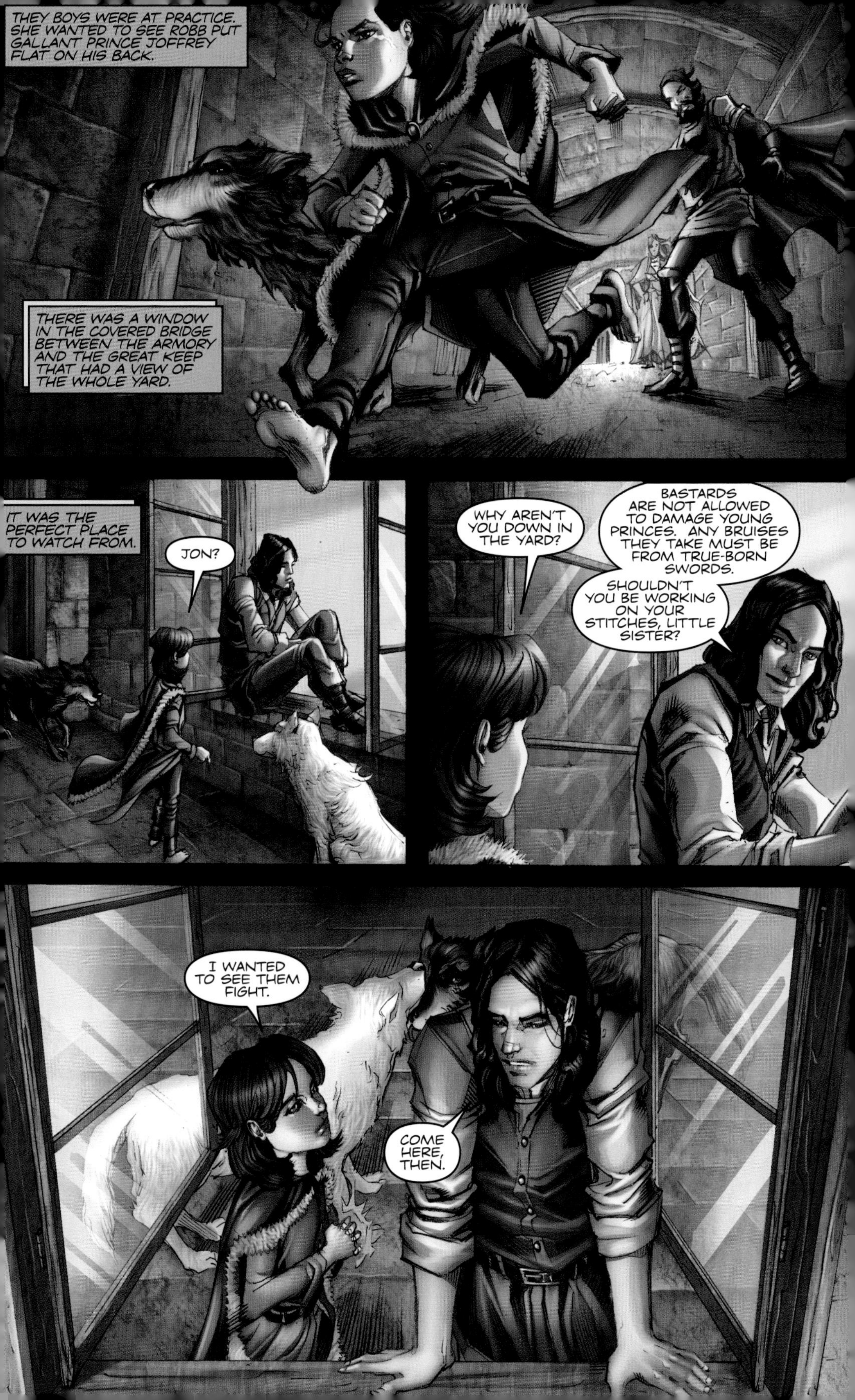
THEY BOYS WERE AT PRACTICE. SHE WANTED TO SEE ROBB PUT GALLANT PRINCE JOFFREY FLAT ON HIS BACK.
THERE WAS A WINDOW IN THE COVERED BRIDGE BETWEEN THE ARMORY AND THE GREAT KEEP THAT HAD A VIEW OF THE WHOLE YARD.
IT WAS THE PERFECT PLACE TO WATCH FROM.
JON?
WHY AREN'T YOU DOWN IN THE YARD?
BASTARDS ARE NOT ALLOWED TO DAMAGE YOUNG PRINCES. ANY BRUISES THEY TAKE MUST BE FROM TRUE-BORN SWORDS.
SHOULDN'T YOU BE WORKING ON YOUR STITCHES, LITTLE SISTER?
I WANTED TO SEE THEM FIGHT.
COME HERE, THEN.

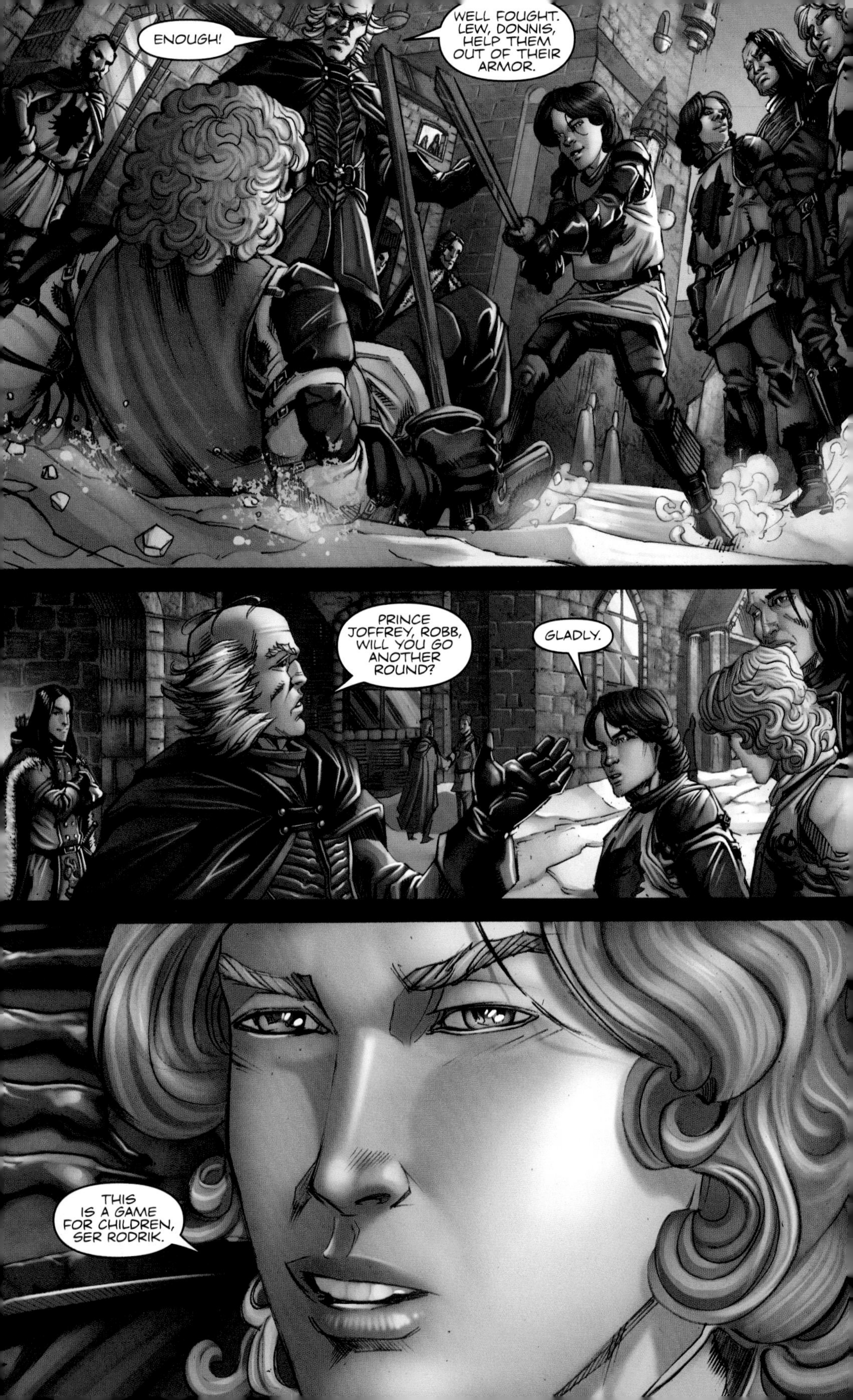
ENOUGH!
WELL FOUGHT. LEW, DONNIS, HELP THEM OUT OF THEIR ARMOR.
PRINCE JOFFREY, ROBB, WILL YOU GO ANOTHER ROUND?
GLADLY.
THIS IS A GAME FOR CHILDREN, SER RODRIK.

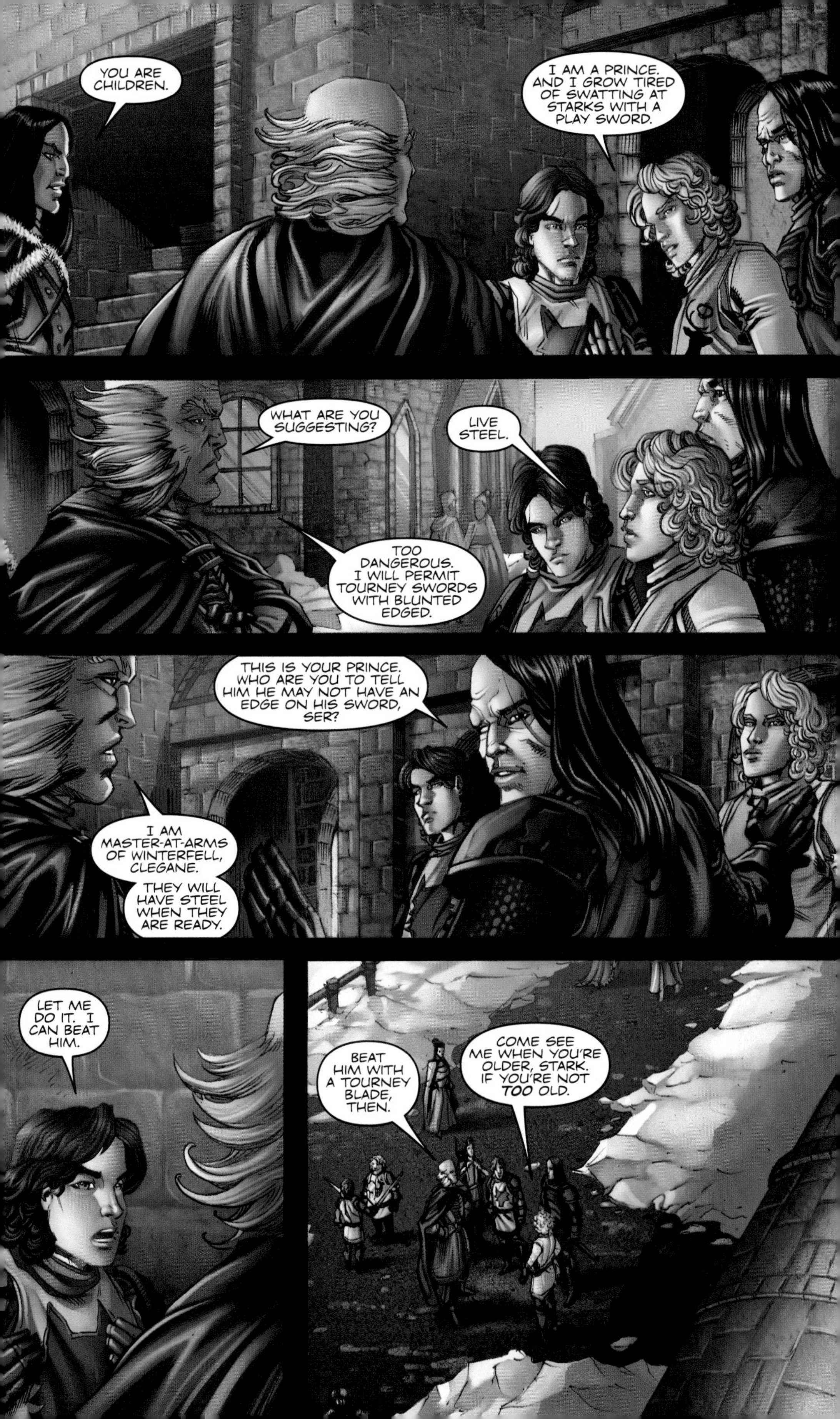
YOU ARE CHILDREN.
I AM A PRINCE. AND I GROW TIRED OF SWATTING AT STARKS WITH A PLAY SWORD.
WHAT ARE YOU SUGGESTING?
LIVE STEEL.
TOO DANGEROUS. I WILL PERMIT TOURNEY SWORDS WITH BLUNTED EDGED.
THIS IS YOUR PRINCE. WHO ARE YOU TO TELL HIM HE MAY NOT HAVE AN EDGE ON HIS SWORD, SER?
I AM MASTER-AT-ARMS OF WINTERFELL, CLEGANE.
THEY WILL HAVE STEEL WHEN THEY ARE READY.
LET ME DO IT. I CAN BEAT HIM.
BEAT HIM WITH A TOURNEY BLADE, THEN.
COME SEE ME WHEN YOU'RE OLDER, STARK. IF YOU'RE NOT *TOO* OLD.

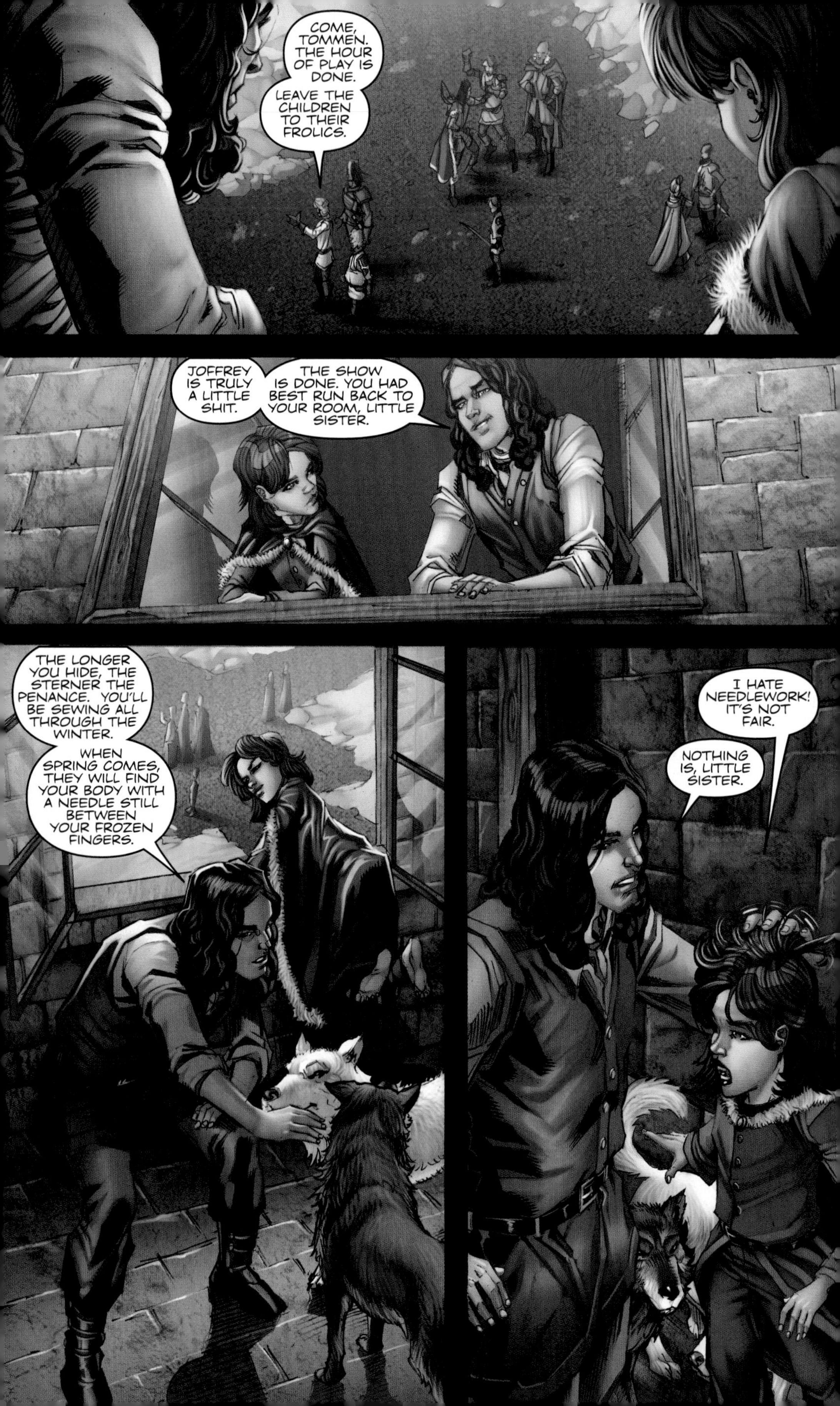
COME, TOMMEN. THE HOUR OF PLAY IS DONE.
LEAVE THE CHILDREN TO THEIR FROLICS.
JOFFREY IS TRULY A LITTLE SHIT.
THE SHOW IS DONE. YOU HAD BEST RUN BACK TO YOUR ROOM, LITTLE SISTER.
THE LONGER YOU HIDE, THE STERNER THE PENANCE. YOU'LL BE SEWING ALL THROUGH THE WINTER.
WHEN SPRING COMES, THEY WILL FIND YOUR BODY WITH A NEEDLE STILL BETWEEN YOUR FROZEN FINGERS.
I HATE NEEDLEWORK! IT'S NOT FAIR.
NOTHING IS, LITTLE SISTER.

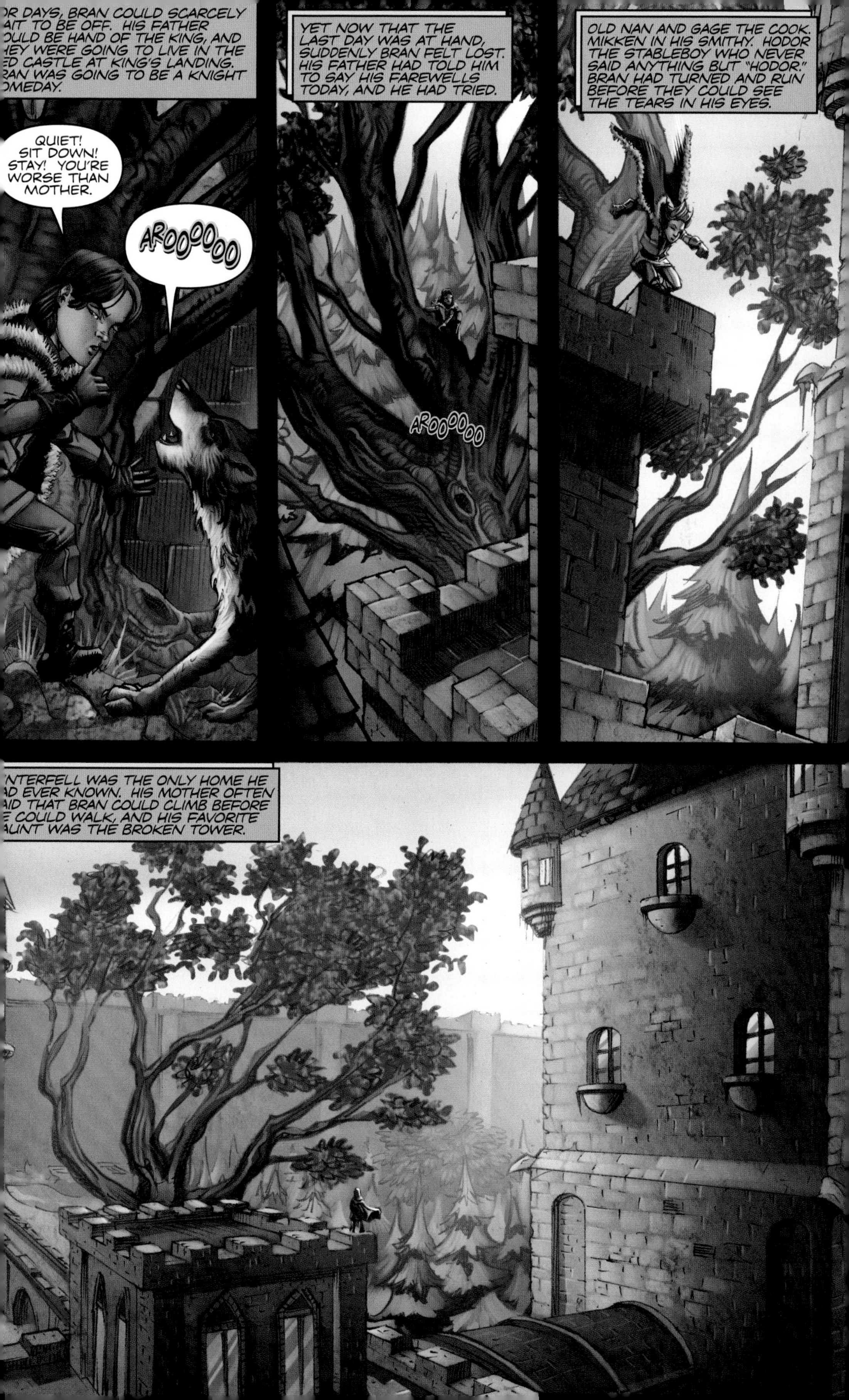
OR DAYS, BRAN COULD SCARCELY AIT TO BE OFF. HIS FATHER OULD BE HAND OF THE KING, AND HEY WERE GOING TO LIVE IN THE ED CASTLE AT KING'S LANDING. RAN WAS GOING TO BE A KNIGHT OMEDAY.
QUIET! SIT DOWN! STAY! YOU'RE WORSE THAN MOTHER.
AROOOOOOO
YET NOW THAT THE LAST DAY WAS AT HAND, SUDDENLY BRAN FELT LOST. HIS FATHER HAD TOLD HIM TO SAY HIS FAREWELLS TODAY, AND HE HAD TRIED.
AROOOOOO
OLD NAN AND GAGE THE COOK. MIKKEN IN HIS SMITHY. HODOR THE STABLEBOY WHO NEVER SAID ANYTHING BUT "HODOR." BRAN HAD TURNED AND RUN BEFORE THEY COULD SEE THE TEARS IN HIS EYES.
NTERFELL WAS THE ONLY HOME HE AD EVER KNOWN. HIS MOTHER OFTEN AID THAT BRAN COULD CLIMB BEFORE E COULD WALK, AND HIS FAVORITE AUNT WAS THE BROKEN TOWER.

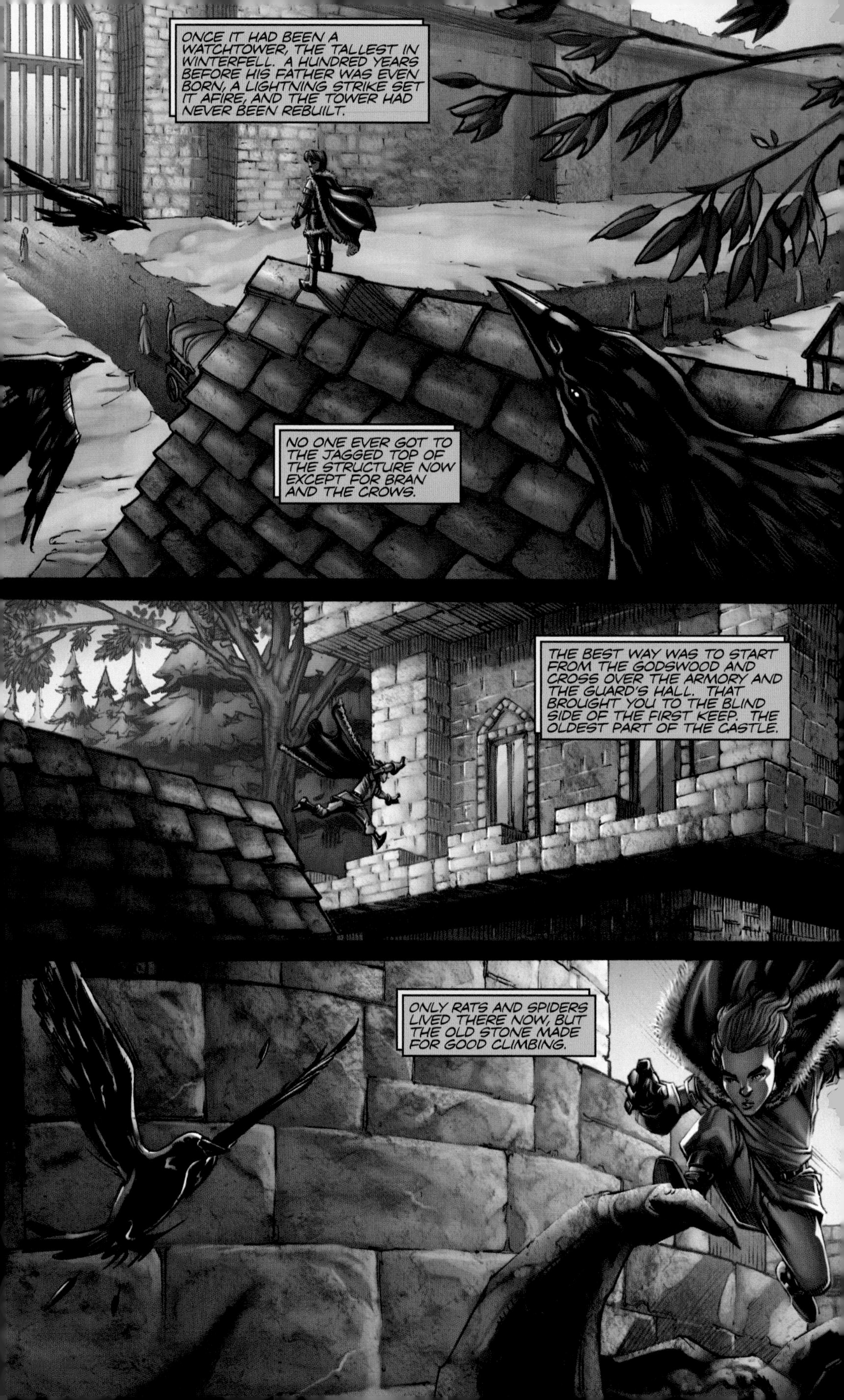
ONCE IT HAD BEEN A WATCHTOWER, THE TALLEST IN WINTERFELL. A HUNDRED YEARS BEFORE HIS FATHER WAS EVEN BORN, A LIGHTNING STRIKE SET IT AFIRE, AND THE TOWER HAD NEVER BEEN REBUILT.
NO ONE EVER GOT TO THE JAGGED TOP OF THE STRUCTURE NOW EXCEPT FOR BRAN AND THE CROWS.
THE BEST WAY WAS TO START FROM THE GODSWOOD AND CROSS OVER THE ARMORY AND THE GUARD'S HALL. THAT BROUGHT YOU TO THE BLIND SIDE OF THE FIRST KEEP. THE OLDEST PART OF THE CASTLE.
ONLY RATS AND SPIDERS LIVED THERE NOW, BUT THE OLD STONE MADE FOR GOOD CLIMBING.

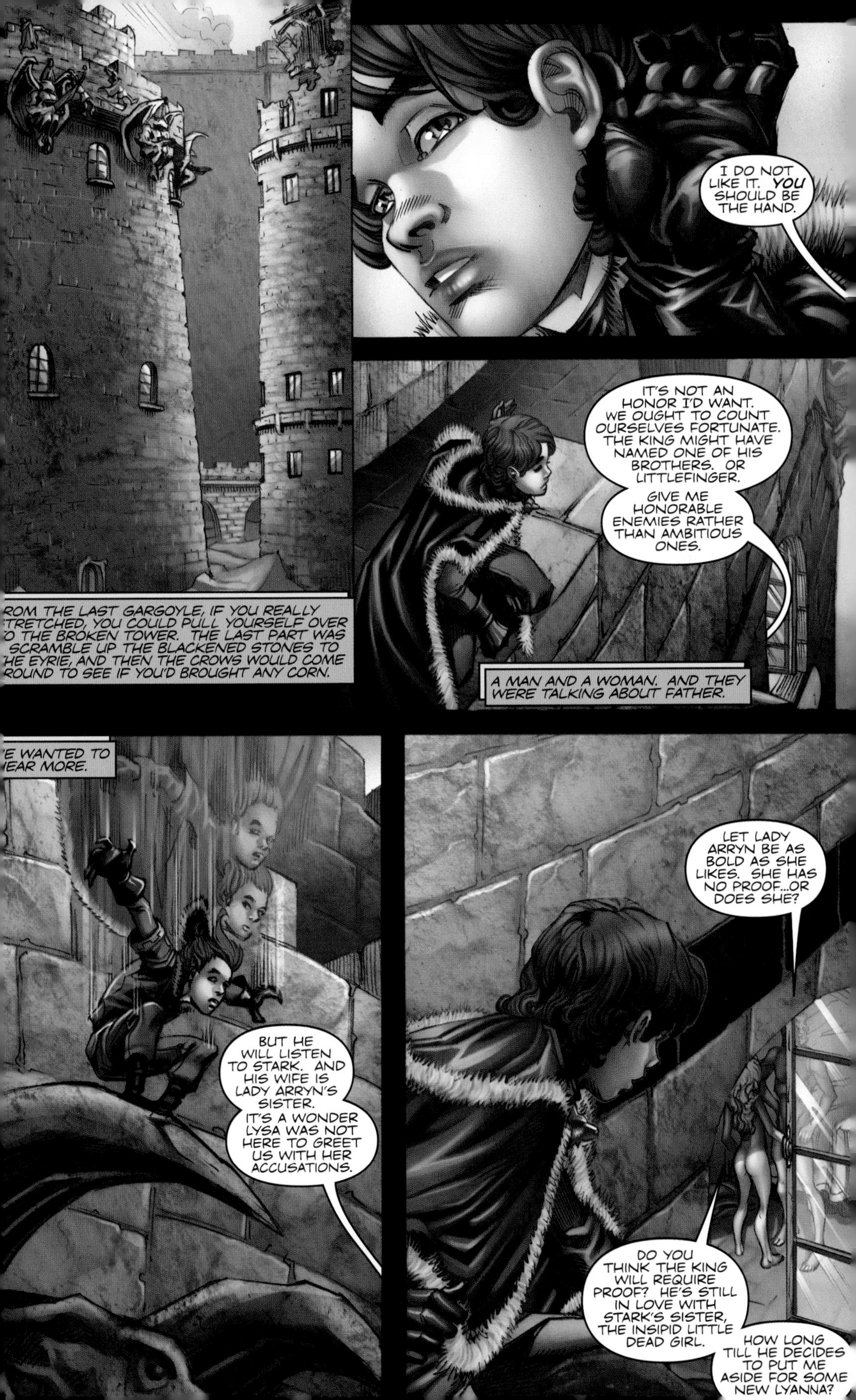
ROM THE LAST GARGOYLE, IF YOU REALLY TRETCHED, YOU COULD PULL YOURSELF OVER O THE BROKEN TOWER. THE LAST PART WAS SCRAMBLE UP THE BLACKENED STONES TO HE EYRIE, AND THEN THE CROWS WOULD COME ROUND TO SEE IF YOU'D BROUGHT ANY CORN.
I DO NOT LIKE IT. *YOU* SHOULD BE THE HAND.
IT'S NOT AN HONOR I'D WANT. WE OUGHT TO COUNT OURSELVES FORTUNATE. THE KING MIGHT HAVE NAMED ONE OF HIS BROTHERS. OR LITTLEFINGER.
GIVE ME HONORABLE ENEMIES RATHER THAN AMBITIOUS ONES.
A MAN AND A WOMAN. AND THEY WERE TALKING ABOUT FATHER.
'E WANTED TO EAR MORE.
BUT HE WILL LISTEN TO STARK. AND HIS WIFE IS LADY ARRYN'S SISTER.
IT'S A WONDER LYSA WAS NOT HERE TO GREET US WITH HER ACCUSATIONS.
LET LADY ARRYN BE AS BOLD AS SHE LIKES. SHE HAS NO PROOF...OR DOES SHE?
DO YOU THINK THE KING WILL REQUIRE PROOF? HE'S STILL IN LOVE WITH STARK'S SISTER, THE INSIPID LITTLE DEAD GIRL.
HOW LONG TILL HE DECIDES TO PUT ME ASIDE FOR SOME NEW LYANNA?

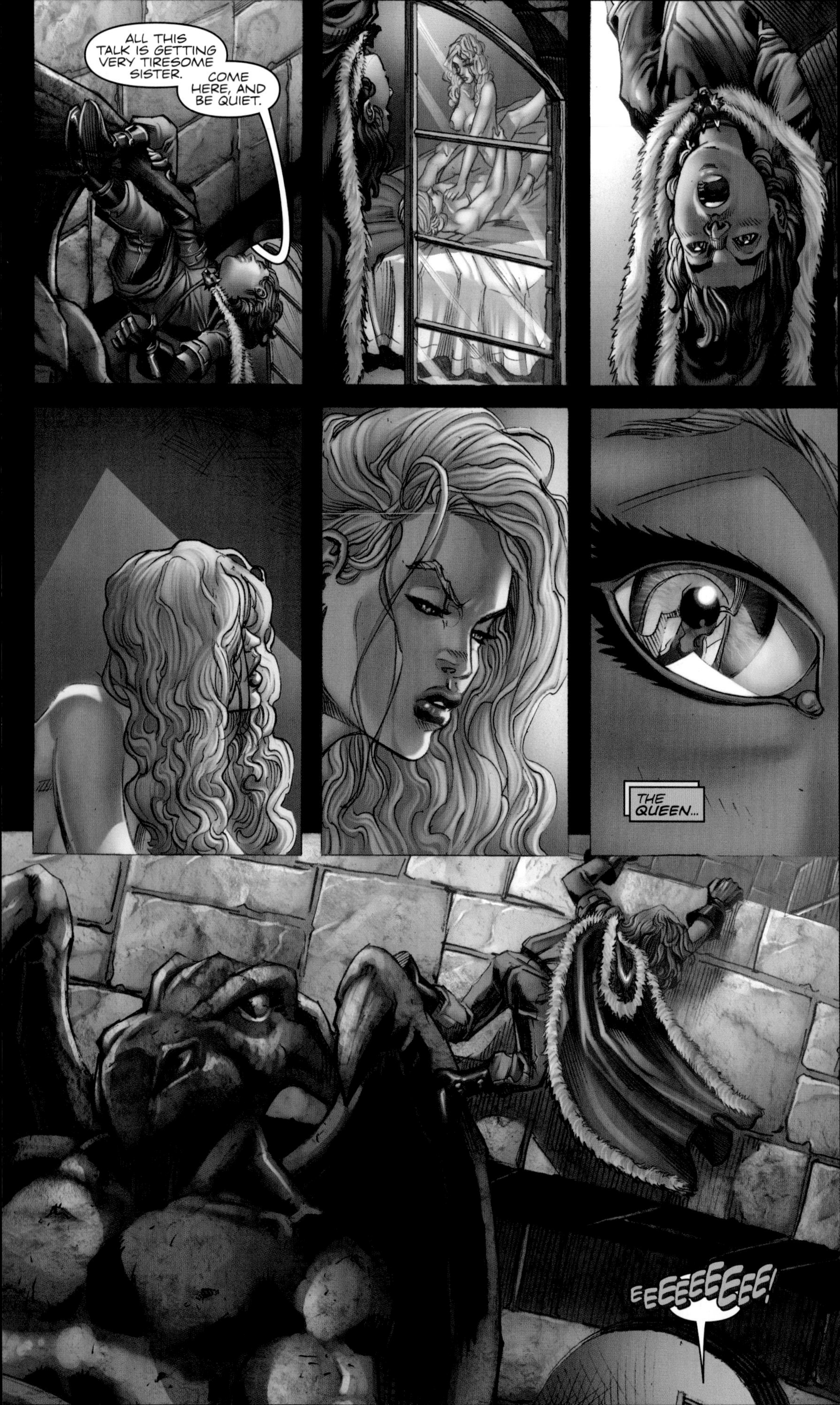
ALL THIS TALK IS GETTING VERY TIRESOME SISTER.
COME HERE, AND BE QUIET.
THE QUEEN...
EEEEEEEEEE!

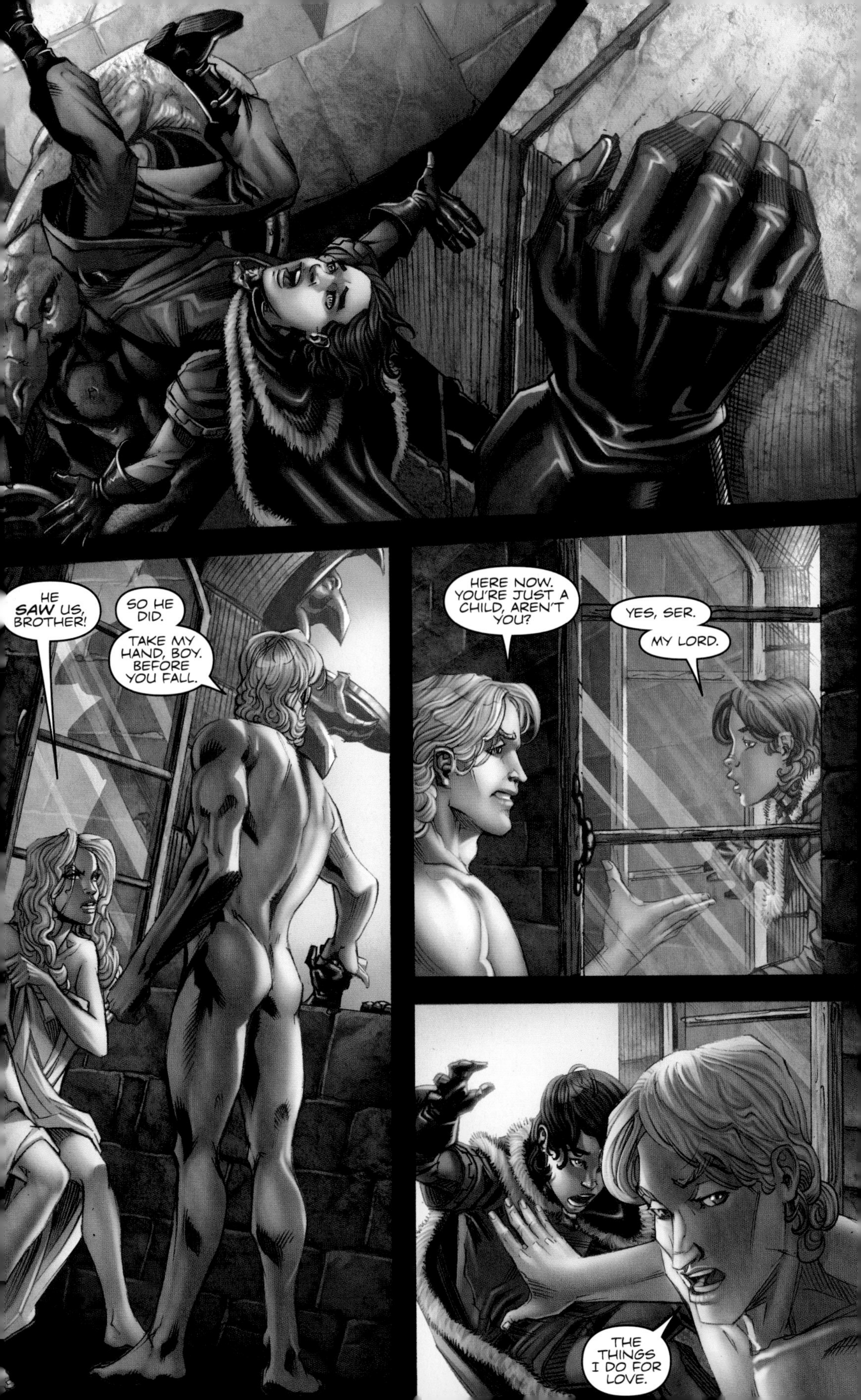
HE SAW US, BROTHER!
SO HE DID.
TAKE MY HAND, BOY. BEFORE YOU FALL.
HERE NOW. YOU'RE JUST A CHILD, AREN'T YOU?
YES, SER.
MY LORD.
THE THINGS I DO FOR LOVE.

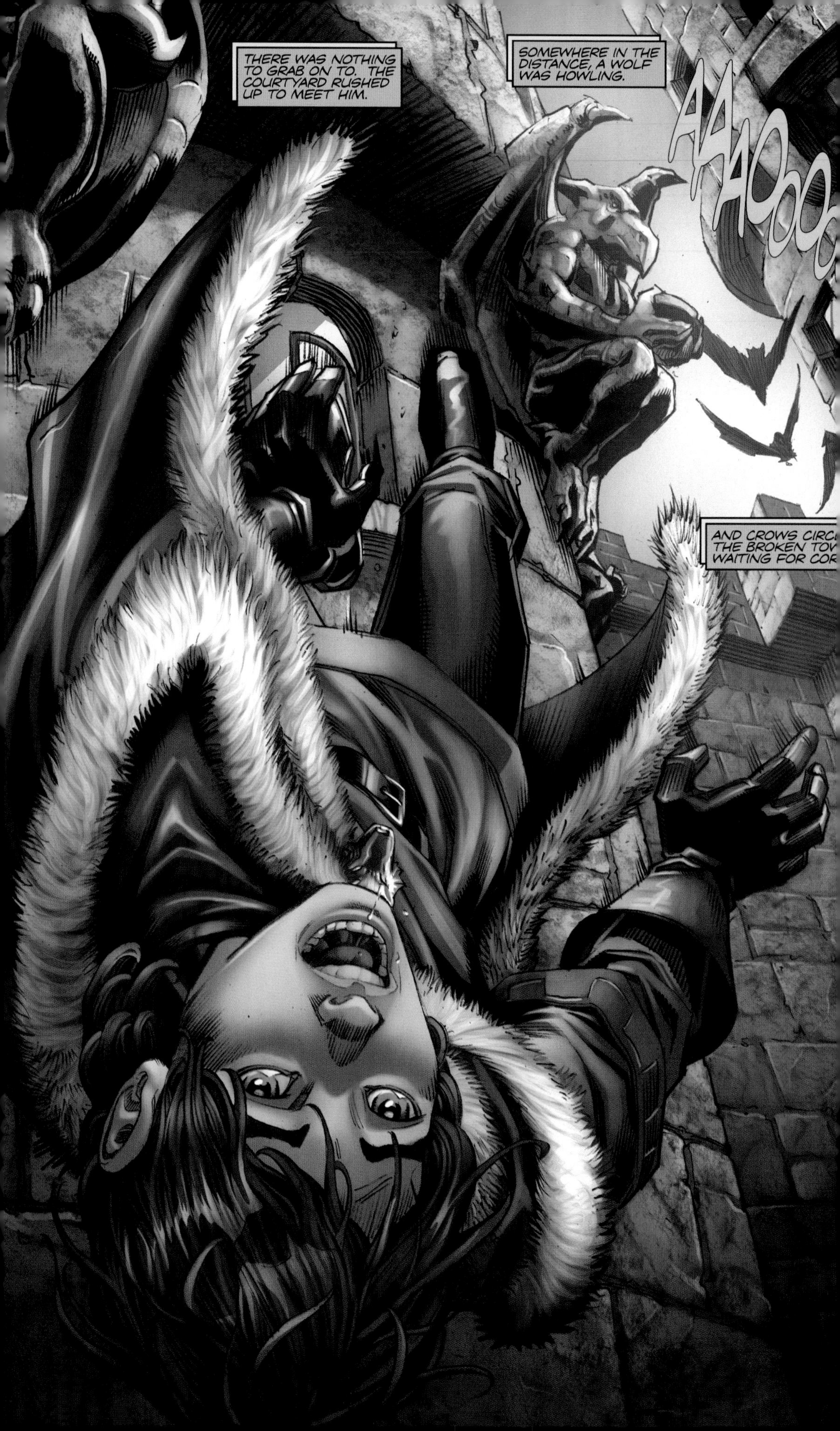
THERE WAS NOTHING TO GRAB ON TO. THE COURTYARD RUSHED UP TO MEET HIM.
SOMEWHERE IN THE DISTANCE, A WOLF WAS HOWLING.
AAAOOOO

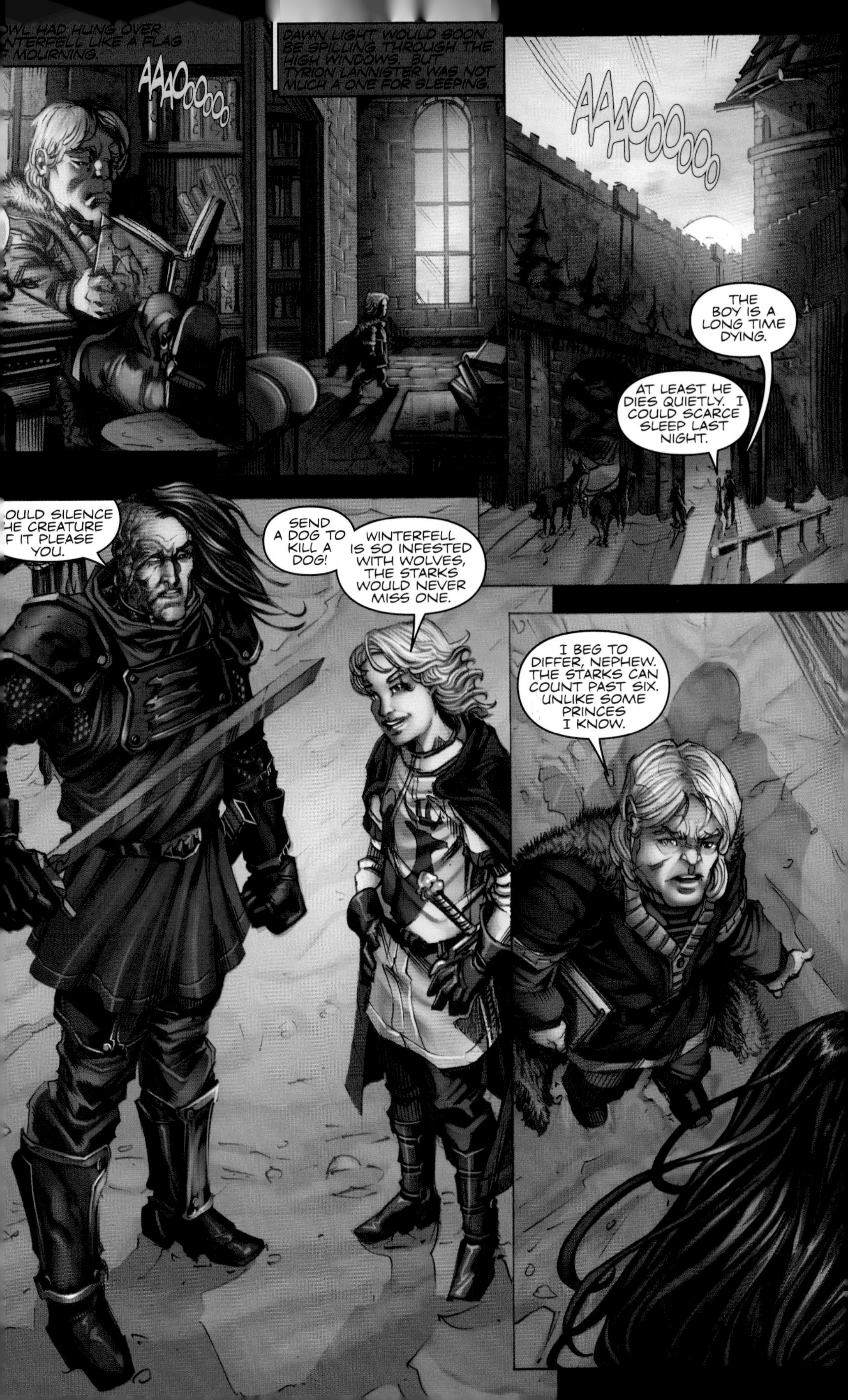

OWL HAD HUNG OVER INTERFELL LIKE A FLAG F MOURNING.
AAAOOOOO
DAWN LIGHT WOULD SOON BE SPILLING THROUGH THE HIGH WINDOWS. BUT TYRION LANNISTER WAS NOT MUCH A ONE FOR SLEEPING.
AAAOOOOOO
THE BOY IS A LONG TIME DYING.
AT LEAST HE DIES QUIETLY. I COULD SCARCE SLEEP LAST NIGHT.
OULD SILENCE HE CREATURE F IT PLEASE YOU.
SEND A DOG TO KILL A DOG!
WINTERFELL IS SO INFESTED WITH WOLVES, THE STARKS WOULD NEVER MISS ONE.
I BEG TO DIFFER, NEPHEW. THE STARKS CAN COUNT PAST SIX. UNLIKE SOME PRINCES I KNOW.

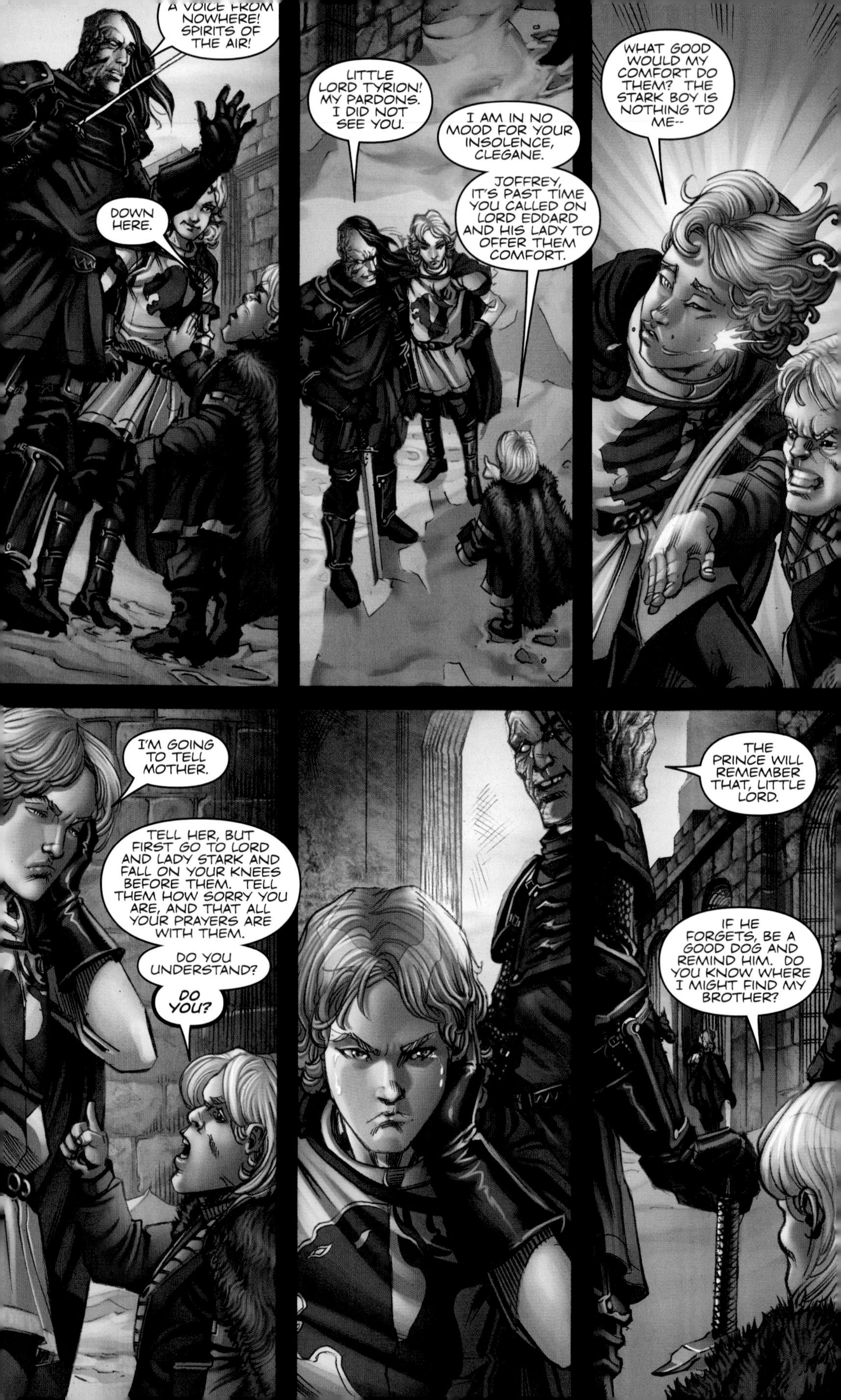

A VOICE FROM NOWHERE! SPIRITS OF THE AIR!
DOWN HERE.
LITTLE LORD TYRION! MY PARDONS. I DID NOT SEE YOU.
I AM IN NO MOOD FOR YOUR INSOLENCE, CLEGANE.
JOFFREY, IT'S PAST TIME YOU CALLED ON LORD EDDARD AND HIS LADY TO OFFER THEM COMFORT.
WHAT GOOD WOULD MY COMFORT DO THEM? THE STARK BOY IS NOTHING TO ME--
I'M GOING TO TELL MOTHER.
TELL HER, BUT FIRST GO TO LORD AND LADY STARK AND FALL ON YOUR KNEES BEFORE THEM. TELL THEM HOW SORRY YOU ARE, AND THAT ALL YOUR PRAYERS ARE WITH THEM.
DO YOU UNDERSTAND?
DO YOU?
THE PRINCE WILL REMEMBER THAT, LITTLE LORD.
IF HE FORGETS, BE A GOOD DOG AND REMIND HIM. DO YOU KNOW WHERE I MIGHT FIND MY BROTHER?

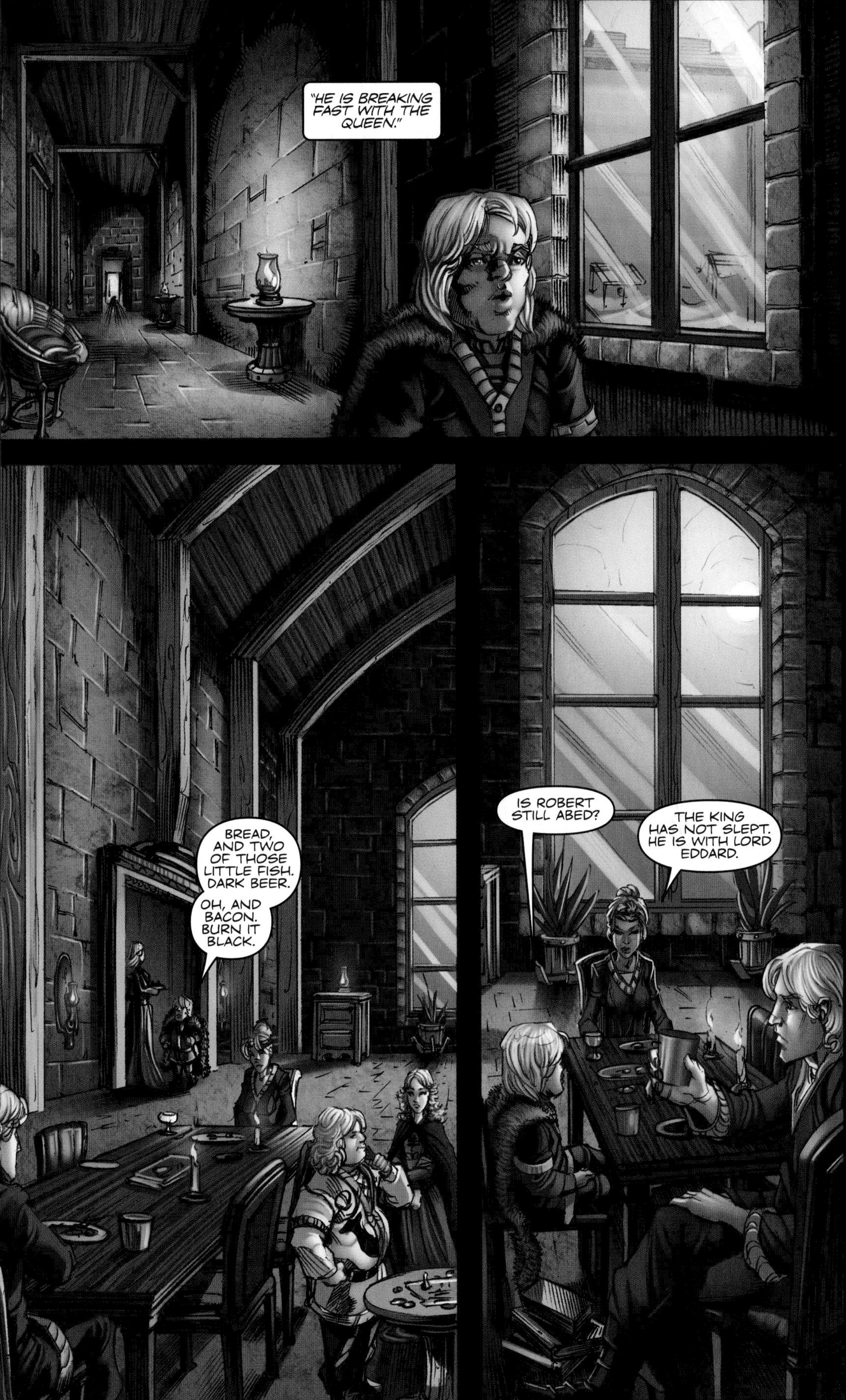
"HE IS BREAKING FAST WITH THE QUEEN."
BREAD, AND TWO OF THOSE LITTLE FISH. DARK BEER.
OH, AND BACON. BURN IT BLACK.
IS ROBERT STILL ABED?
THE KING HAS NOT SLEPT. HE IS WITH LORD EDDARD.

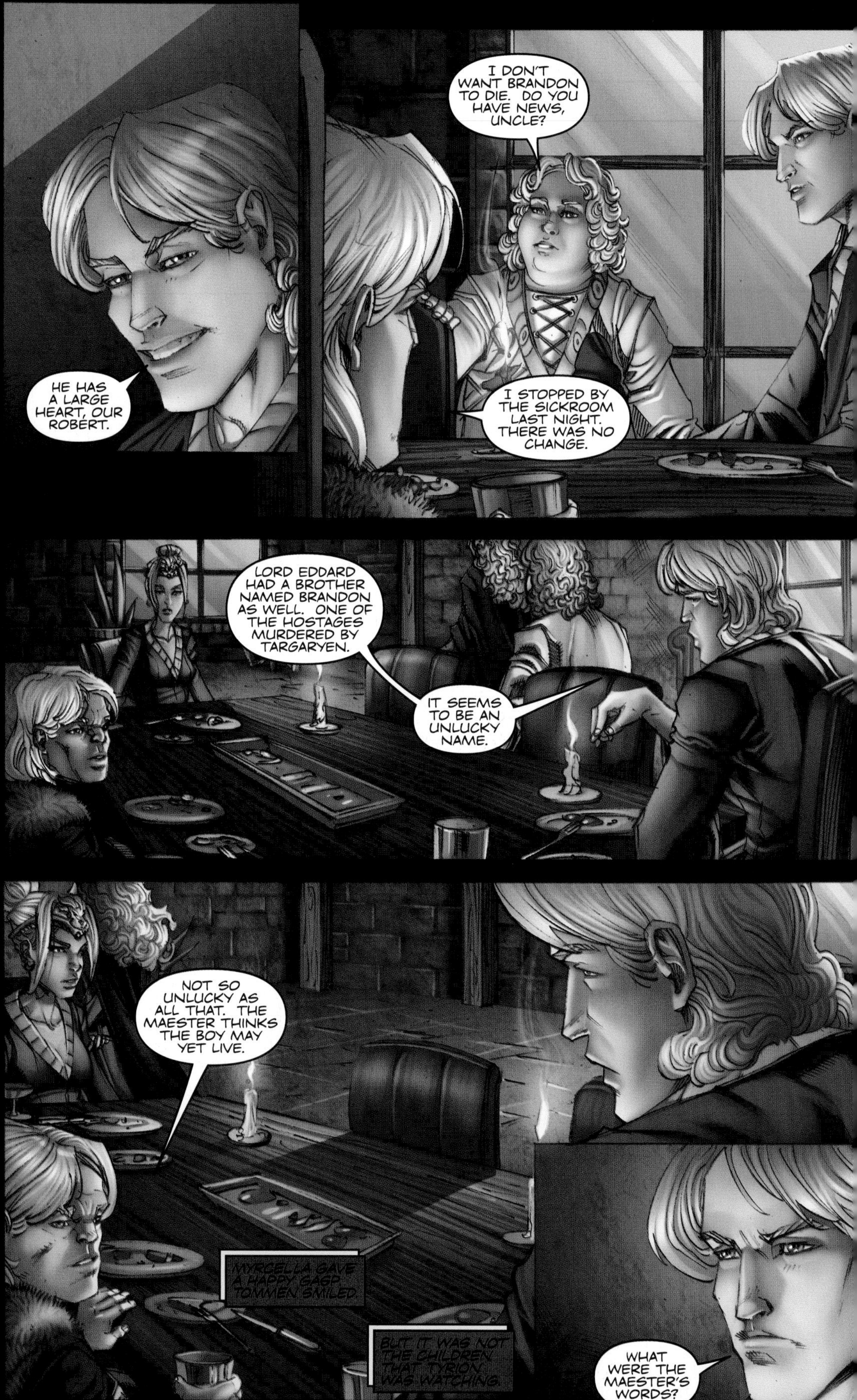
HE HAS A LARGE HEART, OUR ROBERT.
I DON'T WANT BRANDON TO DIE. DO YOU HAVE NEWS, UNCLE?
I STOPPED BY THE SICKROOM LAST NIGHT. THERE WAS NO CHANGE.
LORD EDDARD HAD A BROTHER NAMED BRANDON AS WELL. ONE OF THE HOSTAGES MURDERED BY TARGARYEN.
IT SEEMS TO BE AN UNLUCKY NAME.
NOT SO UNLUCKY AS ALL THAT. THE MAESTER THINKS THE BOY MAY YET LIVE.
MYRCELLA GAVE A HAPPY GASP. TOMMEN SMILED.
BUT IT WAS NOT THE CHILDREN THAT TYRION WAS WATCHING.
WHAT WERE THE MAESTER'S WORDS?

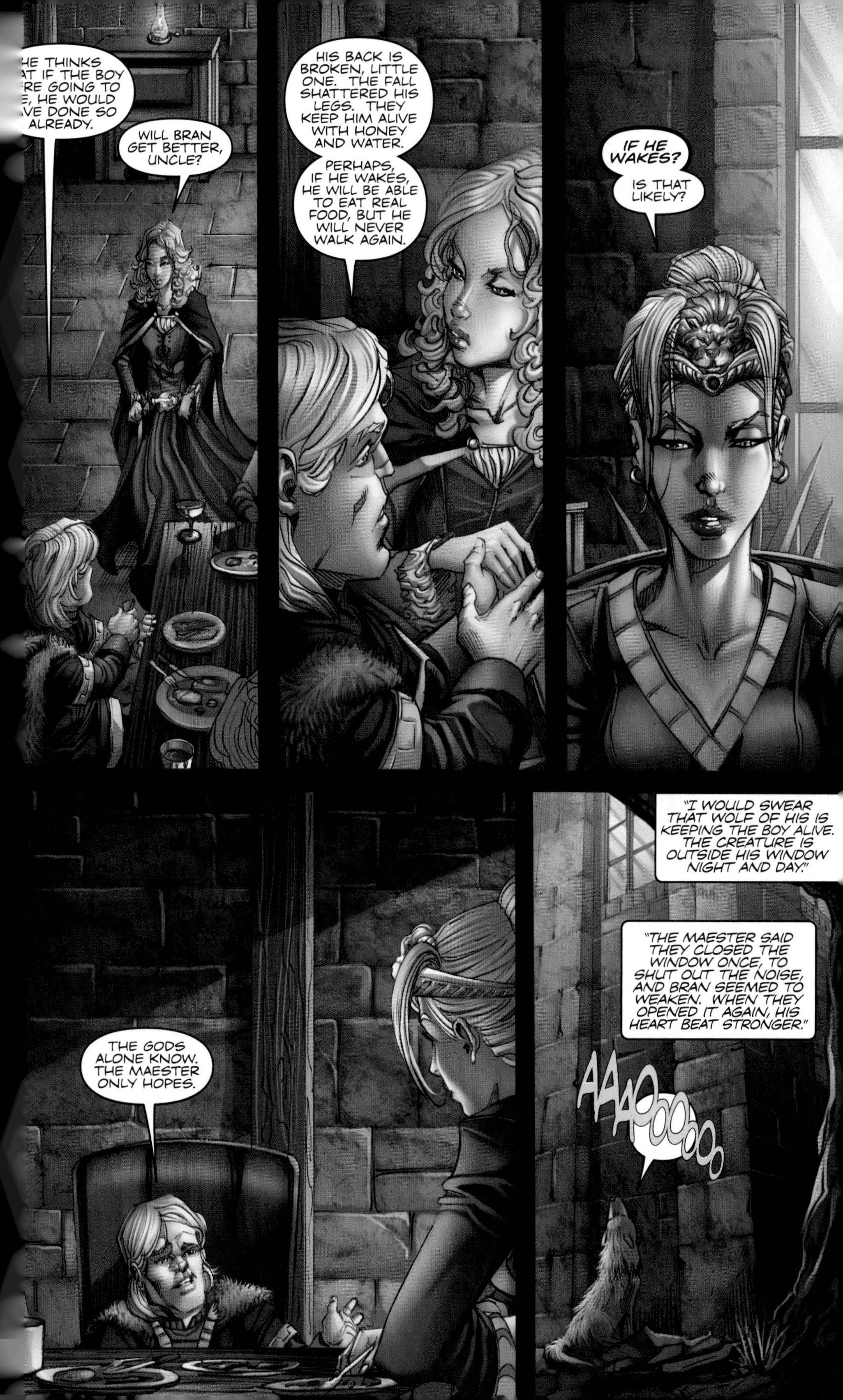
HE THINKS
AT IF THE BOY
RE GOING TO
E, HE WOULD
VE DONE SO
ALREADY.
WILL BRAN GET BETTER, UNCLE?
HIS BACK IS BROKEN, LITTLE ONE. THE FALL SHATTERED HIS LEGS. THEY KEEP HIM ALIVE WITH HONEY AND WATER.
PERHAPS, IF HE WAKES, HE WILL BE ABLE TO EAT REAL FOOD, BUT HE WILL NEVER WALK AGAIN.
IF HE WAKES?
IS THAT LIKELY?
THE GODS ALONE KNOW. THE MAESTER ONLY HOPES.
"I WOULD SWEAR THAT WOLF OF HIS IS KEEPING THE BOY ALIVE. THE CREATURE IS OUTSIDE HIS WINDOW NIGHT AND DAY."
"THE MAESTER SAID THEY CLOSED THE WINDOW ONCE, TO SHUT OUT THE NOISE, AND BRAN SEEMED TO WEAKEN. WHEN THEY OPENED IT AGAIN, HIS HEART BEAT STRONGER."
AAAOOOOOOO

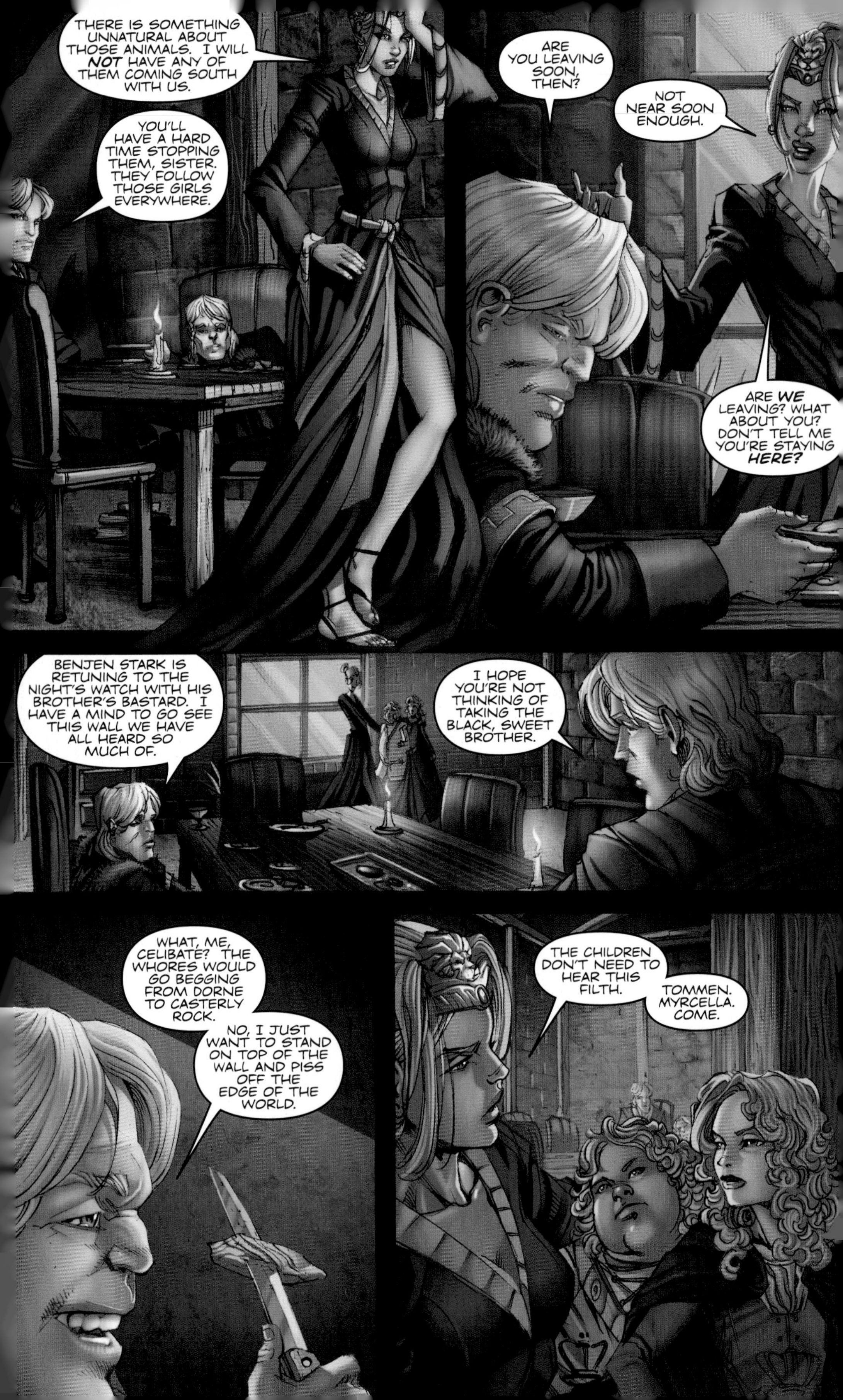
THERE IS SOMETHING UNNATURAL ABOUT THOSE ANIMALS. I WILL **NOT** HAVE ANY OF THEM COMING SOUTH WITH US.
YOU'LL HAVE A HARD TIME STOPPING THEM, SISTER. THEY FOLLOW THOSE GIRLS EVERYWHERE.
ARE YOU LEAVING SOON, THEN?
NOT NEAR SOON ENOUGH.
ARE **WE** LEAVING? WHAT ABOUT YOU? DON'T TELL ME YOU'RE STAYING **HERE?**
BENJEN STARK IS RETUNING TO THE NIGHT'S WATCH WITH HIS BROTHER'S BASTARD. I HAVE A MIND TO GO SEE THIS WALL WE HAVE ALL HEARD SO MUCH OF.
I HOPE YOU'RE NOT THINKING OF TAKING THE BLACK, SWEET BROTHER.
WHAT, ME, CELIBATE? THE WHORES WOULD GO BEGGING FROM DORNE TO CASTERLY ROCK.
NO, I JUST WANT TO STAND ON TOP OF THE WALL AND PISS OFF THE EDGE OF THE WORLD.
THE CHILDREN DON'T NEED TO HEAR THIS FILTH.
TOMMEN. MYRCELLA. COME.

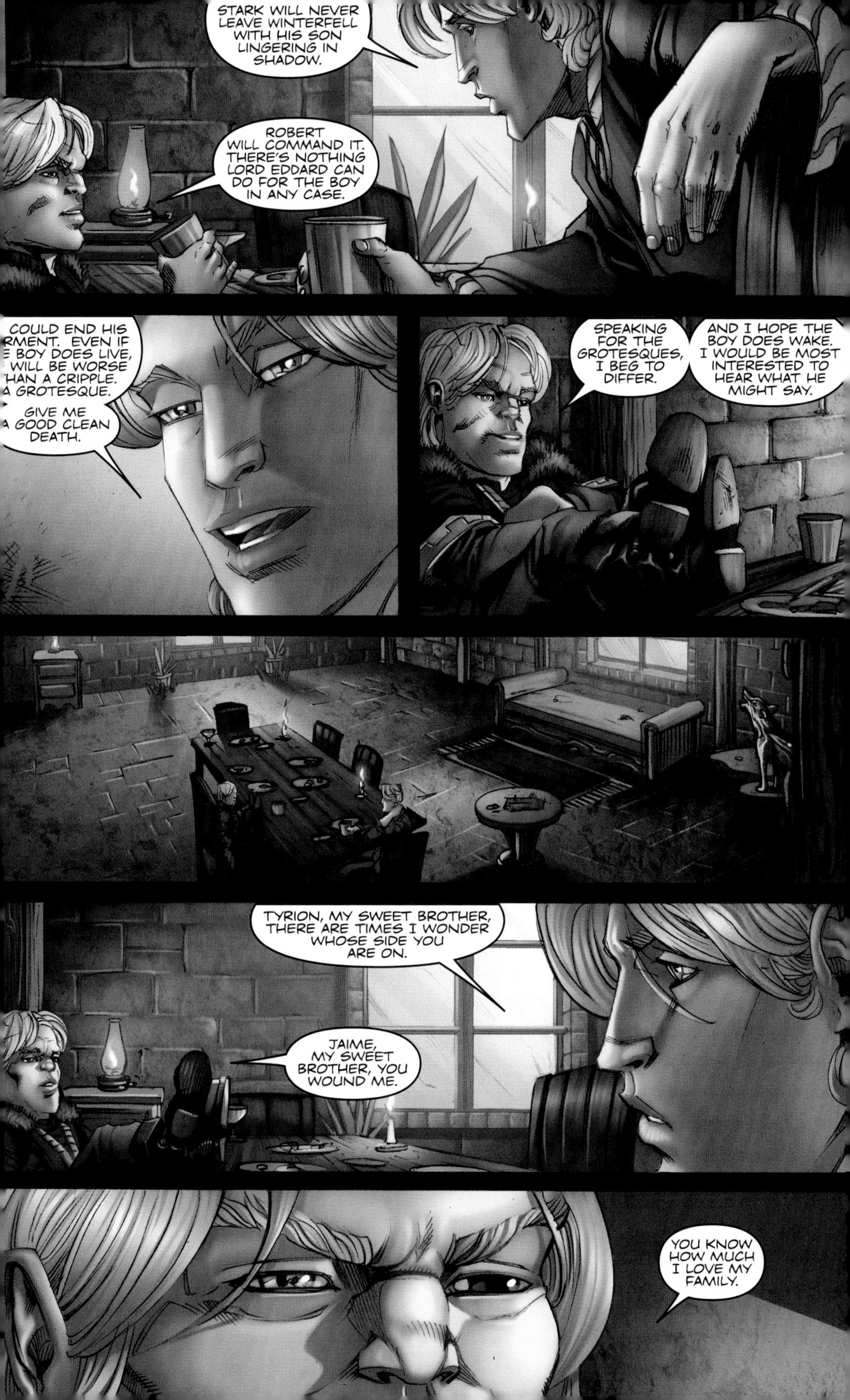
STARK WILL NEVER LEAVE WINTERFELL WITH HIS SON LINGERING IN SHADOW.
ROBERT WILL COMMAND IT. THERE'S NOTHING LORD EDDARD CAN DO FOR THE BOY IN ANY CASE.
COULD END HIS RMENT. EVEN IF E BOY DOES LIVE, WILL BE WORSE HAN A CRIPPLE. A GROTESQUE.
GIVE ME A GOOD CLEAN DEATH.
SPEAKING FOR THE GROTESQUES, I BEG TO DIFFER.
AND I HOPE THE BOY DOES WAKE. I WOULD BE MOST INTERESTED TO HEAR WHAT HE MIGHT SAY.
TYRION, MY SWEET BROTHER, THERE ARE TIMES I WONDER WHOSE SIDE YOU ARE ON.
JAIME, MY SWEET BROTHER, YOU WOUND ME.
YOU KNOW HOW MUCH I LOVE MY FAMILY.

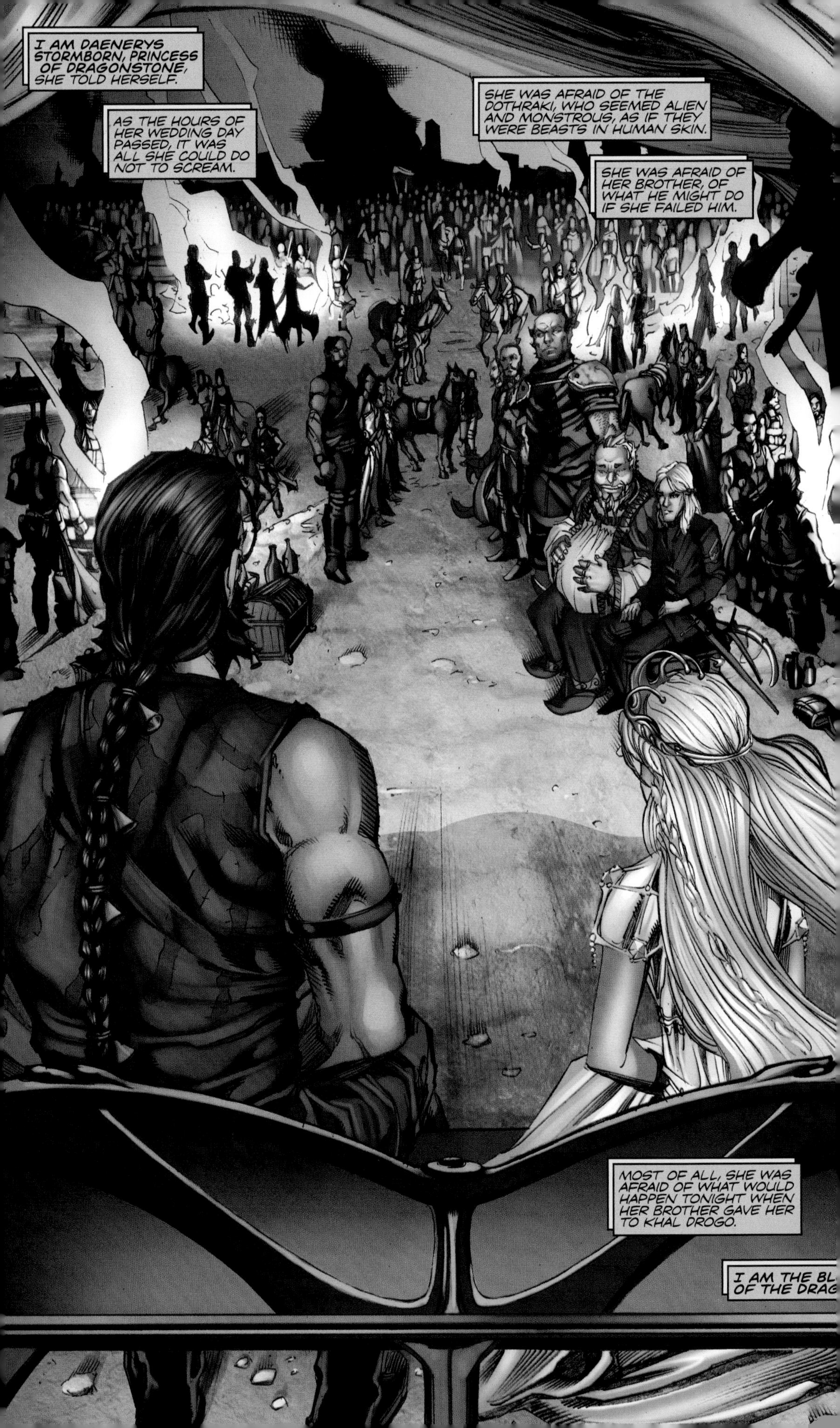
I AM DAENERYS STORMBORN, PRINCESS OF DRAGONSTONE, SHE TOLD HERSELF.
AS THE HOURS OF HER WEDDING DAY PASSED, IT WAS ALL SHE COULD DO NOT TO SCREAM.
SHE WAS AFRAID OF THE DOTHRAKI, WHO SEEMED ALIEN AND MONSTROUS, AS IF THEY WERE BEASTS IN HUMAN SKIN.
SHE WAS AFRAID OF HER BROTHER, OF WHAT HE MIGHT DO IF SHE FAILED HIM.
MOST OF ALL, SHE WAS AFRAID OF WHAT WOULD HAPPEN TONIGHT WHEN HER BROTHER GAVE HER TO KHAL DROGO.
I AM THE BL
OF THE DRAG

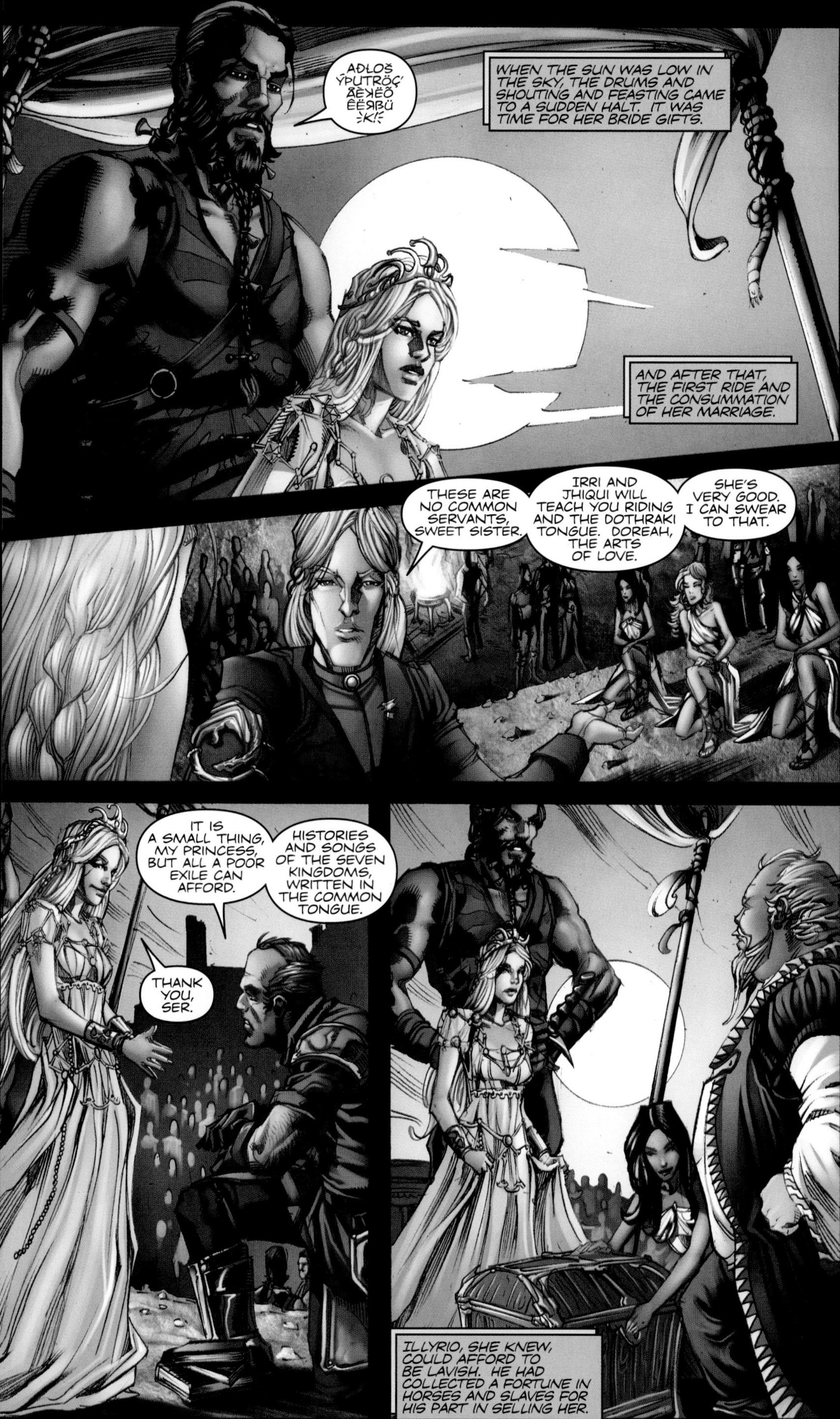

WHEN THE SUN WAS LOW IN THE SKY, THE DRUMS AND SHOUTING AND FEASTING CAME TO A SUDDEN HALT. IT WAS TIME FOR HER BRIDE GIFTS.
AND AFTER THAT, THE FIRST RIDE AND THE CONSUMMATION OF HER MARRIAGE.
THESE ARE NO COMMON SERVANTS, SWEET SISTER.
IRRI AND JHIQUI WILL TEACH YOU RIDING AND THE DOTHRAKI TONGUE. DOREAH, THE ARTS OF LOVE.
SHE'S VERY GOOD. I CAN SWEAR TO THAT.
IT IS A SMALL THING, MY PRINCESS, BUT ALL A POOR EXILE CAN AFFORD.
HISTORIES AND SONGS OF THE SEVEN KINGDOMS, WRITTEN IN THE COMMON TONGUE.
THANK YOU, SER.
ILLYRIO, SHE KNEW, COULD AFFORD TO BE LAVISH. HE HAD COLLECTED A FORTUNE IN HORSES AND SLAVES FOR HIS PART IN SELLING HER.

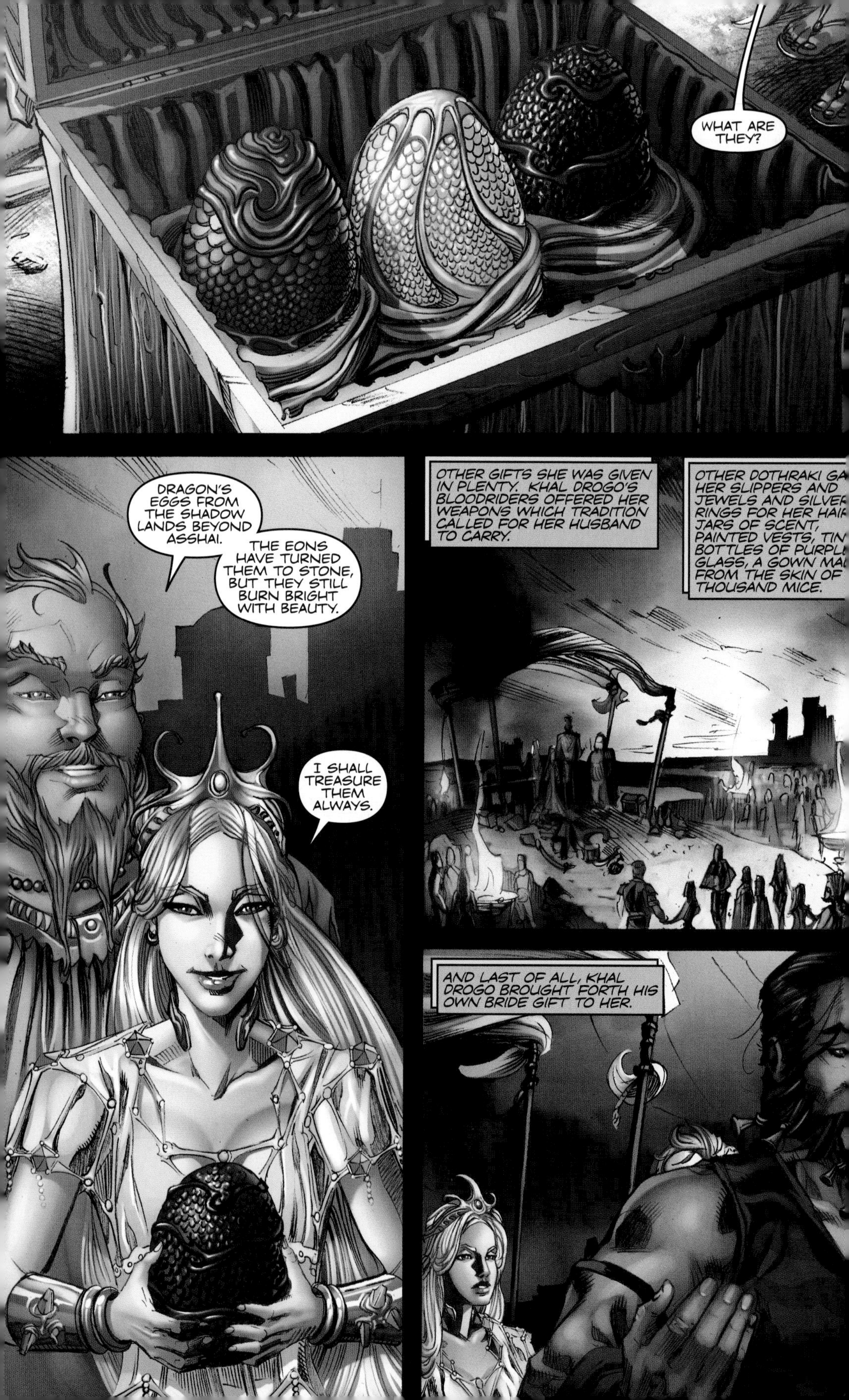
WHAT ARE THEY?
DRAGON'S EGGS FROM THE SHADOW LANDS BEYOND ASSHAI.
THE EONS HAVE TURNED THEM TO STONE, BUT THEY STILL BURN BRIGHT WITH BEAUTY.
I SHALL TREASURE THEM ALWAYS.
OTHER GIFTS SHE WAS GIVEN IN PLENTY. KHAL DROGO'S BLOODRIDERS OFFERED HER WEAPONS WHICH TRADITION CALLED FOR HER HUSBAND TO CARRY.
OTHER DOTHRAKI GA HER SLIPPERS AND JEWELS AND SILVER RINGS FOR HER HAIR JARS OF SCENT, PAINTED VESTS, TIN BOTTLES OF PURPLE GLASS, A GOWN MA FROM THE SKIN OF THOUSAND MICE.
AND LAST OF ALL, KHAL DROGO BROUGHT FORTH HIS OWN BRIDE GIFT TO HER.

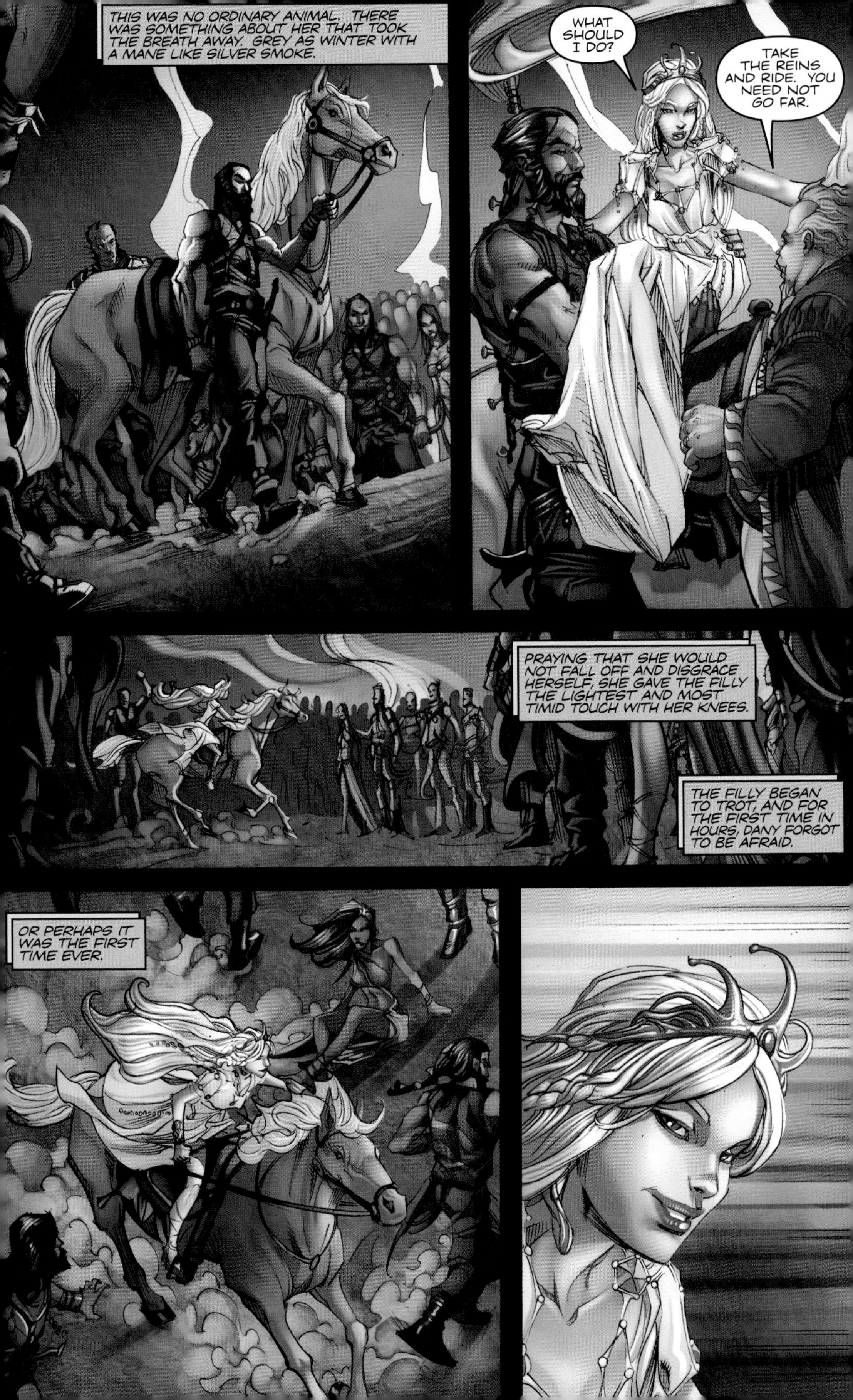
THIS WAS NO ORDINARY ANIMAL. THERE WAS SOMETHING ABOUT HER THAT TOOK THE BREATH AWAY. GREY AS WINTER WITH A MANE LIKE SILVER SMOKE.
WHAT SHOULD I DO?
TAKE THE REINS AND RIDE. YOU NEED NOT GO FAR.
PRAYING THAT SHE WOULD NOT FALL OFF AND DISGRACE HERSELF, SHE GAVE THE FILLY THE LIGHTEST AND MOST TIMID TOUCH WITH HER KNEES.
THE FILLY BEGAN TO TROT, AND FOR THE FIRST TIME IN HOURS, DANY FORGOT TO BE AFRAID.
OR PERHAPS IT WAS THE FIRST TIME EVER.

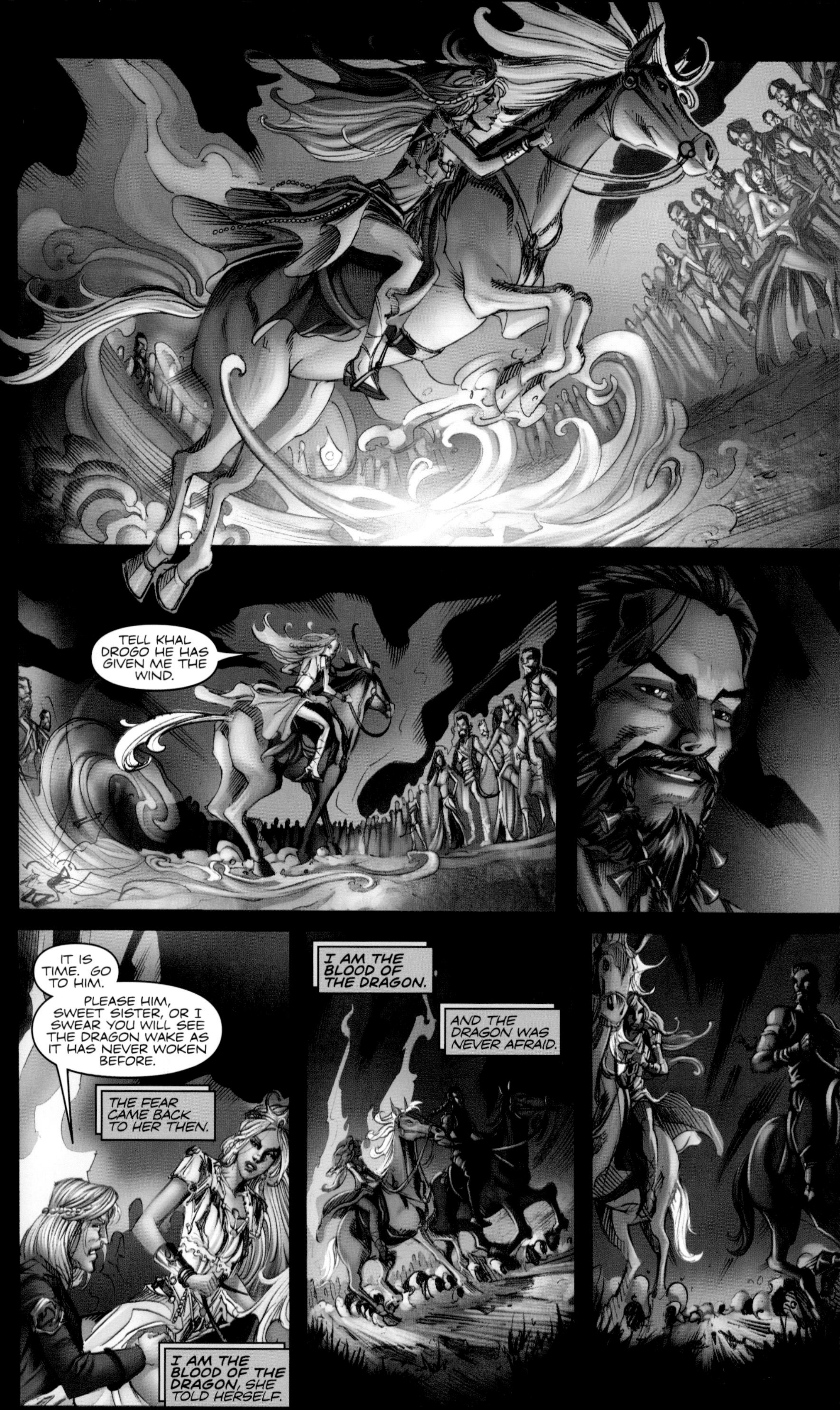
TELL KHAL DROGO HE HAS GIVEN ME THE WIND.
IT IS TIME. GO TO HIM.
PLEASE HIM, SWEET SISTER, OR I SWEAR YOU WILL SEE THE DRAGON WAKE AS IT HAS NEVER WOKEN BEFORE.
THE FEAR CAME BACK TO HER THEN.
I AM THE BLOOD OF THE DRAGON, SHE TOLD HERSELF.
I AM THE BLOOD OF THE DRAGON.
AND THE DRAGON WAS NEVER AFRAID.

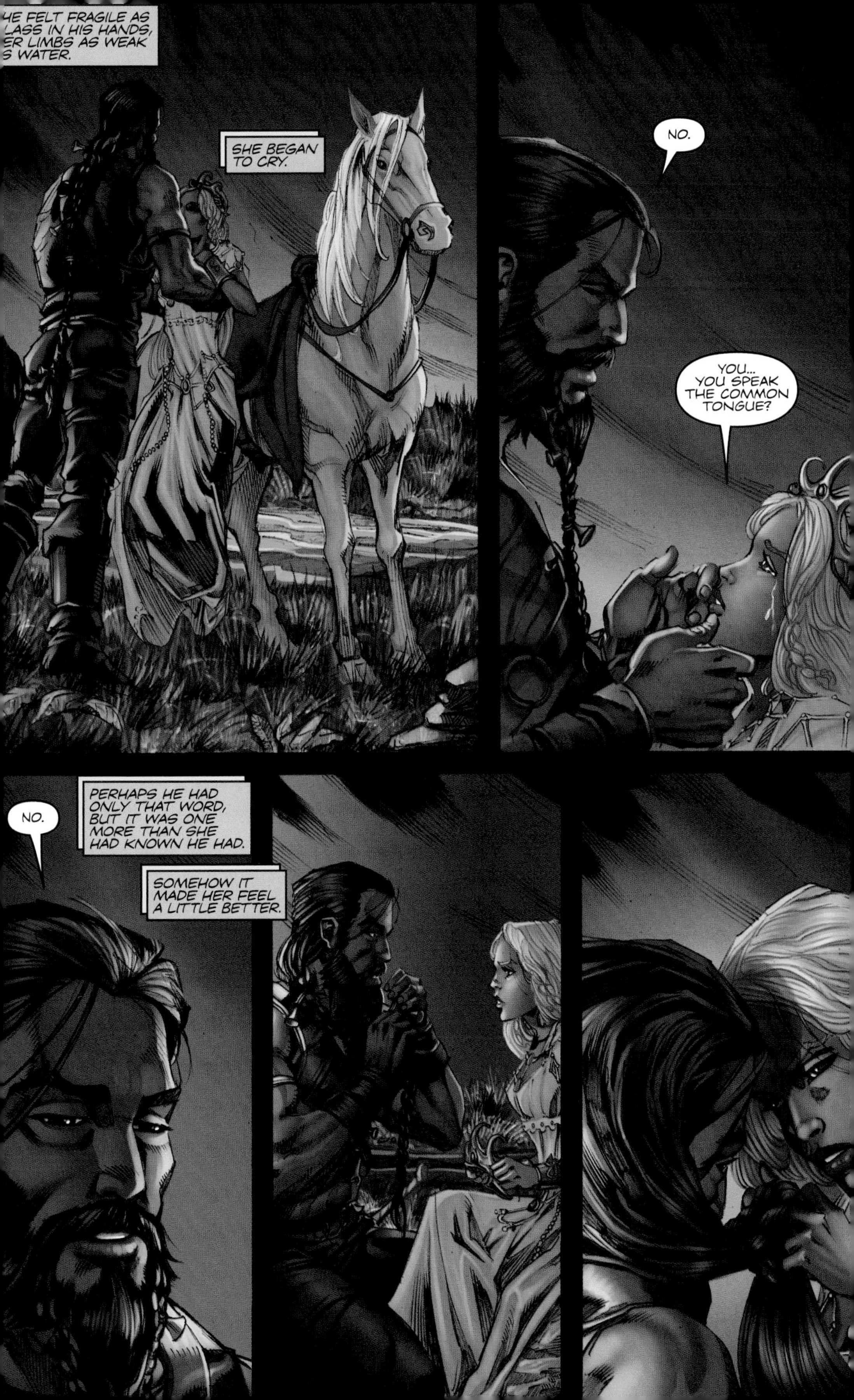
HE FELT FRAGILE AS
LASS IN HIS HANDS,
ER LIMBS AS WEAK
S WATER.
SHE BEGAN TO CRY.
NO.
YOU... YOU SPEAK THE COMMON TONGUE?
NO.
PERHAPS HE HAD ONLY THAT WORD, BUT IT WAS ONE MORE THAN SHE HAD KNOWN HE HAD.
SOMEHOW IT MADE HER FEEL A LITTLE BETTER.

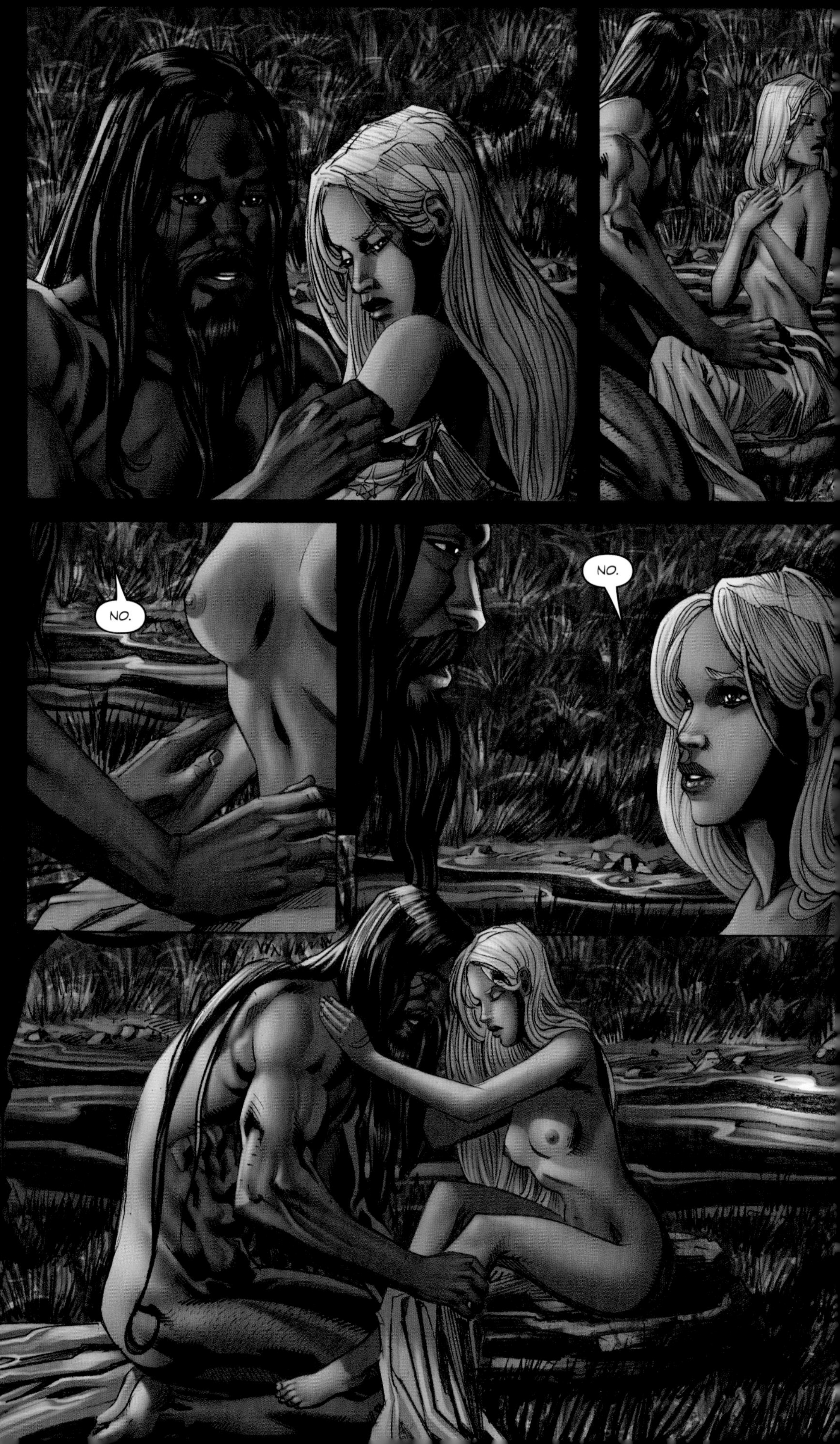
NO.
NO.

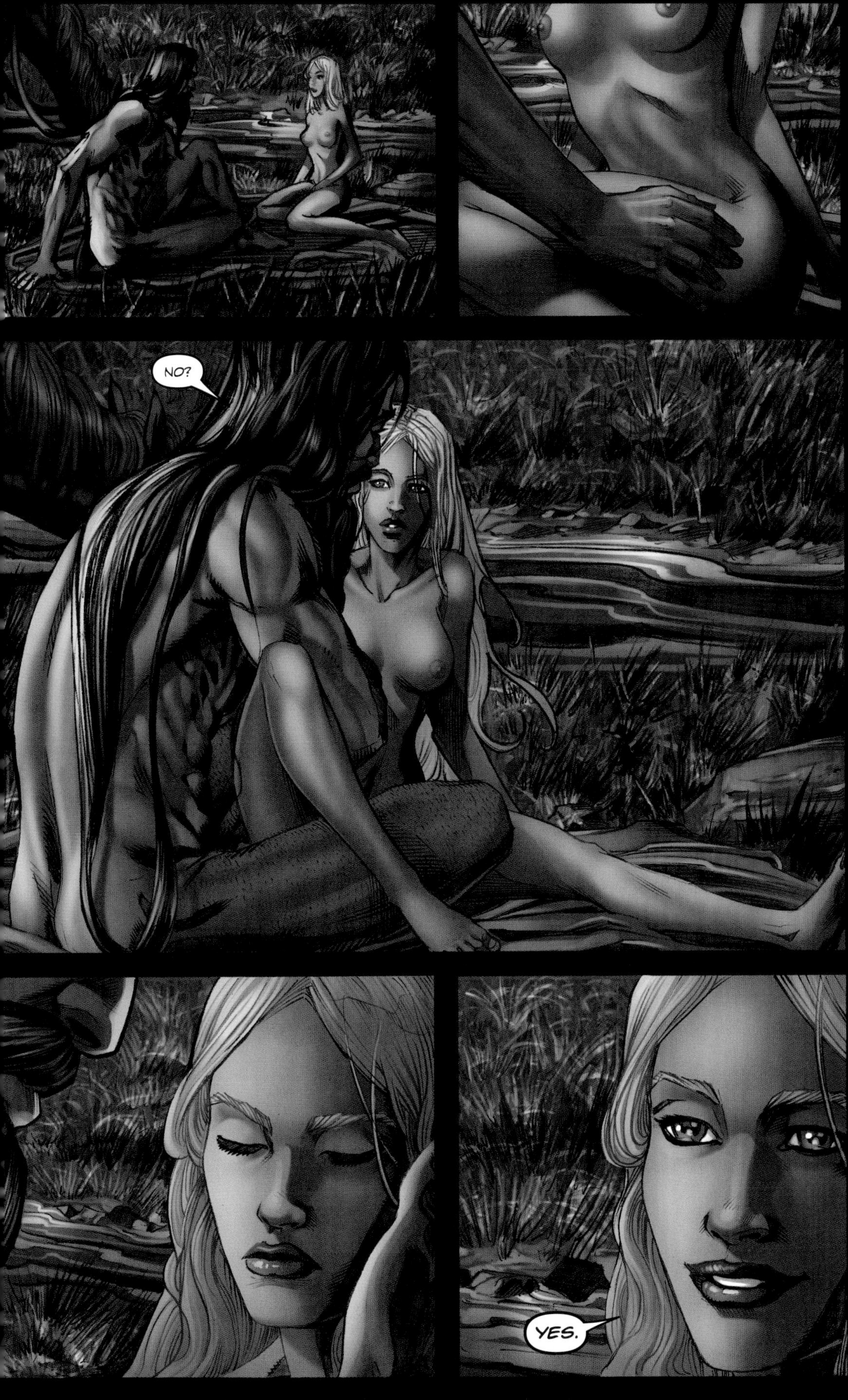
NO?
YES.

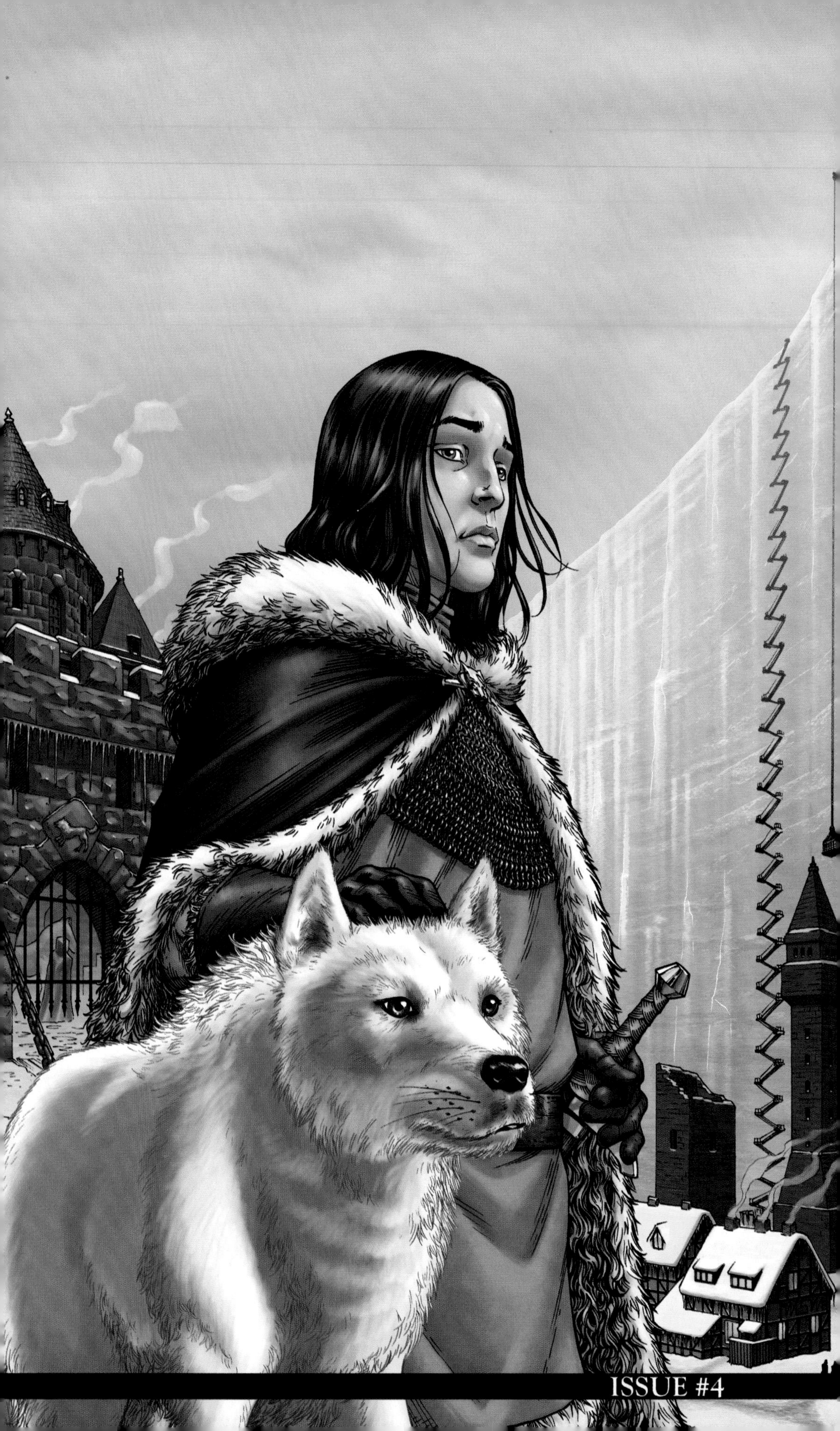
ISSUE #4

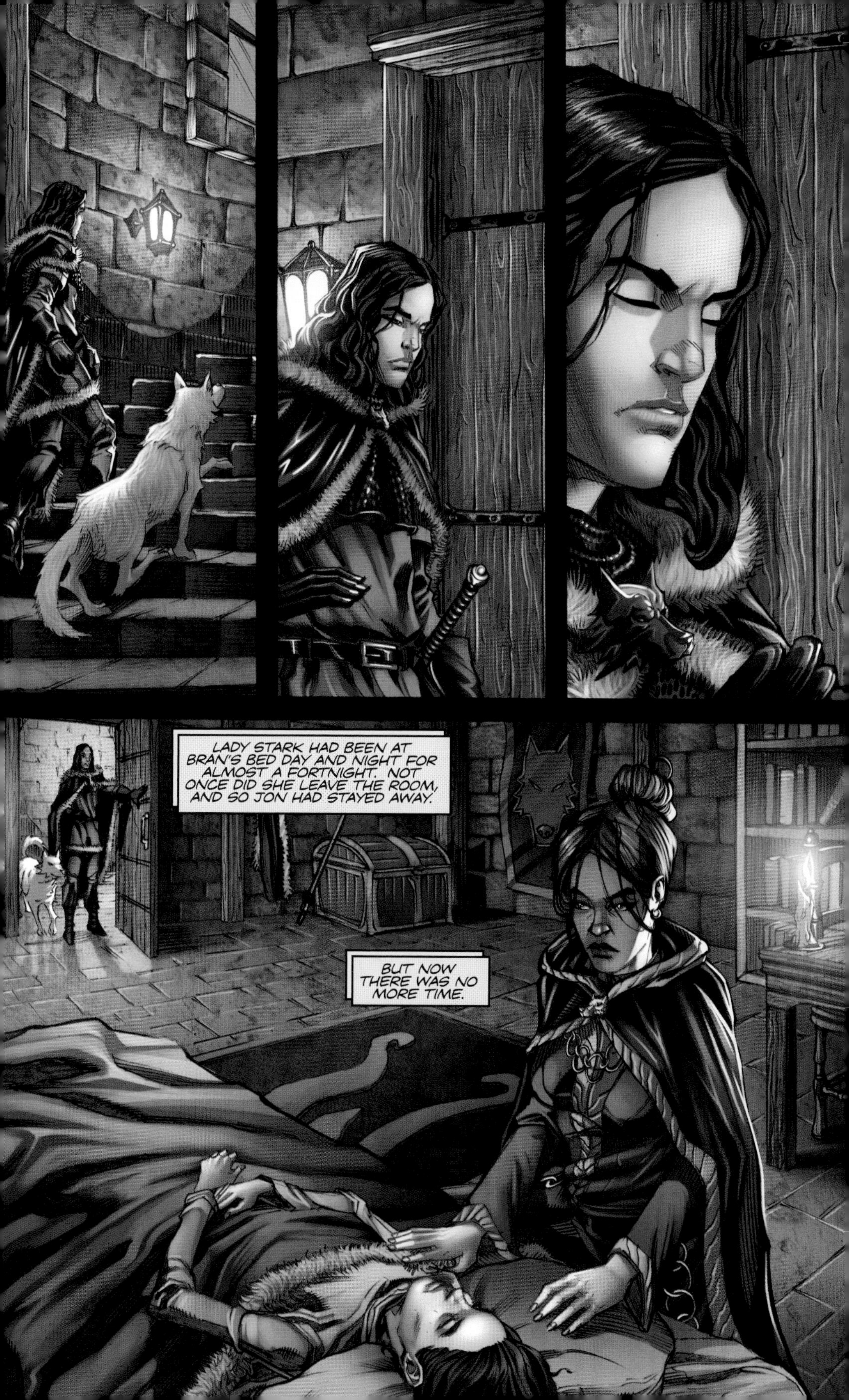
LADY STARK HAD BEEN AT BRAN'S BED DAY AND NIGHT FOR ALMOST A FORTNIGHT. NOT ONCE DID SHE LEAVE THE ROOM, AND SO JON HAD STAYED AWAY.
BUT NOW THERE WAS NO MORE TIME.

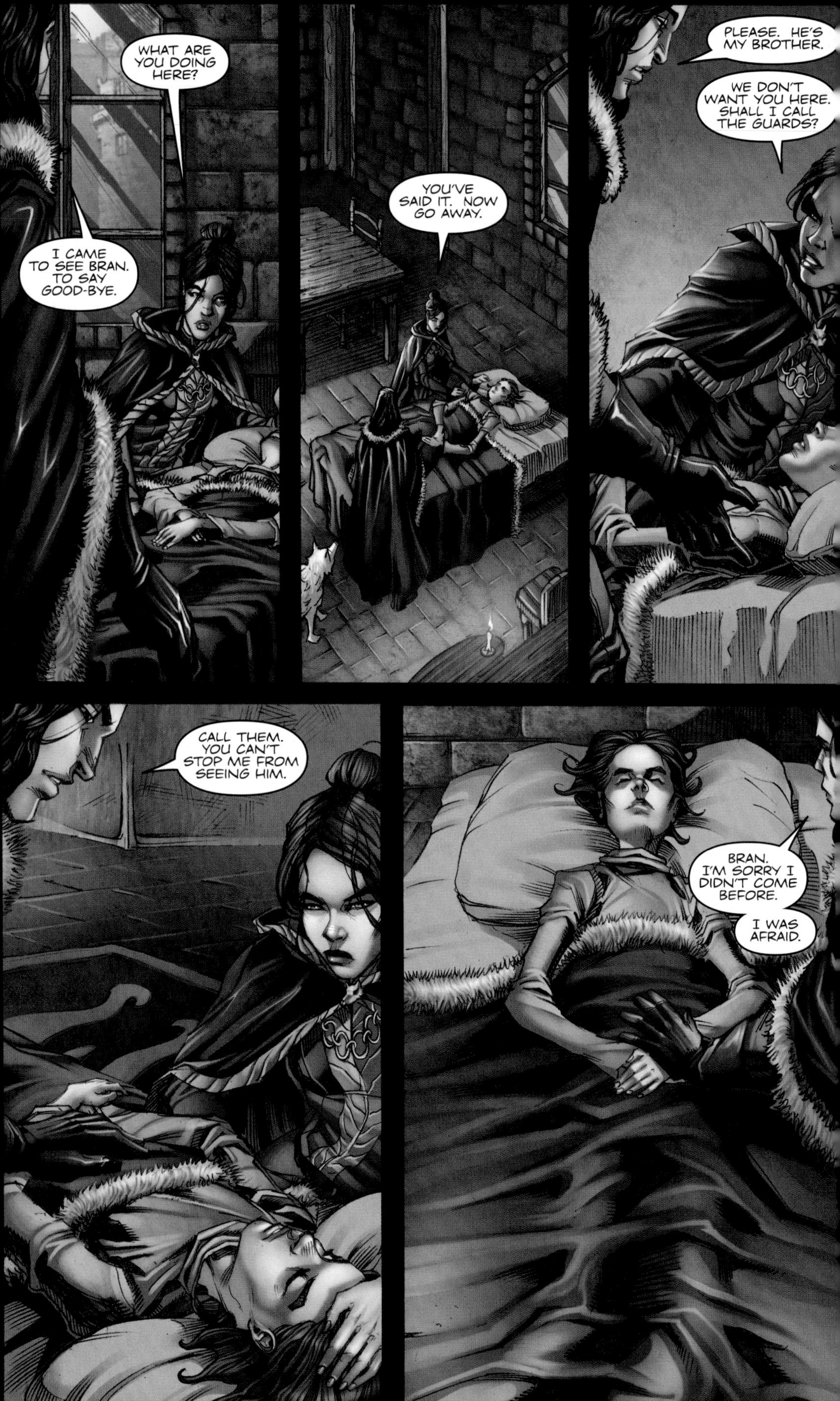
WHAT ARE YOU DOING HERE?
I CAME TO SEE BRAN. TO SAY GOOD-BYE.
YOU'VE SAID IT. NOW GO AWAY.
PLEASE. HE'S MY BROTHER.
WE DON'T WANT YOU HERE. SHALL I CALL THE GUARDS?
CALL THEM. YOU CAN'T STOP ME FROM SEEING HIM.
BRAN. I'M SORRY I DIDN'T COME BEFORE.
I WAS AFRAID.

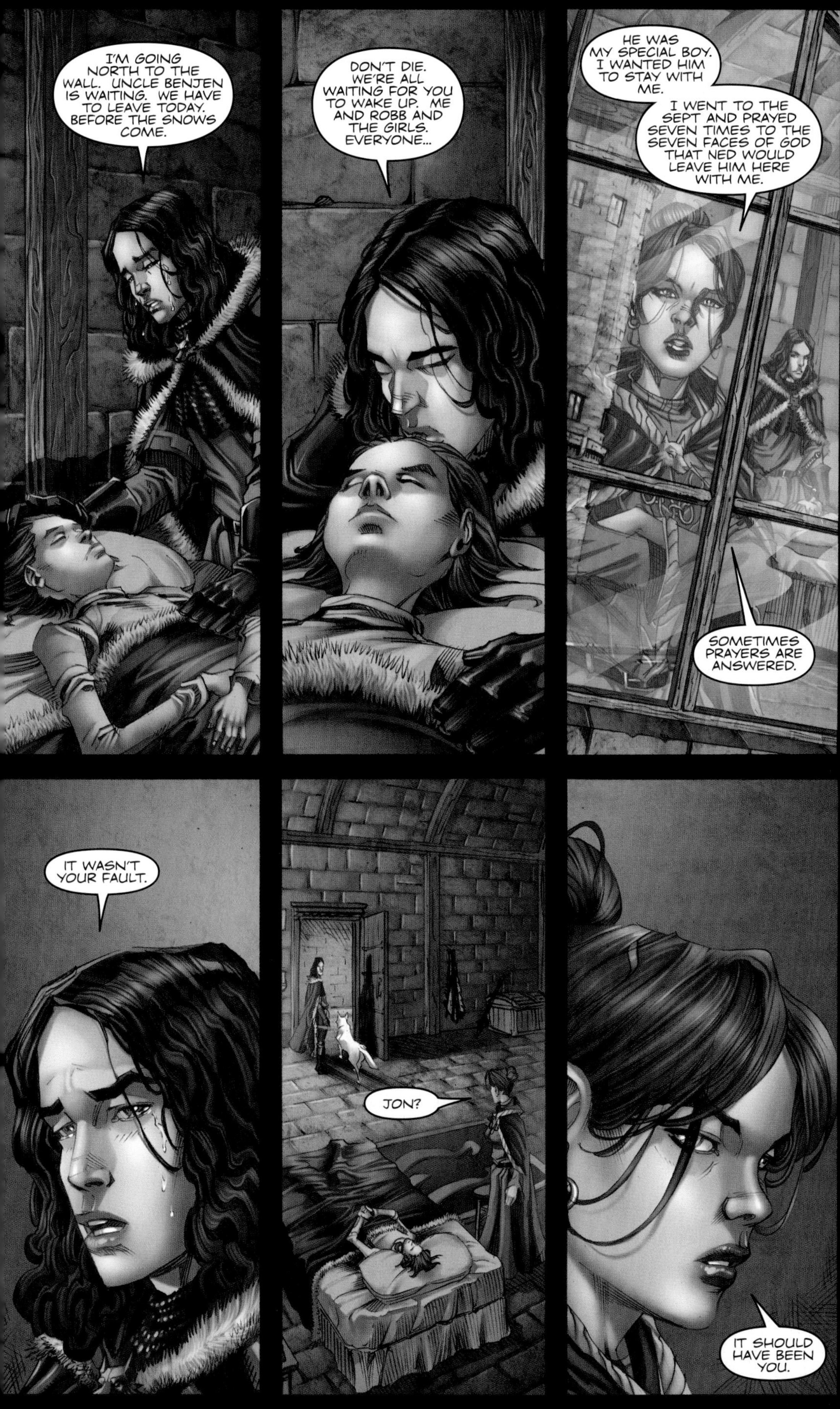
I'M GOING NORTH TO THE WALL. UNCLE BENJEN IS WAITING. WE HAVE TO LEAVE TODAY. BEFORE THE SNOWS COME.
DON'T DIE. WE'RE ALL WAITING FOR YOU TO WAKE UP. ME AND ROBB AND THE GIRLS. EVERYONE...
HE WAS MY SPECIAL BOY. I WANTED HIM TO STAY WITH ME.
I WENT TO THE SEPT AND PRAYED SEVEN TIMES TO THE SEVEN FACES OF GOD THAT NED WOULD LEAVE HIM HERE WITH ME.
SOMETIMES PRAYERS ARE ANSWERED.
IT WASN'T YOUR FAULT.
JON?
IT SHOULD HAVE BEEN YOU.

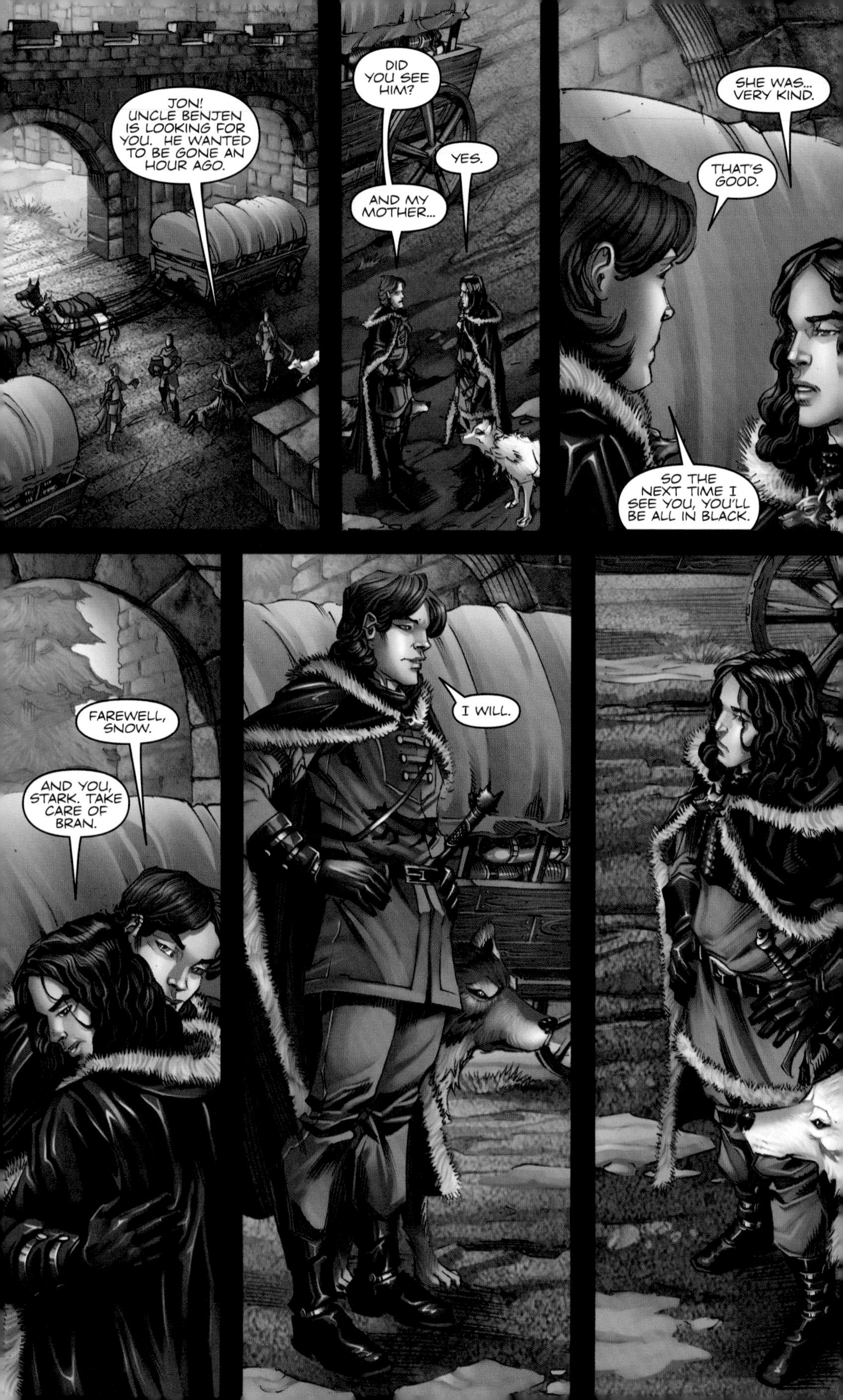
JON! UNCLE BENJEN IS LOOKING FOR YOU. HE WANTED TO BE GONE AN HOUR AGO.
DID YOU SEE HIM?
YES.
AND MY MOTHER...
SHE WAS... VERY KIND.
THAT'S GOOD.
SO THE NEXT TIME I SEE YOU, YOU'LL BE ALL IN BLACK.
FAREWELL, SNOW.
AND YOU, STARK. TAKE CARE OF BRAN.
I WILL.

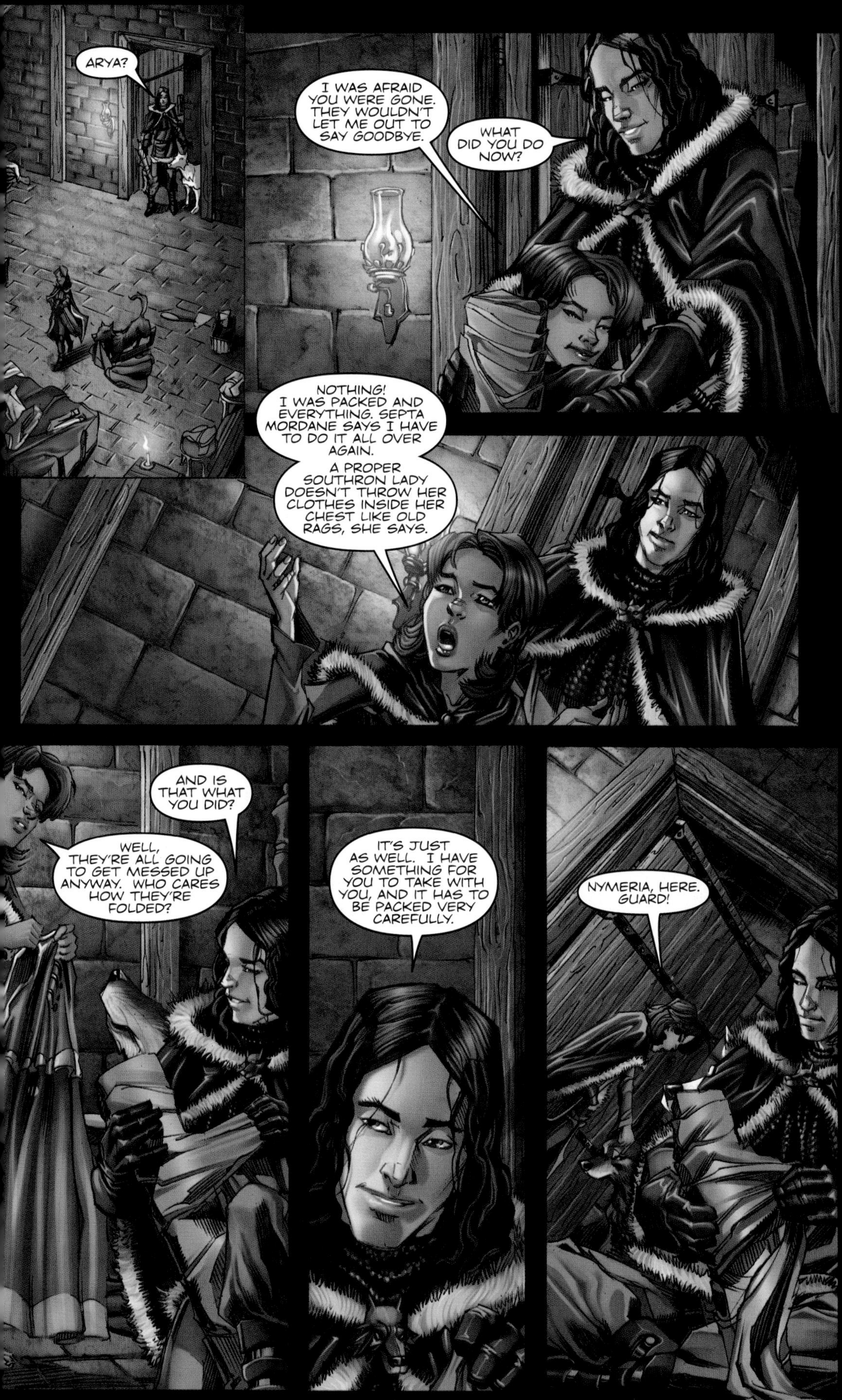
ARYA?
I WAS AFRAID YOU WERE GONE. THEY WOULDN'T LET ME OUT TO SAY GOODBYE.
WHAT DID YOU DO NOW?
NOTHING! I WAS PACKED AND EVERYTHING. SEPTA MORDANE SAYS I HAVE TO DO IT ALL OVER AGAIN.
A PROPER SOUTHRON LADY DOESN'T THROW HER CLOTHES INSIDE HER CHEST LIKE OLD RAGS, SHE SAYS.
AND IS THAT WHAT YOU DID?
WELL, THEY'RE ALL GOING TO GET MESSED UP ANYWAY. WHO CARES HOW THEY'RE FOLDED?
IT'S JUST AS WELL. I HAVE SOMETHING FOR YOU TO TAKE WITH YOU, AND IT HAS TO BE PACKED VERY CAREFULLY.
NYMERIA, HERE. GUARD!

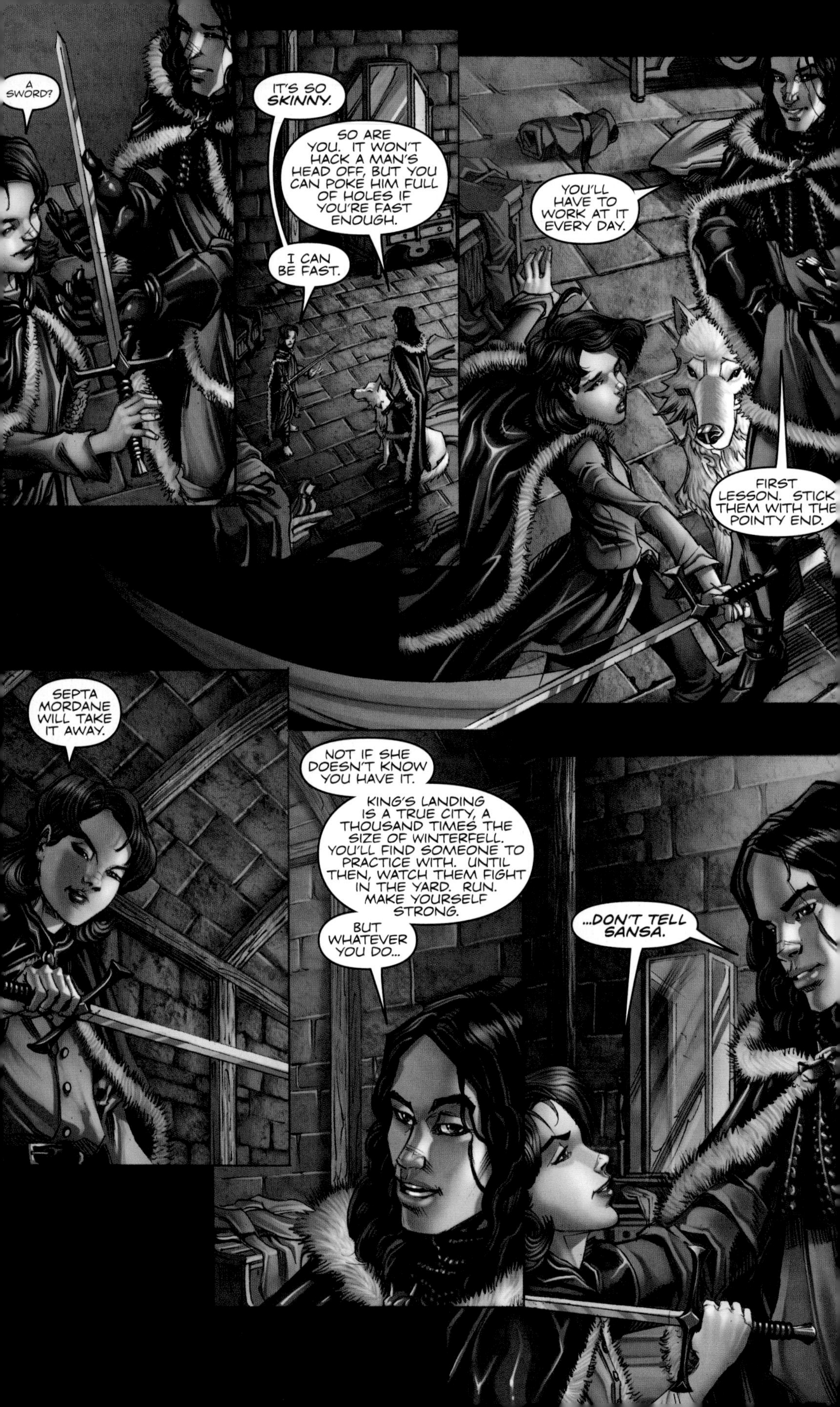
A SWORD?
IT'S SO **SKINNY**.
SO ARE YOU. IT WON'T HACK A MAN'S HEAD OFF, BUT YOU CAN POKE HIM FULL OF HOLES IF YOU'RE FAST ENOUGH.
I CAN BE FAST.
YOU'LL HAVE TO WORK AT IT EVERY DAY.
FIRST LESSON. STICK THEM WITH THE POINTY END.
SEPTA MORDANE WILL TAKE IT AWAY.
NOT IF SHE DOESN'T KNOW YOU HAVE IT.
KING'S LANDING IS A TRUE CITY, A THOUSAND TIMES THE SIZE OF WINTERFELL. YOU'LL FIND SOMEONE TO PRACTICE WITH. UNTIL THEN, WATCH THEM FIGHT IN THE YARD. RUN. MAKE YOURSELF STRONG.
BUT WHATEVER YOU DO...
...**DON'T TELL SANSA.**

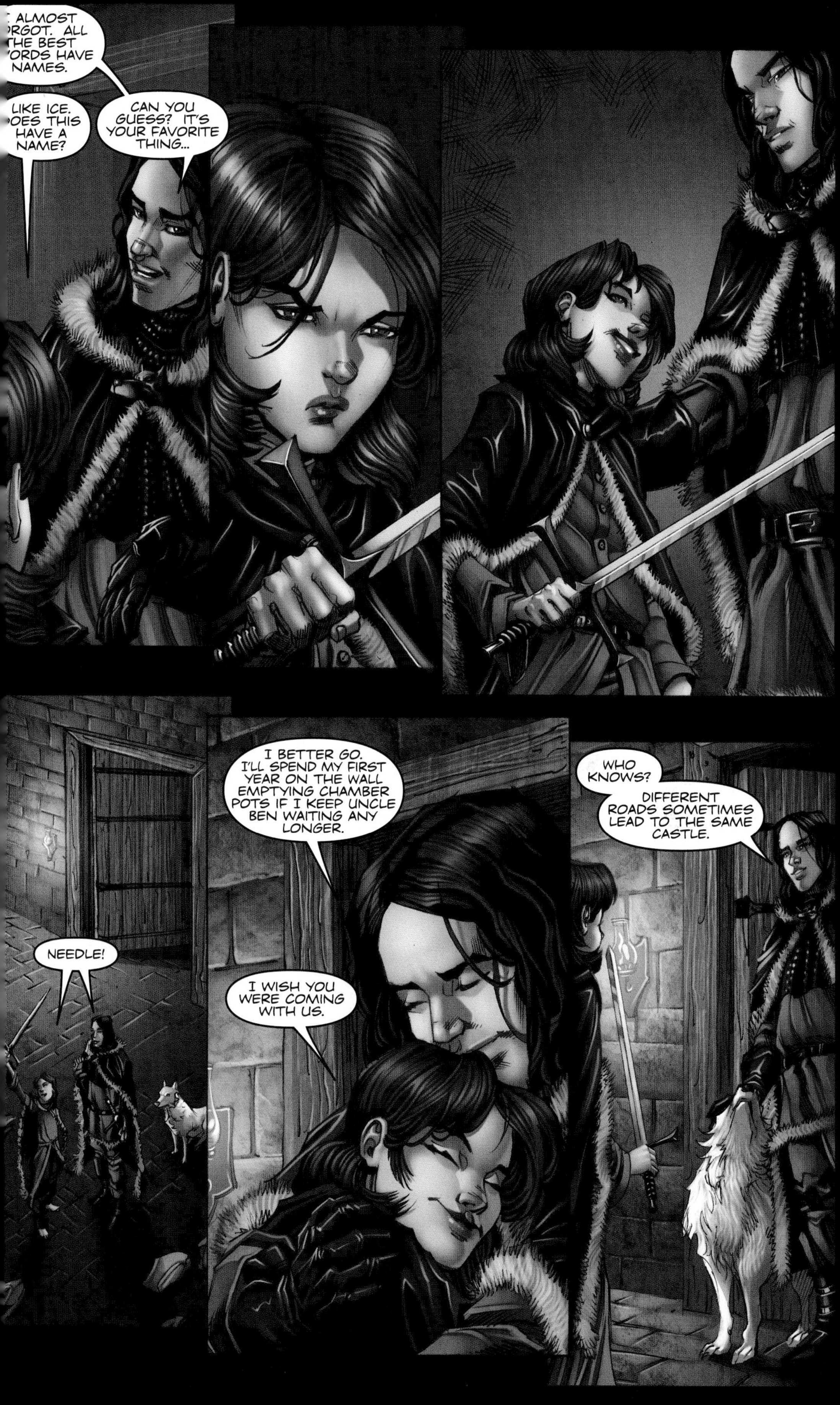
ALMOST RGOT. ALL THE BEST ORDS HAVE NAMES.
LIKE ICE. OES THIS HAVE A NAME?
CAN YOU GUESS? IT'S YOUR FAVORITE THING...
NEEDLE!
I BETTER GO. I'LL SPEND MY FIRST YEAR ON THE WALL EMPTYING CHAMBER POTS IF I KEEP UNCLE BEN WAITING ANY LONGER.
I WISH YOU WERE COMING WITH US.
WHO KNOWS?
DIFFERENT ROADS SOMETIMES LEAD TO THE SAME CASTLE.

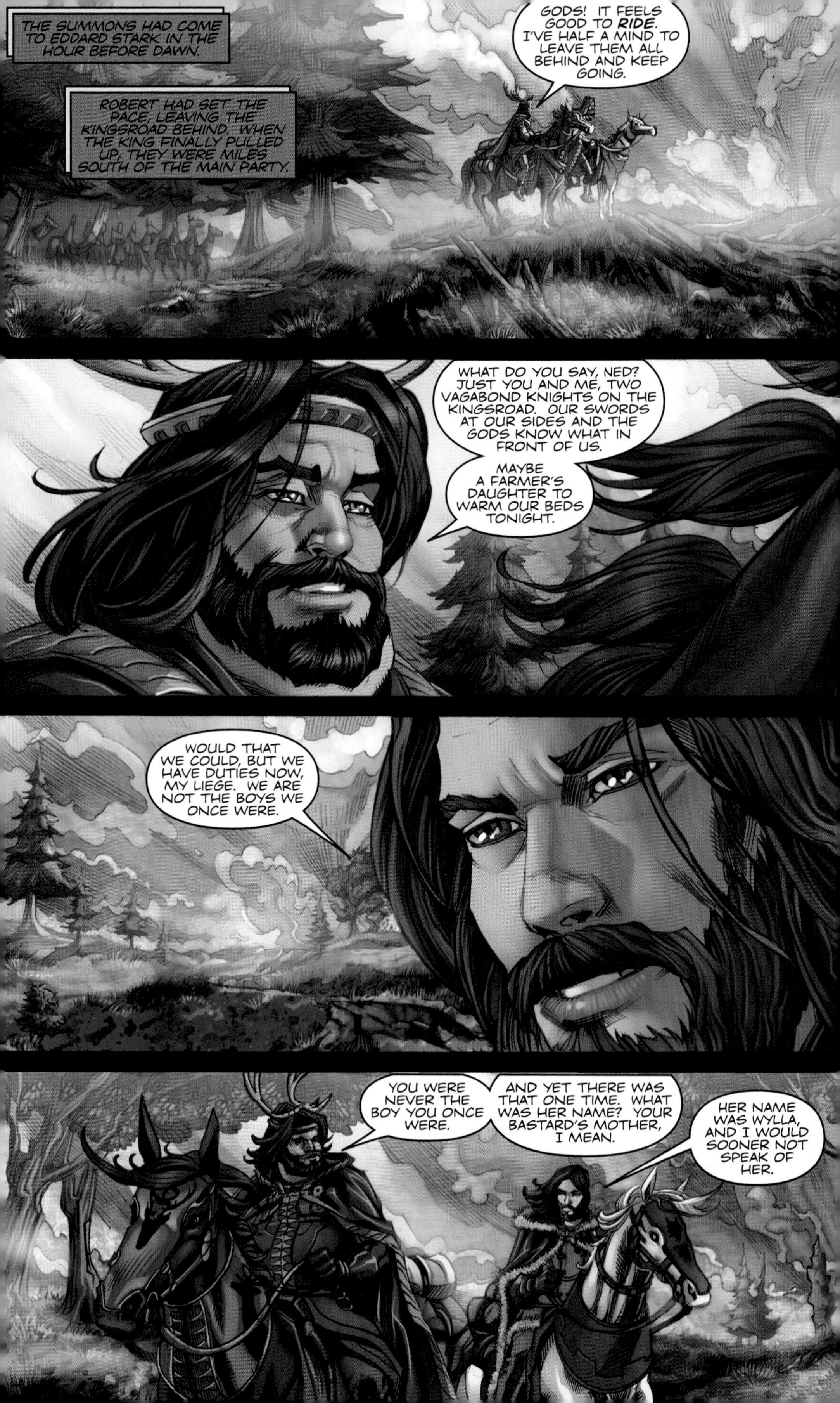
THE SUMMONS HAD COME TO EDDARD STARK IN THE HOUR BEFORE DAWN.
ROBERT HAD SET THE PACE, LEAVING THE KINGSROAD BEHIND. WHEN THE KING FINALLY PULLED UP, THEY WERE MILES SOUTH OF THE MAIN PARTY.
GODS! IT FEELS GOOD TO RIDE. I'VE HALF A MIND TO LEAVE THEM ALL BEHIND AND KEEP GOING.
WHAT DO YOU SAY, NED? JUST YOU AND ME, TWO VAGABOND KNIGHTS ON THE KINGSROAD. OUR SWORDS AT OUR SIDES AND THE GODS KNOW WHAT IN FRONT OF US.
MAYBE A FARMER'S DAUGHTER TO WARM OUR BEDS TONIGHT.
WOULD THAT WE COULD, BUT WE HAVE DUTIES NOW, MY LIEGE. WE ARE NOT THE BOYS WE ONCE WERE.
YOU WERE NEVER THE BOY YOU ONCE WERE.
AND YET THERE WAS THAT ONE TIME. WHAT WAS HER NAME? YOUR BASTARD'S MOTHER, I MEAN.
HER NAME WAS WYLLA, AND I WOULD SOONER NOT SPEAK OF HER.

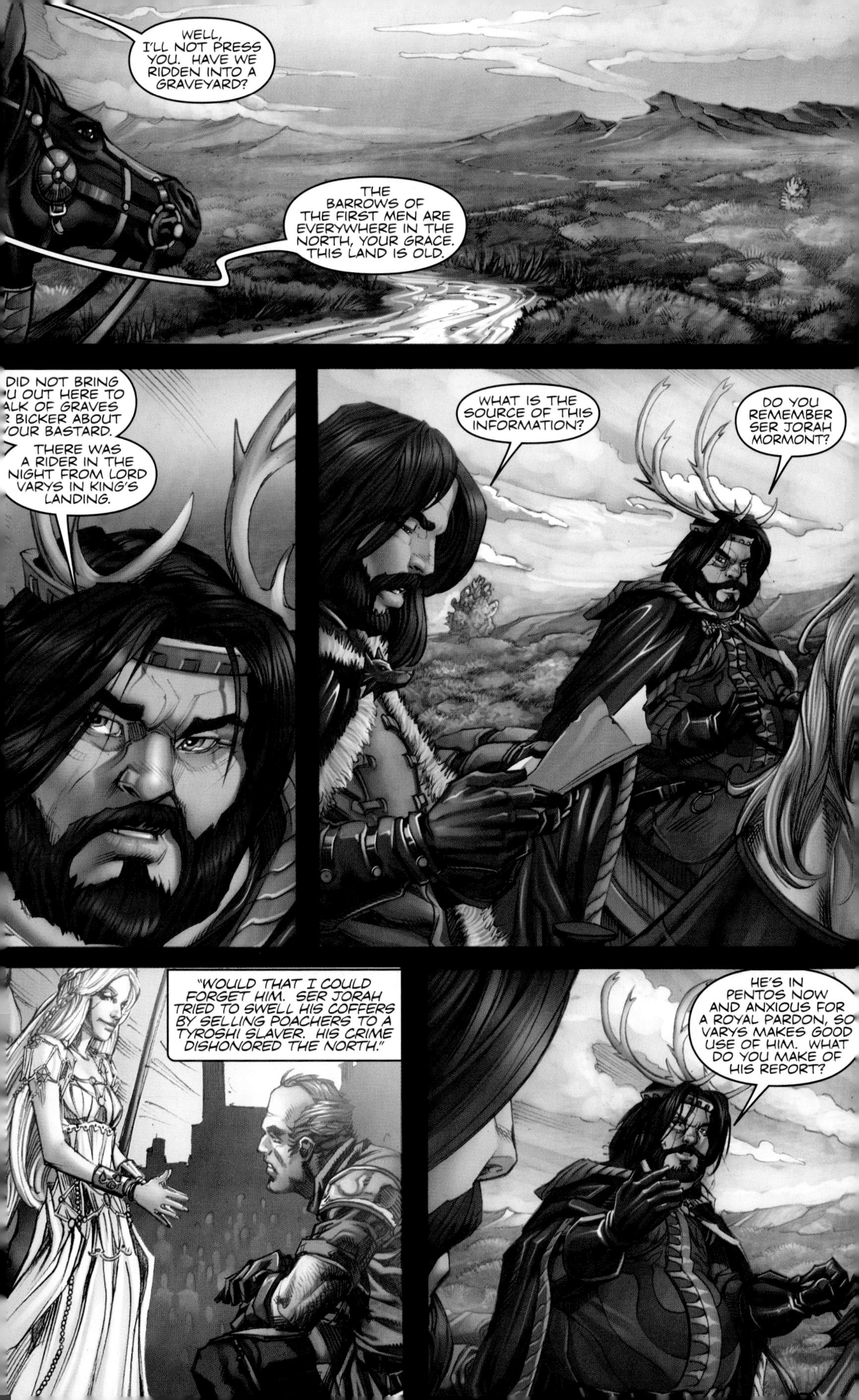
WELL, I'LL NOT PRESS YOU. HAVE WE RIDDEN INTO A GRAVEYARD?
THE BARROWS OF THE FIRST MEN ARE EVERYWHERE IN THE NORTH, YOUR GRACE. THIS LAND IS OLD.
DID NOT BRING U OUT HERE TO ALK OF GRAVES R BICKER ABOUT YOUR BASTARD.
THERE WAS A RIDER IN THE NIGHT FROM LORD VARYS IN KING'S LANDING.
WHAT IS THE SOURCE OF THIS INFORMATION?
DO YOU REMEMBER SER JORAH MORMONT?
"WOULD THAT I COULD FORGET HIM. SER JORAH TRIED TO SWELL HIS COFFERS BY SELLING POACHERS TO A TYROSHI SLAVER. HIS CRIME DISHONORED THE NORTH."
HE'S IN PENTOS NOW AND ANXIOUS FOR A ROYAL PARDON, SO VARYS MAKES GOOD USE OF HIM. WHAT DO YOU MAKE OF HIS REPORT?

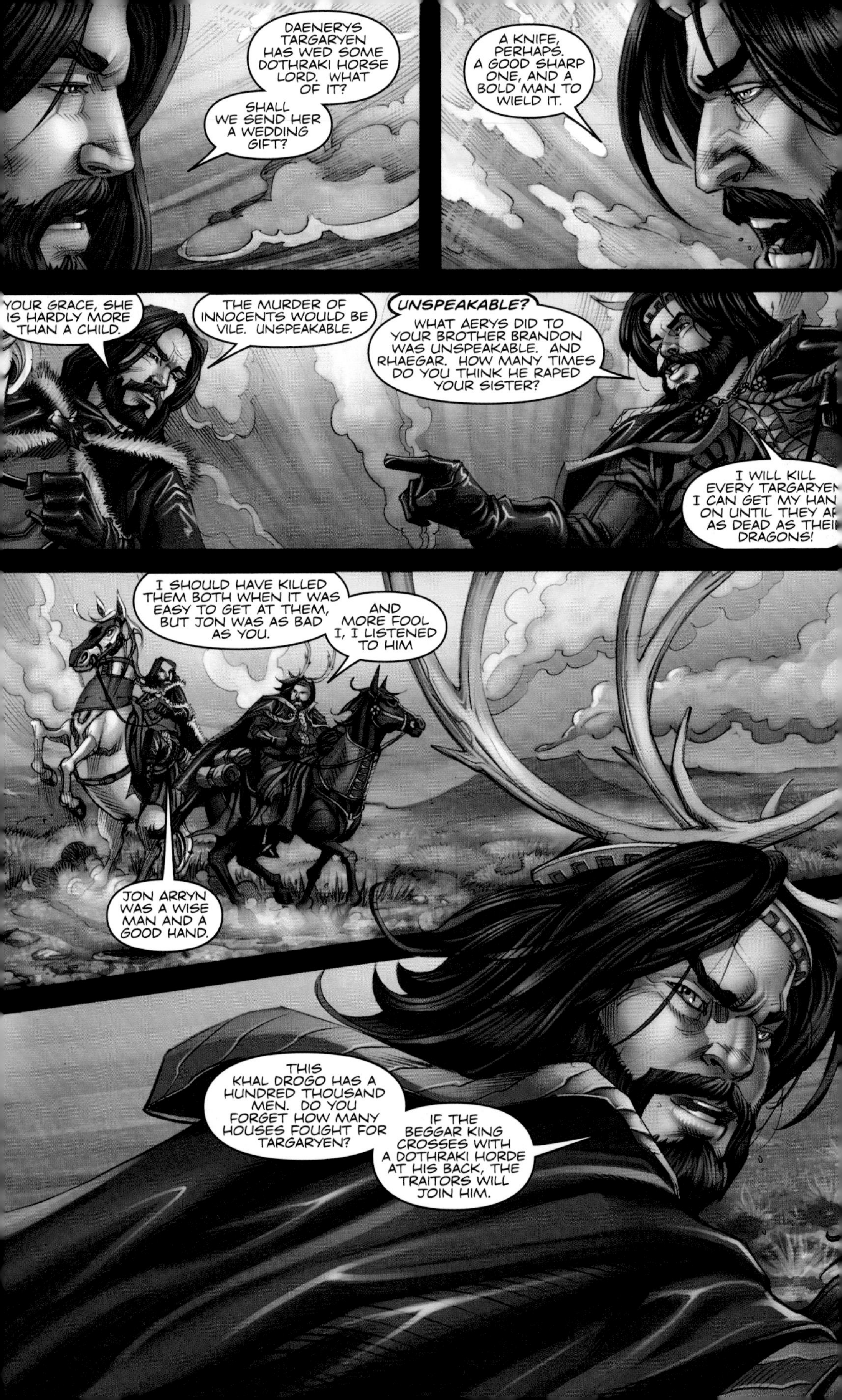

DAENERYS TARGARYEN HAS WED SOME DOTHRAKI HORSE LORD. WHAT OF IT?
SHALL WE SEND HER A WEDDING GIFT?
A KNIFE, PERHAPS. A GOOD SHARP ONE, AND A BOLD MAN TO WIELD IT.
YOUR GRACE, SHE IS HARDLY MORE THAN A CHILD.
THE MURDER OF INNOCENTS WOULD BE VILE. UNSPEAKABLE.
UNSPEAKABLE?
WHAT AERYS DID TO YOUR BROTHER BRANDON WAS UNSPEAKABLE. AND RHAEGAR. HOW MANY TIMES DO YOU THINK HE RAPED YOUR SISTER?
I WILL KILL EVERY TARGARYEN I CAN GET MY HAN ON UNTIL THEY A AS DEAD AS THEI DRAGONS!
I SHOULD HAVE KILLED THEM BOTH WHEN IT WAS EASY TO GET AT THEM, BUT JON WAS AS BAD AS YOU.
AND MORE FOOL I, I LISTENED TO HIM
JON ARRYN WAS A WISE MAN AND A GOOD HAND.
THIS KHAL DROGO HAS A HUNDRED THOUSAND MEN. DO YOU FORGET HOW MANY HOUSES FOUGHT FOR TARGARYEN?
IF THE BEGGAR KING CROSSES WITH A DOTHRAKI HORDE AT HIS BACK, THE TRAITORS WILL JOIN HIM.

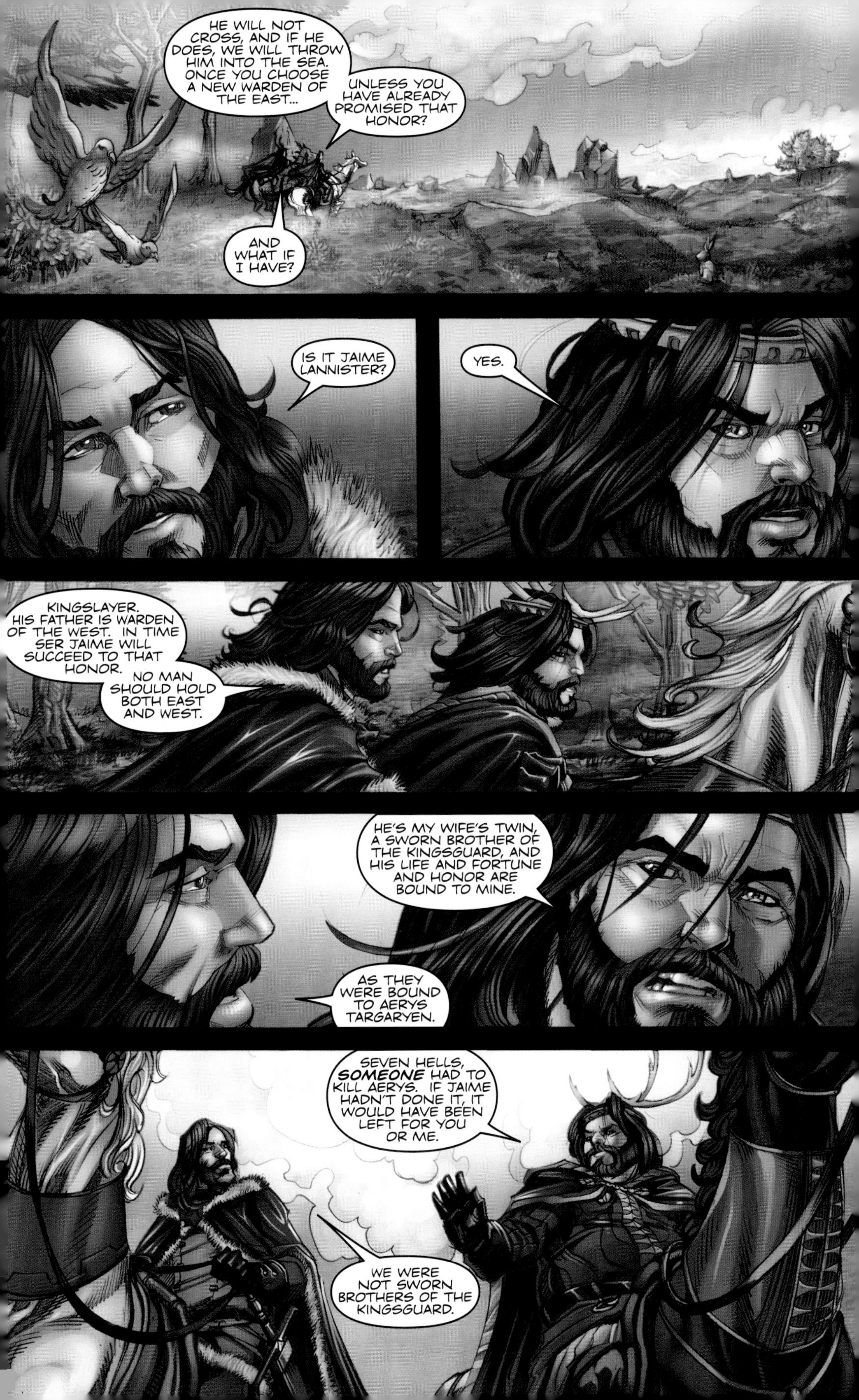
HE WILL NOT CROSS, AND IF HE DOES, WE WILL THROW HIM INTO THE SEA. ONCE YOU CHOOSE A NEW WARDEN OF THE EAST...
UNLESS YOU HAVE ALREADY PROMISED THAT HONOR?
AND WHAT IF I HAVE?
IS IT JAIME LANNISTER?
YES.
KINGSLAYER. HIS FATHER IS WARDEN OF THE WEST. IN TIME SER JAIME WILL SUCCEED TO THAT HONOR.
NO MAN SHOULD HOLD BOTH EAST AND WEST.
HE'S MY WIFE'S TWIN, A SWORN BROTHER OF THE KINGSGUARD, AND HIS LIFE AND FORTUNE AND HONOR ARE BOUND TO MINE.
AS THEY WERE BOUND TO AERYS TARGARYEN.
SEVEN HELLS, **SOMEONE** HAD TO KILL AERYS. IF JAIME HADN'T DONE IT, IT WOULD HAVE BEEN LEFT FOR YOU OR ME.
WE WERE NOT SWORN BROTHERS OF THE KINGSGUARD.

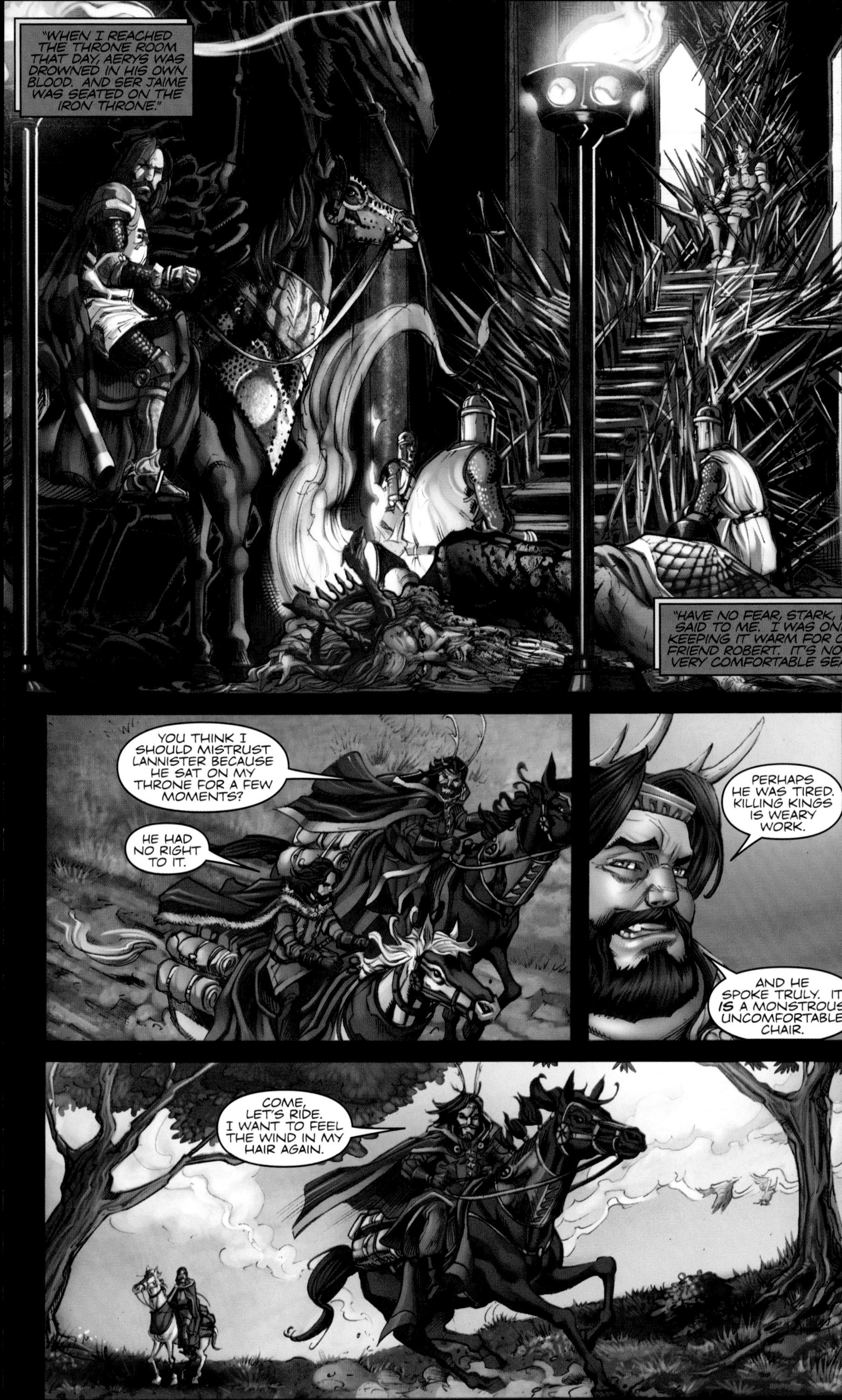

"WHEN I REACHED THE THRONE ROOM THAT DAY, AERYS WAS DROWNED IN HIS OWN BLOOD. AND SER JAIME WAS SEATED ON THE IRON THRONE."
"HAVE NO FEAR, STARK," SAID TO ME. I WAS ON KEEPING IT WARM FOR FRIEND ROBERT. IT'S NO VERY COMFORTABLE SEA
YOU THINK I SHOULD MISTRUST LANNISTER BECAUSE HE SAT ON MY THRONE FOR A FEW MOMENTS?
HE HAD NO RIGHT TO IT.
PERHAPS HE WAS TIRED. KILLING KINGS IS WEARY WORK.
AND HE SPOKE TRULY. IT IS A MONSTROUS UNCOMFORTABLE CHAIR.
COME, LET'S RIDE. I WANT TO FEEL THE WIND IN MY HAIR AGAIN.

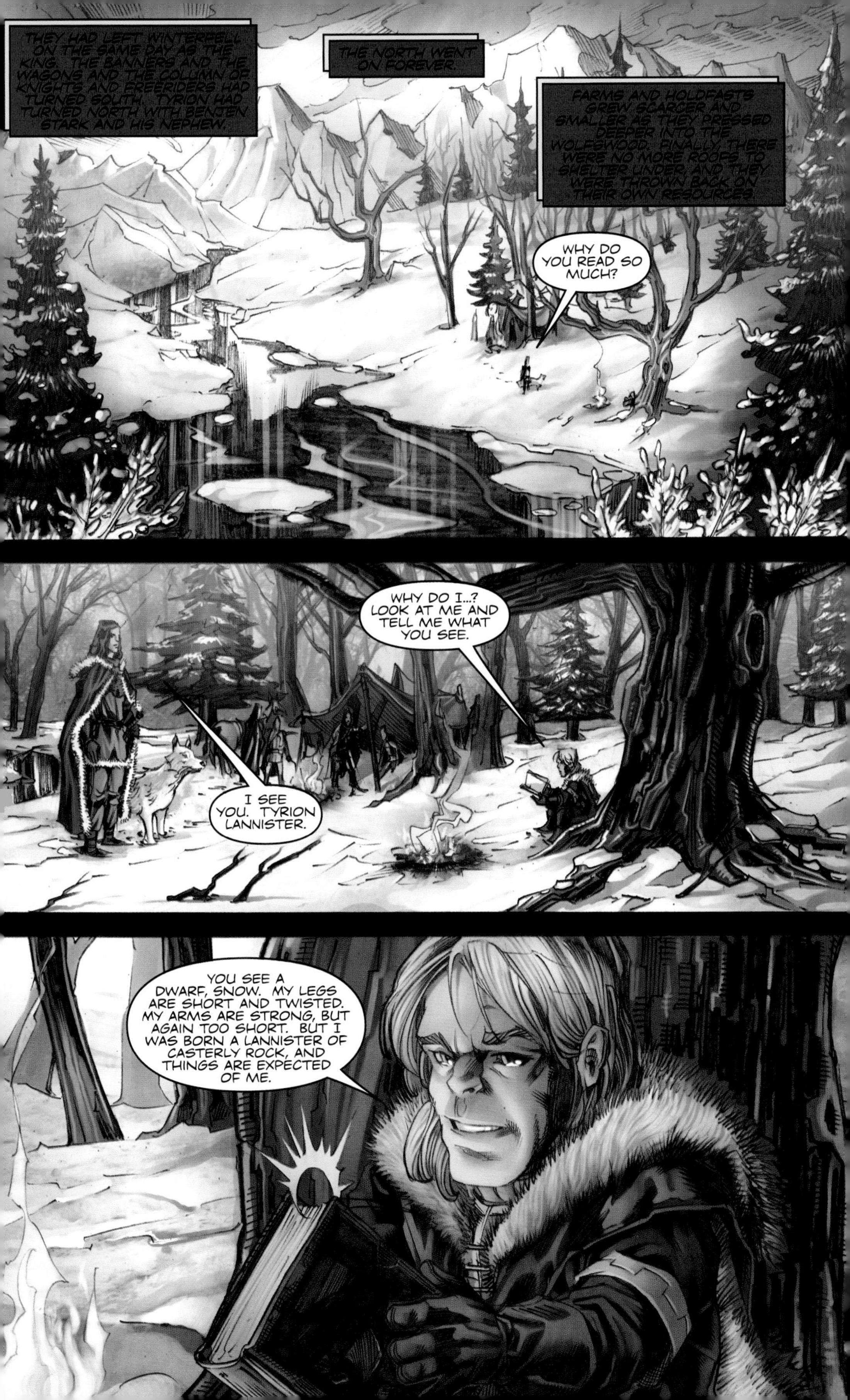
THEY HAD LEFT WINTERFELL ON THE SAME DAY AS THE KING. THE BANNERS AND THE WAGONS AND THE COLUMN OF KNIGHTS AND FREERIDERS HAD TURNED SOUTH. TYRION HAD TURNED NORTH WITH BENJEN STARK AND HIS NEPHEW.
THE NORTH WENT ON FOREVER.
FARMS AND HOLDFASTS GREW SCARCER AND SMALLER AS THEY PRESSED DEEPER INTO THE WOLFSWOOD. FINALLY, THERE WERE NO MORE ROOFS TO SHELTER UNDER, AND THEY WERE THROWN BACK ON THEIR OWN RESOURCES.
WHY DO YOU READ SO MUCH?
WHY DO I...? LOOK AT ME AND TELL ME WHAT YOU SEE.
I SEE YOU. TYRION LANNISTER.
YOU SEE A DWARF, SNOW. MY LEGS ARE SHORT AND TWISTED. MY ARMS ARE STRONG, BUT AGAIN TOO SHORT. BUT I WAS BORN A LANNISTER OF CASTERLY ROCK, AND THINGS ARE EXPECTED OF ME.

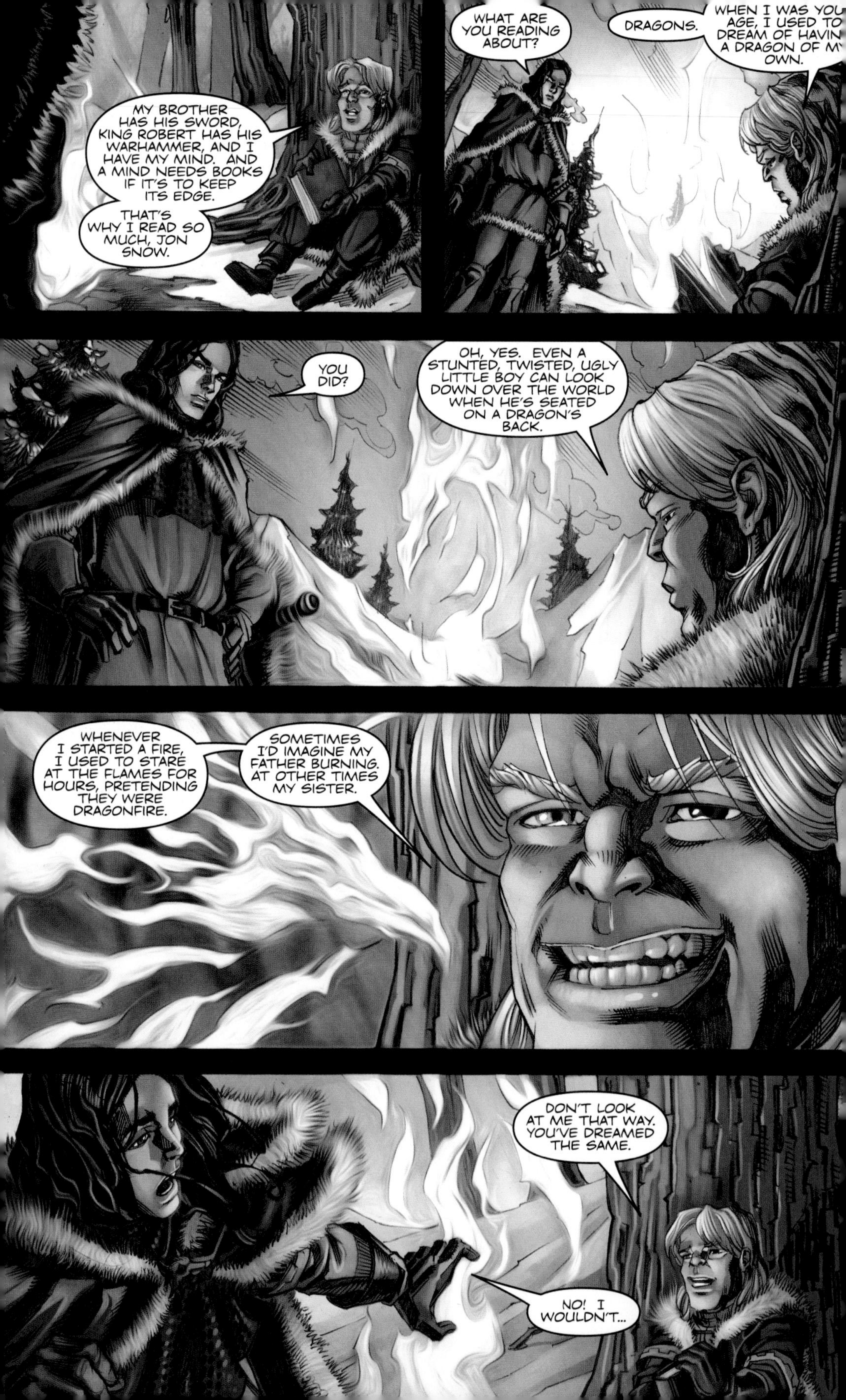
MY BROTHER HAS HIS SWORD, KING ROBERT HAS HIS WARHAMMER, AND I HAVE MY MIND. AND A MIND NEEDS BOOKS IF IT'S TO KEEP ITS EDGE.
THAT'S WHY I READ SO MUCH, JON SNOW.
WHAT ARE YOU READING ABOUT?
DRAGONS.
WHEN I WAS YOU AGE, I USED TO DREAM OF HAVIN A DRAGON OF MY OWN.
YOU DID?
OH, YES. EVEN A STUNTED, TWISTED, UGLY LITTLE BOY CAN LOOK DOWN OVER THE WORLD WHEN HE'S SEATED ON A DRAGON'S BACK.
WHENEVER I STARTED A FIRE, I USED TO STARE AT THE FLAMES FOR HOURS, PRETENDING THEY WERE DRAGONFIRE.
SOMETIMES I'D IMAGINE MY FATHER BURNING. AT OTHER TIMES MY SISTER.
DON'T LOOK AT ME THAT WAY. YOU'VE DREAMED THE SAME.
NO! I WOULDN'T...

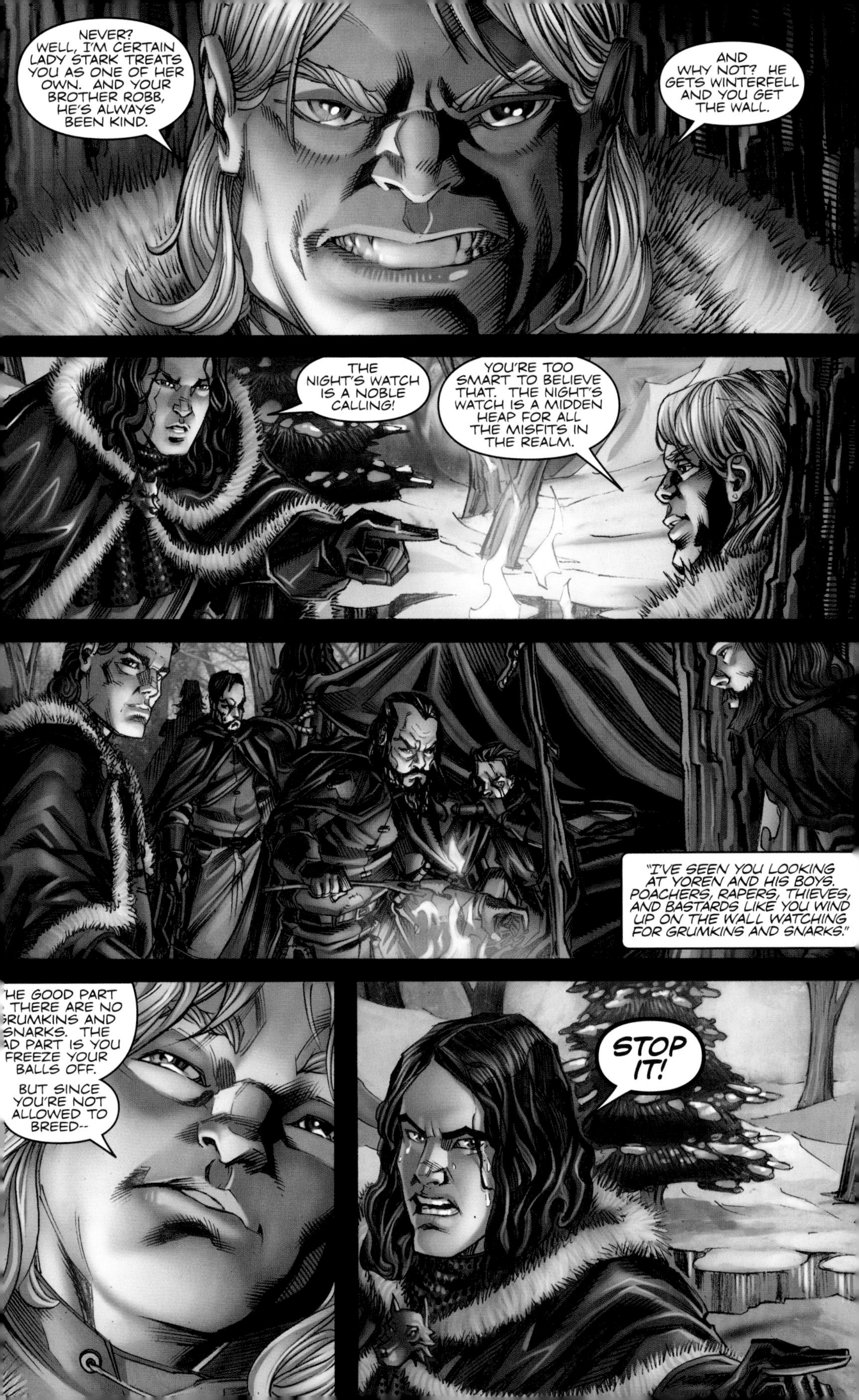
NEVER? WELL, I'M CERTAIN LADY STARK TREATS YOU AS ONE OF HER OWN. AND YOUR BROTHER ROBB, HE'S ALWAYS BEEN KIND.
AND WHY NOT? HE GETS WINTERFELL AND YOU GET THE WALL.
THE NIGHT'S WATCH IS A NOBLE CALLING!
YOU'RE TOO SMART TO BELIEVE THAT. THE NIGHT'S WATCH IS A MIDDEN HEAP FOR ALL THE MISFITS IN THE REALM.
"I'VE SEEN YOU LOOKING AT YOREN AND HIS BOYS. POACHERS, RAPERS, THIEVES, AND BASTARDS LIKE YOU WIND UP ON THE WALL WATCHING FOR GRUMKINS AND SNARKS."
HE GOOD PART THERE ARE NO GRUMKINS AND SNARKS. THE AD PART IS YOU FREEZE YOUR BALLS OFF.
BUT SINCE YOU'RE NOT ALLOWED TO BREED--
STOP IT!

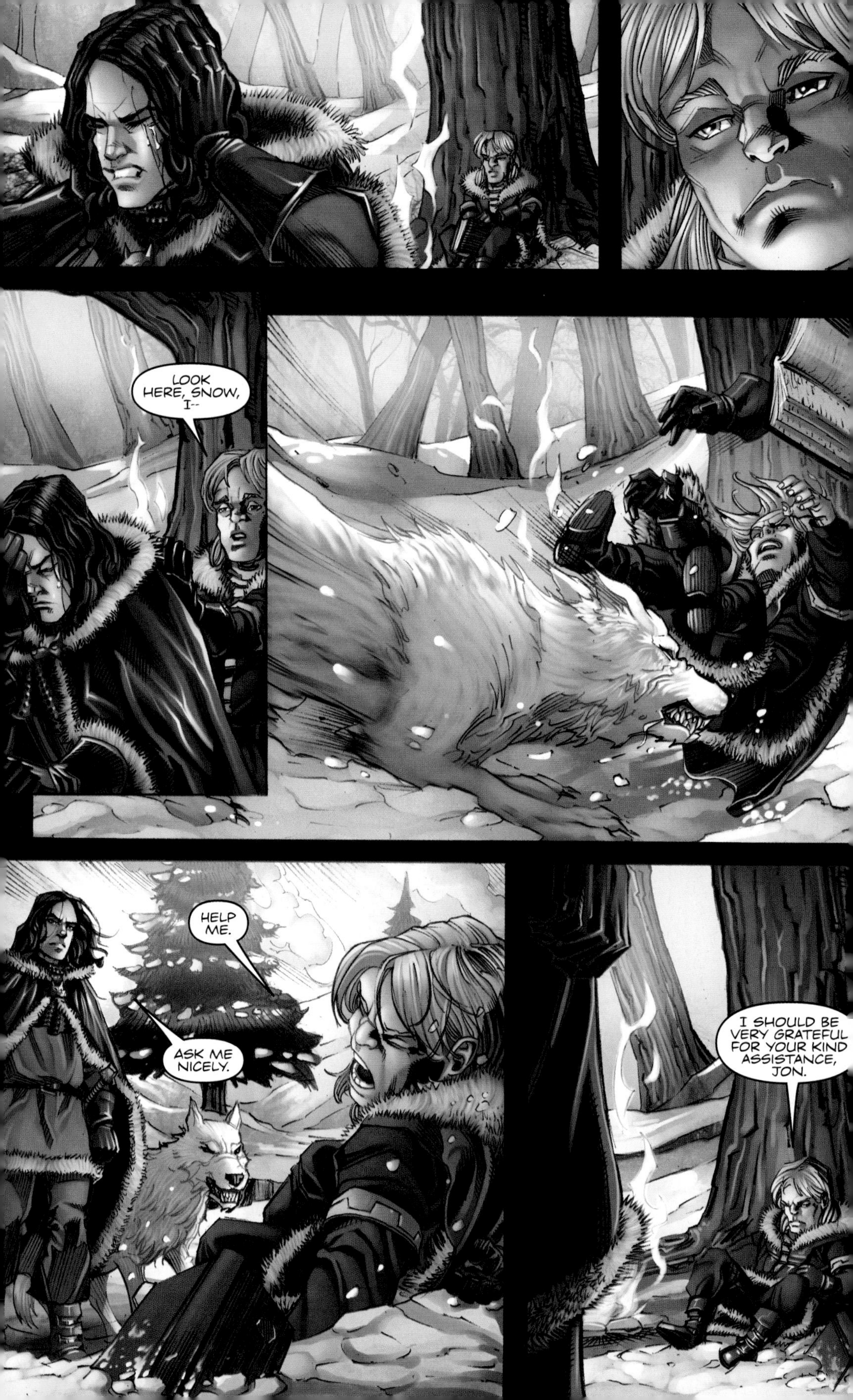
LOOK HERE, SNOW, I--
HELP ME.
ASK ME NICELY.
I SHOULD BE VERY GRATEFUL FOR YOUR KIND ASSISTANCE, JON.

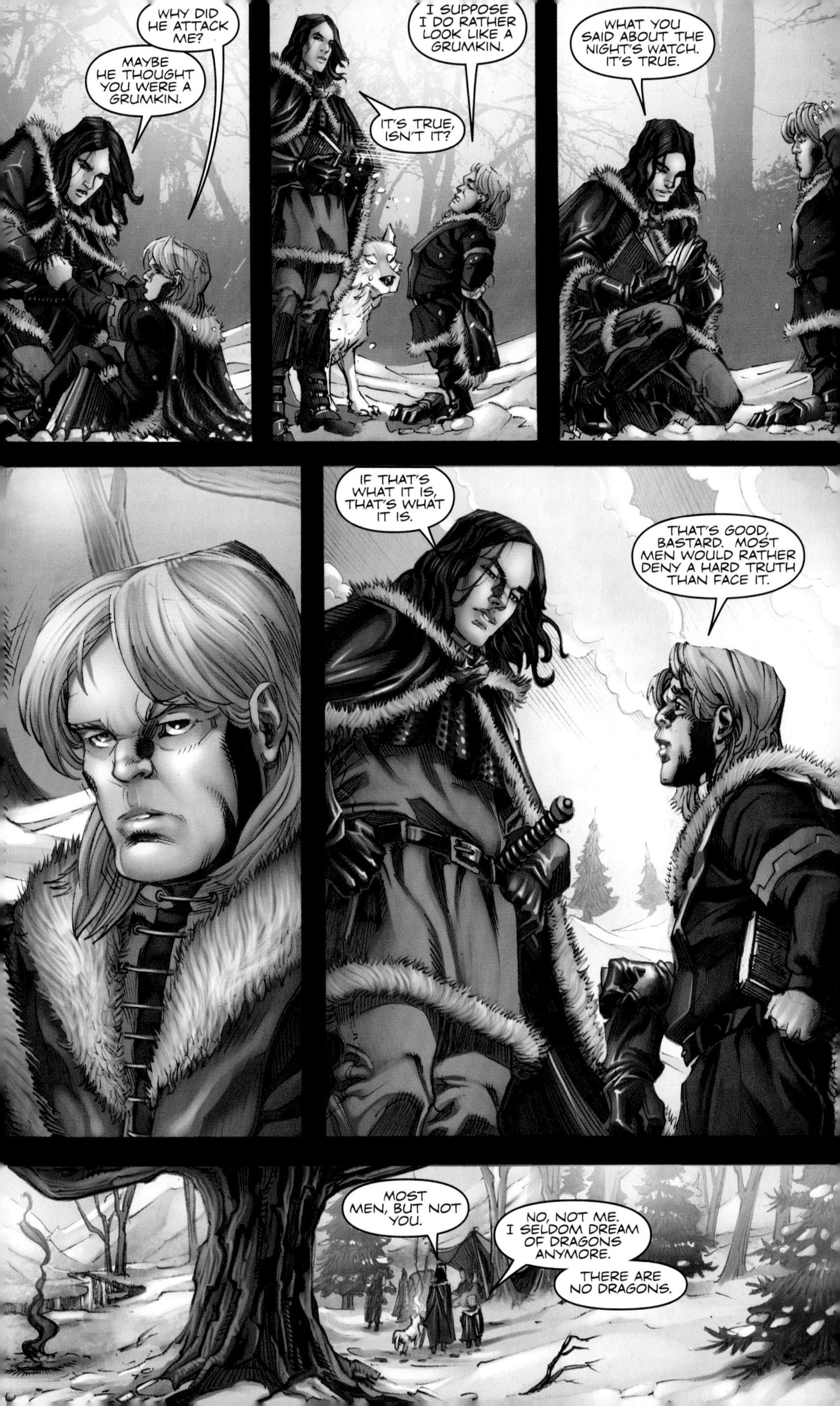

WHY DID HE ATTACK ME?
MAYBE HE THOUGHT YOU WERE A GRUMKIN.
I SUPPOSE I DO RATHER LOOK LIKE A GRUMKIN.
IT'S TRUE, ISN'T IT?
WHAT YOU SAID ABOUT THE NIGHT'S WATCH. IT'S TRUE.
IF THAT'S WHAT IT IS, THAT'S WHAT IT IS.
THAT'S GOOD, BASTARD. MOST MEN WOULD RATHER DENY A HARD TRUTH THAN FACE IT.
MOST MEN, BUT NOT YOU.
NO, NOT ME. I SELDOM DREAM OF DRAGONS ANYMORE.
THERE ARE NO DRAGONS.

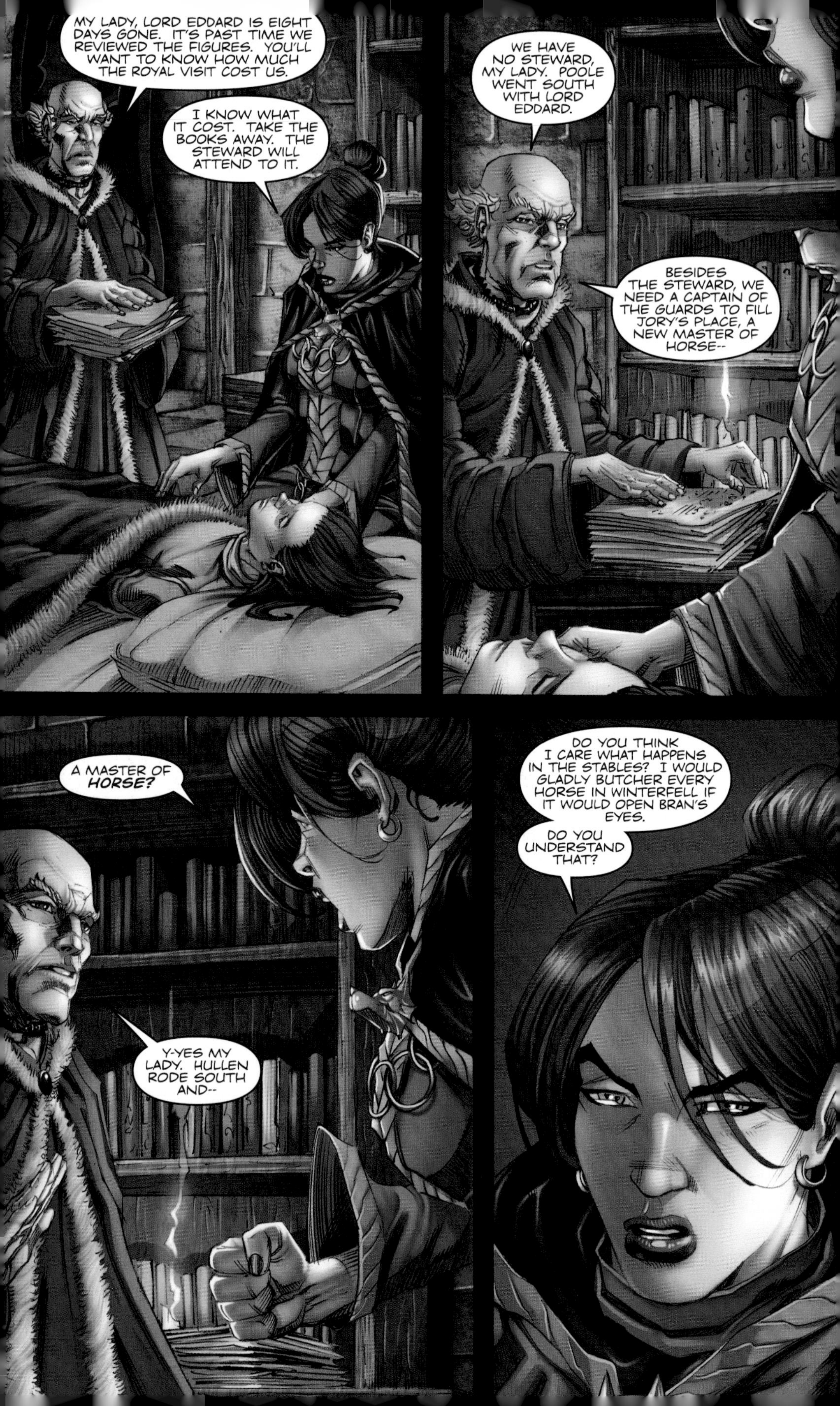
MY LADY, LORD EDDARD IS EIGHT DAYS GONE. IT'S PAST TIME WE REVIEWED THE FIGURES. YOU'LL WANT TO KNOW HOW MUCH THE ROYAL VISIT COST US.
I KNOW WHAT IT COST. TAKE THE BOOKS AWAY. THE STEWARD WILL ATTEND TO IT.
WE HAVE NO STEWARD, MY LADY. POOLE WENT SOUTH WITH LORD EDDARD.
BESIDES THE STEWARD, WE NEED A CAPTAIN OF THE GUARDS TO FILL JORY'S PLACE, A NEW MASTER OF HORSE--
A MASTER OF ***HORSE?***
Y-YES MY LADY. HULLEN RODE SOUTH AND--
DO YOU THINK I CARE WHAT HAPPENS IN THE STABLES? I WOULD GLADLY BUTCHER EVERY HORSE IN WINTERFELL IF IT WOULD OPEN BRAN'S EYES.
DO YOU UNDERSTAND THAT?

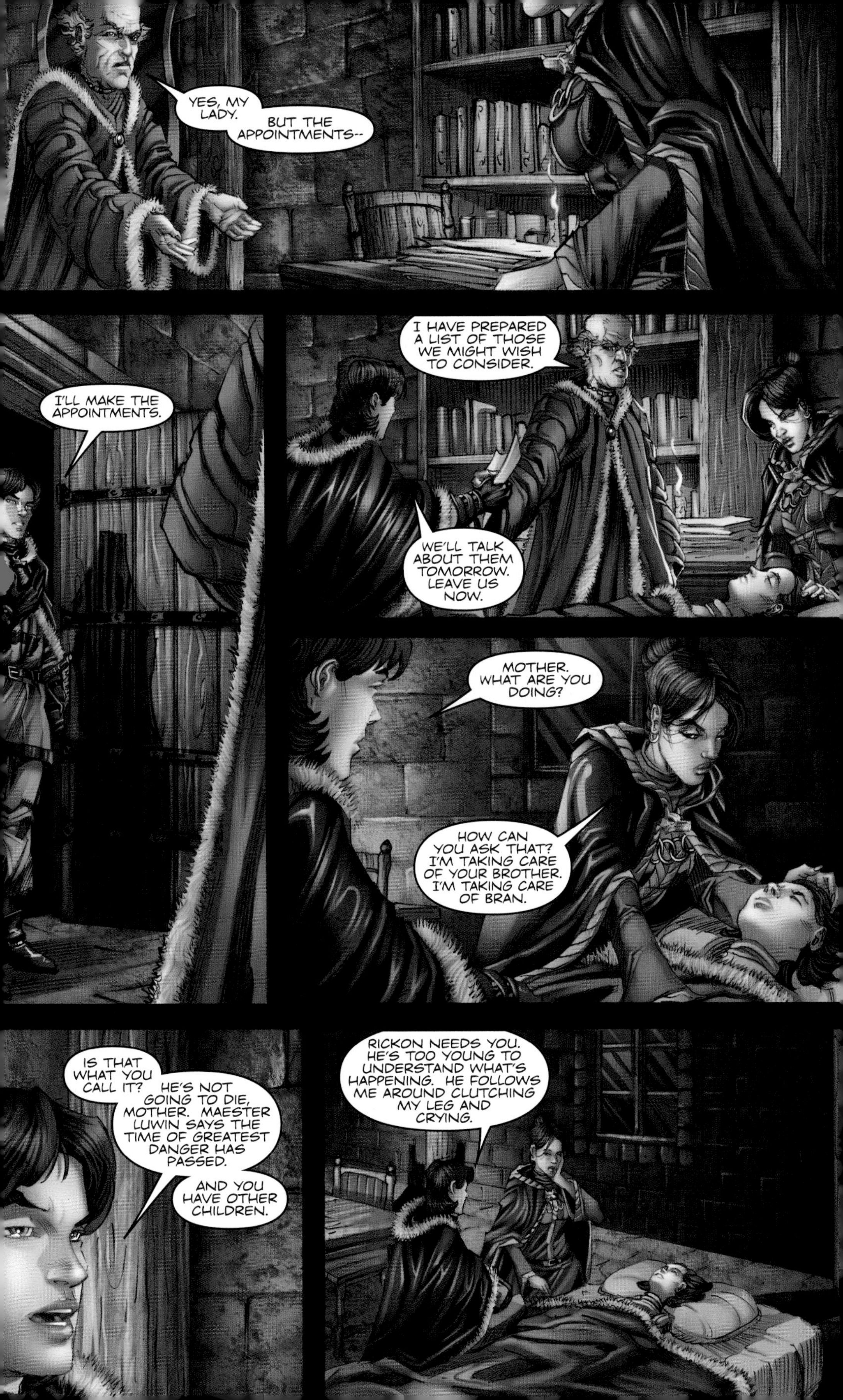
YES, MY LADY.
BUT THE APPOINTMENTS--
I'LL MAKE THE APPOINTMENTS.
I HAVE PREPARED A LIST OF THOSE WE MIGHT WISH TO CONSIDER.
WE'LL TALK ABOUT THEM TOMORROW. LEAVE US NOW.
MOTHER. WHAT ARE YOU DOING?
HOW CAN YOU ASK THAT? I'M TAKING CARE OF YOUR BROTHER. I'M TAKING CARE OF BRAN.
IS THAT WHAT YOU CALL IT?
HE'S NOT GOING TO DIE, MOTHER. MAESTER LUWIN SAYS THE TIME OF GREATEST DANGER HAS PASSED.
AND YOU HAVE OTHER CHILDREN.
RICKON NEEDS YOU. HE'S TOO YOUNG TO UNDERSTAND WHAT'S HAPPENING. HE FOLLOWS ME AROUND CLUTCHING MY LEG AND CRYING.

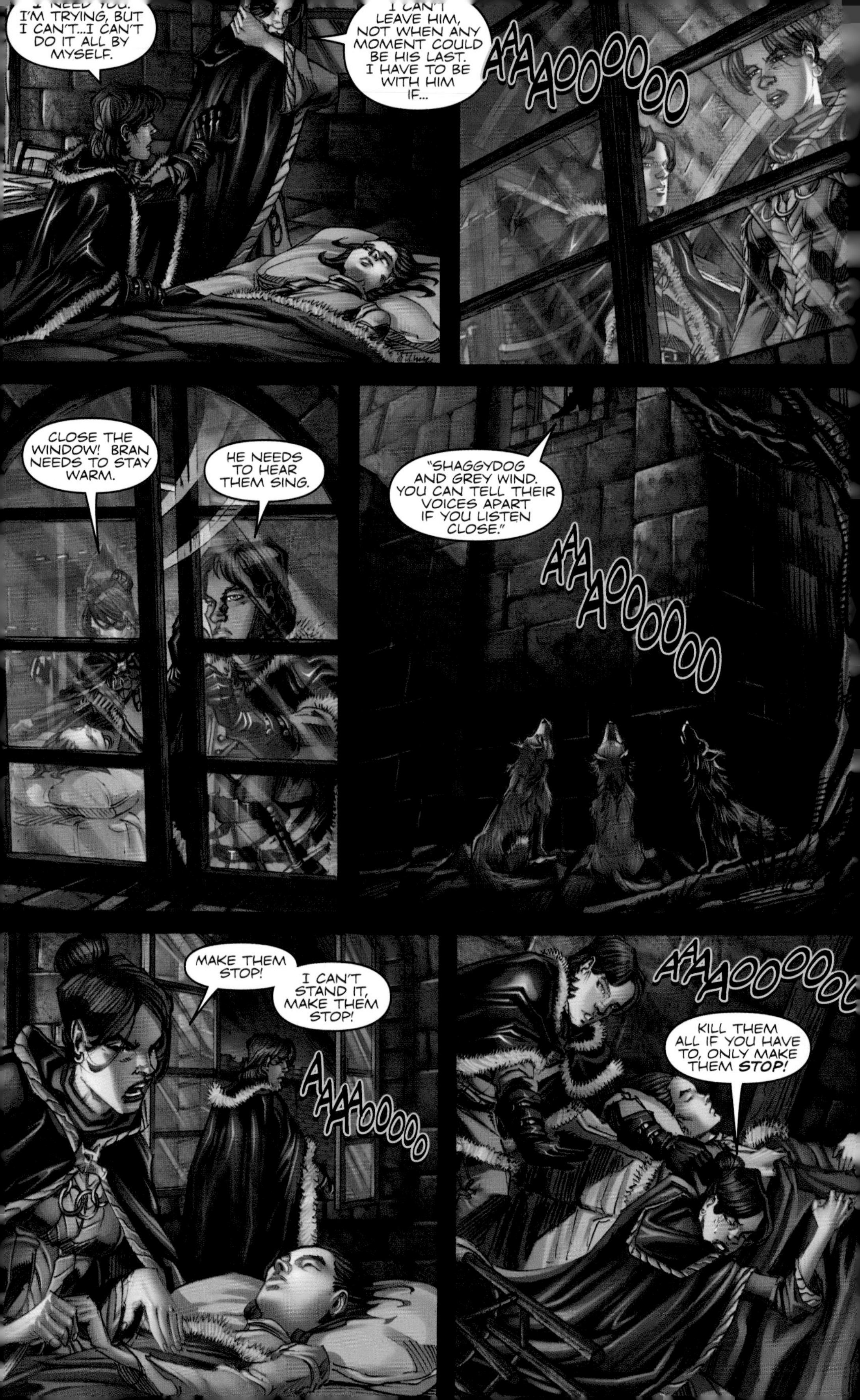
I NEED YOU. I'M TRYING, BUT I CAN'T...I CAN'T DO IT ALL BY MYSELF.
I CAN'T LEAVE HIM, NOT WHEN ANY MOMENT COULD BE HIS LAST. I HAVE TO BE WITH HIM IF...
AAAAOOOOOOO
CLOSE THE WINDOW! BRAN NEEDS TO STAY WARM.
HE NEEDS TO HEAR THEM SING.
"SHAGGYDOG AND GREY WIND. YOU CAN TELL THEIR VOICES APART IF YOU LISTEN CLOSE."
AAAAOOOOOOO
MAKE THEM STOP!
I CAN'T STAND IT, MAKE THEM STOP!
AAAAOOOOO
AAAAOOOOOO
KILL THEM ALL IF YOU HAVE TO, ONLY MAKE THEM *STOP!*

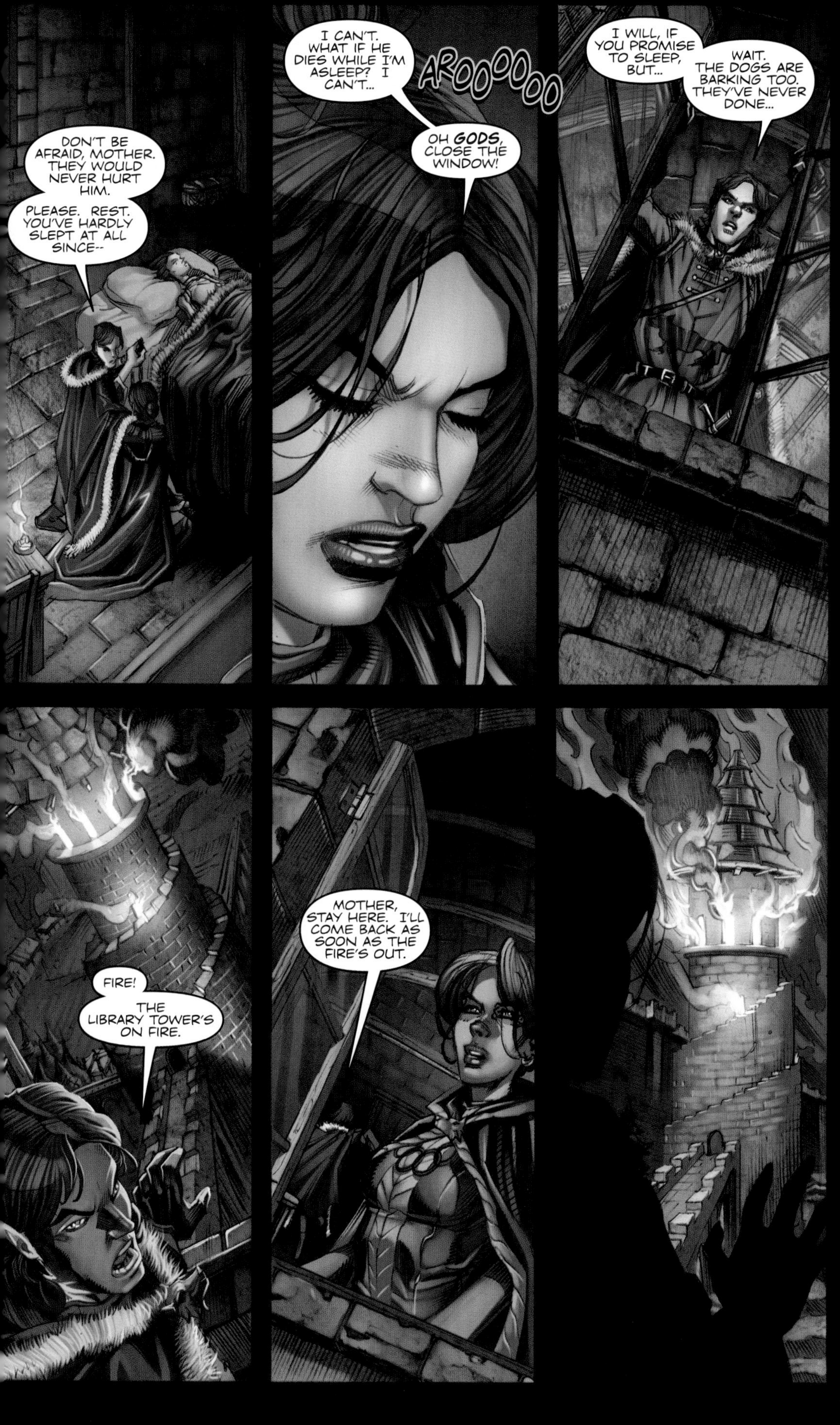
DON'T BE AFRAID, MOTHER. THEY WOULD NEVER HURT HIM.
PLEASE. REST. YOU'VE HARDLY SLEPT AT ALL SINCE--
I CAN'T. WHAT IF HE DIES WHILE I'M ASLEEP? I CAN'T...
AROOOOOOO
OH GODS, CLOSE THE WINDOW!
I WILL, IF YOU PROMISE TO SLEEP, BUT...
WAIT. THE DOGS ARE BARKING TOO. THEY'VE NEVER DONE...
FIRE!
THE LIBRARY TOWER'S ON FIRE.
MOTHER, STAY HERE. I'LL COME BACK AS SOON AS THE FIRE'S OUT.

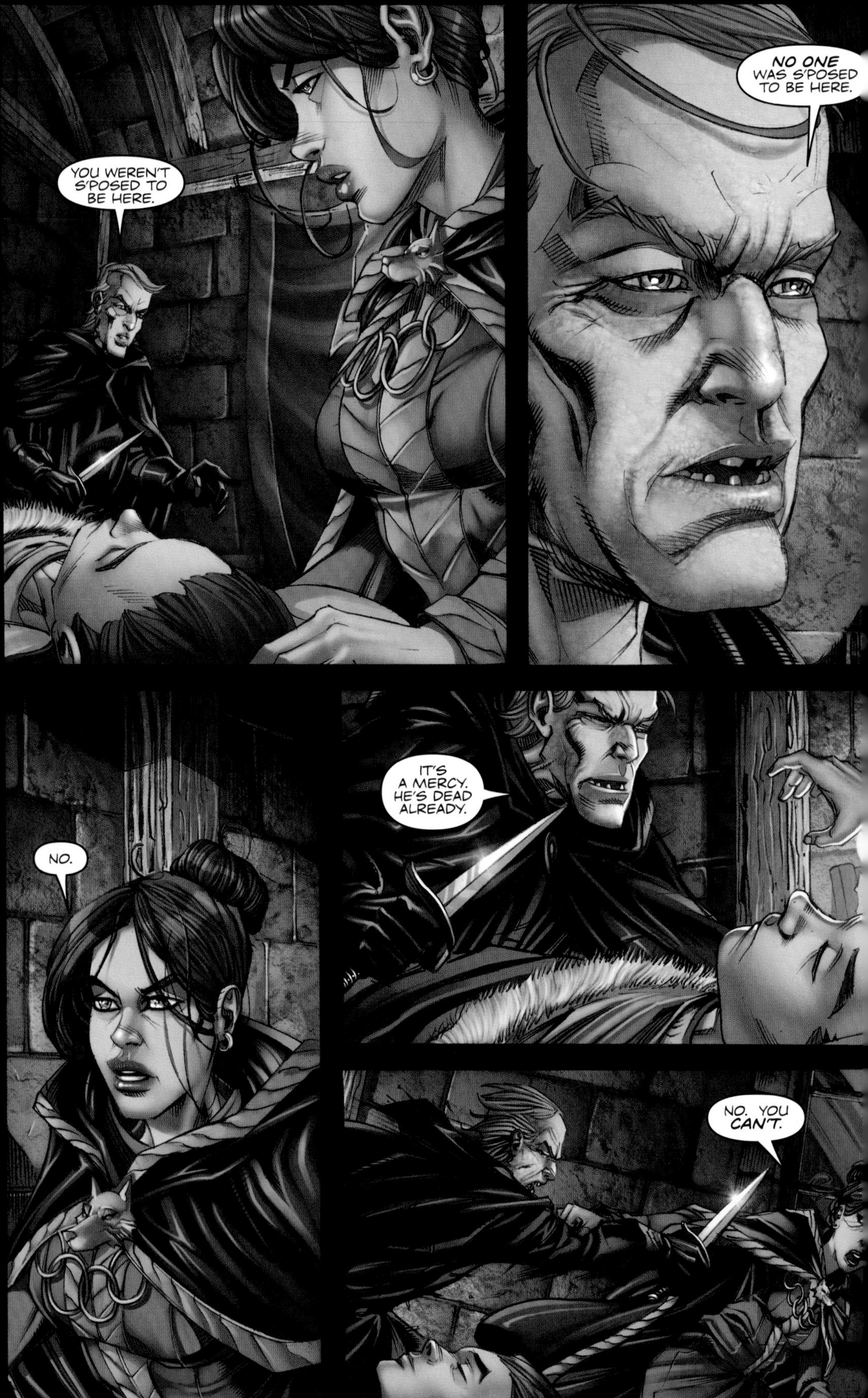
YOU WEREN'T S'POSED TO BE HERE.
NO ONE WAS S'POSED TO BE HERE.
NO.
IT'S A MERCY. HE'S DEAD ALREADY.
NO. YOU CAN'T.

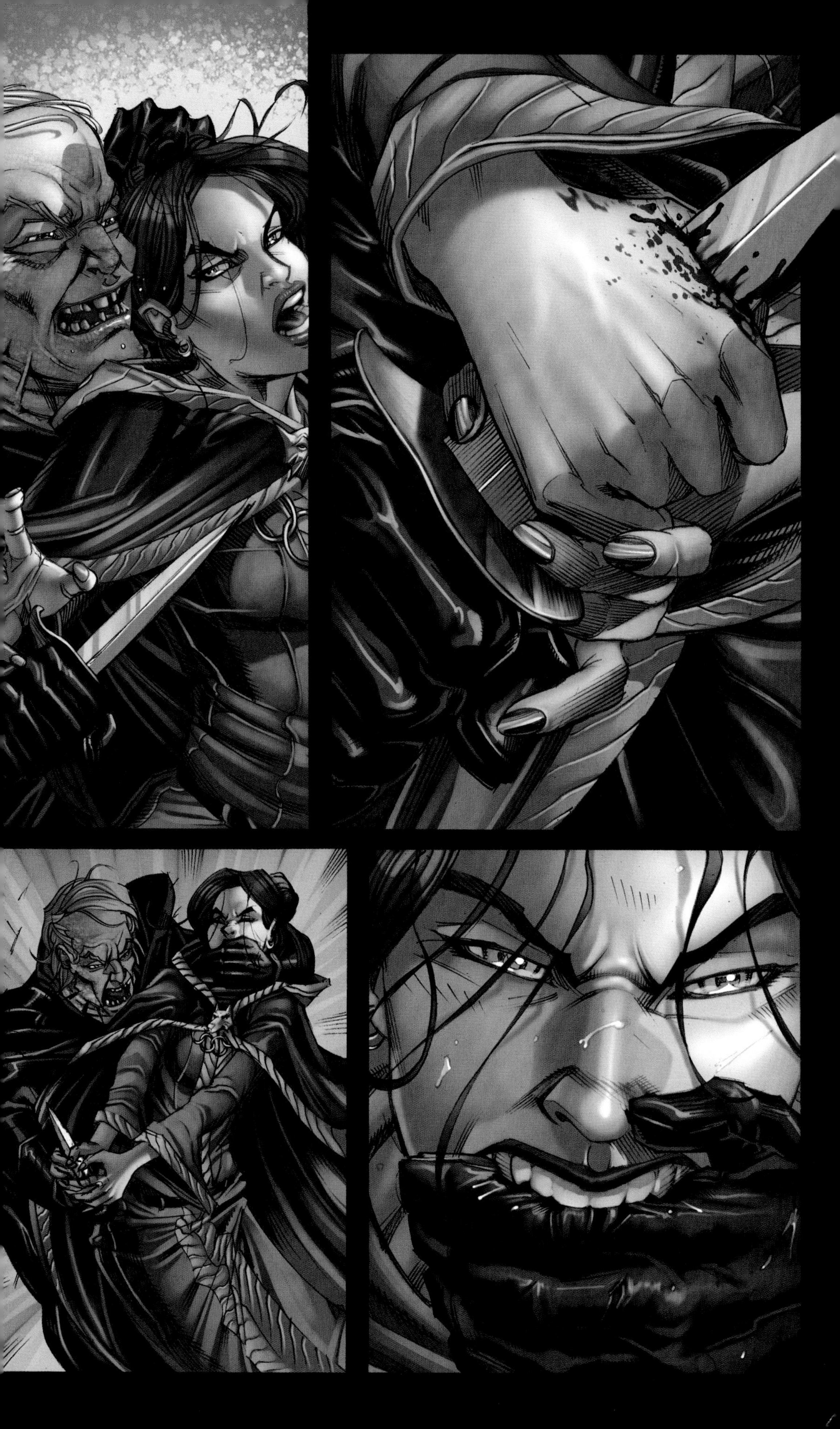

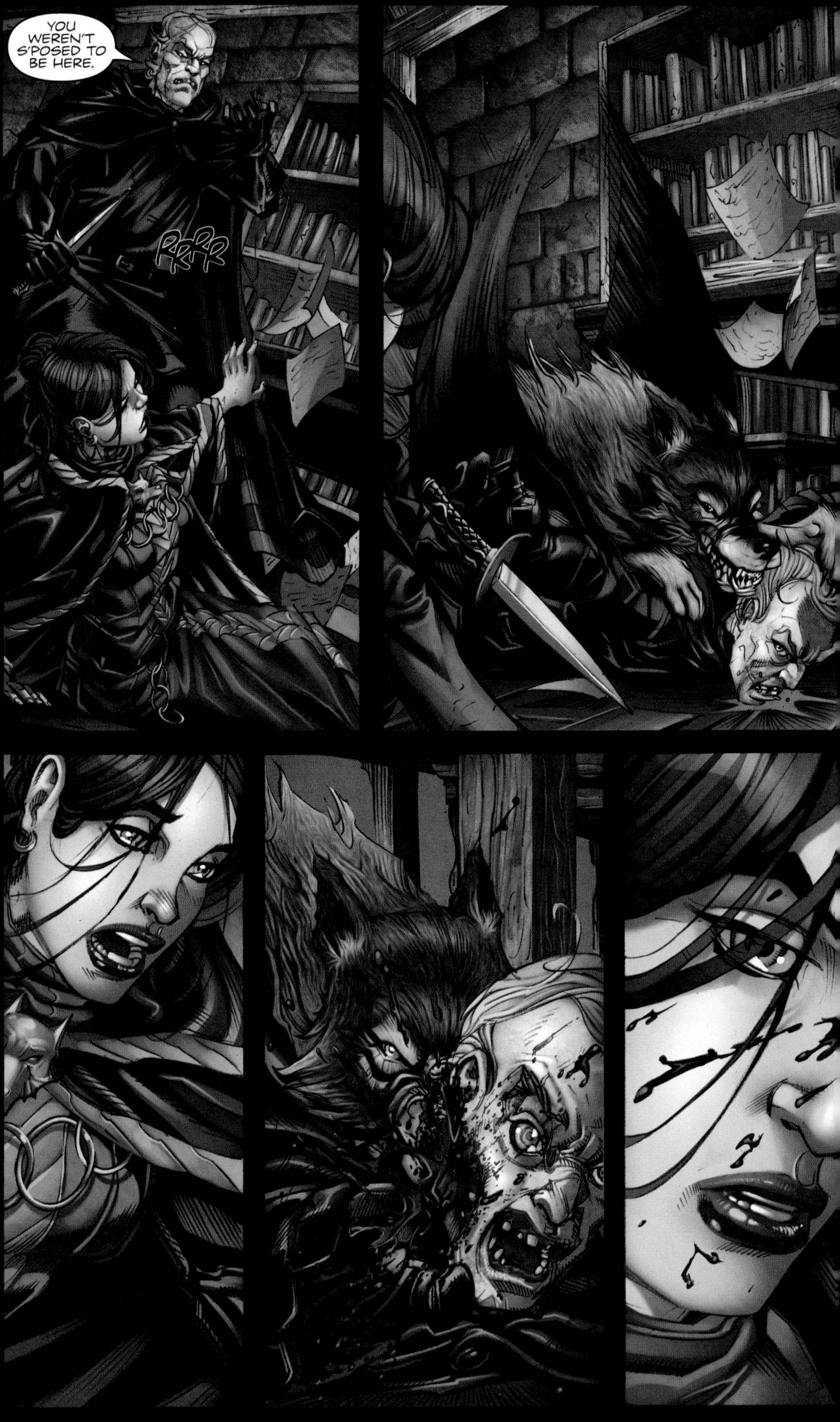
YOU WEREN'T S'POSED TO BE HERE.
RRRR

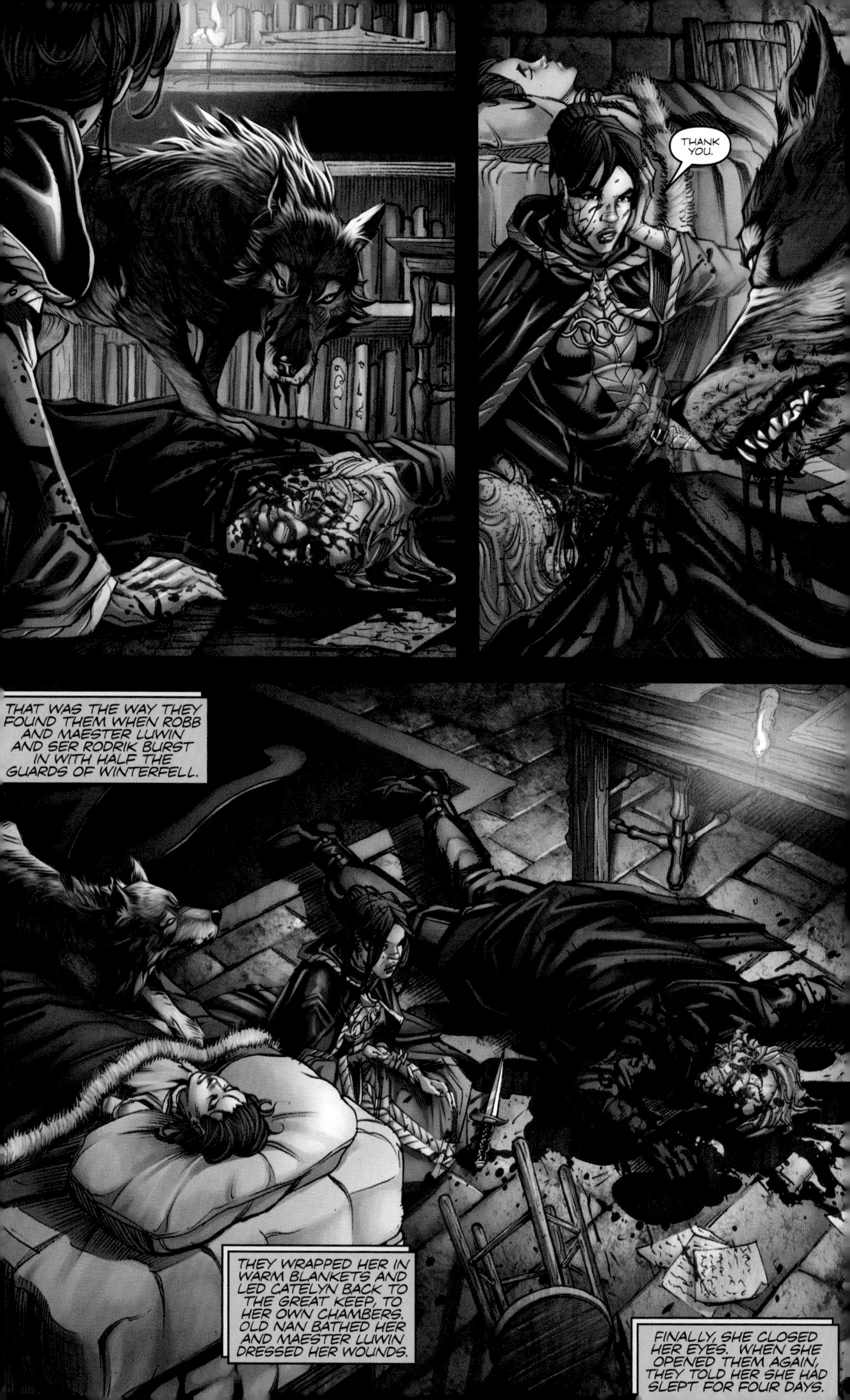
THANK YOU.
THAT WAS THE WAY THEY FOUND THEM WHEN ROBB AND MAESTER LUWIN AND SER RODRIK BURST IN WITH HALF THE GUARDS OF WINTERFELL.
THEY WRAPPED HER IN WARM BLANKETS AND LED CATELYN BACK TO THE GREAT KEEP, TO HER OWN CHAMBERS. OLD NAN BATHED HER AND MAESTER LUWIN DRESSED HER WOUNDS.
FINALLY, SHE CLOSED HER EYES. WHEN SHE OPENED THEM AGAIN, THEY TOLD HER SHE HAD SLEPT FOR FOUR DAYS.

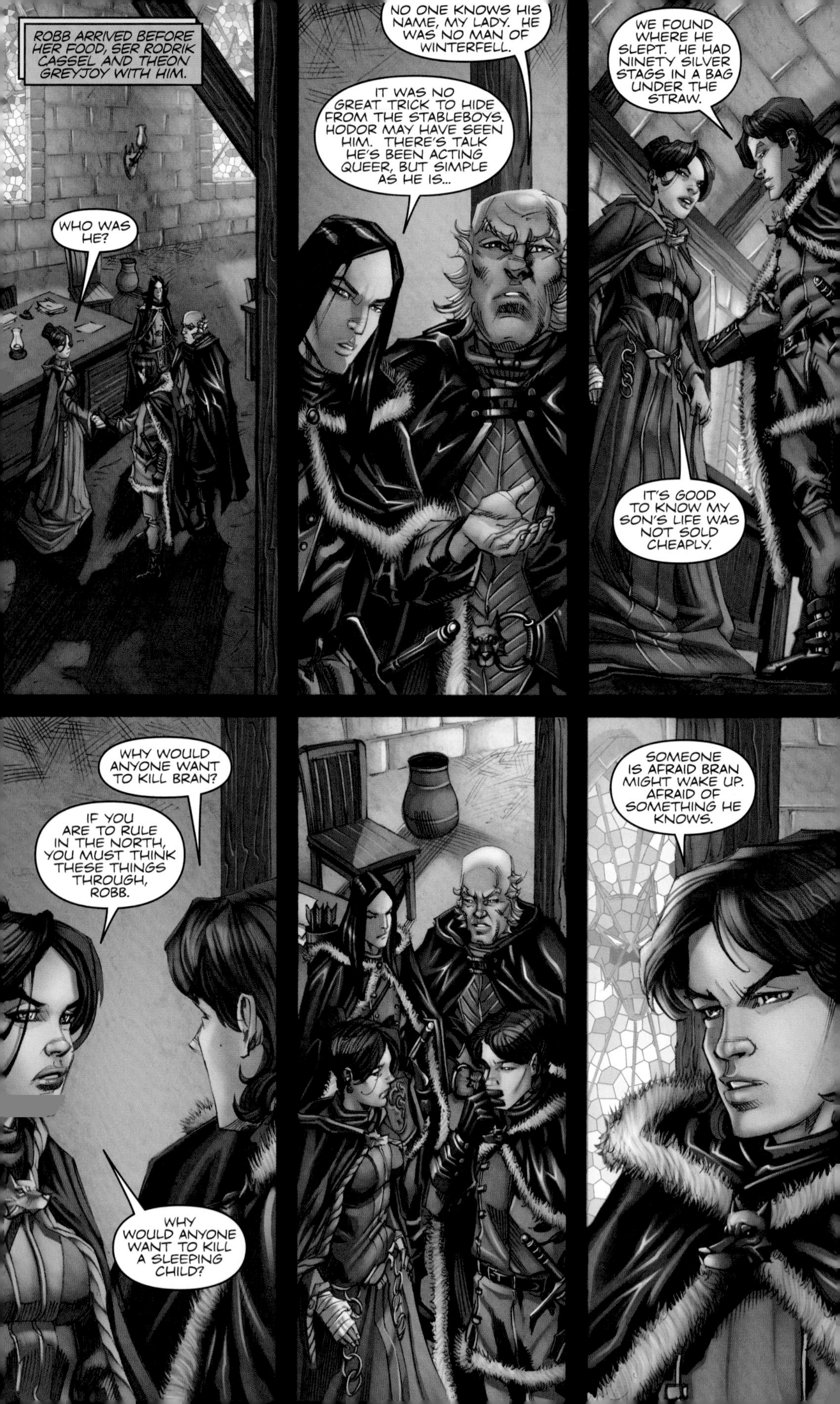
ROBB ARRIVED BEFORE HER FOOD, SER RODRIK CASSEL AND THEON GREYJOY WITH HIM.
WHO WAS HE?
NO ONE KNOWS HIS NAME, MY LADY. HE WAS NO MAN OF WINTERFELL.
IT WAS NO GREAT TRICK TO HIDE FROM THE STABLEBOYS. HODOR MAY HAVE SEEN HIM. THERE'S TALK HE'S BEEN ACTING QUEER, BUT SIMPLE AS HE IS...
WE FOUND WHERE HE SLEPT. HE HAD NINETY SILVER STAGS IN A BAG UNDER THE STRAW.
IT'S GOOD TO KNOW MY SON'S LIFE WAS NOT SOLD CHEAPLY.
WHY WOULD ANYONE WANT TO KILL BRAN?
IF YOU ARE TO RULE IN THE NORTH, YOU MUST THINK THESE THINGS THROUGH, ROBB.
WHY WOULD ANYONE WANT TO KILL A SLEEPING CHILD?
SOMEONE IS AFRAID BRAN MIGHT WAKE UP. AFRAID OF SOMETHING HE KNOWS.

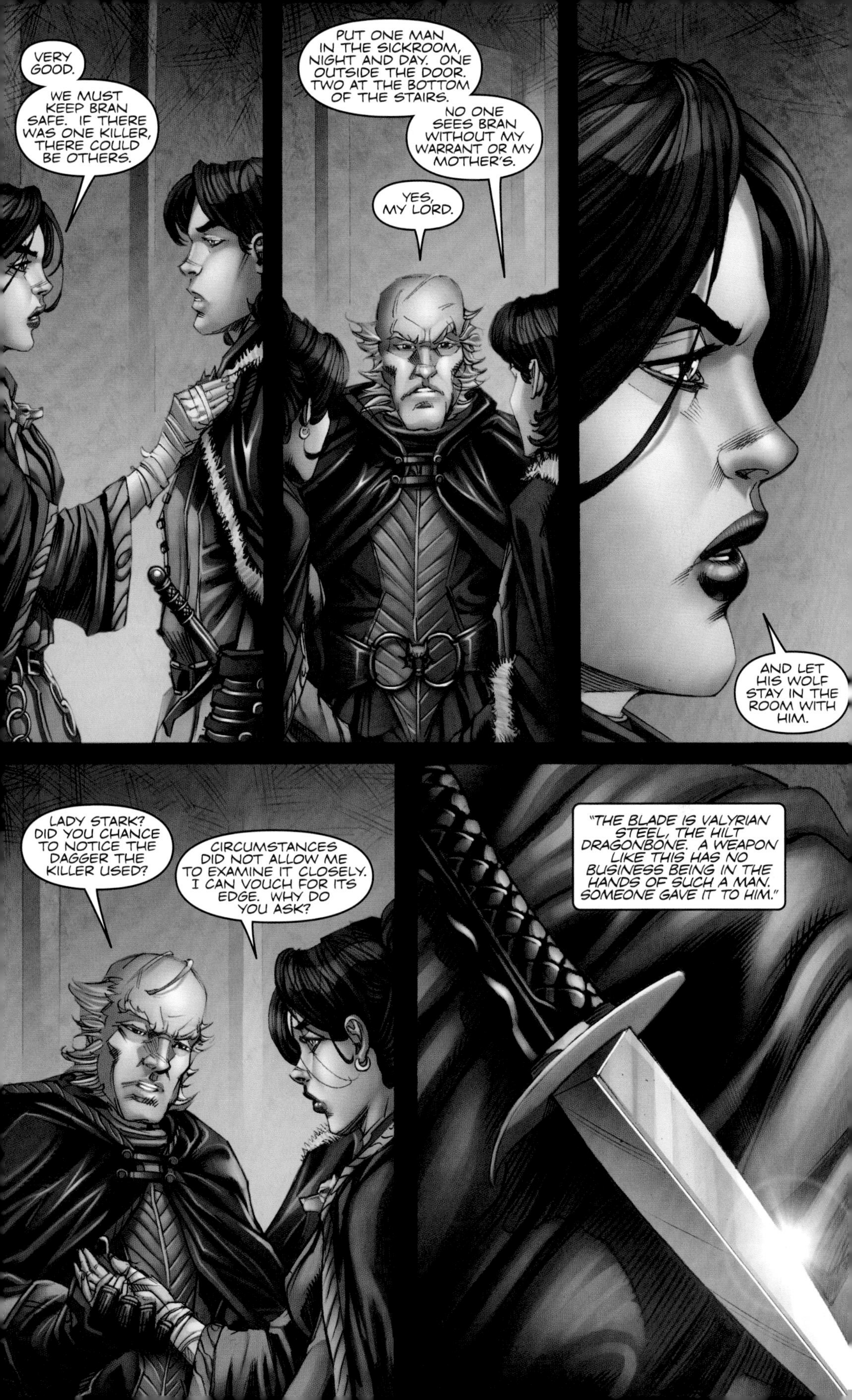
VERY GOOD.
WE MUST KEEP BRAN SAFE. IF THERE WAS ONE KILLER, THERE COULD BE OTHERS.
PUT ONE MAN IN THE SICKROOM, NIGHT AND DAY. ONE OUTSIDE THE DOOR. TWO AT THE BOTTOM OF THE STAIRS.
NO ONE SEES BRAN WITHOUT MY WARRANT OR MY MOTHER'S.
YES, MY LORD.
AND LET HIS WOLF STAY IN THE ROOM WITH HIM.
LADY STARK? DID YOU CHANCE TO NOTICE THE DAGGER THE KILLER USED?
CIRCUMSTANCES DID NOT ALLOW ME TO EXAMINE IT CLOSELY. I CAN VOUCH FOR ITS EDGE. WHY DO YOU ASK?
"THE BLADE IS VALYRIAN STEEL, THE HILT DRAGONBONE. A WEAPON LIKE THIS HAS NO BUSINESS BEING IN THE HANDS OF SUCH A MAN. SOMEONE GAVE IT TO HIM."

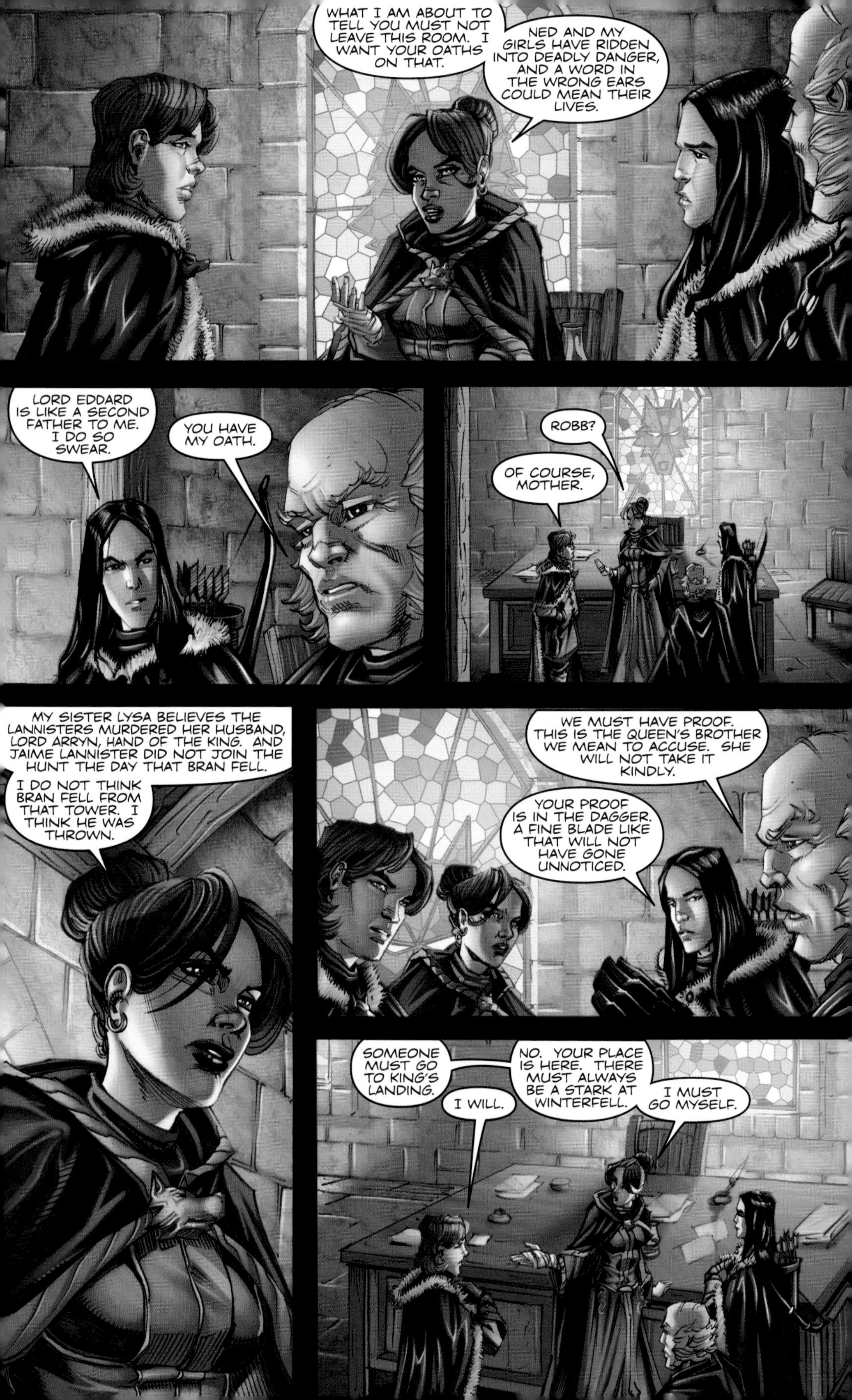
WHAT I AM ABOUT TO TELL YOU MUST NOT LEAVE THIS ROOM. I WANT YOUR OATHS ON THAT.
NED AND MY GIRLS HAVE RIDDEN INTO DEADLY DANGER, AND A WORD IN THE WRONG EARS COULD MEAN THEIR LIVES.
LORD EDDARD IS LIKE A SECOND FATHER TO ME. I DO SO SWEAR.
YOU HAVE MY OATH.
ROBB?
OF COURSE, MOTHER.
MY SISTER LYSA BELIEVES THE LANNISTERS MURDERED HER HUSBAND, LORD ARRYN, HAND OF THE KING. AND JAIME LANNISTER DID NOT JOIN THE HUNT THE DAY THAT BRAN FELL.
I DO NOT THINK BRAN FELL FROM THAT TOWER. I THINK HE WAS THROWN.
WE MUST HAVE PROOF. THIS IS THE QUEEN'S BROTHER WE MEAN TO ACCUSE. SHE WILL NOT TAKE IT KINDLY.
YOUR PROOF IS IN THE DAGGER. A FINE BLADE LIKE THAT WILL NOT HAVE GONE UNNOTICED.
SOMEONE MUST GO TO KING'S LANDING.
I WILL.
NO. YOUR PLACE IS HERE. THERE MUST ALWAYS BE A STARK AT WINTERFELL.
I MUST GO MYSELF.

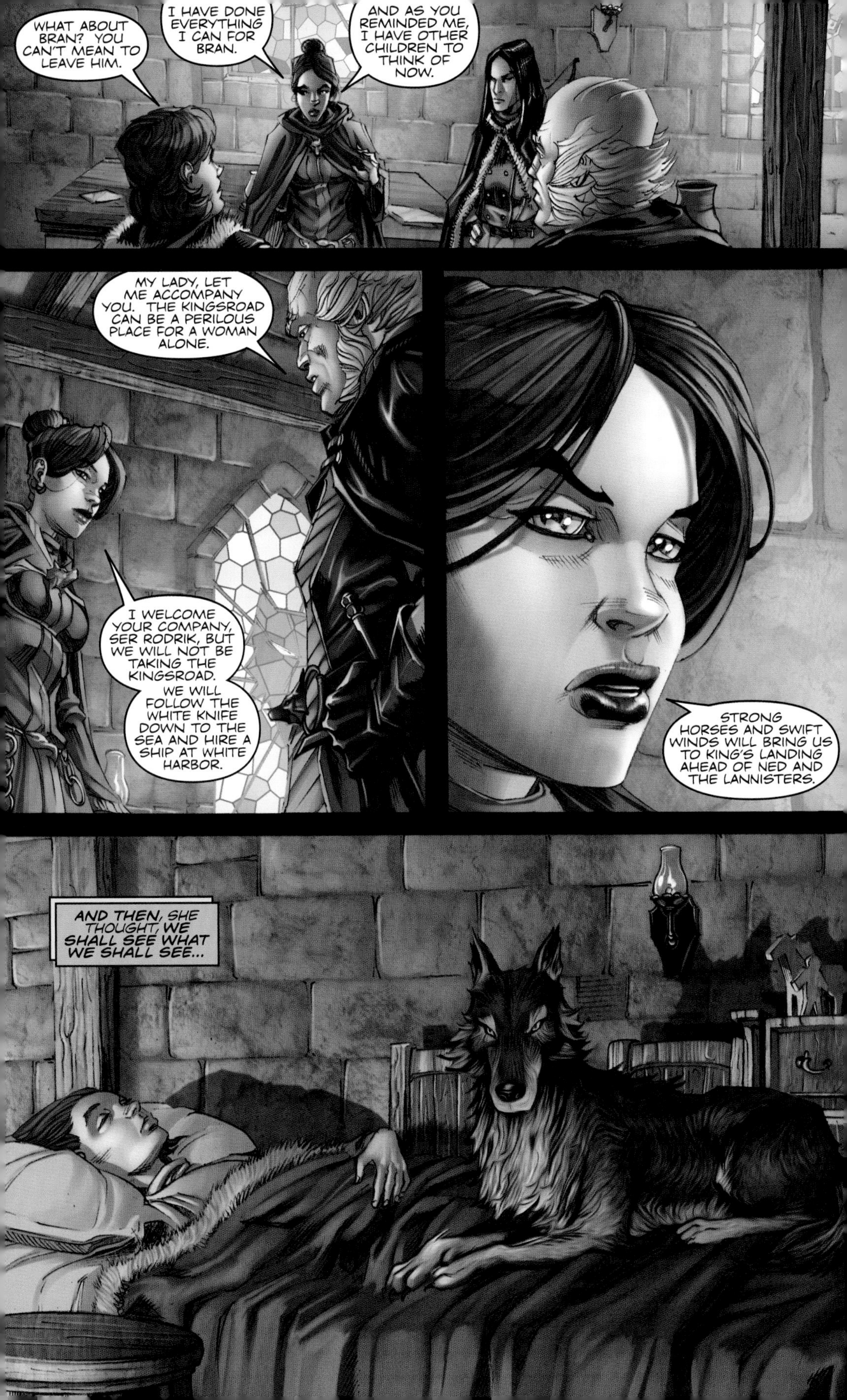
WHAT ABOUT BRAN? YOU CAN'T MEAN TO LEAVE HIM.
I HAVE DONE EVERYTHING I CAN FOR BRAN.
AND AS YOU REMINDED ME, I HAVE OTHER CHILDREN TO THINK OF NOW.
MY LADY, LET ME ACCOMPANY YOU. THE KINGSROAD CAN BE A PERILOUS PLACE FOR A WOMAN ALONE.
I WELCOME YOUR COMPANY, SER RODRIK, BUT WE WILL NOT BE TAKING THE KINGSROAD.
WE WILL FOLLOW THE WHITE KNIFE DOWN TO THE SEA AND HIRE A SHIP AT WHITE HARBOR.
STRONG HORSES AND SWIFT WINDS WILL BRING US TO KING'S LANDING AHEAD OF NED AND THE LANNISTERS.
AND THEN, SHE THOUGHT, WE SHALL SEE WHAT WE SHALL SEE...

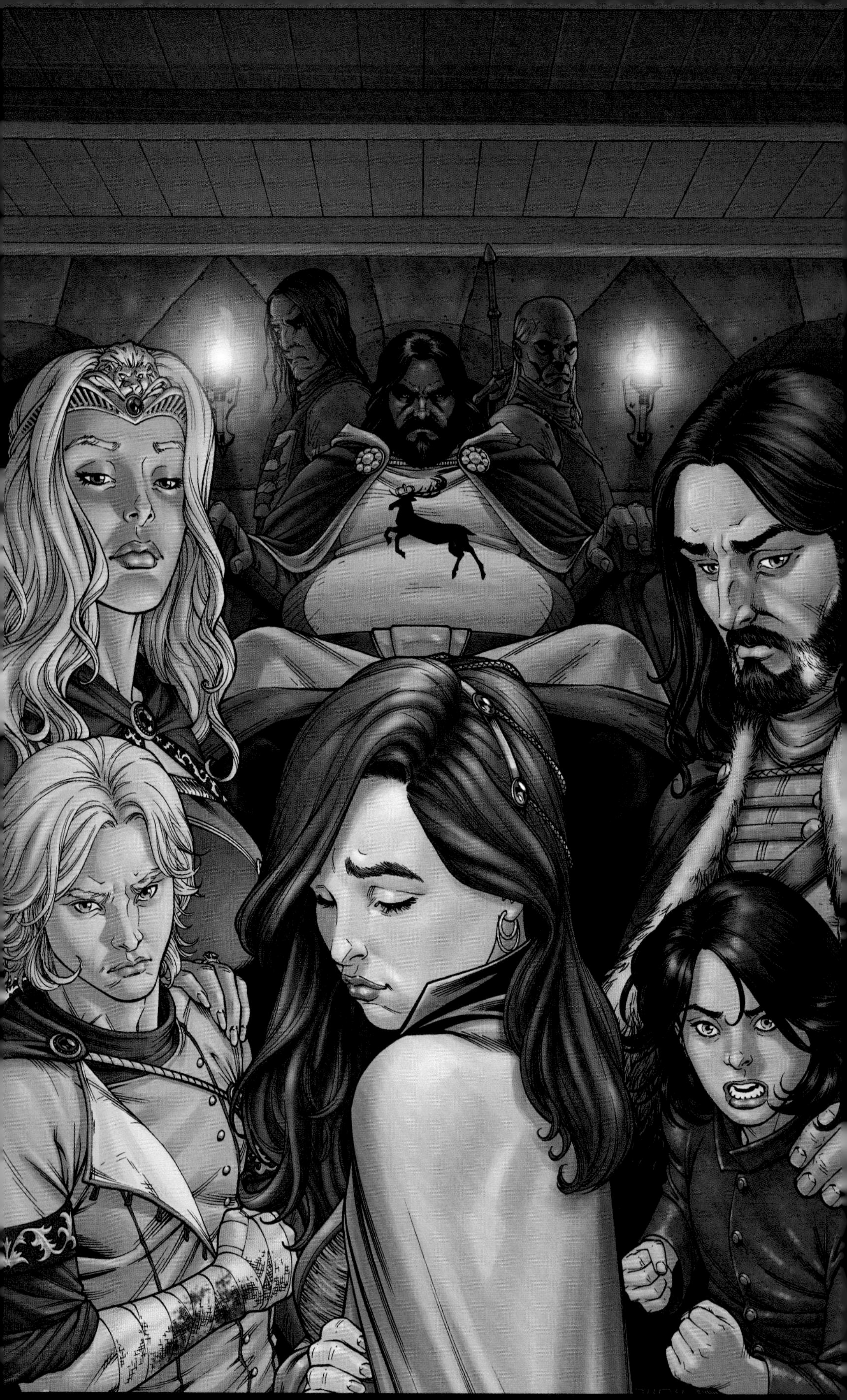

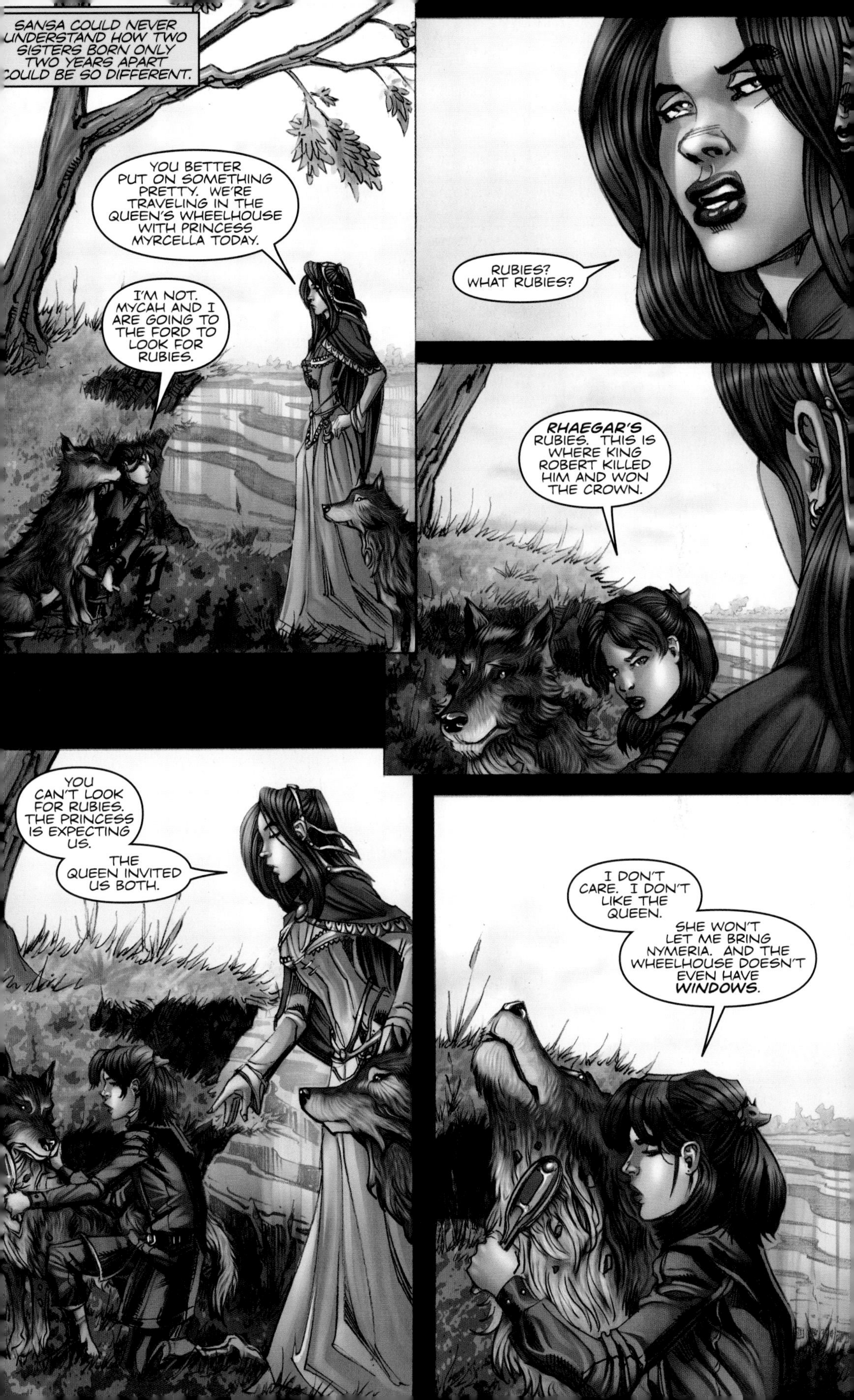
SANSA COULD NEVER UNDERSTAND HOW TWO SISTERS BORN ONLY TWO YEARS APART COULD BE SO DIFFERENT.
YOU BETTER PUT ON SOMETHING PRETTY. WE'RE TRAVELING IN THE QUEEN'S WHEELHOUSE WITH PRINCESS MYRCELLA TODAY.
I'M NOT. MYCAH AND I ARE GOING TO THE FORD TO LOOK FOR RUBIES.
RUBIES? WHAT RUBIES?
RHAEGAR'S RUBIES. THIS IS WHERE KING ROBERT KILLED HIM AND WON THE CROWN.
YOU CAN'T LOOK FOR RUBIES. THE PRINCESS IS EXPECTING US.
THE QUEEN INVITED US BOTH.
I DON'T CARE. I DON'T LIKE THE QUEEN.
SHE WON'T LET ME BRING NYMERIA. AND THE WHEELHOUSE DOESN'T EVEN HAVE WINDOWS.

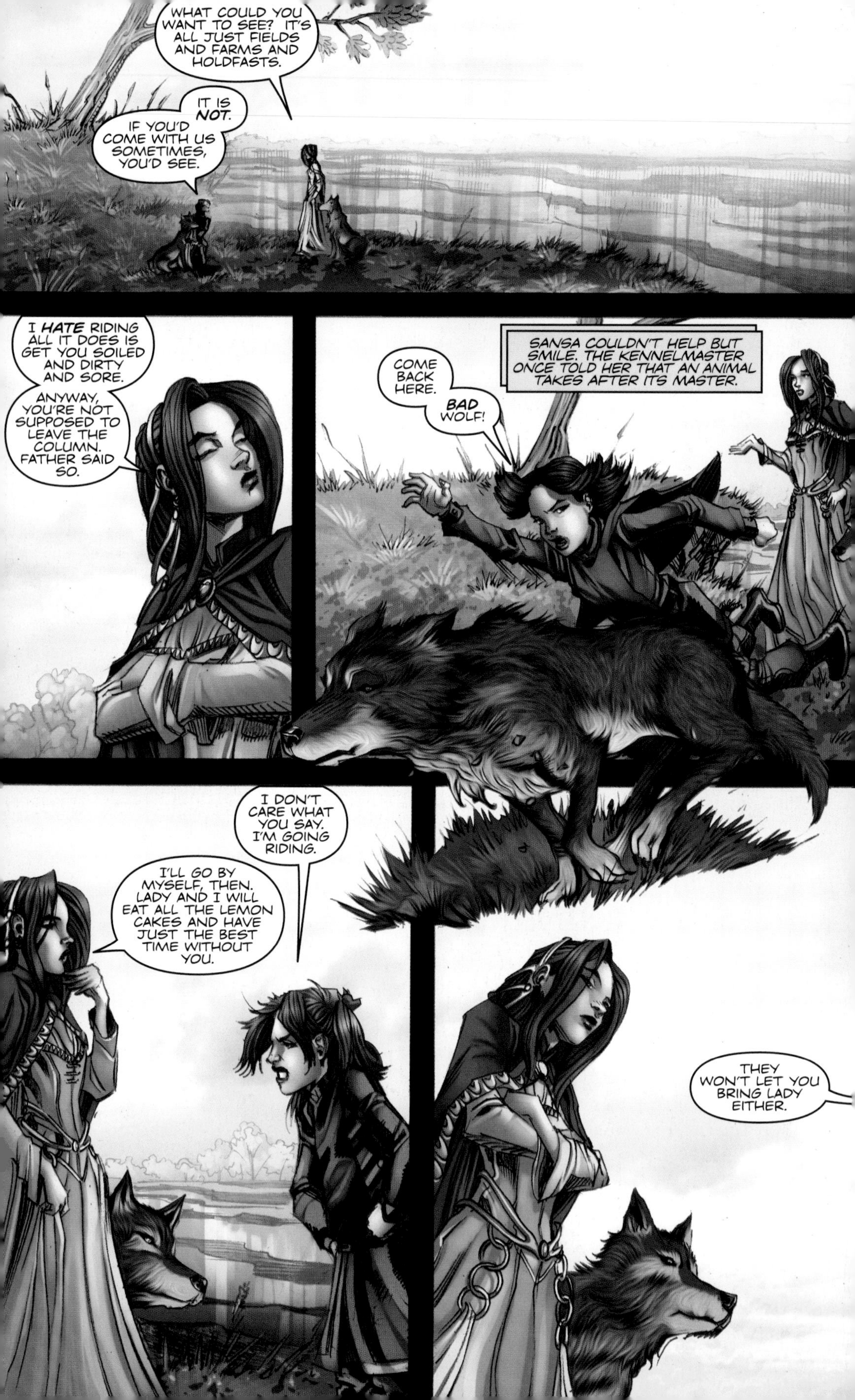
WHAT COULD YOU WANT TO SEE? IT'S ALL JUST FIELDS AND FARMS AND HOLDFASTS.
IT IS **NOT**.
IF YOU'D COME WITH US SOMETIMES, YOU'D SEE.
I **HATE** RIDING ALL IT DOES IS GET YOU SOILED AND DIRTY AND SORE.
ANYWAY, YOU'RE NOT SUPPOSED TO LEAVE THE COLUMN. FATHER SAID SO.
SANSA COULDN'T HELP BUT SMILE. THE KENNELMASTER ONCE TOLD HER THAT AN ANIMAL TAKES AFTER ITS MASTER.
COME BACK HERE.
BAD WOLF!
I DON'T CARE WHAT YOU SAY. I'M GOING RIDING.
I'LL GO BY MYSELF, THEN. LADY AND I WILL EAT ALL THE LEMON CAKES AND HAVE JUST THE BEST TIME WITHOUT YOU.
THEY WON'T LET YOU BRING LADY EITHER.

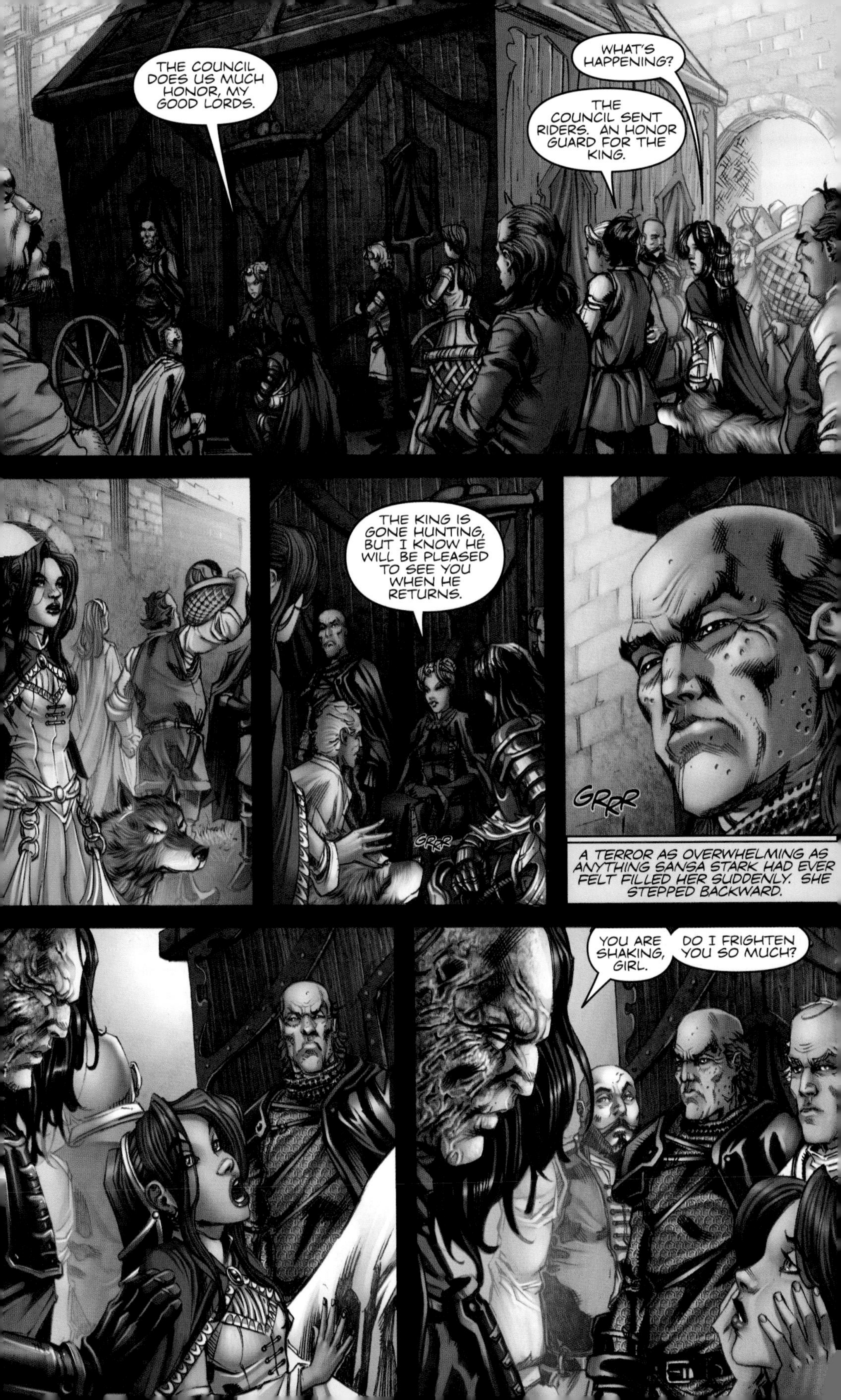
THE COUNCIL DOES US MUCH HONOR, MY GOOD LORDS.
WHAT'S HAPPENING?
THE COUNCIL SENT RIDERS. AN HONOR GUARD FOR THE KING.
THE KING IS GONE HUNTING, BUT I KNOW HE WILL BE PLEASED TO SEE YOU WHEN HE RETURNS.
GRRR
GRRR
A TERROR AS OVERWHELMING AS ANYTHING SANSA STARK HAD EVER FELT FILLED HER SUDDENLY. SHE STEPPED BACKWARD.
YOU ARE SHAKING, GIRL.
DO I FRIGHTEN YOU SO MUCH?

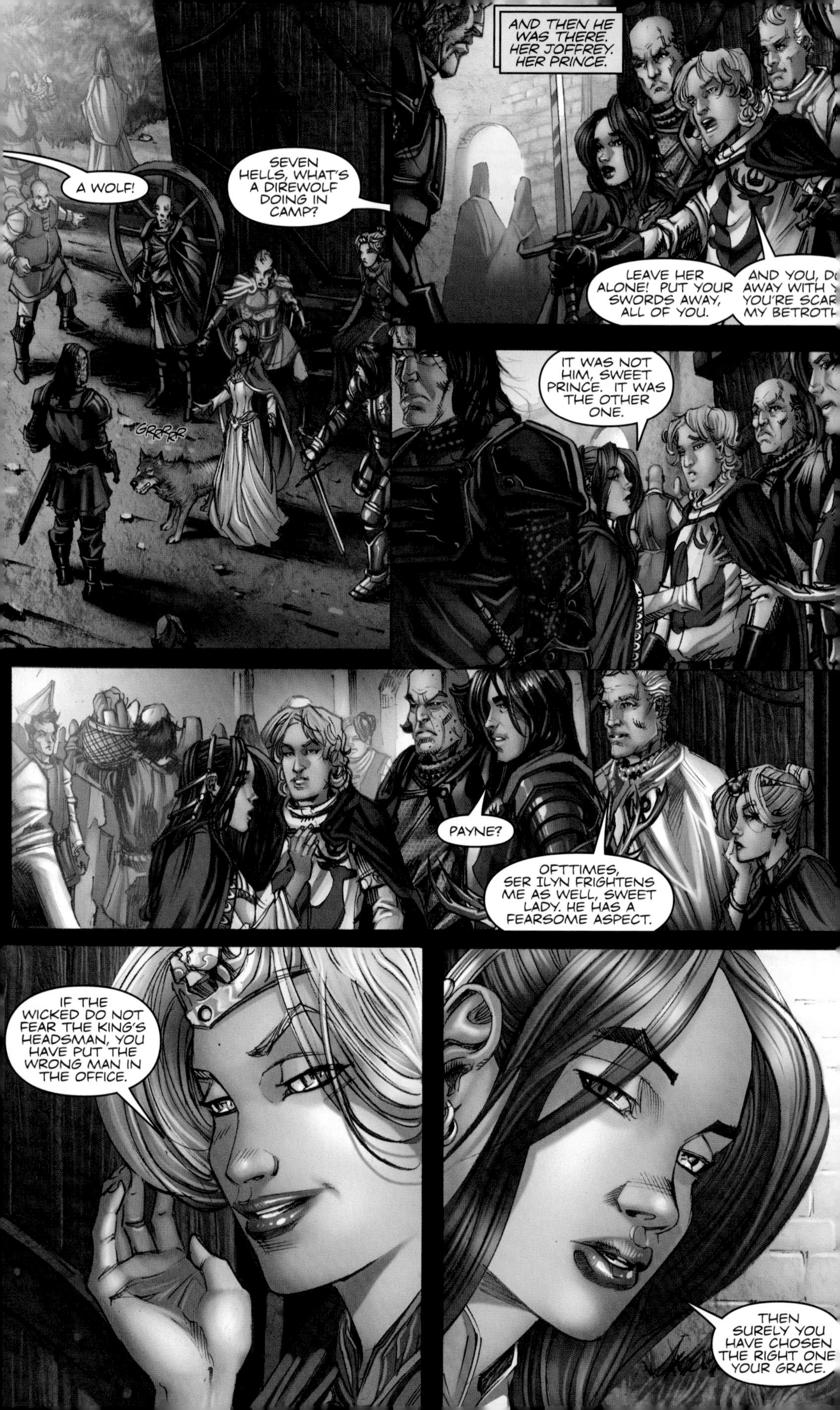
A WOLF!
SEVEN HELLS, WHAT'S A DIREWOLF DOING IN CAMP?
GRRRRR
AND THEN HE WAS THERE. HER JOFFREY. HER PRINCE.
LEAVE HER ALONE! PUT YOUR SWORDS AWAY, ALL OF YOU.
AND YOU, D
AWAY WITH Y
YOU'RE SCAR
MY BETROTH
IT WAS NOT HIM, SWEET PRINCE. IT WAS THE OTHER ONE.
PAYNE?
OFTTIMES, SER ILYN FRIGHTENS ME AS WELL, SWEET LADY. HE HAS A FEARSOME ASPECT.
IF THE WICKED DO NOT FEAR THE KING'S HEADSMAN, YOU HAVE PUT THE WRONG MAN IN THE OFFICE.
THEN SURELY YOU HAVE CHOSEN THE RIGHT ONE YOUR GRACE.

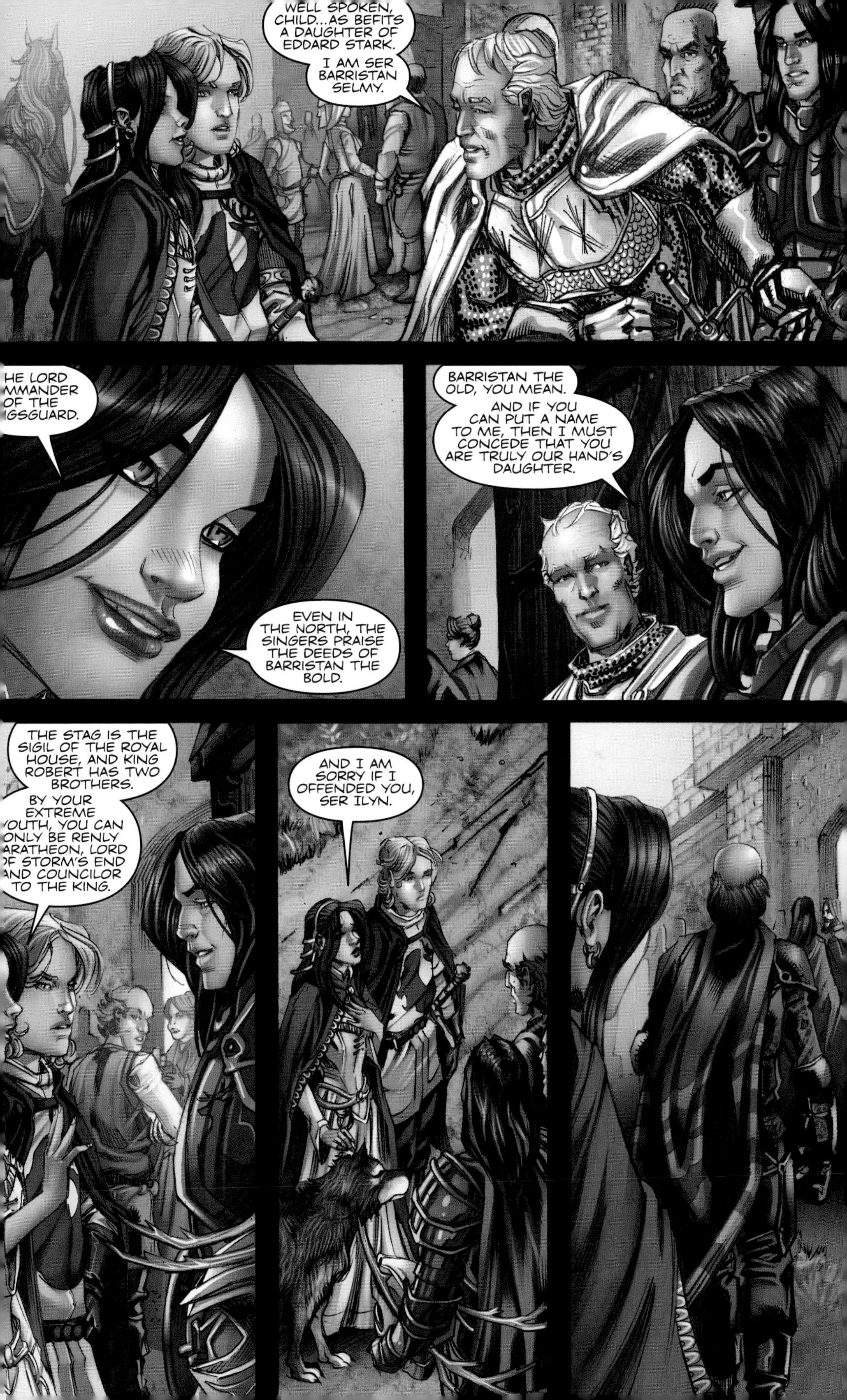
WELL SPOKEN, CHILD...AS BEFITS A DAUGHTER OF EDDARD STARK.
I AM SER BARRISTAN SELMY.
HE LORD MMANDER OF THE IGSGUARD.
EVEN IN THE NORTH, THE SINGERS PRAISE THE DEEDS OF BARRISTAN THE BOLD.
BARRISTAN THE OLD, YOU MEAN.
AND IF YOU CAN PUT A NAME TO ME, THEN I MUST CONCEDE THAT YOU ARE TRULY OUR HAND'S DAUGHTER.
THE STAG IS THE SIGIL OF THE ROYAL HOUSE, AND KING ROBERT HAS TWO BROTHERS.
BY YOUR EXTREME YOUTH, YOU CAN ONLY BE RENLY ARATHEON, LORD OF STORM'S END AND COUNCILOR TO THE KING.
AND I AM SORRY IF I OFFENDED YOU, SER ILYN.

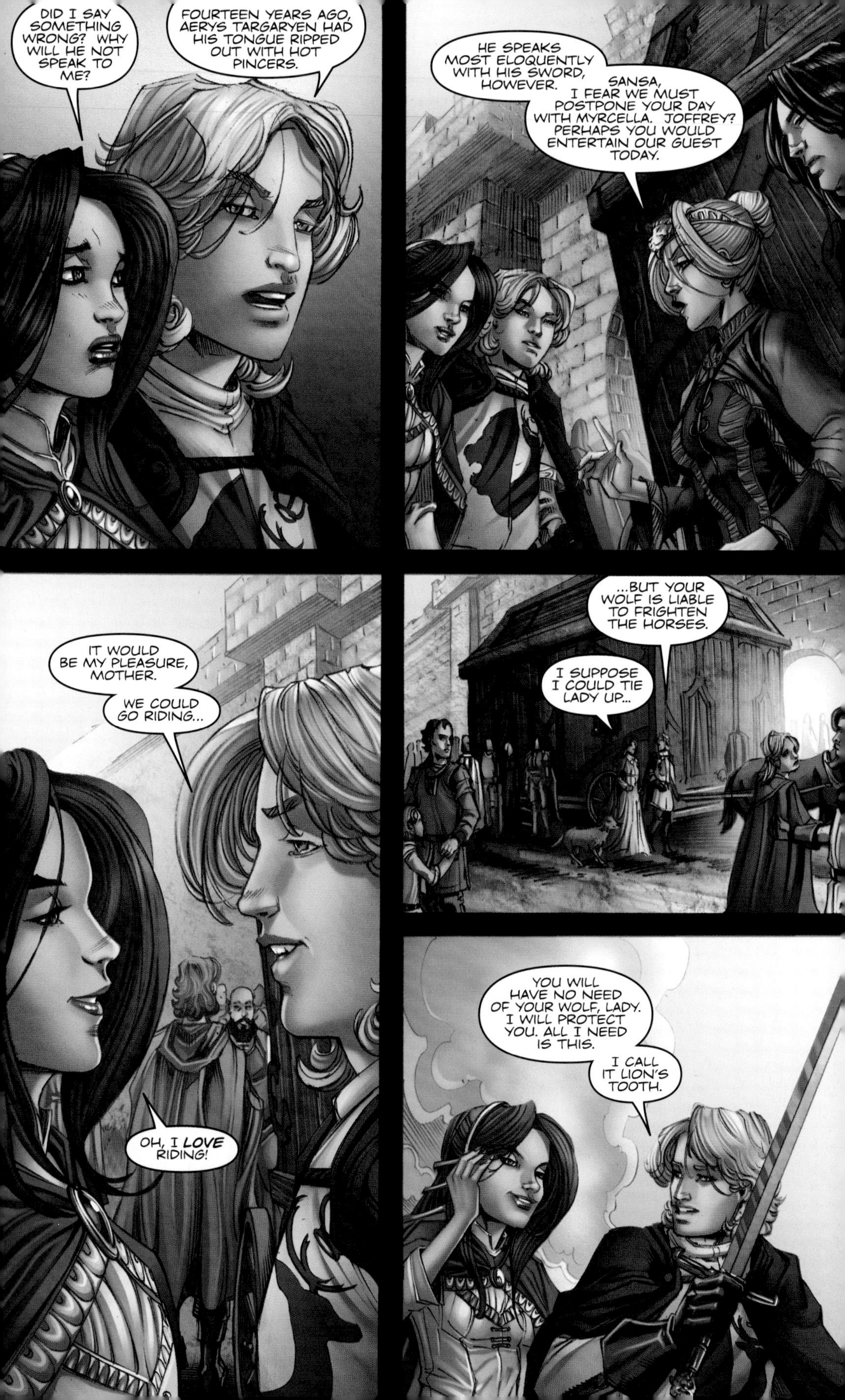
DID I SAY SOMETHING WRONG? WHY WILL HE NOT SPEAK TO ME?
FOURTEEN YEARS AGO, AERYS TARGARYEN HAD HIS TONGUE RIPPED OUT WITH HOT PINCERS.
HE SPEAKS MOST ELOQUENTLY WITH HIS SWORD, HOWEVER.
SANSA, I FEAR WE MUST POSTPONE YOUR DAY WITH MYRCELLA. JOFFREY? PERHAPS YOU WOULD ENTERTAIN OUR GUEST TODAY.
IT WOULD BE MY PLEASURE, MOTHER.
WE COULD GO RIDING...
OH, I **LOVE** RIDING!
...BUT YOUR WOLF IS LIABLE TO FRIGHTEN THE HORSES.
I SUPPOSE I COULD TIE LADY UP...
YOU WILL HAVE NO NEED OF YOUR WOLF, LADY. I WILL PROTECT YOU. ALL I NEED IS THIS.
I CALL IT LION'S TOOTH.

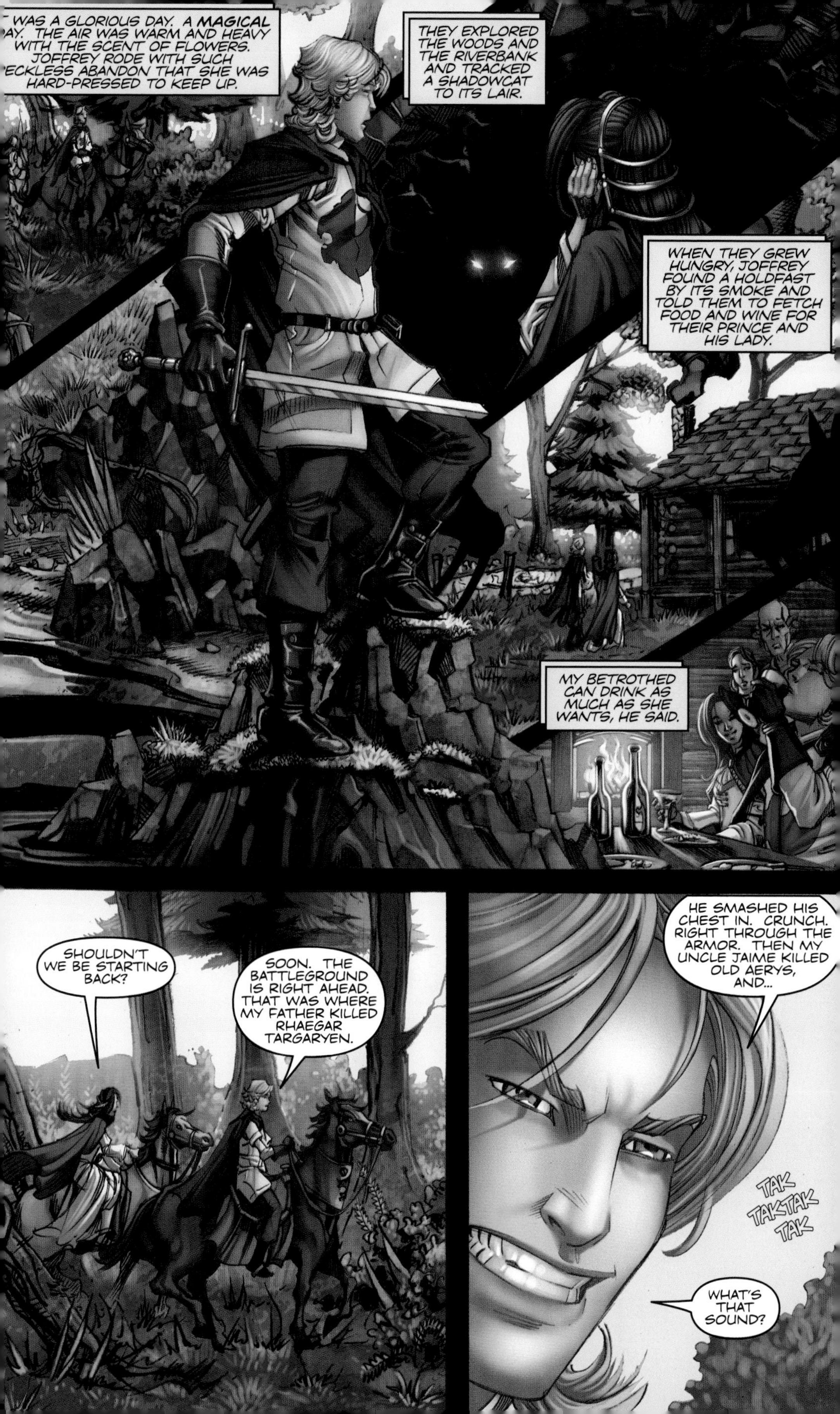
IT WAS A GLORIOUS DAY. A MAGICAL DAY. THE AIR WAS WARM AND HEAVY WITH THE SCENT OF FLOWERS. JOFFREY RODE WITH SUCH RECKLESS ABANDON THAT SHE WAS HARD-PRESSED TO KEEP UP.
THEY EXPLORED THE WOODS AND THE RIVERBANK AND TRACKED A SHADOWCAT TO ITS LAIR.
WHEN THEY GREW HUNGRY, JOFFREY FOUND A HOLDFAST BY ITS SMOKE AND TOLD THEM TO FETCH FOOD AND WINE FOR THEIR PRINCE AND HIS LADY.
MY BETROTHED CAN DRINK AS MUCH AS SHE WANTS, HE SAID.
SHOULDN'T WE BE STARTING BACK?
SOON. THE BATTLEGROUND IS RIGHT AHEAD. THAT WAS WHERE MY FATHER KILLED RHAEGAR TARGARYEN.
HE SMASHED HIS CHEST IN. CRUNCH. RIGHT THROUGH THE ARMOR. THEN MY UNCLE JAIME KILLED OLD AERYS, AND...
TAK TAKTAK TAK
WHAT'S THAT SOUND?

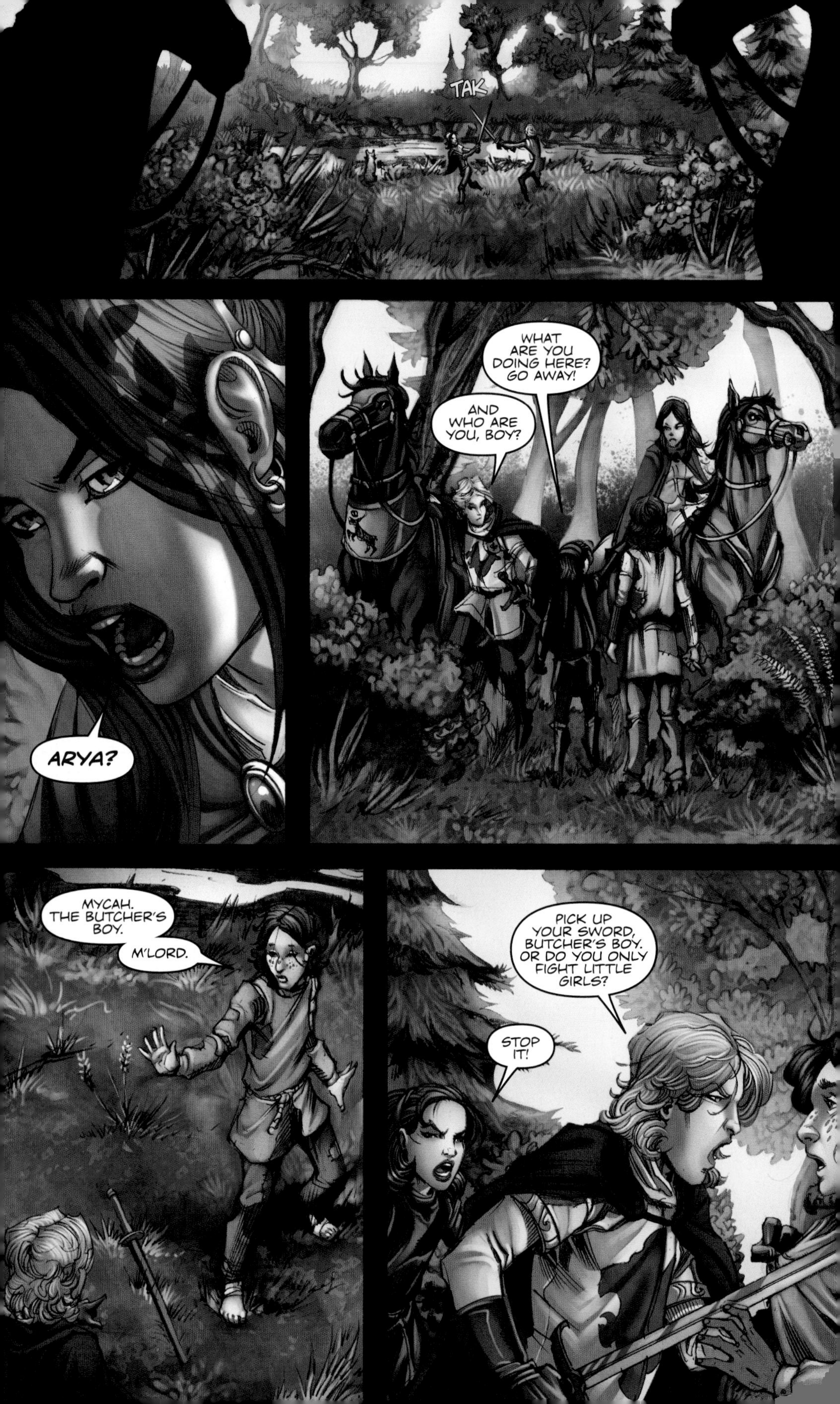
TAK
ARYA?
WHAT ARE YOU DOING HERE? GO AWAY!
AND WHO ARE YOU, BOY?
MYCAH. THE BUTCHER'S BOY.
M'LORD.
PICK UP YOUR SWORD, BUTCHER'S BOY. OR DO YOU ONLY FIGHT LITTLE GIRLS?
STOP IT!

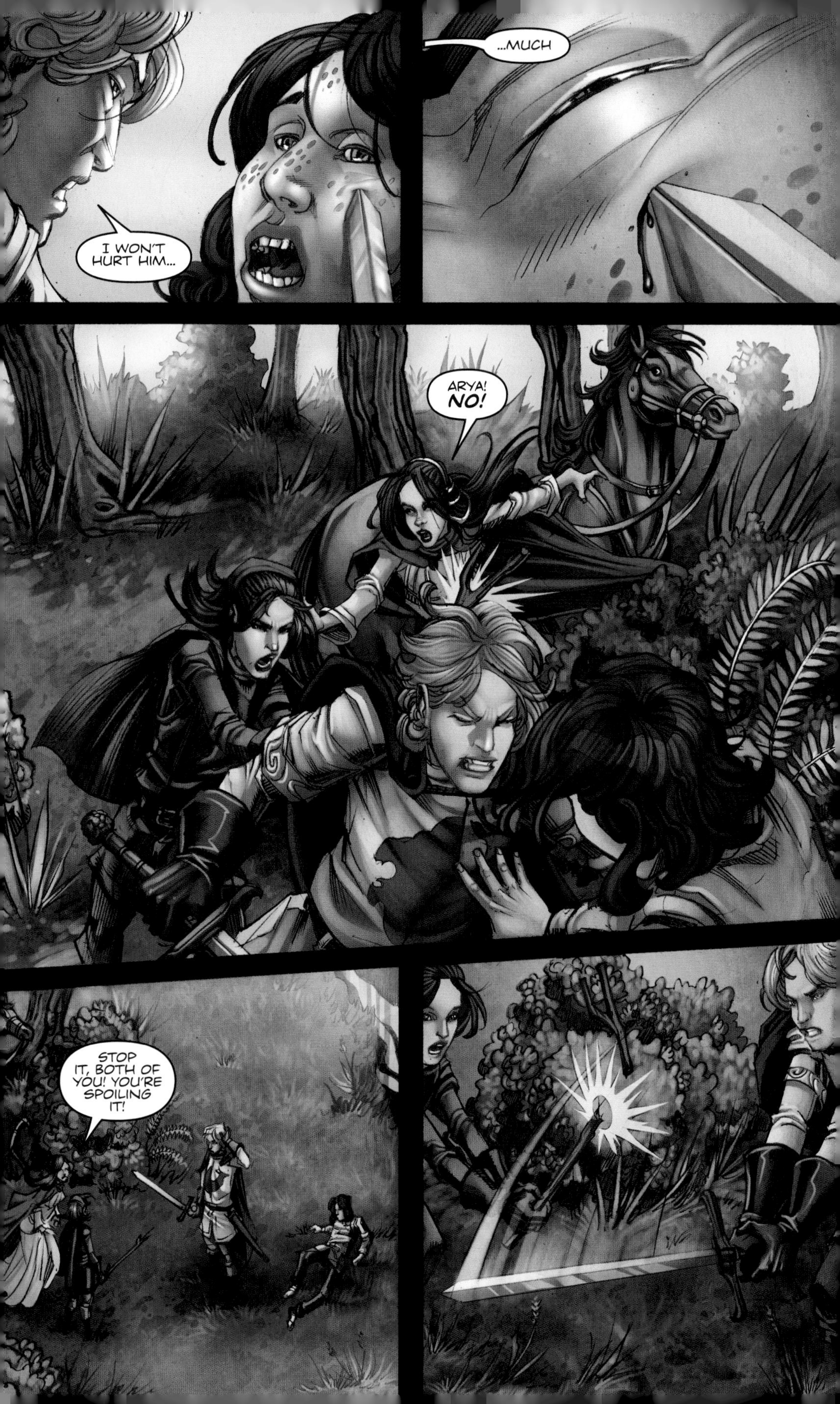
I WON'T HURT HIM...
...MUCH
ARYA! NO!
STOP IT, BOTH OF YOU! YOU'RE SPOILING IT!

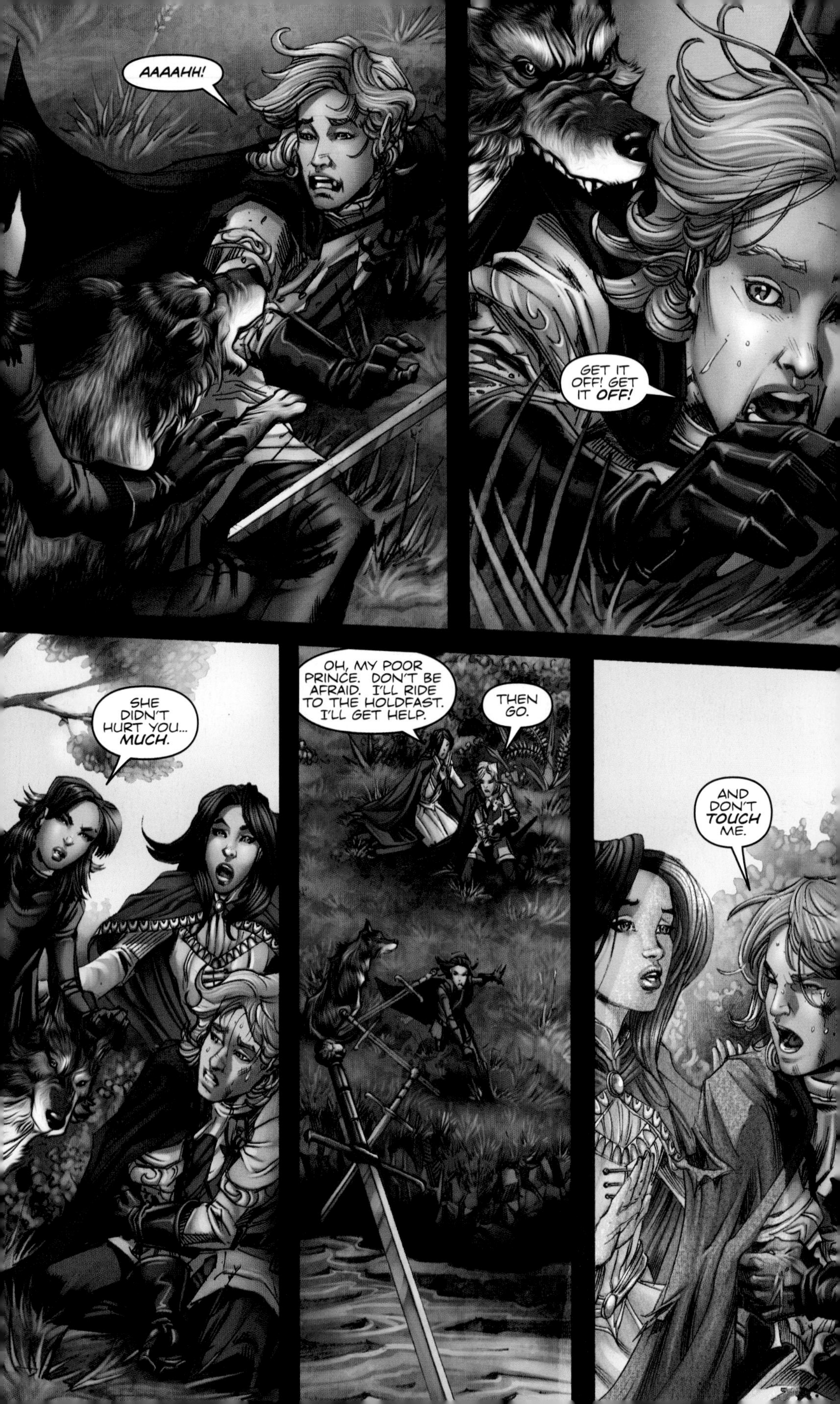
AAAAHH!
GET IT OFF! GET IT OFF!
SHE DIDN'T HURT YOU... MUCH.
OH, MY POOR PRINCE. DON'T BE AFRAID. I'LL RIDE TO THE HOLDFAST. I'LL GET HELP.
THEN GO.
AND DON'T TOUCH ME.

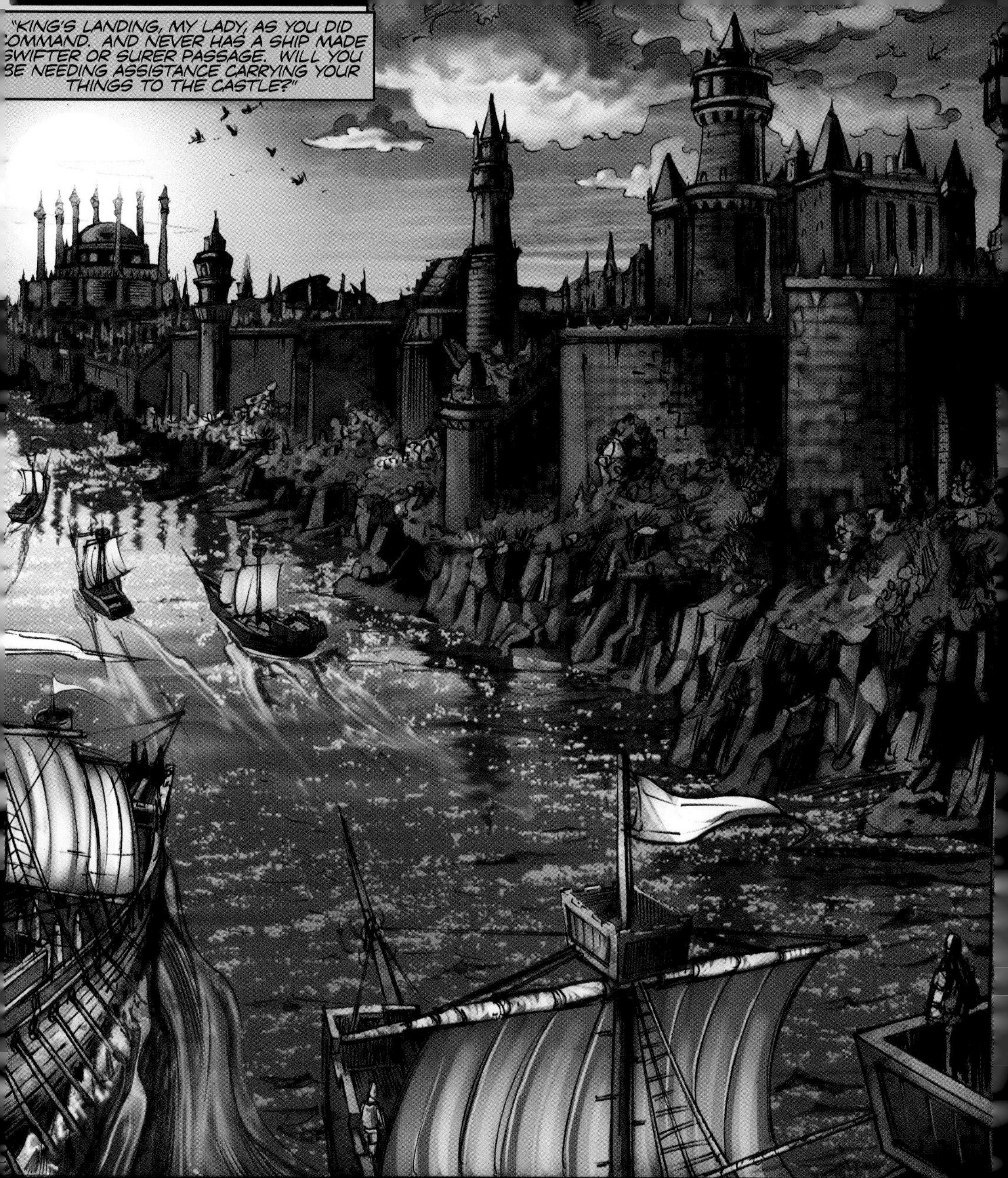
"KING'S LANDING, MY LADY, AS YOU DID COMMAND. AND NEVER HAS A SHIP MADE SWIFTER OR SURER PASSAGE. WILL YOU BE NEEDING ASSISTANCE CARRYING YOUR THINGS TO THE CASTLE?"

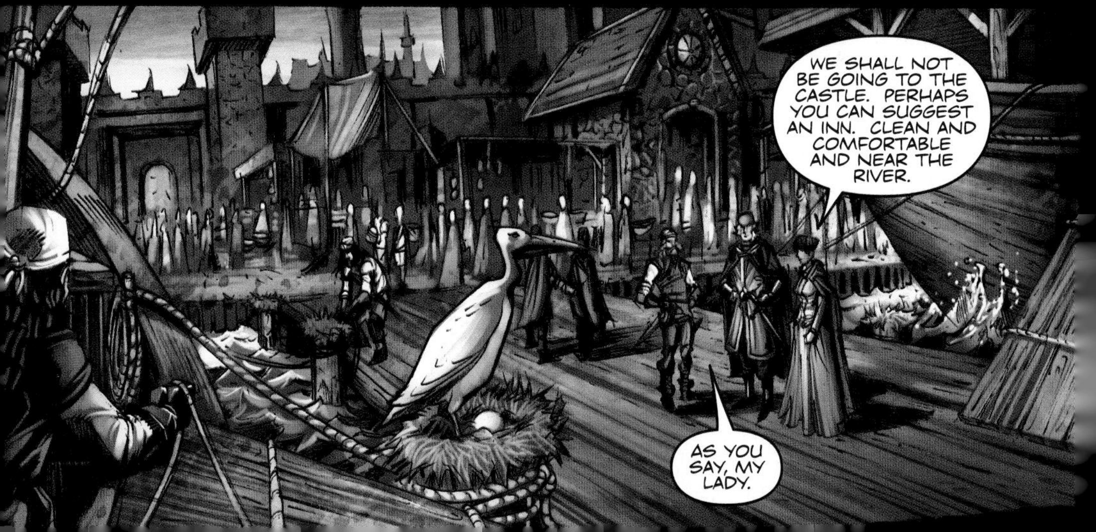
WE SHALL NOT BE GOING TO THE CASTLE. PERHAPS YOU CAN SUGGEST AN INN. CLEAN AND COMFORTABLE AND NEAR THE RIVER.
AS YOU SAY, MY LADY.

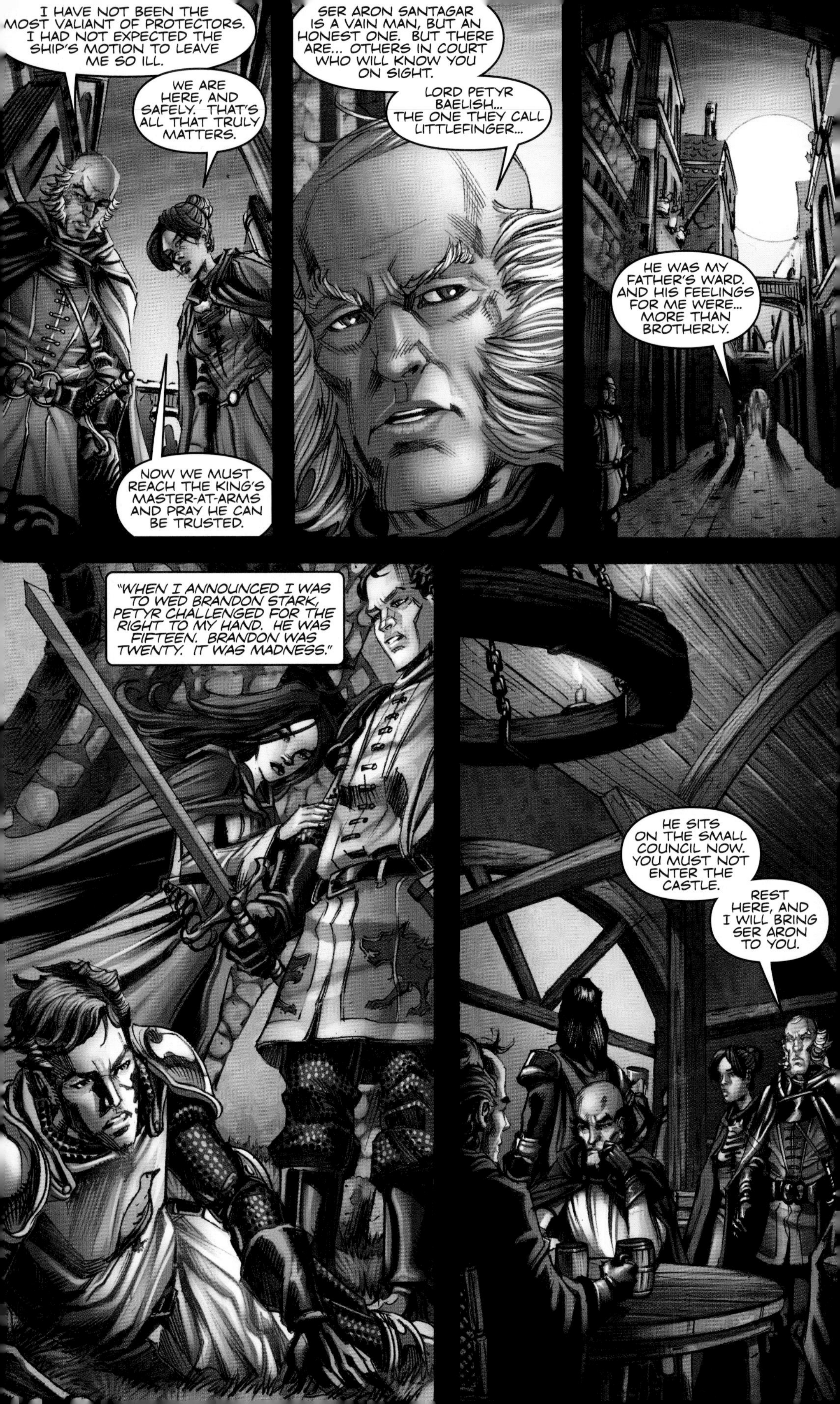

I HAVE NOT BEEN THE MOST VALIANT OF PROTECTORS. I HAD NOT EXPECTED THE SHIP'S MOTION TO LEAVE ME SO ILL.
WE ARE HERE, AND SAFELY. THAT'S ALL THAT TRULY MATTERS.
NOW WE MUST REACH THE KING'S MASTER-AT-ARMS AND PRAY HE CAN BE TRUSTED.
SER ARON SANTAGAR IS A VAIN MAN, BUT AN HONEST ONE. BUT THERE ARE... OTHERS IN COURT WHO WILL KNOW YOU ON SIGHT.
LORD PETYR BAELISH... THE ONE THEY CALL LITTLEFINGER...
HE WAS MY FATHER'S WARD. AND HIS FEELINGS FOR ME WERE... MORE THAN BROTHERLY.
"WHEN I ANNOUNCED I WAS TO WED BRANDON STARK, PETYR CHALLENGED FOR THE RIGHT TO MY HAND. HE WAS FIFTEEN. BRANDON WAS TWENTY. IT WAS MADNESS."
HE SITS ON THE SMALL COUNCIL NOW. YOU MUST NOT ENTER THE CASTLE.
REST HERE, AND I WILL BRING SER ARON TO YOU.

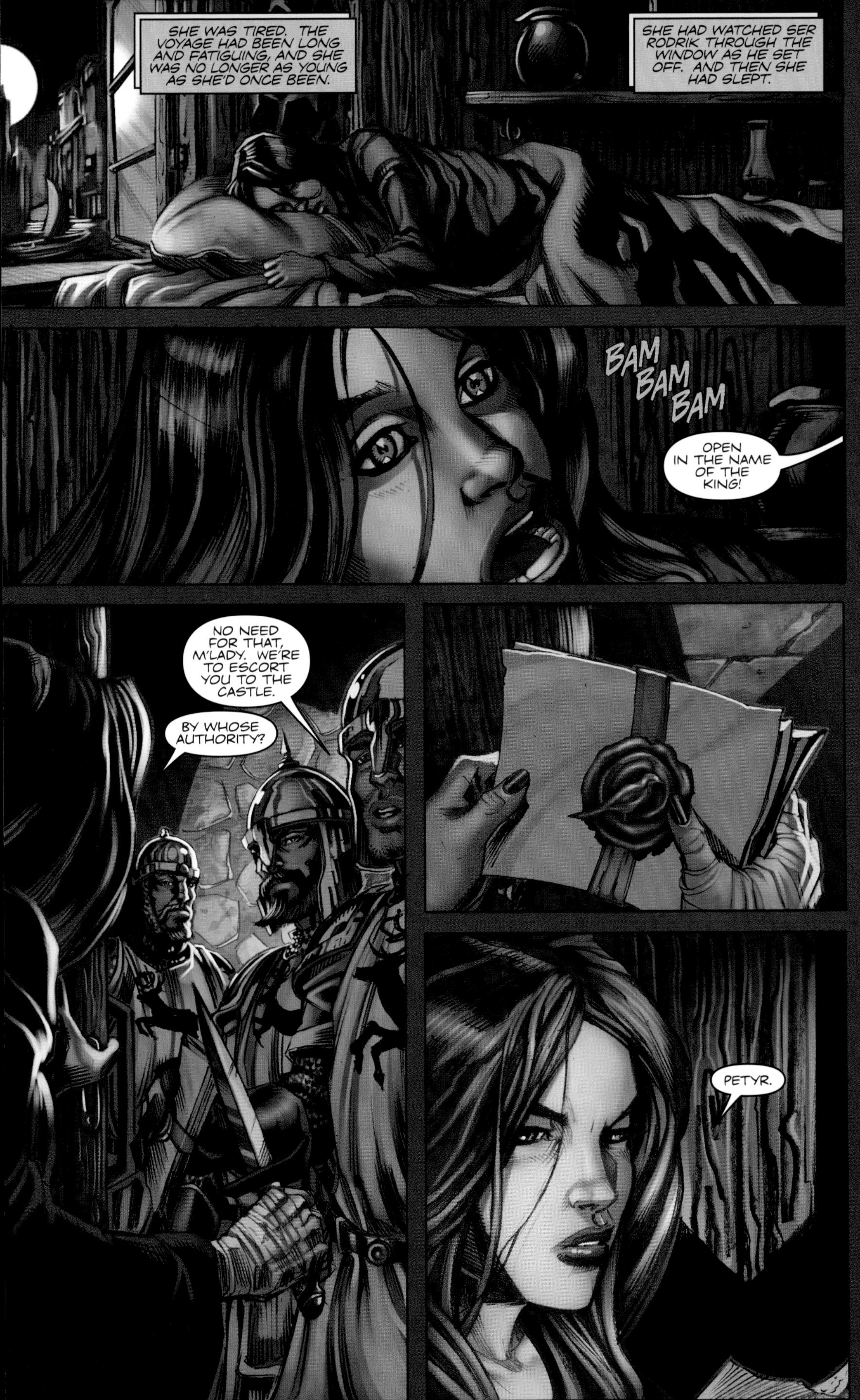
SHE WAS TIRED. THE VOYAGE HAD BEEN LONG AND FATIGUING, AND SHE WAS NO LONGER AS YOUNG AS SHE'D ONCE BEEN.
SHE HAD WATCHED SER RODRIK THROUGH THE WINDOW AS HE SET OFF. AND THEN SHE HAD SLEPT.
BAM BAM BAM
OPEN IN THE NAME OF THE KING!
NO NEED FOR THAT, M'LADY. WE'RE TO ESCORT YOU TO THE CASTLE.
BY WHOSE AUTHORITY?
PETYR.

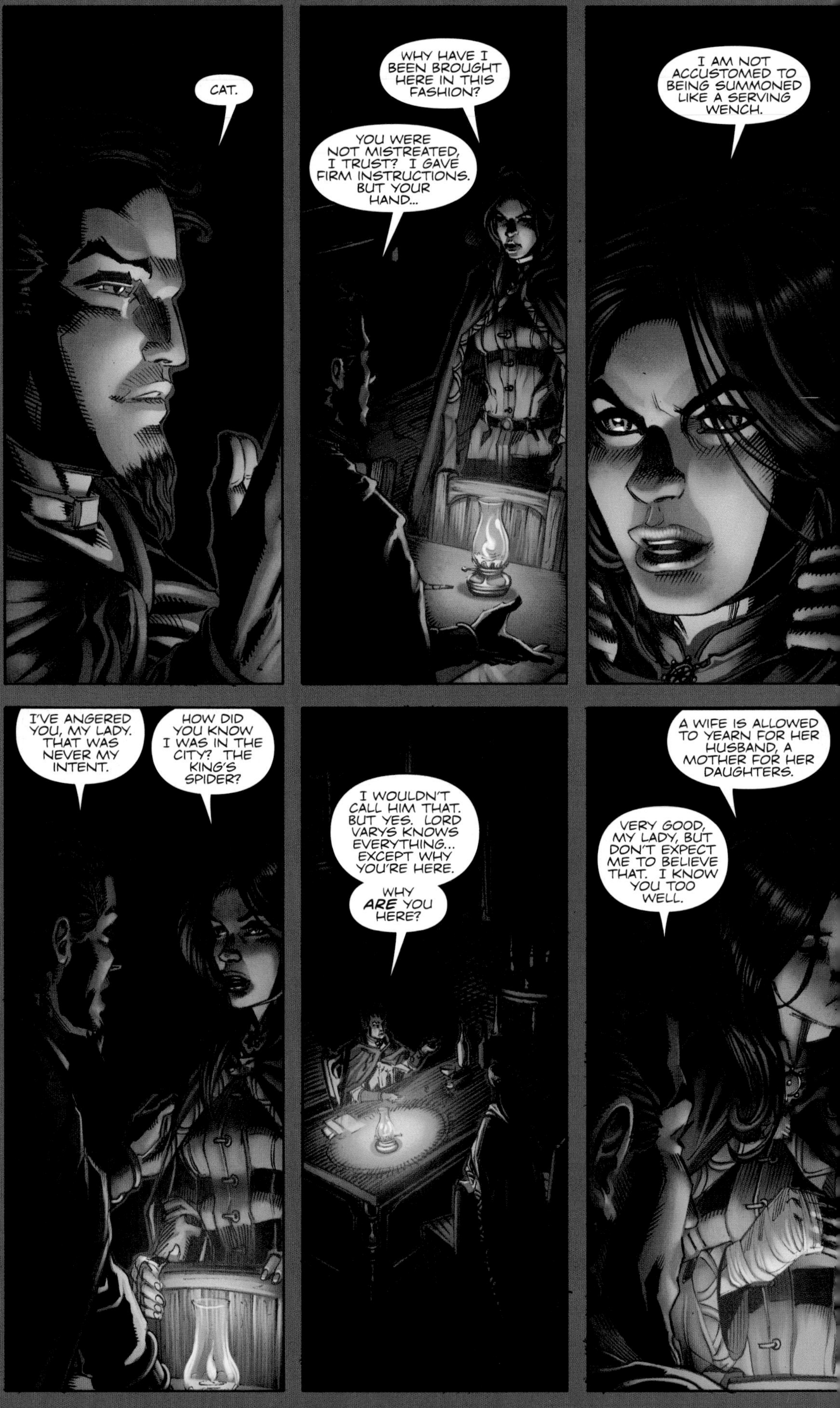
CAT.
WHY HAVE I BEEN BROUGHT HERE IN THIS FASHION?
YOU WERE NOT MISTREATED, I TRUST? I GAVE FIRM INSTRUCTIONS. BUT YOUR HAND...
I AM NOT ACCUSTOMED TO BEING SUMMONED LIKE A SERVING WENCH.
I'VE ANGERED YOU, MY LADY. THAT WAS NEVER MY INTENT.
HOW DID YOU KNOW I WAS IN THE CITY? THE KING'S SPIDER?
I WOULDN'T CALL HIM THAT. BUT YES. LORD VARYS KNOWS EVERYTHING... EXCEPT WHY YOU'RE HERE.
WHY **ARE** YOU HERE?
A WIFE IS ALLOWED TO YEARN FOR HER HUSBAND, A MOTHER FOR HER DAUGHTERS.
VERY GOOD, MY LADY, BUT DON'T EXPECT ME TO BELIEVE THAT. I KNOW YOU TOO WELL.

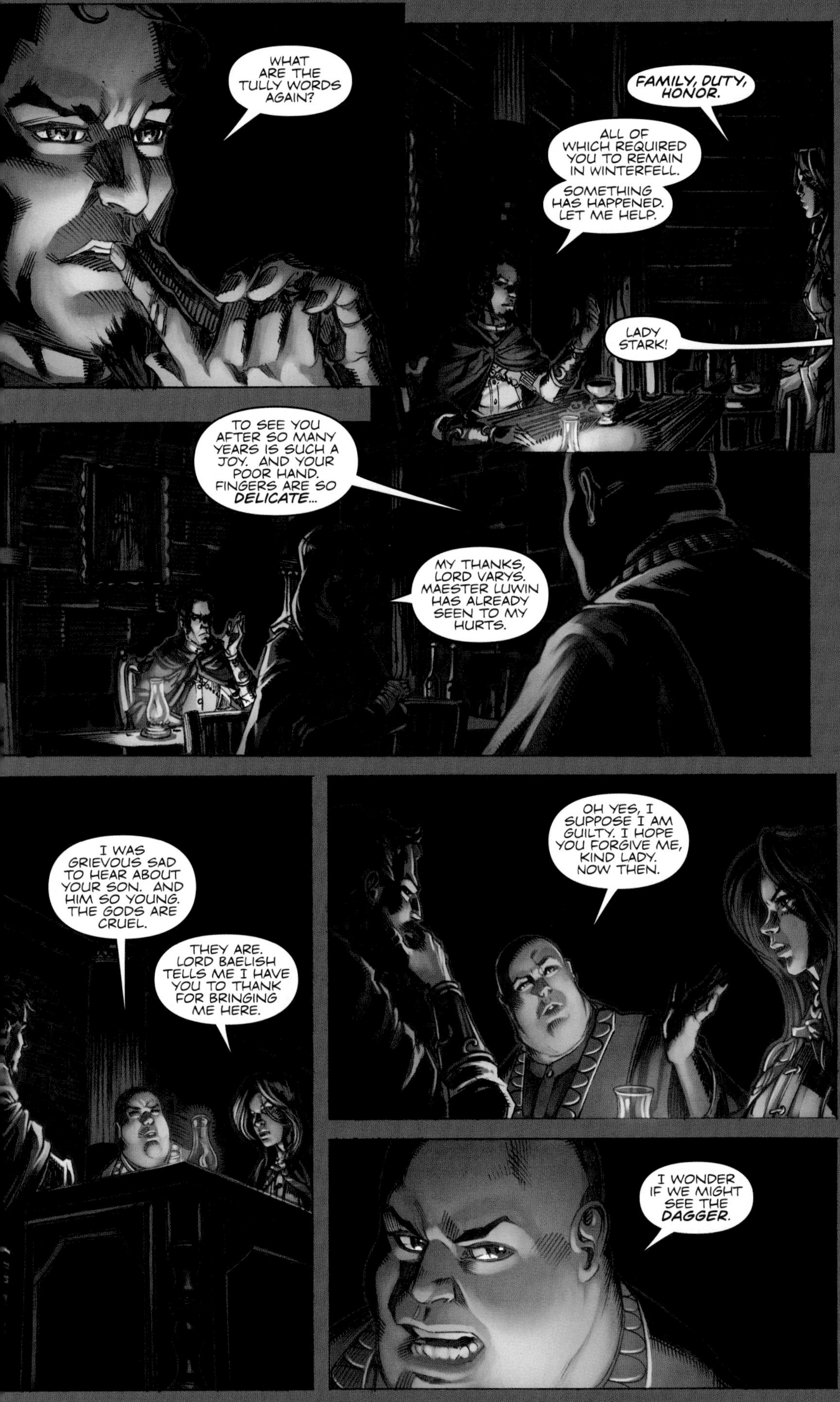
WHAT ARE THE TULLY WORDS AGAIN?
FAMILY, DUTY, HONOR.
ALL OF WHICH REQUIRED YOU TO REMAIN IN WINTERFELL.
SOMETHING HAS HAPPENED. LET ME HELP.
LADY STARK!
TO SEE YOU AFTER SO MANY YEARS IS SUCH A JOY. AND YOUR POOR HAND. FINGERS ARE SO DELICATE...
MY THANKS, LORD VARYS. MAESTER LUWIN HAS ALREADY SEEN TO MY HURTS.
I WAS GRIEVOUS SAD TO HEAR ABOUT YOUR SON. AND HIM SO YOUNG. THE GODS ARE CRUEL.
THEY ARE. LORD BAELISH TELLS ME I HAVE YOU TO THANK FOR BRINGING ME HERE.
OH YES, I SUPPOSE I AM GUILTY. I HOPE YOU FORGIVE ME, KIND LADY. NOW THEN.
I WONDER IF WE MIGHT SEE THE DAGGER.

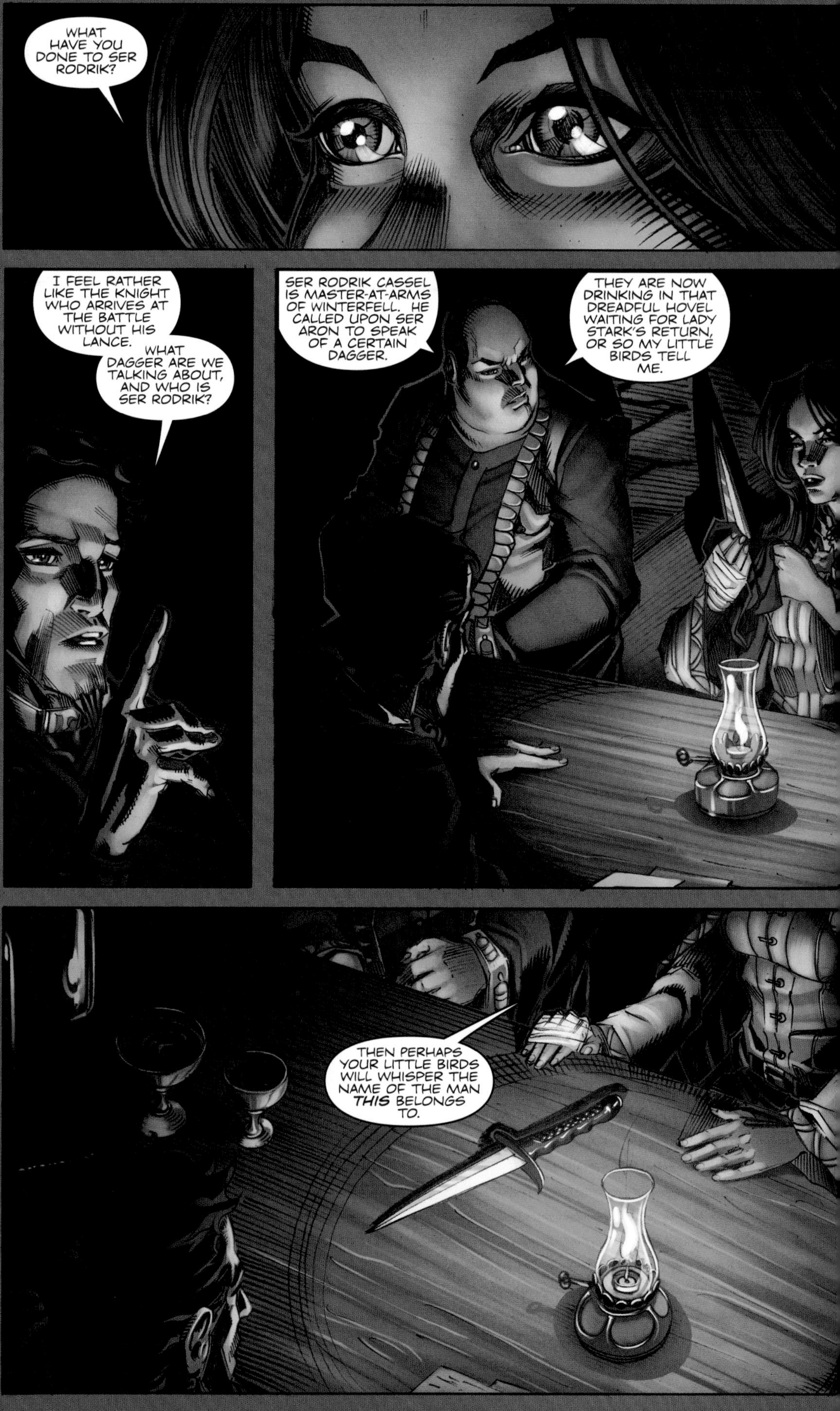
WHAT HAVE YOU DONE TO SER RODRIK?
I FEEL RATHER LIKE THE KNIGHT WHO ARRIVES AT THE BATTLE WITHOUT HIS LANCE.
WHAT DAGGER ARE WE TALKING ABOUT, AND WHO IS SER RODRIK?
SER RODRIK CASSEL IS MASTER-AT-ARMS OF WINTERFELL. HE CALLED UPON SER ARON TO SPEAK OF A CERTAIN DAGGER.
THEY ARE NOW DRINKING IN THAT DREADFUL HOVEL WAITING FOR LADY STARK'S RETURN, OR SO MY LITTLE BIRDS TELL ME.
THEN PERHAPS YOUR LITTLE BIRDS WILL WHISPER THE NAME OF THE MAN *THIS* BELONGS TO.

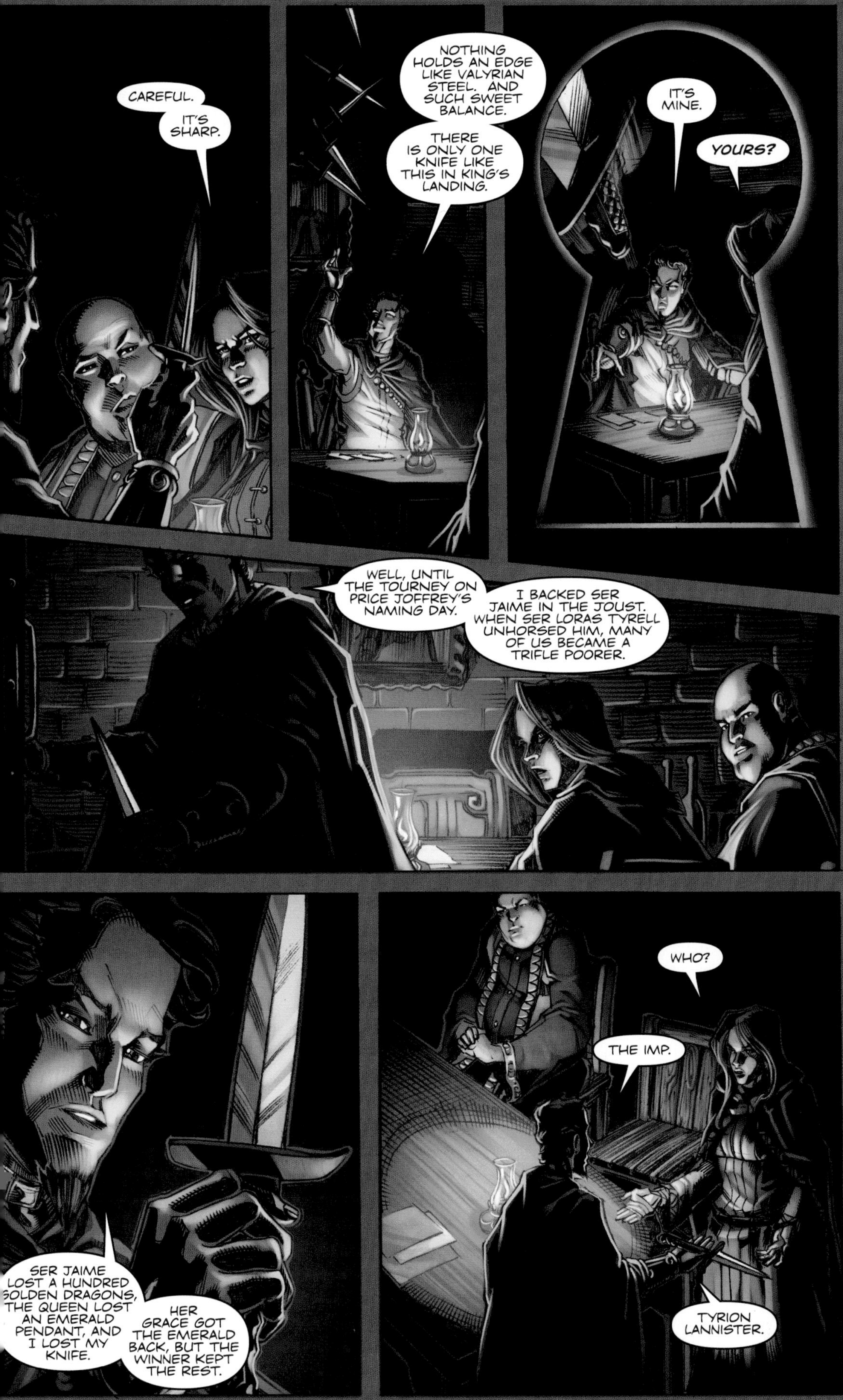
CAREFUL.
IT'S SHARP.
NOTHING HOLDS AN EDGE LIKE VALYRIAN STEEL. AND SUCH SWEET BALANCE.
THERE IS ONLY ONE KNIFE LIKE THIS IN KING'S LANDING.
IT'S MINE.
YOURS?
WELL, UNTIL THE TOURNEY ON PRICE JOFFREY'S NAMING DAY.
I BACKED SER JAIME IN THE JOUST. WHEN SER LORAS TYRELL UNHORSED HIM, MANY OF US BECAME A TRIFLE POORER.
SER JAIME LOST A HUNDRED GOLDEN DRAGONS, THE QUEEN LOST AN EMERALD PENDANT, AND I LOST MY KNIFE.
HER GRACE GOT THE EMERALD BACK, BUT THE WINNER KEPT THE REST.
WHO?
THE IMP.
TYRION LANNISTER.

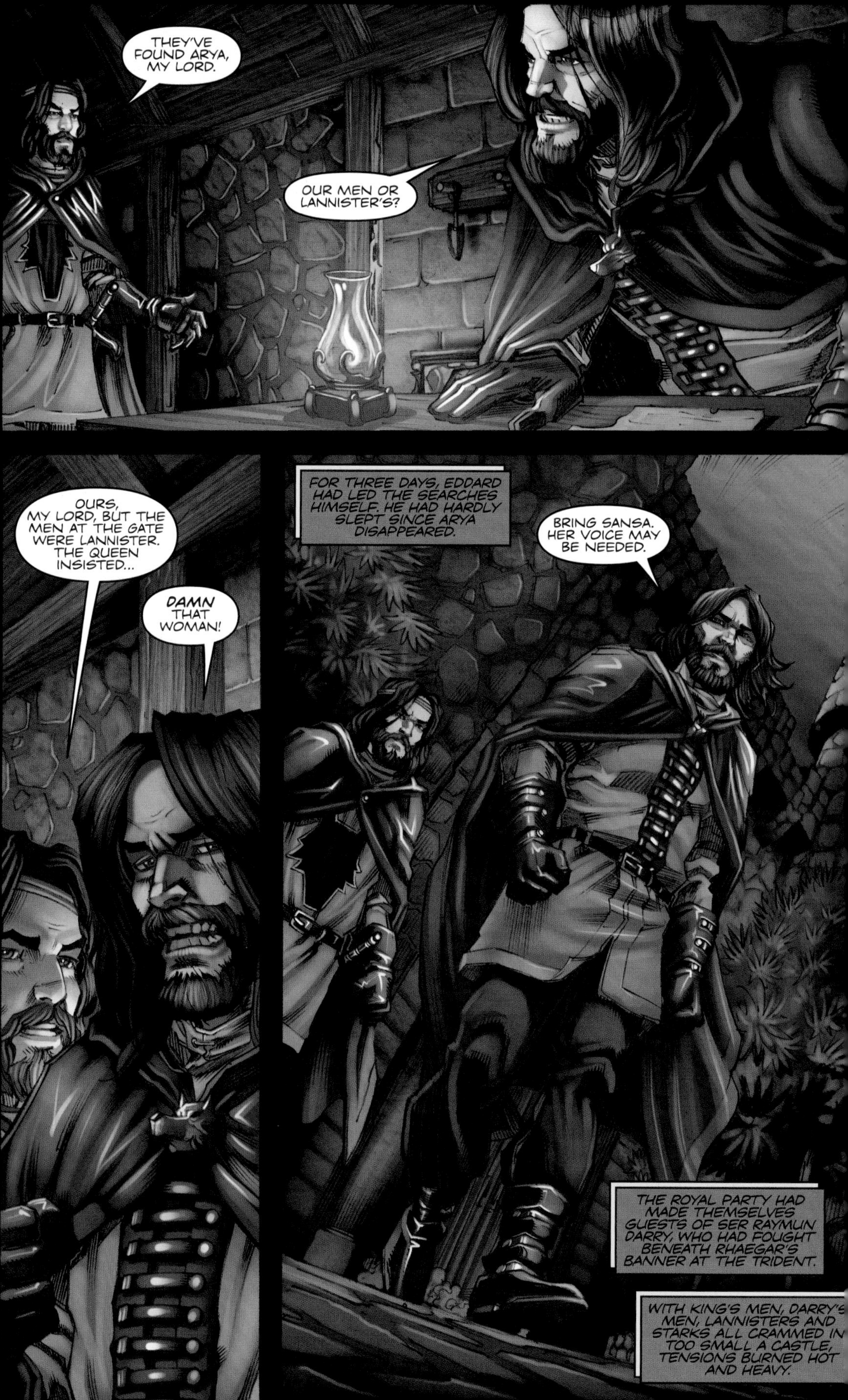
THEY'VE FOUND ARYA, MY LORD.
OUR MEN OR LANNISTER'S?
OURS, MY LORD, BUT THE MEN AT THE GATE WERE LANNISTER. THE QUEEN INSISTED...
DAMN THAT WOMAN!
FOR THREE DAYS, EDDARD HAD LED THE SEARCHES HIMSELF. HE HAD HARDLY SLEPT SINCE ARYA DISAPPEARED.
BRING SANSA. HER VOICE MAY BE NEEDED.
THE ROYAL PARTY HAD MADE THEMSELVES GUESTS OF SER RAYMUN DARRY, WHO HAD FOUGHT BENEATH RHAEGAR'S BANNER AT THE TRIDENT.
WITH KING'S MEN, DARRY'S MEN, LANNISTERS AND STARKS ALL CRAMMED IN TOO SMALL A CASTLE, TENSIONS BURNED HOT AND HEAVY.

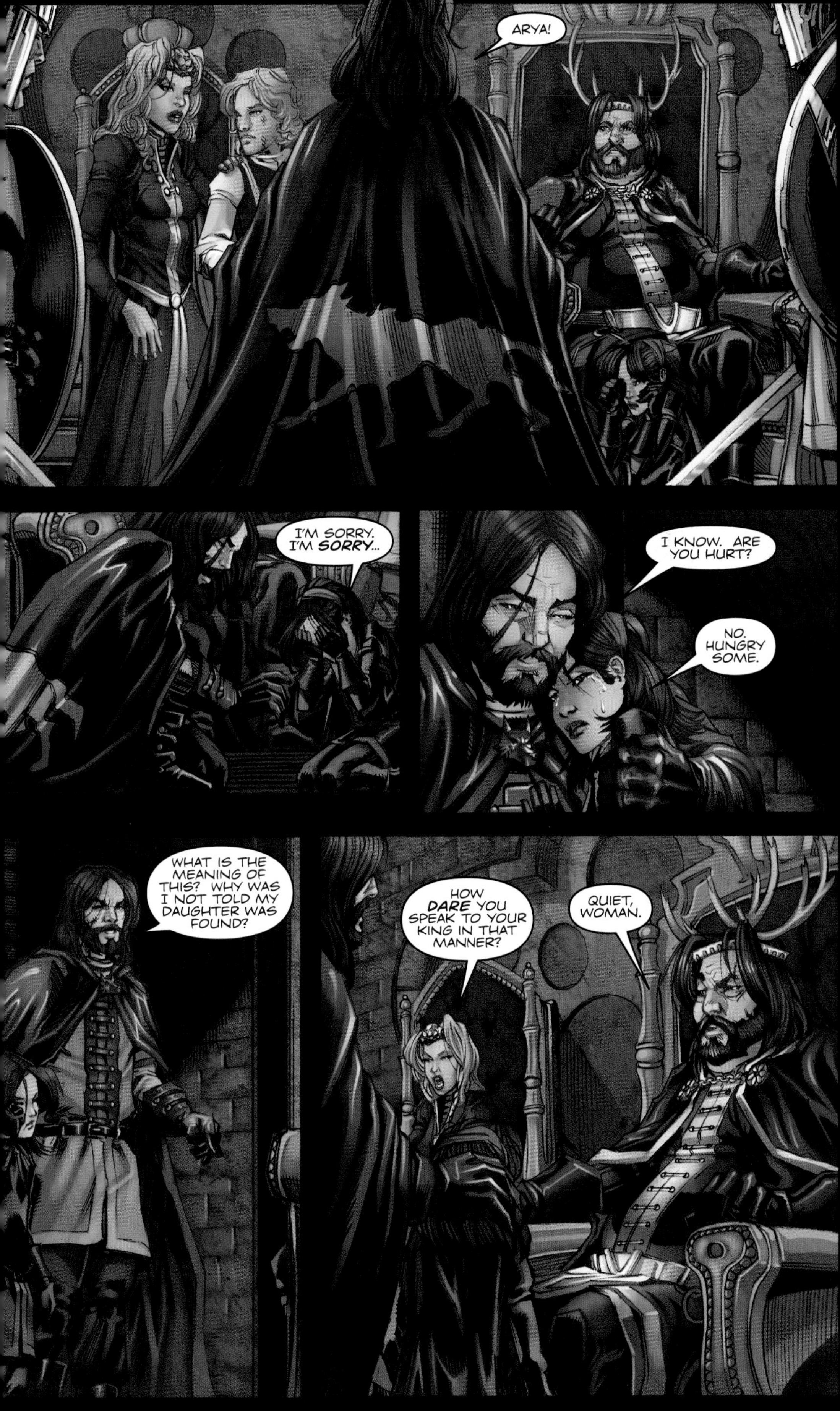
ARYA!
I'M SORRY. I'M **SORRY**...
I KNOW. ARE YOU HURT?
NO. HUNGRY SOME.
WHAT IS THE MEANING OF THIS? WHY WAS I NOT TOLD MY DAUGHTER WAS FOUND?
HOW **DARE** YOU SPEAK TO YOUR KING IN THAT MANNER?
QUIET, WOMAN.

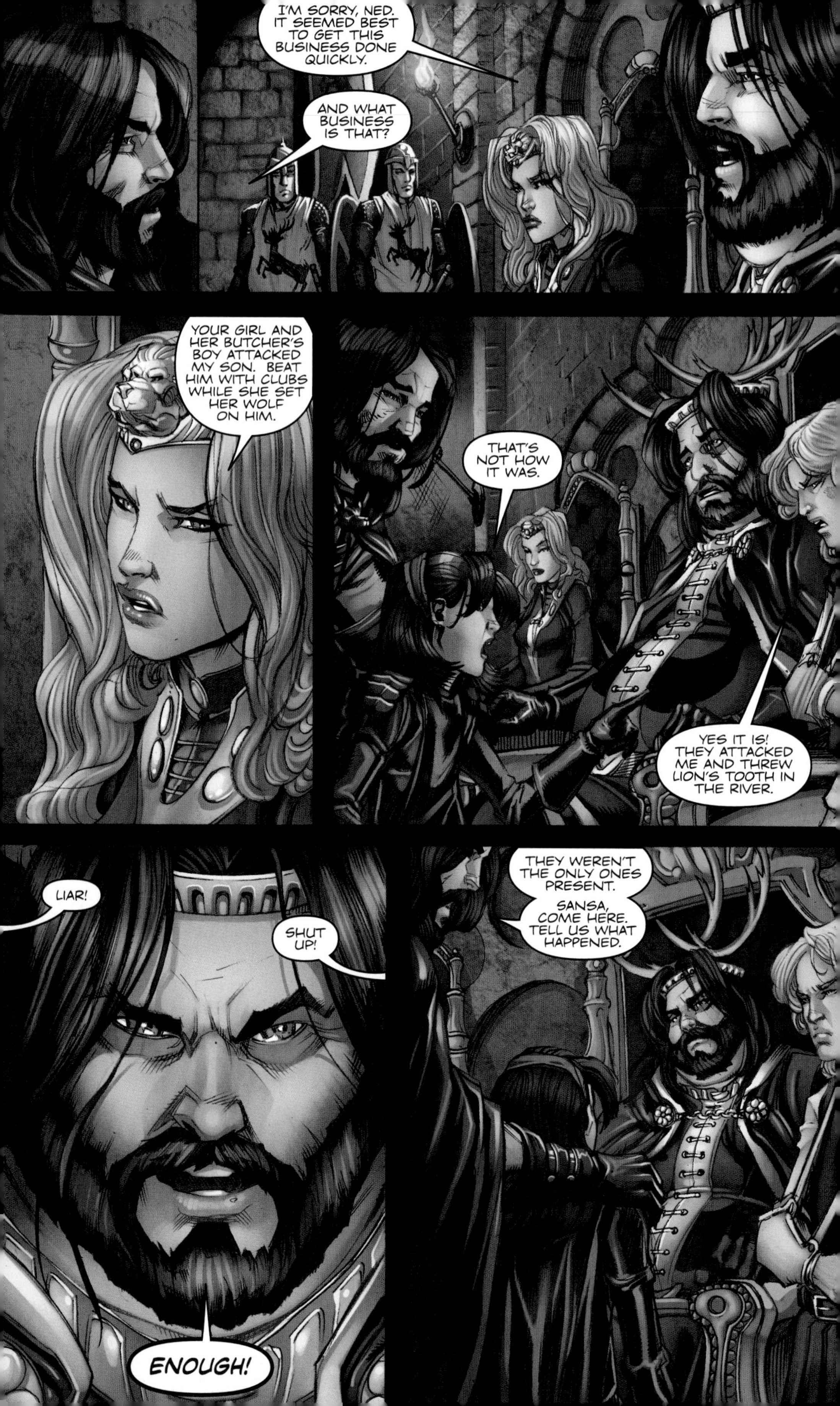
I'M SORRY, NED. IT SEEMED BEST TO GET THIS BUSINESS DONE QUICKLY.
AND WHAT BUSINESS IS THAT?
YOUR GIRL AND HER BUTCHER'S BOY ATTACKED MY SON. BEAT HIM WITH CLUBS WHILE SHE SET HER WOLF ON HIM.
THAT'S NOT HOW IT WAS.
YES IT IS! THEY ATTACKED ME AND THREW LION'S TOOTH IN THE RIVER.
LIAR!
SHUT UP!
ENOUGH!
THEY WEREN'T THE ONLY ONES PRESENT.
SANSA, COME HERE. TELL US WHAT HAPPENED.

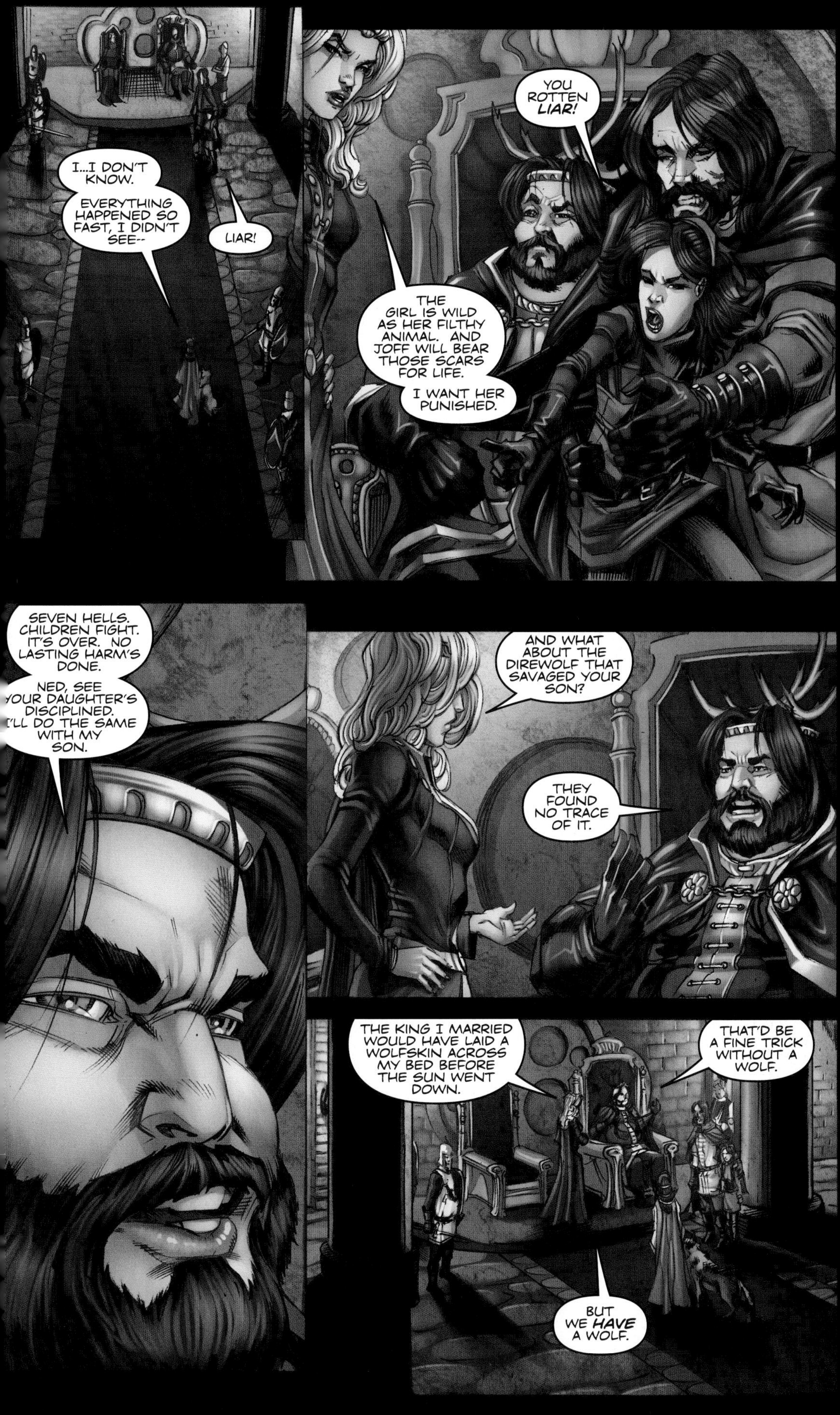
I...I DON'T KNOW.
EVERYTHING HAPPENED SO FAST, I DIDN'T SEE--
LIAR!
YOU ROTTEN LIAR!
THE GIRL IS WILD AS HER FILTHY ANIMAL. AND JOFF WILL BEAR THOSE SCARS FOR LIFE.
I WANT HER PUNISHED.
SEVEN HELLS. CHILDREN FIGHT. IT'S OVER. NO LASTING HARM'S DONE.
NED, SEE YOUR DAUGHTER'S DISCIPLINED. I'LL DO THE SAME WITH MY SON.
AND WHAT ABOUT THE DIREWOLF THAT SAVAGED YOUR SON?
THEY FOUND NO TRACE OF IT.
THE KING I MARRIED WOULD HAVE LAID A WOLFSKIN ACROSS MY BED BEFORE THE SUN WENT DOWN.
THAT'D BE A FINE TRICK WITHOUT A WOLF.
BUT WE *HAVE* A WOLF.

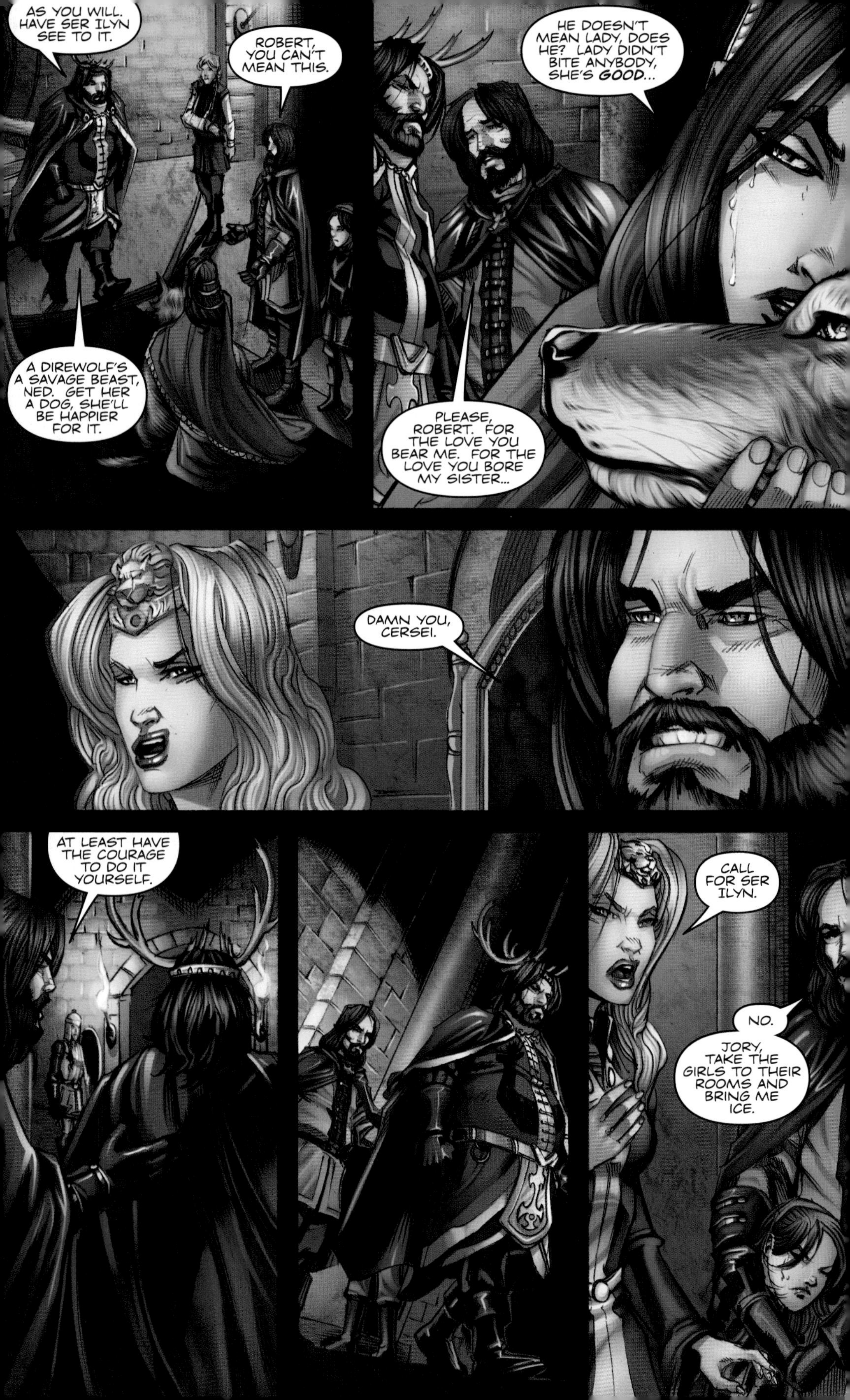
AS YOU WILL. HAVE SER ILYN SEE TO IT.
ROBERT, YOU CAN'T MEAN THIS.
A DIREWOLF'S A SAVAGE BEAST, NED. GET HER A DOG, SHE'LL BE HAPPIER FOR IT.
HE DOESN'T MEAN LADY, DOES HE? LADY DIDN'T BITE ANYBODY, SHE'S **GOOD**...
PLEASE, ROBERT. FOR THE LOVE YOU BEAR ME. FOR THE LOVE YOU BORE MY SISTER...
DAMN YOU, CERSEI.
AT LEAST HAVE THE COURAGE TO DO IT YOURSELF.
CALL FOR SER ILYN.
NO.
JORY, TAKE THE GIRLS TO THEIR ROOMS AND BRING ME ICE.

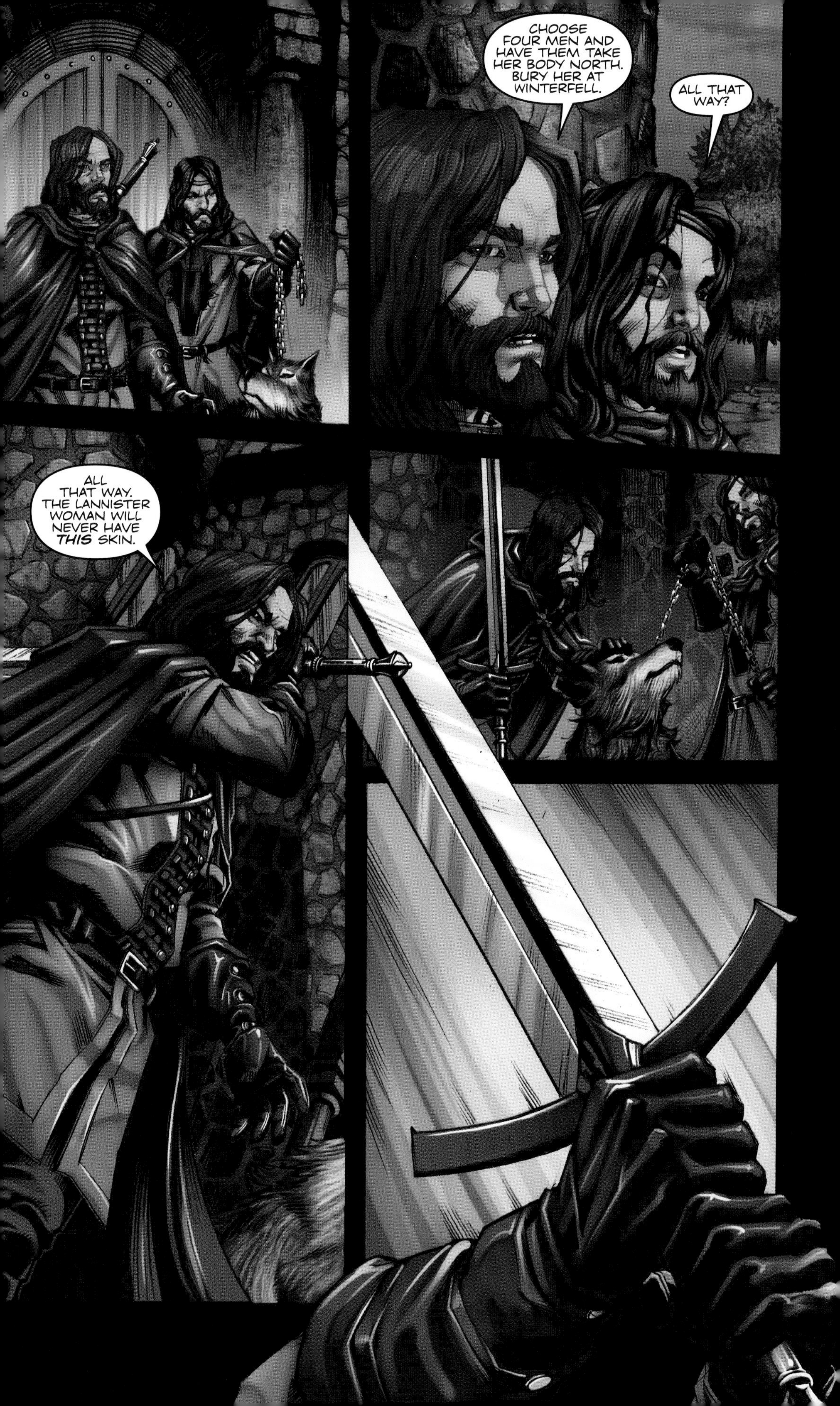
CHOOSE FOUR MEN AND HAVE THEM TAKE HER BODY NORTH. BURY HER AT WINTERFELL.
ALL THAT WAY?
ALL THAT WAY. THE LANNISTER WOMAN WILL NEVER HAVE THIS SKIN.

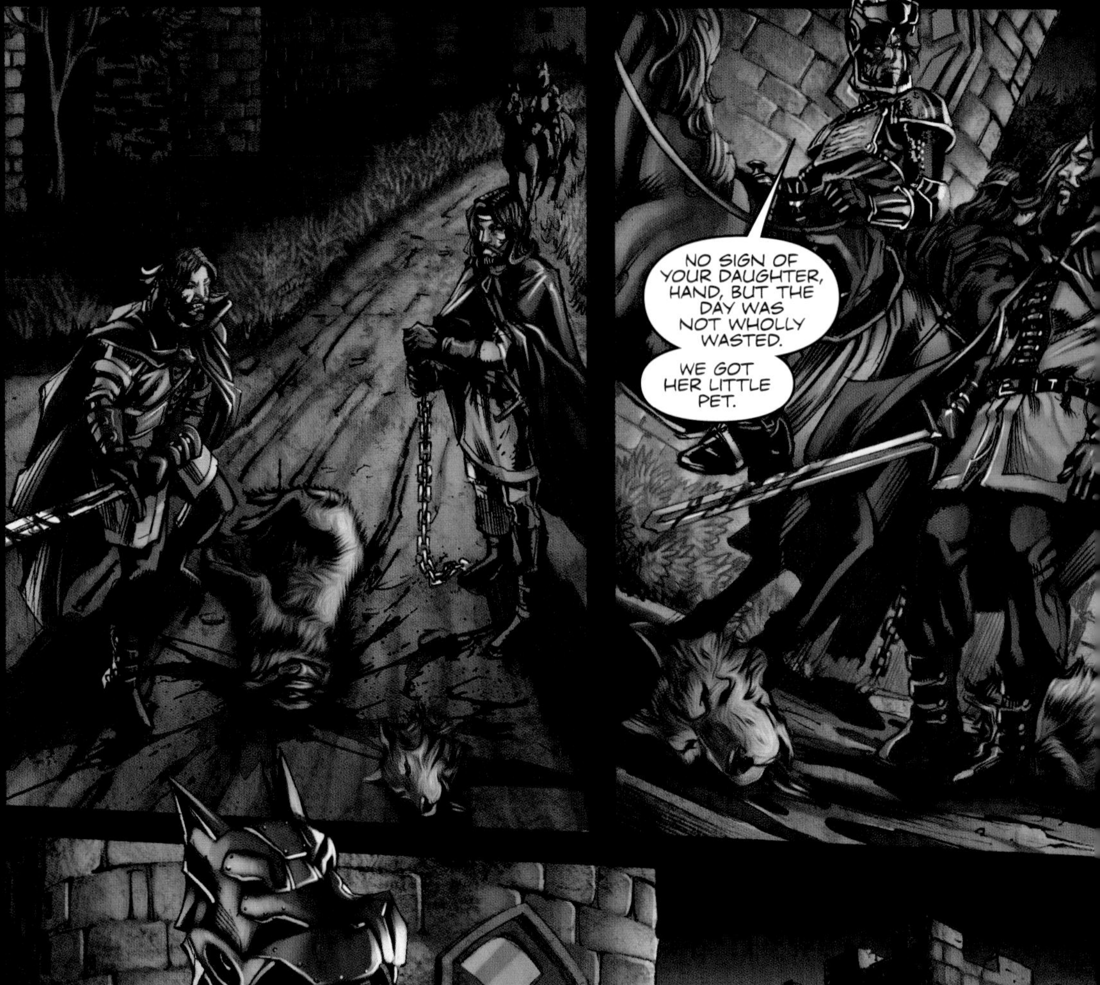
NO SIGN OF YOUR DAUGHTER, HAND, BUT THE DAY WAS NOT WHOLLY WASTED.
WE GOT HER LITTLE PET.
YOU RODE HIM DOWN.
HE RAN.
BUT NOT VERY FAST.

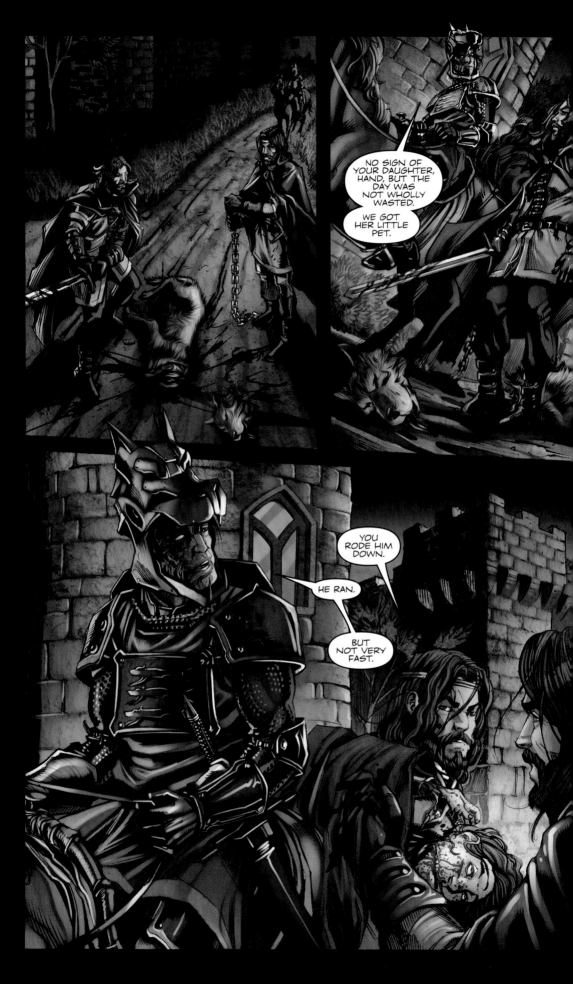

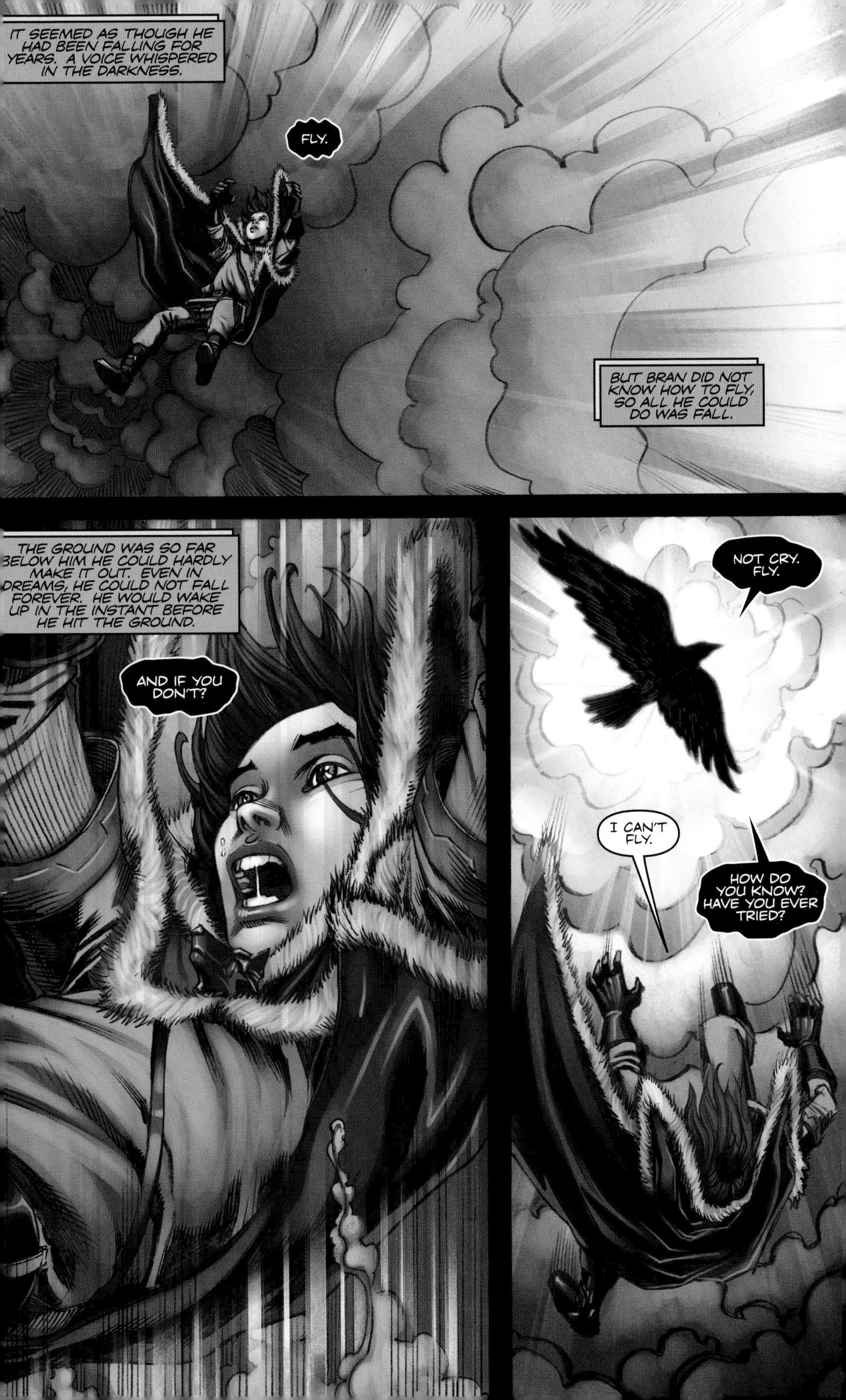
IT SEEMED AS THOUGH HE HAD BEEN FALLING FOR YEARS. A VOICE WHISPERED IN THE DARKNESS.
FLY.
BUT BRAN DID NOT KNOW HOW TO FLY, SO ALL HE COULD DO WAS FALL.
THE GROUND WAS SO FAR BELOW HIM HE COULD HARDLY MAKE IT OUT. EVEN IN DREAMS, HE COULD NOT FALL FOREVER. HE WOULD WAKE UP IN THE INSTANT BEFORE HE HIT THE GROUND.
AND IF YOU DON'T?
NOT CRY. FLY.
I CAN'T FLY.
HOW DO YOU KNOW? HAVE YOU EVER TRIED?

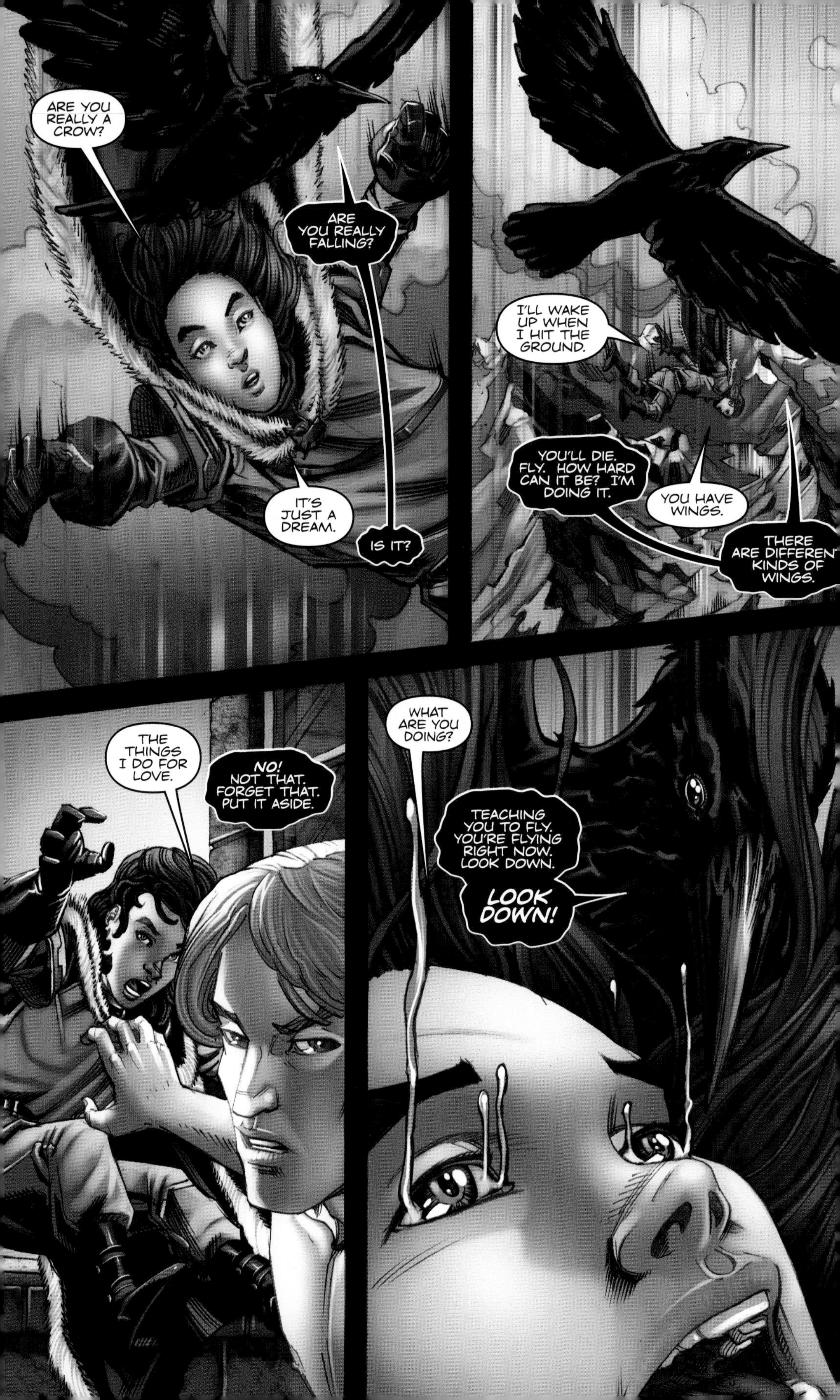
ARE YOU REALLY A CROW?
ARE YOU REALLY FALLING?
IT'S JUST A DREAM.
IS IT?
I'LL WAKE UP WHEN I HIT THE GROUND.
YOU'LL DIE. FLY. HOW HARD CAN IT BE? I'M DOING IT.
YOU HAVE WINGS.
THERE ARE DIFFEREN KINDS OF WINGS.
THE THINGS I DO FOR LOVE.
NO! NOT THAT. FORGET THAT. PUT IT ASIDE.
WHAT ARE YOU DOING?
TEACHING YOU TO FLY. YOU'RE FLYING RIGHT NOW. LOOK DOWN.
LOOK DOWN!

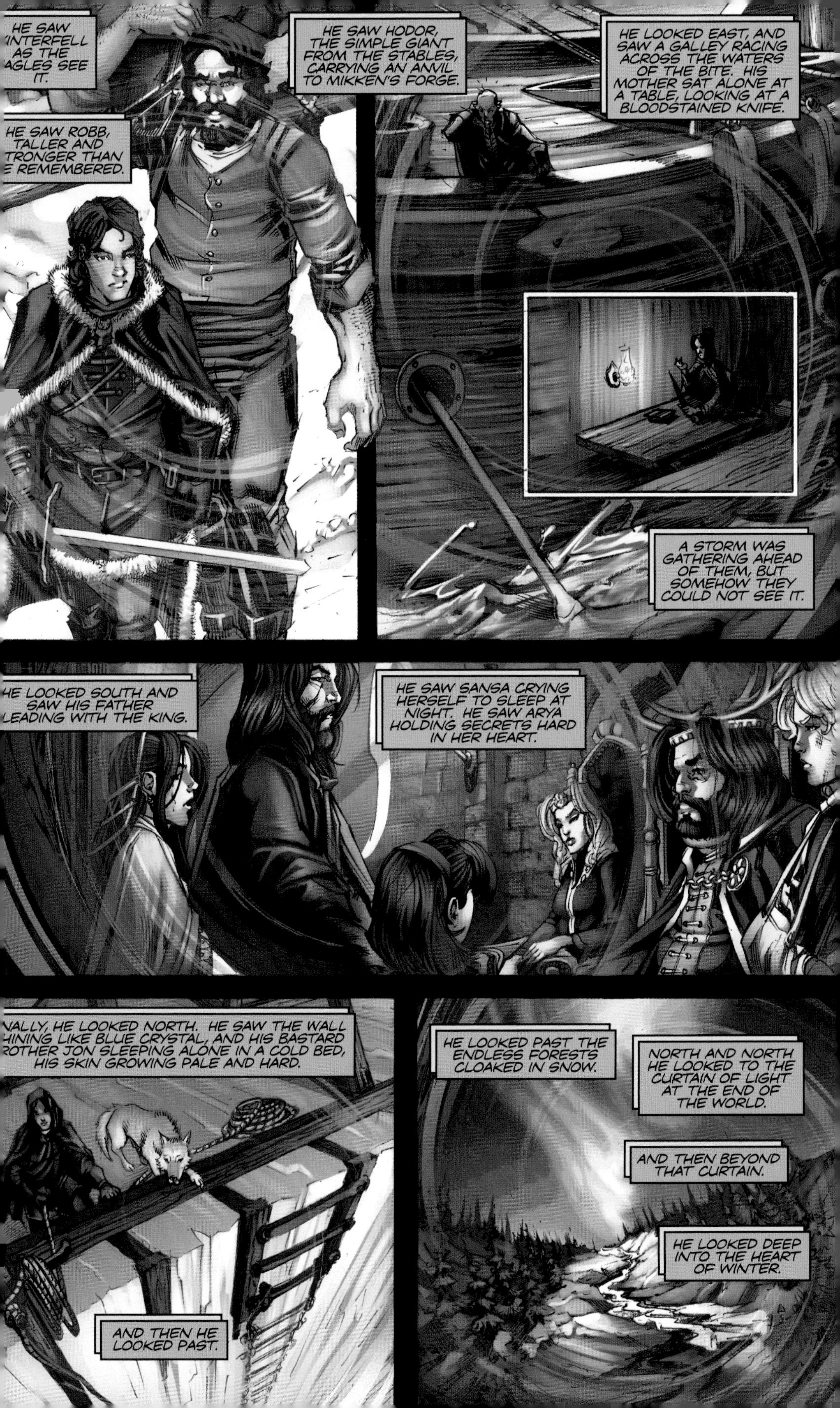

HE SAW
VINTERFELL
AS THE
AGLES SEE
IT.
HE SAW ROBB,
TALLER AND
TRONGER THAN
E REMEMBERED.
HE SAW HODOR, THE SIMPLE GIANT FROM THE STABLES, CARRYING AN ANVIL TO MIKKEN'S FORGE.
HE LOOKED EAST, AND SAW A GALLEY RACING ACROSS THE WATERS OF THE BITE. HIS MOTHER SAT ALONE AT A TABLE, LOOKING AT A BLOODSTAINED KNIFE.
A STORM WAS GATHERING AHEAD OF THEM, BUT SOMEHOW THEY COULD NOT SEE IT.
HE LOOKED SOUTH AND SAW HIS FATHER LEADING WITH THE KING.
HE SAW SANSA CRYING HERSELF TO SLEEP AT NIGHT. HE SAW ARYA HOLDING SECRETS HARD IN HER HEART.
NALLY, HE LOOKED NORTH. HE SAW THE WALL HINING LIKE BLUE CRYSTAL, AND HIS BASTARD ROTHER JON SLEEPING ALONE IN A COLD BED, HIS SKIN GROWING PALE AND HARD.
AND THEN HE LOOKED PAST.
HE LOOKED PAST THE ENDLESS FORESTS CLOAKED IN SNOW.
NORTH AND NORTH HE LOOKED TO THE CURTAIN OF LIGHT AT THE END OF THE WORLD.
AND THEN BEYOND THAT CURTAIN.
HE LOOKED DEEP INTO THE HEART OF WINTER.

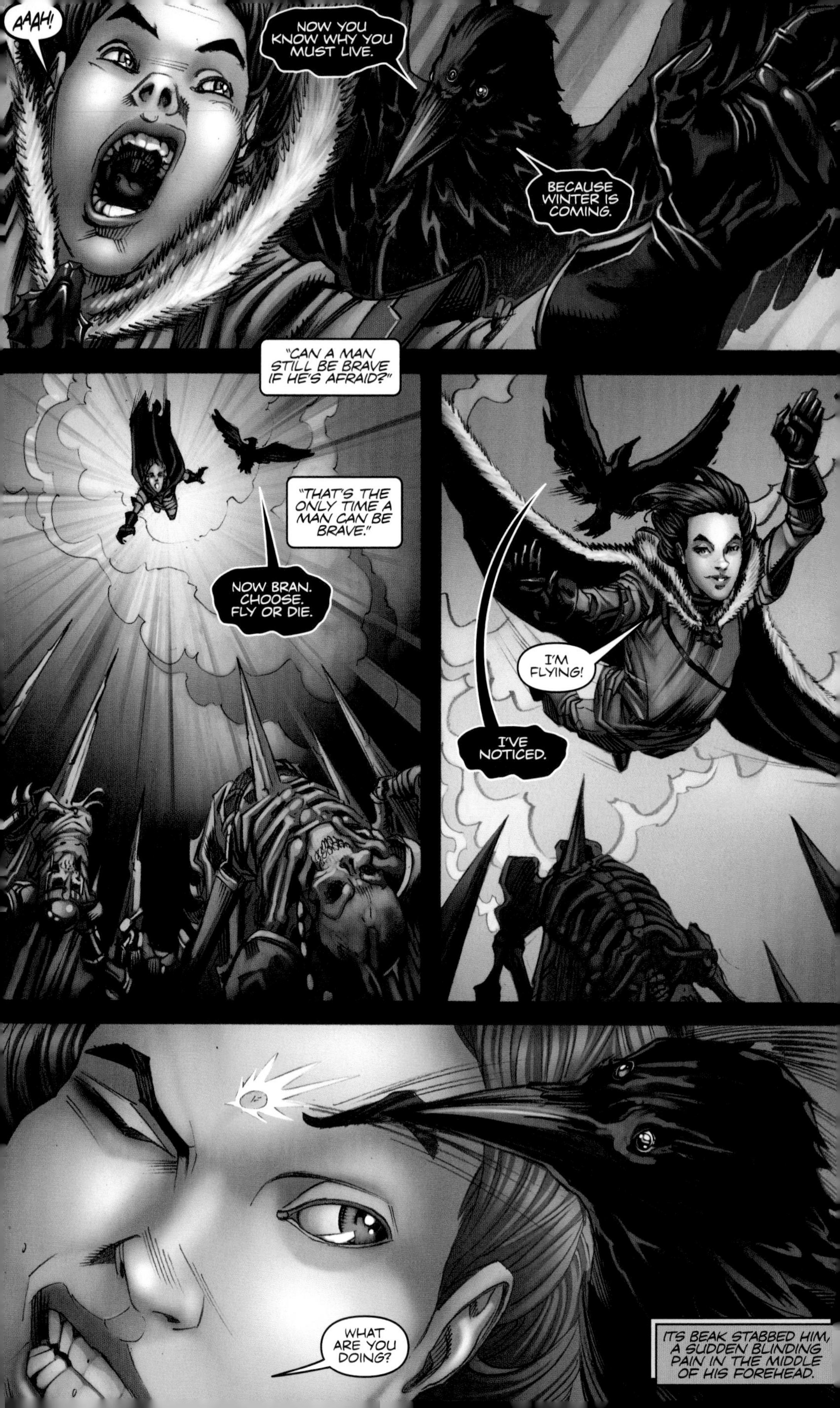
AAAH!
NOW YOU KNOW WHY YOU MUST LIVE.
BECAUSE WINTER IS COMING.
"CAN A MAN STILL BE BRAVE IF HE'S AFRAID?"
"THAT'S THE ONLY TIME A MAN CAN BE BRAVE."
NOW BRAN. CHOOSE. FLY OR DIE.
I'M FLYING!
I'VE NOTICED.
WHAT ARE YOU DOING?
ITS BEAK STABBED HIM, A SUDDEN BLINDING PAIN IN THE MIDDLE OF HIS FOREHEAD.

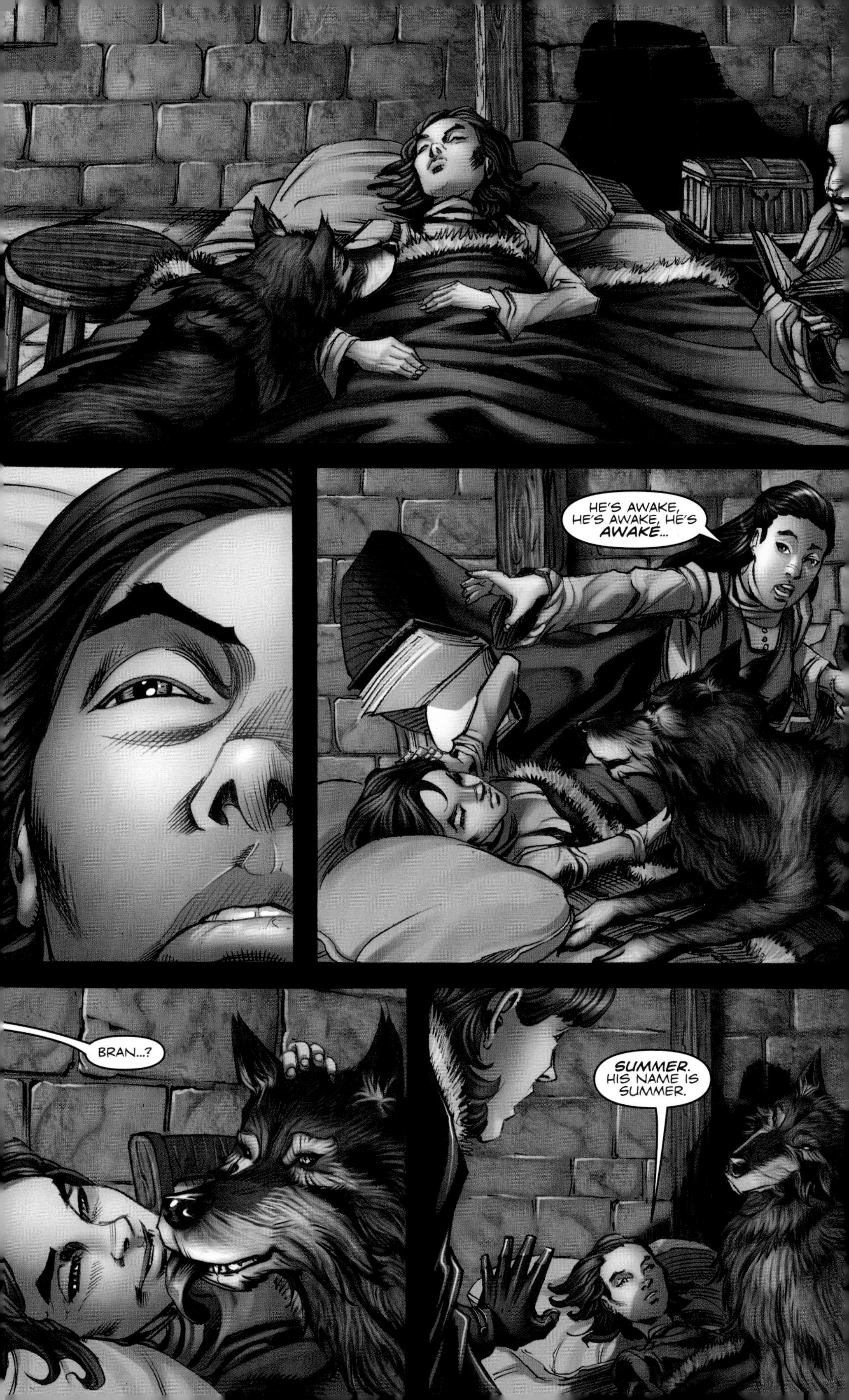
HE'S AWAKE, HE'S AWAKE, HE'S AWAKE...
BRAN...?
SUMMER. HIS NAME IS SUMMER.

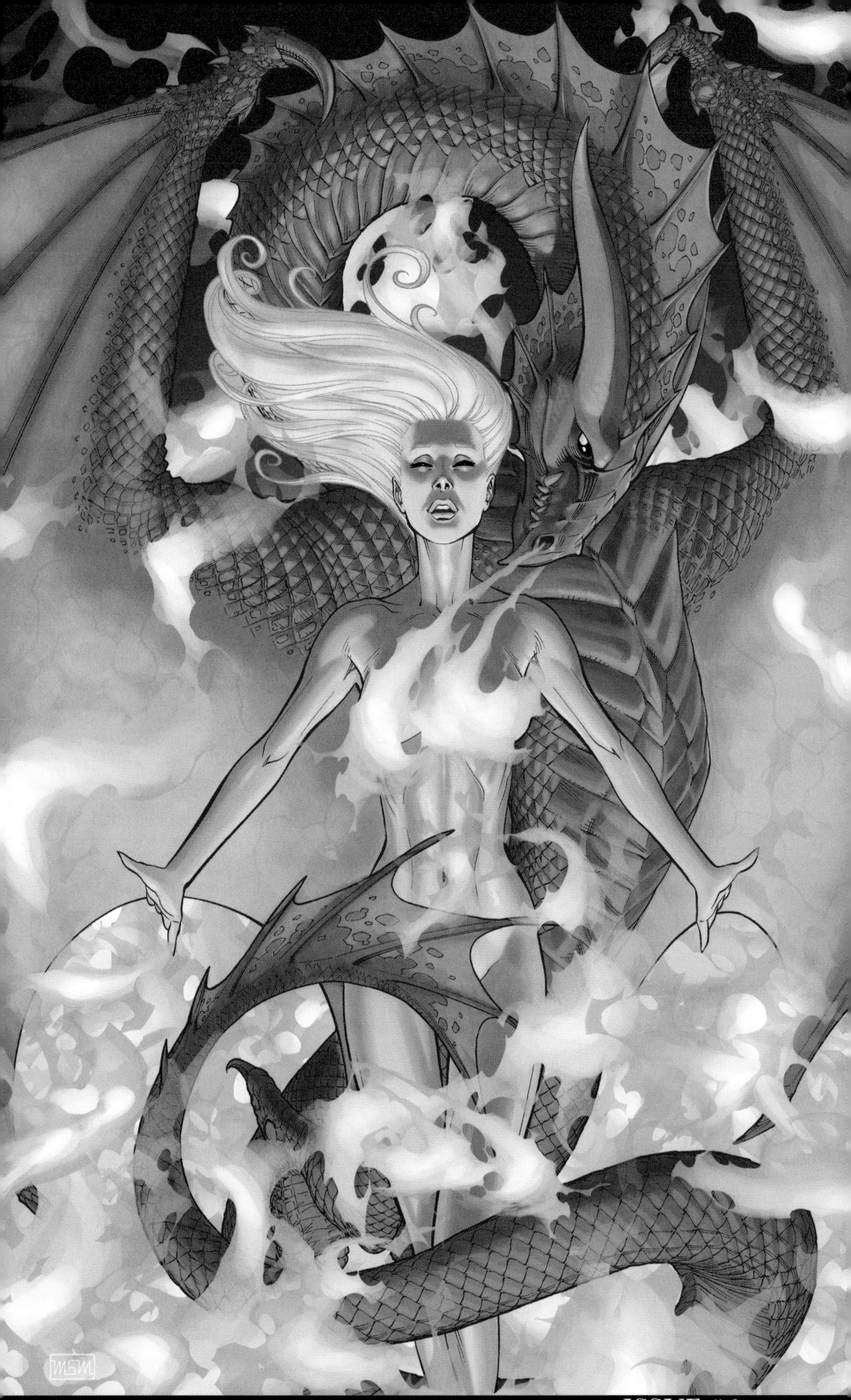

ISSUE #6

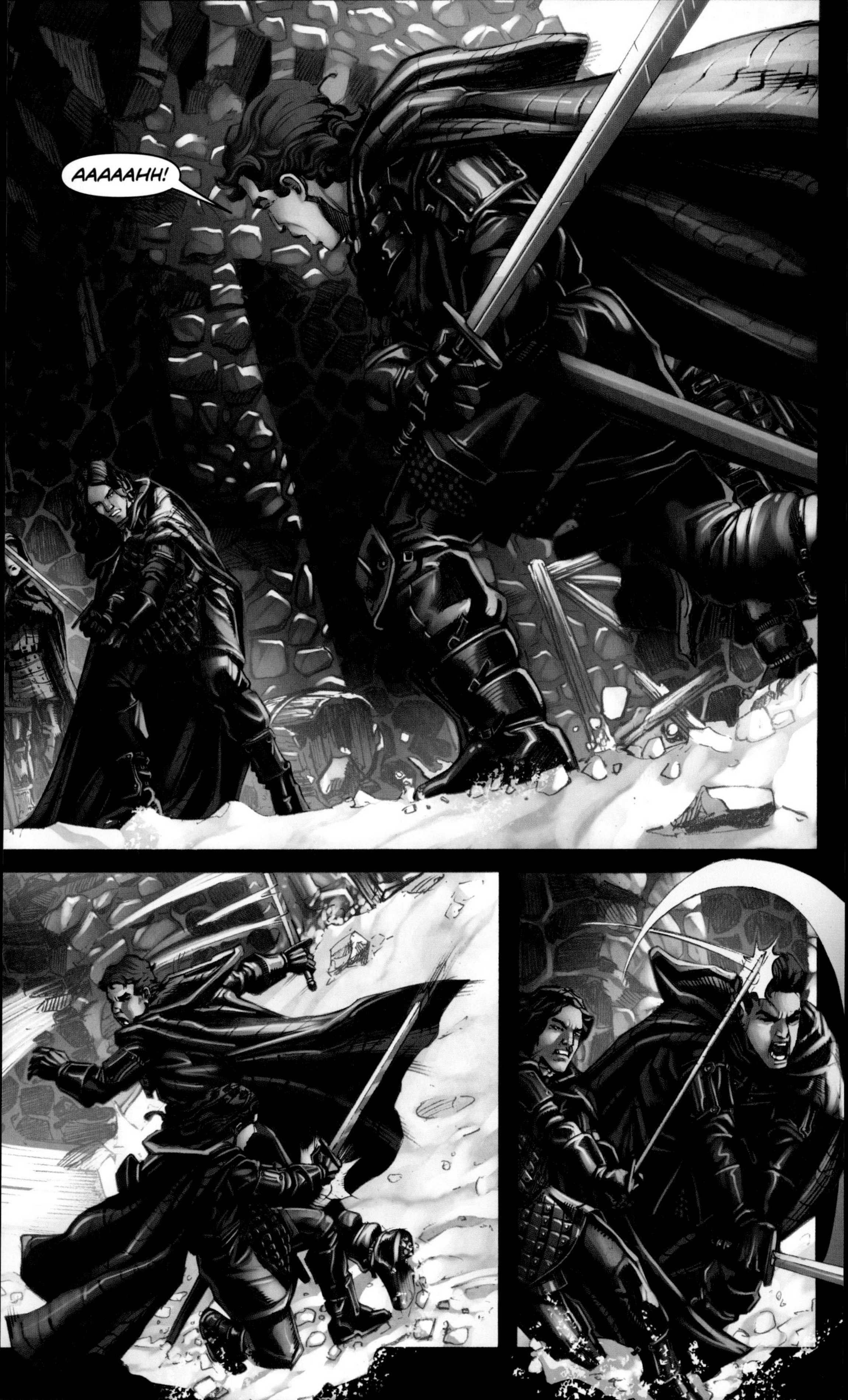
AAAAAHH!

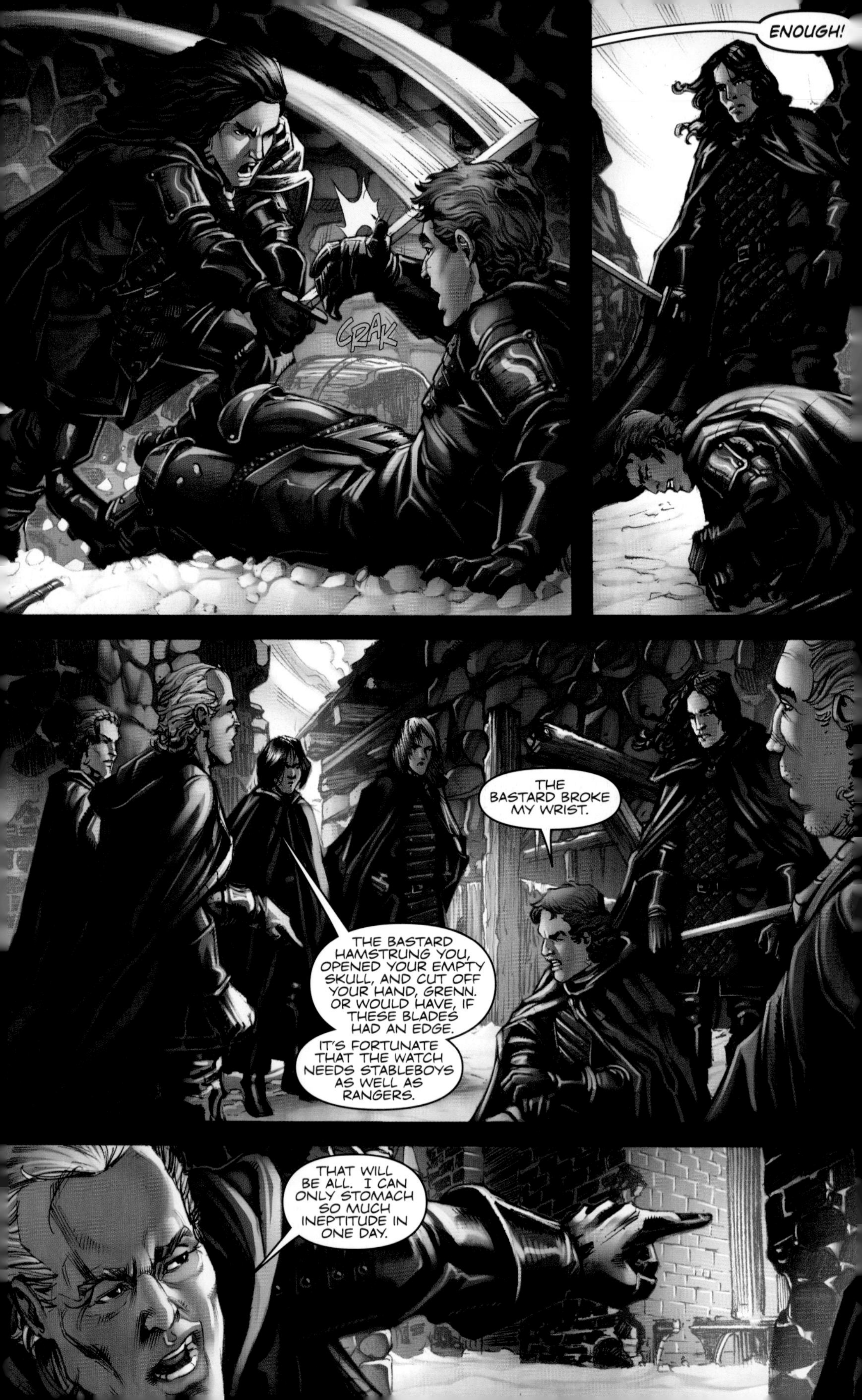
CRAK
ENOUGH!
THE BASTARD BROKE MY WRIST.
THE BASTARD HAMSTRUNG YOU, OPENED YOUR EMPTY SKULL, AND CUT OFF YOUR HAND, GRENN. OR WOULD HAVE, IF THESE BLADES HAD AN EDGE.
IT'S FORTUNATE THAT THE WATCH NEEDS STABLEBOYS AS WELL AS RANGERS.
THAT WILL BE ALL. I CAN ONLY STOMACH SO MUCH INEPTITUDE IN ONE DAY.

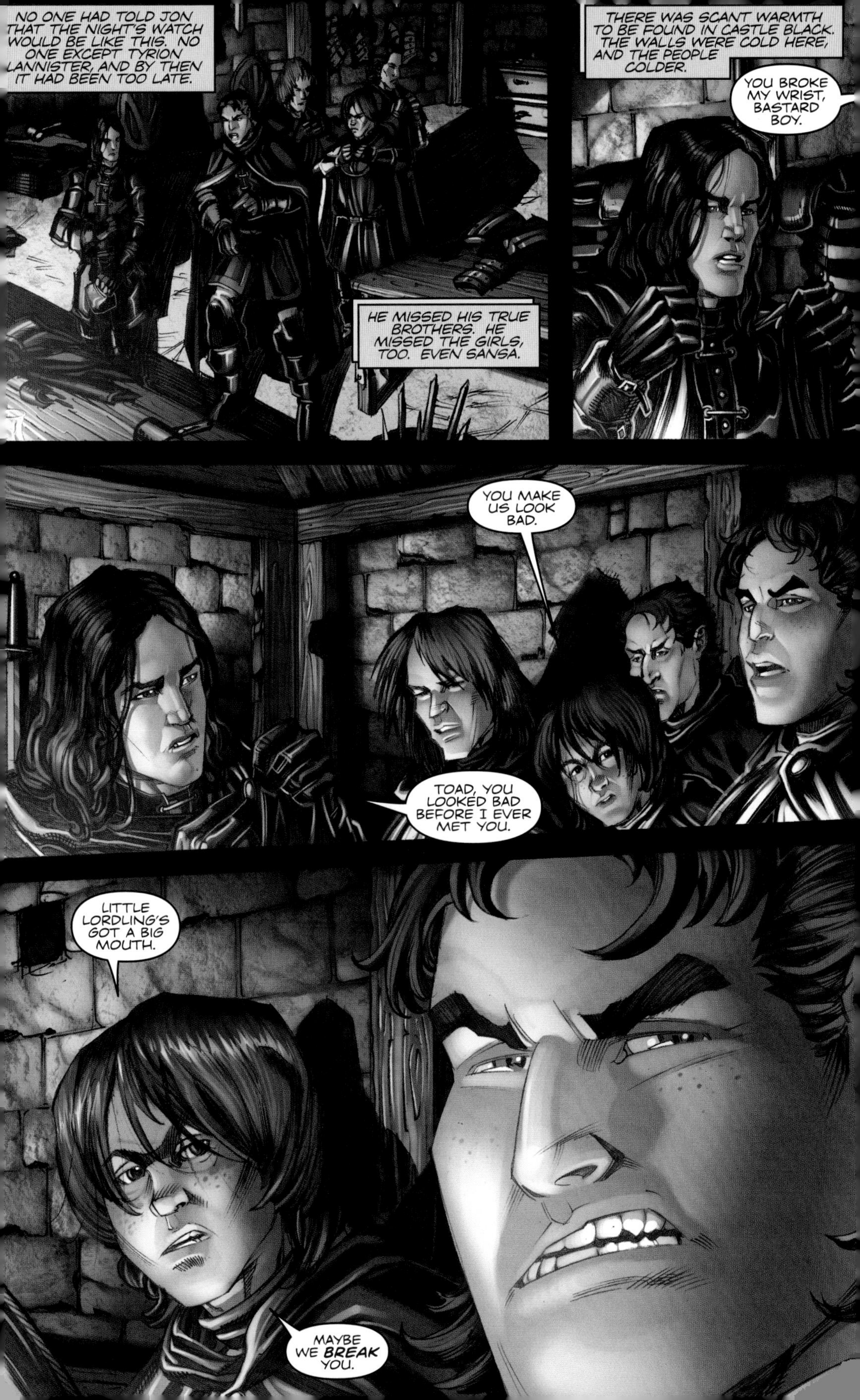
NO ONE HAD TOLD JON THAT THE NIGHT'S WATCH WOULD BE LIKE THIS. NO ONE EXCEPT TYRION LANNISTER, AND BY THEN IT HAD BEEN TOO LATE.
HE MISSED HIS TRUE BROTHERS. HE MISSED THE GIRLS, TOO. EVEN SANSA.
THERE WAS SCANT WARMTH TO BE FOUND IN CASTLE BLACK. THE WALLS WERE COLD HERE, AND THE PEOPLE COLDER.
YOU BROKE MY WRIST, BASTARD BOY.
YOU MAKE US LOOK BAD.
TOAD, YOU LOOKED BAD BEFORE I EVER MET YOU.
LITTLE LORDLING'S GOT A BIG MOUTH.
MAYBE WE **BREAK** YOU.

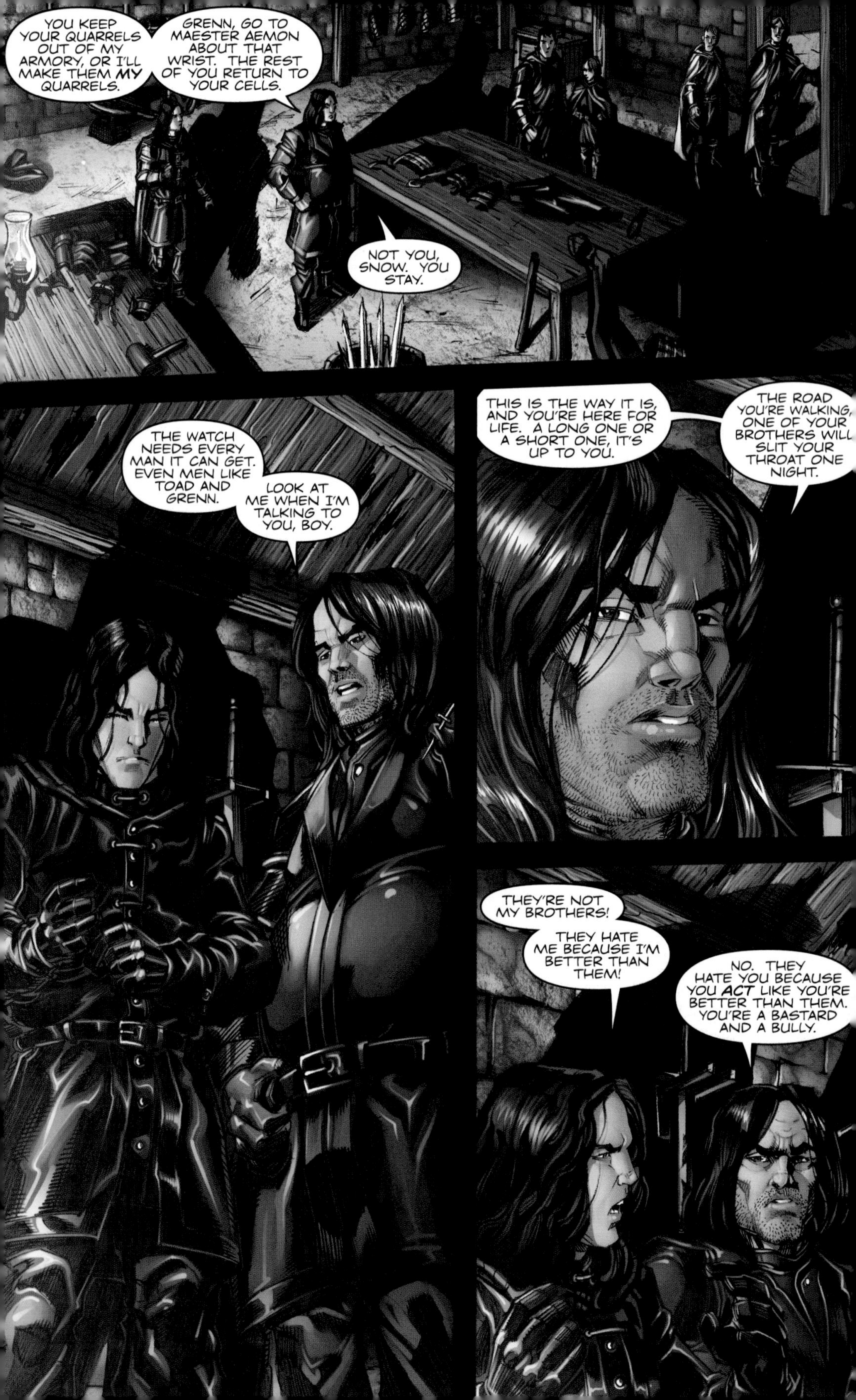
YOU KEEP YOUR QUARRELS OUT OF MY ARMORY, OR I'LL MAKE THEM **MY** QUARRELS.
GRENN, GO TO MAESTER AEMON ABOUT THAT WRIST. THE REST OF YOU RETURN TO YOUR CELLS.
NOT YOU, SNOW. YOU STAY.
THE WATCH NEEDS EVERY MAN IT CAN GET. EVEN MEN LIKE TOAD AND GRENN.
LOOK AT ME WHEN I'M TALKING TO YOU, BOY.
THIS IS THE WAY IT IS, AND YOU'RE HERE FOR LIFE. A LONG ONE OR A SHORT ONE, IT'S UP TO YOU.
THE ROAD YOU'RE WALKING, ONE OF YOUR BROTHERS WILL SLIT YOUR THROAT ONE NIGHT.
THEY'RE NOT MY BROTHERS!
THEY HATE ME BECAUSE I'M BETTER THAN THEM!
NO. THEY HATE YOU BECAUSE YOU **ACT** LIKE YOU'RE BETTER THAN THEM. YOU'RE A BASTARD AND A BULLY.

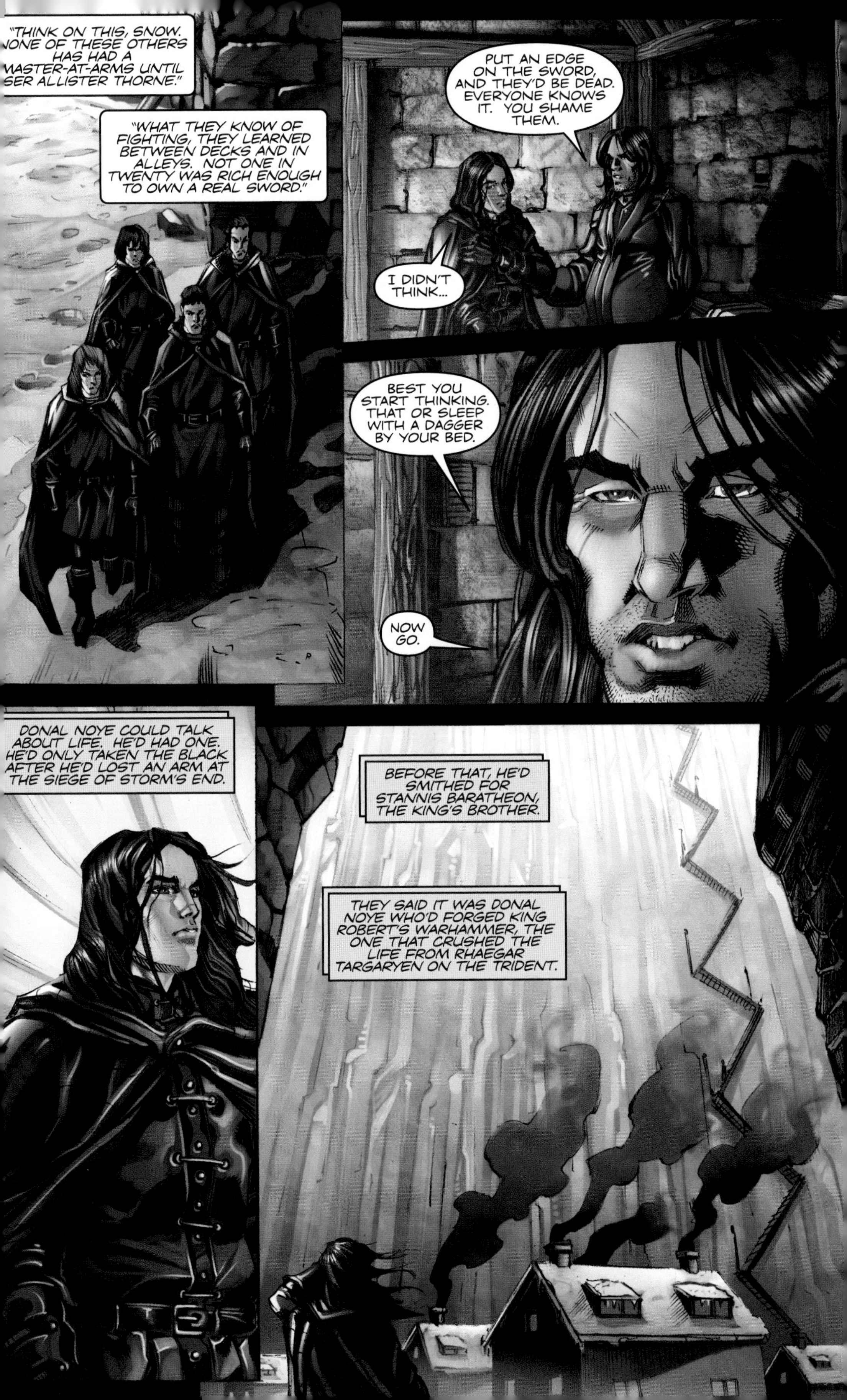
"THINK ON THIS, SNOW. NONE OF THESE OTHERS HAS HAD A MASTER-AT-ARMS UNTIL SER ALLISTER THORNE."
"WHAT THEY KNOW OF FIGHTING, THEY LEARNED BETWEEN DECKS AND IN ALLEYS. NOT ONE IN TWENTY WAS RICH ENOUGH TO OWN A REAL SWORD."
PUT AN EDGE ON THE SWORD, AND THEY'D BE DEAD. EVERYONE KNOWS IT. YOU SHAME THEM.
I DIDN'T THINK...
BEST YOU START THINKING. THAT OR SLEEP WITH A DAGGER BY YOUR BED.
NOW GO.
DONAL NOYE COULD TALK ABOUT LIFE. HE'D HAD ONE. HE'D ONLY TAKEN THE BLACK AFTER HE'D LOST AN ARM AT THE SIEGE OF STORM'S END.
BEFORE THAT, HE'D SMITHED FOR STANNIS BARATHEON, THE KING'S BROTHER.
THEY SAID IT WAS DONAL NOYE WHO'D FORGED KING ROBERT'S WARHAMMER, THE ONE THAT CRUSHED THE LIFE FROM RHAEGAR TARGARYEN ON THE TRIDENT.

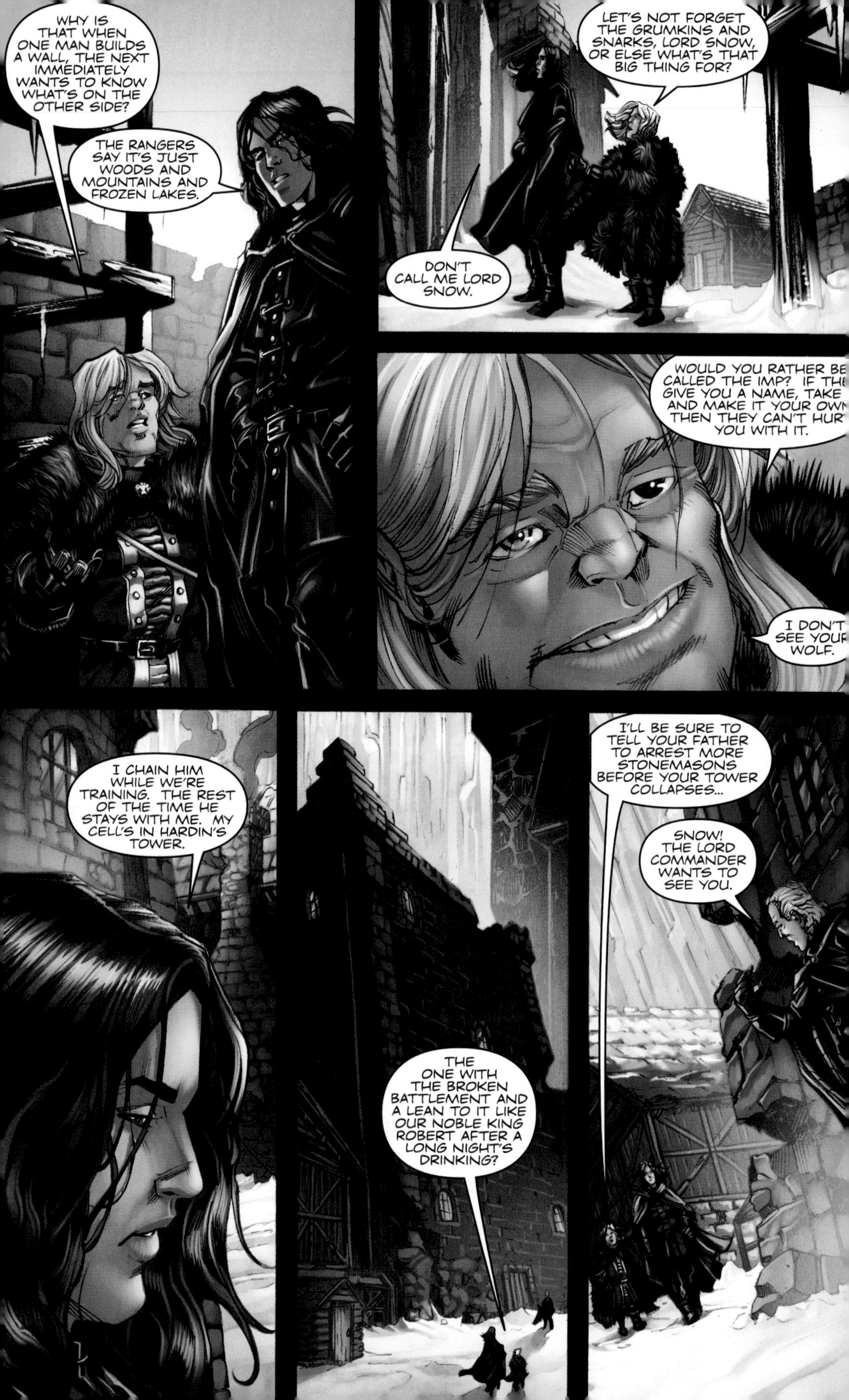
WHY IS THAT WHEN ONE MAN BUILDS A WALL, THE NEXT IMMEDIATELY WANTS TO KNOW WHAT'S ON THE OTHER SIDE?
THE RANGERS SAY IT'S JUST WOODS AND MOUNTAINS AND FROZEN LAKES.
LET'S NOT FORGET THE GRUMKINS AND SNARKS, LORD SNOW, OR ELSE WHAT'S THAT BIG THING FOR?
DON'T CALL ME LORD SNOW.
WOULD YOU RATHER BE CALLED THE IMP? IF THE GIVE YOU A NAME, TAKE AND MAKE IT YOUR OWN THEN THEY CAN'T HURT YOU WITH IT.
I DON'T SEE YOUR WOLF.
I CHAIN HIM WHILE WE'RE TRAINING. THE REST OF THE TIME HE STAYS WITH ME. MY CELL'S IN HARDIN'S TOWER.
THE ONE WITH THE BROKEN BATTLEMENT AND A LEAN TO IT LIKE OUR NOBLE KING ROBERT AFTER A LONG NIGHT'S DRINKING?
I'LL BE SURE TO TELL YOUR FATHER TO ARREST MORE STONEMASONS BEFORE YOUR TOWER COLLAPSES...
SNOW! THE LORD COMMANDER WANTS TO SEE YOU.

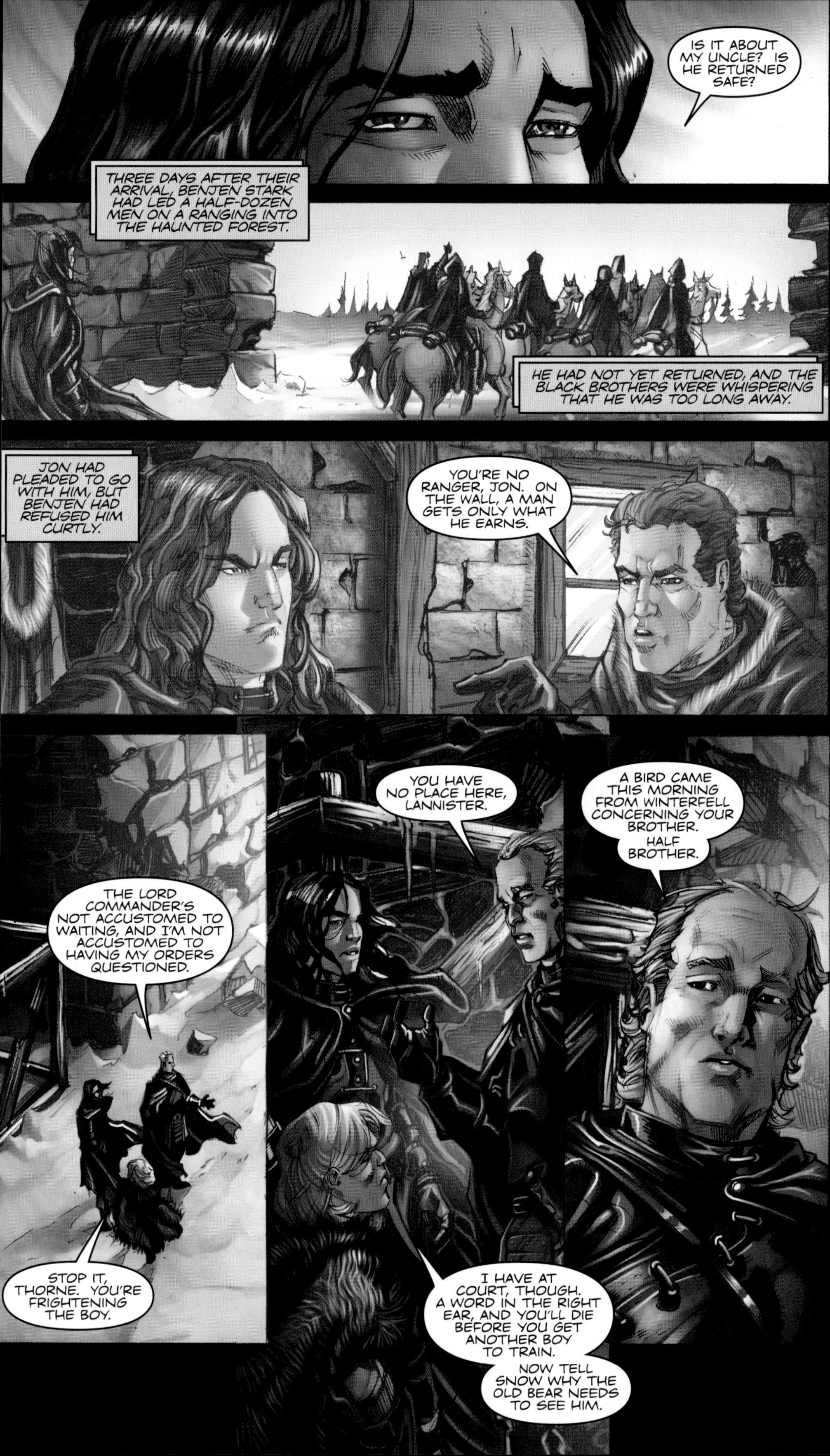
IS IT ABOUT MY UNCLE? IS HE RETURNED SAFE?
THREE DAYS AFTER THEIR ARRIVAL, BENJEN STARK HAD LED A HALF-DOZEN MEN ON A RANGING INTO THE HAUNTED FOREST.
HE HAD NOT YET RETURNED, AND THE BLACK BROTHERS WERE WHISPERING THAT HE WAS TOO LONG AWAY.
JON HAD PLEADED TO GO WITH HIM, BUT BENJEN HAD REFUSED HIM CURTLY.
YOU'RE NO RANGER, JON. ON THE WALL, A MAN GETS ONLY WHAT HE EARNS.
THE LORD COMMANDER'S NOT ACCUSTOMED TO WAITING, AND I'M NOT ACCUSTOMED TO HAVING MY ORDERS QUESTIONED.
STOP IT, THORNE. YOU'RE FRIGHTENING THE BOY.
YOU HAVE NO PLACE HERE, LANNISTER.
I HAVE AT COURT, THOUGH. A WORD IN THE RIGHT EAR, AND YOU'LL DIE BEFORE YOU GET ANOTHER BOY TO TRAIN.
NOW TELL SNOW WHY THE OLD BEAR NEEDS TO SEE HIM.
A BIRD CAME THIS MORNING FROM WINTERFELL CONCERNING YOUR BROTHER.
HALF BROTHER.

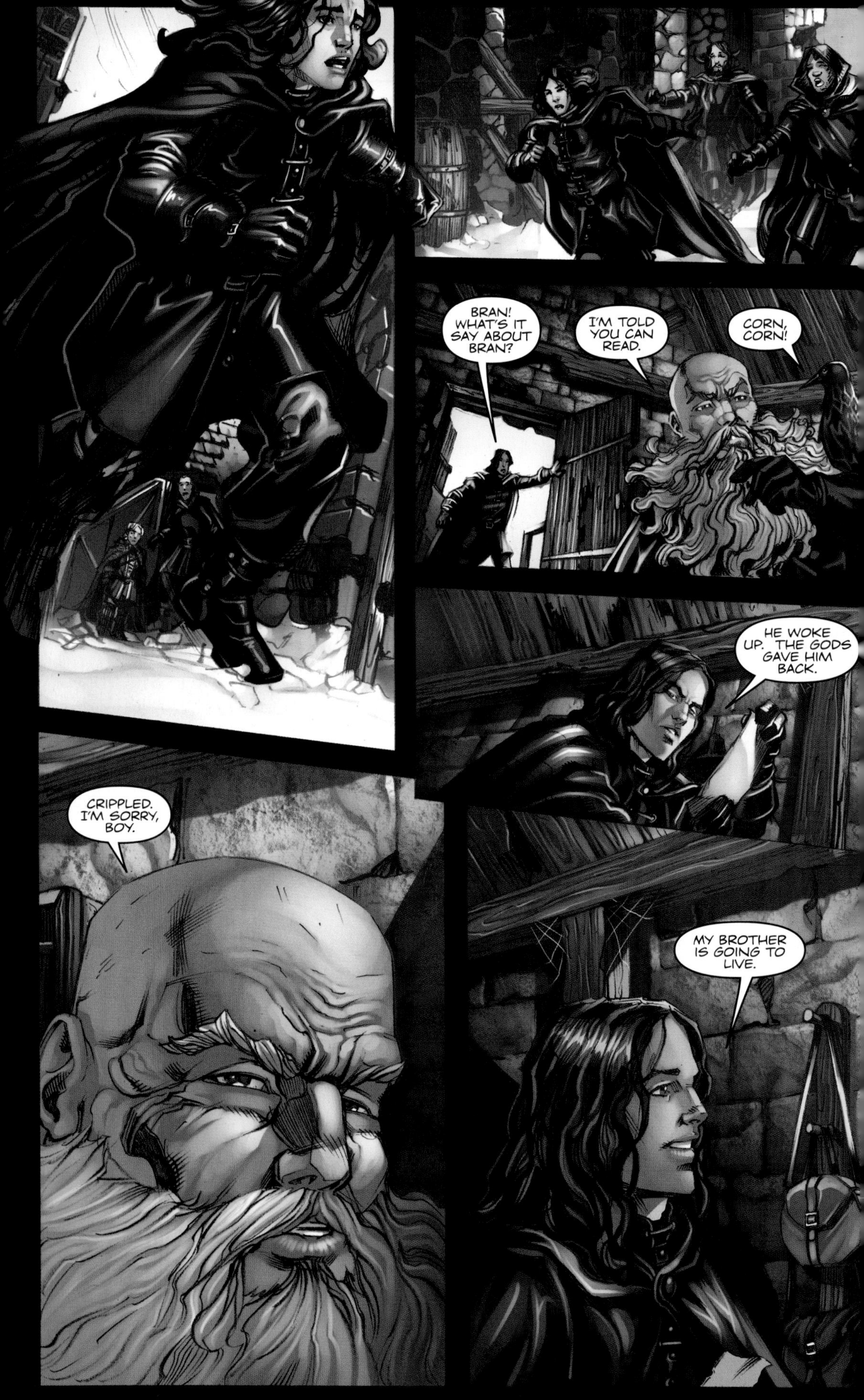
BRAN! WHAT'S IT SAY ABOUT BRAN?
I'M TOLD YOU CAN READ.
CORN, CORN!
HE WOKE UP. THE GODS GAVE HIM BACK.
CRIPPLED. I'M SORRY, BOY.
MY BROTHER IS GOING TO LIVE.

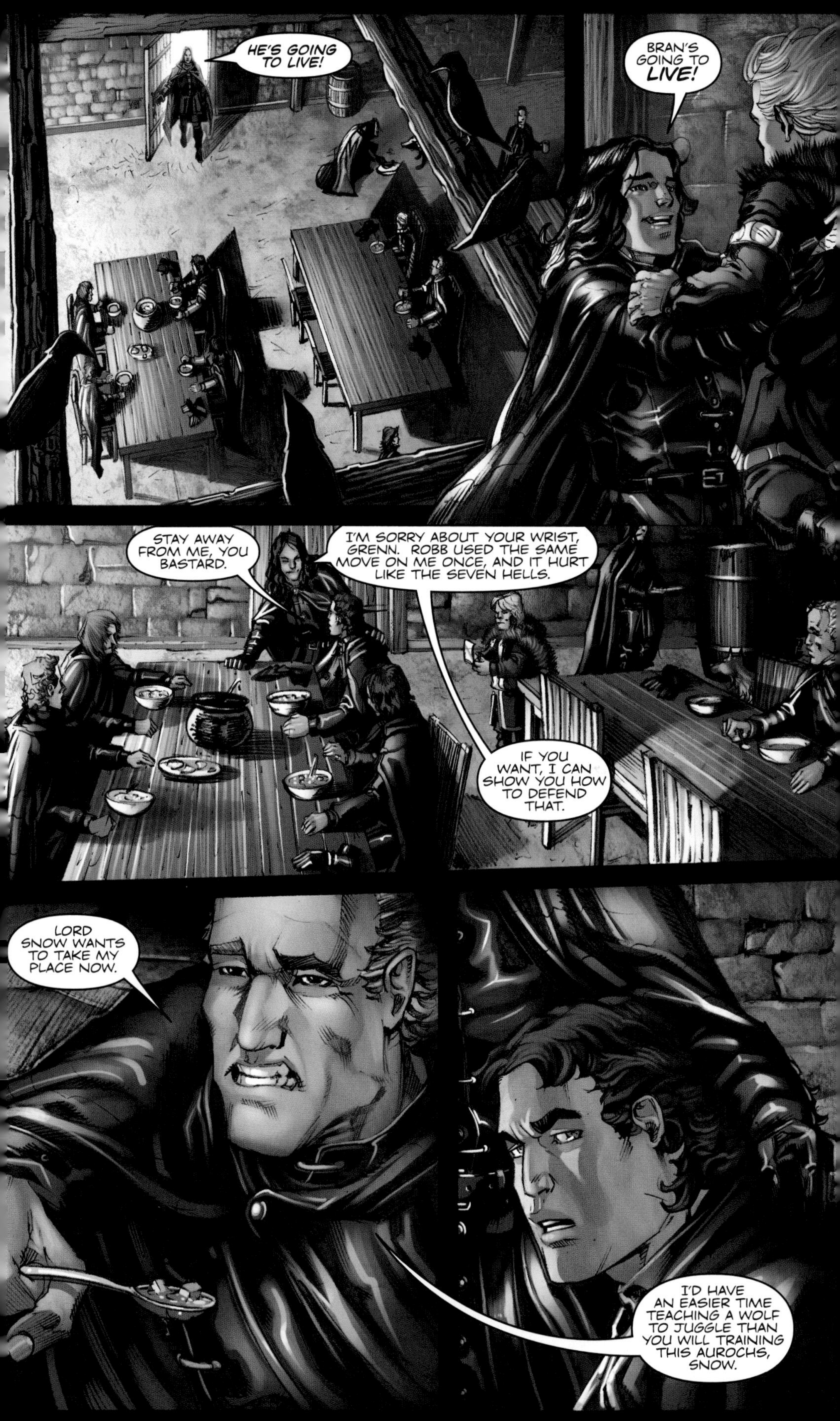
HE'S GOING TO LIVE!
BRAN'S GOING TO LIVE!
STAY AWAY FROM ME, YOU BASTARD.
I'M SORRY ABOUT YOUR WRIST, GRENN. ROBB USED THE SAME MOVE ON ME ONCE, AND IT HURT LIKE THE SEVEN HELLS.
IF YOU WANT, I CAN SHOW YOU HOW TO DEFEND THAT.
LORD SNOW WANTS TO TAKE MY PLACE NOW.
I'D HAVE AN EASIER TIME TEACHING A WOLF TO JUGGLE THAN YOU WILL TRAINING THIS AUROCHS, SNOW.

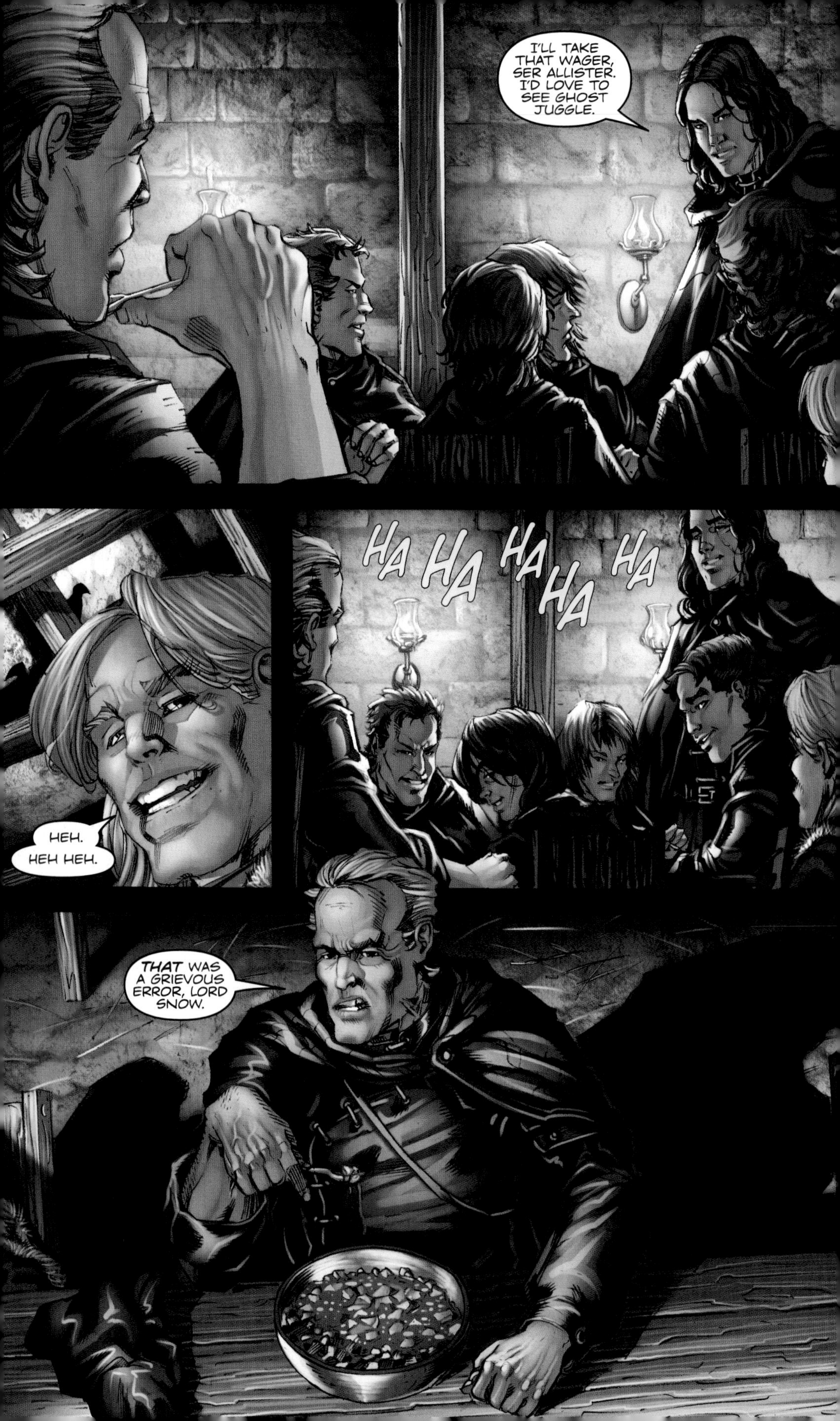
I'LL TAKE THAT WAGER, SER ALLISTER. I'D LOVE TO SEE GHOST JUGGLE.
HA HA HA HA HA
HEH. HEH HEH.
THAT WAS A GRIEVOUS ERROR, LORD SNOW.

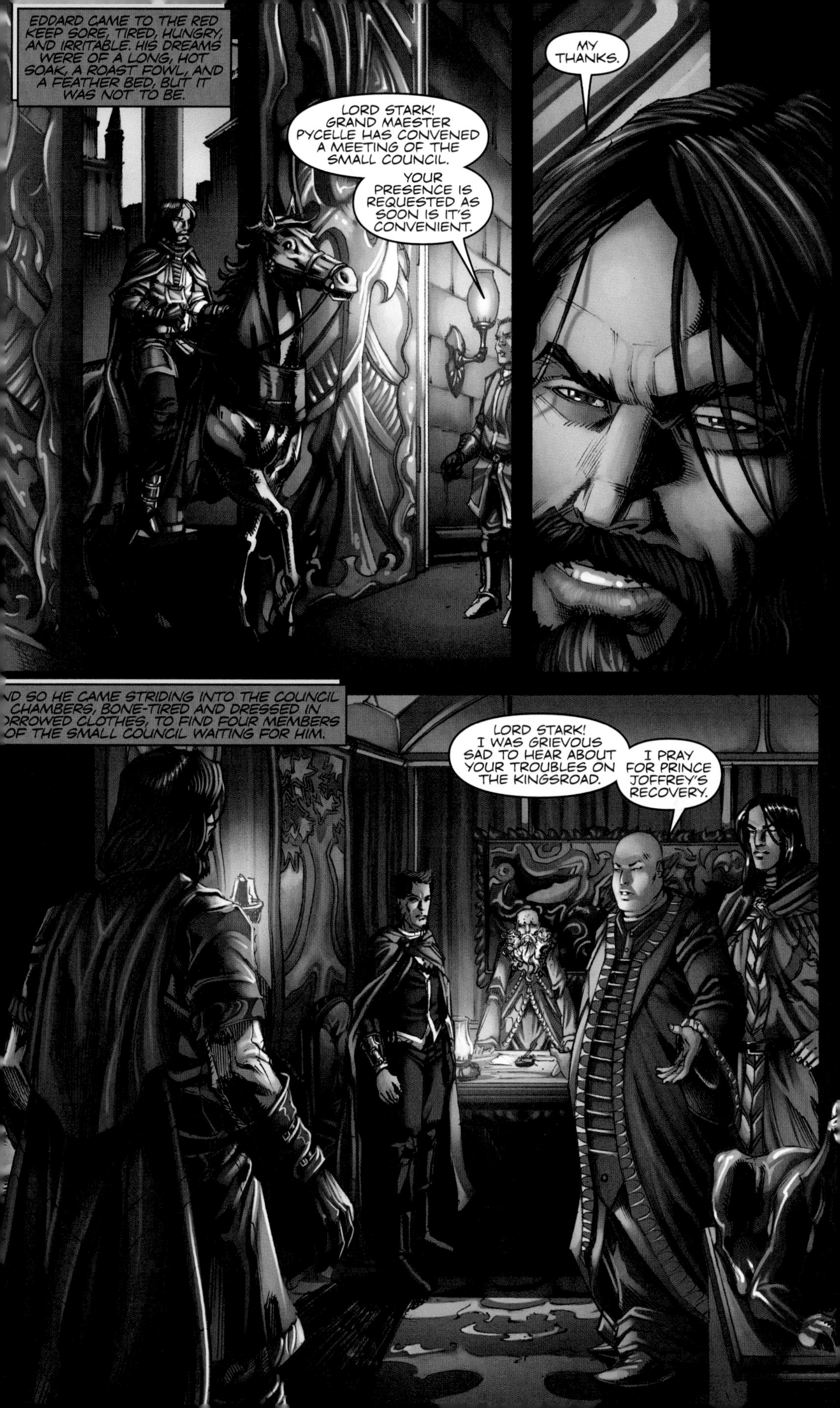
EDDARD CAME TO THE RED KEEP SORE, TIRED, HUNGRY, AND IRRITABLE. HIS DREAMS WERE OF A LONG, HOT SOAK, A ROAST FOWL, AND A FEATHER BED, BUT IT WAS NOT TO BE.
LORD STARK! GRAND MAESTER PYCELLE HAS CONVENED A MEETING OF THE SMALL COUNCIL.
YOUR PRESENCE IS REQUESTED AS SOON IS IT'S CONVENIENT.
MY THANKS.
ND SO HE CAME STRIDING INTO THE COUNCIL CHAMBERS, BONE-TIRED AND DRESSED IN ORROWED CLOTHES, TO FIND FOUR MEMBERS OF THE SMALL COUNCIL WAITING FOR HIM.
LORD STARK! I WAS GRIEVOUS SAD TO HEAR ABOUT YOUR TROUBLES ON THE KINGSROAD.
I PRAY FOR PRINCE JOFFREY'S RECOVERY.

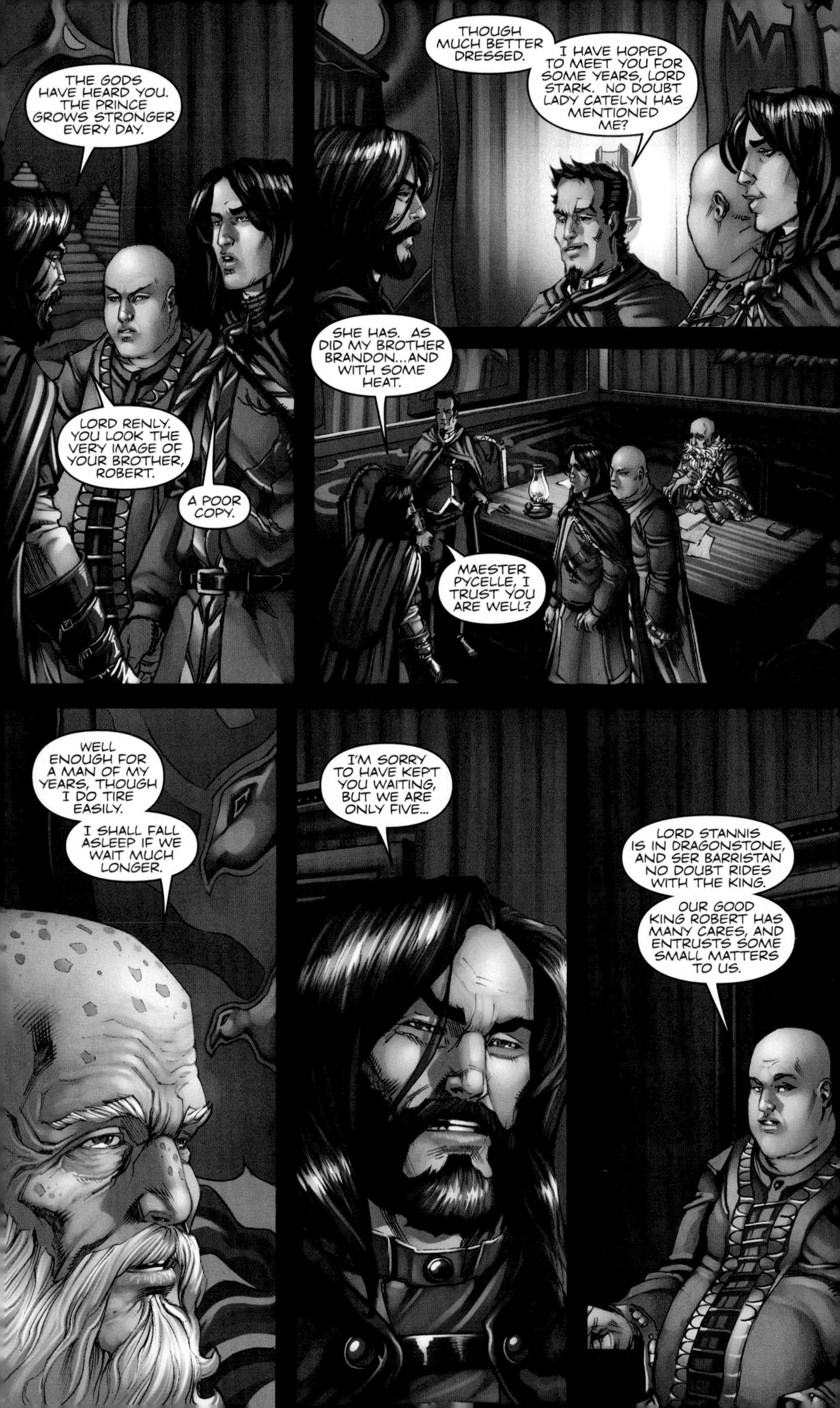
THE GODS HAVE HEARD YOU. THE PRINCE GROWS STRONGER EVERY DAY.
LORD RENLY. YOU LOOK THE VERY IMAGE OF YOUR BROTHER, ROBERT.
A POOR COPY.
THOUGH MUCH BETTER DRESSED.
I HAVE HOPED TO MEET YOU FOR SOME YEARS, LORD STARK. NO DOUBT LADY CATELYN HAS MENTIONED ME?
SHE HAS. AS DID MY BROTHER BRANDON...AND WITH SOME HEAT.
MAESTER PYCELLE, I TRUST YOU ARE WELL?
WELL ENOUGH FOR A MAN OF MY YEARS, THOUGH I DO TIRE EASILY.
I SHALL FALL ASLEEP IF WE WAIT MUCH LONGER.
I'M SORRY TO HAVE KEPT YOU WAITING, BUT WE ARE ONLY FIVE...
LORD STANNIS IS IN DRAGONSTONE, AND SER BARRISTAN NO DOUBT RIDES WITH THE KING.
OUR GOOD KING ROBERT HAS MANY CARES, AND ENTRUSTS SOME SMALL MATTERS TO US.

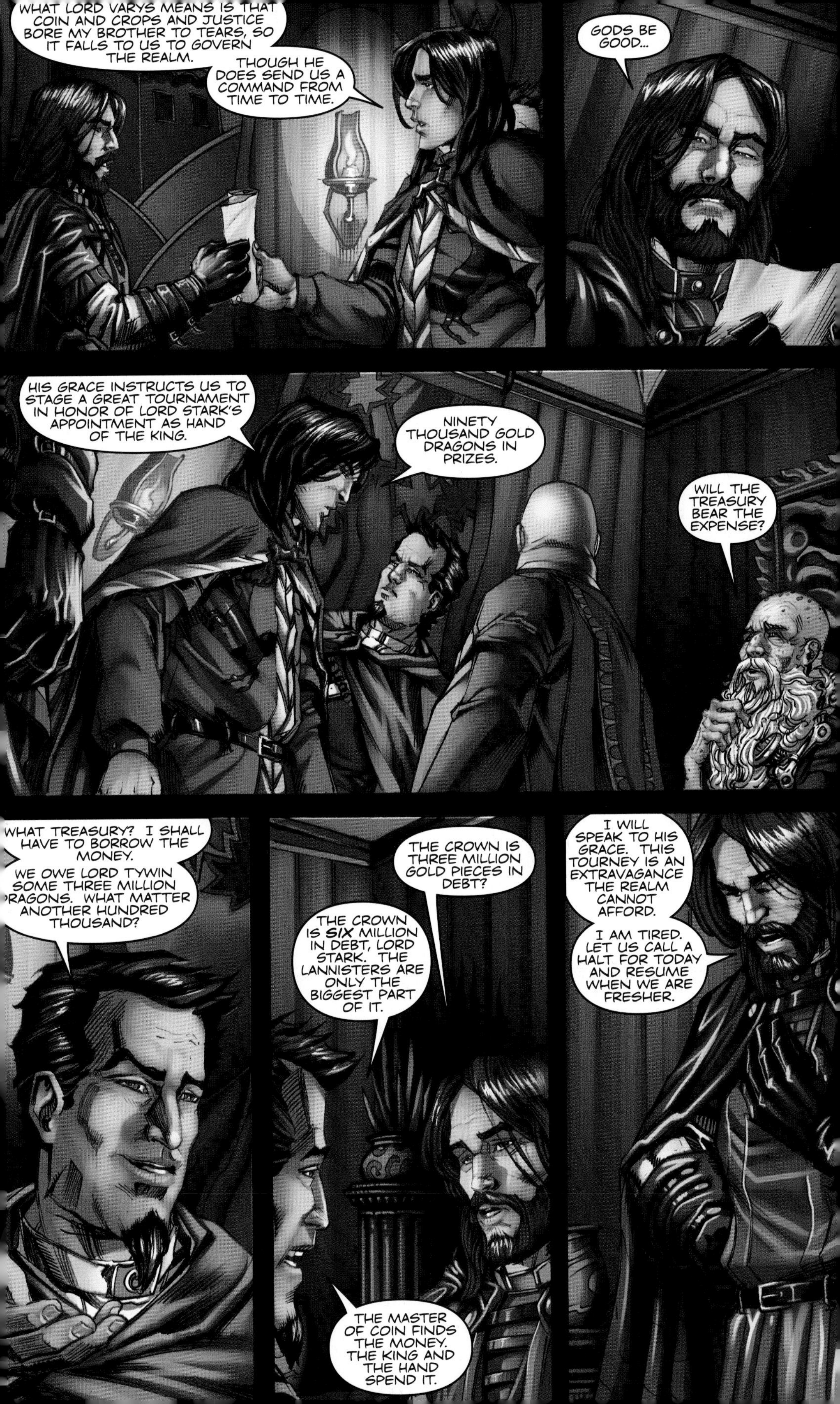
WHAT LORD VARYS MEANS IS THAT COIN AND CROPS AND JUSTICE BORE MY BROTHER TO TEARS, SO IT FALLS TO US TO GOVERN THE REALM.
THOUGH HE DOES SEND US A COMMAND FROM TIME TO TIME.
GODS BE GOOD...
HIS GRACE INSTRUCTS US TO STAGE A GREAT TOURNAMENT IN HONOR OF LORD STARK'S APPOINTMENT AS HAND OF THE KING.
NINETY THOUSAND GOLD DRAGONS IN PRIZES.
WILL THE TREASURY BEAR THE EXPENSE?
WHAT TREASURY? I SHALL HAVE TO BORROW THE MONEY.
WE OWE LORD TYWIN SOME THREE MILLION DRAGONS. WHAT MATTER ANOTHER HUNDRED THOUSAND?
THE CROWN IS THREE MILLION GOLD PIECES IN DEBT?
THE CROWN IS **SIX** MILLION IN DEBT, LORD STARK. THE LANNISTERS ARE ONLY THE BIGGEST PART OF IT.
THE MASTER OF COIN FINDS THE MONEY. THE KING AND THE HAND SPEND IT.
I WILL SPEAK TO HIS GRACE. THIS TOURNEY IS AN EXTRAVAGANCE THE REALM CANNOT AFFORD.
I AM TIRED. LET US CALL A HALT FOR TODAY AND RESUME WHEN WE ARE FRESHER.

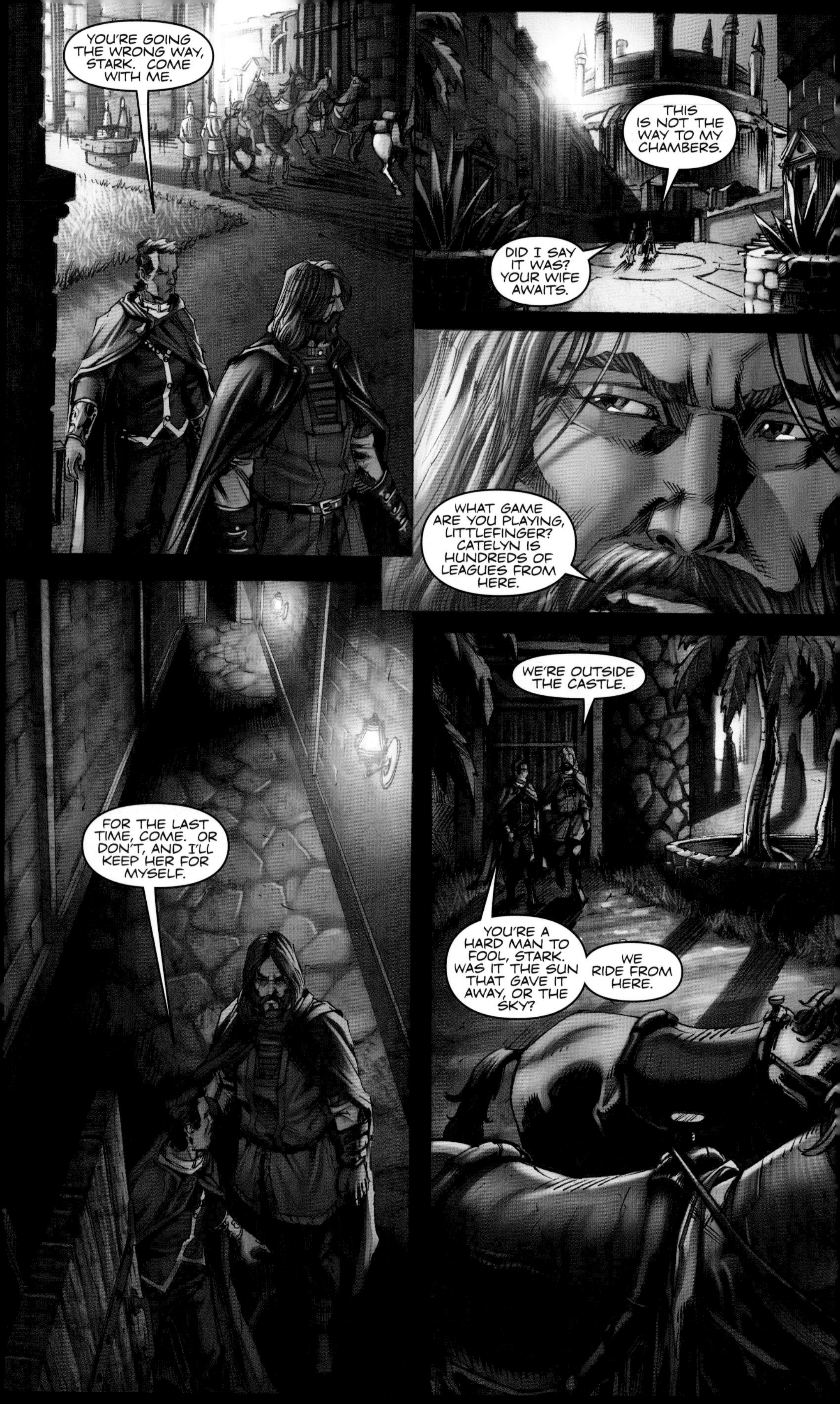
YOU'RE GOING THE WRONG WAY, STARK. COME WITH ME.
THIS IS NOT THE WAY TO MY CHAMBERS.
DID I SAY IT WAS? YOUR WIFE AWAITS.
WHAT GAME ARE YOU PLAYING, LITTLEFINGER? CATELYN IS HUNDREDS OF LEAGUES FROM HERE.
FOR THE LAST TIME, COME. OR DON'T, AND I'LL KEEP HER FOR MYSELF.
WE'RE OUTSIDE THE CASTLE.
YOU'RE A HARD MAN TO FOOL, STARK. WAS IT THE SUN THAT GAVE IT AWAY, OR THE SKY?
WE RIDE FROM HERE.

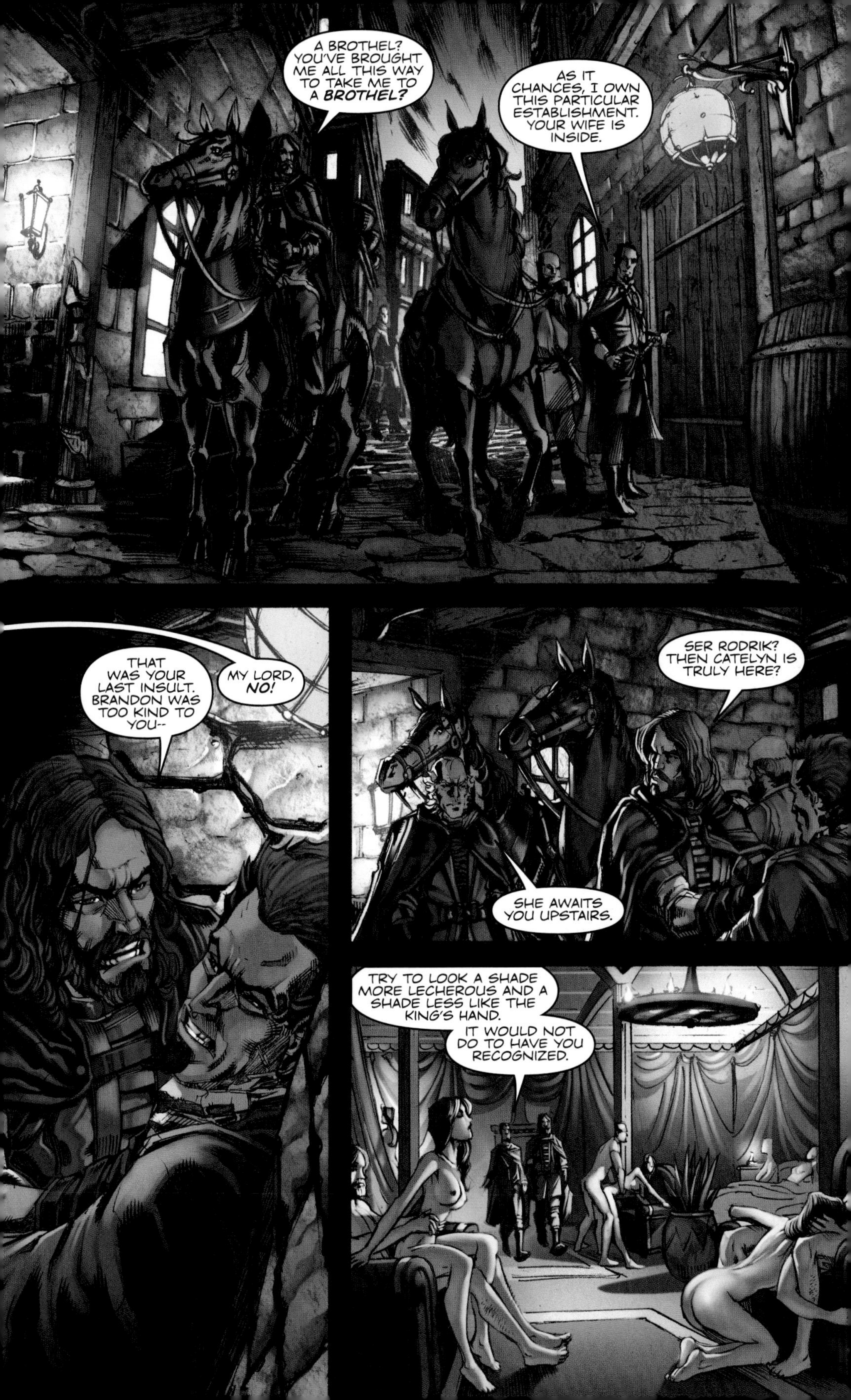
A BROTHEL? YOU'VE BROUGHT ME ALL THIS WAY TO TAKE ME TO A **BROTHEL?**
AS IT CHANCES, I OWN THIS PARTICULAR ESTABLISHMENT. YOUR WIFE IS INSIDE.
THAT WAS YOUR LAST INSULT. BRANDON WAS TOO KIND TO YOU--
MY LORD, **NO!**
SER RODRIK? THEN CATELYN IS TRULY HERE?
SHE AWAITS YOU UPSTAIRS.
TRY TO LOOK A SHADE MORE LECHEROUS AND A SHADE LESS LIKE THE KING'S HAND.
IT WOULD NOT DO TO HAVE YOU RECOGNIZED.

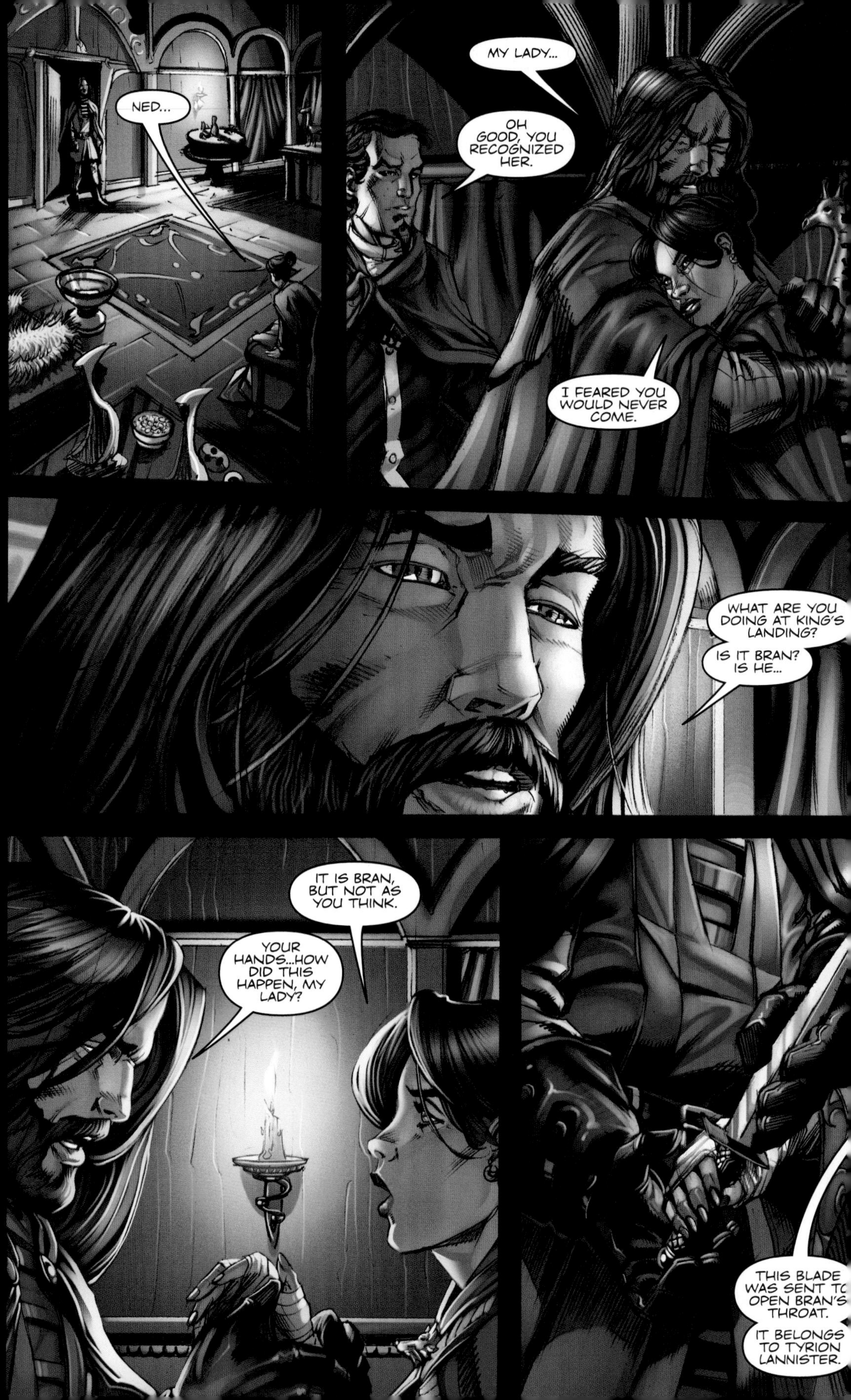
NED...
MY LADY...
OH GOOD, YOU RECOGNIZED HER.
I FEARED YOU WOULD NEVER COME.
WHAT ARE YOU DOING AT KING'S LANDING?
IS IT BRAN? IS HE...
IT IS BRAN, BUT NOT AS YOU THINK.
YOUR HANDS...HOW DID THIS HAPPEN, MY LADY?
THIS BLADE WAS SENT TO OPEN BRAN'S THROAT.
IT BELONGS TO TYRION LANNISTER.

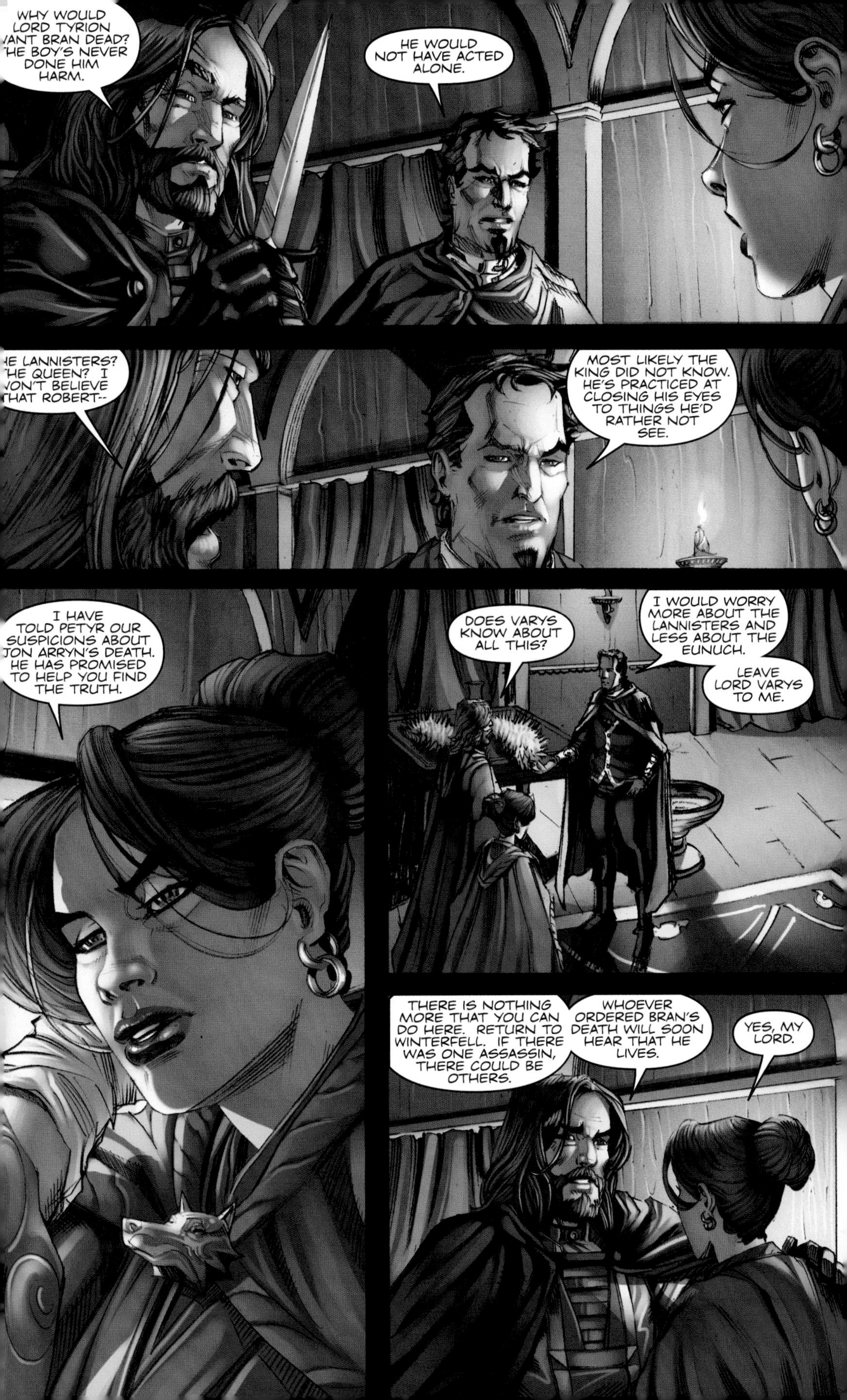
WHY WOULD LORD TYRION ANT BRAN DEAD? HE BOY'S NEVER DONE HIM HARM.
HE WOULD NOT HAVE ACTED ALONE.
HE LANNISTERS? HE QUEEN? I ON'T BELIEVE HAT ROBERT--
MOST LIKELY THE KING DID NOT KNOW. HE'S PRACTICED AT CLOSING HIS EYES TO THINGS HE'D RATHER NOT SEE.
I HAVE TOLD PETYR OUR SUSPICIONS ABOUT JON ARRYN'S DEATH. HE HAS PROMISED TO HELP YOU FIND THE TRUTH.
DOES VARYS KNOW ABOUT ALL THIS?
I WOULD WORRY MORE ABOUT THE LANNISTERS AND LESS ABOUT THE EUNUCH.
LEAVE LORD VARYS TO ME.
THERE IS NOTHING MORE THAT YOU CAN DO HERE. RETURN TO WINTERFELL. IF THERE WAS ONE ASSASSIN, THERE COULD BE OTHERS.
WHOEVER ORDERED BRAN'S DEATH WILL SOON HEAR THAT HE LIVES.
YES, MY LORD.

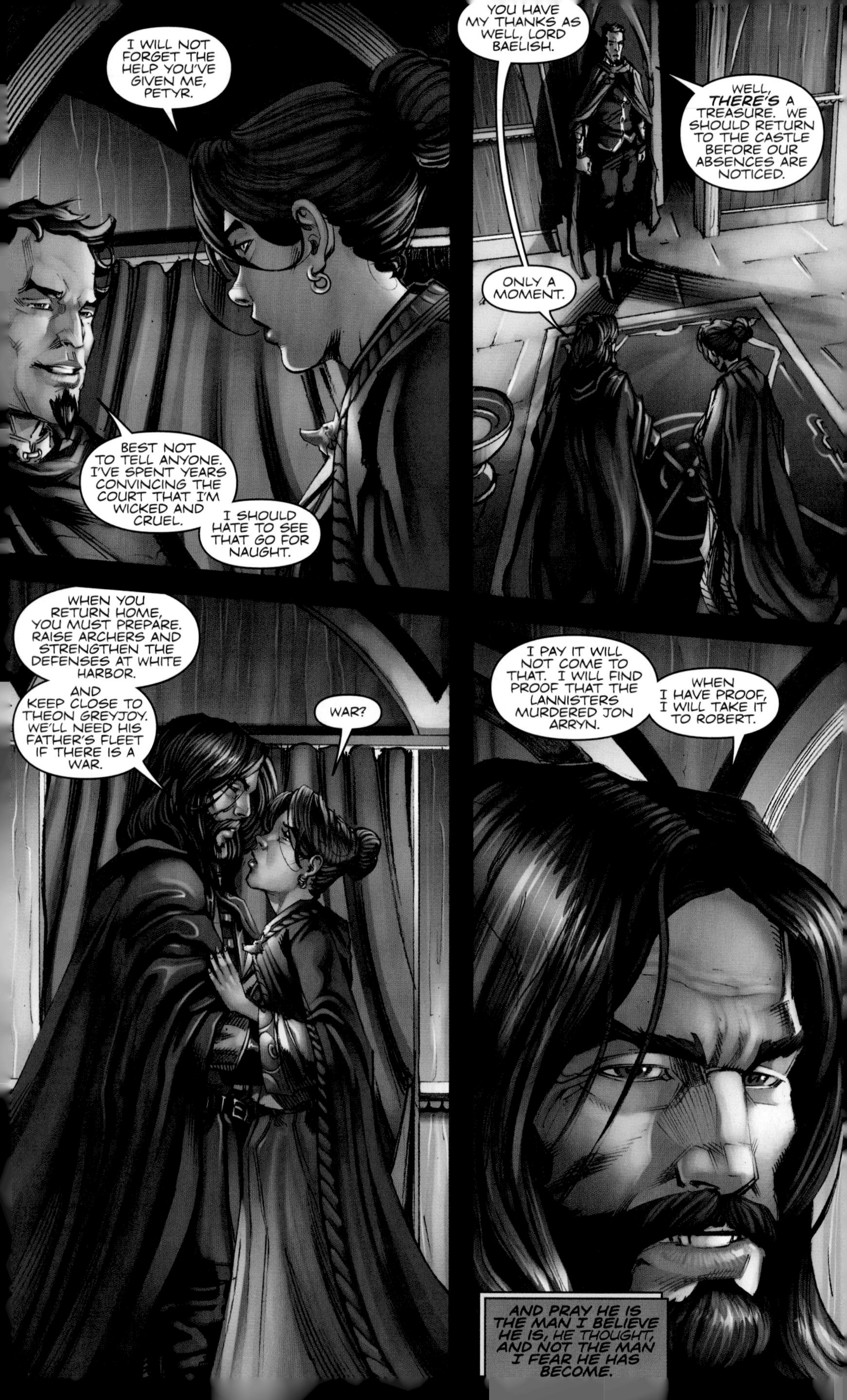
I WILL NOT FORGET THE HELP YOU'VE GIVEN ME, PETYR.
BEST NOT TO TELL ANYONE. I'VE SPENT YEARS CONVINCING THE COURT THAT I'M WICKED AND CRUEL.
I SHOULD HATE TO SEE THAT GO FOR NAUGHT.
YOU HAVE MY THANKS AS WELL, LORD BAELISH.
WELL, *THERE'S* A TREASURE. WE SHOULD RETURN TO THE CASTLE BEFORE OUR ABSENCES ARE NOTICED.
ONLY A MOMENT.
WHEN YOU RETURN HOME, YOU MUST PREPARE. RAISE ARCHERS AND STRENGTHEN THE DEFENSES AT WHITE HARBOR.
AND KEEP CLOSE TO THEON GREYJOY. WE'LL NEED HIS FATHER'S FLEET IF THERE IS A WAR.
WAR?
I PAY IT WILL NOT COME TO THAT. I WILL FIND PROOF THAT THE LANNISTERS MURDERED JON ARRYN.
WHEN I HAVE PROOF, I WILL TAKE IT TO ROBERT.
AND PRAY HE IS THE MAN I BELIEVE HE IS, HE THOUGHT, AND NOT THE MAN I FEAR HE HAS BECOME.

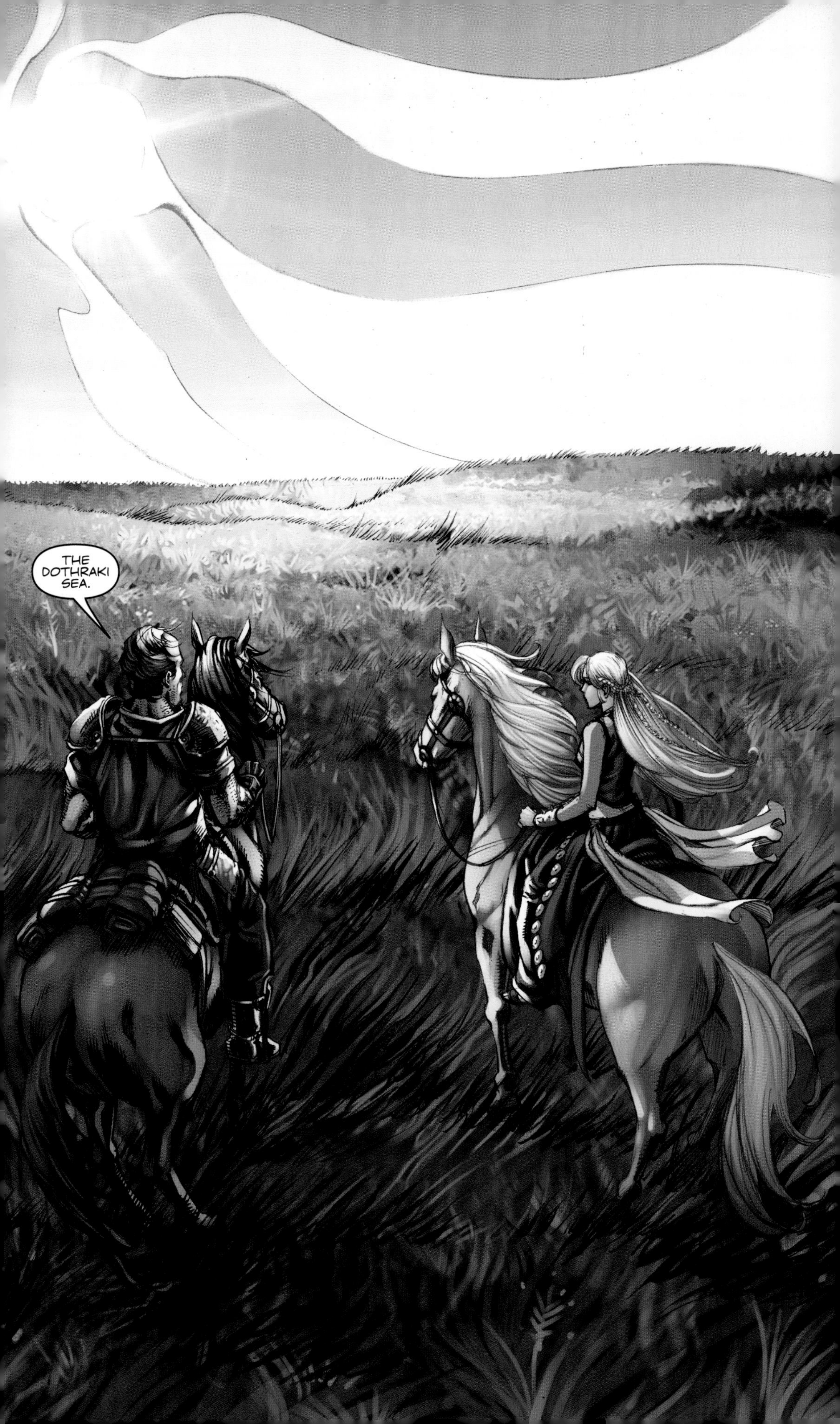
THE DOTHRAKI SEA.

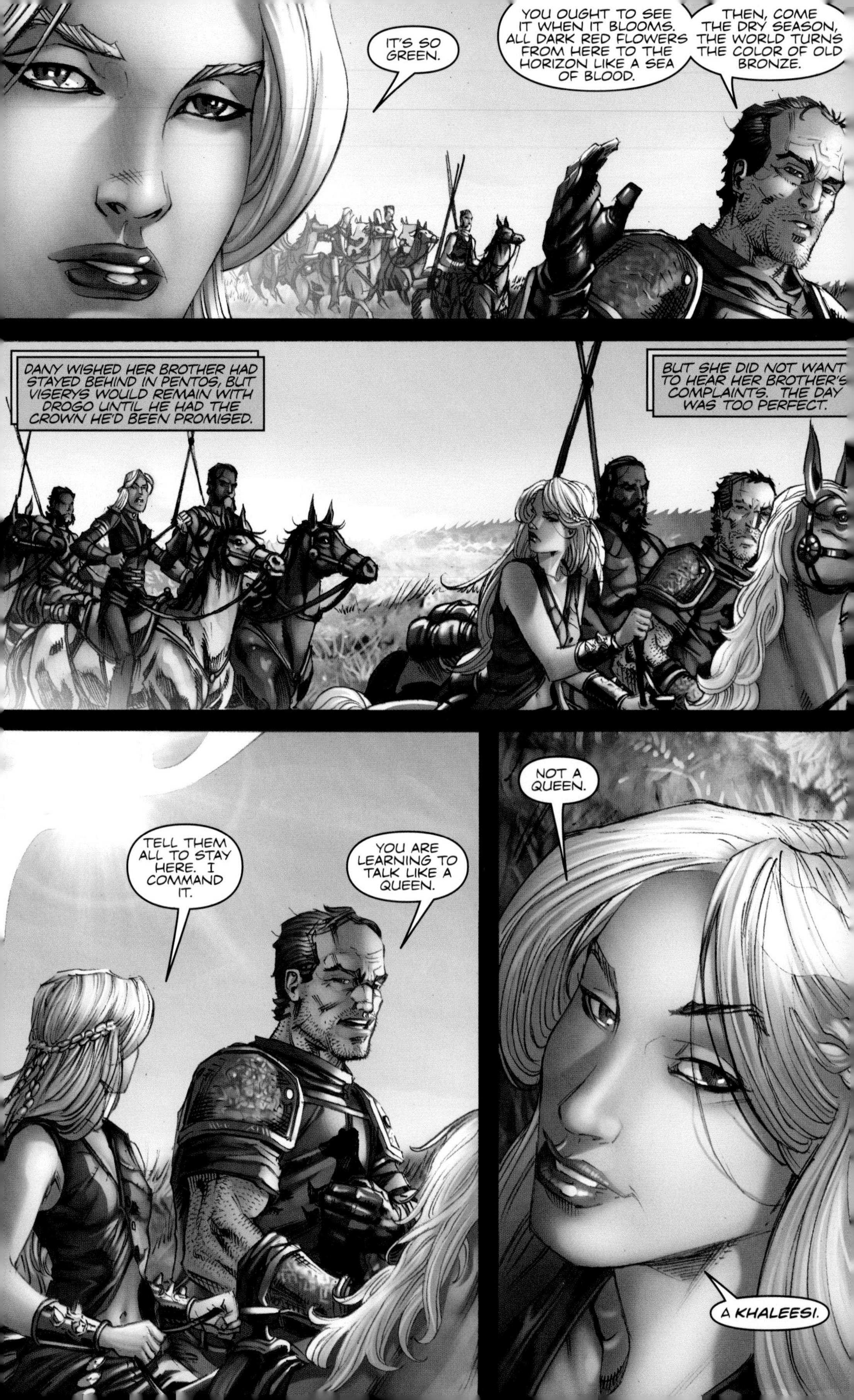
IT'S SO GREEN.
YOU OUGHT TO SEE IT WHEN IT BLOOMS. ALL DARK RED FLOWERS FROM HERE TO THE HORIZON LIKE A SEA OF BLOOD.
THEN, COME THE DRY SEASON, THE WORLD TURNS THE COLOR OF OLD BRONZE.
DANY WISHED HER BROTHER HAD STAYED BEHIND IN PENTOS, BUT VISERYS WOULD REMAIN WITH DROGO UNTIL HE HAD THE CROWN HE'D BEEN PROMISED.
BUT SHE DID NOT WANT TO HEAR HER BROTHER'S COMPLAINTS. THE DAY WAS TOO PERFECT.
TELL THEM ALL TO STAY HERE. I COMMAND IT.
YOU ARE LEARNING TO TALK LIKE A QUEEN.
NOT A QUEEN.
A KHALEESI.

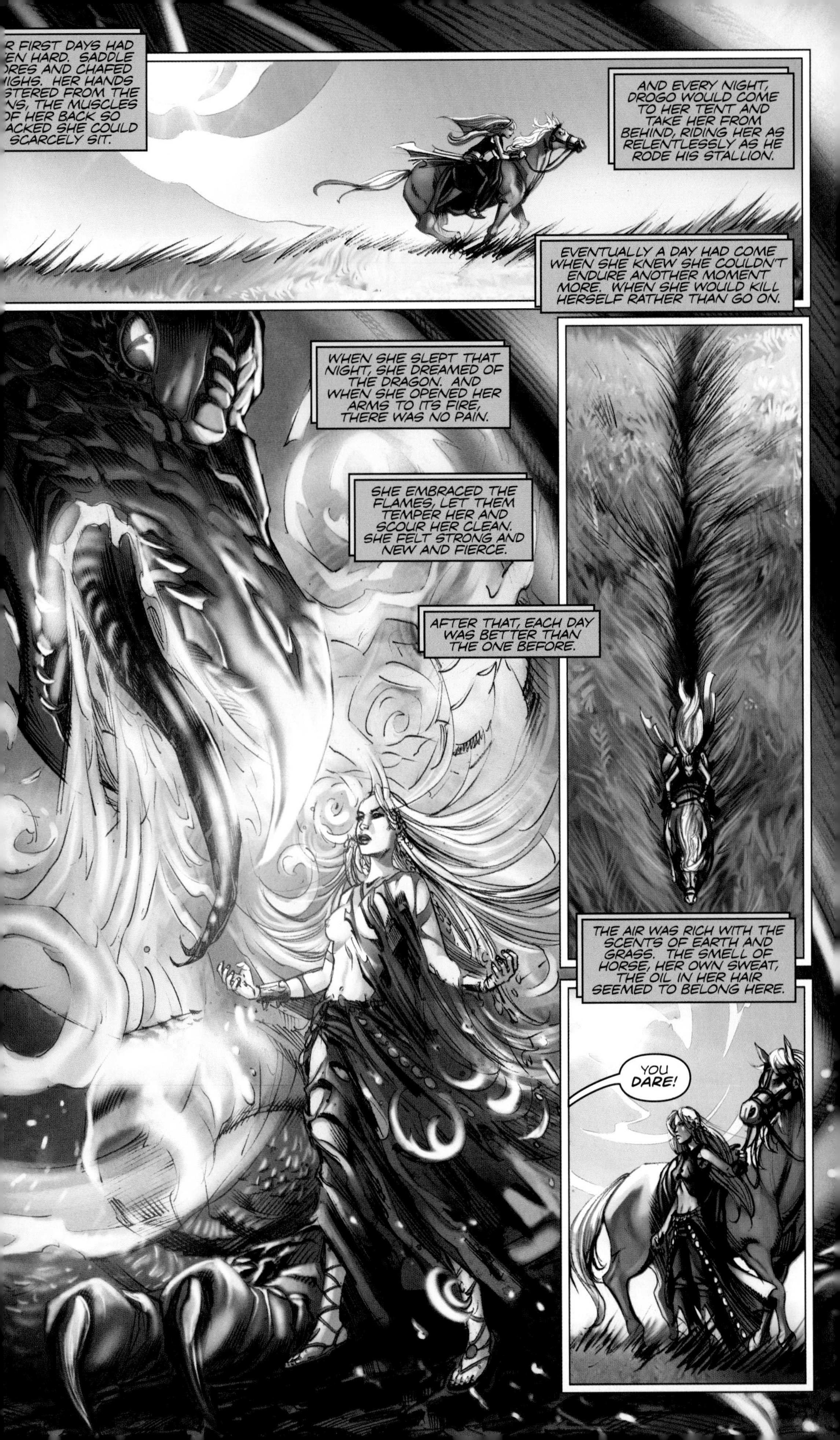

R FIRST DAYS HAD EN HARD. SADDLE ORES AND CHAFED IGHS. HER HANDS STERED FROM THE NS, THE MUSCLES OF HER BACK SO ACKED SHE COULD SCARCELY SIT.
AND EVERY NIGHT, DROGO WOULD COME TO HER TENT AND TAKE HER FROM BEHIND, RIDING HER AS RELENTLESSLY AS HE RODE HIS STALLION.
EVENTUALLY A DAY HAD COME WHEN SHE KNEW SHE COULDN'T ENDURE ANOTHER MOMENT MORE. WHEN SHE WOULD KILL HERSELF RATHER THAN GO ON.
WHEN SHE SLEPT THAT NIGHT, SHE DREAMED OF THE DRAGON. AND WHEN SHE OPENED HER ARMS TO ITS FIRE, THERE WAS NO PAIN.
SHE EMBRACED THE FLAMES, LET THEM TEMPER HER AND SCOUR HER CLEAN. SHE FELT STRONG AND NEW AND FIERCE.
AFTER THAT, EACH DAY WAS BETTER THAN THE ONE BEFORE.
THE AIR WAS RICH WITH THE SCENTS OF EARTH AND GRASS. THE SMELL OF HORSE, HER OWN SWEAT, THE OIL IN HER HAIR SEEMED TO BELONG HERE.
YOU **DARE!**

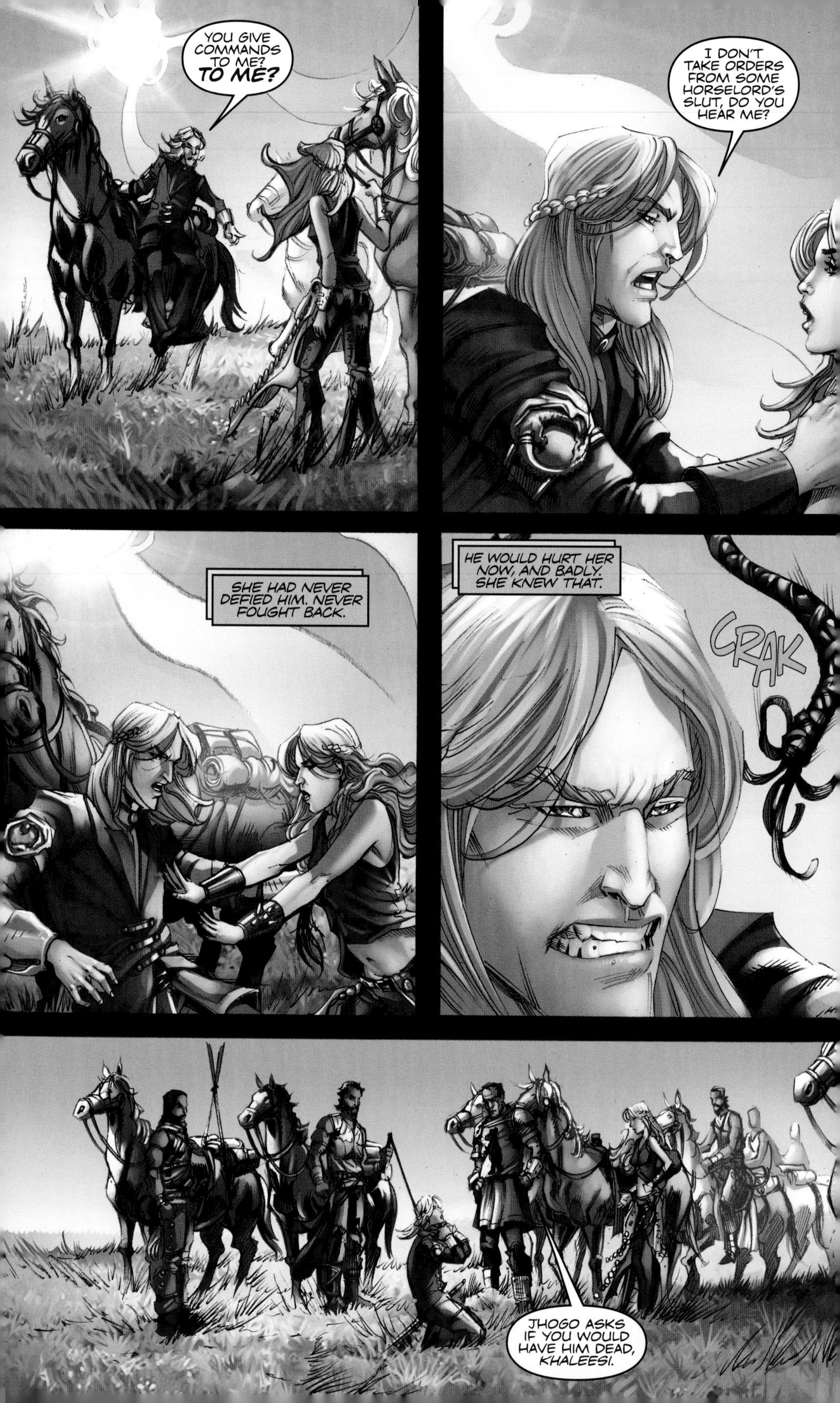
YOU GIVE COMMANDS TO ME? TO ME?
I DON'T TAKE ORDERS FROM SOME HORSELORD'S SLUT, DO YOU HEAR ME?
SHE HAD NEVER DEFIED HIM. NEVER FOUGHT BACK.
HE WOULD HURT HER NOW, AND BADLY. SHE KNEW THAT.
CRAK
JHOGO ASKS IF YOU WOULD HAVE HIM DEAD, KHALEESI.

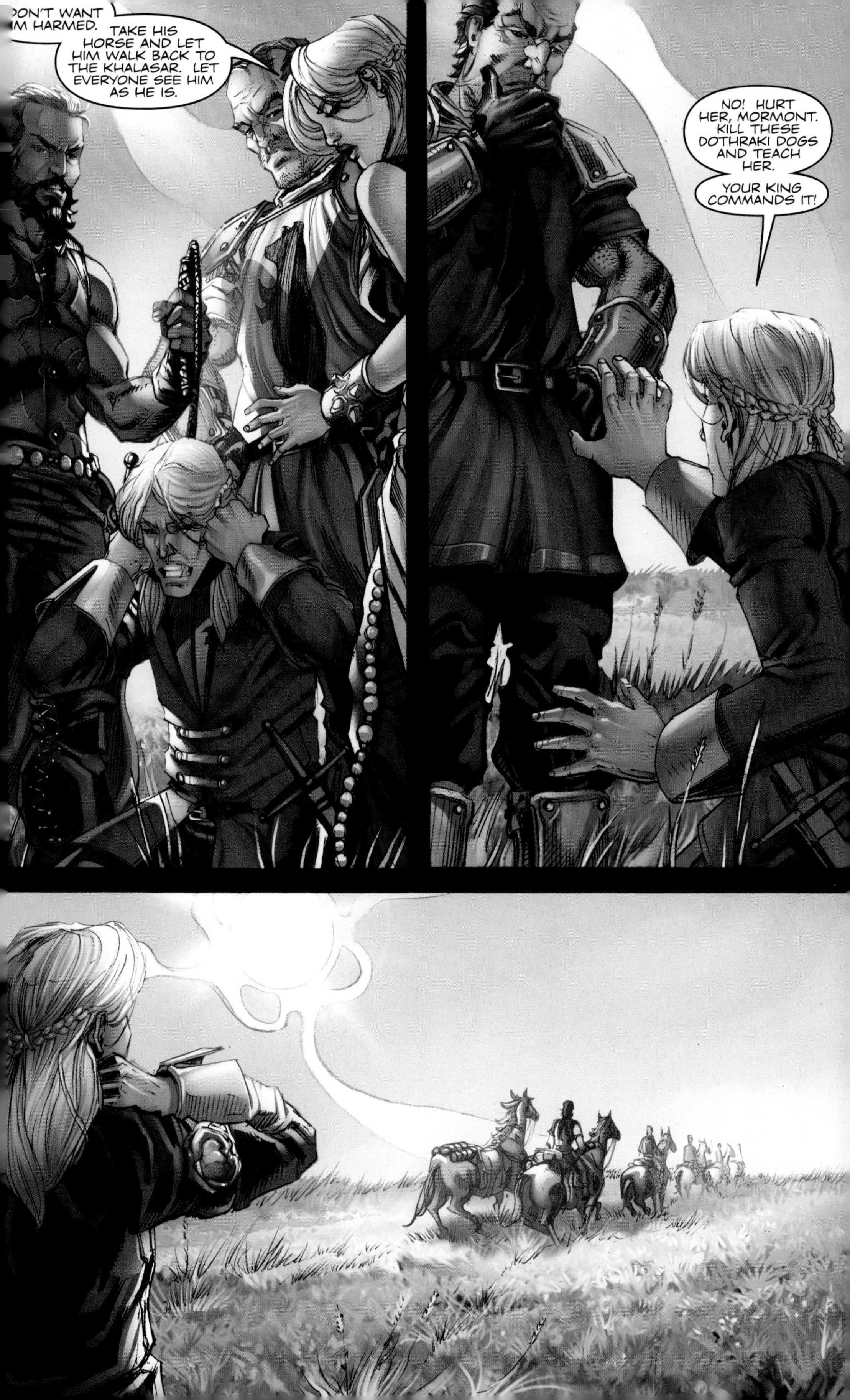
DON'T WANT
IM HARMED.
TAKE HIS HORSE AND LET HIM WALK BACK TO THE KHALASAR. LET EVERYONE SEE HIM AS HE IS.
NO! HURT HER, MORMONT. KILL THESE DOTHRAKI DOGS AND TEACH HER.
YOUR KING COMMANDS IT!

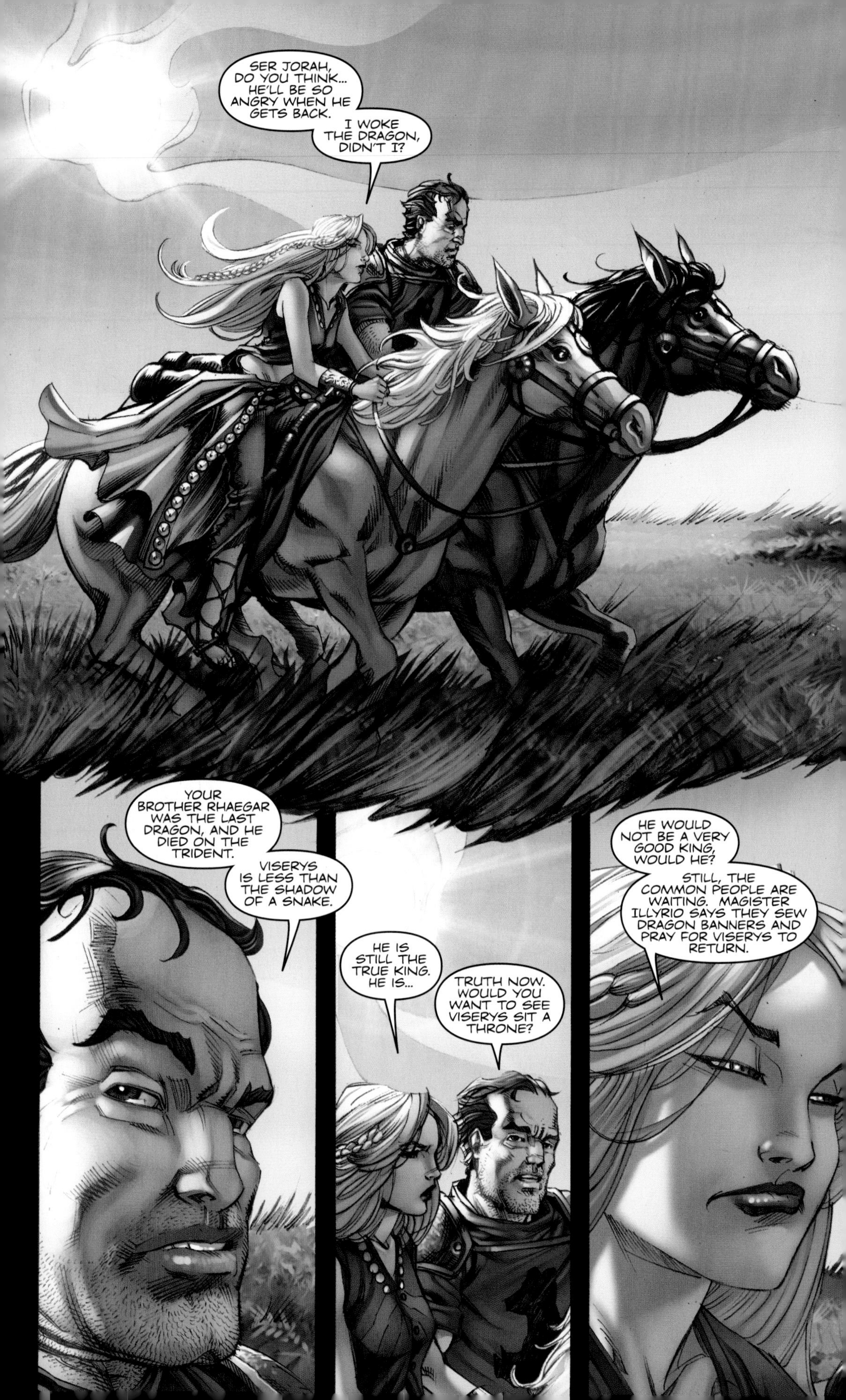
SER JORAH, DO YOU THINK... HE'LL BE SO ANGRY WHEN HE GETS BACK.
I WOKE THE DRAGON, DIDN'T I?
YOUR BROTHER RHAEGAR WAS THE LAST DRAGON, AND HE DIED ON THE TRIDENT.
VISERYS IS LESS THAN THE SHADOW OF A SNAKE.
HE IS STILL THE TRUE KING. HE IS...
TRUTH NOW. WOULD YOU WANT TO SEE VISERYS SIT A THRONE?
HE WOULD NOT BE A VERY GOOD KING, WOULD HE?
STILL, THE COMMON PEOPLE ARE WAITING. MAGISTER ILLYRIO SAYS THEY SEW DRAGON BANNERS AND PRAY FOR VISERYS TO RETURN.

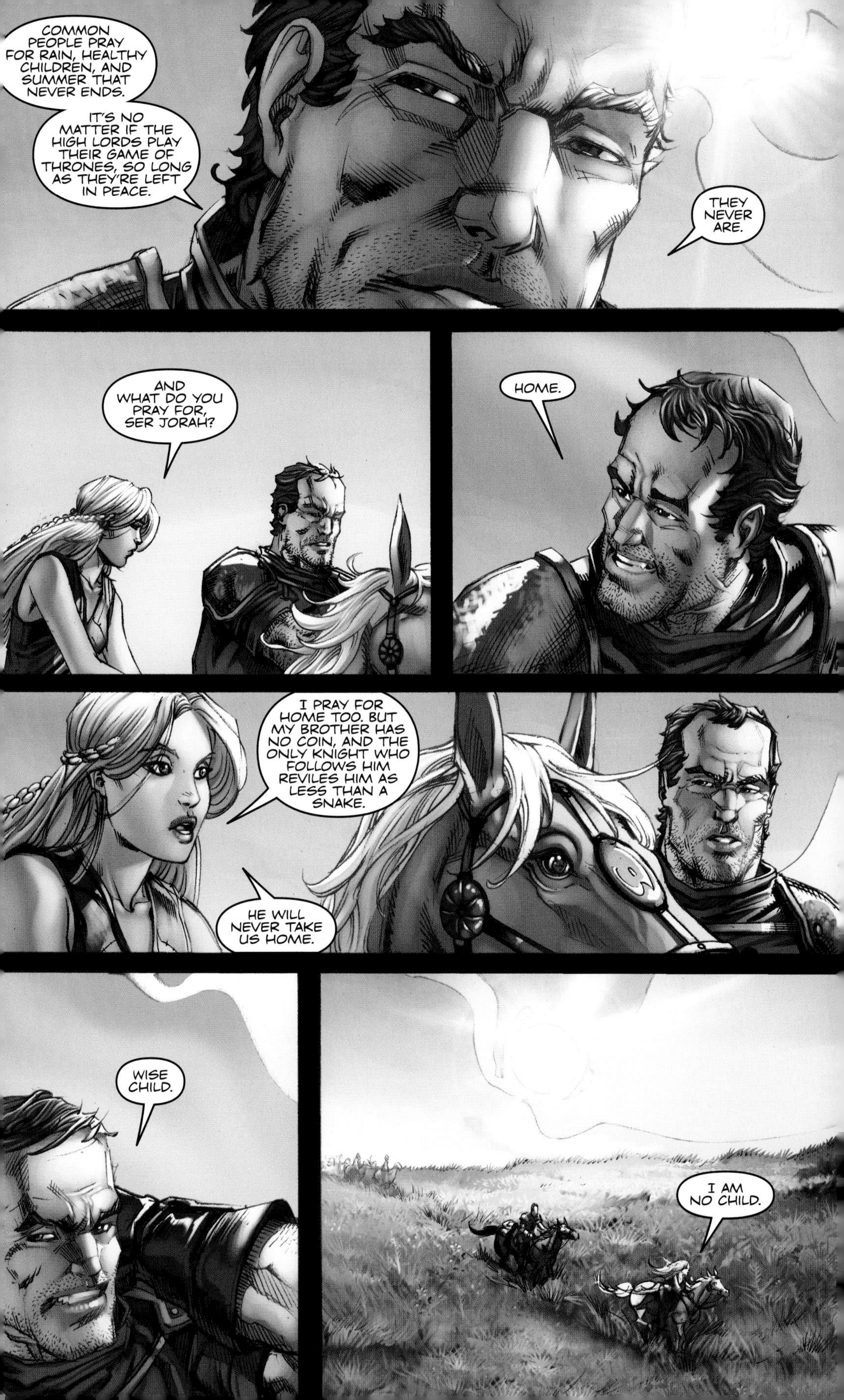
COMMON PEOPLE PRAY FOR RAIN, HEALTHY CHILDREN, AND SUMMER THAT NEVER ENDS.
IT'S NO MATTER IF THE HIGH LORDS PLAY THEIR GAME OF THRONES, SO LONG AS THEY'RE LEFT IN PEACE.
THEY NEVER ARE.
AND WHAT DO YOU PRAY FOR, SER JORAH?
HOME.
I PRAY FOR HOME TOO. BUT MY BROTHER HAS NO COIN, AND THE ONLY KNIGHT WHO FOLLOWS HIM REVILES HIM AS LESS THAN A SNAKE.
HE WILL NEVER TAKE US HOME.
WISE CHILD.
I AM NO CHILD.

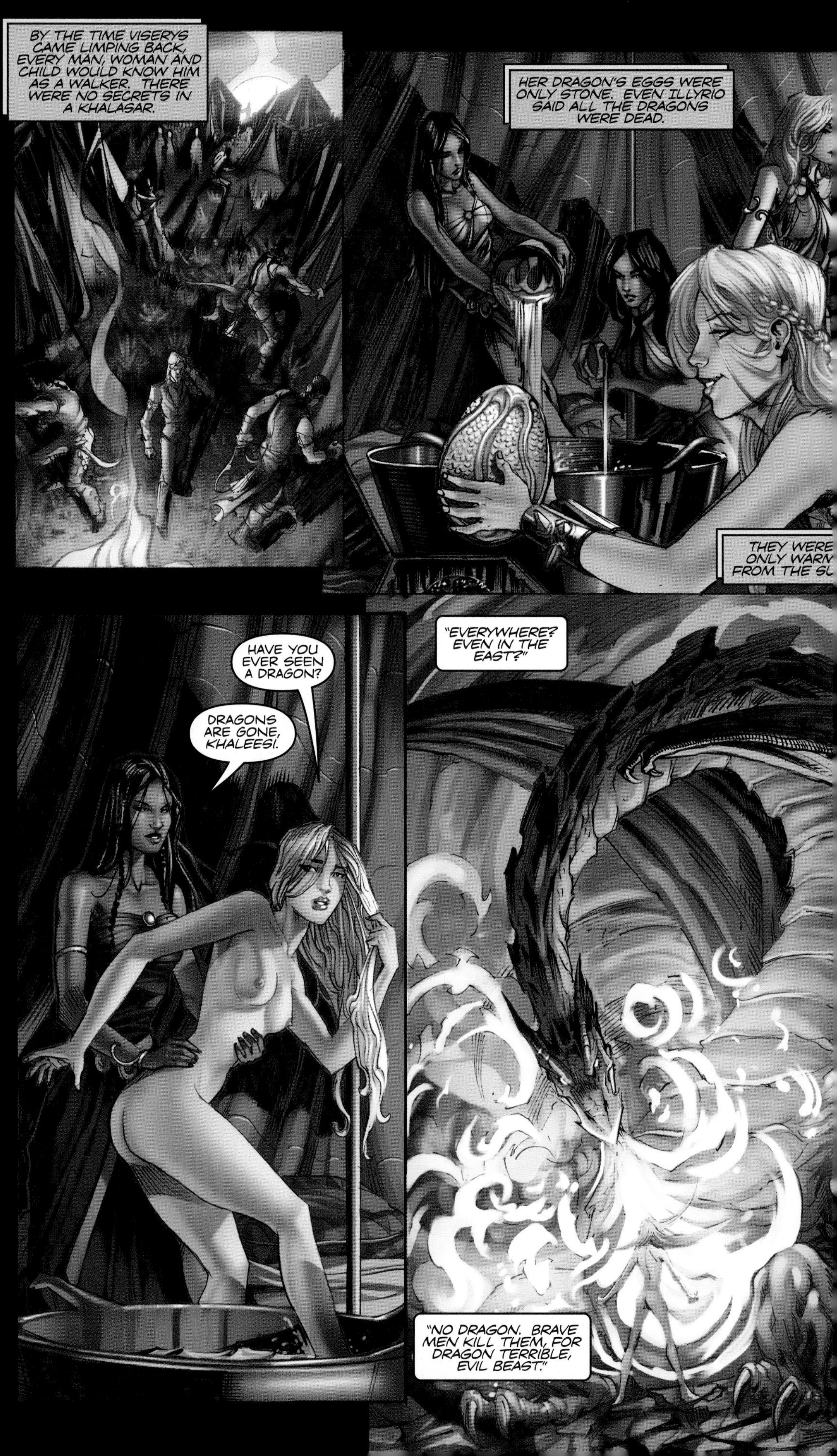
BY THE TIME VISERYS CAME LIMPING BACK, EVERY MAN, WOMAN AND CHILD WOULD KNOW HIM AS A WALKER. THERE WERE NO SECRETS IN A KHALASAR.
HER DRAGON'S EGGS WERE ONLY STONE. EVEN ILLYRIO SAID ALL THE DRAGONS WERE DEAD.
THEY WERE ONLY WARM FROM THE SU
HAVE YOU EVER SEEN A DRAGON?
DRAGONS ARE GONE, KHALEESI.
"EVERYWHERE? EVEN IN THE EAST?"
"NO DRAGON. BRAVE MEN KILL THEM, FOR DRAGON TERRIBLE, EVIL BEAST."

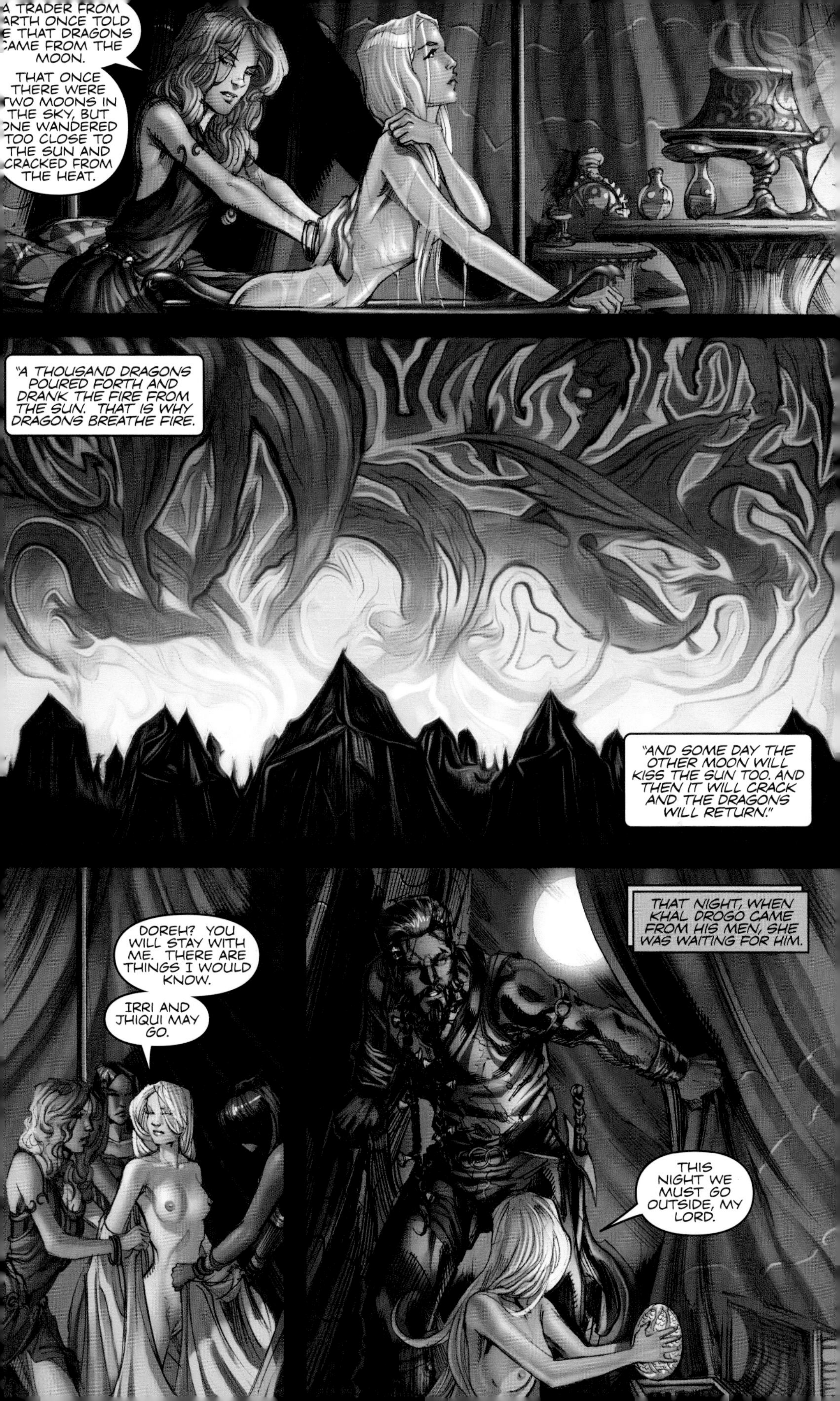
A TRADER FROM ARTH ONCE TOLD E THAT DRAGONS CAME FROM THE MOON.
THAT ONCE THERE WERE TWO MOONS IN THE SKY, BUT ONE WANDERED TOO CLOSE TO THE SUN AND CRACKED FROM THE HEAT.
"A THOUSAND DRAGONS POURED FORTH AND DRANK THE FIRE FROM THE SUN. THAT IS WHY DRAGONS BREATHE FIRE.
"AND SOME DAY THE OTHER MOON WILL KISS THE SUN TOO. AND THEN IT WILL CRACK AND THE DRAGONS WILL RETURN."
DOREH? YOU WILL STAY WITH ME. THERE ARE THINGS I WOULD KNOW.
IRRI AND JHIQUI MAY GO.
THAT NIGHT, WHEN KHAL DROGO CAME FROM HIS MEN, SHE WAS WAITING FOR HIM.
THIS NIGHT WE MUST GO OUTSIDE, MY LORD.

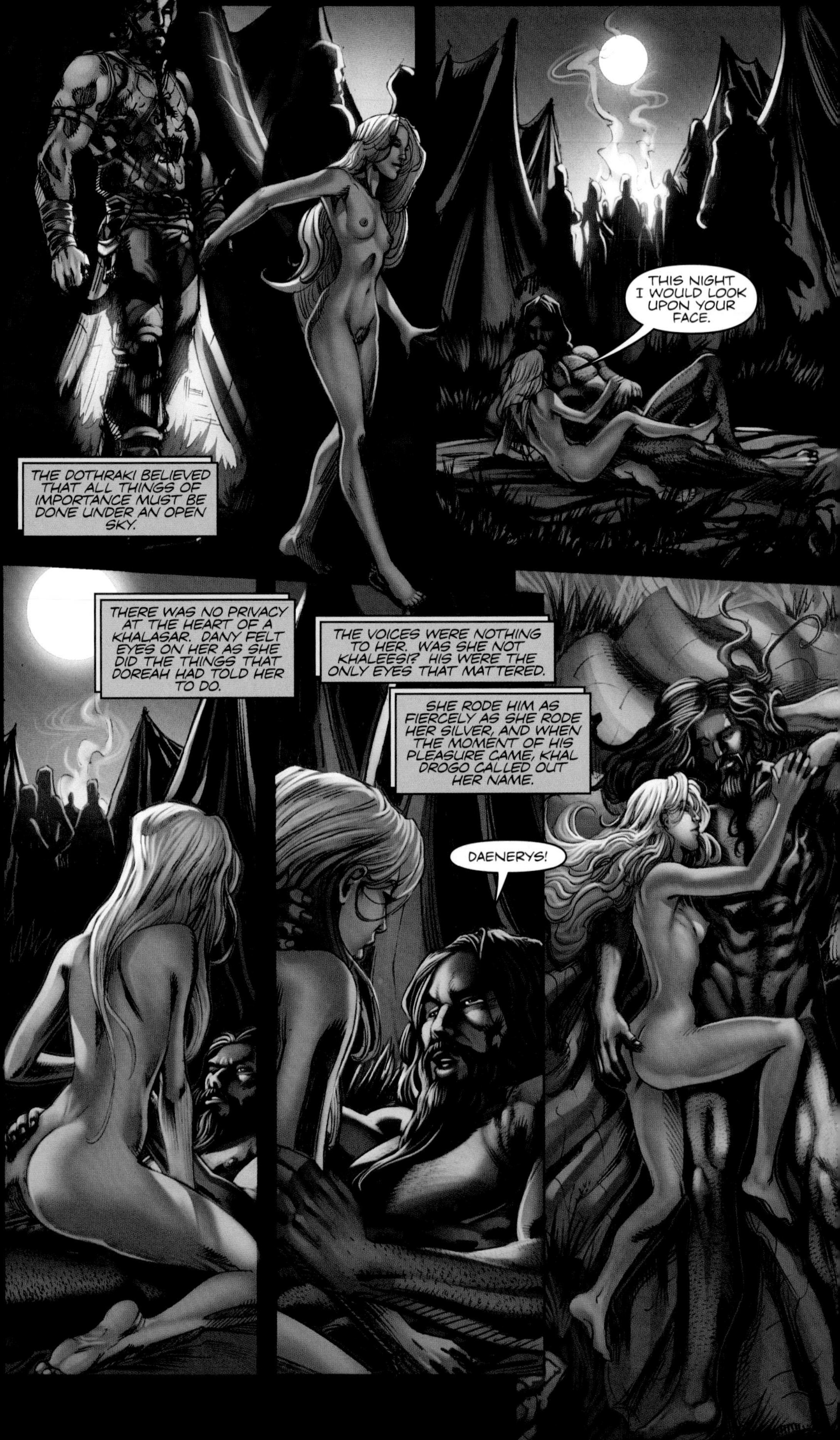
THE DOTHRAKI BELIEVED THAT ALL THINGS OF IMPORTANCE MUST BE DONE UNDER AN OPEN SKY.
THIS NIGHT I WOULD LOOK UPON YOUR FACE.
THERE WAS NO PRIVACY AT THE HEART OF A KHALASAR. DANY FELT EYES ON HER AS SHE DID THE THINGS THAT DOREAH HAD TOLD HER TO DO.
THE VOICES WERE NOTHING TO HER. WAS SHE NOT KHALEESI? HIS WERE THE ONLY EYES THAT MATTERED.
SHE RODE HIM AS FIERCELY AS SHE RODE HER SILVER, AND WHEN THE MOMENT OF HIS PLEASURE CAME, KHAL DROGO CALLED OUT HER NAME.
DAENERYS!

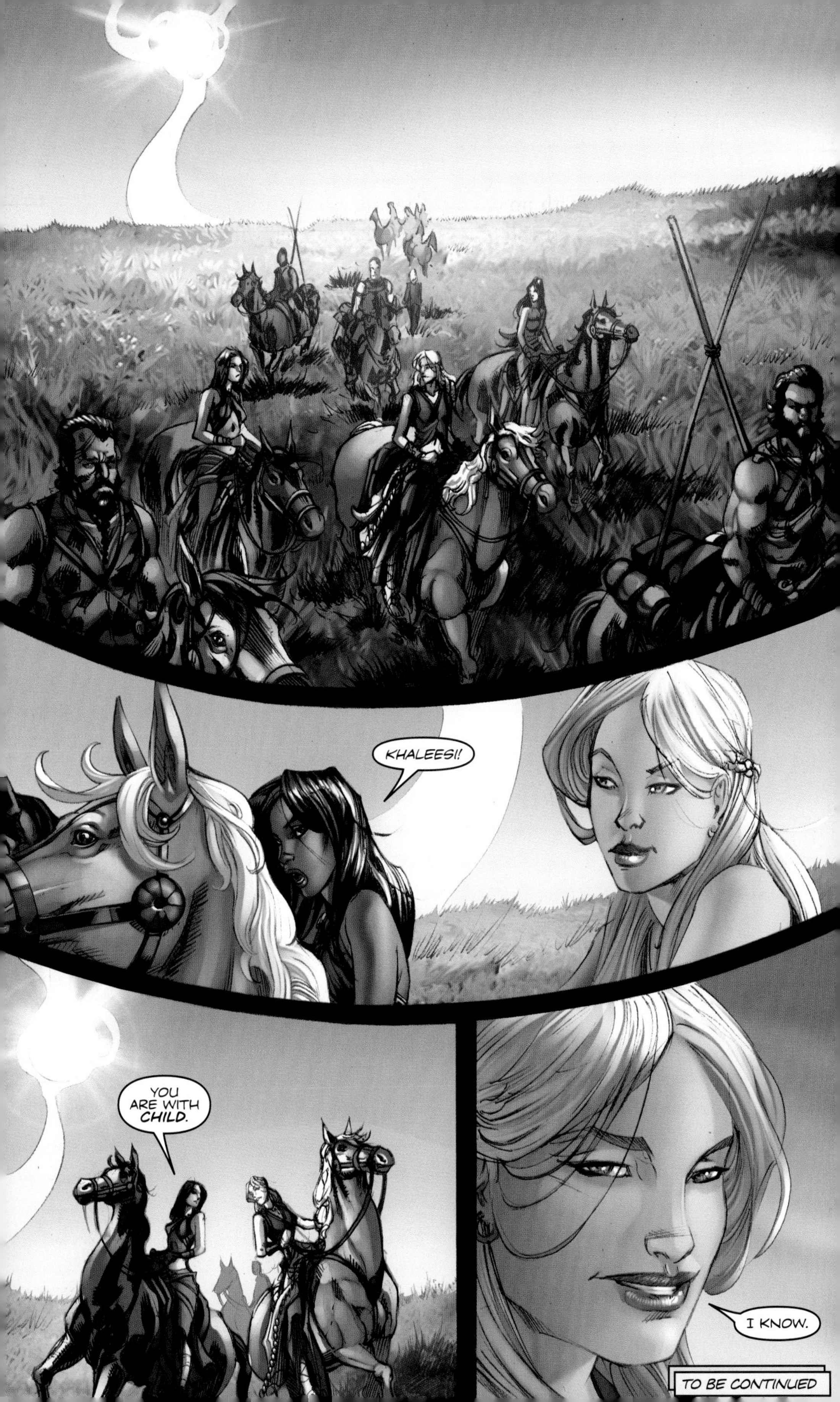
KHALEESI!
YOU ARE WITH CHILD.
I KNOW.
TO BE CONTINUED

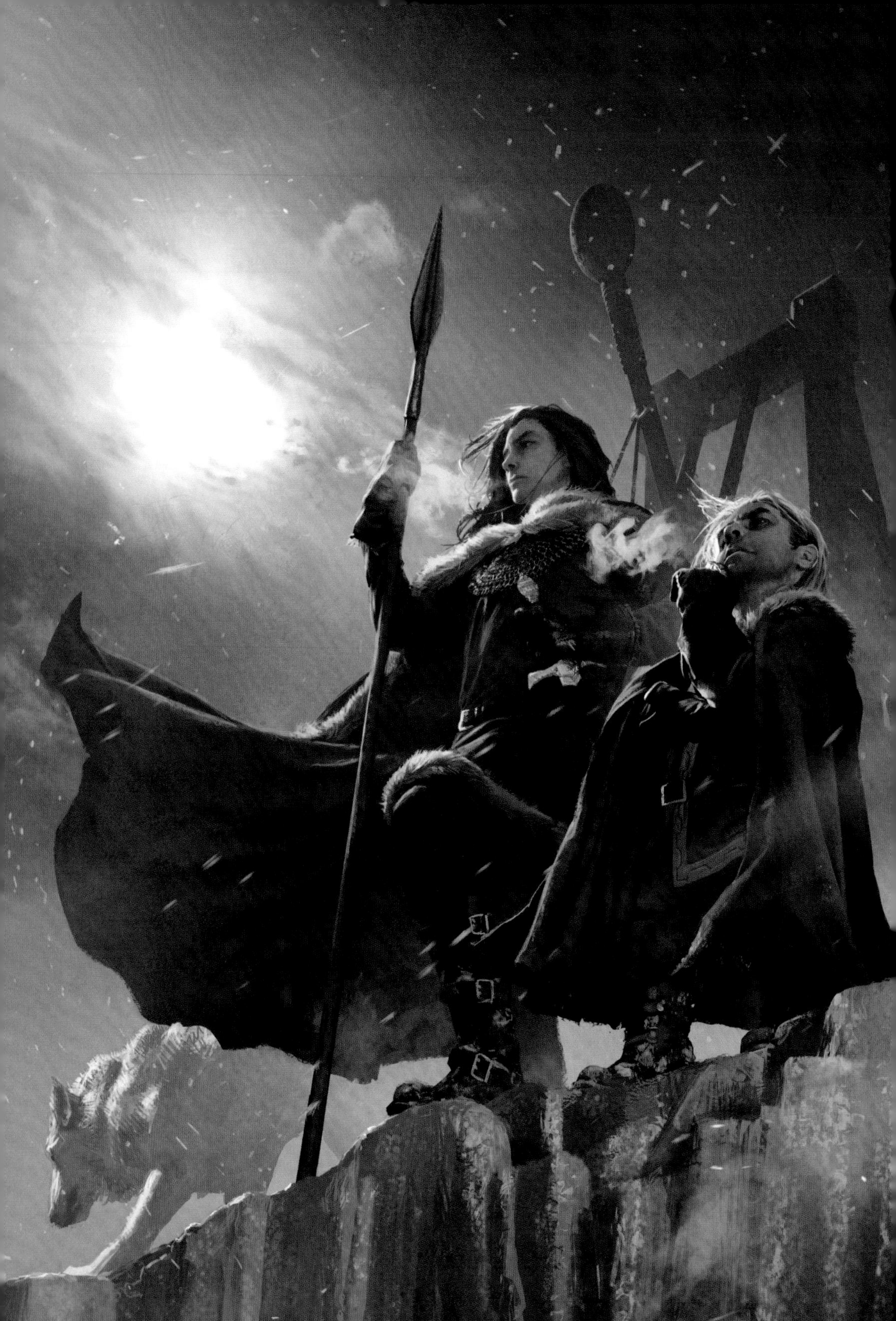

AND NOW...
HERE IS A SPECIAL, INSIDER'S LOOK AT

THE MAKING OF

A GAME OF THRONES

THE GRAPHIC NOVEL
VOLUME 1

WITH COMMENTARY BY:
ANNE GROELL (SERIES EDITOR)
TOMMY PATTERSON (ARTIST)
DANIEL ABRAHAM (ADAPTER)

I think I can speak for all of us when I say that this has been a truly amazing experience to be a part of. And definitely one with a steep learning curve for me, personally.

I have been George's editor since the bulk of the first draft of *A Game of Thrones* (somewhere in the 1,200-page range, as I recall) first hit my desk in early 1995. Mind you, I was not the acquiring editor for Bantam. That honor belongs to Jennifer Hershey. I was merely the extremely anxious (and, later, *extremely* disappointed) underbidder for the project, over at Avon Books. But six months later, Jennifer hired me on at Bantam, then six months after that, she left for Avon, and suddenly I was—at long last—the official editor for this project I had been itching to work on since I had first read the 170 pages and synopsis for this proposed trilogy that George had submitted to his agent in October of 1993.

When the full draft of *A Game of Thrones* finally arrived a year or so later, I was over the moon, because it was every bit as good—and better!—as the promise of that partial manuscript and synopsis I had fallen so in love with before.

Now, seventeen years later, all of you know what I knew then—that this book, and this series, are something truly remarkable. Yes, we are far beyond the original proposed trilogy, and I have done things like gotten married and had a kid in the intervals between George's various book deliveries. But I have been with Westeros almost since its inception, so when the opportunity came to adapt this book to the graphic format, I jumped at the chance, despite the fact that I had never really been a dedicated reader of graphic novels.

George's world is intensely visual, so in that sense, it is a perfect fit for this new medium. It is also complex and detailed, which has led to its own set of problems. Even with twenty-four twenty-nine-page issues, we cannot cover every word of the book. Some stuff must be cut, boiled down, conflated. (It was especially fun and challenging to be adapting this alongside the first season of the HBO show. I loved watching the choices that they had made, and measuring those against the choices we were—and still are—actively making.)

For myself, I have had to learn how to edit pictures as well as words—though I remain staggered by the consistent high quality of Tommy Patterson's work. I have learned a ton about the fine art of adaptation from the ever-talented Daniel Abraham, who has a real knack for getting right to the heart of a scene. And my fellow series editor, Tricia Pasternak—who actually had edited graphic novels before—has basically taught me everything I now know about this format with grace and style.

Daniel, Tommy, Tricia, and I have all worked extremely hard trying to create a product that was as true to the book as we could make it—and mostly because we know that you, the fans, expect no less of us. We are all enormously proud of the six issues you hold in your hand now, and strive to get even better as the series continues. So we hope you have all enjoyed your first visual foray into Westeros, and will continue to share this amazing ride with us in the months and years ahead.

—Anne Groell
Executive Editor, Random House, Inc.

Coming to *A Game of Thrones* as an adaptor was surprisingly different from coming to is as a reader or a writer. George is so readable that it's easy to go fast and miss some of the finer details. Reading it with this particular perspective, I've been able to slow down and really consider every scene closely. It's been fascinating to read a text that I've known for over a decade and see new things in it. The hardest thing has been to omit things. A lot of things don't translate gracefully from text to sequential art, but it's still hard to keep the discipline to cut them out.
—Daniel Abraham

Illustrating *A Game of Thrones* has been extremely fulfilling. It's been everything that I had hoped it would be. It allows me to grow as an artist and focus 100 percent of my energy on my craft. I feel very fortunate to be attached to a world such as Westeros and the many, many great fans who take part in George R. R. Martin's creation.

A Song of Ice and Fire fans have been welcoming and extremely supportive; they don't mind providing details when I find myself in need of guidance. I consider them part of the essence that is A Song of Ice and Fire. I am surprised every day by their love and dedication to the world of Westeros and all its inhabitants. And this pushes me to draw to the absolute best of my ability, in the hopes that my imagery can bring this world to life for them.

Being spun from a medieval world, this project has additionally allowed me a chance to study an intriguing period in history. I have added numerous skills to my repertoire, such as medieval engineering, weaponry, buildings and clothing, as well as animals like the horse, bird, and—you guessed it—the wolf.

For me, the hardest thing has been giving the characters a distinct look while also keeping family traits recognizable. I then have to give them each their own expressions and mannerisms…which I am still in the process of doing. Juggling the ideal appearance of each character based on how George and the fans perceive them while avoiding similarities to the HBO series has been a bit challenging.

But most of all, I am in awe of how real the world feels. I feel like I am making a documentary about a pivotal moment in history. I enjoy knowing how much time George put into this world to make it feel that way. I love the intrinsic reward of seeing all my hard work land on the page. I love designing this all 90 percent from scratch, then taking a step back to see the sheer volume of drawings around me. I love knowing that I have to give my very best because all those involved are doing the exact same thing.
—Tommy Patterson

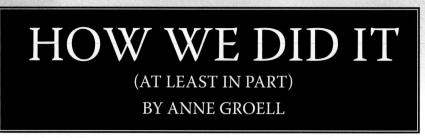

HOW WE DID IT
(AT LEAST IN PART)
BY ANNE GROELL

In the sections that follow, we will show you a little of the behind-the-scenes magic (or fumbles) that went into the making of this graphic novel. We all had a lot to learn about working both with each other and with this rich-but-challenging world, but we also had a lot of fun along the way.

THE AUDITION

Our first order of business, after signing the contract that gave us the right to publish the graphic novels (and getting Daniel on board as the adapter), was to find the artist who could best bring Westeros to life. We needed someone who would work for a reasonable rate, but—more critically—someone who was willing to give us, exclusively, over two years of their creative life. We wanted a single artist's vision driving the book, but we also needed the issues to come out on a strict monthly basis. And with twenty-four monthly issues…well, you do the math. It's a *giant* commitment.

To audition our artists, we first chose five characters that we felt could best give us a feel for the range of their talents, then asked each artist to submit sketches of the five characters. Our choices were: Eddard Stark, Jon Snow, Tyrion Lannister, Daenerys Targaryen, and Arya Stark. Male and female, young and old, short and tall; a good cross section of George's world, we felt.

Here is what Tommy gave us:

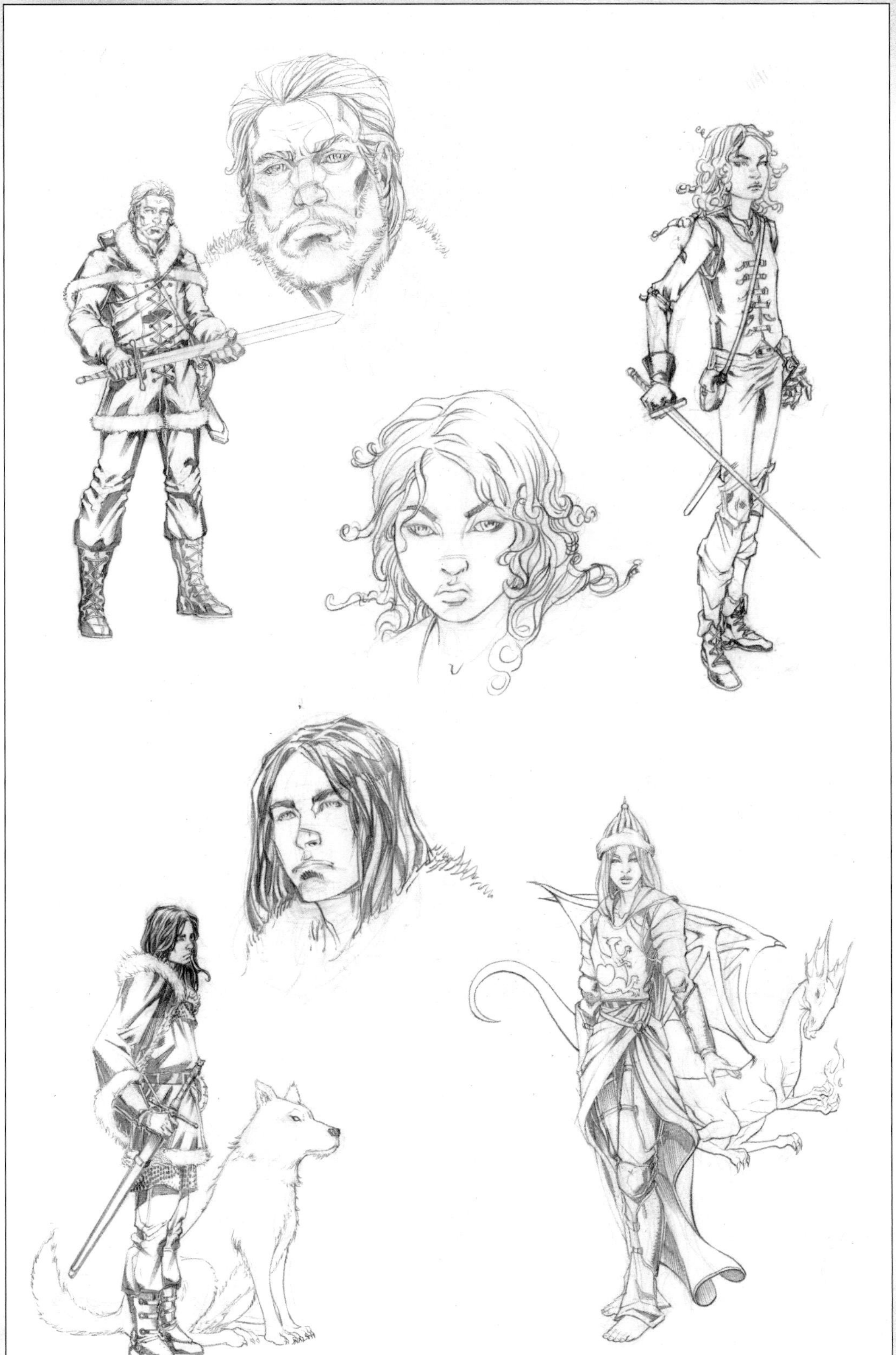

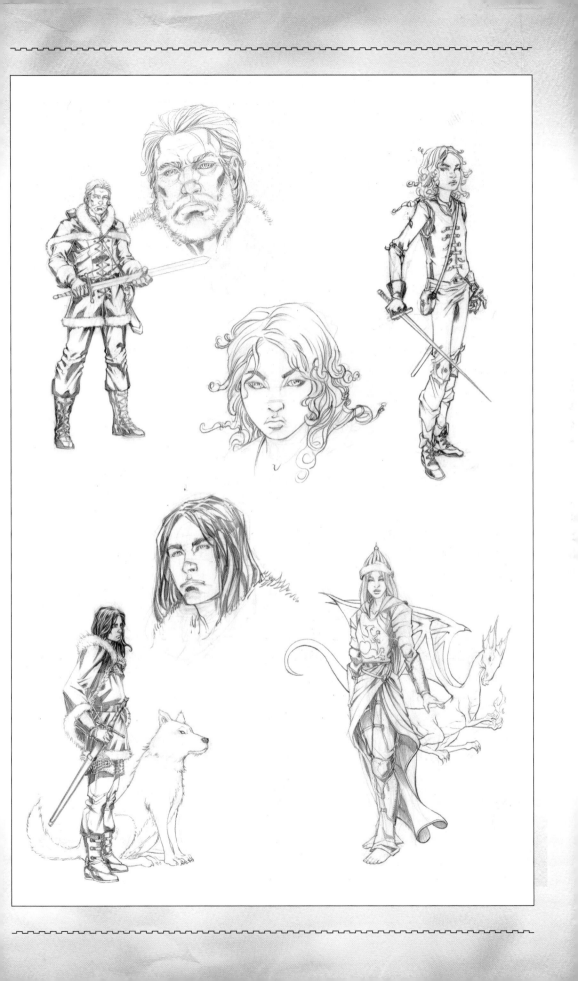

Tommy turned in some fabulous initial designs—some of the strongest, overall, we felt. And he was definitely one of the few who got Tyrion correct right off the bat. But before we and George made our final decision, we asked the semifinalists from this round to submit two sample pages for the actual first issue, which Daniel had already written.

For this, we asked for page 5 (Ser Waymar Royce's battle with the Others, see below) and page 24 (Dany contemplating her past, see next page). We felt, again, that these two pages would show us a wide range of the artist's abilities. On page 5, we have an action scene: swords, fighting, and the winter cold of the northern forests. With page 24, we have a quietly contemplative moment set in the far warmer climes of the world. And with both, we had a chance to let the artist really play with the details of the world.

One of the most important things to George, in choosing the artist, was to make sure that the richness of the world came across. Every panel needed a fully detailed background. ("If they're walking though a hall," he told me, "I want to see the hall.") Page 24 especially—with Dany gazing out over Pentos—gave us a chance to see what our artists could do with scenery and background.

In Tommy's initial take on page 24, I think you can see why his detail work instantly catapulted him to the top of our list and won him the job.

This went straight into the final issue with no changes—a sign in and of itself!

Astute readers will notice that Tommy's sample for page 5 is pretty much the identical structure for the finished page, save for one element: the Others. Which leads me to my next topic…

THE BATTLE FOR THE OTHERS

This was one of the two hardest tasks we had to do, conceptually. Those familiar with the books will know that George barely describes these beings in the text, except extremely cryptically. (And I should know; I did the document searches.) They need to be creepy and scary and numinous and essentially unseen...while also being very much on the page, since this is a visual medium.

George, Daniel, Tricia, and I knew the robotic look was not right, but as for what was? I had many talks with George. He told me of the ice swords, and the reflective, camouflaging armor that picks up the images of the things around it like a clear, still pond. He spoke a lot about what they were not, but what they were was harder to put into words. Here is what George said, in one e-mail: "The Others are not dead. They are strange, beautiful...think, oh...the Sidhe made of ice, something like that...a different sort of life...inhuman, elegant, dangerous."

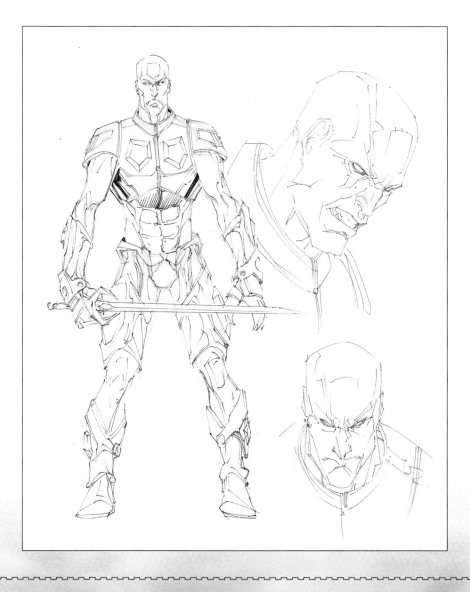

Tommy adds:

"My first take on the Others didn't take into account the ethereal nature of the beings. I had them a bit too rigid to start. So my next couple of takes tried to add a bit of movement to them. I started by adding some wispy clothes. That wasn't quite right either. I next had them as wild, icey-looking creatures. The ice would form perpetually and shed as they moved about. The next version had a Halloween gothic female sort of take."

But again, it still did not match George's vision—proving, not for the last time, how hard it is to actually get into someone's head and see what he is seeing. Even when that someone is a master at putting words to paper, like George.

However, in one of those great concatenations of circumstances, George and I were also working on the 2012 A Song of Ice and Fire calendar, featuring the art-

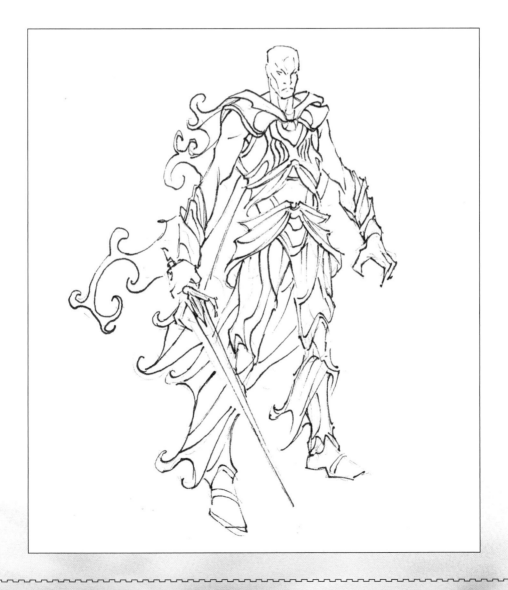

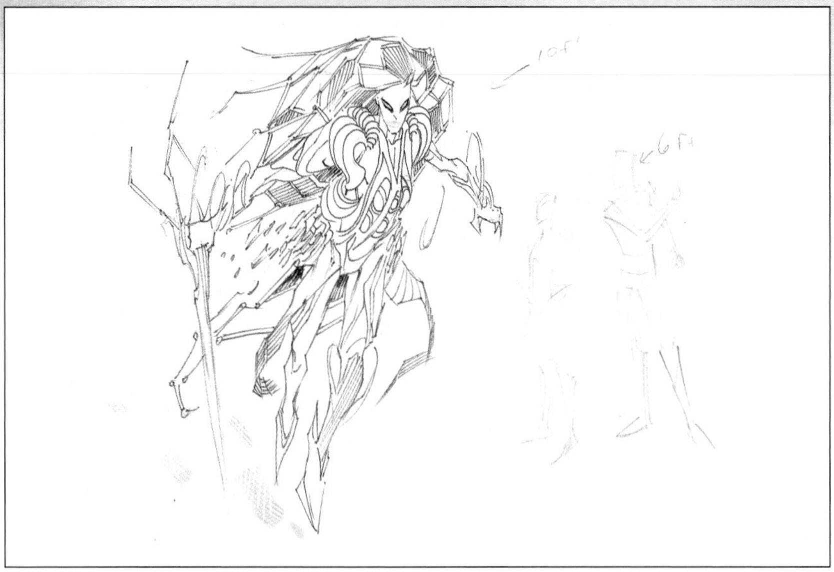
10ft
6ft

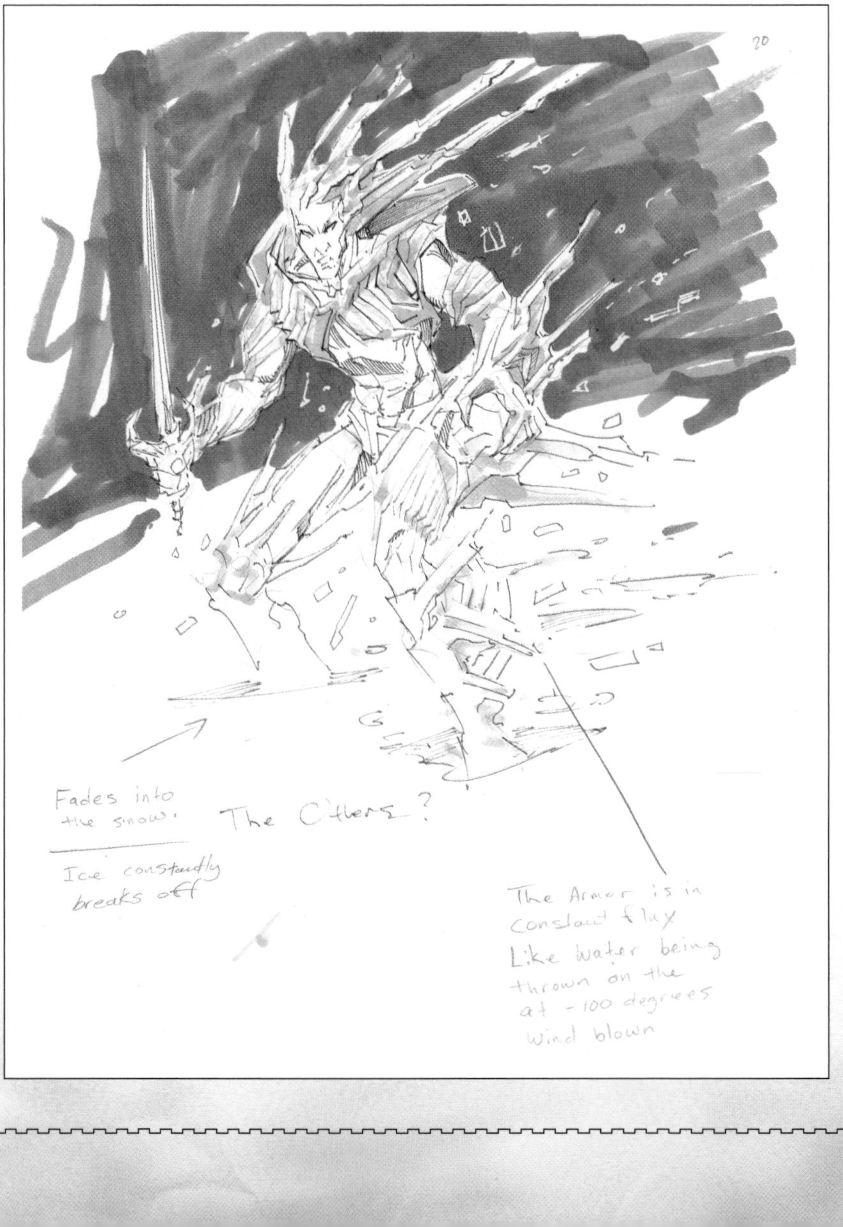
20
Fades into the snow.
The Others?
Ice constantly breaks off
The Armor is in constant flux Like Water being thrown on the at -100 degrees wind blown

work of the wonderful John Picacio, at the same time. John, George felt, had done a very nice recent take on the Others.

Tommy says:

"At this point, George sent over a painting John Picacio did for the calendar (below). He mentioned a couple of tweaks I might make. I finally worked up the final version derived from John's painting. I had a different take on the sword that George thought was cool. I couldn't figure out how to draw the smoky contrails

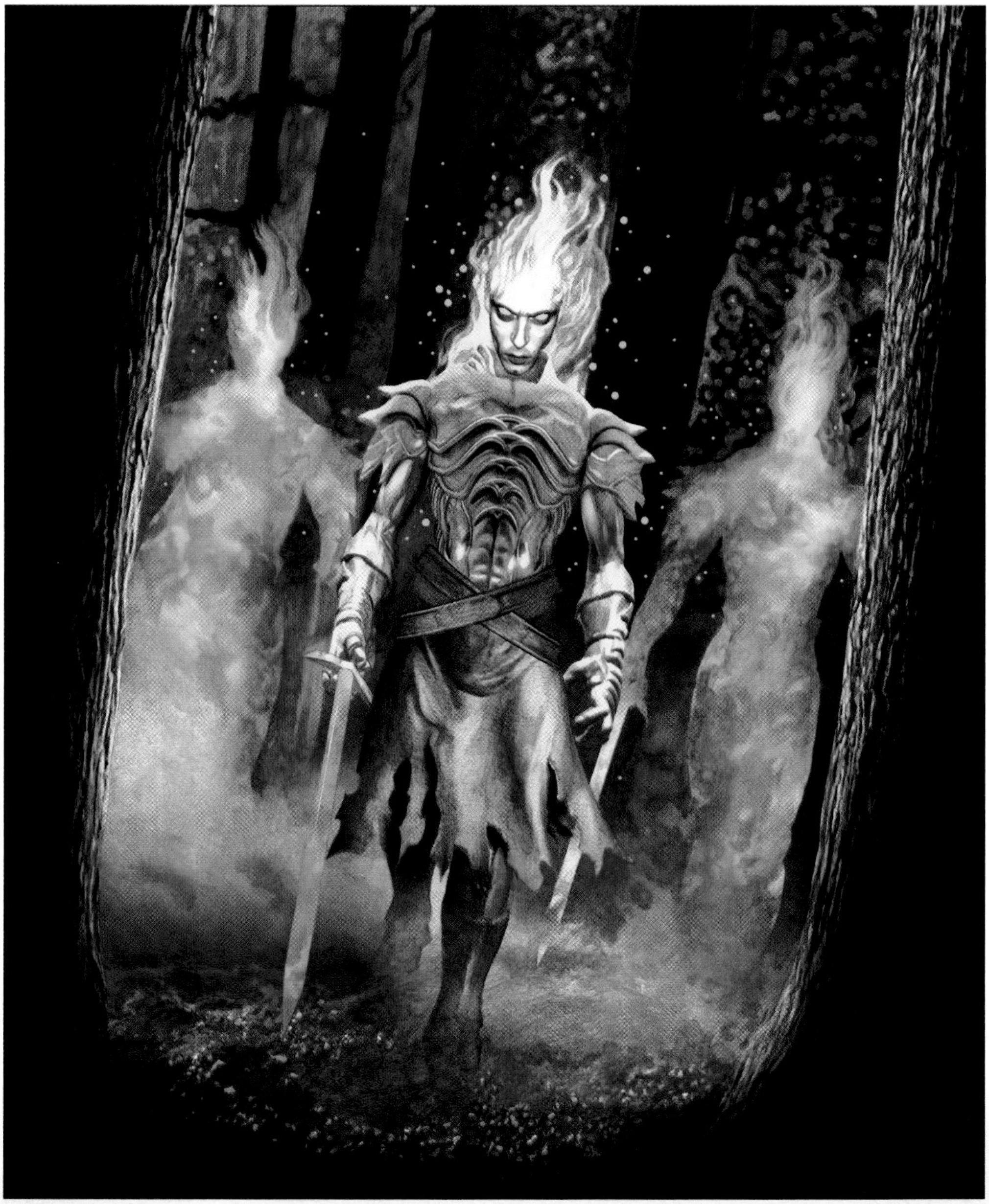

that John pulls off in the painting. I ended up with delicate flourish on the armor instead. As of Issue #7, I have tweaked the design just a bit more. I'm learning new techniques all the time, and lately I'm drawing more with the side of my pencil. I get a soft but very expressive line. It just happens to look great for drawing the contrails instead of the hair and the stringy armor that made the first go-round."

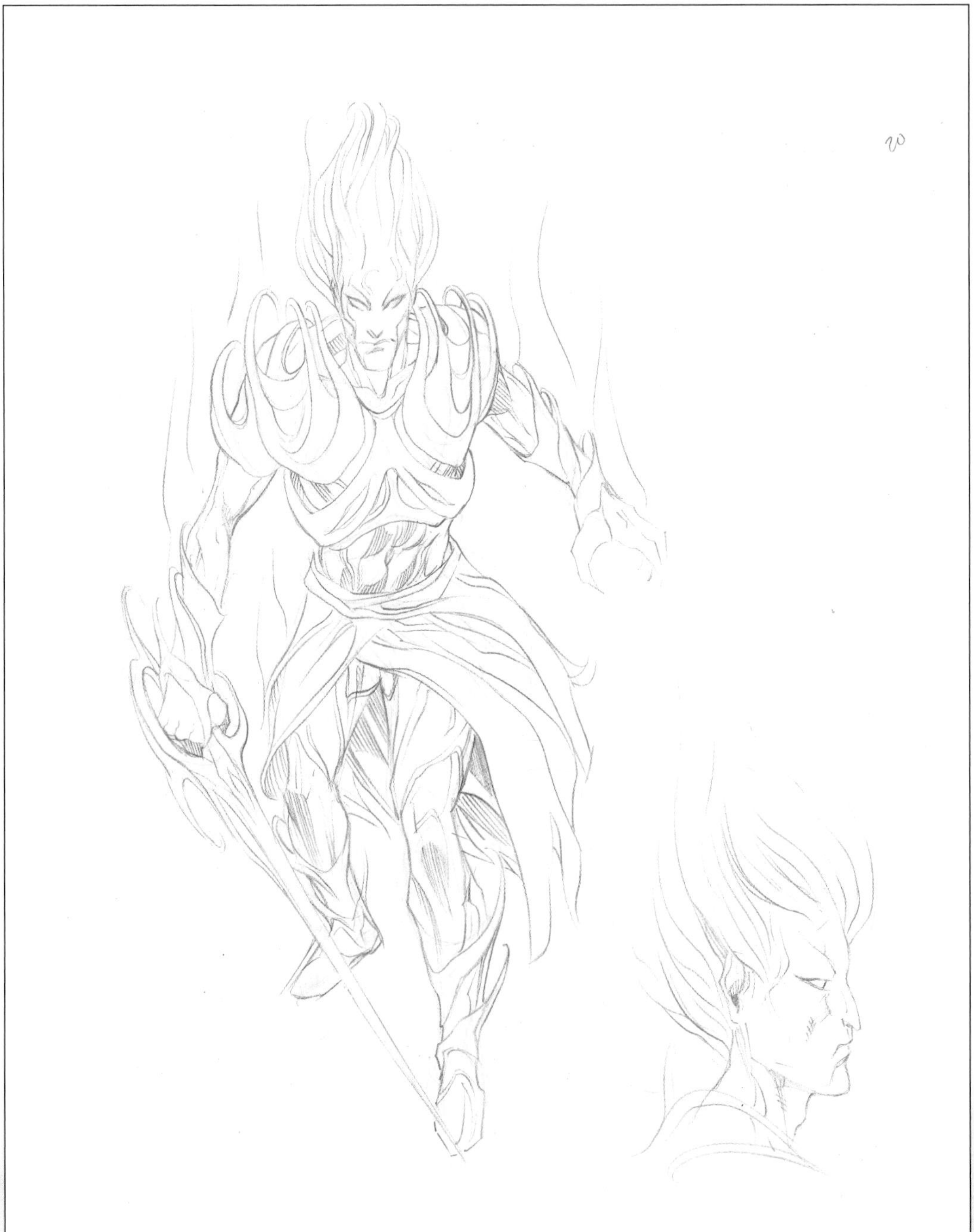

Of course, we were still dependent on the considerable talents of colorist Ivan Nunes to create the necessary, numinous now-you-see-me-now-you-don't quality. But we think Ivan did a terrific job in rounding out—and fading back—the Others.

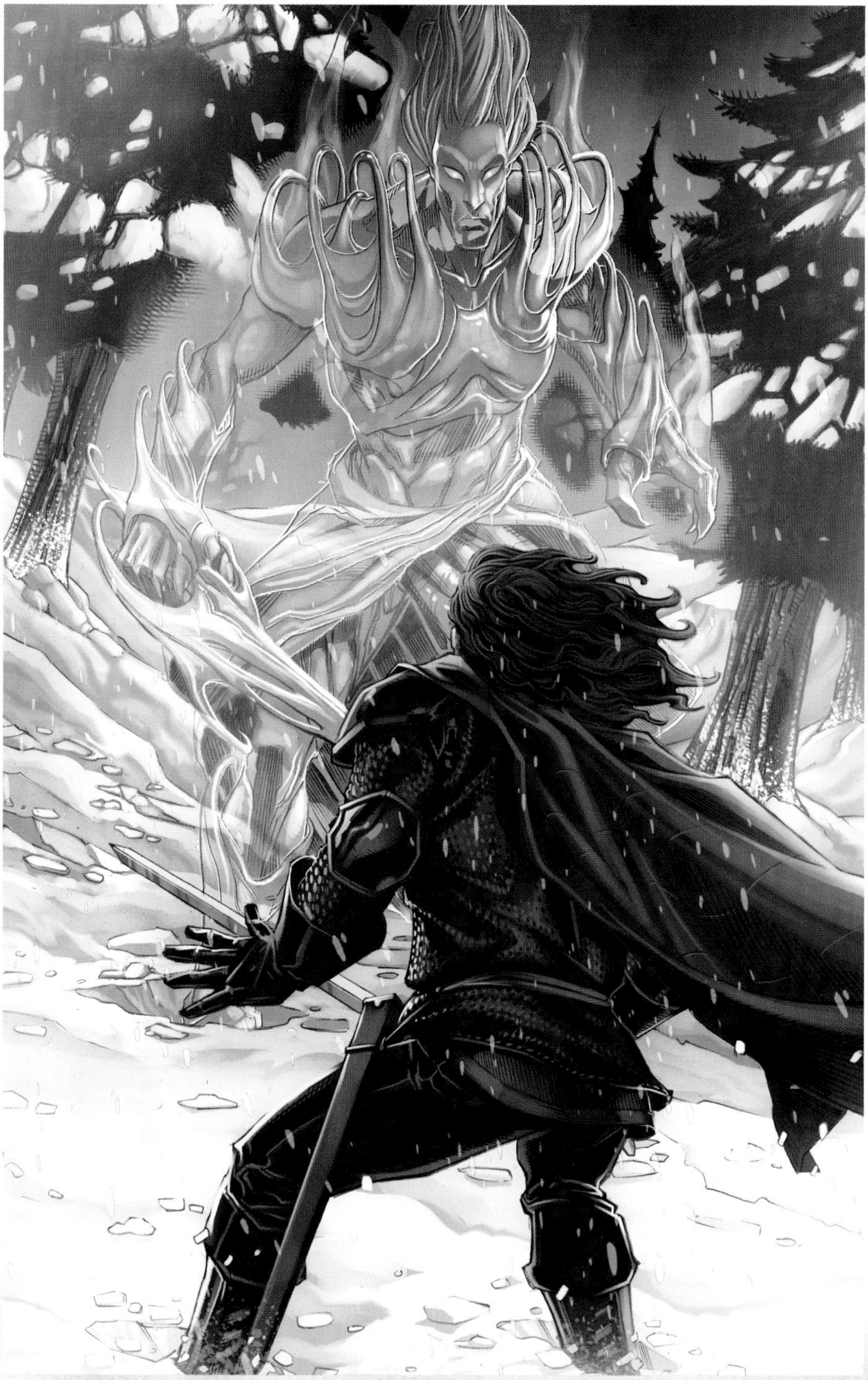

THE CHARACTERS

Another reason this project was initially so daunting was the sheer volume of characters we needed to create to populate this world. Sure, Tommy had done some fabulous character studies...of five characters. And, yes, two of these—Ned and Tyrion—were deemed perfect, with no changes needed.

Two more needed minor fixes. Jon needed to look a bit younger, with a bigger sword, and a scarier wolf. Dany went into a softer costume.

Arya, who looked too cute and girly, needed to be more substantially reworked, until she looked more like herself.

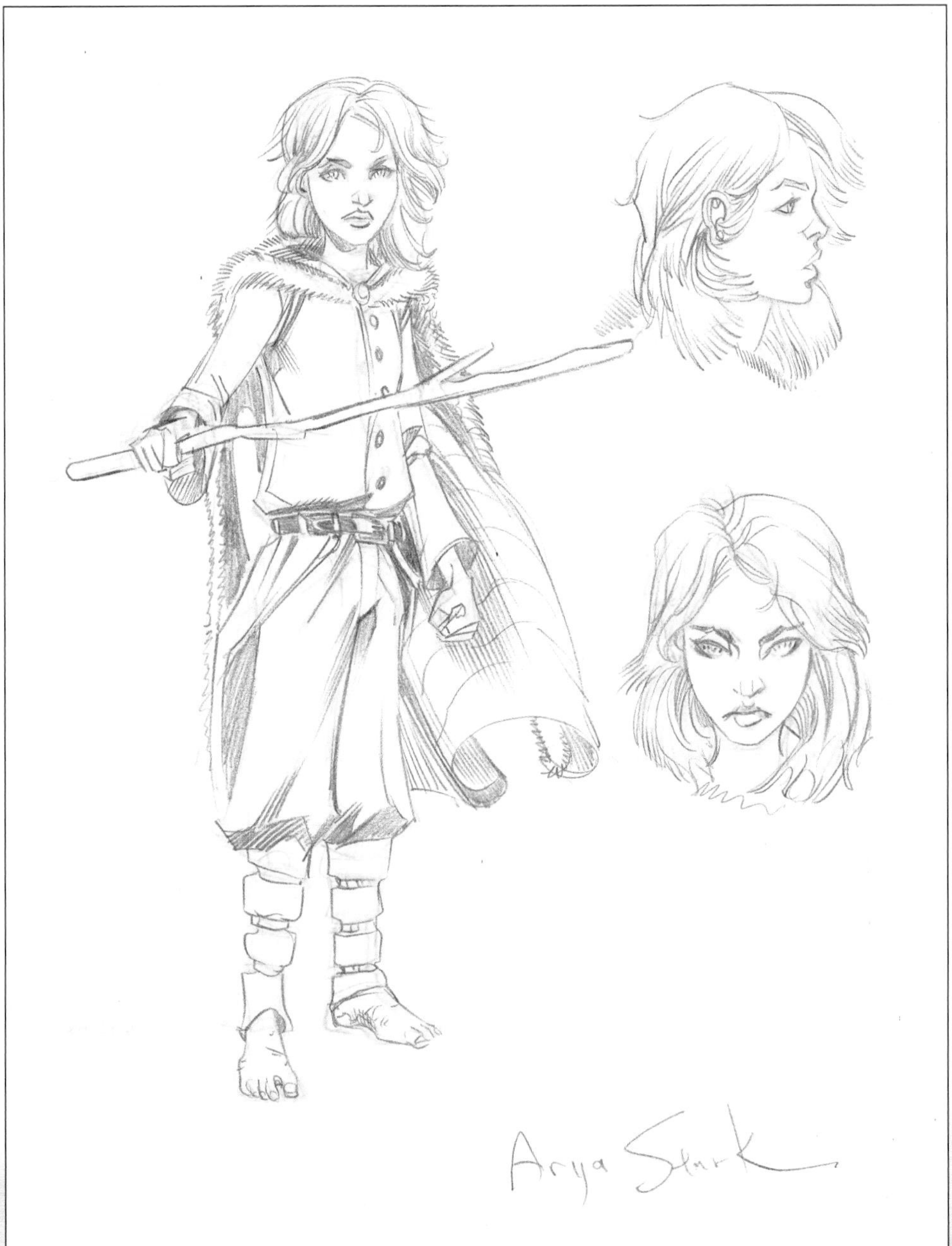
Arya Stark

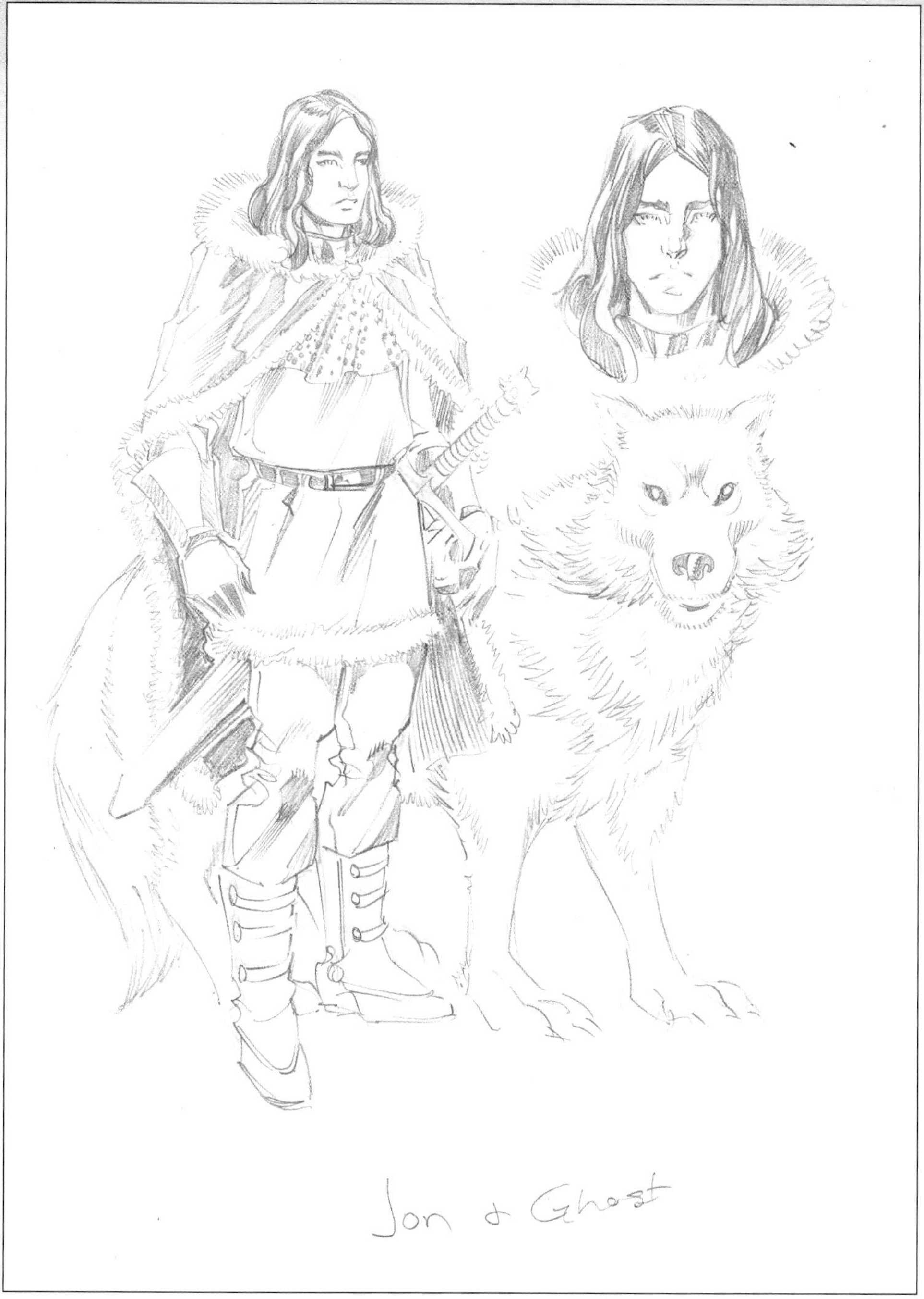
Jon & Ghost

But this was but the tip of a *very* large iceberg! To help Tommy out, I started drawing up character lists, with descriptions culled from the books, for each issue, for characters that George would need to see and approve before they could go into a scene. Issue #1 had twenty-five characters that needed to be created, and Issues #2 and #3 had fourteen each. So, fifty-three distinct characters, and this just for the first three issues! (And this is not to mention all the minor characters, which didn't need to be preapproved, but still needed to have their own distinctive looks.)

We decided to give Tommy three months to work on all the character designs for Issues #1 to #3 together, before even starting to draw another panel.

Tommy says:

"This is one of the highlights of drawing the book. The first couple of issues I had to design fifty-plus characters. Each issue after that has on average eight. George spent so much time fleshing everyone out that it's not hard to get a visual that works after one or two tries. I also try to incorporate a character's sigil when possible. The fans love that sort of detail.

"I have to do the designs at the start of each issue, but I usually have a page or two I can start on with previously designed characters so downtime isn't needed. I love the variety in shape, size, and demeanor the characters have because it keeps me fresh. I have experienced next to no creative lulls or burnout. That's all an artist could ever want besides finding all those missing pencils. Where did they go?"

What are Tommy's five favorite characters to draw and/or create? Says Tommy:

1) "Tyrion all day, every day. He isn't handsome so mistakes almost never happen. He has the widest range of events happening to him. I get to have him act out so many emotions and quips. He is a riot in action scenes, too."

2) "Arya is great because I get to use my daughter for expressions and poses. That sort of practice translates into other characters, and that helps the book overall. Arya is all over the map just like Tyrion. Plus, she whacks Joffrey. Who wouldn't enjoy drawing that?"

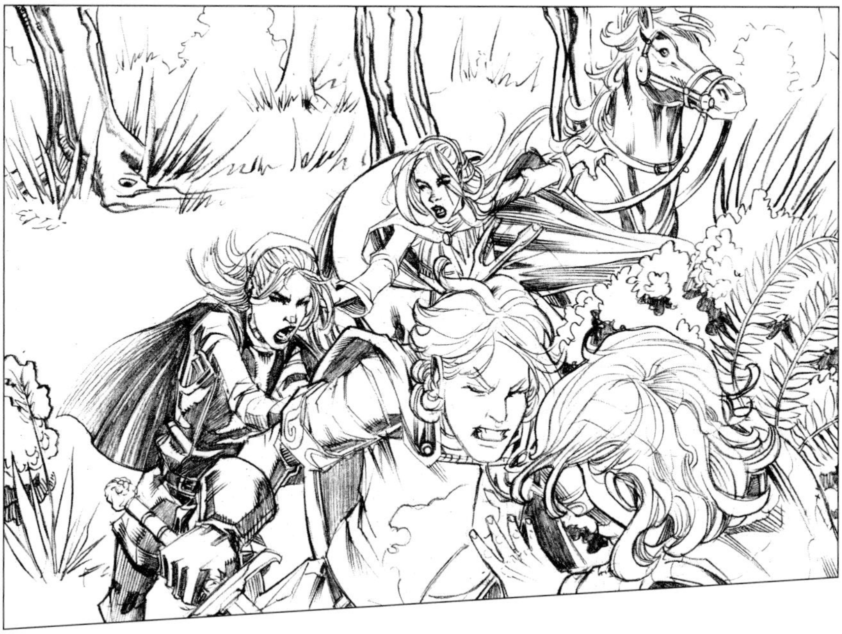

3) "Bran so far has been fun, but since the accident, things have changed. Now he is riding on the back of HODOR! He went from climbing around like Spider-Man to being part of a two-headed monster."

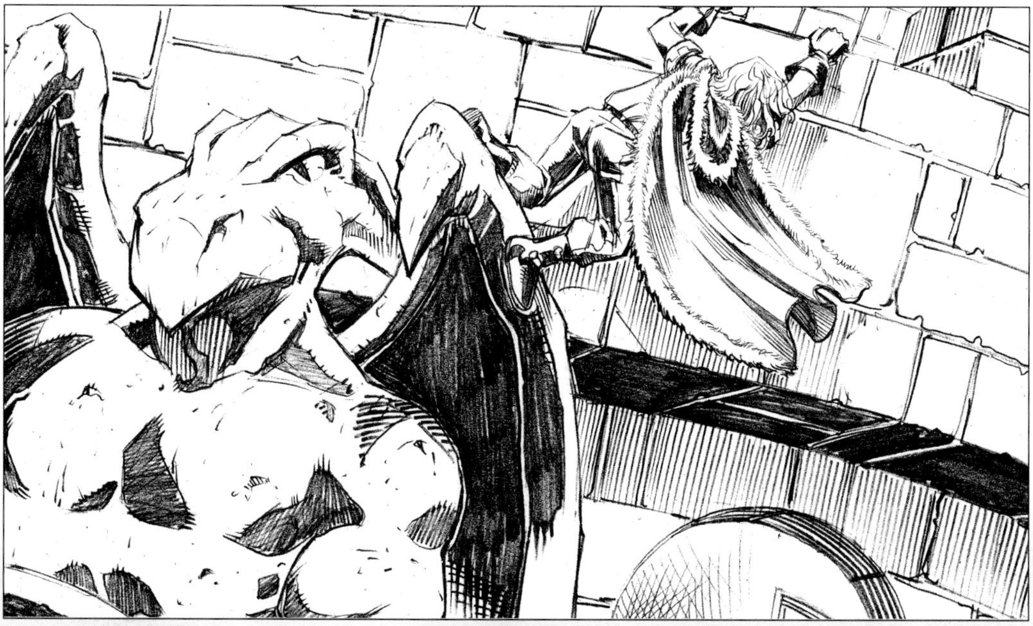

4) "Drogo is classic comic-book fun. He is a beast of a man with all kinds of fun details. When he is on a page, he DOMINATES it. Drawing muscled-up dudes will forever and always be fun. If you hate it, you are in the wrong business."

5) "Horses. Hey, this sort of thing has ended some artists. But I love drawing them. The challenge alone keeps me sharp. They will never get their due, but they add so much character to the environment."

THE STORY

While Tommy was busy auditioning and drawing his characters, Daniel was industriously writing the scripts. Daniel was, in many ways, the perfect candidate for the job. Not only was he George's top choice, but he is a phenomenal writer in his own right (I was also the underbidder on his most recent fantasy trilogy; there seems to be a theme, here!), and he also lives near enough to George to be able to consult in person, if needed.

He was the first person we called when we signed the contract with George, and we were thrilled when he accepted the job.

Here is how Daniel describes his process:

"I started with a master outline that shows what we're covering in each of the issues and graphic novels. At the beginning of the issue, I'll read the text that we're covering four or five times, and start picturing how it might look on the page, playing with ideas and approaches. Sometimes I'll doodle a little, though I'm nothing like an artist. Then I can build a page-by-page outline for the issue. I try to keep as true to the original text as I possibly can. Most of the words on the page are George's, and I think you can hear his voice in them."

"She was more beautiful than that," the king said after a silence. His eyes lingered on Lyanna's face, as if he could will her back to life. Finally he rose, made awkward by weight. "Ah, damnit, Ned, did you have to bury her in a place like this?" His voice was hoarse with remembered grief. "She deserves more than darkness."

"She was a Stark of Winterfell," Ned said quietly. "This is her place."

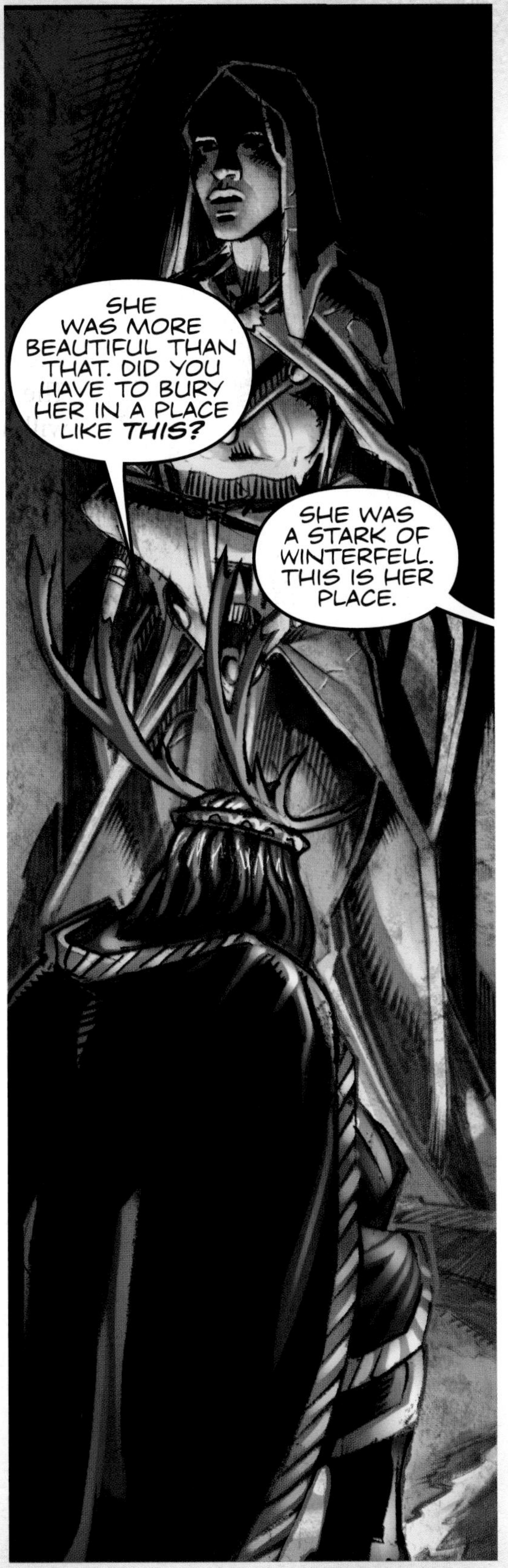
SHE WAS MORE BEAUTIFUL THAN THAT. DID YOU HAVE TO BURY HER IN A PLACE LIKE *THIS?*
SHE WAS A STARK OF WINTERFELL. THIS IS HER PLACE.

Then I come in. Before I even look at Daniel's script, I read the chapters from the book through once slowly and kind of file away what I think some of the key moments and words in the scenes and chapters are. Then I start reading the script. Usually, Daniel has gotten all of them. In a few instances, I sneak a few things in that I think are critical to character development, or just because I like them.

For example, George was bemoaning the fact that HBO cut the scene with Sansa and Arya, in which Sansa declares that she hates riding, then later declares to Joffrey that she *loves* it. The scene between the two girls won both the actresses their parts, but then it was cut for length, rendering Sansa's subsequent flip-flop moot. So I made sure it all stayed in our script—and you will see it now in Issue #5.

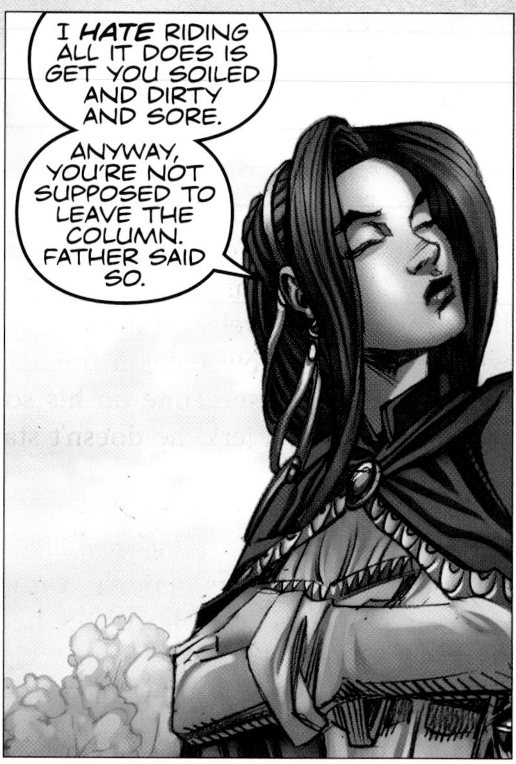
I HATE RIDING ALL IT DOES IS GET YOU SOILED AND DIRTY AND SORE.
ANYWAY, YOU'RE NOT SUPPOSED TO LEAVE THE COLUMN. FATHER SAID SO.

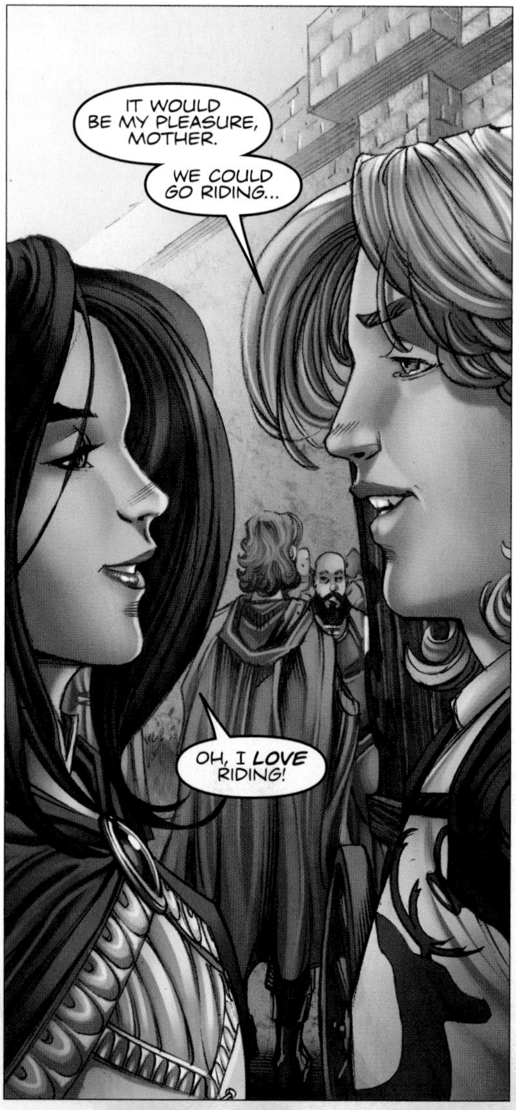
IT WOULD BE MY PLEASURE, MOTHER.
WE COULD GO RIDING...
OH, I LOVE RIDING!

I also check if characters are introduced properly by name and how the scene flows and catch typos, and minor things like that. I mark up Daniel's electronic file with Track Changes, shoot it to Tricia for her comments, then send it off to Daniel, and he revises it as needed. And from there, we have an approved script.

Says Daniel:

"I most enjoyed adapting the scene where Tyrion instructs Joffrey to offer sympathy about Bran (right). Tyrion is a great character, and this sequence is like a showcase of everything that makes him sympathetic and admirable. When the Hound mocks him, he shrugs it off. When Joffrey gets out of line, Tyrion stands up to him. It's brilliant on so many levels. He doesn't rise to anger when someone below him on the social ladder is rude, but when someone on his social plane or more is being a jerk, he doesn't stand for it."

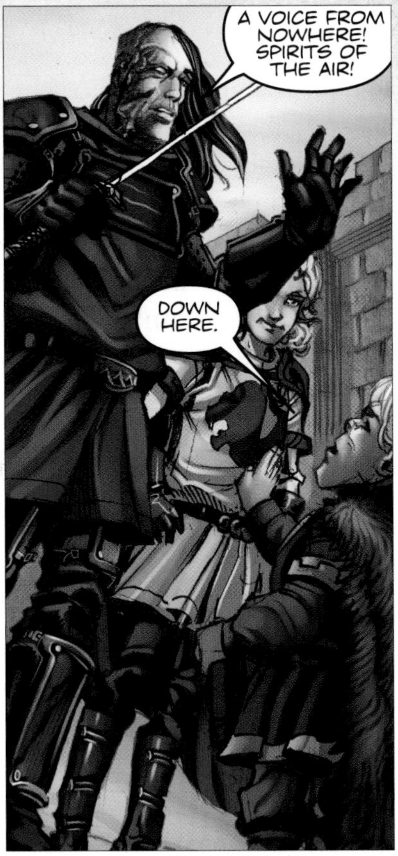
A VOICE FROM NOWHERE! SPIRITS OF THE AIR!
DOWN HERE.

As for what was the most challenging scene of this volume to adapt? Daniel says:

"Probably the most difficult was Jon Snow's departure from Winterfell for the Wall (below). It's a tremendously moving chapter and the pain and complexity of it is important. But so much of it is internal to Jon that it's hard to show it. He's putting on a brave face, and so the literal image is of that bravery and restraint. Getting to the soul underneath that was important and difficult."

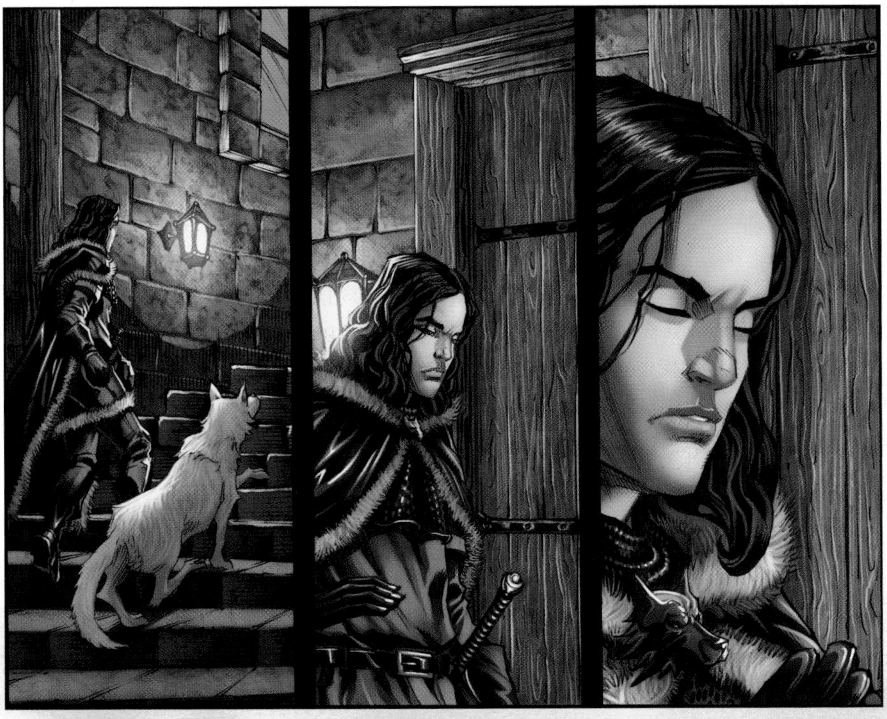

PANELS AND PAGES

Once the initial round of character designs were done, Tommy started drawing the actual issues. Here is how Tommy describes his process:

"I usually read the script and thumbnail as I go. Laying out the pages takes the most brain power of anything I do. I do twenty-nine layouts over two days, and I am zapped the next day. As an artist who likes to draw because it's fun, this is true labor. I'm in the process of convincing my whiny butt that it's good for me and the story to do them all up front. The work flow is way easier, so Anne, Tricia, and Daniel can find errors BEFORE they get drawn on the actual page. So much of being a pro is working through bad days or working on corrections. I'm still in the process of developing productive habits. I'll figure out an easy way one day.

"I do have a steady method of drawing a page. I pull up the script and read the page two or three times. When doing the layouts over two days, they can end up generic. I look at the thumbnail and decide if I need to tweak or totally change a panel. Sometimes, I will flip or mirror a panel for a better flow when reading. Sometimes, I need to rethink the panel entirely. It's rare, but it does happen. I rely on the thumbnail as a guide, but it's not set in stone. I analyze panel size and debate if any panels need to be enlarged for effect or to make space for text. I rule out the page on 11 x 17 smooth bristol (Strathmore 400 series, it can take a beating), and start drawing it in with a Col-erase Light Blue pencil. This saves tons of time because I don't have to erase my underdrawing. I can drop it out in Photoshop after I scan it. I like blue for the underdrawing because when I come in with graphite, it's like correcting someone else's drawing. I find errors are easier to see that way. After the page is done, I scan it in and print it out at reduced size. Again, it's like seeing someone else's drawing. Artists are blind to their own work, so you have to trick yourself to see what is really there and not what you think is there."

Then Tricia, Daniel and I come in. I do the first round, both comparing the panel to the script and looking for inconsistencies, then looking through the panel on its own for anything I might see that needs fixing. Then I send a list to Daniel and Tricia, and they cast their eyes over the panels, adding anything additional that I have missed.

Tommy's favorite page so far:

"Arya and Needle (next page). I felt the characters had settled in on their looks and it was time to punch up the expressions. You have to have confidence to do expressions and this page was the first one where I feel the characters looked and acted exactly how I wanted. It's a turning point for me as an artist. It's neat to be able to point to the exact page it happened."

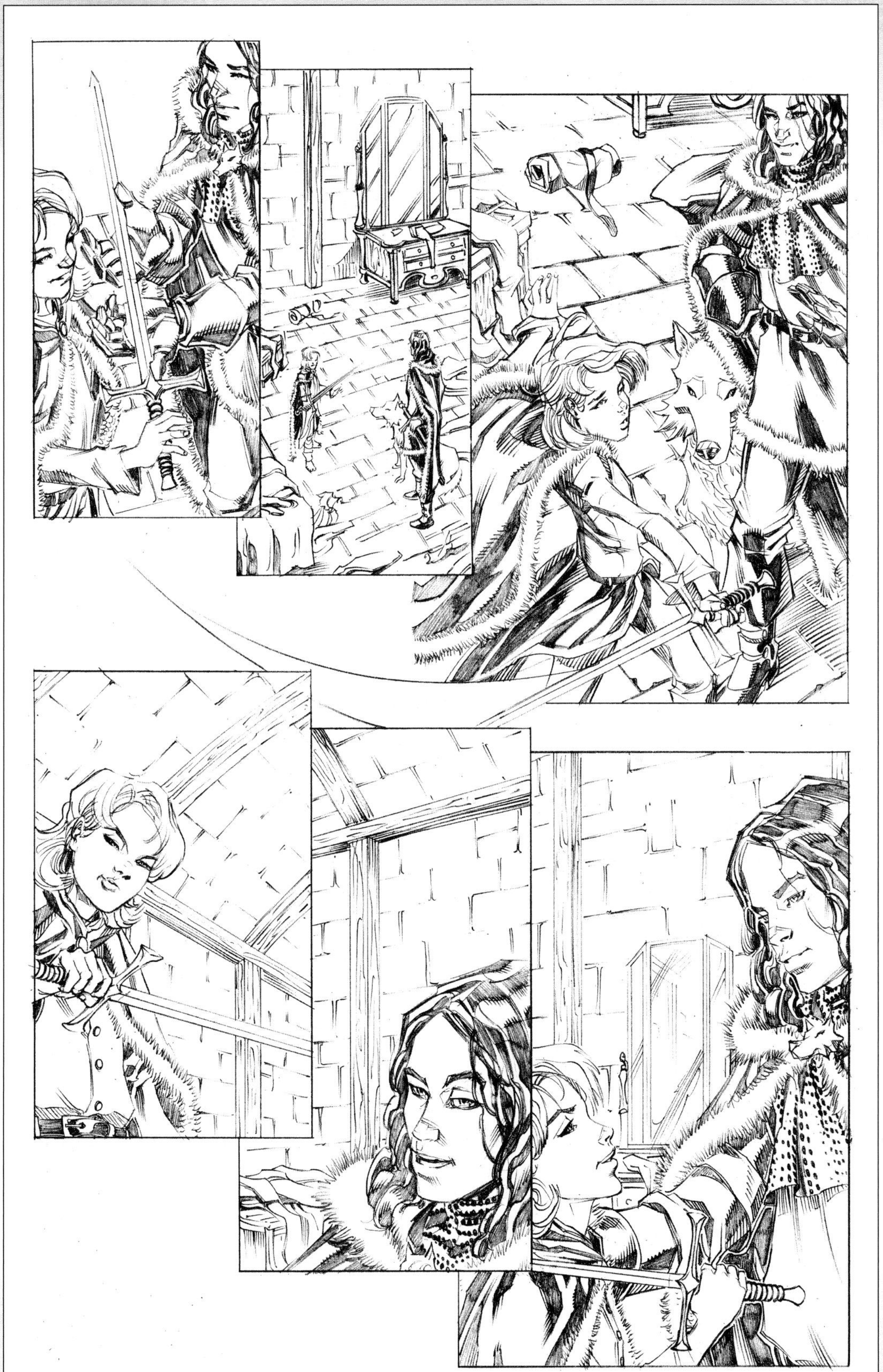

Tommy's most-sweated-over page so far:

"The Great Hall. SO. MANY. PEOPLE. It took two days to complete. I kinda wanted to show off my ability to punish myself. It's like an episode of *Man vs. Wild*. You find yourself in a tough situation and you sink or swim. Nobody said it was easy. That page nearly ruined me, ha-ha-ha."

However, as we can testify, the effort was absolutely worth it. See page 42 for the completed panel, which ranks as one of Tricia's and my favorites so far.

THE IRON THRONE

I mentioned before how the Others were one of our main visual challenges. Well, the other was the Iron Throne. Initially, Tommy had turned in something looking very much like the HBO throne.

This was a problem for two reasons. First, we not only wanted, but needed (for legal reasons) our graphic novel to have its own distinct look, apart from what HBO was doing so beautifully. This was not to be an adaptation of the HBO series, wonderful and gorgeous as it was, but our own interpretation of George's novel.

But, more critically, this HBO-type throne was not at all what George had envisioned. And we wanted our book to match George's vision as much as possible in as many respects as we could.

George and I talked. "Bigger," he said. "Much bigger." So Tommy did this:

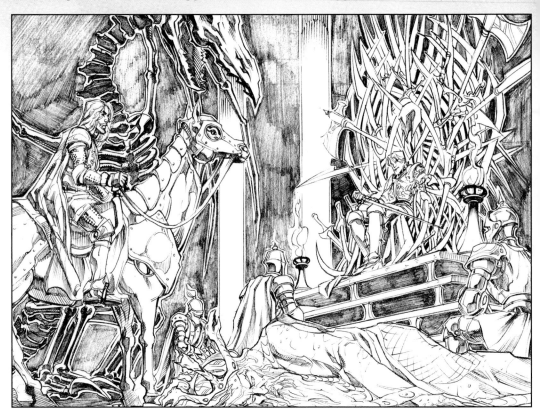

Once again, that was not right, either. It was too short, not hulking or bestial enough. And, yes, it was only made of swords. I pulled what descriptions there were from the book; there were not a lot. ("A hunched black beast made of razor edges and barbs and ribbons of sharp metal" is the most specific description in the whole of *A Game of Thrones*.)

So Tommy gave us these two, which had the hulking look of dragons on top.

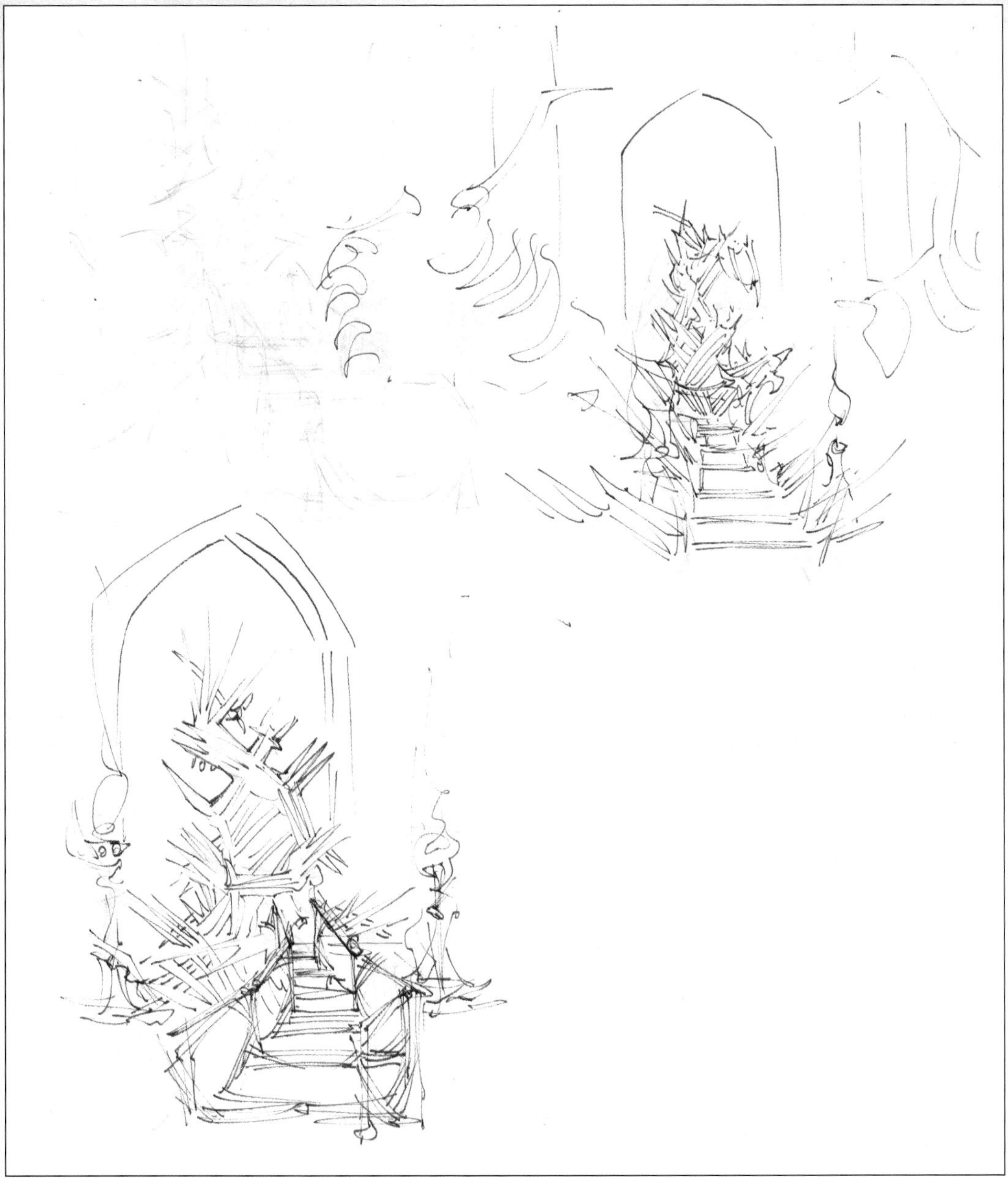

No, too designed, George said. The throne was not crafted, but melded together in dragonfire, which is very hard to get clever with. George and I talked some more. A few more iterations came and went. Then I think I finally began to ask the right questions, because I suddenly learned it was probably about ten feet off the ground, and had narrow steps leading up to it like up to the top of a slide. Eureka!

Here, at last, is the Iron Throne, as close to what George envisoned as we could make it:

Tommy adds:

"I was totally influenced by the show and previous takes on the throne, so I had to work away from that. George wanted something far more...sinister or imposing. The throne had to represent the struggle for its very existence. Taking all that in, I finally twisted and forged something that met George's vision. I can't wait to draw it again in all its glory. It's one gnarly chair!"

WHERE TOMMY UTTERLY
BLEW US OUT OF THE WATER

Sometimes, just seeing the raw pencil drawings coming in gave us chills—seeing George's world brought to life so vividly and so gorgeously! So Daniel, Tricia, and I want to show you just a few of our favorite pages and panels as they first arrived in our in-boxes.

First, here are five of Tricia's and my favorite panels.

ROBERT ARRIVING IN WINTERFELL

Why? The sheer detail is amazing! Plus, the unusual rakish tilt. We both remember gasping at this one, until we got to…

THE BANQUET AT WINTERFELL

The details may nearly have killed Tommy, but we love it! I am particularly enamored of Theon's turn, which either has him ogling the girl, weighing up Jon, or both. Such a genuine Theon moment, in the midst of someone else's scene!

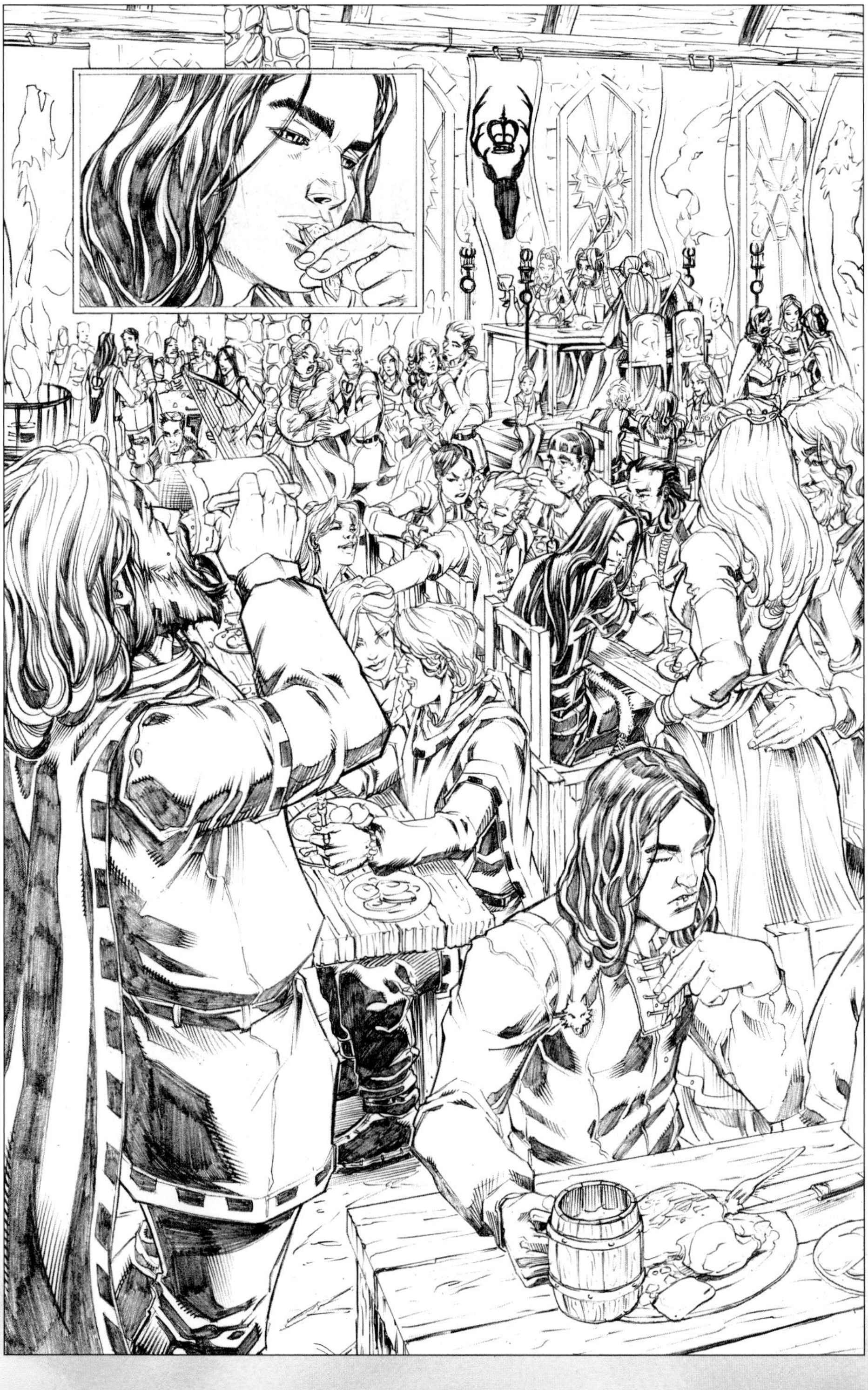

THE FIRST VIEW OF THE DRAGON EGGS

We adore Tommy's design for the eggs—enhanced so wonderfully by Ivan's colors.
Who wouldn't want to own them?

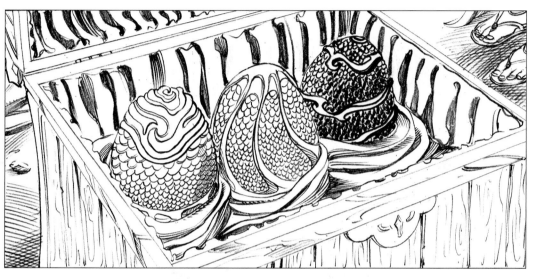

CATELYN'S ARRIVAL IN KING'S LANDING

Tommy truly excels at the huge architectural shots, and nothing showcases that better than our first view of King's Landing.

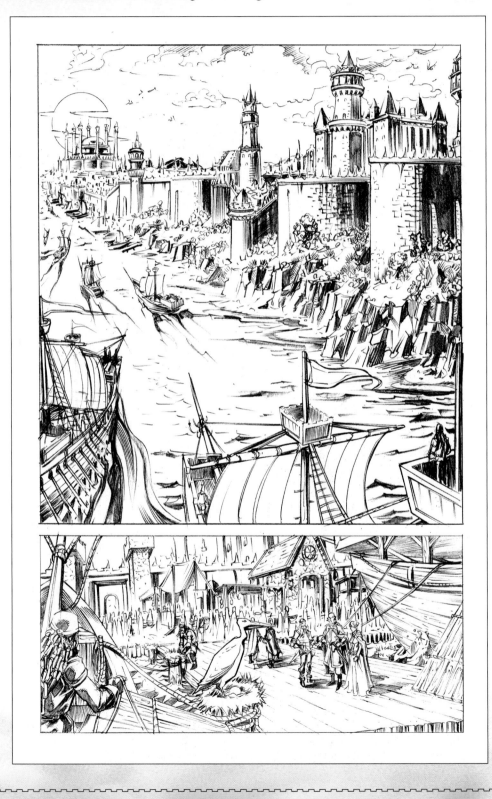

DANY'S DRAGON DREAM ON THE DOTHRAKI SEA

How do you convey a character's inner journey in visual medium? This page is the perfect example of Daniel and Tommy working in perfect synchrony—and it is gorgeous, to boot!

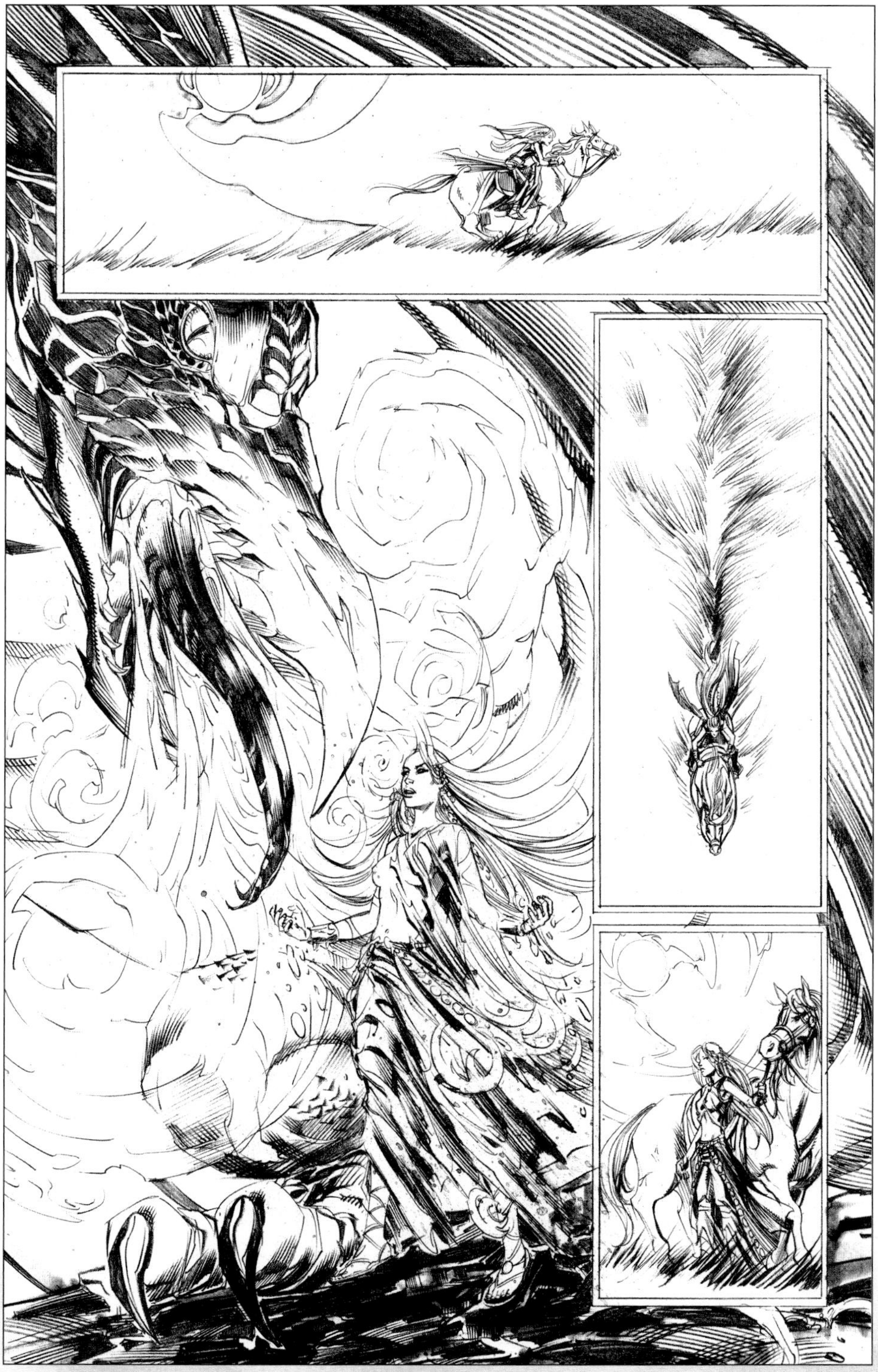

And here are five of Daniel's favorite pages/panels:

THE FLASHBACKS DURING DANY'S BATH

One of the really hard things when you're moving from prose to a graphic novel is how to handle exposition and backstory. The way that Tommy was able to capture all these iconic moments in Dany's life and without it getting cluttered or confusing was great.

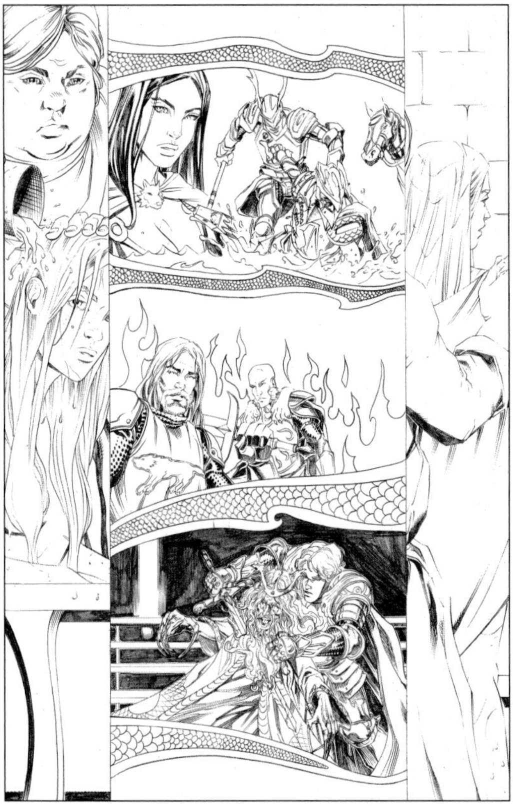

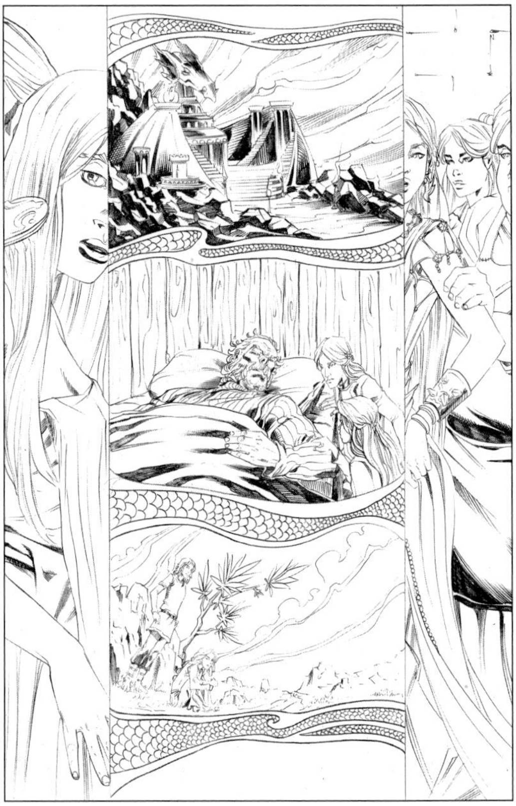

DANY AND KHAL DROGO MEETING FOR
THE FIRST TIME AT THE END OF ISSUE #1

So much of Dany's story is about power. This moment, where she meets the man she's essentially being sold to, and he's this monstrously huge, threatening guy, carried a lot of the story. Seeing the two of them paired off that way was great.

JON AND TYRION'S ENCOUNTER IN ISSUE #2: "NOT ALL BASTARDS NEED BE DWARFS."

This was a hard moment to capture from the book. In prose, it's easy to kind of say what it means, with Tyrion's shadow stretching out like a giant. We can see how it would impress Jon. Tommy caught it in the image. They say a picture's worth a thousand words. I think one carried at least a fifteen hundred.

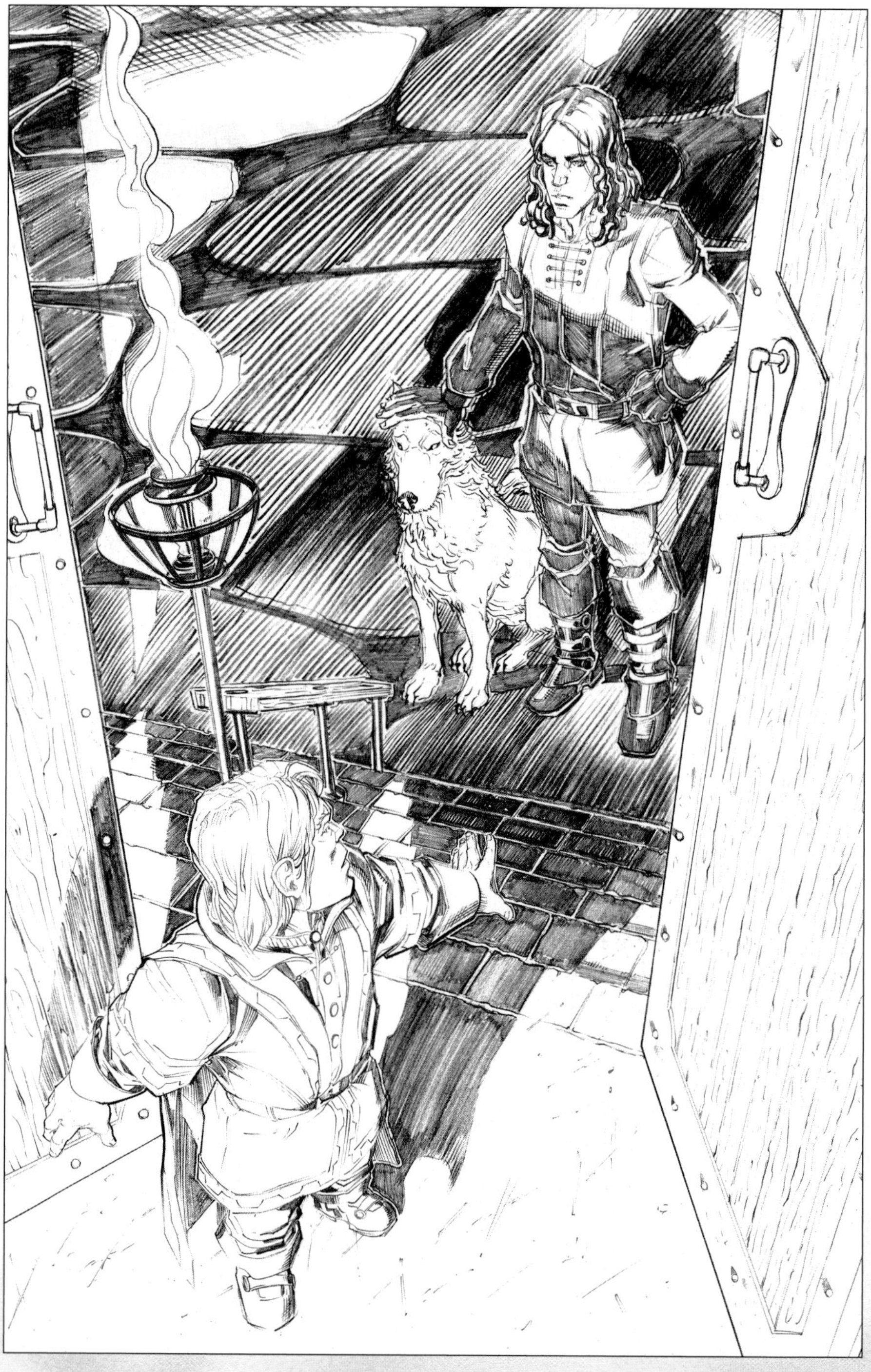

JON FIGHTING GRENN

This was one of the first places I really saw Tommy mastering action. Swordplay and violence is so much a part of the story, it was great seeing this combat and having a real sense of what the fight was and how it felt. It was immediate.

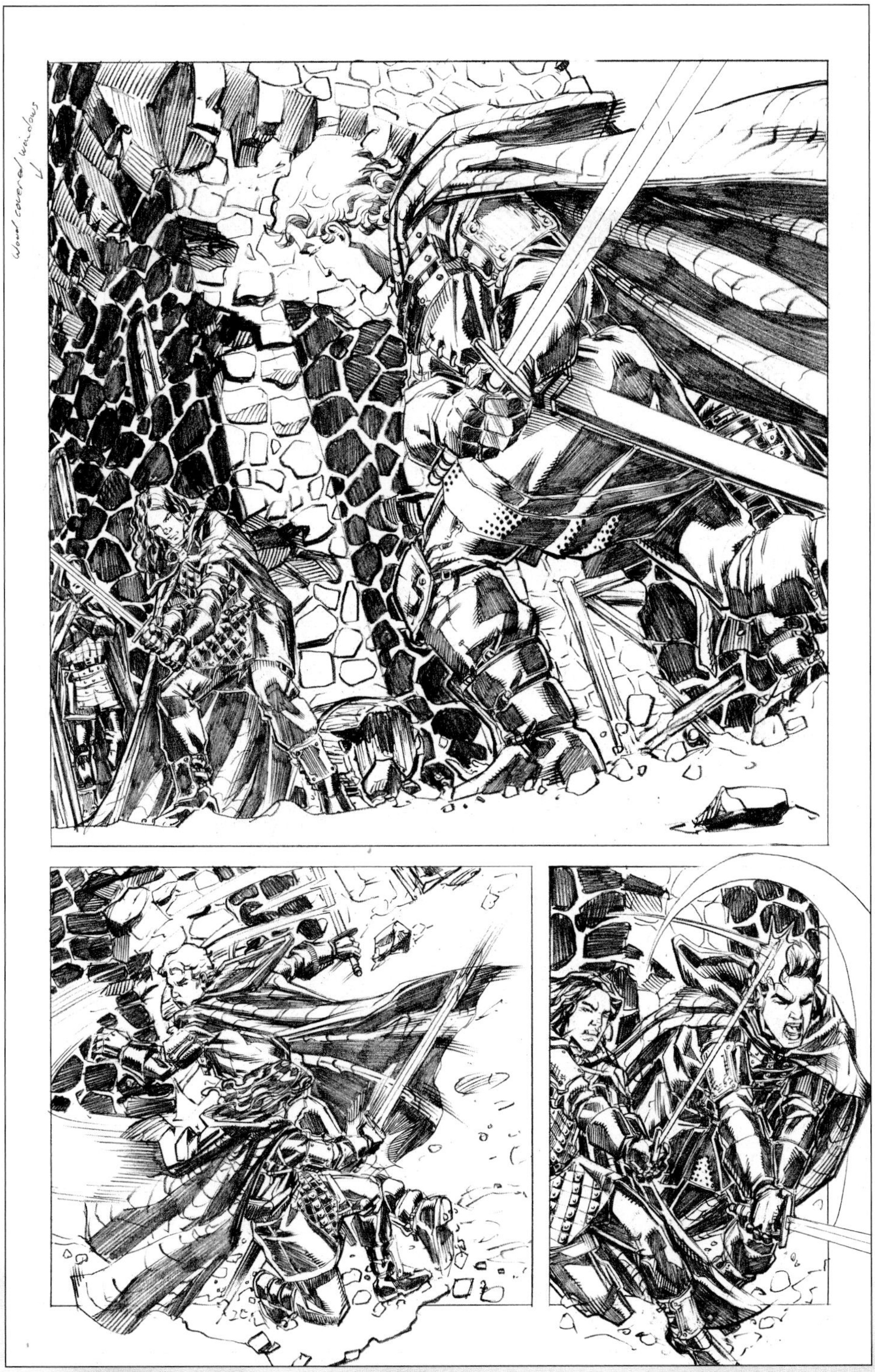

AND WE THINK THE ARTIST HAD FUN, TOO

Despite the fact that I know that we have eaten Tommy's life, here are some of the panels and pages he most enjoyed drawing, along with his reasons why:

THE VERY FIRST PAGE

I wanted to start off on the right foot. I put in more time than it would seem. Stage fright is a hell of an obstacle.

LITTLEFINGER'S DARK ROOM KEYHOLE PAGE

I read a review where it was mentioned that my take was a little on the bright side. A perfectly constructive critique. I read it while drawing this particular scene: a dark room. Synchronicity? The throwing of the knife into the door AND showing the characters made this funky keyhole shot the best way, in my opinion, to solve the spatial dilemma.

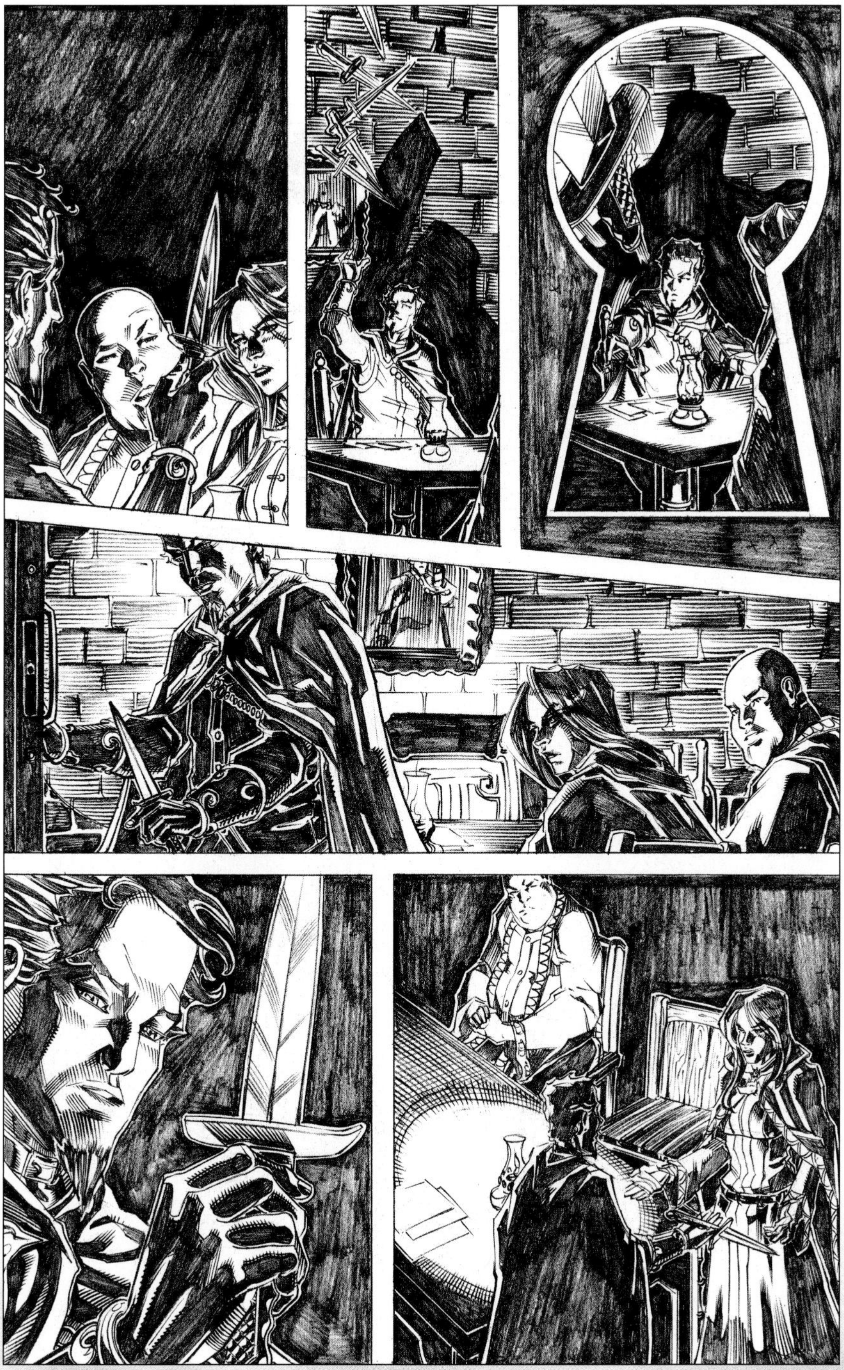

TYRION'S SINISTER FACE AT CAMP ON THE WAY TO THE WALL

This is one of the better performances I've drawn. Jon reached an emotional pitch. The Night's Watch gang in panel 3 took a good four hours to draw.

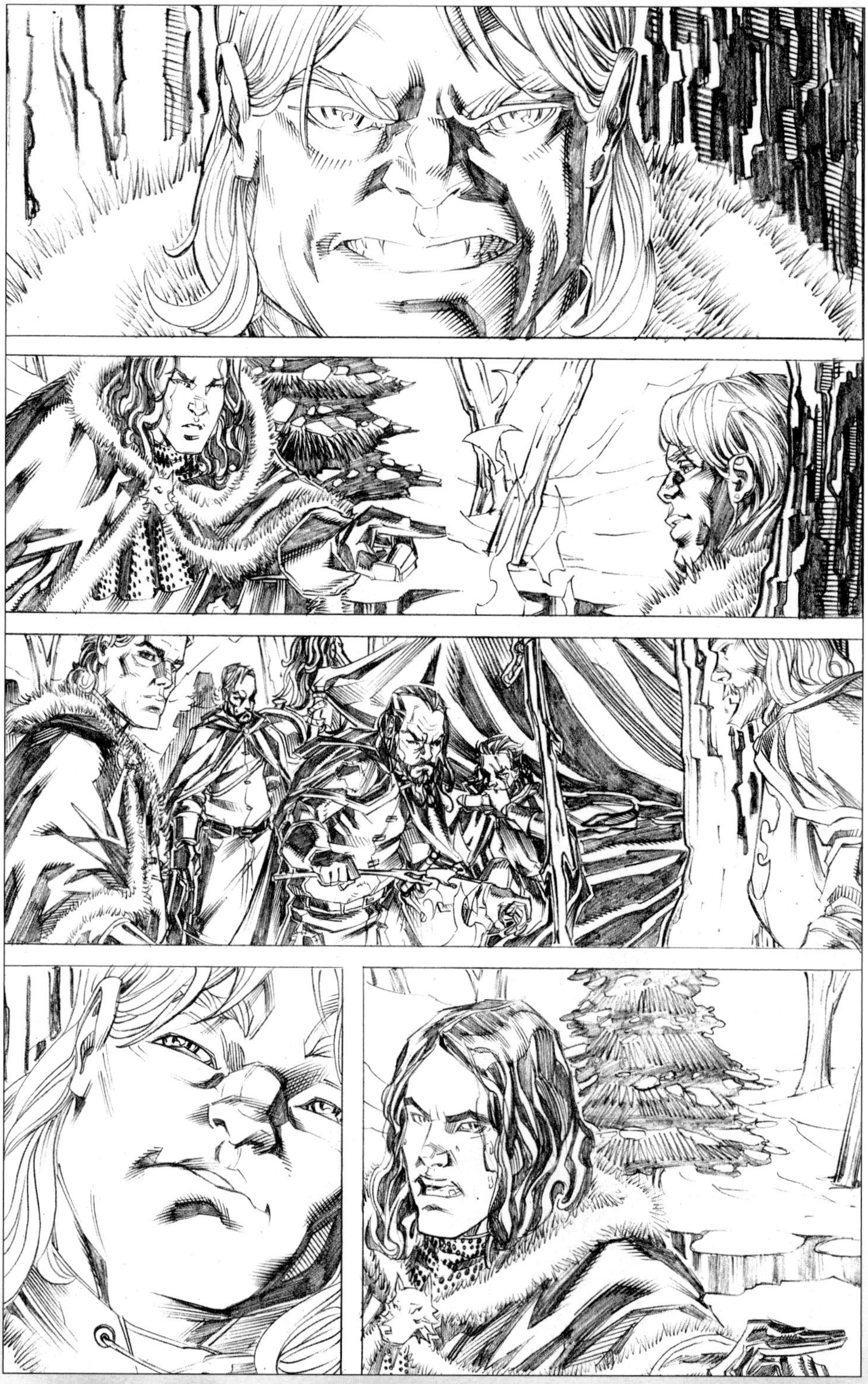

NED WALKING INTO THE COUNCIL CHAMBER, TO MEET LITTLEFINGER AND THE GANG

I'm still pushing for a darker take on everything. Spotting more black areas takes a ton of time, but I feel it looks great. The bottom panel was a monster. So much needed to be shown.

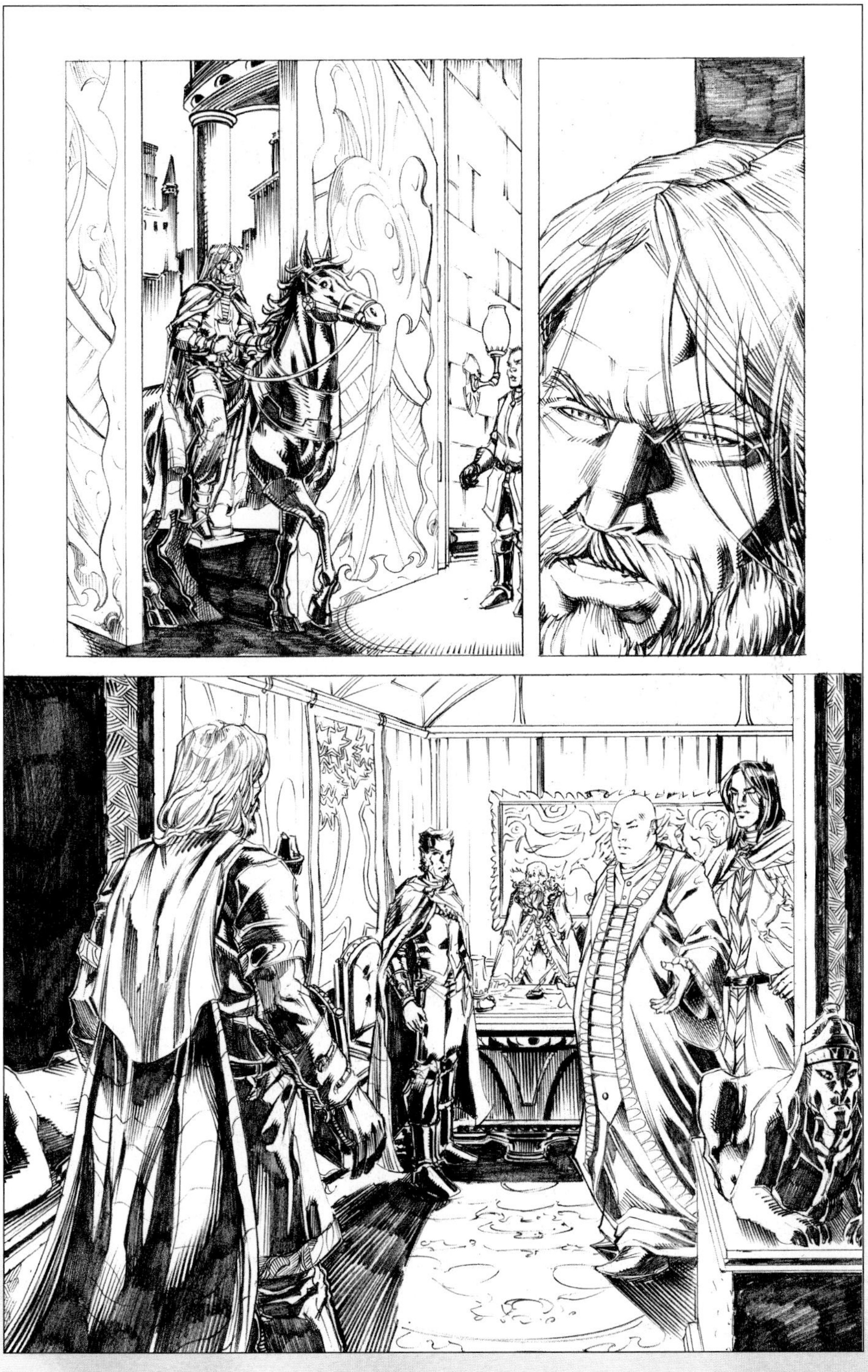

CROW'S-EYE VIEW AT CASTLE BLACK DINING HALL

Framing panels is really fun to do. You can make a panel exponentially cooler with foreground objects. When I read a comic and run across a panel like this, you feel like—if you move your head around—you can peek over and around stuff. It engages the reader

COLORS AND LETTERS

We looked at the work of a few colorists at the audition stage, and Ivan Nunes was far and away our top choice, for his ability to insert instant atmosphere into a panel. Mist, shadows, lighting effects...they are truly impressive, and have added a lot to the feeling of the graphic novel.

I also don't want you to think that we are giving short shrift to the wonderful work of Ivan on the colors, and Marshall Dillon on the letters. They are both invaluable parts of the team, and so flawless at execution that by the time we get to this point, our work is mostly done. The revisions at this point are minor, and mostly involve moving misplaced speech bubbles, correcting typos we overlooked in the scripts, and tweaking a few hair/eye/costume colors, thanks to both of their meticulous work.

In the next volume, we'll run you through the stage-by-stage making of a single page, from the text of *A Game of Thones* through to the finished graphic page, but to give you but a quick taste here, we did have to pay attention to things like Tyrion's mismatched eye color...and keep track of which eye was which. (George did not care, so we decided.)

Probably the pickiest I got with the color-tweaking was for Dany's silver, in Issue #3. Initially, the horse was looking a bit too generically gray...and this is a special beast. So we darkened the body a bit and lightened the mane—a subtle change, but one that totally makes the horse pop.

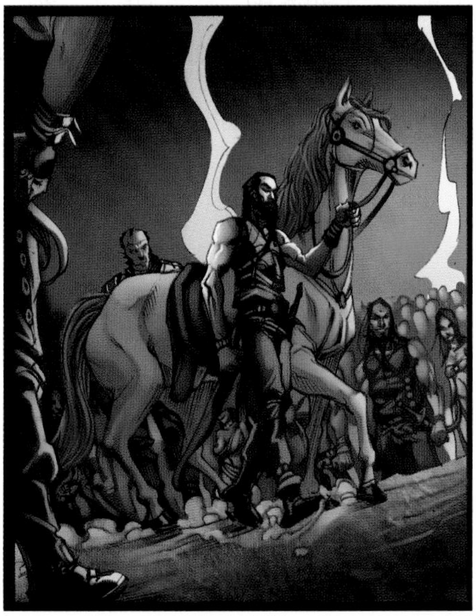

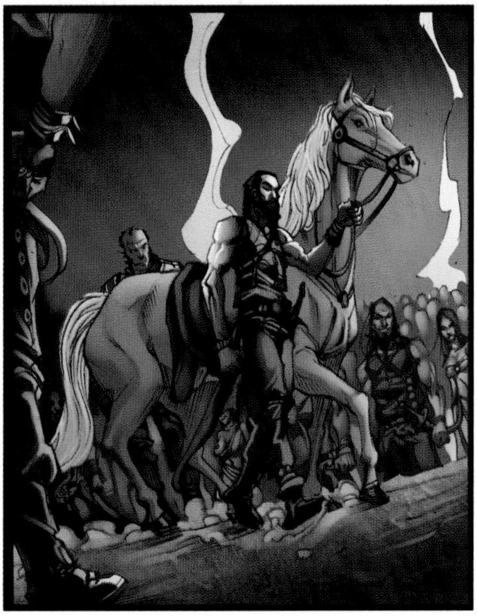

Tommy adds:

"Ivan and Marshall are great. I sneak-peek Ivan's colors to some of my comic-book peers (don't tell anyone) and they are stunned every time. He has saved me so many times, adding atmosphere and detailing. Check out the wrinkles he adds to the banners on the dining-hall page, or the stained glass he takes up a notch. Marshall is awesome at not covering up the cool parts. I occasionally clutter things up, but you will never miss an important moment because of a misplaced balloon."

We hope you've enjoyed this look inside the process, and that you continue to have as much fun on this visual journey as we have!

GEORGE R. R. MARTIN is the #1 *New York Times* bestselling author of many novels, including the acclaimed series A Song of Ice and Fire—*A Game of Thrones, A Clash of Kings, A Storm of Swords, A Feast for Crows*, and *A Dance with Dragons*. As a writer-producer, he has worked on *The Twilight Zone, Beauty and the Beast*, and various feature films and pilots that were never made. He lives with the lovely Parris in Santa Fe, New Mexico.

DANIEL ABRAHAM is the author of the critically acclaimed fantasy novels *The Long Price Quartet* and *The Dagger and The Coin*. He's been nominated for the Hugo, Nebula, and World Fantasy awards, and has won the International Horror Guild award. He also writes as M. L. N. Hanover and (with Ty Franck) as James S. A. Corey.

TOMMY PATTERSON'S illustrator credits include *Farscape* for Boom! Studios, the movie adaptation *The Warriors* for Dynamite Entertainment, and *Tales from Wonderland: The White Night, Red Rose*, and *Stingers* for Zenescope Entertainment.

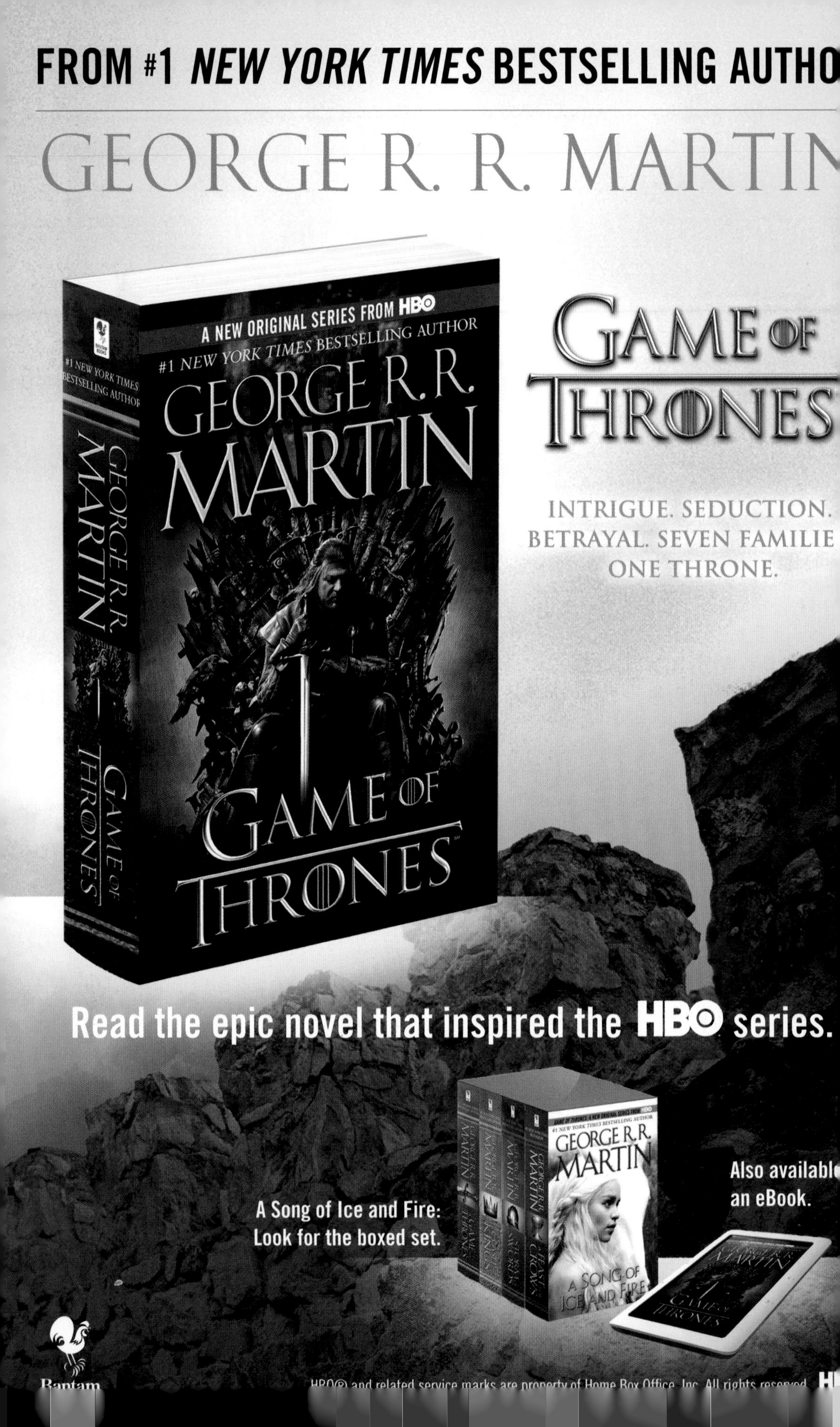
FROM #1 NEW YORK TIMES BESTSELLING AUTHO
GEORGE R. R. MARTIN
A NEW ORIGINAL SERIES FROM HBO
#1 NEW YORK TIMES BESTSELLING AUTHOR
GEORGE R. R. MARTIN
GAME OF THRONES
GAME OF THRONES
INTRIGUE. SEDUCTION.
BETRAYAL. SEVEN FAMILIE
ONE THRONE.
Read the epic novel that inspired the HBO series.
A Song of Ice and Fire:
Look for the boxed set.
Also availabl
an eBook.
GEORGE R.R. MARTIN
A SONG OF ICE AND FIRE
Bantam
HBO® and related service marks are property of Home Box Office, Inc. All rights reserved.